T0161089

BUY THE TICKET TAKE THE RIDE

A NOVEL

BRIAN SWEANY

This is a Genuine Barnacle Book

A Barnacle Book | Rare Bird Books
453 South Spring Street, Suite 302
Los Angeles, CA 90013
rarebirdbooks.com

FIRST TRADE PAPERBACK ORIGINAL EDITION

Set in Dante
Printed in the United States

Book design by STARLING

Illustration by Alexandra Infante

10 9 8 7 6 5 4 3 2 1

Publisher's Cataloging-in-Publication data

Names: Sweany, Brian, author.

Title: Buy the ticket , take the ride : a novel / Brian Sweany.

Description: First Trade Paperback Original Edition | A Barnacle Book | Los Angeles [California] , New York [New York] : Rare Bird Books, 2016.

Identifiers: ISBN 978-1-942600-38-1

Subjects: LCSH Family—Fiction. | Indianapolis (Ind.)—Fiction. | Bildungsroman. | Rock music—Fiction. | Relationships—Fiction. | Publishing—Fiction. | Biographical fiction. | Humorous fiction. | Satire. | BISAC FICTION/General.

Classification: LCC PS3619.W42 B49 2016 | DDC 813.6—dc23

PART I

1986-1989

CHAPTER ONE

My morning gets off to its usual start. I wake up. Masturbate. Eat some bacon and eggs. Drink a cup of creamed and sugared coffee. Have a frank discussion with my father about his testicles.

"A vasectomy *reversal*? Are you kidding me?"

"Oh come on, son. It's not that big of a deal." A bi-folded pamphlet sits on the table. Dad opens and reads the pamphlet aloud: "'A small incision is made in the scrotal skin over the old vasectomy site. The two ends of the vas deferens are found and freed from the surrounding scar tissue.'"

He offers me the pamphlet. Something resembling a beat up three-wood taunts me on page two. I shake my head. "No, thanks."

"That right there is the vas..." Dad runs his finger along the shaft of the three-wood. He taps once on the top of the club. "Then you have your epididymis and your testicle." He points to the three-wood's shaft one more time. "My vas is currently severed, and they're going in and sewing it back together, more or less."

I cringe at the thought of Dad's nutsack getting sliced open. Mom hovers off to the side of the kitchen. She sips on her coffee in between bites of toast, reluctant to enter the fray. I don't let her off that easy.

"You put him up to this?"

"Henry, your father and I have been talking about this for years."

"Oh, really?" I cringe at the sound of my given name. I hate the name Henry. Hank is the only name to which I've answered for pretty much my entire fifteen years on this planet, having cast aside "Henry David" and my mother's literary pretense—she's never even fucking read *Walden*—at the precise moment I split her vagina with my freakishly oversized melon.

Dad sips his coffee. "Yes, really. Besides, if anyone's at risk, it's your mother, not me."

"Okay then, Mom, why the sudden interest in suicide?"

"Suicide?" Mom shrugs. She's wearing her old cotton bathrobe and Dad's slippers. She shuffles across the linoleum floor and sits next to me at the kitchen table. "They've made a lot of advances in prenatal care since I had you and your sister."

"They have?"

"Sure."

"Jesus, Mom! Last time I checked, I was born in *nineteen* seventy-one, not *eighteen* seventy-one. You had all kinds of problems with me and Jeanine. And Grandma Louise, what did she have, eight miscarriages or something?"

"My mother only had three miscarriages."

"Only three? That's a relief. How's that twin sister of yours doing by the way?" It's a callous reference to the premature twin my mother never knew. I'm curious as to how Mom's twin would have turned out. It's hard to picture anyone else looking back at me with that round, cherub-like face and its fountain of teased, hair sprayed, and overly dyed blondish hair. Harder still to imagine another woman dumb enough to contemplate reentering a world measured in dirty diapers and ear infections at the age of forty-one.

But Mom is unwavering.

"Women with much worse track records than mine are having babies nowadays."

"Worse? Have you looked in the mirror lately?"

"As a matter of fact, I have."

"When's the last time you just went for a walk?"

"Can't recall."

"You can't recall because you *don't* walk. You don't really take care of yourself."

"Oh, Hank, stop it!" Mom shakes her head, as if merely denying she's sedentary and bookish might alter reality.

"Stop what?" I reach over and grab her wrist. She's wearing a gold watch Dad gave her for their fifteenth anniversary two years ago. I turn her wrist so she can see the face of the watch. "What time you got? Because I'm looking at someone's biological clock, and it says about quarter 'til midnight!"

"Quarter 'til midnight, my ass." Grandpa George throws the morning newspaper on the table. Although our family has been in America for close to two hundred years, Grandpa looks fresh off the boat—a freckled, strawberry blond Irishman even at age eighty-one. His thick, Coke-bottle glasses magnify the size of his eyes to comical proportions. He's more blind than far-sighted at this point in his life.

Grandpa sips his coffee. "If that goddamn kid throws my paper in the bushes one more goddamn time..."

"Thanks, Dad," Mom says.

"'Thanks nothing," Grandpa says. "Boy shouldn't be talking to his mother like that."

We moved Grandpa into our first floor guest room last year. Dad said it was the right thing to do. Grandpa had lived alone since Grandma Eleanor died of cancer in '81, but sometime after the beginning of Reagan's second term, he started forgetting things. He'd go out to meet his friends for breakfast, walking the same route along Kentucky Avenue on the southwest side of Indianapolis that he'd been walking for fifty years, and he'd get lost. Kentucky Avenue was no longer the best place to get lost. The old neighborhood wasn't safe anymore. His favorite neighborhood stores—Murphy's Mart, Woolworth's, and Linder's Ice Cream—had all gone out of business and been replaced by Mega Liquor World, Instamatic Cash Checking, and Rent-to-Own Furniture and Appliance Store. The Laundromat that used to have quarter washes and the machine that dispensed free popcorn now had ten-dollar hookers and a machine that dispensed fifty-cent condoms, and the house across the street that used to leak puppies and shirtless toddlers now leaked meth addicts and shirtless adults.

Within months, Dad's selfless act started backfiring. Incontinence, feebleness, dementia—Grandpa George's body and mind has been giving out on him, but we're always there to patch him up. The other night, I caught Dad hovering over Grandpa's bed when he slept. I asked him what he was doing. He told me he was praying for God to make his father whole again. Even though we keep starting over with a puzzle that's missing another piece, Dad refuses to entertain the idea of a nursing home or assisted care living. Our house has started to reek of urine—the smell of mortality and a son's well-intentioned but misguided love.

A part of me cherishes Grandpa George living with us, and not just because he's a convenient scapegoat when Mom and Dad discover half-empty bottles in the liquor cabinet. Grandpa was my best friend for the first ten years of my life, and we had our rituals. Every Saturday morning when I was a kid, we'd walk to Mr. Dan's Diner for breakfast. We'd sit with Grandpa's World War II buddies—guys with inexplicable nicknames like Beef, Old Crow, Buddha, and Skeckel—and we'd order biscuits and gravy with coffee. The gravy at Mr. Dan's had too much pepper for most people, but that was the way Grandpa and I liked it. After our breakfast, we'd hop on a bus to downtown. Our schedule was pretty much the same every Saturday. We walked through the Children's Museum and ate lunch at Shapiro's, the old Jewish deli in downtown Indianapolis—Grandpa George's favorite restaurant. After lunch, we stopped in at St. John's to kneel down and say some Hail Mary's, and then Grandpa would buy me a model airplane at L. S. Ayres department store.

At the end of the day, Grandpa and I would get on a bus and then hop off a couple miles short of his house. This gave us time to pick boysenberries from the bushes growing alongside the railroad tracks on Kentucky Avenue for Grandma Eleanor's pies. The crickets chirping and that creosote smell of railroad ties would always make me think of summer. One day Grandpa told me the boysenberry bushes had come from the seeds left by passenger trains "dumping out their crappers." I stopped picking boysenberries after that.

But back to the kitchen and my father's testicles.

Grandpa George sets his coffee cup down on the table. "Now you listen here, Johnny, uh, Hank. What your mom and dad do behind closed doors is their own business."

"Johnny-uh-Hank" has been Grandpa's unintentional nickname for me my whole life, as he never quite remembers that I'm his grandson instead of his son until halfway into my name.

"Well, Grandpa, I assumed Dad made it my business when he shoved his vas deferens in my face."

"Take it easy, son," Dad says, smiling. Smiling! And it isn't just any smile. It's one of those irrepressible John Fitzpatrick smiles that lights up a room while at the same time diffusing any situation. Dad tilts his head down, still smiling. He arches his dark, I-know-better-than-you eyebrows and points his pronounced Fitzpatrick nose at me.

"I'm going in for the procedure on Monday morning, and your Mom and I are taking this one day at a time. I only have a fifty-fifty shot at even regaining my fertility."

He says *fertility* with an unmistakable reverence in his voice, as if his sperm is akin to the holiest of holy oils as opposed to what I dispense daily like party confetti. Chrism, jism—what's the fucking difference?

"Whatever, Pops. They're your balls."

"Henry David Fitzpatrick!"

She nails me across the back of my bedhead with her open palm. It's more annoying than punitive, but it gets the job done. "Dammit, Mom!"

She smacks me again. "Don't think you're too old for me to wash your mouth out with soap," Mom says.

Dad shoves two pieces of bacon into his mouth, smothering his laughter. Grandpa left the room unnoticed, shuffling out for his morning walk around the neighborhood with his sassafras cane.

"Well, if we're talking about another kid," I say, "can we have the dog conversation again?"

My mother hates animals. In my first fifteen years of life, various people—no fewer than three babysitters, Aunt Claudia, even a couple girlfriends—conspired to get me a dog. And each time, Mom was steadfast in her opposition.

"Hank, as long as you live under this roof..."

"I know, I know. Fish are the only pets I'll ever get."

Dad washes down his bacon with a swallow of coffee. He looks out the kitchen window at our backyard. Our lawn is bordered on the left by a willow tree stump, and on the right by a purple martin house. The ankle-high bluegrass waves in the morning breeze, its silver-green tapering off at the edge of the pond behind our house. "That lawn isn't going to cut itself," he says.

I GRUMBLE AS I walk outside. I raise the garage door, step out onto the driveway. The morning dew on the grass mocks me with its promise of matted clumps clogging the lawnmower and two hours of frustration and engine-masked profanity. The mower greets me with predictable ambivalence. A dozen futile pulls on the starter send me back into the house.

I don't know when Dad ceded lawn duties over to me. The transition was imperceptible. Yesterday, I was a little kid sitting in the family room wearing my Miami Dolphins helmet and cursing the New York Jets—this was back in the late seventies when Shula was God in my world, long before the Colts came to town—while Dad was outside coating himself in layers of grass, fertilizer, and gasoline. Today, I'm a teenager, no longer a Dolphins fan but still not enough of a Colts fan to care, bursting in on Mom and Dad coating themselves in pre-sex sweat.

I wish I could say this is the first time I've walked in on them. Hell, I wish I could say this is the first time I've walked in on them this week.

"Seriously, you two? I'm outside for five minutes, and you're already dry-humping on the couch?" The inherent repulsiveness of parental copulation sends an acidic bacon and coffee burp up from my stomach.

"What's the problem, son?" Dad stands up, erection in tow, trying to cover himself. His robe leaves little to the imagination, so he turns sideways with his back to me.

"Well, other than my disintegrating psyche, the stupid lawnmower won't start."

"You prime her?" Dad asks.

"A bunch of times."

"You probably flooded the engine. Is the sparkplug connected?"

"Yeah, Dad."

"She have plenty of gas in her?"

I shake my head. "You do realize I'm *not* retarded, right?"

"Understood." Dad adjusts his robe over his still noticeable bulge. Mom gives his butt a squeeze as he walks past, pouring salt into my psychological wounds. "Let's have a look, then."

There are few more timeless traditions than men yelling at inanimate objects. We stand in the driveway pleading with the four-wheeled, two-cycle engine to obey our commands. Dad can't get the mower started either, but he loves the old machine. Grandpa George bought it when Dad was in high school. It's one of those yellow metal Lawn-Boys from the mid-sixties that manages to hurl everything it finds—sticks, rocks, dog poop, bird carcasses—back in your face. I don't like the mower so much.

Dad gives the starter a few more tugs. He comes as close as he's capable to cussing, managing a "sheee-oot."

Mom yells out the garage door, interrupting our exercise in futility with the news that she's put on a second pot of coffee.

"Sounds good to me." Dad pushes the mower back into the garage.

I nod. "Don't have to ask me twice."

My father looks at me. I look at him. We exchange wordless smiles. I enjoy Dad's company more than I'm willing to admit.

CHAPTER TWO

My family is sorta semi-nomadic. When I was born, we lived in an apartment on the south side of Indianapolis off Thompson Road. It shared a parking lot with a Red Lobster. Our next door neighbor, Uncle Angelo, was a fat, bald guy with black-rimmed glasses and a salt-and-pepper mustache. He tended bar at the Milano Inn but moonlighted as the Fitzpatrick family's guardian angel. When someone broke into our apartment when Dad was out of town, Mom grabbed me and went straight to Uncle Angelo's place.

"Debbie, you-anna-uh-Hank stay here with-uh-yur Aunt-uh-Pat," he said with his thick Italian brogue. He went over to our place in full crime-stopping gear—white ribbed tank top, stained boxer shorts, loaded rifle on his hip. Uncle Angelo's wife's name was Pasqualina, or "Aunt Pat" to everyone who knew her. She fed me my first solid food—pasta in marinara sauce.

After the place on Thompson, we moved a couple miles south to Southport, an incorporated town inside Indianapolis that got the *South* part of its name because it's on the far Southside of Indy and the *port* part of its name apparently because the town's founders had a perverse sense of irony about having a port in the middle of a waterless stretch of farmland. Our backyard overlooked the playground at St. Ambrose, the Catholic parish my family attended for most of the first ten years of my life. My sister, Jeanine, was born when I was three years old. Mom wrapped our piss-yellow, velvety living room couch in white sheets for Jeanine's first formal photo shoot. She was too fat to smile.

After I turned four, we moved outside the city. Claiming it was "an unbelievable opportunity," Dad took a sales job with a Chrysler dealership in Kokomo. Mom had to pull up the olive-green shag carpet in our two-bedroom ranch because the floors smelled like cat urine, while Dad found out the deal he got on our house had less to do with his negotiating skills and more to do with the previous owner hanging herself in the garage.

There was a large gray gas tower crowned by red-and-white checkers that served as Mom's primary guidepost when she drove around Kokomo. She spent most of her day at the mall with me and Jeanine in lieu of fraternizing with our neighbors who had cigarettes permanently attached to their lips and drank Budweiser for breakfast. Mom was so depressed she started taking belly dancing lessons. It would be the only time in my mother's life she would feel inclined to do anything that could be interpreted as *exercise*, so essentially we should have been on suicide watch.

On some afternoons, Mom would take me to see Dad at the dealership. Dad showed me off to the wrinkled suits and grease monkeys, who I thought were the coolest bunch of guys I'd ever met. But mostly I stayed at home and did my best to stay out of the way of my mom's misery. My favorite thing to do was skip rocks across the creek running through our backyard, at least until a mosquito bit Grandma Eleanor and she almost died from encephalitis. We fled Dad's "unbelievable opportunity" after less than six months. As we were driving out of town for the last time, Dad thought Jeanine and I were sleeping when he pointed to his rearview mirror and said to Mom, "Hey, Debbie, did you know *Kokomo* pronounced backward is *oh muh cock*?"

After Kokomo, Dad got a job selling Mercedes while his family sought refuge in a newer neighborhood back in Southport just off Meridian Street called Clematis Gardens. No matter how many times Mom pointed out "clematis" was a flower and not a sexually transmitted disease, Dad still snickered at the name.

The summer after my sixth birthday, we moved into an old farmhouse north of County Line Road, during which time I attended St. Ambrose through all of elementary school. St. Ambrose had separate girls' and boys' monkey bars on opposite sides of the playground. The boys would "launch" periodic attacks into the girls' monkey bars, pretending with our outstretched arms and fake propeller noises to be fighter planes as we weaved in and out of the biting and scratching flurry of plaid skirts and white oxfords.

In the first grade, I fell in love with Kimberly Thompson after she rescued me, bloodied and torn, following a kamikaze dive into the girls' monkey bars. As a token of my devotion, I stole a silver tin of consecrated hosts from the church sacristy for Kimberly. Stealing the body of Christ for love—where does a guy go from there to impress the ladies?

Kimberly refused my gift. She always did the right thing, except for the time she swallowed aspirin when she had chicken pox and died of Reye's syndrome. Mom made me wear my First Communion suit to Kimberly's funeral. It was navy-blue polyester wrapped around a butterfly-collared shirt of powder blue. I remember standing at the funeral and Mom whispering to me that Kimberly would have thought I was handsome. I remember thinking her casket was too small and that I hated my haircut.

We moved to Louisville, Kentucky, the summer before my fifth-grade year. Dad felt bad about moving out of state, what with his mother, Grandma Eleanor, getting sick and all. But the financial security afforded him as general manager of a BMW franchise in northern Kentucky was too good to pass up.

Our new house stood on a wooded hilltop just off Highway 42. Uncle Mitch and Aunt Ophelia drove down from Indianapolis to help us unpack. Uncle Mitch was not my real uncle, but Dad was an only child and Mitchell Hass had been Dad's best friend since they were kids. A month after I was born, Mom and Dad asked Mitch to be my godfather, so calling him "Uncle" became an afterthought. Three years after that, they extended the same courtesy to his wife, "Aunt" Ophelia, after Jeanine was born.

Our first night in the house, there was a thunderstorm that knocked out our power. Dad went down into the basement to check the fuse box. He left me alone with Uncle Mitch in my bedroom. It wasn't the first time or the last time Dad left me alone with him, and it wasn't the first or last time Uncle Mitch took advantage of the situation. My godfather handed me his beer and moved next to me on my bed. He winked at me and said, "Our little secret, Hank." It was my first beer. It tasted awful, but I kept the beer on my lips and drank the whole thing. I stared at the ceiling while Uncle Mitch put his hands down the front of my underwear. He liked touching me. A godfather's love measured by the length of his godson's erection.

Our little secret, Hank.

DAD CRIED WHEN HE told us the news. The owner of the BMW franchise fired Dad because his employees preferred Dad's leadership to that of the guy signing their checks—plus Dad busted said owner for having drinks with his mistress. Dad was rewarded a nice severance package from a judge who agreed Dad's former boss was a complete asshole. It was the second time I ever saw my father cry. The other time was when Grandma Eleanor died. Our Pentecostal cleaning lady, Charlotte Fayne, sang "The Old Rugged Cross" at the funeral. Charlotte wore her hair and skirts long because the Devil had a place reserved in hell for shorthaired women who wore pants.

We moved from Louisville back to the south side of Indianapolis—Greenwood this time, a town that's of course more grey colored and relatively devoid of trees. Dad took a job as a stockbroker for Paine Webber, commuting back and forth to downtown Indy. He worked sixteen hour days in a three by five cubicle doing a job that a monkey flipping a coin could perform with equal competence. Dad's new career came and went in a span of less than two years.

Those two years were much kinder to me. In addition to being the home of the Grand Wizard of the Ku Klux Klan, Greenwood staked its claim to a Chinese restaurant with the state's largest indoor Koi pond and a Catholic school with the state's largest pool of pubescent hormones. My seventh and eighth grade years at Our Lady of Perpetual Help were what I classify as my awkward, albeit enriching, years. Faced with the prospect of fading into adolescent obscurity, I compensated better than most for bad acne and twenty extra pounds. I quit football and became a wrestler, a sport my singlet-wearing fat ass inexplicably peddled into a higher-than-deserved social status. My sly sense of humor disarmed my peers and teachers into thinking I was harmless, and thanks to a couple years of cotillion, I could pull out dance moves that embarrassed the guys and enflamed the girls.

After a three-month flirtation with an eighth grade volleyball player during which I was crowned King of All Seventh Graders, I became drawn to Twyla Levine, a tall, brunette vixen who sat next to me in Mr. Marker's seventh grade class. On an overnight field trip to St. Louis, Twyla and I made out during a game of spin the bottle. Later, on the bus ride home to Greenwood, I put my hand up Twyla's skirt and managed to fiddle with the elastic on her panties. Someone witnessed the panties episode, so by the time we got back to Greenwood, Twyla had given me a hand job while

I fingered her in the back of the bus. None of this was true, but over the years, as the story followed me and took on a life of its own, I never tried very hard to deny the rumors. Years later, I would have sworn on a stack of Bibles I lost my virginity in the back of that bus. True or not, you have to admit the image of a thirteen-year-old stumbling around a bus looking for a place to stick his dick has a humorously scandalous quality to it.

The truth was Twyla did give me an orgasm. After I got back from St. Louis I locked myself in the bathroom with Twyla—or at least, Twyla's seventh grade class picture cut out of my yearbook and taped to the body of 1984 Playboy Playmate of the Year, Barbara Edwards. Twyla's ambitions were "To fulfill my dream as a promising artist and actress and to contribute my share of help to the starving children of the world." Her turn-ons were "Being a Sigma Chi sister of USC, drawing, traveling, and attending musicals."

Even though I was a Notre Dame fan, I let the USC comment slide. Anything for Twyla.

In the wake of Dad's stock broker experiment, a couple investors whose portfolios quite miraculously quadrupled on his watch set up my father as president of his own car dealership. We moved, again, putting down what turned out to be permanent roots in Empire Ridge, a mill town about halfway to Cincinnati. We said our driveway goodbyes to our Greenwood neighbors, a brand-new Oldsmobile Custom Cruiser station wagon hunched low over the tires with the weight of a couple more years of memories. I mailed a goodbye letter to Twyla, outing myself as the town pervert with the affecting words, "How about you take a picture of yourself naked and send it to me?" And in the fall of 1985, with the "Fitzpatrick Olds-Cadillac-Subaru" marquee hoisted and lit and my family settling down after our eighth move in twelve years, I enrolled as a freshman at Empire Ridge Public High School.

It's been more than two infant-free years since Dad reversed his sterility. Much like his failed attempts to cajole disinterested sperm cells in the general direction of my mother's worn-out uterus, I'm still finding my stride in Empire Ridge. I grew ten inches without gaining a pound, my complexion cleared up, and I carry one hundred and seventy pounds of taut muscle over a five foot ten inch frame. Student council, the wrestling team, Catholic youth group—everything to me is an opportunity for initiation.

And there is no faster road to acceptance in a sleepy Indiana town than getting drunk, something I try to do as much as possible.

I hold the shot of Jim Beam to the light. Its amber glow is the color of hope—my hope it will somehow magically disappear without having to touch my lips. A goofy-looking guy sits next to me. He's skinny, skinnier than me at least, and maybe a half inch taller, with a round face and a head sprouting random cowlicks rather than curls.

"Drink it, you fucking pussy," he says.

"Hatch," I reply, "shut the fuck up."

Elias Hatcher has been my best friend since I met him at freshman orientation. Hatch is your typical child of divorce. His mother is a recovering hippie who now raises free-range ostriches somewhere in Oklahoma, his father a Vietnam vet turned semipro sport fisherman who's spent the better part of the eighties chain smoking clove cigarettes and crawling out from the bottom of a liquor bottle. Hatch's every move, at least in public when he has an audience, is a premeditated, loud, and more often than not obnoxious attempt to draw attention to himself. He is overly protective and sentimental toward his closest friends to the point of making you feel uncomfortable. Stick Jimmy Buffett's "A Pirate Looks at Forty" in the tape deck, and Hatch is hugging you while bawling his eyes out—guaranteed. If you're unwilling to commit any impulsive act—shotgun six beers in a row, jump off high bridges into shallow water, or drop everything and take a road trip because you've snagged some warm Natty Light with your fake ID and need an excuse to drink it—Hatch invokes the word "pals" and you have no say in the matter.

Like tonight.

"We've almost downed this entire half gallon." I hold up the nearly empty bottle of Jim Beam save for an inch of bourbon—the remains of a sobriety lost hours earlier. "How about we take a break?"

"Pals, Fitzy." Hatch grabs the half gallon from me. He finishes it, drinking it straight from the bottle. "Bring it!"

"Come on, Hatch."

"Pals!"

"But I can't feel my legs."

"Pals!"

"Ah, fuck it." I open my mouth and raise the shot glass to my lips. I throw the warm brown liquid down the back of my throat, doing whatever

I can to prevent the harsh, woody bite of cheap whiskey from gagging me. I slam the empty shot glass down.

"That's what I'm talking about!" Hatch offers me a large cup of Mountain Dew. "Chaser?"

I nod, grabbing the cup. I drink the lemony soda until it runs out the sides of my mouth and down my face.

Last weekend Hatch and I got kicked out of the big hockey matchup versus Prep. Half-cocked on a bottle of Jägermeister we split before the game, we started taking liberties with the last names of the Prep players. By the middle of the third period, Mrs. Pocock tired of the demonstrative harassment of her son and had us removed.

Founded as Whiskeyville by a couple drunken Scotch-Irish trappers in the eighteenth century, Empire Ridge was renamed in the nineteen-twenties in honor of the large quarry just outside of town that supplied every inch of limestone to the Empire State Building's exterior. Empire Ridge Preparatory Academy and Empire Ridge Public High School, or simply "Prep" and "The Ridge," are separated by a mere three and a half miles.

If the stereotypes are to be believed—and given that I have neither the time nor inclination to get to know most people beyond their subjectively imposed stereotypes—Prep is a bastion of entitled fucksticks. The school's coffers are lined by old money trust funds and new money CEOs who buy their "Prepsters" Beamers on their sixteenth birthdays. Meanwhile we "Ridgies" aspire to little more than attending the next pig roast, slugging pure grain alcohol, and shouting as racecars make left turns for three hours. Excepting the fact I have my own personal automobile pipeline courtesy of Dad, most of us Ridgies drive fifteen-year-old cars inherited from an older sibling—Camaros, Firebirds, Dodge Royal Monacos, and trucks. Lots and lots of trucks.

After the hockey game, we were eating our way to sobriety at the McDonald's down the street when two Prep girls, one a petite brown-haired girl named Carrie, the other a taller brunette named Mary, introduced themselves. They were new in town, their fathers both engineers who'd transferred in from the East Coast. After a half hour of dedicated flirting on both sides, Mary invited us to her house that following Saturday on Gotham Lake, punctuating her invitation with four very unfortunate words: "Bring whoever you want."

Hatch has procured a new half-gallon of Beam. He pours himself another shot. "Some party," he says.

I wipe the traces of Mountain Dew from my mouth. "Yeah."

By my rough calculations, "Bring whoever you want" has translated into two hundred and fifty people since the party started. Hatch and I sit at a table on the second floor balcony overlooking the carnage. Every potted plant is dumped out on the floor, creating a carpet of peace lilies, rubber trees, philodendrons, and potting soil. There are zero exposed surfaces. Wine cooler bottles line the fireplace, cigarette butts floating in every third or fourth bottle. A case or so of shot-gunned beer cans are piled high in the kitchen sink, and multiple decks of playing cards are crawling amongst the refuse.

I've been drinking off and on since we got here this morning, some eight hours ago. I'm wearing nothing but a towel. Someone bet me twenty bucks to walk out to the middle of Gotham Lake, which is half-frozen at best. Formed by two limestone quarries adjacent to Empire Quarry that were later connected and flooded, Gotham Lake is shaped like a horseshoe. The bet was to walk out to the middle of the widest part of the lake, which is in the middle of the right curve of the horseshoe. I won the bet, but I lost my clothes, plunging chest-deep into the horseshoe just as I was nearly back to shore.

Steve Miller Band's *Greatest Hits 1974–1978* starts up on the back deck of the house, replacing *Fore!* by Huey Lewis and the News, which inexcusably made the playlist. "Swingtown" is a few chords old before someone skips to "Jungle Love." The techno introduction echoes across Gotham Lake. Hatch and I simultaneously mimic the whistle with our fingers in our mouths, transitioning to dueling air guitars, and then dueling air drums. Aside from us both flubbing the second line and saying "you thought you'd been lonely before" instead of "you thought you had known me before," we sound pretty good.

Hatch ducks into the bathroom, reemerging with two beers in one hand and a set of car keys in the other. "Shotgun?" He pretends as if I even have the option of saying no.

This time around I don't even bother going through the motions. "Give it here."

Hatch hands me the beer. We each take turns cutting a quarter-sized hole in the bottom half of our cans with his dirty car key.

Hatch drives a serious piece-of-shit Volkswagen Beetle that burns through a couple fan belts every month. His idea of a car stereo is me holding a boom box in my lap and making sure his fourth copy of Van Halen's *OU812* doesn't get eaten by his ravenous tape player. Hatch and I have developed a growing affection for Sammy Hagar, much to the distaste of our diehard David Lee Roth friends. Although Van Halen's self-titled '78 debut has to be considered one of rock's all-time great albums, lately I look to Roth less for his debatable musicianship and more for the gratuitous D-cups and G-strings in his music videos.

Hatch asks if I'm ready. Grunting in reply, I put my mouth on the opening of the can, careful not to cut my lips on the jagged aluminum edges. I pop the tab on the other side of the can and suck the beer through the opening. One full beer down in maybe five seconds. I let out a relieved belch. Hatch leaves a good three or four swallows in his can as he crushes it and throws it on the floor.

We work our way through three more beers. I point to the foam dripping out of his third can. "Fucking cheater." I punctuate the accusation with a loud, wet belch.

As is the natural order of a party in southern Indiana, Johnny Cougar's *Uh-huh* finds its way to the front of the playlist. The opening guitar riff of "Pink Houses" commands a wave of dutiful shouts and catcalls in the house. Although most Ridgies choose to defer to the more sentimental "Jack and Diane" or the more obvious "Small Town," for me and Hatch it doesn't get any better than "Pink Houses." This is our "New York, New York," our "Yellow Rose of Texas," our "Old Kentucky Home."

Hatch and I stand up. When "Pink Houses" plays, you're required to stand up. We hold our beers high in the air, crooning to no one in particular.

"Ahh, but ain't that America, for you and me..."

"Hank?"

Hatch and I turn to the sound of the voice. It's coming from the master bedroom. It's Mary.

"Yeah?"

Mary steps out of the room, my shirt and pants in her right hand. "I think your clothes are dry. You want to come in and, uh, get dressed?"

"You tired of me walking around half-naked or something?"

Mary smiles and winks. "I'm hardly tired of that, Henry." She turns and walks back into the bedroom.

I stand up. Hatch stands up as well, shaking his head. "Henry?" He punches me in the shoulder, then sings, *"Little pink houses, for my pal, Fitzy!"*

"Oh, shut up." I pretend as if the girl who has just invited me into her room to get undressed has not been flirting with me all day.

"Don't forget this." Hatch picks my Velcro Def Leppard *Pyromania* wallet off the table and throws it at me. "Try to be careful in there."

"Careful?" I feel the impression of the off-brand condom I bought out of a machine in a gas station bathroom. "It's not like she's going to eat me."

"She might only be sixteen, but she's an East Coast girl," Hatch says. "There's no telling what she'll do to you."

I ENTER THE BEDROOM. Mary is sitting on the edge of the bed, smoking a cigarette. With her brunette hair she looks like a much younger, tanning bed version of Erin Gray—the *Buck Rogers in the 25th Century* Erin Gray as opposed to the *Silver Spoons* Erin Gray. I try to picture her in one of Erin Gray's signature skintight bodysuits, although the elongated cigarette in Mary's left hand and the bottle of Heineken in her right skews the fantasy.

"Here," Mary says, patting the bed with her left hand. "Have a seat."

I stumble forward. The alcohol in my system has made the outer edges of her face fuzzy. I manage to find my way to the bed and sit down beside her.

"Smoke?" Mary hands me a long, peculiarly thin cigarette.

"Sure." I roll the cigarette between my fingers. I grab the pack off the bed and hold it up to the light. "Virginia Slims?"

Mary nods toward the closet to her right. "My mom's stash."

I can feel the butterflies in my stomach. I'm nervous. "My friends and I call these Vagina Slimes," I say, chuckling.

She doesn't laugh, which makes me even more nervous. I fumble around with the cigarette, managing to get it in my mouth by sheer dumb luck.

"Please, allow me." Mary holds the lighter to my face. With a quick roll of her thumb, a small tongue of fire ticks the end of my cigarette. She never looks at the cigarette, staring into my eyes and then down to my lips—textbook flirting. I stare at the cigarette—textbook avoidance.

Mary leans off the side of the bed. I hear the rattle of ice cubes. She produces another bottle of Heineken. The bottle is already open, like she was expecting me. "Beer?"

"Of course." I take a quick swig. The beer tastes like canned corn, like all Heineken does in my opinion, but I pretend to like it. "Pretty fancy beer. Part of the parents' stash, too?"

"Uh-huhhhh." Her affirmative is more of a moan than a response. She sips her beer and then licks her lips. Her hand has somehow found its way onto my leg.

"Look, Mary, I—"

"You want to watch a movie?" Mary grabs my beer and sits it on the floor. She nods at the videos stacked on top of the television.

"Sure." I cross one arm over my bare chest, squeeze my shoulder in awkward modesty. "Whatever."

"Here you go." Mary hands me my boxers and jeans but not my shirt.

"Thanks." I pull my boxers and jeans on with my towel still attached at the waist. I stuff my wallet in my back pocket.

Mary is neither awkward nor modest in her intent. "Oh, you're no fun."

MARY SUGGESTED *PEGGY SUE Got Married*. I suggested *Hoosiers*. Somehow we decided *Crocodile Dundee* was a good compromise. We sit on the floor in front of the bed. A half hour into the film, Mary has wedged herself under my arm, wrapping her right leg around my left leg. We are at the part when Sue Charlton tells Mick Dundee she can make it in the Outback on her own. Mick lets her go, but hangs back out of sight. Sue gets tired, takes a break by a watering hole, and undoes her pants. She's wearing a black one-piece swimsuit, but with a thong back that's all but swallowed up by her beautiful rotund ass.

As if that moment could have gotten any better, a crocodile lunges at Sue Charlton. Mary flinches, burying her face in my chest. She isn't scared so much as looking for her opening. She runs her pursed lips up my chest, and then starts nibbling the side of my neck. She presses her chest against mine. I can feel Mary's erect nipples beneath her shirt because she isn't wearing a bra. Mary finds her way to my fly as Mick Dundee saves his lady-in-distress. She unbuttons one button, then two, then a third. She is inside my jeans and past the slit in my boxers before I even know what's happening. We kiss, but just for a second or two before she goes back to work on my neck. She kisses my neck and then starts to move down my chest. She bites my nipples, licks my navel, then…

"Wait a second, Mary." I push her away with my forearm and tuck myself inside my boxers, all in the same motion. "We can't do this."

"What?" Mary says.

The blood coursing through my drunk, engorged erection is equally taken aback with my decision. But this is not going to happen.

"I don't know what to say." I stand up, buttoning my fly. "I'm sorry."

Mary folds her arms in front of her chest. She seems more sad than angry. "Is it me? Did I do something wrong? I thought this is what you—"

"Oh no, Mary, it's not you at all." I offer my hand to her. She takes it, standing. We sit face-to-face on the bed."

"Then what's the problem?"

I scratch my chin. I grab the pack of cigarettes off the bed and pull out a cigarette. I offer it to Mary and light it for her. She takes a long, frustrated drag.

"My problem isn't so much a *what*," I say. "It's a *who*."

"A who?" Mary blows her Vagina Slimes disgust in my face. I wave it off, eyes squinting.

"Yeah, see, the thing is, I kind of have a girlfriend."

"Fuck you, Hank!"

"Mary, wait. Can I just—"

"Can you just what?"

"Can I, umm, have my shirt?"

Mary slams the door behind me as I walk out of the bedroom. I put on my clothes, scanning my general vicinity. No one is upstairs. Hatch has disappeared, which is a good thing. I'm not in the mood for him fucking with me, not to mention I still have an erection. I see the bathroom just to my right. I walk in, shut the door, and lock it.

I test the door, making sure the lock is secure. I pull my wallet out of my pants pocket. Inside is a picture of a headless belly dancer.

I was casually introduced to the record album *Exotic Music of the Belly Dancer* in the nineteen-seventies, back when my mom took belly dancing lessons in Kokomo. Soon thereafter, the album went into exile until Dad invested an obscene amount of money in a new stereo system and pulled his dusty old record collection out of the attic to justify his new investment.

The year was 1983. I had just finished listening to the *Urban Cowboy* movie soundtrack, an album I played on a regular basis from when I was nine years old until the LP disintegrated sometime in the mid-eighties. I loved the album because it had the unedited version of the Charlie Daniels

Band's "The Devil Went Down to Georgia" and my parents let me get away with screaming "son of a bitch" during the song. Granted, it isn't quite the glorious, profane karaoke experience of the *Grease* soundtrack and its signature song, "Greased Lightning," which since 1978 has afforded me the opportunity to shout, without so much as a head-shaking reprisal, things like "you know that ain't no shit we'll be getting lots of tit," "you are supreme the chicks'll cream," and "you know that I ain't bragging she's a real pussy wagon."

For whatever reason that April day, only a few days after my twelfth birthday, I decided to stick *Urban Cowboy* toward the back of the collection rather than its usual place near the front with my parents' favorites: *Kenny Rogers Greatest Hits, Barry Manilow Live, Larry Gatlin & The Gatlin Brothers Greatest Hits, Helen Reddy's Greatest Hits (And More),* the original Broadway cast recording of *Annie*, and of course Dad's prized Chuck Mangione albums. Aside from *Urban Cowboy* and *Grease*, some Jim Croce, the soundtracks to *Hair* and *Jesus Christ Superstar*, a few Eagles albums, and exactly one Beatles album—*A Hard Day's Night*—my parents' taste in music sucks balls. When I slid my hand between the albums to make room for John Travolta in a black cowboy hat, a sexy headless belly dancer invited me into her world.

Even the album's title was fucking sexy: *Exotic Music of the Belly Dancer* by Mohammed El-Bakkar and His Oriental Ensemble. A voluptuous belly dancer shimmied up the left side of the album cover, her hands raised above her head and her right hip thrusting out. The album's title bar cut off the belly dancer's face at the chin and her raised arms just above the elbows, giving her an air of mystery. A shadow covered half of the belly dancer's body like a question mark, bisecting her creamy-white skin at the navel, running up from her waist, around the bottom of her left breast and then across her underarms and chin. Below her navel, she wore a multi-layered silk skirt fastened low on her hips with a pearl-encrusted belt, all of the ensemble in various shades of gold to match her pasties. The pasties themselves were pointed teacups. Shiny, metallic moons ending in gold tassels that crowned the smoothest, most perfectly rounded breasts I'd ever seen. They became the standard by which all breasts were compared for the rest of my life.

I took the belly dancer to my bedroom and had my way with her.

When Dad told me he was phasing out his vinyls to make way for a cassette collection—a collection that, in continuing the Fitzpatrick musical tradition of sucking balls, would be dominated by compilations of movie and television theme songs—I took a box cutter to the front sleeve of *Exotic Music of the Belly Dancer*. I was very careful to separate the image from the cardboard corrugation. For being folded and refolded into my wallet on multiple occasions over the last five years, my girl has held up pretty well. I hold on to her for emergency situations, like today.

The sink and toilet are to my left, a washer and dryer tucked in a closet to my right. Bright white crown moldings and baseboards trim walls of barn red. I reach for some toilet paper and undo my pants. Taking my erection in my hands, I look at my belly dancer.

Thanks to Mary, I'm pretty well primed, but I try to hold on as long as I can. I hover over the toilet, my pelvis thrusting, my pants pulled down to my knees. I close my eyes right when it starts.

I tuck the belly dancer snuggly back into my wallet. I have to piss so bad I can almost feel it coming out my ocular cavities, but I'm still hard as a rock. I try to push my erection down so I can piss on the back of the toilet seat. A few drops trickle out, but I can't piss unless my penis is bent well below perpendicular to my body. And I know if I hazard an attempt at anything close to perpendicular, my urine is destined for multiple and varied locales maybe or maybe not in the general vicinity of the toilet.

I finally decide to sit on the toilet seat backwards. I straddle the seat with my legs while leaning over the back of the toilet. My penis is still hard, touching the inside of the toilet bowl. The cold toilet water gets things going. The clear liquid comes out in multiple streams, like a sprinkler. It burns. It feels toxic, punitive. The bleachy odor of ejaculate hovers in the bathroom. An unmistakable odor of adolescence. Like sweaty polyester athletic uniforms, dirty ashtrays, cheap beer, vomit, and too much Drakkar Noir cologne. Like the inside of a girl.

I gather myself. With a hand towel I wipe the sweat off my face. Pausing one last time to wipe some errant sperm off the wall above the toilet, I exit the bathroom and head downstairs.

Hatch is sitting on the family room couch watching a movie on the big screen projection television. Most of the crowd has cleared out. I try to sneak by him into the kitchen.

"Where the hell you think you're going?" Hatch asks.

"Me?" I veer toward the couch, pretending as if this were my intention all along. I sit down. "Just looking for you."

Hatch hands me a lukewarm, already opened Natty Light. I force down a swallow of it. I wipe my mouth, looking at the animated image on the projection television. "What are you watching?"

"Some kind of cartoon."

"That's no ordinary cartoon. That's *Fritz the Cat.*"

"Fritz the what?"

"*Fritz the Cat*. It was the first ever X-rated animated film."

Hatch scratches his head. "Well, that explains a lot. I thought the dope was just making me see things. So this cartoon has a lot of psychedelic colors?"

"Yep."

"And the occasional cow, pig, cat, or crow with enormous tits getting fucked by, what's his name again?"

"Yep, a lot of big-breasted farm animals getting fucked by Fritz."

"And a lot of them smoking weed?"

"Lots of weed smoking."

"Okay, then…" Hatch pauses. He stares at the television. An effeminate crow shouts an expletive onscreen. Hatch sips his beer, sits it down on the coffee table. "But it still freaks me out."

I force out one of those fake laughs, the kind you do when you're thankful full frontal nudity, even the animated feline kind, can distract your buddy enough that he doesn't remember to ask you—

"How'd it go with Mary, stud man?"

I play dumb. "What do you mean?"

"Don't be a jackass." Hatch punches me in the shoulder. "How was she?"

"Relax, dude." I pull a long white cigarette out of my back pocket. I light it with the still-burning ember of a butt nesting in an ashtray on the coffee table. "We just watched a movie."

Hatch opens his mouth, speechless, but not for long, I suspect. He stands with his hands on his hips. "You've gotta be fist fucking me!"

"Nope." I hold in a long drag of smoke. Man, I was one lame piece of shit.

Hatch points at me. "Man, you're one lame piece of shit."

"She's just not my type."

"Since when is drunk, hot, and naked not your type?"

He has a point. "I don't know. I guess since…well, I don't know."

"Since Laura maybe?"

Her name breaks the tenuous peace. "Listen, shithead." I lurch up from the couch, so sudden and awkward the top of my head smacks the bottom of Hatch's chin on the way up. "Leave her out of this!"

Hatch staggers back onto the couch. I hover over him, fists clenched, face reddening. He rubs his chin. "Jesus Christ, Fitzy. I'm just fucking with you."

I relax my shoulders, the color already fading from my face. As always, this is the extent to which we argue, never beyond this point. I extend my hand to help him up. Hatch accepts the gesture.

"Sorry, buddy." I pat him on the back. "Got any of that pot left?"

Hatch straightens his shirt. "Hello, remember me? I'm your best friend, Hatch, son of an alcoholic marine who'd whip my fucking ass if he ever found that shit on me."

"So you're *not* high right now?"

"I didn't say that, did I? Yours truly is fucked up as a football bat." Hatch motions to the backdoor. "Hockey team is out back lighting up."

For whatever reason, our hockey team always has the best pot. I step aside, offering Hatch a path to the backdoor. "Ladies first, then."

Hatch shakes his head, waves me off. "No, thanks. You go ahead. I need to come down off this buzz a little."

"You sure?"

"Yeah. I'm going to watch the rest of this movie, try to get my feet back under me."

Hatch eyes the door to the upstairs bedroom as he says this. I pretend not to notice, but I know what he's thinking. "Suit yourself."

CHAPTER THREE

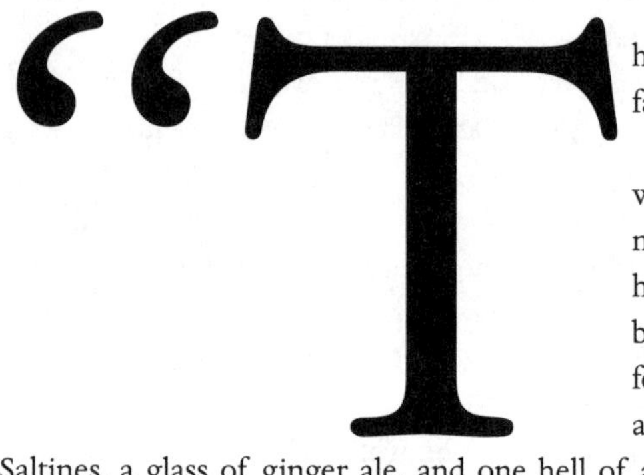

“This is really all Hatch’s fault, isn’t it?”

Dad made sure to wake me up early this morning, before my sister had to see anything. I’ve been back from the party for about five hours. I’m armed with a sleeve of Saltines, a glass of ginger ale, and one hell of a hangover. The smell of smoke and liquor is still on my breath, in my hair, in my clothes—the clothes I wore and slept in last night.

“Ease up, Dad.” I lift the ginger ale to my lips, drinking half the glass in one gulp. “Believe it or not, I’m perfectly capable of getting in trouble all by myself.”

The party at Gotham Lake ended badly, at least for me. After I got high with the hockey team, I walked in on Hatch losing his virginity to Mary on the bathroom floor. I hitched a ride home with the third-string goalie, trying not to replay in my mind the image of Hatch’s bare, sweaty ass bouncing up and down against Mary’s splayed legs, her feet propped against the edge of the toilet and the bathroom wall. I walked through the front door of my house around 2:00 a.m. to find Mom sitting in the family room. She told me my father was driving around Gotham Lake looking for me. I tried to string a few words together before falling face first at her feet. Dad came home an hour later to find me passed out on the family room floor.

“How much did you drink yesterday?” Dad asks.

I bite down on a cracker. “Beats me. A case maybe?”

"A case…of beer?"

I look at my father like he's one step away from the short bus. "Yes, it was beer."

"Did you happen to think about anyone else but yourself last night?"

My throat constricts, the cracker sticking to the roof of my mouth. "What's that supposed to mean?"

"I'll tell you what it means." Dad points at me. "Your father spent six hours driving around town to three different houses that you or your friends were supposedly spending the night at, until he ended up at a house on Gotham Lake at two in the morning."

I can tell Dad is pissed off. He always speaks in the third person when he's pissed off.

I'm reminded of how bad we fucked things up. Yesterday morning, I told Mom and Dad I was going sledding all day and then spending the night at Nicholas Truman's house, Nick being my wrestling teammate. Nick told his parents he was going sledding and then spending the night at Joel Trudeau's house, another wrestling teammate who I didn't even hang out with. Joel, not in on the conspiracy, stayed home for family movie night and told his parents and my father sometime around midnight that he had no idea where we were. Meanwhile, a West German foreign exchange student named Marcus—name pronounced mar-KOOS who, like all European foreign exchange students, smells like dirty armpit, swears in English at inappropriate times, and wears ugly bowling shoes—told his sponsor family he was going sledding and then spending the night at my house. From what I can surmise from Dad's manic rambling, he drove out to Gotham Lake, walked in on Hatch and Mary in an amorous state, figured out I'd already left, and then snagged Nick Truman as a consolation prize.

"Six hours." Dad points to my mother. She sits across the table from me, arms folded. "Meanwhile, a four-months pregnant mother was up all night worried sick about her boy. I wonder when her son was drinking that twenty-fourth beer if he ever thought about the possibility of his mother losing another baby."

I can't believe Dad has the balls to even say this. Hell, his balls are the whole problem. I thought those few months before and after the vasectomy reversal were as close as the Fitzpatrick household would ever come to being dysfunctional, but Dad fucking Dixie cups and talking about sperm counts was nothing compared to Mom's miscarriage.

She got pregnant three months after the operation, lost the baby three months after that. Dad stumbled through a disaffected malaise. His interaction with the family was measured by the stack of greasy boxes on the kitchen counter and the hours he spent fishing alone in our backyard pond for largemouth bass and channel cats. Mom wasn't getting pregnant mainly because Dad wasn't trying to get her pregnant. And I came to the realization that when faced with death, at least the sudden and tragic kind, the invincible John Fitzpatrick threw in the cards just as fast as anyone else.

"Are you listening to me, Hank?"

If we were playing a game of euchre, Dad probably thinks he has the high card, the right bower. But, at best, he's holding a guarded left, three low trumps at the most. *I was there with Mom in the days and weeks after her miscarriage. You remember that, Dad? Those nights when you couldn't handle it? When Mom's son, not her husband, crawled in bed with her and stroked her hair until she fell asleep?*

I look at the hand I've been dealt. I don't have an obvious play here, but I go for it anyway. "Don't you need to go fishing or something?"

It's the equivalent of throwing out an off-suite ace to sneak a point early in the game or else force your opponent to burn trump. Mom looks at me with her don't-go-there eyes.

In Dad's defense, he did put down the fishing pole. Although maybe not as soon as I would have liked, one day he put down the pole, scooped Mom up in his arms, and gave her an uncomfortably long kiss on his way out the door to work. That night, he stopped ordering pizza. The night after that, he stopped ordering Chinese. The night after that, Mom made us our first home cooked meal in a month. And the night after that, mere hours after Mom came back from her obstetrician with a clean bill of health, my parents starting locking their bedroom door again. They assumed I didn't notice, just as I assume they don't notice a son who goes through a box of Kleenex every other week without ever having a cold.

"What did you say, Hank?"

"Nothing, Dad." Even with all this trump in my hand, I have no choice but to fold. "I guess I said I was sorry."

"You guess?" Dad raises his open palm next to his head, closes it, and covers his mouth with his fist. He gets up from the table, refills his coffee, stands at the kitchen sink. He looks out the window at the willow tree stump in our backyard, its decaying roots at the water's edge breaking the pond's frozen surface. Dad stands there for what seems like a long time but is no more than ten seconds. He turns around and sits back down, pulls his chair closer to mine. "Look, son, I know kids will be kids. And I know there are a lot of temptations out there your mother and I never faced."

"That's an understatement."

I've made it through the worst part of the storm, but Dad isn't in the mood for banter. "Don't start with me, Hank."

Of course, what I hear is, *Start with me, Hank.*

"You and Mom met each other at your college freshman orientation," I say. "You dated exclusively for five years, and you both lost your virginity on your wedding night. Never mind zip code, you two weren't in the same universe as me growing up."

"Don't be so glib, Hank."

"How many times have you been drunk, Dad?"

"I don't see what that has to do with—"

"How many?"

"Maybe three or four times."

"In your whole life?"

"Okay, son." Dad dips his chin in deference to me. "For the sake of argument, I'll concede your point."

"Thank you."

"Your point that you're just a stupid kid."

"Hey!"

I see the makings of a smile on Dad's face. "Tell me, oh wise one, would you ever sit down and drink twenty-four Cokes in one sitting?"

"Is that a trick question?"

"Just answer it."

"Of course not. I'd get sick." I try to pretend the irony escapes me.

"Here's the deal." Dad stands up, walks around the table, and places his hands on Mom's shoulders. "You're grounded for four weeks. No phone, no going out on weekends, and you come home straight from wrestling practice after school."

A slap on the wrist as punishments go, and yet what comes out of my mouth is, "No phone?"

"Except for..." Mom raises her hand in the air, index finger pointing back at my father.

Dad rolls his eyes as he sits back down. "Except for Laura."

"Really?" I say.

Mom nods. "You can call Laura. No sense taking away the best part of your life just because the worst part got you in trouble. But no dates for four weeks."

My eventual escape is secured. If things hold true to form, my parents will cave around the two, two-and-a-half-week mark. I push my chair back from the table, stand up. I try to look repentant, but I can't help smiling. I walk around to stand between my parents. "I'm sorry." Mom and Dad hug me, but briefly, as if to maintain the punitive illusion.

I reach down and place my hand on my mother's distended belly beneath her old cotton robe. "Really…" I choke up a little, Dad's earlier miscarriage allusion sneaking a punch into my midsection for real this time. "I am *very* sorry."

Mom understands. "We know."

I need to throw Dad some kind of bone, too. "Hey, Pops, how about I go shovel the driveway?"

Dad rustles the newspaper, not nearly as appreciative of my gesture as I had hoped. "Uncle Mitch is outside already doing it."

"Uncle Mitch?" I say. "What's he doing here?"

"I ended up buying that nineteen forty Series ninety from that farmer down in Kentucky."

"That beat up old Oldsmobile?"

"That *classic* Oldsmobile. And yeah, that's the one. Mitch volunteered to be my co-pilot. He and Aunt Ophelia are still going through a bit of a rough patch. I just thought a road trip would be a nice distraction."

"Oh," I say, pretending to care. Uncle Mitch and Aunt Ophelia have been separated for a year. Ophelia is seeking an annulment, but no one seems to know why. I have my theories.

"Is that a problem, Hank?" Dad asks.

Is that a problem? It's a simple question without a simple answer. A part of me thinks I've imagined it all. Okay, so maybe there was some skin-on-skin heavy petting, but how awful is that? It's not like I ever wake up in the middle of the night in a cold sweat as the repressed memories come rushing back to me. So he touched me. Big deal. I touch myself all the fucking time. Can the memories of a five-year-old or even a ten-year-old be trusted? I got past the flying monkeys in *The Wizard of Oz*, the Oompa Loompas in *Willy Wonka and the Chocolate Factory,* even that fucked up episode of *Little House in the Prairie* where the girl gets raped by the guy in the clown mask. Maybe I need to stop looking underneath the bed for a reason to be afraid. What's there to fear under that bed anyway? My dad's discarded Playboys? Those old penny loafers, two sizes too small and scuffed beyond the reach of any polish? That paperback edition of *Zen and the Art of Motorcycle Maintenance* I've tried to read because I want the artsy college chick who moved in across the street to think I'm cool, and yet I never seem to get past the last sentence of Chapter Six: "But he took on so much and went so far in the end his real victim was himself."

Who am I fucking kidding? That clown mask episode of *Little House in the Prairie* still scares me shitless.

"Need a hand?" I ask.

My godfather is a little underdressed for the weather, wearing a jean jacket, a pair of faded jeans, and old tennis shoes. "Sure I can't interest you in a beer or something?" he says.

"You're just so fucking funny," I say.

"I'd like to think I am." He laughs, handing me the shovel. His laugh starts in his throat and comes out of his mouth and nose at the same time, like a pig. He has a dark black receding hairline that frames a pitted face and a complexion made darker by his five o'clock shadow. A lit cigarette hangs out of his mouth. As he exhales, I can see and smell his three-packs-a-day breath.

Uncle Mitch smokes Merits. In the early eighties, he switched brands from Kool because someone told him menthol cigarettes were bad for you. The sound of crinkling plastic reminds me of Uncle Mitch and his Merits. Whenever I slept over, he'd spoon with me on the living room floor while we watched Charlie Chan movies. He always forgot to take his Merits out of his front pants pocket. I could hear the crinkling plastic during the whole movie.

"You gave your parents a scare last night."

"I realize that."

"You think you've learned your lesson?"

"Probably not."

"I'm guessing John and Debbie want a bit more assurance."

"Come on, Uncle Mitch, you're a high school teacher. As the song goes, I am sixteen, going on seventeen."

"Yeah, but your parents can't hide you away from the real world in an Austrian castle and dress you in curtains."

I shovel the snow in strips running parallel to the street as opposed to perpendicular. It's an old trick Grandpa Fred taught me to keep the snow from piling up at the end of the driveway. He was a good teacher. Better than my godfather.

Uncle Mitch follows me. I point to the house. "You can go in now if you want."

He extracts another Merit, lights it, and inhales long and deep. "I like the fresh air."

I keep shoveling. I'm not comfortable around him, but I've had a lot of practice faking it. "How's the job?" I ask. "You're teaching health and driver's education at East Catholic, right?"

"That's right," he answers.

"And you're an assistant coach for the girls' basketball team?"

"Assistant for the boys' team," Uncle Mitch says. "Great bunch of kids. After being lost for a really long time, I finally feel like I'm making a difference."

"Lost? Is that what you call it?" I don't know where the question comes from, but the fact is, I say it, and I've wanted to say it for years.

Uncle Mitch takes a tentative step toward me. "Hank, I don't know what you're trying to get at, but you know—"

"Don't bullshit me, Mitch!" I turn the shovel in my hands until I'm holding it like a baseball bat.

"Please, Hank." Uncle Mitch holds up his hand and waves it back and forth in a placating motion. "Life hasn't been easy for me. Your aunt Ophelia and I are trying really hard to work things out. Give me some credit."

"Give you some credit? For what?"

"I was a sick man." He holds the Merit to his mouth with one hand, reaches for my shoulder with the other. "But I'm better now."

"Sick?" I can feel my hands tightening around the shovel's handle. "It's not like you had a fucking cold."

"Hank..." Uncle Mitch looks down, noticing my hands. "I need you to put the shovel down."

"And I needed you to not give me hand jobs when I was ten years old."

"Look, I don't know what you think I did, but that never happened."

"It didn't?"

"No, it didn't. I mean, yeah, I know I'm overly affectionate, but that's just me. I'd never do something so horrible, so…"

"Monstrous?"

"You know Ophelia can't have kids. For all intents and purposes, you are my son."

Uncle Mitch draws closer, his steps more committed. I raise the shovel in the air, preparing to swing. "Don't take another step, asshole," I say.

We stand there for a minute or two, not even inches apart. A physical and emotional standoff.

Uncle Mitch hazards the waters. "What is it you want me to do, Hank?"

I look at the shovel in my hands. I shake my head, taking a few steps back. I throw the shovel on the ground. "Well, since you're taking requests."

"Yes, anything."

"Get the fuck out of here."

"What?"

"I know what you've done. You know what you've done. If you don't want me to let Dad in on 'our little secret,' get in your car, drive out of this town and out of our lives."

Uncle Mitch starts crying. "You can't do this, Hank. You have no right. I was John's best friend twenty years before you were even born. What am I supposed to tell him?"

"Tell him whatever you want. Tell him nothing. I suspect whatever you come up with will be preferable to what I have to say."

"So that's what this has come down to, son? You're willing to break your father's heart just like that?"

"No," I say. "You are."

He stands there for five minutes while I finish shoveling the driveway. But finally, irrevocably, Uncle Mitch gets in his car. I knock on the passenger-side window. He rolls it down.

"There's just one more thing," I say.

Red-faced and beaten-down, Uncle Mitch doesn't even look at me. "What?"

"The next time you call me 'son' to my face, I'll kill you."

That comment catches him right on the jaw. He staggers a little, but he shakes it off. Now Uncle Mitch is looking at me. "What did you say, Hank?"

"Do you really want me to repeat it?"

Another standoff. I can see the conflict in his eyes. Dad's best friend is itching for a fight, but it is a fight the monster Uncle Mitch has become knows he would lose.

CHAPTER FOUR

Love is fucking stupid.

Oh sure, there's parental love, sibling semi-tolerance, grade school crushes, idol obsessions—innocent shit like that. But the whole idea of drowning in the idea of someone, and what's worse, not knowing you're drowning until you're underwater and you open your mouth to take a breath and realize, *Hey, something isn't quite right here*—well, until it happens to you, it sounds fucking stupid.

Laura Elliot is my fucking stupid.

I call her right when I wake up, still hungover more than thirty hours after my last sip of alcohol.

"Four weeks?" She makes that cooing, mopey sound with her voice that always gets me. "I can't go that long without seeing you."

"You see me every day at school."

"But that's not the same."

"Look, I have study hall last period three times a week. Maybe I can snag a couple hall passes from my mom. We can hang out before I go to wrestling practice or something."

"But I want to be with you…" She trails off. "Alone."

A flash of her parents' basement. The dueling dryer and dehumidifier each trying to upstage the other, the smells of fabric softener and musty throw rugs, a scratchy old couch relegated to rec room duty but enjoying a most active retirement. Laura's head bent awkwardly against the couch's armrest.

"Hank, you still there?"

I nod like she can see me. "Yeah," I say. "I'm here."

I realized I liked Laura about a month ago. She's a senior and a year older than me. It just kind of happened. Two hours after the Christmas

Dance ended, our dates kicked to the curb, we were making out on her front porch. Laura introduced me to her mom and dad. They went to bed. We made out on the couch in her family room. We made out in the kitchen. We made out in the dining room. She stopped me as I was pulling out of the driveway, jumped in my car, and we made out in my car. Two weeks ago, we fooled around all night in a hot tub at a New Year's party and missed *Dick Clark's New Year's Rockin' Eve.* And I never fucking miss *Dick Clark's New Year's Rockin' Eve.*

"Hank? Hello?"

"I said I'm still here."

"Well, you're not talking much."

Sixty minutes into a phone conversation, and she wants to ratchet up the chit chat. I could tell her about the guilt I feel over the whole Mary thing, if I felt any. Thanks to Hatch's sweaty bare ass, I've managed to rationalize away any culpability.

"I'm just bummed out, I guess."

"Yeah, me too."

She does it again, that cooing thing with her voice. I can't take it any longer. "Hey, Laura."

"Yeah?"

"You working tonight?"

"Sure am."

"When's the last show end?"

"Midnight-ish."

"I'll be there."

Laura giggles. "See you then."

Mom fixes us spaghetti for dinner. She makes the sauce from scratch, with ground-up Italian sausage instead of meatballs, because the sauce tastes better that way. Grandpa George is visiting some cousins in Kentucky for the week, so she only makes half as much as normal. After dinner, Dad asks Mom to join him for a walk around the block. Mom doesn't want to. The thirty pounds she's put on not even halfway through her pregnancy tells me she's won this argument once or twice. But Dad insists. He issues instructions to his progeny.

"Clean the kitchen, son."

I nod. "Sure thing, Dad."

"And, Jeanine?"

"What?" my sister asks. She has a tendency to whine more than talk when she's annoyed by the world. She whines a lot.

"Help your brother."

"But, Dad, I cleaned after lunch."

I look at Jeanine. She's the one most opposed to the new baby, for fear of breaking her stranglehold on the getting-away-with-murder privileges afforded her as the youngest child. "We went out to eat for lunch today," I say to her. "You were the one who begged us to go to Taco Bell."

"Did not."

"Did, too."

"Do you or don't you want to go to the New Kids on the Block concert?" I ask. "Because I can always back out as your chaperone."

"Uh…" I can see the horror in Jeanine's face. "I guess I just forgot."

"Just do it!" Dad orders, shutting the door.

My sister thinks I'm doing her a favor when I tell her I'll take care of the kitchen and she should go watch a movie. But the truth is I don't want any witnesses.

I clear the dinner table and wipe it down with a wet rag. I carry the butter to the refrigerator, open the refrigerator door, and place the butter on its plastic shelf inside the door. I grab the gallon of milk and the carton of large eggs. The milk is just opened. Two eggs are missing from the dozen. I carry the milk and the eggs over to the sink.

"I want a snack."

I jump, startled. Jeanine stands behind me. Her mop of curly blonde hair makes her look younger than thirteen.

Between us, I most resemble Dad—the longer face, the prominent nose, the large eyes setting off a more straight than curved smile. Jeanine is her mother's daughter, the eyes smaller and closer together in the middle of a more circular face, the nose not as obvious, all of which sit perched above a deep sickle-shaped smile that overwhelms all her features whenever she laughs.

I turn to block the evidence. "You just ate."

"What about dessert?" Jeanine asks.

"How's ice cream sound?"

"With Magic Shell?"

"Yes, with Magic Shell."

"I want the stuff that gets hard. Not Hershey's Syrup."

"I know the difference between the two."

My sister leaves the kitchen. I start to unscrew the cap to the milk when I hear the sound of feet sliding on oak hardwood floors.

Jeanine peeks into the kitchen.

"What?" I say.

"I changed my mind. I don't want Magic Shell now. I want Hershey's Syrup."

"Okay."

"And another thing."

I grab the edge of the sink in exasperation. "Good Lord, what now?"

"I think we're out of Hershey's Syrup."

"So you want Magic Shell?"

"No..." Jeanine pauses, taps her finger on her mouth. "If we're out of Hershey's Syrup, and if all we have is chocolate ice cream, I'll have mine plain. But if we have vanilla, I'll have Hershey's Syrup."

"You mean Magic Shell?"

"I don't like Magic Shell."

"Get out of here!" I push her out of the kitchen. "You'll eat what I bring you."

I pour out the gallon of milk. I grab the eggs, shove them one by one down the drain, then turn on the disposal. I throw away the empty milk jug, and wait.

MOM GOES TO BED around nine. At ten o'clock Dad takes his exalted place on the couch in front of the television. Halfway into the Channel 13 weather forecast, I "suddenly" realize we don't have any milk or eggs for breakfast. Dad asks if I wouldn't mind making a late night grocery run.

The five screen Regency 5 Theater sits behind my neighborhood on the corner of Regence and Farr, a mile from my house. I look at my Swatch as I pull into the theater parking lot, trying to discern the time. The face of the Swatch has no numerals. The small hand is pointing to a mint-green triangle in the upper left corner, and the big hand is about halfway between a fluorescent-orange squiggly line and a yellow circle near the bottom of the watch. 11:35 p.m. is my best guess. Dad is falling asleep right about now in the middle of Carson's monologue.

Regency 5 used to be a two-screen theater, a nondescript brick building tacked onto the south end of a Hills department store. Then, two screens became three, and then they skipped four and went straight to five. The biggest mystery is how they managed to add three extra screens without ever expanding the building itself.

I drive a cheap-ass, late-seventies Subaru even though my father has an entire parking lot of brand-new Oldsmobiles, mostly because I have an affinity for wrecking brand-new Oldsmobiles. I park my red Subaru wagon in a handicap spot at the front of the theater. A row of glass doors wrap the front of the theater below the marquee. I give the doors a shake. They're locked. The lights are dimmed inside, but I see someone walking toward me. She opens the doors.

"You're early." She closes the door behind me and locks it again.

"I know. Just thought I'd surprise—"

Her arms are around my neck, her lips already pressed against my own. She pretends to rub her lipstick off my lips but leaves it there. Laura likes to mark her territory. I can't get enough of her: her smell, her taste, her touch, that smoky lilt in her voice when she pouts to get what she wants. We kiss again.

"Sorry, but I just want to eat you up," Laura says, nibbling my neck. She rests her cleft chin on my shoulder.

Laura's long, brown hair is pulled back into a ponytail, a few stray curls sneaking out the sides. Even smelling of popcorn oil and garbed in her Regency 5 standard issue uniform—white oxford, red vest, blue pants—I find her irresistible. Her shirt looks a size too small, but that's just her breasts. I'm not going to lie, they're the first thing I ever noticed about her—soft and big, with a slight downward slope to them, almost too large for her age. Not belly dancer perfect, but as perfect as I've ever felt. Next to her substantial rack, her most striking feature is her mass of brown curls she spends hours teasing and spraying into something that emerges, quite miraculously, gorgeous. Laura is more confident about her looks than most girls her age but not in an obvious way. She's coy in public, taking the sexy route behind closed doors.

I grin. "No apologies necessary."

Laura grabs my hand. "Want to catch the last ten minutes of a flick?"

"What's on?"

"*Working Girl.*"

"The movie isn't on my must-see list. Anything else?"

"Nope," Laura says. "Last show of the night."

"Why don't we just stay out here?"

Laura pushes me. "You're no fun."

I grab her by the hips and pull her toward me. "It's not that."

"Then what is it?"

"Unless it involves an alien popping out of someone's chest cavity or a giant marshmallow man, I don't care for Sigourney Weaver."

"And I suppose you don't like Melanie Griffith, either?"

"I happen to like Melanie Griffith very much, at least when she plays a stripper and when Brian De Palma is her director."

She doesn't catch the reference.

"You know, *Body Double*?"

Still nothing.

"Holly Body? Frankie Goes to Hollywood? *Relax, don't do it, when you wanna go to it*? Not quite legendary B-movie actor Craig Wasson?"

Laura hasn't seen the movie. By the time we finish arguing about it, *Working Girl* is over. Three couples file out the front door of the theater to the tune of Carly Simon's "Let the River Run." I refuse to admit I like this song, although it is quite catchy. Any acknowledgment of its positive attributes takes me right back to that impressionable four-year-old boy whose mother played *Helen Reddy's Greatest Hits (And More)* so many times he memorized the lyrics. Mom would invite friends over and have me sing "I Am Woman" and "Ain't No Way to Treat a Lady," and they'd all tell me how cute I was. Yeah, Mom, it's cute to emasculate your four-year-old son for the neighbors' amusement.

"Time to close up." Laura starts to segue into another subject. I pretend I'm listening, but the only thing in my head at the moment are the lyrics to "Delta Dawn."

"What do you think?" she asks.

I have no idea what I'm about to agree to, but nonetheless I nod eagerly. "Sounds good."

Laura hands me a broom and dustpan, so I'm guessing I agreed to help her sweep down the aisles of Screen 3. At least Helen Reddy has stopped singing. Scraping Dots and Milk Duds off a sticky, cola-stained floor of a movie theater is not what I had in mind for tonight. I tell myself it's all for the cause.

Laura walks by and gives me a peck on the check. "You're such a cutie."

Hopefully somewhere down the road, "the cause" involves a little more than a peck on the cheek and being cute.

CHAPTER FIVE

Laura hands me an oversized red-and-pink cardboard heart stuffed with chocolates. "They're coconut-filled," she says. "Your favorite, right?"

"Yeah, right." I think about all those Halloweens waiting for Jeanine to empty her treat basket and hand over her discarded Almond Joy and Mounds bars. Have I already told Laura that story? Fuck, what haven't I told her?

We sit on Laura's front porch, the two dozen red roses on her dresser visible through her bedroom window. I had them delivered by a local florist, courtesy of the Fitzpatrick Olds-Cadillac-Subaru expense account. Laura told me the roses were the most beautiful flowers anyone had ever given her. I told her I paid for them with my own money and then ended with the exclamatory flourish, "Two dozen roses for two months of being in love."

Yes, I said *it*. Fucking goddamn right I said it.

The Valentine's Day dance was last night. Laura and I were on the dance floor. I floated the word out there for public consumption sometime during Aerosmith's "Angel." She floated the word back at me during Patrick Swayze's "She's Like the Wind." We said it together during George Harrison's "Got My Mind Set on You."

The chasm separating the act of being in love and the act of making love is filled with the nervous sweat and rendered tears of my many unconsummated relationships. I'm a junior, of course, turning seventeen in April. Laura is a senior, and turned eighteen right before we started dating. Up until now, we have acted under the tacit assumption that neither of us are virgins. More to the point, I know she isn't a virgin, and she has bought into my bullshit sexual history.

Laura puts her head in my lap. She reaches up and runs her hand through my hair. "You were such a gentleman last night."

We ended up in Laura's basement after the dance, both of us a little tipsy on purple passion—a noxious mix of grape soda and Everclear. I got her naked on the old couch. Loose change kept rattling inside the clothes dryer behind our heads. She gave me a hickey and a hand job. I buried my face in her bare chest, squeezed her nipples until they turned red, and fingered her until she came. A lesser girl would come right out and say, "Why didn't you fuck me last night?" But for whatever reason, Laura seems intent on mistaking my awkwardness for chivalry.

"What's all that?" I nod at the stack of letters in her other hand.

"These?" Laura throws the letters aside. "Nothing but junk mail. Ever since we booked a room down in Panama City, I'm guessing my name got on a ton of spring break mailing lists. I sift through a half dozen of these things every day."

"Spring break?"

"Hell yeah! Senior year, rite of passage, the last hurrah."

Senior spring break has been looming on the horizon. With Laura being a senior and me a junior, it's the one thing that has scared me more than anything else in our relationship. She will go to Florida my girlfriend, and she will come back single. That is just how the world works.

"This is news to me." I reach over and grab one of the letters. I pull out and unfold a full color poster of sunburned frat boys with bulges in their pants ogling drunken bikini-clad girls.

Laura scoots right up next to me and takes my hand in hers. She kisses me on the cheek. I want to say, "I love you," or, "don't go," or something, but anything comprehensible or appropriate defers to an internal reel of Laura climbing out of a pool Phoebe Cates-like in a red-string bikini to The Cars' "Moving in Stereo."

"Hank?" Laura grabs my chin with her hand, pulling me around until we were facing one another. "You okay?"

If *okay* means watching my girlfriend's bare breasts burst out of her bikini top while Benjamin Orr serenades her, I'm fine. I nod but don't say anything.

I've never been jealous. Is this what it feels like? Is this what love feels like? Panic. Mistrust. Paranoia. Life gives you every reason to be happy, and you're all, "Fuck it, bring on the misery."

I stand, taking Laura in my arms. I reach around and grab her ass, pulling her hard into me. I kiss her, my tongue pushing into her mouth, prying open her teeth. It's an obvious kiss, at least to me. More desperate than passionate.

Whitesnake is in my head as I kiss her. And why wouldn't Whitesnake be in my head? For one, their '79 album *Lovehunter* is graced by the greatest piece of cover art in rock history—a naked, bare-assed Amazonian warrior princess astride a giant snake. For another, it is both a blessing and a curse of my generation that we set our lives to a constant soundtrack of suspect music and even more suspect decisions, the pitiful made indescribable by David Coverdale's cautionary serenade that *I should have known better, than to let you go aloooone.*

I just now realize that Whitesnake is a euphemism for penis.

CHAPTER SIX

Mom lost another baby again. Her doctor told her that the first trimester was the most critical time for the viability of the fetus, but he made the mistake of counting on my mom's uterus. She almost made it to six months this time, three months longer than the first miscarriage.

My father was better this time around. He has been an absolute rock, if I'm being honest. Yesterday, Uncle Mitch called to tell him the annulment with Aunt Ophelia was final and that he was relocating to the West Coast. Dad seemed more angry than sad. I was more resentful than grateful that he didn't want to talk about it.

CHAPTER SEVEN

Laura squeezes my shoulder. "How's your mom doing?"

"Good."

"Really?"

"Almost too good. Mom and Dad say they're trying again as soon as they get the okay from the doctor."

"Wow."

"I know—crazy, right?"

"I was thinking more like courageous."

"What's the difference?"

"Cut her some slack, Hank. She's just a mom who wants to be a mom again."

"I guess." I hand Laura her bottle of Sea Breeze. "Is this the last of them?"

"I think so," Laura answers.

I've spent most of our last night together before spring break helping Laura pack. For the last hour, we've emptied and washed a large assortment of shampoo, mouthwash, and hair gel bottles, which we then refilled with an even greater assortment of alcohols in the clear family: schnapps, vodka, gin. The Sea Breeze bottle is filled with tequila, its amber color passing for the skin astringent. Laura's suitcase comprises these dozen or so bottles, two pairs of frayed jean shorts, three pairs of underwear, three T-shirts, and a white bikini. She modeled the bikini top for me earlier, her large breasts overwhelming the white cups. At least it isn't red.

The opening chords of "Moving in Stereo" ring again in my ears. "This all you taking, honey?"

Laura bats her eyes. She softens her smoky lilt down to a feminine and sexy tone. "I was thinking about packing just my bikini and the booze."

I don't see the humor in this, and Laura notices. "Come here, sweetie," she says, her hand extended towards mine.

I step cautiously toward her. She grabs my hand and pulls me into her. She gives me a deep kiss, one of those kisses that's so long and intense you start gasping through your nose to breathe.

"What was that for?" I say.

Laura puts her head on my shoulder. "Reassurance?"

I want to be comforted, but I can't tell if she's talking to me or herself.

CHAPTER EIGHT

"I'm not going on no fucking retreat."

"Watch your mouth," Mom says. "I already paid for it, and you don't have a choice in the matter. It's with some kids from East Catholic up at the CYO center in Indianapolis. It'll do you some good to meet new people. Get out of the Ridge social circle for a few days, get your mind off Laura."

"I don't want to get my mind off Laura." I stare at the television. For the last week, MTV has been broadcasting live from Panama City Beach, and I've spent every waking hour since Laura left watching the coverage in lieu of eating, showering, or engaging with the world on even a rudimentary level.

"If I have to watch you mope around this house for even one more day, I'm going to go nuts. It's pathetic."

"I hate to burst your bubble, but going on a three day religious retreat for my spring break isn't much of an upgrade on the pathetic scale."

Future Cardinal Joseph E. Ritter started the Catholic Youth Organization back in the thirties or forties. The "CYO" supports a variety of youth activities—anything that keeps our dicks in our pants. And nowhere is this brainwashing more acute than the retreats.

Retreat. The word carries with it a certain connotation in Catholic circles: rebirth, resurrection, renewal…retarded. You disappear for a few days, get all hopped up on Jesus, then spend the next few months trying to clear him out of your system. Jesus is like bad lunchmeat, I guess.

I went to my first retreat last year as a sophomore. They corralled a thousand of us into the East Catholic High School gymnasium. The motivational speaker was a "rock 'n roll priest," a guy who tried to validate his coolness by using contemporary music during Mass. Father Don was his name. He played Mr. Mister's "Kyrie" as an entrance hymn. I made out with a girl who had a Mohawk and smelled like peaches and marijuana, which, come to think of it, wasn't a totally horrible experience.

"You're going," Mom says. "End of discussion."

CHAPTER NINE

I enter the house. Mom is huddled over the stove in the kitchen, coffee mug in her left hand, sharp knife in her right. She looks up at me.

"There's our good Catholic boy," Mom says. "Glad to have you back."

I smile. "Glad to be back."

"That's not what I mean." She leans over and kisses me on the cheek, leans back, and points at my face with the knife. "Haven't seen that smile around this house in more than a week. Nice to have *you* back. How was it?"

"It was okay."

Mom's eyes perk up. "Okay?"

"Kind of fun, actually."

"Tell me about it," Mom says.

I humor my mother. I tell her the retreat began like any Catholic retreat, with a procession of pep talks, a Bible study, a group sing, and a daily Mass that numbed the brain and cleansed the soul. I tell her about our retreat leader, this guy in his mid-twenties who in the span of an hour fought drug addiction, dropped out of high school, was ostracized by family and friends, found Jesus, went back and got his GED, and was now in his second year of trade school where he was studying to become an electrical engineer. The second speaker, months removed from his last "Christian Awakening" retreat and still pretty much Lorded up, gave his own stirring account of how the Holy Spirit had changed his life for the better. He interspersed Top 40 songs in with his presentation to keep us interested. He was an ex-jock, just turned twenty, who had turned his back on the four S's—"Stroh's, Smoking, Sex, and Satan." He played "I Won't Back Down" by Tom Petty and the Heartbreakers and "Calling on You" by the Christian rock band Stryper. Seriously, *fucking Stryper*? All the girls thought he was deep. I wanted to punch him in the face, or else buy him a beer.

What I don't tell my mother is how on the first night in the dorms we stole the Gatorade cooler out of the rec room, spiked it with vodka, and hid it in a broom closet. Or how after we ran out of dirty jokes, I read from the Book of Leviticus.

With all due respect to Orthodox Jews, the Book of Leviticus is the most fucked up thing I've ever read, an inane list of do and do nots that reads like a long practical joke from God:

"When a man has an emission of seed, he shall bathe his whole body in water and be unclean until evening." (By my rough calculations, I've been unclean since the invasion of Grenada.)

"You shall not disgrace your father by having intercourse with your mother." (Don't fuck your mom. Good advice.)

"If a man has carnal relations with a female slave who has already been living with another man but has not yet been redeemed or given her freedom, they shall be punished but not put to death, because she is not free." (As always in the Bible, slavery is cool. Got it.)

"If a man commits adultery with his neighbor's wife, both the adulterer and the adulteress shall be put to death." (Yeah, but have they *seen* my neighbor's wife?)

"If a man lies with a male as with a woman, both of them shall be put to death for their abominable deed…" (Love your neighbor as yourself, but kill him if he's a goddamn homo. Understood.)

"A man or a woman who acts as a medium or fortune-teller shall be put to death by stoning…" (I'll have my pile of rocks at the ready next Halloween when some six-year-old dressed as the Wicked Witch of the West comes to my door and tries to get her satanic paws on my Reese's Pieces. "Trick or treat," she'll say, with that cute, sugar-edgy voice. "Happy Halloween," I'll reply in kind, only to raise my rock-filled fists of vengeance, shouting, "Death to the infidels!")

The Book of Leviticus's sage advice notwithstanding, I still thought about Laura.

Our group leaders woke us up at dawn on the last day of the retreat, April Fool's Day. Most of us had less than four hours of sleep under our belts. They were still pushing us nineteen hours later.

After midnight, they separated us into our small groups, sending each group into a private classroom in the old Latin School building. Our classroom was illuminated by a small circle of candles, with a crucifix in the middle of the circle. Our group leader asked everyone to take turns holding the crucifix and talking to Jesus. Slap happy and defenseless, we coughed up some serious shit.

The girl across the circle had a bad experience when she lost her virginity and had sworn to give up sex forever. Given that she was hot, I thought this was a rash decision. The guy to my left buried his infant brother two days before he got there, and this made me cry because I thought about Mom's miscarriages.

I was fucking exhausted. They broke me. I devolved into a lovesick pussy pining away for Laura. None of the guys in the room liked me for the rest of the night, while I was certain all the girls wanted to fuck me.

We had an extended farewell Mass the following morning, which pissed me off because Saturday morning was too early to count as Sunday service. Two priests, three guitars, and a triangle—they pulled out all the stops. We were each given a medal—a cheap chain that ended in a medallion resembling a German Iron Cross—and an American Bible Society mass market paperback edition of the New Testament entitled *Good News New Testament: Today's English Version*. We all signed each other's New Testaments, like a yearbook, adding a cliché sentiment or two.

There was the requisite exclamation point overkill:

> *Hank,*
>
> *You know you're such a special person! I say that because you opened up to total strangers! That takes guts, and I admire you! Stay as special as I know you are!*
>
> *Love! Leanne*

The not-even-close-to-subtle flirting:

> *Hank,*
>
> *You're such a charmer and sooooo cute. I only wish this wasn't the only time we could hang out. Good luck in whatever it is you do. Keep that charming personality.*

Peace & lots of Enjoyment, Samantha

The lone person with perspective:

Hank,

What's up, dude? Whew, glad we're done with this. I hope we'll go party together because I think it will be a unique experience. I need your phone number.

Friends, Pete

And then of course the big-breasted girl who read way too much into something I said to her during last night's séance because it afforded me multiple hugs and therefore multiple exposures to her enormous rack:

Hank,

I'm really glad I got an opportunity to get to know you because you're one heck of a person. If you ever need someone, I'm here and I hope we can keep a friendship going even after we leave here. It helped to know that you were going through the same thing with your girlfriend that I am with my boyfriend. We both obviously love them very much and I'm glad I didn't have to go through that by myself. Thanks a lot for being yourself.

Love, Theresa

P.S. I need to get something cleared up with you as soon as possible, OK? OK.

Yeah, about that. After the séance, Theresa and I may have snuck into Holy Rosary and made out in an empty confessional booth. And I may have gotten her top off and fondled her breasts for a solid half hour.

"Sounds like you had a good time despite yourself, Hank."

I hover over Mom's shoulder, peering down at the breakfast spread. "Yeah, I guess I did."

"Good," Mom says. "How does ham and eggs sound?"

"My favorite."

"I know."

I notice Mom is using leftover grilled ham steak, from last night's supper, no doubt. The ham harbors a distinct pineapple odor from the marinade. For me this is usually, to borrow some recently reacquired Vatican parlance, *victus non grata*. I don't mix my salts and sweets, ever. I make it a point to eat all my bacon or sausage before I put syrup on my pancakes, so as not to get syrup on the meat. I consider things like grapes in chicken salad and salt on watermelon affronts to my existence.

But I don't mind the pineapple flavored ham in my eggs, at least not today.

I watch as Mom cuts the ham into little squares and drops it in a skillet with a couple tablespoons of butter. She pauses every so often to stretch her back and give a slow, mournful rub to her belly. She thinks no one notices.

While the ham is sautéing, I beat three eggs and a quarter-cup of milk together. I hand the egg mixture to Mom, and she pours it over the ham. Ham and eggs was the first thing I ever learned how to cook. I was seven years old when I made it for Mom and Dad. I remember the harvest gold appliances, the ornate vinyl flooring, the trash compacter, and Mom and Dad not complaining about the large pieces of egg shell.

The phone rings. Mom points her spatula at me. "Can you get that? I'm guessing it's for you anyway."

I pick up the phone. "Hi, Hank."

"Laura? Hey there, baby." I try to temper my enthusiasm. "I didn't expect to hear from you this early."

"Yeah, well we drove straight through. Got in about three this morning. I couldn't really sleep."

"Poor thing," I say, more sarcastic than sympathetic.

We exchange a few forced pleasantries. I give her a hard time for not calling me since Wednesday and sending me one postcard the entire week. She talks about the days getting away from her and how she already wishes she could go back.

"Go back? But aren't you glad to—"

"Can you meet me in front of the library this afternoon?" Her tone is impatient.

"Not any sooner?" I ask.

"Look, Hank…" A pause on the other end of the line. "I'm going to try to get some rest, clear the cobwebs. I don't think my body can figure out whether it's hungover or still drunk."

"Three o'clock, then?"

"How about five thirty?"

"I guess I can wait 'til then. I love y—"

Laura hangs up on me.

I PARK THE SUBIE in front of the Empire Ridge Public Library. I'm early, so I wait in the lobby. As soon as I walk in, the receptionist, who I don't know but who of course recognizes me as "John's boy," says hello. Another loyal Oldsmobile driver. A Delta 88 looks about her speed.

I flip through the sports section of today's *Empire Daily,* and then glance at my watch. Laura is late. She's never late for anything. I'm already bothered that she hung up on me. And my cock still hurts from masturbating in the shower this morning. Twice.

I have this waterproof poster of a bikini-clad Brenda Dickson, the original Jill Foster from *The Young and the Restless*. With its special self-adhesive backing that sticks to wet surfaces, the poster has been my on-again, off-again bathing companion for a while now. The combination of Brenda's cleavage and knowing Laura was getting back from spring break gave me the rare dual orgasm—once early on, after having popped an erection the moment the oscillating spray hit me, and a second time a half hour later after I'd drained the house of all hot water.

Multiple single-session ejaculations in the shower, waxing sentimental about waterproof posters of soap opera stars…these things beg the question: why haven't Laura and I had sex yet?

I guess at some point in time over the last couple months, the awkwardness between us became safe. That line I was once all too ready to cross became a wall—a comfort zone behind which I retreated when things got too intense. We always got most of our clothes off. I always got my mouth on her breasts or my fingers inside her. And yet the nights always ended with me alone in a bathroom, trying to rub out a debilitating case of blue balls, my chastity preserved.

My chastity preserved? What the hell is my problem? I accrued more "hands-on" sexual experience by the time I was ten years old than most teenagers. I am the ultimate hormonally dysfunctional example of a Catholic upbringing that did not take. And I can't pull off something as simple as fucking a girl? What does my penis see in my left hand that it doesn't see in my girlfriend's vagina?

"Hey there, Hank."

Laura startles me. I smell traces of aloe and suntan lotion on the hand that grabs my shoulder. I turn to her. Her skin is bronzed, her cheeks sunburned, her nose peeling. Her hair is windblown, bleached sandy blonde by a week in the Panama City sun. She looks fresh off the beach: hair pulled back in a half ponytail, minimal makeup for her, no jewelry save for a large, white hemp bracelet on her left wrist. She's sexy as hell.

"Laura," I say, embracing her. She hugs me back, but it's cursory and cold, more like how my sister would hug me. As she backs away, I see him standing about ten yards back.

"You bring a friend?" My question is rhetorical. There's a lump in my throat. I feel sick.

"Hank, I'm sorry. It just kind of happened."

The "it" in our discussion is the asshole standing behind Laura. His name is Lee Barnes. I fucking know him! She didn't just hook up with some random guy—she hooked up with a Prepster.

"Lee Barnes?" I shout his name as if he isn't even there. "Lee fucking Barnes?"

"I couldn't just come back home and pretend nothing happened."

"Sure you could," I respond. "I did."

"And what's that supposed to mean?"

"You don't think I went to a retreat for my fucking salvation, did you?"

Laura seems offended by my candor. "What was her name?"

"Miss None Of Your Goddamn Business," I say. "I was in a church confessional with a pair of needy Catholic breasts in my face. You were with Lee Barnes. The end."

Truth is, I don't really know Lee Barnes. He's stocky, but still leaner than me. He has a square jaw and coal-black hair that looks to be permed rather than naturally curly. He used to date Tammy Dwyer, one half of the Dwyer sisters, gorgeous fraternal twins who rule the junior class at the Ridge. I had a crush on Tammy for the first two years of high school, although not so much now that she's become a chain smoker and whiskey drinker who dates guys partial to ripping out your spleen for even looking at her. Sammy is the sweeter of the two, the shrinking violet you'd throw yourself in front of a bus for. I'm protective of Sammy, even though we aren't all that close, at least not as close as I pretend we are. She was in my sophomore English class. We flirted. We still flirt, now that I think about it.

"Please, Laura." I hold back tears. Man, I am one enormous pussy. *Please?* Is that all I can come up with?

Laura, though noticeably flustered, is steadfast. She keeps her distance, committed to not giving any pretense of hope. "We're obviously no good for one another."

My voice cracks. "And when did that become a unilateral decision?"

"Please, Hank." Laura reaches out to me. She squeezes my arm, more calculating than compassionate. "You're still the sweetest guy I know."

"Sweet!" I give her a sarcastic thumbs-up. "Good to know I got that going for me."

Laura continues to hold on to my arm. "Don't say that." She gives my arm a patronizing shake. "Come on, guy. I'm a senior, you're a junior. You and I knew this was inevitable."

"Bullshit!" I wrench my arm out of her grasp. "You could have fucking clued me in on the inevitable part before I wasted the last four months of my life."

"They were special to me too, Han—"

"Don't you fucking say that!" My finger is in her face, almost touching her nose. "You've lost the right to say that."

"I'm sorry."

"You sure are fucking sorry."

"What do you want me to say?"

"What do you want *me* to say?"

All I can do is throw it back in her face. Laura wants to feel okay about what she's done. She wants absolution. Fuck her. I'm not her fucking priest. She isn't even Catholic. I'm not getting dumped by a slut—I'm getting dumped by a Protestant slut.

I finally turn my back on Laura after another profanity-riddled diatribe. By the time I settle down enough to face her again, she's halfway to Lee Barnes. He puts his arm around her. Just as they start to walk away he glances back at me with a smarmy look of satisfaction on his face. He tries to pull Laura in for a kiss, but she pushes him off. "Not now, Lee," she says.

Not now. I walk past the front passenger side of the Subie. I see the rose I brought for Laura in the front seat. I brought Laura a red rose, and she brought me a fucking pink slip.

Not now. I approach the rear of my car. A scene is looping in my head. Laura is naked, playing with her tits, pumping her bare ass up and down

Lee's shaft and screaming, "Now, now, now!" I cock my fist back and then bring it forward, straightening my arm as I hit the tailgate. I get my hips into it for good measure. I remove my hand to reveal a dent in the back hatch of my car. My knuckles are bleeding. I know Dad is going to be mad, but I don't think about that. I think about how much this hurts. And I'm not talking about my hand.

My stomach clenches. The ham and eggs come up in three rushes of bilious fluid. I drop to one knee and steady myself with my good hand. The vomit covers my shoes. It smells of ham, pineapple, and vinegar.

All I can think about is Laura's bare skin. The tears. The blood. The vomit. Her touch. Why can't I get a handle on this? She could turn around, walk up to me, reach down my pants and say, "One hand job for the road?" and I'd readily accept the invitation.

What the fuck is wrong with me?

CHAPTER TEN

Dad was cool about the dent, although I lied and told him I backed into a tree at the 7-Eleven. Monday at school was unbearable. I couldn't handle seeing Laura in the hallways—trading bronzed smiles and inside jokes with her girlfriends, all of them wearing their matching white hemp bracelets and airbrushed T-shirts reminding us all to "Never Forget Room two-oh-four." So, I got Mom to let me skip class on Tuesday.

No big deal. She'll walk into the office today and tell one of the deans, "Hank's not feeling well," and they'll mark me down as absent, no questions asked. She'll run into one of my teachers later and say, "I think he has that flu bug that's going around." Never mind we're a good three months beyond flu season. Mom has lied for me my whole life.

I'm so depressed I didn't even have the heart to masturbate this morning. I tried. I pulled the big guns out of my father's *Playboy* stash—the January Holiday Anniversary issue with Kimberly Conrad, the just opened April "Star-Studded Spring Spectacular" issue with Vanity. But nothing. Flaccid city.

I sit at the kitchen table. The smells wafting up from my stained white undershirt and torn jeans beg me in vain for a shower. I yawn, scratch my face. I've already started into Dad's Maker's Mark. I pick at the red wax on the bottleneck. I haven't eaten since Sunday, so I'm buzzing three drinks in. After about a dozen shots, I get bored with whiskey. My balls itch, so I scratch them. I unscrew the cap off the Popov, an inexpensive vodka packaged in a plastic half-gallon bottle. Evidently I'm not too drunk to get disgusted by cheap vodka. I gag after one shot. With nothing but an unopened bottle of vermouth left in my parents' liquor cabinet, my options are limited.

I remember the bottle under my bed.

I'm back at the kitchen table. I remove the family-size bottle of cough syrup from the plastic bag. I had bought it a couple weekends ago. Someone told me that drinking a whole bottle had the same effect on you as dropping acid. I figured I was still a couple years away from my serious experimentation phase, so I went to the drugstore and scored me some cough syrup.

I struggle with the top of the box for a few seconds before I rip the box in half. An empty bottle of whisky and a full bottle of vermouth bear witness to my inebriated struggle. I remove the bottle from the box. I push down and rotate the childproof cap with the palm of my hand and remove it. I notice my nails need trimming. Ten crescents of dirt work to pull back the childproof seal.

Improved taste promises the label on the bottle. I doubt the manufacturer anticipated someone drinking a full twelve ounces in one sitting when they were touting its palatability. My first swallow is a big one. I gag a little. The taste of so much cough syrup in my mouth is just as I imagined—stale maraschino cherries mixed with Listerine, only not as pleasant. The cough syrup is thick and warm on my throat.

My second swallow is almost as big. I already feel a little drunk from the alcohol. It takes me three more pulls at the bottle to finish the entire twelve ounces. I think about raiding the medicine cabinet, but I've heard a cough syrup buzz takes about a half hour to kick in. That gives me time to think about her. Too much time. My heart races. My chest hurts.

I STUMBLE DOWN THE upstairs hallway. How long has it been? A half hour? An hour, maybe? I feel like I'm rolling along the side of a wall. Did I chase that last swallow of cough syrup with vermouth? My mouth has a dry sweetness to it. Yep, vermouth. Definitely vermouth. I'm in Dad's closet now. I know where he keeps his gun.

The gun is on the top shelf to the left, beneath a stack of sweaters. I reach under the sweaters, feel the cold steel of the Smith & Wesson .357 Magnum. I bring the gun down to eye level, look at myself in the mirror as I hold the revolver to my head.

The gun isn't loaded. It's never loaded. Except for maybe once. That one time in Louisville when the basketball rolled into the log pile and a copperhead snake had coiled itself around the ball. Dad ran upstairs to his bedroom. It took him at least five minutes to find the bullets and load the gun. He came outside and blasted the snake—and the basketball—into oblivion.

I've pulled the gun out and looked at myself in the mirror holding it easily a hundred times. I don't even know where Dad keeps the bullets. I'm not angry. Just sad. Just thinking about what it would be like to pull the trigger for real. But not acting on it. I just want to be somewhere else.

MOM WAKES ME UP. My head is in a pool of saliva and bile on the kitchen table. "I'm fine, Mom." At least that's what I think I say. Judging by the look on Mom's face, my diction is less than precise.

Mom is no toastmaster herself. I can't understand a word she's saying. I giggle. "Whatever."

Mom leaves the room. Wait a second. Am I in a hospital? What the fuck? I thought I was in my kitchen. What happened to Dad's gun? I'm confused.

I hear voices outside the drawn curtain around my bed, bits and pieces of a conversation:

"His pupils are still very dilated…"

"He ingested a tremendous amount of alcohol…"

"…no telling what it's doing to his system."

"…stomach pumped."

"…stupid."

"…teach him a lesson."

"…father."

I don't know who's saying what. I try to concentrate. The more I relax and let it take over, the worse I feel. The room is rubbery, waxy, everything in it contracting and melting at the same time. I find a fixed spot—the wall clock—and stare at it.

Ten seconds… Twenty seconds… Thirty seconds… One minute…

Two minutes…

I talk myself off the ledge by the time Mom and Dad enter the room. An ugly nurse follows behind them carrying a metal tray. On the tray are two white plastic bottles and a large paper cup.

Mom approaches me, but Dad doesn't. She runs her hand through my hair. "How you feeling, honey?"

"Fine, Mom." I'm more sluggish than intoxicated by this point. "Really, all of this isn't necessary."

I catch the nurse out of the corner of my eye pouring one of the plastic bottles into the paper cup. A black, tar-like substance rolls out of the bottle. Dad walks over to the nurse and takes the cup. He turns, handing the cup to me.

I grab the cup. "What am I drinking here?"

She picks up the empty bottle and looks at the label as if she forgot why she was here. "It's activated charcoal in liquid form."

Dad bites his lip, nods his head, and exhales like he's been holding in a breath the whole time he's been in the room. "Bottom's up, son."

The nurse sets the bottle down. "It's not that bad, Hank. More or less tasteless, really."

I hold the rim of the cup to my lips and tilt it. The black ooze starts to roll down my tongue.

Yeah, nurse, if this shit is tasteless, you're attractive. The twelve ounces of cough syrup was impressive enough, but that's nothing compared to a nice room temperature cup of liquid charcoal. The concoction is slightly sweet and very gritty. It tastes as if someone mixed sand and melted black licorice. My teeth are soon charred black. I can't swallow.

Mom starts toward the door. Dad has already left.

CHAPTER ELEVEN

After the hospital discharged me, and after my fifth pure black shit in as many hours—which henceforth I shall refer to as The Great Black Butt Incident of 1988—I find myself walking down the hallway toward my bedroom. My body is covered in beads of sweat.

"How you feeling?" Mom asks, ascending the stairs with a cup of decaf in hand. She's wearing Dad's old blue robe, his initials "JHF" on the left lapel.

"I'm okay." I shrug. "One more stupid-ass stunt for you to tell the world about, I guess."

"Hank!" Mom says. She switches her cup of coffee to her opposite hand as her right hand grabs me by the elbow. "Is that what you call yesterday? A stunt?"

"Come on, Mom."

"You could have killed yourself!"

"Jesus Christ."

"I'm being very serious here."

"Glad to see someone cares."

"And what's that supposed to mean?"

"You tell me."

Dad hasn't spoken a word to me since he left my hospital room. He volunteered his trumpet at a Tuesday evening mass at St. Benjamins and then snuck out of the house early this morning for the dealership. And I noticed.

"What'd you expect, Hank?"

"Anything," I say. "Being pissed off as hell is better than no reaction at all."

"Oh, he reacted," Mom says. "You just didn't see it."

I roll my eyes. Mom squeezes my elbow harder. "Don't you for a second question your father's love," she says.

"Take it easy, Mom." I shake her hand loose.

She's crying now, her tears more angry than sad. "Do you have any idea what he said to the doctor yesterday?"

"What do you mean?"

"They were going to pump your stomach!" Mom shouts. "I think they wanted to teach you a lesson."

I'm quiet.

"And you know what your dad said?"

Still quiet.

"He looked that doctor straight in the eyes…"

My throat hurts a little.

"And he said, 'You stick to being a doctor, and I'll stick to being a father.'"

I look down at the floor's dark oak hardwood planks. You can see hundreds of footprint watermarks if you catch the floor in the right light. A casualty of living on a pond. Mom keeps saying she's going to carpet over everything. I wipe the sweat off my brow. The room is cooling down, the hangover passing.

"Dad really said that?" I say.

Mom sips her coffee, nodding. "Yep."

I don't know what to say next. My martyr complex is subtle, nuanced. It usually works for me. The eldest son, trying to live up to his father's expectations, woe is me—I can do the damn thing in my sleep. But Mom's bullshit meter is pretty sensitive today.

"Can I stay home one more day?"

Mom scowls, walks by me and into her room. She starts to shut the door behind her and then stops herself at the last second. She peeks through the crack. "Not a chance, mister." She shuts the door.

CHAPTER TWELVE

I'm the son of a car dealer, and I don't know a dipstick from a chopstick. I have a surprising disregard for automobiles in general.

I got my driver's license the Monday after my sixteenth birthday. By that Thursday, I had totaled my first car. It was the family car even—a brand-new '87 Oldsmobile Custom Cruiser station wagon with simulated wood grain paneling. I took a turn at about thirty-five miles-per-hour in a rainstorm, hit the sidewalk on my right, the median, and a Bradford pear tree on my left. I busted three of the four axles. I worked half the summer at the dealership pro bono to pay it off. And yet Dad still saw fit to give me Grandpa's restored '68 Oldsmobile 442 Coupe.

"The Beast" isn't your average Oldsmobile. A couple years back, Grandpa Fred traded it in for a newer Cutlass Supreme. Dad sent the old car over to the community college so the students could experiment on it. They had plenty to work with, most notably the 455 CID engine backed by a modified W-45 rated at 390 horsepower. In order to generate more rpms, they retrofitted her with cylinder heads from the W-30 and the camshaft from the W-31. They also installed new bucket seats and a Hurst Dual-Gate shifter in her walnut mini-console. Granted, I have no fucking clue if what I just said is accurate, but Dad kept a laminated copy of the'68 442 brochure in the top drawer of his office desk that I halfway memorized just so I would sound cool. The Beast's finishing touches were largely cosmetic: her deep-maroon paint job restored to its factory-original sheen, her faded vinyl top replaced with a textured black lid that smelled of shoe polish and great expectations. A white vertical stripe ran up both sides of the car just behind her front wheel wells, the number "442" bisecting the stripe like a watch on a watchband as if to say, "Time to get some pussy and kick some ass." If only Dad had not installed an obnoxious air horn that played the chorus to "In My Merry Oldsmobile," each note fractionally diminishing your pussy-getting, ass-kicking potential until you were just another lonely teenage boy with a cool car and a cramped hand.

Dad took the Beast away from me before the summer was even over. A doctor had run a stop sign in front of me. The police report and the insurance companies said he was at fault. No argument from me. But I could have been going a little slower than sixty-five down a residential street, and I could have let off the gas in lieu of cutting the good doctor's Honda Accord in half. Although it didn't look it, the Beast was almost as unlucky with a cracked engine block and a buckled frame.

The Subie is a fire-engine red '77 Subaru DL Station Wagon; her distinctive feature a massive white steel brush guard running the full width of her front bumper. I've had her almost a year. When we got our first real snow in December, some friends and I tested out the four-wheel drive by sneaking onto the airfield at the Empire Ridge Municipal Airport. We hit the iced-over runway at about sixty miles an hour, at which time I jerked the wheel hard to my left. The Subie stayed on her feet, but she slid off the runway a good hundred yards into a cornfield. I found random pieces of cornhusks under my car for weeks.

I have to hand it to the Subie. Up until a lovesick dumbshit tried to punch a hole in her ass last month, she's survived me fairly unscathed. Four of us are piled into her at the moment. There's a party tonight at Martin Neff's house. Neff is our age, but he lives with his older brother. Translation? Booze, and lots of it. There's even rumor of a keg.

"How's your hand?" Beth asks.

Hatch and I started hanging out with Beth Burke and Claire Sullivan a couple weeks ago. We've known them since we were freshmen together but, like all high school boys, endured our customary two-year waiting period during which freshmen and sophomore girls hang out exclusively with upperclassmen. The irony, of course, is that Hatch and I are now those upperclassmen making time for them *and* the freshmen and sophomore girls.

Our first night out together started after Claire flagged us down at McDonald's. Beth was trying to break up with her boyfriend in the parking lot of the First Baptist Church, and he was being, according to Claire, "uncooperative." Hatch and I swooped in to the rescue. Beth's boyfriend was berating her, refusing to get out of her face. Tyler was his name, yet another Prepster. After a couple veiled threats, spoken while I held a not-so-veiled baseball bat, Beth was soon very much single.

Hatch sits in the front passenger seat of the Subie. Beth and Claire sit in back. Beth sits behind me.

"How's my hand?" I echo.

Beth leans forward and points at my hand. "Yeah. How's it feel?"

I flex my fingers, but I know Beth's question is not exclusive to my hand. "I feel good."

The doggedness of youth. A plunger, a half bottle of peroxide, and a couple cute girls can repair your car, your hand, and your self-esteem.

We've been at the party maybe ten minutes, and Claire is already flirting with somebody from Prep, a hockey player I don't recognize. This annoys Hatch, because Claire is the great love of his life even though she'll never think of him as anything more than an annoying, overprotective brother.

I can see the attraction, not just to Claire but to her whole family. From top to bottom, Claire has inherited everything from her mother—smallish breasts, a tight ass, some slight curves below the waist, slender legs, long but delicate feet. Claire's sister is a year behind her in school and almost as hot. I've had several fantasies involving the three Sullivan women, the mother in a supporting role as her daughters' wise, and always naked, teacher.

Beth hasn't left my side. The music is turned low, as one would expect from a party of underage drinkers in the middle of town. Too bad. The song playing right now is Scorpions's "Rock You Like a Hurricane."

"Turn this shit up!" Martin Neff says. He's drunk and loud, but hey, it's his party. He cranks the volume, following it up with some air guitar. He sees me and toasts his beer to the ceiling.

I toast Neff back. "You fucking know it!" He rocks like a hurricane down the hallway.

Beth hooks my arm with her hand. "What was that all about?"

"Monsters of Rock."

"You got tickets?"

"Yeah, Neff and I, couple other guys."

"Who's playing?"

"Kingdom Come..." I pause for a sip of beer, halfway into my third drink already. "Dokken, Metallica, Scorpions, and Van Halen. Noon to midnight, baby."

"Kingdom Come?"

"Zeppelin cover band. Decent."

"Sounds exhausting."

"Exhaustingly kick ass." My bravado impresses no one, least of all Beth. "He's a genius, you know."

"Who, Neff?"

"No, Klaus Meine, Scorpions's lead singer."

"How so?"

"It's his vocals. The guy is a miraculous wordsmith." I lift a single finger in the air, turning my ear toward the stereo. "Hear that?"

"The chorus?"

"Not just any chorus. If you or I spoke the words, 'Here I am, rock you like you a hurricane,' it would sound clunky. And yet Klaus magically rhymes 'here I am' with 'hurricane.' A lot of Scorpions' songs are like this."

Beth indulges me. "Name another."

"How about 'Bad Boys Running Wild'?"

"Not familiar with the song."

"*Bad boys running wild*—bump bummmp—*if you don't play along with their geeeems*." I sing the Rudolph Schenker guitar to great effect. "*Bad boys running wild*—bump bummmp—*and you better get out of their weeee*."

"Is that even English?"

"That's Klaus Meine. Except in this example, the actual words *games* and *way* do kind of rhyme, and Klaus still molds them into completely new words—*geeeems* and *weeee*—not found in any language."

"And that makes him a lyrical genius?"

"A genius with a fucking killer skullet!"

"A skullet?"

"That's when someone with a receding hairline grows a mullet." I point to the balding thirty something standing by the stereo. "Like Big Neff over there."

Big Neff is Martin's much older half-brother. I can't recall his real name. His hair begins at a widow's point a good three inches back from his forehead and ends in a ponytail that runs down to his waist. If possible, his goatee is even worse, the mustache Burt Reynolds-thick but the beard uneven and growing in patches all the way down to his chest hair. Skullet or no skullet, Big Neff is a saint on Earth; he's purchased at least half the beer I've consumed in high school.

At the moment, Big Neff is pissed at Little Neff. "Shit, Martin. Why don't I just mount a neon sign on the roof saying, 'arrest our fucking asses'?"

Neff garbles something from the front porch. He's pissing on a bush. His brother disappears without a response. What the hell is his name anyway?

I NUDGE THE VOLUME back up again. No one notices. I pause before the fourth beer hits my lips. Beth is still standing next to me. She starts bouncing to the music. She looks bored.

"You don't have to babysit me. I'll be fine."

Beth's smile disappears. "Is that what you think I'm doing?"

"Well, I just figured that, you know…"

"I came out with you to have some fun, Hank." She yanks my fourth beer from my hand, takes about half of it down in one swallow, and leaves the other half on both our shirts. "And have some fun is exactly what we're going to do."

"Did someone say *fun*?"

It's Hatch. He has in his hands an unopened fifth of Jim Beam and a shot glass. I respond with a mock puking noise.

"Relax, Fitzy. I brought us a chaser. Fire in the hole!" Hatch zips a two liter of Mountain Dew at me. It hits me in the balls, as was intended.

"Hatch…" I gasp for air. "You're a fucking dick."

The unrecognizable Prep hockey player and Claire join us. Claire sits on the hockey player's lap. This bugs the shit out of Hatch. He drinks two shots of Beam for no apparent reason other than the jealousy he wears on his sleeve like an oversized cufflink.

"Scoot back." Beth turns her ass to me and starts to bend over.

A fifth of whiskey between five people is just enough to be dangerous. I'm not full-on wasted, but I'm getting there. "What?"

"I said scoot back. Let me sit on your lap."

I like Beth, a petite but athletic blond, five feet tall, and a full four or five inches shorter than Laura. She has an omnipresent smile framed by high cheekbones and straight blonde hair taht ends just below the small of her back. She's more cute than sexy, more natural than made-up. Whereas

Laura's bare skin, though tanned, hides behind a sheen of cosmetics, Beth has to remind herself to put on makeup. She's a state champion gymnast, as advertised by her figure—small but firm breasts, noticeable hips and rounded buttocks, muscular thighs, and obscenely defined calves.

I push my chair away from the table. I nod to Beth, bowing almost. "I'm all yours."

Hatch suggests a game of euchre to Claire. "Fitzy and I versus you two."

The hockey player and Claire move to opposite sides of the table. Beth's ass remains attached to my lap.

Hatch peels the beer-sodden cards off the table. He and I exchange the barest hint of a smirk. Nobody catches it but me. *Well played, my friend.*

We're up 2–0 before I even know what's happening. The hockey player, whom we've now identified as Bobbie, comes out of the gates way too aggressive. Hatch turns up the nine of hearts. Bobbie orders him up, gets euchred with the first three tricks.

Bobbie looks at Claire. "I was two-suited with the left and the queen. You'd think I could count on my partner for one."

Claire does not appreciate the condescension, and Hatch notices. "Or in this case, Bobbie, two or three," he says, handing the deck of cards over to Claire. He smiles at her. She smiles back. Claire shuffles the deck, offering a cut to Hatch.

"No, thanks. I trust you."

Another exchange between friends, only this time Hatch and I are more obvious about it. I have a legitimate smirk on my face. *Nicely played again.* Claire turns up a jack of hearts. I have a crappy hand: one low trump and an ace of hearts, plus an off-suit ten, queen, and jack. My best bet is to see what my partner has, or else hope it goes around again and maybe bait Bobbie into making it diamonds, smack him with another euchre, or else call black for my partner.

I don't really care about my hand. All I care about is that Beth is dry humping me.

"What do you call, Hank?" Claire says.

"What?"

She takes a shot of Jim Beam, wipes her mouth with the back of her hand that's holding her cards. "I said, what's your call?"

Maybe it's the whiskey, but I missed a lot during that first game of euchre. I missed Beth sliding her ass a little farther back into me. I missed her propping her foot against the table leg. I missed her pushing against the table leg with her foot. I missed her relaxing her foot. *Push and relax.*

Bobbie is irritated, too. "Hank, do you want to fucking pass or pick it up?"

Push and relax.

All I know is I want out of this game. Beth looks at my cards, contemplates. It's an awful hand: no trump, no support, no nothing. "Your call," I say.

"Hmm..." Beth says, pushing against the table leg and holding this time, while rotating her ass harder into me. "I think we'll—"

"Pick it up!" I shout, my raised shot glass affirming my transparent conviction.

Push and relax.

Hatch's eyes open wide. "Really? You sure about that, Fitzy?"

Push and relax.

Bobbie leers at Hatch. "No fucking table talk."

Push and relax.

Hatch almost pulls the hand out all by himself. But Bobbie drops the hammer down on the fifth trick.

"Euchre, bitches!"

THAT'S HOW THE NEXT five games went. A few whiskey shots, me going out of my way to lose hands. *Push and relax.* A few more whiskey shots, Hatch growing despondent with my recklessness. *Push and relax.* Bobbie and Claire were in the barn, up 9–2 and only one point away from victory, when the whiskey ran dry. Hatch dealt himself a loner to get the game to 9–6. *Push and relax.* Claire turned up another red jack, this one a diamond. *Push and relax.* I had no diamonds in my hand and looked at Beth, who saw my cards, squeezed my knee, and shouted, "Pick it up!" We were predictably euchred in the first three tricks. Beth and I were already halfway out the front door as Hatch yelled behind us, "What the fuck did you call that on?"

We walk toward the Subie. Beth hooks her arm inside mine again. I struggle with my keys, dropping them on the ground.

Neither of us is in any shape to drive, but that's not the plan. Beth picks up the keys and unlocks the front door. She opens the door, reaches around, and unlocks the back door. We hop into the back seat together. I still have one foot outside the car when she kisses me.

Beth is a much more aggressive kisser than Laura. Laura was always frugal with her tongue. Beth's tongue is all over the place. Laura's kisses were light, uncertain. Beth's lips are strong, committed. She smells like lavender.

This isn't Beth's first time in the backseat of a car. She grabs my left hand and shoves it under her shirt. She slides my hand up to her right breast. My thumb grazes her left nipple, and Beth moans between kisses. I open my hand, encompassing her small breast, and slide my fingers underneath her bra strap. Something bites me.

"Ouch!" I jerk my hand out of her shirt.

"What's the matter?" Beth leans forward, panting a little.

"I pinched my finger on your underwire thingy…" I'm panting, too. "On your bra."

"Oh, is that all?" Beth reaches inside her shirt and behind her back with both hands. She brings her hands forward, her bra in her right hand. "Is that better?"

I nod, smirking more than smiling. We start kissing again. Beth is playful, nothing at all like Laura.

"Okay, you fucking horndogs!"

Hatch's timing, as usual, sucks.

Claire says she hasn't been drinking, which is a lie. I let her drive anyway. She and Hatch are screaming at each other in the front seats. Hatch caught her making out with Bobbie on the kitchen table.

Beth nibbles on my ear. She reaches down with her left hand to my crotch.

"What are you doing?" I ask.

"Relax. They're too drunk and pissed off to even know we're back here." Beth unfastens my pants. Her index finger teases the elastic of my boxers.

She reaches inside my underwear and takes me in her hand. I'm hard. I've been hard since that first game of euchre. Beth slides her hand up and down, stopping at both ends to rub the tip of my cock and squeeze my balls.

Beth's kisses are rougher now. She bites my tongue a couple times. Her breasts are smashed up against me. I come in minutes.

We pull into Beth's driveway. Claire slams her car door while telling Hatch to fuck off. Beth kisses me goodbye, with just a hint of tongue.

"I'd walk you to your door, but…you know."

Beth gets out of the car. She shuts the door, leans in, and kisses me on the cheek, smiling. "Yeah, I know."

Hatch drives us back to my house. My underwear is unsalvageable. I'm reluctant to shower, comforted in a perverse way by sitting in my own aftermath.

Hatch tries to collapse on the family room sofa, but I drag him down a flight of stairs to the ugly red, brown, and white convertible couch that used to be in my Grandpa George's living room.

I strip down to nothing, wrap my boxers in newspaper, and stuff them in the garage trash can. I go upstairs to shower in the laundry room shower. I hate that shower, all cramped and smelling like my Grandpa George's urine. The water pressure is anemic thanks to a newly installed energy-saver showerhead. But the other shower is upstairs, and I've given up my room to the still-hypothetical nursery to avoid these potential drunken encounters.

Not that I'm drunk, at least not anymore. The warm water helps, but my tolerance is getting ridiculous. I dry off, wrap a towel around my waist, and tiptoe across the main floor of the house. I open the door to the basement, but not before the stairway light catches a pile of mail on the kitchen table. On top is a letter addressed to me with no return address. But I recognize the handwriting.

I grab the letter. If Hatch were awake he'd tell me, "Burn that son of a bitch." My towel falls to the floor. Expectant and naked, with maybe a hint of another erection, I open the envelope.

Dear Hank, it begins, *I miss you...*

CHAPTER THIRTEEN

I pull into the library parking lot. Laura is already there in the silver Oldsmobile Calais her parents bought from my dad. The "Fitzpatrick Oldsmobile-Cadillac-Subaru" license plate frame on the back of the car almost dares me to be nice to her.

No fucking way that's happening.

I get out of the Subie. Its dented rear hatch does its best to remind me I'm still dented as well. I step over to the passenger side door of Laura's car. I open the door and sit down without waiting to be invited.

"Fancy meeting you here again," I say.

"Hi, Hank," Laura says. She looks like she's been crying.

I swear, she's leaning in to hug me. I shrink back toward the door. The car feels small, even for a Calais. Laura is wearing that white denim miniskirt that hugs her ass. The remnants of her Florida tan have faded into a soft glow. I've missed her smell. I've missed hearing her voice. We broke up a month ago, and it's as if that month never happened, and all because she said, *Hi, Hank*?

Holy fucking Christ, this was a bad idea.

"Laura." I nod. That's more like it. My tone is short, assured. Not even a "hi" or "hello."

Laura backs away. She squeezes her steering wheel as if to steady herself. "You hungry?"

"Excuse me?"

"You want to go somewhere for dinner?"

"Why would I want to do that?"

"Just asking."

"Look, Laura. I didn't come here for dinner or a date or whatever it is you have rolling around in that fucked-up head of yours."

"Fair enough. I guess I had that coming."

"You guess?"

"Okay, I deserve every mean and cruel thing you plan on saying to me. Is that better?"

"No, but you're getting there. And please save the martyr bit for somebody who gives two shits about you."

I set the over–under for when she'd start crying at two minutes. I nail the under without even trying. I don't feel as good as I thought I'd feel when I see her cry. In fact, I don't feel good at all.

Laura pulls a tissue out of her pocket and blows her nose. "I might deserve every awful thing you plan on saying to me, Hank. But that doesn't mean it feels good to hear you say them."

The temptation to pile it on is just too great. "You want a fucking medal?"

"You son of a bitch. I still love you!"

"Oh, shut the fuck up!"

It's the loudest I've ever raised my voice to a woman. I'm poking her in the shoulder before I even know what I'm doing. "You've lost the right to cuss me out. And you've certainly lost the right to love me."

"Do you love me?"

Laura is fast on the trigger. "Do I *what*?"

"Do you still love me?"

"Did I ever?" Answering questions with questions. Smart strategy, Hank. Keep her on the defensive.

"You said I was your first true love."

"And you were." Well played again, throwing a confident, positive answer her way, conveying the sincerity of your feelings without betraying the weakness of your convictions.

"Then I think you're the cruel one here, Hank."

"How do you figure?"

"Because if I was good enough to be the first girl you ever loved…" Laura grabs my poking hand before I can pull it away. "Why can't I be good enough to be the first girl you ever gave a second chance?"

Fucking shit. Where'd that come from? Here I am just trolling the waters, and she goes and harpoons my ass. *Why can't I be good enough to be the first girl you ever gave a second chance?* Either that's the most brilliant line I've ever heard, or Laura is for real.

"Laura, I-I can't…I can't do, whatever this is we're doing."

"Here, take this." She hands me a mix tape and tells me what's on it. She reiterates some of her letter—how she was watching the video to Gloria Estefan's "Anything for You" and broke down in tears at the *But don't you ever think that I don't love you, that for one minute I forgot you* part. How she was working out the day after we broke up, and after hearing Boston's "We're Ready," knew she'd made a mistake.

I laugh. My laughter is loud—almost too loud, like I'm trying too hard.

"What's so funny?" Laura asks.

I keep laughing. I lean back into my seat, reach back, and squeeze the headrest. "So, what you're saying is that me telling you I loved you was never enough. You needed to hear it from Gloria Estefan and Tom Scholz before you were convinced."

"That's not what I'm saying at all, Hank."

"The hell it isn't."

"The hell it is. Don't you see that all I want is for us to be—"

I cut her last sentence off. When all else fails, kissing a girl shuts her up faster than anything else.

CHAPTER FOURTEEN

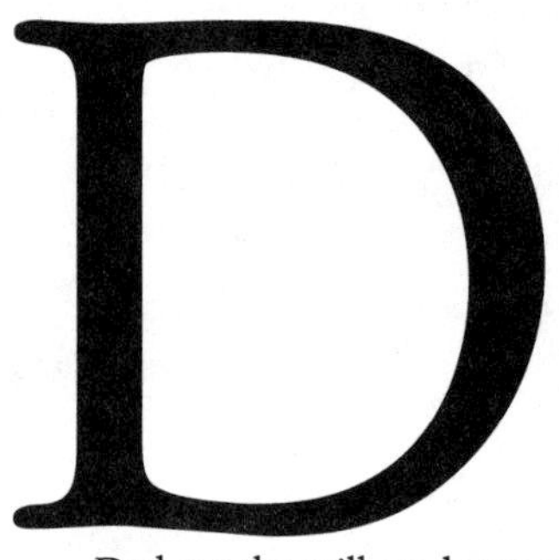
ad leans against the willow tree stump in our backyard, in the middle of his post-run stretch. He's wearing running shorts and an old Adidas tank top. A sweatshirt, a fishing pole, and a foam cup of grubs sit at his feet. He presses his hands onto the stump, arms straight, one foot forward, and one foot back, keeping his back leg straight with his heel on the ground.

Dad cut the willow down at the end of our first summer in the house. He said he was tired of tripping over its roots and having to deal with its constantly shedding limbs. But if the sun hits him just right when he's shirtless, you can make out the faint scars on his back from when Grandma Eleanor took a switch to him as a child.

My father has the pronounced calves of a marcher-turned-runner. Mom once even said, "I married your father for his calves." I don't know whether it's ironic, hereditary, or just weird, but calves are the first thing I notice in girls, too. Calves can make or break the deal for me. I don't ask for much—a slight athletic curve about halfway down the calf, the mere suggestion of something beyond just weekend laps around the mall. Not too skinny, so waifish eating disorder types need not apply, but not too big either, especially those thick, knee-to-feet, vintage Catholic nun "cankles."

Okay, that's weird.

The air has a cold edge to it. Dad puts his sweatshirt back on. He's owned this sweatshirt, hooded and navy blue with "Notre Dame" scrolled in faded orange-yellow across the chest, as long as I can remember. I had a matching sweatshirt when I was about five or six years old, back when Dad and I used to bundle up for our early morning walks on his aunt's tobacco farm in Kentucky. At the end of our walks, we'd sometimes spend hours at a time just sitting in the barn. Black and white dairy cows would poke their heads around the barn door to say hello. Tomcats would chase mice across the straw-covered floor. There would be rows upon rows of sweet-scented tobacco leaves curing in the rafters.

I miss those childhood years; those years when in the depths of quietness the world seemed to talk to me more.

"You're up early, son."

"It's a big day." I yawn, stepping off the porch. Our lawn slopes into the water, so I walk sideways toward my father. I hold two cups of black coffee in my hands.

"Big day as in the first day of your last week as a junior?"

"No." I hand Dad his coffee. "My first day as a senior."

"How so?"

"It's kind of a loophole. The seniors get the last week of school off, so the juniors get a head start—"

"At being prima donnas?"

The old man is sharper then I give him credit for. "Exactly, Pops."

Dad finishes his calf stretches. He stands straight up and then crosses his feet. He sets down his coffee, reaches for his toes. A noticeable grunt.

The grunting is something new with him—when he stretches, when he stands up after lying down on the couch, or after a long car ride. I've never perceived Dad or Mom as old or even getting old. Grandparents are old, parents are just...well, parents.

"Still battling those shin splints?"

"Just a little tight. How you doing these days?"

"My shins are fine."

"That's not what I meant, smart aleck."

Smart *aleck?* Early morning. Fishing poles. Black coffee. Grunting. Only my father and his uncompromising sense of goodness can throw out an *aleck* when the sheer maleness of the moment all but requires an *ass.*

"I figured that wasn't what you meant. I'm doing great."

"Really?"

The man looks unconvinced. I've been pretty discreet. Haven't I? "Yeah, Dad. Couldn't be better."

"I'll take your word for it."

Dad picks up the fishing pole and an unopened plastic baggie of fake worms. He breaks open the bag. The sound of crinkling plastic reminds me of Uncle Mitch and his Merits. I smell smoke, even though there isn't any.

"Something on your mind, son?"

"You hear from Uncle Mitch lately?"

"What makes you ask that?"

"He left town in kind of a hurry."

"Just one of those things, I suppose," Dad says. "He got a job offer on the other side of the country the same day Aunt Ophelia served him with annulment papers. Guess he just needed a clean start."

"And you're okay with that?"

"Looks like I have to be."

Just as when Uncle Mitch called him to say he was moving, Dad seems remorseless, cold even.

"Dad, everything all right?"

He raises his chin and takes a deep breath, almost as if he's caught a scent. "You think you know people, and then…"

"And then what?"

Dad is silent. I can't read his face. I don't know if he's searching for the words or refusing to search. He threads the fishing line into the eyehook on the end of the plastic worm.

"Dad?"

"Ahh, don't listen to your old man." He casts out his line. "Time to see what's biting this morning."

The implication here is that today's catch might be some big mystery, but both Dad and I know he has a 125 percent chance of catching a bluegill. Twenty years of hand-feeding has mollified these fish—the near-literal manifestations of fish in a barrel. And yet the bluegills thrive, overwhelming the pond, eating the hatchlings of the largemouth bass and crappie trying to hide in its deeper locales.

I start to make my way back to the house. Dad reaches out, grabs me by the arm. "Hey, you don't want to at least wait for the first catch?"

"No thanks, Dad. Gotta go get dressed, pick up some people."

He flicks the pole, reels in the line a couple feet. "At least wait a few minutes."

"Where's Grandpa?"

"Still in bed."

"His hip?"

"His hip, his knees, his blood pressure, his cholesterol—take your pick."

A small moment of recognition. "He's not going down without a fight, Dad."

Dad nods, gazes out across the water. Our house sits on the north side of the pond. The location affords us a nice view, especially now with the sun dropping lower in the sky on summer's eve.

"Seeing your grandpa go downhill so fast is tough to watch," he says. "I feel so powerless."

I pat him on the shoulder. "You're doing all that you can, Dad."

"Am I?" he asks. "My hope and prayer for you is that you never have to see me like that, after life has beaten me down."

"Speaking of down," I say, pointing to the red-and-white bobber dipping below the surface. "Looks like you got one."

CLAIRE LIVES IN MY neighborhood, so I picked her up first. Beth was next, then Hatch. The Subie ferries us to McDonald's to meet the rest of the seniors, or at least the ones that matter.

It's been an interesting few weeks leading up to today. Prom was awkward at best. A complex confluence of events led me to take the Johnson County Fair Queen as my date. Not that complex—Laura had ripped my heart out of my chest cavity and thrown it in a Cuisinart, Beth had said yes to her ex-boyfriend Tyler before they broke up and didn't have the heart to back out, and Dad's sales manager at the dealership had a hot seventeen-year-old daughter who happened to be the Johnson County Fair Queen.

Zoe Applefeld had above-average calves, she was one hell of a dancer, and I was certain she'd have slept with me if I had asked her. What is the proper etiquette in regards to losing your virginity to daughters of your father's employees anyway? We got drunk after prom, stayed out all night, split a plate of biscuits and gravy at Bob Evans, and I kissed her goodbye sometime around 8:00 a.m. The kiss was more innocent than I wanted it to be, just a quick peck on the lips, although I did try to pry open her teeth with my tongue. I'm a giver.

"Thanks for choosing McDonald's this morning, May I take your order?"

I recognize the cashier's bad bowl cut and pencil-thin mustache. His name is Chip Funke. He's in our class. Nice guy but keeps to himself at school and plays trombone in the band. A little on the delusional side—drives go-karts on the weekends, talks about one day winning the Indy 500.

"Morning, Chip."

"Oh, hi there, Hank."

"You plan on going to school today?"

"I pulled a twelve-hour shift last night. Thought I'd stay and help the morning crew before I head out."

"That's mighty charitable of you. How's the racing going?"

"Doing pretty well in three-quarter midgets."

"Does that involve race cars or actual midgets that are seventy-five percent as tall as normal midgets?"

"Shut up, Hank. What do you want to eat?"

"I'm just fucking with you, Chip. Egg McMuffin and a coffee, please."

Hatch orders two sausage biscuits and a Coke. Claire and Beth both just order coffees, their appetites curbed by the most popular of high school diet pills, cigarettes. Claire, Beth, Hatch, and I sit at our regular booth in the far corner of the restaurant. The Dwyer twins sit a couple booths away with their boyfriends.

"Tammy, Sammy."

"Hi, Hank!" Their Prepster boyfriends don't even raise their heads to look at us. Hatch and I call them "Steff-1" and "Steff-2," in honor of their feathered hair, glassy eyes, expensive suits, and cotton shirts unbuttoned down to their navels that were more than a little derivative of James Spader's character in *Pretty in Pink*. Steff-1, Tammy's boyfriend, is the guy who likes to rip out spleens. Steff-2, Sammy's boyfriend, has slept around behind Sammy's back for almost their entire relationship.

Beth looks at all of us. "I can't believe we're seniors."

Claire nods. "This year is going to be one to remember."

"I plan on not remembering much of it." Hatch laughs. He passes the invisible baton to me. "How about you, Fitzy?"

"Umm..." I can't think of anything to say, which of course means I'm about to say everything. Even better, I'll probably phrase it as a question, as if to mitigate the moment with uncertainty.

"Laura and I are back together?" The sound of a cash register...

Thanks for choosing McDonald's this morning. May I take your order...

The cash register again…

Your order number is fifty-seven…

"What?" Hatch slams his hands on the table. "You've gotta be fist fucking me."

Claire shakes her head. "Unbelievable."

"Seriously, Fitzy." Hatch grabs my shoulder, squeezing. "You better be yanking my chain, or else you can just go suck a fat baby's dick."

I try to ignore Hatch's metaphor onslaught. I stare at Beth. She hasn't said anything.

Number fifty-five…

I look at the receipt in my hand. "That's us." My eyes do a quick back-and-forth glance from Beth to the cash register. She picks up on the hint, stands up, and walks with me.

"Well?" I say to Beth.

"Well, what?"

"You okay?"

"W-when did this…" She stutters, her first hint of recognition.

"It didn't all of a sudden happen. Laura sent me a letter a few weeks ago. We talked. And it just sort of went from there."

I leave out the details of course. About our stolen smiles and "accidental" bumps in the hallways that each became a new promise to one another. About every forbidden late night rendezvous that by day could turn me into a social pariah. About every after-hours phone call made after Mom fell asleep so she wouldn't know I was again talking to the girl who reduced her little boy to a pool of liquid charcoal and self-pity. About my desperate attempt to erase the pain, rationalizing that love and anguish just went hand-in-hand.

"Did you see her before or after that night we—"

"After, definitely after." I grab the tray off the counter.

"You sure?" Beth's eyes narrow, testing me, trying to catch me in a lie. I'm not lying, but she overestimates her ability to tell one way or the other. I'm a very good liar.

I throw a handful of ketchup packets onto my tray. Beth follows with some creamers and sugars. I sense some disbelief.

"Beth, I think you know me well enough by now. I swear to you, I thought Laura and I were done. I got the first letter from Laura, the one that said she wanted me back, right after you and I hooked up."

"That same night?"

"Yes, I'm talking minutes after we dropped you and Claire off at your house."

"Jesus, Hank, that was like six weeks ago. Have you two been back together ever since?"

"More or less."

"Is that why you've been so weird lately? Why you haven't been returning my calls?"

"I'm sorry."

"What are you apologizing for?"

"I-I don't know." My turn to stutter. "You know, you and I, w-we..."

"You and I weren't ever a couple, if that's what you're getting at."

We sit back down at the table. I ready my concession speech. "Guys, don't think for a second anything's going to change this summer. We're still going to have a blast." My tone conveys the opposite of my original intent, like I'm trying to convince myself more than anybody else. But they play along. That's what friends do.

Claire reaches across the table and squeezes my hand. "You bet we're going to have some fun."

Hatch slaps me on the back. "Even if I have to drag your whipped ass out of the house to do it."

Again, Beth is quiet. She's tying a discarded straw wrapper in multiple knots. She looks past us, out the window.

I catch myself staring at her for the second time this morning. As good as Beth looks in a gymnastics leotard, never mind her bikini, her usual wardrobe reads like someone in a witness protection program, like those *National Enquirer* photos of movie actresses who go out in public in old sweat suits, baseball caps, and sunglasses. Most of the time, at least when she's sober, Beth doesn't want to be noticed. Like this morning, a blue jean miniskirt that's more maxi than mini, and an unflattering long-sleeved rugby shirt untucked and draped halfway to the end of her skirt.

But there's something about Beth—if not a confidence, a boldness to her. She never asks to be taken too seriously. She has a hellion side to her personality. About seventy-two ounces of barley and hops separate the girl who drove your grandfather to Sunday night bingo from the girl who'll give you a hand job in the backseat of your car. She's a refreshing change from Laura, who tends to grow detached and sullen in direct proportion to the number of drinks she consumes. With Laura, there's just so much emotion—too much emotion—tied up in even the smallest of affections. In a lot of meaningful ways, Beth is the antidote to Laura.

Whoa. Did I just think that?

"Hank?"

I'm busted. How long have I been staring at her? "Yeah, Beth?"

She discards the straw wrapper and grabs a napkin. She reaches up to my face and wipes a piece of egg off the corner of my mouth. She smiles. "Something on your mind?"

"Nope." I shake my head. "Nothing at all." I'm a very good liar.

CHAPTER FIFTEEN

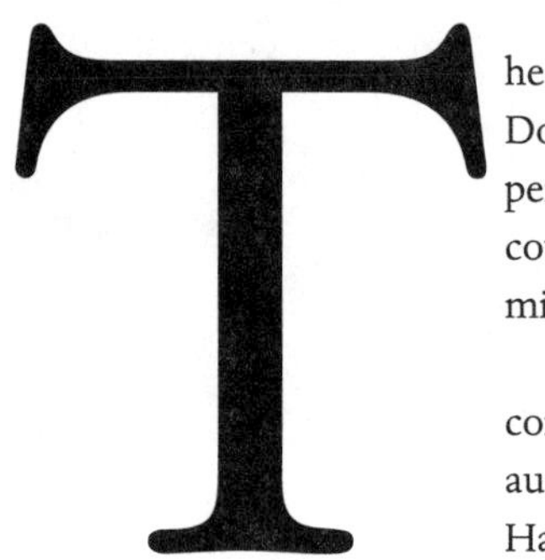he Monsters of Rock. Kingdom Come, Dokken, Metallica, Scorpions, and Van Halen performing consecutively on stage over the course of twelve straight hours from noon to midnight.

Halfway into Dokken, I traded my concert tee for a few joints. The shirt looked authentic—black and red, flying "VH" Van Halen logo on the front, tour dates on the back—but it was a cheap knockoff I got in the parking lot for five bucks.

The weed isn't a cheap knockoff. Fifteen rows up on the second level of the Hoosier Dome, through the soupy haze of tobacco and marijuana smoke, I'm pretty sure Metallica has just come off an extended version of "Sanitarium."

James Hetfield steps to the front of the stage, long stringy hair, goatee, pitted face, wearing black from head to toe. He pumps his fist in the air, grabs the microphone. "Fuck yeah!"

Sixty-seven thousand fists raised in unison respond, "Fuck yeah!"

"I hope you fucking know that we're just getting fucking started, because..."

Cue Kirk Hammett on guitar...

Camera two on about sixty-seven thousand bobbing heads... Camera one back on James... Go James, go...

"I got something to say-ayyy!!!"

Metallica's signature cover of the Misfits's "Last Caress/Green Hell" sends the crowd into a chorus of frothing-at-the-mouth shouts. The careening, paralyzing, manic headbanging is a perfect accompaniment to the song's affirming themes of killing babies, raping mothers, and cold, sweet death.

Mom and Dad gave me a free pass for the night. Knowing the concert wasn't supposed to end until midnight, they said, "Call us sometime later just to let us know you're okay, and be home before we wake up in the morning."

My parents' misplaced trust stems from my grades—straight As for the semester, again. Tonight is their reward for me "keeping my head in the game despite everything." Logic dictates a kid that smart can't simultaneously be that stupid. But then again, logic has nothing to do with drinking a six-pack of beer and most of a fifth of whiskey, followed by three joints and a hit off an opium pipe administered by a biker chick who wanted to take my "cute little ass" home with her.

Van Halen squeezed out an anticlimactic twelfth-hour encore that sent us home mute, deaf, drunk, and stoned. Kent Hagen invited us to his apartment for a post-concert party, his invitation made more enticing by the fact that Neff and I were too fucked up to argue or consider our other options. That, and our car was parked in front of Kent's apartment.

Kent's party is like any high school party in which you don't know anyone, hovering between cool and alienating. Kent used to live in Empire Ridge, but he moved up to Indianapolis after his freshman year. Some of Kent's Indy friends have been there all night—a couple of freakishly tall black dudes from the North Central High School basketball team, and a handful of girls way out of my league. Kent and Neff and their feathered heads of parted-down-the-middle hair entertain from behind the bar, serving weak drinks and even weaker jokes. As if a half-day of their music wasn't enough, a Kingdom Come-Dokken-Metallica-Scorpions-Van Halen mix tape plays on the stereo.

I've been alternating between waters and Diet Coke for at least an hour. I'm still pretty drunk. I think I already called my parents. I know I called somebody when I got here.

There's a knock at the door.

Kent turns down the stereo. "Who is it?"

Another knock.

Not a one of us in the apartment is eighteen, let alone twenty-one. I remind myself that this is the west side of Indianapolis, a place where underage drinking ranks somewhere beneath armed robbery, drive-by shootings, and good ol' fashioned homicide on the list of things cops have to worry about.

"It's Laura," the disembodied voice says. "Is Hank here?"

Kent throws me a look, his feathered bangs, furrowed brow, and thin mustache running in almost parallel lines across his face. He opens the door. "You about gave me a heart attack."

"Sorry, Kent." Laura sees me over his shoulder and flashes me a dimpled smile. She's wearing her favorite white miniskirt with a teal off-the-shoulder sweater, matching teal socks, and white flats. Her hair, its Florida gold taunting me still, is teased out to her shoulders.

Laura approaches me. "So you're the one I called?" I say, smiling a little too hard.

Her lips are on mine before I know what's happening. Our kiss is long, wet, and tactless, right there in the middle of the living room. Laura kisses me hard, her teeth biting and pulling my bottom lip as she backs away from me. She smells of peach schnapps.

"Yeah, I'm the one you called." She kisses and bites me again.

Kent slams the front door. "Get a room, you two."

We force a laugh but keep kissing.

"No, seriously." Kent pushes us toward the stairs. "Go to my room. Top of the stairs. Second door on your left."

I turn to Kent, letting go of Laura. "Thanks, Kent, but we're fine right here. Aren't we, babe?"

I look up and notice my girlfriend is gone. She's already at the top of the stairs.

Laura locks the door behind us. The room is dark. We feel our way to the corner of the room and start to sit down on what I hope is a bed. I hear a cracking sound and jump up, startled. "What the hell was that?"

"Your back pocket."

"My what?"

"Something's in your back pocket." Laura walks behind me, her left hand on my shoulder. She stands between me and the bed, pulling Scorpions's *Savage Amusement* cassette out of my back pocket.

"Shit," I say.

"No worries." Laura holds the cassette up to me for inspection. "You just cracked the case. Tape is fine." She throws the cassette on the bed. In one fluid motion, her lips are on my ear and her left hand drops down the front of my pants.

Laura runs her hand up and down between my legs. She rubs it a little. I don't know what to do next. I push her down toward the bed.

"Not so fast." She bites me for a third time, this time on the ear. She grabs my Scorpions tape, walks around me to the stereo on the opposite corner of the room. My eyes are still adjusting to the darkness. A mini-blind wraps Laura's silhouette in horizontal stripes of moonlight. She pulls off her shirt and reaches back to unfasten her bra with one hand, her back still to me. She pops in *Savage Amusement,* presses play, and spins on the ball of her right foot to face me, bare-chested. Her breasts seem to stare at me, but only briefly. She crosses her arms in front of her chest from force of habit—hiding what she regards as more blight than beautiful.

I acknowledge and counter her insecurity. "You're hot, you know that, right?"

"You're just trying to get in my pants."

"Maybe, but you're still smoking hot. I hate to break this to you, but I'm very superficial. If you were ugly, I wouldn't go out with you."

That gets a smile out of her. She drops her arms by her side. "You know just what to say to a girl, don't you?"

Her breasts are staring at me again, like the cover of *Exotic Music of the Belly Dancer*. For a second, I see only my longtime headless companion. Things seemed so much easier when she didn't have a face.

My cock is so hard it hurts. Same with my balls. At this rate, I'm not going to even get the damn thing out of my pants.

"Are you sure, Laura?" I ask.

"Yes, Hank," she answers. "I'm sure."

Laura approaches the bed to the tune of "Don't Stop at the Top," the first song on the *Savage Amusement* album. One of my favorites. She is already stripped down to her cotton panties and her teal socks. In my drunken and bumbling state, I'm still clothed from head to toe.

"Allow me," Laura says. She grabs the bottom of my Monsters of Rock T-shirt, then pulls it up and over my head. She leans down and kisses me hard on the lips, even harder than before, her tongue daring mine to put up a fight. She bites me for a fourth time, this time concentrating on my left nipple. Just when the sensation is about to become more painful than pleasurable, she opens her mouth a little wider, soothing the nipple with a dozen quick flicks of her tongue.

Laura then guides my hands down the front of her panties. I slide my middle and index fingers in and out of her, our lips biding their time with soft kisses on one another's necks. Laura's hands find their way inside my boxer shorts.

"I want you inside me." She says this in a decibel just below a whisper, so quiet I almost think I'm hearing things.

"What?" I feel my pockets, looking around the room like a contractor who just misplaced his tape measure. "But, Laura, I don't know where my wallet is. I don't have any..."

"Protection?"

I'm thinking "experience," but I run with it. "Yeah, I didn't bring anything."

"You don't need it."

"Why not?"

"I'm due to start my period any day now. I'm okay."

She slinks onto the bed and rolls over to her back. She spreads her legs. I crawl on top of her, naked and engorged, eager. My arms are on either side of her—straight, extended, like I've just finished a pushup and am about to go down for another.

Below my waist is the comic relief part of the exercise, my naked white ass bouncing in the air as my penis tries in vain to find my girlfriend's vagina. I'm like the guy who refuses to get directions. "The key is to act like you belong here," Dad likes to say whenever he gets us lost on vacation, which is every vacation. I don't care if I belong here or not, but somebody needs to give my dick a map.

Laura reaches down and clasps me in hand. "It's okay, Hank, I can do it."

She clasps me in her hand, pulls me inside her. I push for the first time, but way too hard. "Ouch," she says under her breath. "Careful."

"Sorry," I say.

"It's okay."

I reenter her as "Don't Stop at the Top" segues to "Rhythm of Love." I try to be gentle this time, cupping Laura's left breast in my right hand and propping myself over her with my left forearm to her side. Our bodies move in an awkward harmony, forgiving one another's missteps. I can already tell positioning myself higher is more pleasurable for her, less so for me, and that when I drop my torso below hers, the reverse is true. My lips get carried away on her left nipple, remembering Beth's sharp teeth and maybe returning the favor with a little too much relish.

"Easy, Hank."

"Sorry."

"Just relax."

Easy for her to say. She's not the one about to unleash sixteen years of pent-up hormones and testosterone into the world. As Klaus Meine serenades us with "Passion Rules the Game," I move my arms around Laura's body, reaching down to dig my fingers into her bare ass. I lift her into me. Laura arches her back and moans.

I shudder, releasing myself inside her.

I stay inside Laura for what seems like forever. Or at least, I wish it was forever. Holy shit, this is awesome. For the last five years, I've chosen masturbation over this? I'm a fucking idiot.

We stare into each other's eyes, panting and sweating. I pull out and roll off her only after my wrists go numb. We both try to catch our breath as the guitar solo kicks in for "Media Overkill."

"You practically made it through four songs," Laura says.

"Is that good?" I ask.

"I would think four *seconds* is impressive for a sixteen-year-old."

"I might have masturbated earlier in the day."

"When?"

"Whenever. Keeps me sane."

"So you do it a lot?"

"Define a lot."

"Two or three times."

"In a day? Yeah, that's about right."

"I was thinking in a week."

I lean in, kiss Laura on the cheek. I can feel the room starting to exhale.

"I take it everybody knows then?" Laura asks.

"That I masturbate two or three times a day?"

"No, dumbass. That we're back together."

"Yeah, I told everyone Monday morning before school."

"How'd Beth take it?"

And the room puckers up one more time. "Why do you care what Beth said?"

"Well..." Laura says. "You know."

"I know *what*?"

"She and you were..."

"We were friends," I say. "We *are* friends."

"Friends with benefits?"

"Jesus Christ, Laura. Can we just enjoy tonight?"

"Time's up, lovebirds!" Kent pounds on the door.

We turn on the lights. I watch Laura get dressed. I see her naked back and the curve of her ass in full view for the first time.

"Are you sneaking a peek at me, Mr. Fitzpatrick?"

"That depends."

"On what?"

"Are you going to stop being a jealous hose beast?"

WE SNUCK BACK INTO Kent's room and had sex two more times that night. I attended the greatest rock concert of my life, and yet, of the five bands and twelve hours' worth of music, aside from a vague image of a choreographed human pyramid involving Scorpions's Klaus Meine, Rudolf Schenker, and Matthias Jabs during the intro to "The Zoo," I can't recall one song from the show. What's more, I don't give a shit. My amnesia is glorious. My smile is so big it hurts.

Virgins have no fucking clue how good life can be.

CHAPTER SIXTEEN

Laura meets me at the door wearing cutoff jean shorts and her white bikini top. She pulls me into the house, standing on her bare tiptoes. She kisses me while squeezing my ass. Her aggressiveness surprises me. I push her away.

"What's wrong?" Laura asks.

"No 'hello,' or 'I've missed you' first?"

Laura smiles, grabs me by the front belt loops on my jeans and pulls me into her. "And here I thought I was the one who needed to be romanced."

"What about your parents?" I ask, our lips nearly touching.

"Gone for the weekend," she answers.

"You're kidding me."

"Nope."

"So we have the whole house…"

"To ourselves."

I stare at her eyes, then at the area in question below her waist. "And I suppose you're going to tell me you're free and clear to, uh…"

"Hank…" Laura unzips her shorts. "I've been open for business since Friday morning."

Losing your virginity the day before your girlfriend starts her period is like winning the lottery and being forced to wait a week to cash in your ticket. Contrary to popular belief, "blue balls" is not a figment of a teenage boy's imagination, much less some psychosomatic last-ditch effort to get some action. I did the research after Dad's vasectomy reversal. There's a medical term for it—*epididymitis*, defined as an inflammation of the epididymis, or scrotal sac. Blue balls occur, more or less, when the scrotal sac is stopped up with sperm that left the testes but not the penis. The vas deferens is the conduit for the sperm from the testes to the urethra, and whenever it's blocked it feels like someone is wailing on your balls with a Louisville Slugger.

Laura leads me by the hand into her bedroom. The walls, bed linens, and window treatments are all pink. Pictures line various bookshelves, bedside tables, and a lone tall dresser on the wall to the left of her bed. Parents, brothers, grandparents, classmates, and various younger incarnations of Laura stand shoulder to shoulder, angling for a better view.

Today is nothing like last Saturday. Last Saturday we were drunk. It was dark. Even now, a week after having sex and some seven odd months into our relationship, we're in a way still alien to one another. For today, at least, there's a reckless immodesty to us both. Two windows stand perpendicular to one another, one on Laura's north wall and the other on the west wall. Laura doesn't bother drawing the shades. The sun pours into the room. We strip each other naked, pausing after each discarded piece of clothing, as if we've never seen bare skin in the light of day. As Laura slips out of her panties, first her left foot then her right, she rests her head on my chest. We sway back and forth, synchronizing our breaths, each of us getting used to the feel of the other's skin against our own.

We walk over to the bed. Laura wants me on top again. I fumble with the condom, trying to put it on inside out.

"Here, let me get that." Laura pulls off the condom, flipping it over. With her right hand she reaches down and unrolls the condom in one adroit motion.

I CLIMB OFF LAURA and sit up on the edge of the bed. "I'm sorry."

Laura sits up, sweating. She seems to appreciate my endurance more than me. She kisses my bare shoulder. "Oh my God, Hank, what the hell are you apologizing for?"

I silently curse myself for masturbating twice before I got here. "For taking so long."

"I should be thanking *you*."

"Why? Did you, uh..." My eyes dip below her waistline. "Have an orgasm?"

She smiles. "Damn straight I did."

I smile right back at her. "Well, that's good, then. It just felt a little weird on my end. I think it was the condom."

This is my first subtle admission to Laura that I'm new to this. She doesn't pick up on the hint. "It's just one of those things you get used to again, right?"

I play along. "It's been awhile. I guess I just forgot."

Laura wraps her arm around my waist, resting her chin on my shoulder. "I once heard a stand-up comedian say that having sex with a condom is like eating a delicious steak with a balloon on your tongue."

I laugh. "That's fucking hilarious."

"But true?"

"Hell, yes!"

Laura stands up. She walks across the room in the nude, and there's something about her—something more tender than sexual. Her footfalls are soft, like she doesn't want to disturb the moment. She presses the balls of her bare feet against the ground, her calves contracting. The bottom curves of her ass jiggle, like two smiley faces. She reaches down and grabs her pair of jean shorts off the floor. She slips her feet into the shorts, first her right foot, then her left.

I approach her, white bikini top in my hand. "Here you go."

"Thanks." Laura encases her breasts within the cups of her bikini top, pulling it tight and around her back. She turns her back to me. "Can you fasten me?"

I reach for the bikini and hook the two ends together. I kiss her on the neck. "Let's not make a habit of me helping you put your clothes *on*."

"Deal." Laura kisses me on the cheek. "I'm starving. How about you?"

We sit at the kitchen table while splitting a Diet Coke and a plate of microwave nachos. My side of the nachos has jalapenos. Her side is plain. I notice a stack of college applications on the kitchen table.

"You hear from Bucknell yet?"

"No, not yet."

Laura has been trying to get into Bucknell University for about a year, taking and retaking her standardized tests. Her father went there, and she's been counting on the legacy angle to offset her above-average-though-not-quite-excellent academic record. She's on the waiting list.

I always knew being a year behind Laura in school would suck—the senior spring break that so predictably blew up in my face, the long trek toward our inevitable goodbye, the tedious vetting of colleges. But I play along, for her.

"Earlham still the backup plan?" I ask.

Laura forces a half grin. "I suppose. Everything's ready. Got my housing and courses lined up. What about you?"

"College? It's way too soon for me to be thinking—"

"No, silly. Did you hear from Hoosier Boys State?"

"Oh, that. Yeah, I heard from them."

"And?"

"And I got in."

Laura kisses me on the lips, tells me how proud she is of me. I don't get it. Mom just told me it would look good on my college application, so I applied and got accepted. The local Rotary Club is picking up my tab. "'Hoosier Boys State is a week-long learning experience in the operation of our democratic form of government, the organization of a political party, and the practical application of the knowledge gained from both,'" Mom read from the brochure. She told me, "Senator Birch Bayh, Congressman Lee Hamilton, Senator Dick Lugar, and Terry Lester all attended Hoosier Boys State," and I acted impressed. Well, Terry Lester *is* impressive. He originated the role of Jack Abbott on *The Young and the Restless.* Uncle Mitch went to college with Terry at Indiana Central. I wonder if Terry ever shared his dreams with Uncle Mitch of being the heir to a pretend cosmetics conglomerate. I wonder if Uncle Mitch ever shared his dreams with Uncle Mitch of touching little boys' peckers.

"When do you go?"

"Second week in July."

"That's not that far away."

"Nope. And my family's in Hilton Head for the Fourth."

Laura pouts. "We'll hardly get to see each other. If I somehow manage to get into Bucknell, I could leave as early as August. That sucks."

I reach over and rub her arm. "Let's not get all stressed out. How about we agree to just make the most of the summer we have together, okay?"

"Okay."

I pick the jalapeno off the lone nacho left on the plate and pop it in my mouth. I hand the chip to Laura. "Last one's yours."

"For me? You shouldn't have." She cranes her neck, grabs the chip out of my hand...with her mouth.

"You know, Laura, this might all work out for the better."

"What might all work out?"

"College."

"You think I still got a chance with Bucknell?"

"Maybe, but..."

"But what?"

"Well, Bucknell is in east central Pennsylvania. And Earlham is in east central Indiana. By my rough estimate, Earlham is four hundred sixty-two point two-three miles closer to my house than Bucknell."

She purses her lips into a smile. "By your rough estimate?"

"Very rough."

"Four hundred and sixty-two..."

"Point-two-three."

"Point-two-three, of course."

A pause.

The tapping of Laura's bare feet on the leg of her chair.

She lunges across the table, reaches behind my head and grabs me by my hair. She kisses me. Her kiss starts rough, finishing soft. We separate. She takes my hand. Halfway down the hallway, she unfastens her bikini top and lets it drop to the ground.

CHAPTER SEVENTEEN

Laura meets me at the front door of her house. I'm just back from Hilton Head. We haven't seen one another in ten days, our longest time apart since we got back together.

"Heeey, you." Laura yawns.

I give her a hug. "Don't act so excited to see me."

"I was napping." She backs away, leading me into her house. "How was Hilton Head?"

"Before or after I wrecked the van?"

"You got in *another* accident?"

"I don't know if I'd call it a full-fledged accident. The other car was stationary and unoccupied."

"What happened?"

"I cut a corner too tight backing out of a parking space, peeled the side off a Ford Taurus station wagon."

"What about the van?"

"Just a scratch."

"And by 'scratch' you mean?"

"A gaping wound about three inches wide running the full length of the van."

"Your dad had to be pissed off at you."

"Pissed off for sure, but not at me."

"How'd you talk your way out of that one?"

"I lied, said I was a victim of a hit and run in the Winn Dixie parking lot."

"Hank, you didn't."

"It was only a half lie. There was a hit and run in the Winn Dixie parking lot. I just left out the part about me doing the hitting and the running."

"Someday someone's going to see through your bullshit."

"Probably, but enough about me. You ready to go?"

Some of Laura's friends, seniors mostly, are throwing a party tonight. She disappears into the bathroom. "Just give me a few minutes to freshen up."

Laura takes a lot longer than a few minutes. She emerges from the bathroom, still a little bleary-eyed. Her hair is a couple days removed from its last shampoo. She has on a baggy sweatshirt and wrinkled shorts. She looks ragged.

"You okay, honey?" I ask.

Her smile is more rehearsed than genuine. "Never been better."

"You sure?"

"Yeah, I'm sure."

"I love you."

"I love you, too, Hank."

As forced and ordinary as these words sound, they ease my anxiety. Or at least I pretend they do. We walk outside. "You want me to drive?"

"That's okay." Laura walks over to her car and unlocks the driver's side door. "I'm not in the mood to drink."

The party is at Gary Locke's house. Gary is a good guy, a little nerdy maybe. Cross country runner. Thick, dark-rimmed glasses. Drives a Volkswagen Rabbit. Gary was Laura's date to the senior prom, the safety valve in that transitional phase between dumping Lee Barnes and getting back with me. They're like brother and sister.

Two beers into the party, I notice Laura isn't talking to me. If I were the paranoid type—and I am—I'd say she's going out of her way not to engage me. She's floating around the room, hanging a bit too much on Gary's arm, and laughing too hard at his unfunny jokes. I see her talking to people I've never seen in my life, fake laughing at their stories, too. Or she's sipping on a bottle of soda water while standing alone.

"Sheila!" I catch her out of the corner of my eye, cigarette in hand and about to make a break for the back porch.

"Hank." She gives me a hug, a plastic cup of keg beer in one hand, a cigarette in the other. "How was Hilton Head?"

Sheila Fleming lives three blocks down the street from my house. We shared the same bus as underclassmen. Sheila is cute in an unconventional way, thin-figured with a freckled pale complexion, straight orange-red hair, and coffee brown eyes. She was Hatch's girlfriend for like two minutes, so I keep my flirting to a minimum. Sheila is in Laura's circle of friends—maybe not her absolute best friend but close enough.

"Hilton Head was okay," I say.

"How's Hatch doing?" Sheila asks.

I wave off her more courteous than sincere question. "Never mind that, what's up with Laura?"

"Laura?"

"Yeah, Laura."

Sheila takes a drag off her cigarette, exhales. "I don't know what you're talking about."

She's avoiding eye contact with me. When she reaches to open the patio door, I hold the door shut. "Don't play dumb with me."

"Hank, please let go of the door. This isn't something you and I should be talking about."

"What shouldn't we be talking about?"

"Hank!" Laura is right behind me. "Leave Sheila alone."

I release the door, execute a half turn. Sheila flees. "Nice of you to acknowledge my existence tonight."

"Please, Hank." Laura leans in close to me. "We'll go back to my house. I'll explain everything there."

"Explain? Okay, now you're just scaring me."

Laura grabs my hand. "Don't be scared. We're fine. For whatever stupid reason, I just thought I could put off telling you."

"Put off telling me what?"

"I can't tell you now. At least not here."

THE DRIVE BACK TO Laura's house is interminable. She says nothing to me. I can't get over how tired she looks.

Laura pulls into her driveway, beside my car. The family room and kitchen lights are on in her house because her parents are home. She takes the keys out of the ignition and sighs. She leans back in her seat. "I guess we can talk here."

I am now in full panic mode. I feel like I've been here before. "Laura, whatever it is, I'll understand."

"You will?"

"I'll try at least. You're about to go off to college, a college that's your backup choice even. You need to figure out what you want in life. There's a lot of stuff going through your head right now. "

"More than you know."

"I love you, Laura."

Laura raises her hand to my face, runs her fingers though my hair and over my ear. "I love you, too, Hank."

"And I love you enough to give you your space if you want it."

"That's not it."

"You mean this isn't going to be your I-need-to-be-free-and-you're-nothing-but-dead-weight speech?"

"No." Laura shakes her head. "Not at all."

"You didn't get drunk at some party while I was gone and end up mashing with Lee Barnes, just for old time's sake?"

Laura makes the face I make when I drink tequila. "Dear God, no."

"All this time you just pretended to like Scorpions because I told you they were my favorite band? They're not my favorite band, you know. I mean, I love their music obviously, but—"

"This is serious, Hank."

"Is it?"

"Very serious."

"Why don't you let me be the judge of that?"

"I don't quite know how to tell you."

"Just come right out and say it."

"It's not that easy."

"Sure it is."

"No, it isn't."

"I can take it."

"But maybe I can't."

"As long as we're together, that's all that matters."

"You say that now."

"Come on, Laura. We've been through everything these last few months."

"Not everything."

"Okay, maybe not everything. But enough that you and I can handle whatever life throws at—"

"I'm pregnant, Hank."

I PICTURE MYSELF BACK at my Christian Awakening retreat, talking to Jesus. Someone has handed me the crucifix. Jesus speaks to me. *"It's okay, Hank. Let it out. The Lord is listening."*

"Hey there, Jesus. I did something I'm not too proud of. I fell in love with this girl. And, well, Jesus, we got in some trouble, my girlfriend and I."

"Trouble? What kind of trouble?"

"As in 'that girl's in trouble' trouble."

Jesus breaks into song. *"Oh, we got trouble, right here in River City. With a capital T that rhymes with P that stands for 'pregnant.'"*

"I didn't take you for a *Music Man* guy, JC."

"Don't call me JC. And why is it everybody assumes I fucking love Jesus Christ Superstar*?"*

"Well, you are the star and all. Although to be honest, Judas steals the show. Not to mention Mary is one sweet-looking piece of—"

"Hank, that's my mom you're talking about!"

"No, it isn't. I'm talking about Mary Magdalene, as played by the sultry, olive-skinned actress Yvonne Marianne Elliman."

"Same difference."

"No, it isn't."

"Did you not mistake her for the Virgin Mary the first time you saw Jesus Christ Superstar *and fantasize about her for a solid decade?"*

"That's beside the point."

"And what is your point?"

"My point is the whole theory about Mary's perpetual virginity."

"The whole theory?"

"It's bullshit. Are you telling me Joseph never hit that, ever?"

"And now you're blaspheming my stepfather. Terrific, Hank."

"Don't get me started on Joseph. The Patron Saint of Grin and Bear It. Mary says, 'Sure I'll marry you, Joe.' Cue wedding bells. Cue wedding night. 'Silly me, did I forget to mention I've pledged to my God that I will live and die a virgin?' Then lo and behold, a couple months later, Joseph finds a home pregnancy test stashed in the bottom of a trashcan. Mary says, 'Joe, I swear to you I'm not sleepin' around. An angel knocked me up.'"

"In all fairness, Joseph's initial reaction was to have Mom stoned to death. And in some religious traditions, people believe Joseph and Mom did indeed shack up after I was born."

"Did they?"

"Hell no. But either way, I think you're hovering dangerously close to smite territory."

"You still do that?"

"No, not really. That was more Dad's gig, back when Moses was around. Peter and Paul's market research showed a demand for a kinder, gentler Messiah, especially with adulterers ages eighteen to thirty-four. That's a growing demographic for us."

"I've been meaning to talk to you about that. What is up with the Book of Leviticus?

"I get that all the time. Not the Holy Father's best work."

"I should say not."

"I thought this was supposed to be about you, Hank. You're the one holding the crucifix."

"One last point about Joseph. What's he get for his sacrifice?"

"What's he get, Hank? Well, sainthood for one."

"And with that, what? The distinction of being the world's only eternal foster dad? A stand-in who'll never be allowed to call the purest of sons his own?"

"That's a little harsh, Hank. Joseph was a good man."

"I'm sure he was. I'd also like to think that you, at least for the first few years of your life, were childlike and naïve, blissfully unaware of your destiny. I picture you fishing with Joseph, the two of you making the Passover pilgrimage to Jerusalem, you on his shoulder, laughing."

"Those were some good times, Hank."

"I bet they were. I can even picture Joseph tucking you into bed at night and you dreaming dreams of being a carpenter like your dad and taking his tools to show and tell."

"As a matter of fact, I was pretty handy with a hammer."

"See! Is it too much to ask that your eyes were those of a real boy who saw in Joseph a real father—the everything plus a little more that dads, good dads, are supposed to be to their sons, to their children?"

"You got some serious issues."

"And you're thinking to yourself right now, 'Why didn't I become a fucking carpenter?'"

"Touché, *Hank*."

"Pregnant?" I say. "How'd this happen?"

"How?" Laura says. "Well, Hank, when a man and a woman…"

"That's not what I meant. We were careful."

"We weren't careful every time."

"Okay once, but that was our first…" Laura arches her eyebrows.

"No way."

"I've done the math."

"Come on."

"We got pregnant the first time we ever had sex."

"Back in May?"

"That would be when we first had sex, yes."

"A two for one deal I guess."

"A two for what?"

"Never mind," I say. Laura is unfocused. Good. As much as I might want to scrutinize the tragic irony of getting my high school sweetheart pregnant at the exact same moment I lost my virginity, this conversation is best left on the cutting room floor.

"So, what do we do now?"

"Just find a way to get through it."

"What did your parents say?"

"My parents?"

"I assume you told them."

"Are you high?"

"You're going to start showing pretty soon. I'm surprised you aren't showing already. I'm surprised no one has noticed."

"Don't worry. I'll handle it."

"You'll handle it? What's that supposed to mean?"

"It means what it means."

My parochial school teachers gather behind me in the shadow of memory, behind them the images that freak me out above all others from my Catholic education. To the teachers' left is the crucifixion in all its graphic splendor, right down to Jesus' wounds on his hands and feet—the wounds I could never resist fingering on the oversized crucifix that hung over my bed. "The wounds your sins created and continue to infect," the nuns used to be so fond of reminding me. To my teachers' right, a triptych of photos proceeding by trimester—a translucent arm and leg floating on top of a quarter in a pool of amniotic fluid, a pruned corpse placed in a miniature casket for a Pro-Life photo op, and of course the ubiquitous black garbage bag overflowing with the bloodied, grizzled body parts of dead babies.

"No, Laura."

"I've already made up my mind, Hank."

"But how can you get the procedure without…"

"My parents' permission?"

"Yeah."

"I'm eighteen years old. Don't need their permission. I have an appointment in two weeks at a clinic down in Jeffersonville."

"Two weeks? Isn't that moving a little fast?"

"Fast? I've been pregnant since before Memorial Day. I should've done this last mon—"

"I don't want you to get an abortion!"

It takes me awhile to find my way to the words, but I say them. If anything, I think my candor strengthens Laura's resolve.

"It's not your decision to make," Laura says. "I think maybe you just should go home now."

"But I'm heading out for Hoosier Boys State tomorrow morning. We can't just leave things like this."

"My appointment is still fifteen days away, and nothing's going to change in the next week. I'll be here when you get back."

"Laura, I can't leave now. I can't let you do this."

She grabs me and kisses me on the lips. She reaches her arms around me and leans into my ear. "I'm not asking *you* to do anything, so don't say something you're going to regret. I've dropped a lot on you tonight. It's taken me a month to deal with this."

"A month? You've known for a month?"

"At least that long. I've been taking a pregnancy test about every other day since the beginning of June, hoping it'll come up negative or that I've spontaneously miscarried without knowing about it."

"A month, Laura?"

"My point being, I'm sure as hell going to give you more than a half hour to…"

"To come around?" I wiggle from her grasp, open the car door. "Is that what you want me to do?"

"Yes, as a matter of fact."

"And what if I never come around?"

"I don't want to think about that right now."

"Well, maybe you should."

"Come on, Hank."

"This is a huge deal to me."

"Are you trying to make this a *Catholic* thing?"

"It's a little more than a *thing*, Laura. It's my faith."

"I realize that, and I'm trying to be respectful here."

"Well, you're failing miserably."

"Okay then, what's your faith say about premarital sex, condoms, or masturbation?"

"That's different."

"Really? If they keep track of those things, my guess is you've masturbated your way to hell and back by now."

"I'm going to go, Laura."

"To hell?"

"Maybe. But for now, just to my house."

Laura wipes her eyes. "I think that's best."

I get out of the car. I hold the door open, staring at my feet. I want to add something to this moment. Something poignant. Something insightful. Just *something*. But all I can think to do is shut the door.

I step over to the Subie and open the door. I sit in my car, shut the door, and stick the keys in the ignition. The car fires twice before it starts. I sit there for five minutes with the motor running. Laura is still in her car. She's crying.

The Subie is a manual transmission, so I pop the clutch, throwing the stick shift in reverse. I forget to press the accelerator. The car lurches backward a few inches, and then the engine dies.

I hear a car door shut. Laura is out of her car. I open my door. "Laura, I..."

Her back is to me. She slumps her shoulders and leans her back against the driver's side door of her Calais, head down.

I run around the back of the car and embrace her, both of us crying. This is my moment. I can feel it. It's my time to say my piece, one way or the other. Either take a stand or else just support her.

"Laura, I knew this girl in eighth grade..." No, I didn't.

"She got mixed up with an older guy..." I should stop while I'm ahead.

"I was there for her. Saw her go through so much. She had an abortion, and it ruined her. Almost ruined me seeing her go through it..."

A one hundred percent fabrication. All of it. I ramble on for a couple more minutes. My story doesn't register with Laura. Her eyes are vacant and her tears have stopped. She's just hanging in my arms.

Not that it matters.

I was given my chance to step up. My chance to be a good Catholic or a good man or a good boyfriend—to be a good something. And instead, I plagiarized the plot of *The Last American Virgin.*

Jesus might have wanted to be a carpenter, but I got no fucking tools for this.

CHAPTER EIGHTEEN

Hoosier Boys State, Hoosier Boys State
We are one and all for you…

We will fight for, we will strive for
All the things we've pledged to do…

Ever loyal, ever faithful
And we'll always be true blue…

All the rules of right we will follow honor bright,
Hoosier Boys State we're for you!

Laura called me at Hoosier Boys State to tell me she was vomiting a lot and couldn't keep anything down. I told her I was running for governor and was stressed out about the primary election.

I didn't even make it out of the primaries. I lost my party's nomination to a scrawny cross-country runner from Fort Wayne. The guy was a relentless coalition builder. I won our debate, but he had sixty percent of the votes in his pocket before he even opened his mouth. He went on to win the governor's race. I left the campus of Indiana State thoroughly disenchanted with two-party politics.

I drive straight to Laura's house. Her car is the only one in the driveway. The front door is unlocked. I let myself in.

"Laura!"

The house is quiet, the lights turned off, the curtains drawn throughout. I step into the hallway off the foyer. The master bedroom is the only room in the hallway with its door shut. I don't even knock before I open the door.

"Hey, boyfriend, welcome home." She's in her parents' bed, her head peeking out of the top of multiple sheets and quilts, fists clenched beneath her chin. She looks like Dennis Hopper in *Hoosiers* when he was trying to dry out in the clinic.

"Thanks." I make a cautionary descent to a sitting position beside her, leaning in for a kiss. She turns, offering me her cheek.

"Still pissed about the election?" Her voice is aspirated, her complexion pale.

"I'm over it. How you feeling?"

"Horrible."

"Eat anything today?"

"Not today, not yesterday." She closes her eyes, wincing. "What is it?"

"Stomach…out of my way." Laura pushes me aside and rushes to the bathroom.

She shuts the door behind her. I can hear her dry-heaving through the door. A flushed toilet. The sound of running water as she washes her hands and then brushes her teeth. The door opens. Laura emerges wet-faced and weary. She doesn't even try to make eye contact.

"Laura, at least look at me."

"I can't."

She tries to crawl back into bed, but I block her path and grab her by the arms. "Have you seen yourself in the mirror?"

"Don't have to. I'm sure I look exactly like how I feel."

"You're well into your first trimester, and you look as if you've actually *lost* twenty-five pounds."

This is not an exaggeration. Laura's eyes are sunken into her face. Her cheeks, once round and close to plump, are little more than skin-hued cheekbones. I can see the skeletal outline of her ribcage through her T-shirt. Her shorts hang from her now-boney hips. Her ankles, knees, and elbows are all swollen and disproportionate to her legs and arms, the fatty tissue they once rested in sucked dry by weeks of near-starvation.

Laura hazards a quick glance at me. The disconnect between us is palpable. Laura doesn't feel like my girlfriend. She feels like *that* girl. That varsity cheerleader we all felt sorry for last year who couldn't do cartwheels because of a "bruised abdomen" and spent half a semester hounding three guys for paternity tests. That classmate Mom used to tell me about from her high school days, the one who would disappear from St. Mary's Academy, existing only in the hushed whispers of her peers and the stern countenances of a cadre of nuns. That hussy left to her own anguish, a scarlet letter pinned to her left breast, wandering *without rule or guidance into a moral wilderness… where other women dared not tread. Shame, Despair, Solitude!*

"Hank." Laura collapses in my arms, crying. "I just want my life back. I want us back."

I want us back. That's all it takes. As my shirt soaks through to the skin with the sobs of a broken girl not yet ready to be a broken woman, my choice becomes that simple.

I lay Laura down in the bed, pulling the blankets back up around her face. She isn't *that* girl. She isn't an afterschool special or one of those stupid fucking PSAs. She's not Nancy McKeon, telling me in the middle of my Saturday cartoons, *"Hi, I'm Nancy McKeon, and I'll be right back with* One to Grow On." Laura is my girlfriend. She is real. And I love her.

"Laura." I kiss her full on the lips, my thumb and index finger grasping her chin. "I'm driving you to the clinic next week, and I'm paying for it."

"W-what? But I—"

"Shhh…" I put my hand on her lips. "Let me do this one thing for you."

"Hank, it's not that simple."

"Let me be the man in the relationship I should have been when you first told me."

"You don't understand."

"My mind is made up." I pull the sheets up, tucking her in. "I'll show myself out. Get some rest, and try to eat something, anything."

Laura sits up. She throws her covers off. "For God's sake, would you stop and listen to me?"

"But I thought this is what you wanted."

She stands up, folds her hands in front of her chin, measuring her words. "Last week…you told me…not to do it."

"I was being selfish. You took me by surprise, and I didn't know what to say."

"So you said exactly the opposite of what I wanted to hear?"

"Well, yeah I guess. I'm sorry. I should—"

"You should have said something, something before now."

"What difference does it make? The point is I came around."

"No, that's not the point."

"Laura, please." I grab her by the arms. "I'm confused here. Just tell me what you need me to do. I have the money."

"It's taken care of."

"I want to help. It's my responsibility."

"It's done."

"'It's' done. What's done?"

"The abortion," Laura says. "I went to the clinic two days ago."

CHAPTER NINETEEN

Laura's calendar in her room is covered in black Xs. They're counting down to today, August twentieth, which she's circled in bright red permanent marker.

I walked out on her when she told me about the abortion. I managed to hold out for all of twenty-four hours. Like a moth to a flame, like Kenickie jumping right back on that Ferris wheel with Rizzo as if nothing happened, I drove back to her house the very next day and told her we'd get past this.

To be sure, "this" isn't worth much. Our relationship is falling apart. Experiencing the unintended consequences of sex firsthand with a healthy second course of deceit makes for a great chastity belt, and Laura is doing her best to pull that belt in a few more notches. This last month she's been withholding even token affections—the touch of her hand, a kiss, even something as small as a compliment or a wink. She returns maybe every other phone call, if I'm lucky. Wrestling team conditioning has started up and is taking up a lot of my time, but I still try to make time for dates or even to just hang out. And yet, each and every one of these encounters ends with a door in my face, a turned back, a brush-off.

She had an abortion. *I fucking get it!*

As I look back on these last few weeks, I rationalize that Laura has only herself to blame for my late-night phone calls to Beth.

On the bright side, Bucknell called three days ago. And Laura got in.

She leans up against her bursting-at-the-seams Calais. "This time apart will be good for us, Hank."

"I agree."

Our goodbye kiss is short, choreographed. Laura drives away. I don't even cry.

We haven't officially broken up. But I can't shake the feeling that somewhere in the trunk of Laura's silver Oldsmobile Calais with the Fitzpatrick license plate frame, in a box labeled *toiletries*, tucked in between her disposable contacts and disposable tampons, is our disposable love for one other.

CHAPTER TWENTY

Prep beat the Ridge tonight in football 35–0, so Hatch and I have decided to get shitfaced. Truth is, we'd be getting shitfaced even if the Ridge had won 35–0—I'm a wrestler and Hatch is a golfer, so it's not like we really care—but a belligerent drinking binge is always preferable to a melancholy one.

We get to the party at Claire's house just past ten o'clock. The beer and the shots are flowing. I don't see Claire or Beth. Hatch heads straight to the bar.

"Undefeated against Prep for three years," I say. "We had never lost to those fuckers before tonight."

Hatch pats me on the back. "I know, Fitzy. It fucking sucks, man."

Our drink of choice tonight is "triple shots." Hatch lines them up on the bar: a shot of beer, a shot of whiskey, and a shot of cough syrup, the last of which I've hit more than a few times since the Great Black Butt Incident.

Hatch pours a second round of triple shots, which we down in short order. The music is loud, but not loud enough to mask an unmistakable background sound.

Knock, knock, knock.

I turn my head. "You hear that?"

Hatch cocks one ear higher than the other. "Hear what?"

Knock, knock, knock.

"That!" I point to the ceiling and turn my ear to the offending noise. "Somebody's knocking pretty fucking hard on both the front and back doors."

Claire comes running into the room. "Cops!"

A laid-back affair turned frantic. Teenagers scurry around like carpenter ants just after you stepped on their hill.

THE EMPIRE RIDGE POLICE Department moves us into the family room. Hatch sits in front of the fireplace by himself, sobbing and inconsolable. Off the top of his head, he invents a touching story that incorporates "breaking his dad's heart" and "Butler University pulling his football scholarship." Neither of these things are true, given that Hatch's dad has never cared for him, he's going to Indiana University with me, and I doubt Butler is clamoring for the services of a golfer with a fourteen handicap and the arm strength of Karen Carpenter.

The cop motions to Hatch. "Mr. Hatcher, please blow into this." The cop holds in his hand a breathalyzer, a black remote control-like device tipped with a disposable plastic mouthpiece.

The cop's eyes narrow. He grinds his teeth, looking at Hatch. "Again, please."

Hatch blows again.

The cop stands back, eyes still narrowed. "I got a negative here."

According to the Empire Ridge Police Department's breathalyzer, after no less than six shots in the last ten minutes, Elias Hatcher has not consumed a drop of alcohol.

"Negative?" My best friend screams and hugs one of the cops. He leaves the house without so much as a passing glance or cursory "hang in there" to anybody in the room.

Beep.

"Son." The policewoman pulls the breathalyzer out of my mouth. "Step over here please."

THEY ARREST ME AND Claire. We're sitting together in the back of a police car. She appears to be sucking on something.

"Claire, what the fuck is in your mouth?"

"Pennies."

"You know that doesn't work, right? I suppose you gargled with hand soap before you left the house, too?"

Claire blows me a kiss. I catch a perfumed whiff. "Dish soap, actually," she says.

"Jesus," I say.

"You need to relax, Henry David." She winks at me, unfazed by all of this, her green, saucer-like eyes accentuated by the strong jawline and thin neck of her mother. Every guy has his one Hottest Girl I Never Tried to Sleep With, and Claire Sullivan has been my undisputed titleholder for the three years I've known her. She's that one girl all your girlfriends hate because she deems it her prerogative to flirt with you in front of them. That one girl who makes you feel small without even trying and makes you love every second of your unworthiness.

HANDCUFFS ARE WHERE IT begins and ends for us. No fingerprints. Nothing. We're escorted into a room where they administer a more accurate breathalyzer test. I blow into a long, clear tube that ends in a square machine resembling an electronic produce scale.

The police officer looks unconvinced. "Point-zero-two."

He might be unconvinced, but I'm downright disappointed. "Point-oh-two? The least I could've done is make this arrest worthwhile."

I laugh. The cop doesn't.

Claire takes her turn, her breath reeking of dish soap and Abraham Lincoln.

"Point-one-eight," the cop says. Even he seems impressed, and Claire basks in the notoriety.

CHAPTER TWENTY-ONE

My criminal record notwithstanding, lately, Dad has been on a constant emotional high. Hell, he's downright exultant.

Notre Dame is fucking winning football games this year.

All of them.

It started with the home opener versus Michigan. A diminutive walk-on kicker by the name of Reggie Ho kicked four field goals, including one with a minute seventeen left in the game. Dad and I were seven rows up in the south side of the end zone when Michigan's Mike Gillette missed a forty-seven yard field goal as time expired. The final score was Notre Dame 19, Michigan 17. Notre Dame beat its next three opponents—Michigan State, Purdue, and Stanford—by a combined score of 112–24, then the Irish went on the road to beat a dangerous Pitt team 30–20.

Next up was the University of Miami or, as we refer to them in the Fitzpatrick household, "the true evil empire." How evil? My father, the most humble man I know this side of Jesus Christ, told a Miami fan at the Friday night campus pep rally, "If the Soviet Union suited up a team and played you guys, I'd have to flip a coin to decide who to root for." To us, Miami is Satan in shoulder pads. They are everything that's wrong about football—names on the backs of jerseys, the trash talking, the dubious academics and recruiting, and Jimmy "Jackass" Johnson. Notre Dame transcends football. They represent everything upright and good—the gold helmets and nameless jerseys, the Virgin Mary, the 100 percent graduation rate, and Lou Holtz. Blessed, blessed Saint Lou.

Grandpa Fred was in the stands with me and Dad when Notre Dame free safety Pat Terrell deflected a two point conversion from Miami's Steve

Walsh with forty-five seconds remaining. All three of us were crying. Grandpa told me, "This is the best feeling I've had since VE Day." The Canes came to South Bend with the number one ranking and a thirty-six game regular season winning streak. They left with a 31–30 loss, and two weeks later, the Fighting Irish of Notre Dame would rise to an undisputed #1 ranking in the national polls.

ND enters its season-ending battle versus the University of Southern California Trojans still number one and sporting a 10–0 record. USC is also undefeated, ranked second in the country, just behind the Irish. Laura didn't come home for Thanksgiving, so I invited Beth over for the game. Laura and I gave one another permission to date around while she's at school, but to say Beth has been just a casual diversion would be unfair. She's more than that, and I know she is. But by the middle of the fourth quarter, I'm rethinking my decision to invite her over.

Beth stands up, arms in the air. "Do you two ever sit down?"

Dad flashes Beth a look as close to stern as he can humanly muster. I step in and translate, whispering so as not to disturb him. "Beth, this is the ND-USC game. In terms of Catholic holidays, we rank this a strong fourth behind Christmas, Easter, and St. Patrick's Day."

"Easter is only second, Mr. Fitzpatrick?" Beth asks.

I do my best to translate. "Nobody really likes Easter. They just say they do to get into heaven."

"Careful, son. You know the rules. No blasphemy on game day."

"Sorry, Pops." I cross myself, whispering a quick Hail Mary with my eyes closed.

Beth again throws her hands in the air. "Oh for crying out loud."

I open my eyes. "Notre Dame is ranked number one in the country and USC is number two. This is as big as it gets!"

Beth shakes her head. "It's just a game."

I do my best tight-lipped impersonation of my father. "Blasphemer! Notre Dame football is *not* just a game."

Mom pokes her head into the room. "Hey, Beth, how about you help me finish off this banana cream pie I got in the fridge?"

"There's still some left over?"

"You bet, considering you and Hank missed the first round when you were at your house for Thanksgiving."

"Mrs. Fitzpatrick, it would be my pleasure."

I imagine Beth is giving me some sort of look behind my back as she stomps out of the room, not that I give a shit. It's the fucking USC game!

The fourth quarter ends. "Would you look at that?" Dad points at the television as the stats are displayed onscreen. "They had three hundred and fifty-six yards to our two hundred and fifty-three, twenty-one first downs to our eight, they ran thirty-four more plays, and we beat them twenty-seven to ten."

"USC dominated everywhere but the scoreboard."

Dad nods. "Yep."

"That is..." I offer my open palm to my father. "If you don't take into account USC's quarterback getting decapitated after throwing that interception and the four Southern Cal turnovers."

"Heck, yeah!" Dad smacks my hand with his. "Eleven and oh, baby." He holds his bottle of Miller High Life in the air, celebrating ND's undefeated regular season and toasting the football gods. Or should I say *God*—the uppercase, monotheistic variety—since we are talking about Notre Dame.

I walk into the kitchen to make my peace. Beth sits alone at the table with a licked-clean pie pan. She places the pan in the sink and wads up the discarded plastic wrap. The sound of the crinkling plastic reminds me of Uncle Mitch and his Merits. My chest tightens a little.

"Where'd my mom go?"

"Bathroom."

"How's the pie?"

"Gone."

I sit down next to Beth. I kiss her on the lips, more to just sneak a taste of the pie. "Don't be like that."

"Did they win at least?" Beth asks.

"Would I have this cheesy-ass grin on my face if they lost?"

"I don't know." Beth licks the last of the whipped cream off her fork. "All your grins are pretty much cheesy-ass."

"Thanks."

"You're welcome."

"Tell you what..." I run my thumb along the bottom of her chin, picking up a small dollop of banana filling and whipped cream. I stick my thumb in my mouth. "Let's go out and celebrate tonight."

"Celebrate?" Beth's eyes perk up.

"Why not?"

"What are we celebrating?"

"Everything…" I stand up. I take her plate, depositing it in the kitchen sink. "Notre Dame's big win, us."

"Us?" Beth leans over the table and kisses me. I taste the banana cream pie on her lips. "Is there an *us*?"

It's a valid question, for which I don't have a valid answer. Laura is at Bucknell, out of sight and out of mind, but we have been talking on the phone. I've neglected to mention this to Beth. I pretend Beth didn't say anything. "Claire says she and Hatch are talking about going out to Abe's Place tonight. You in?"

"You sure about that?"

"What's wrong with Abe's?" I ask. "It's safe, secluded…"

"And out of control."

I smile. Beth smiles. It's decided. We're going to Abe's Place.

CHAPTER TWENTY-TWO

Abe's Place is a hundred-acre plot of trees and farmland along the Sycamore River, about ten miles outside of town. It's owned by the Abel family but on weekends presided over by their oldest son, a stocky, near-sighted redhead named Horace Abel. Horace, or Abe as we call him, is the Ridge's starting nose tackle. He sticks chewing tobacco inside his mouthpiece at the beginning of every game and swallows the spit. Talking with a pronounced good ol' boy drawl, he hurls indecipherable expletives at his teammates like, "Kick 'em in nuh fuckin' hey-yid."

Abe's Place can get out of hand. But if the knives and guns are locked up before Horace breaks into the whiskey—and granted, that's a big "if"—there isn't much of a problem. Abe's Place sits far back from the highway, accessible only by a two-mile long, winding, and rutted dirt path. It's perhaps the one spot in Empire Ridge where our nothing-better-to-do police force will never visit.

We all come in the Subie—me, Hatch, Claire, and Beth. The party is hopping, what you'd expect for ten o'clock. The real partiers are just finding their groove, while the underclassmen with curfews are starting to peak, especially the girls.

The freshmen and sophomore girls are always the easiest ones to spot—trying too hard to fit in, drinking too fast. About a dozen of them huddle around a large bonfire, plastic cups of keg beer in hand. In the middle of this sea of estrogen, two very average-looking guys are playing guitar. Jerry Randolph and Clem Hogan are their names. Jerry and Clem are downright homely, and yet, solely based upon their ability to strum a few notes on a piece of mahogany, they're poised to walk away with the hottest girls at the party.

The bonfire pulsates in a small clearing of tilled-over corn. Four old aluminum travel trailers rim the campsite where the clearing meets the tree line, tucked among a patch of silvery sycamores. The trailers are small, not one of them longer than ten feet. The green splashes of moss on the faded white siding and the cracked tires speak of their conversion into semi-permanent single room hunting cabins by Abe's family.

Jerry and Clem have started up a group-sing rendition of "Over the Hills and Far Away" with two of their freshmen concubines, one of whom looks to be more of a Taylor Dayne or Salt-N-Pepa fan and knows Led Zeppelin as "that old 'Stairway to Heaven' band from the sixties or something."

I've already lost Beth in the crowd.

"Come on over here, Hy-ink." Abe waves at me from the opposite side of the bonfire.

Abe has always pronounced my first name as "Hy-ink," dragging the word out to two syllables like my Grandma Eleanor's cousins in Kentucky.

I circle the bonfire. Abe stands up. I shake his hand. "Abe, my man. How you doin'?"

"Oh, all right I guess," he says. Abe is wearing an orange hunter's vest over an insulated flannel shirt. The bonfire reflects in his glasses, illuminating the hundreds of freckles that blanket his face and frame a bushy red mustache, all of it crowned by an old Cincinnati Reds baseball cap.

"My mom says your grades are up."

"I s'pose they are." Abe's left cheek is filled with wad of Red Man Loose Leaf Tobacco. He spits a stream of tobacco juice on the ground near his feet. "How's your family doin' these days?"

"Fantastic, couldn't be better."

For someone who hates animals, my mother has a soft spot for lost causes when it comes to her students. She's been Abe's guidance counselor at Empire Ridge since he was a freshman, transforming him from a drunken casualty of a broken home into a straight-C student.

Abe isn't a casualty anymore, but he's still a drunk. He tips his cap to me. "I got somethin' for ya, Hy-ink." He reaches into his coat pocket, pulls out an unopened fifth of Johnnie Walker Red Label.

"What is that?"

"Been savin' it for ya, Hy-ink. Fuck that bourbon shit. Real men drink Scotch whiskey." Abe cracks open the bottle and powers down multiple swallows, the tobacco still firmly entrenched in his left cheek. He hands me the bottle. I take my first cautious sip.

Barring a large cup of Mountain Dew to chase things down with, I'm not a whiskey drinker. I don't care whether it's from Scotland, Ireland, Kentucky, Tennessee, or Bigfoot's ass crack. The peaty flavor of the Johnnie Walker hits my tongue, sliding to the back of my throat. It's an immediate struggle not to vomit it right back up. I cough, trying to clear my throat. I take a slow, deep breath through my nose.

"Clear a path, folks. We got a live one here!"

I raise my hand and shake my head. "Fuck you, Abe." I tilt the bottle and choke down a couple more shots in one drink.

Abe pats me on the back. "Now that's what I wanna see. Fuckin' pony up, Hy-ink!"

By the time Beth makes it over to the bonfire, the bottle of Johnnie Walker Red Label is almost gone. I, on the other hand, am all the way gone. My diction is right there with me. "Whereveyoubeen?"

Beth points to no place in particular, her red eyes and slurring giving her away, too. "Over there somewheres." She sits on my lap and sticks her tongue in my ear. Beth is drunk, maybe even a little stoned. And maybe a lot horny.

Abe nudges me, tilting his head in the direction of the most isolated trailer. "It's empty, and it's the only clean one." He shoots me one of those maniacal, tobacco juice-stained smiles of his that always freaks my shit out.

I lean in to nibble Beth's ear. "Hey."

"Yeah?" she asks.

"Youwungozumplazeprivate?"

Beth's face perks up. Her eyes refocus, as if she's willing herself to sobriety in real time. "With you, Hank? Anywhere."

I open the trailer door for Beth, follow her in and shut the door behind me. The inside of the trailer smells sour, like that washrag or towel that overstays its welcome in your bathroom. A mattress rests in the shadows on the far wall, covered in a loose-fitting sheet. A layer of cold dust clings to everything.

It's forty degrees outside, if that. Beth and I are separated from the elements by nothing more than an inch-thick sheet of aluminum. You'd think nudity would be the last thing on either of our minds.

You would think.

We get naked except for our socks. On cue, Jerry and Clem transition from Zeppelin to Meatloaf. Through the thin walls of the trailer I can hear them singing. Either the girls have a good handle on the lyrics to "Paradise by the Dashboard Light," or else Jerry and Clem have moved on to different girls. I'm guessing the latter. Jerry and Clem go first, nostalgically remembering every little thing as if it happened only yesterday, bragging about their girl being the hottest chick in school and being none-too-subtle about groping her by the light of their automobile's dashboard. Then the girls, shameless sluts that they are, affirm that yes, indeed, they are doubly blessed for being naked minors.

I love this fucking song, a song whose ultimate message is that life is all about being young and naked.

Beth pulls me on top of her. Her movements are sudden and awkward, like she's afraid I might run out on her at any moment.

Things are moving too fast for me. I'm getting the spins.

"Something wrong, Hank?"

I'm still slurring, and the cold is just making things worse. "Izzzreally fff-fuh-fffucking cold." I want this as bad as Beth does. But between the temperature and me sorting out the three different Beth's circling beneath me, I can't get an erection.

"Here, let me help." Beth slides out from under me and pushes me onto my back. She moves down and drops her mouth over me. I pull a condom from my pocket, hand it to her. She does the rest.

She wants to be on top. She takes me inside her. It's warm inside her. She starts pounding up and down on me, springing off her knees, which are hinged under my ribs. The pounding slows to a sliding motion. The angle of this position seems to excite Beth while at the same time prolong my own orgasm.

My bladder has had enough. How long have we been fucking, anyway? Five minutes? Ten minutes? A half hour?

"Beth."

She can't hear me over her moaning. I focus all my energy into making my lips obey me.

"Beth! Rezdroom."

"Rez droom?" Beth is out of breath, still sliding.

"Tryingtuhholdit. Juscantdoit."

"Oh, restroom." Beth frowns. She pushes herself off me with a disappointed sigh.

"Umzorry."

Beth shakes her head, but then smiles. "It's all right, Hank." She crawls onto her stomach and writhes beneath our remnants of clothing, arching her back. "I'll be here…waiting."

I lean over, kiss her on the back of the neck, trying to rediscover the English language one damaged brain cell at a time. "Somethun to membermeebuy, till I gihback."

My bravado is short-lived. The spins are almost incapacitating when I stand up. Free from the coital distraction, the Johnnie Walker Red Label is kicking my ass with an inebriated vengeance. I fumble with the latch on the trailer door.

"You okay, baby?"

"Doors duck."

"Doors duck?"

"Stuck!"

"Oh, the door. It's stuck."

"Yez. Zwuttisaid."

Beth opens the door for me. The trailer faces the river on the opposite side of the bonfire. I'm guessing I can whip it out unnoticed. I walk down the two aluminum steps to a nearby tree. I stand there wearing only my socks. My dick is in my hand.

Either I've drunk myself deaf, or I am the world's quietest pisser.

If you pee in the forest, and no one is there to tell your drunk ass to take your fucking rubber off before you start peeing, does it make a sound?

My eyes look down just in time to see a giant urine balloon hanging off the end of my cock. The balloon grows heavy. It slides slowly down my shaft.

Warm urine is quite comforting on bare skin in forty degree weather, a point of fact I discover as the urine balloon falls off my cock and explodes at my feet with a great big *sploosh* sound.

I step back into the trailer. "Weeshoodgetdrezzd."

"Get dressed? This is a big night for us."

"Notliethis. Notuhnight. Wurdoodrunk."

"You mean you're too drunk." Beth stands in front of me, defiant. She's also naked except her socks. "I'm fine. Speak for yourself."

I point to my flaccid penis, it being the other part of the *wur* in my equation. "I am speeginfurmuhself."

I reach around her to grab my clothes. I trip over my own feet, fall flat on my face.

Beth helps me up. "You really are wasted, aren't you?"

"Yeahhh-uzz."

I tell Beth the urine balloon story, or at least try to. She falls off the bed, laughing. "Okay, the jury concedes you're too drunk to be having sex."

We get dressed—well, Beth dresses both of us. I stumble out of the trailer. My arm is around Beth. My feet are heavy. "Lezzguhhome."

We track down Hatch and Claire, say our goodbyes to Abe. He tells us to wait and comes running back with a plastic, two-gallon milk jug. "Got somethin' for you guys."

I raise my head. "Wuzzatfur?"

"Consider it a goin' way present." Abe pulls a large hunting knife out of a leather sheath attached to his belt. We all take a precautionary step backward. Abe flips the plastic jug upside down, cuts off the bottom. He makes sure the plastic cap is fastened tight and hands the jug to me. "One ho'made portable puke bucket fur my good buddy, Hy-ink."

Hatch steps in. "We don't need that. Fitzy can hold his liquor."

Abe shakes his head. "I don't think so."

"No really, Abe." It's Claire's turn to stand up for me I guess. "Hank will be fine."

"Maybe..." Abe looks at me, pointing at my face. "But judgin' by his color, and the fact I just barfed my brains out 'bout five minutes ago, I'm uh guessin' Hy-ink ain't too far bu'hine me."

Hatch volunteers to drive us back. These days it's all too easy to guilt him into being designated driver. One casual reminder about disintegrating into a weeping pussy and leaving you for the cops, and presto—instant DD. We figure it's best to drive around the country roads outside Empire Ridge until I can string more than three syllables together without needing a translator.

Beth and I take the backseat, my head in Beth's lap. Beth gets all karaoke on me, singing along with the radio while she runs her hands through my hair. A post-Cetera Chicago tune called "Look Away" followed by Phil Collins's "Groovy Kind of Love." Cheesy-ass songs. Beth doesn't have the best voice. But I don't care.

"Beth?" I'm on the road to recovery, or at least cognizant enough to now realize how far away my genuine recovery still is.

Beth pushes back my hair behind my right ear, kisses me on the lips. "Yeah, babe?"

"Can you hand me my puke bucket, please?"

CHAPTER TWENTY-THREE

I've always been a mediocre football player who loves football and a natural-born wrestler who abhors wrestling. Such is my curse.

Wrestling is the hardest, most arduous activity ever invented by man. Three two-minute periods equal six minutes of exhaustive hell on earth. As our coach once said, "There is no more intense combination of aerobic and anaerobic exercise in all of sports." He also told us that Dan Gable, the greatest amateur wrestler ever who compiled a 132–1 record at the University of Iowa, "is regarded by many experts to be the most complete human specimen in the history of athletics." *Most complete?* What the fuck does that mean?

And did I mention I hate wrestling?

I tipped off my coaches about my latent ability early on. I was a sophomore when one of our varsity wrestlers decided to get mono. Weighing in at 155 pounds soaking wet and with a grand total of five practices under my belt, I was the Ridge's last minute substitution in the 171-pound weight class in our dual meet versus Prep. Not only were we facing our archrivals, but my opponent was Kevin Stark, the undefeated #6–ranked wrestler in the state at 171 pounds, a guy who two nights prior (against wrestling powerhouse Perry Meridian) pinned the #3 wrestler in the state in the first twenty seconds of the first period. I lost the match, by a wide margin. By rule, if one wrestler gains a fifteen-point lead over his opponent at any point, that wrestler is declared the winner of the match by technical fall. Stark whooped my ass 18–3, but it took him until the third period to beat me, and he didn't pin me.

Three years later, that match against Kevin Stark continues to be the highlight of my career. I throw matches during big tournaments so I can have the weekend to myself. I fake bronchitis for weeks at a time to rationalize losing to my coach. I've lost more matches than I've won. And the only reason I don't quit is because my arms and legs look fucking awesome.

About three feet away from me, Mom and Dad sit in the bleachers at the Major Taylor Memorial Gymnasium in downtown Taylor. On any other day, I might pause to note the perverse irony of Taylor, a racist southern Indiana hollow whose namesake was a turn-of-the-century elite cyclist and the world's first great black athlete, but right now I'm just warming up for my match. Per the program, "Hank Fitzpatrick's 9–8 record earned him the fourth seed in the 171-pound weight class of the 1989 Indiana High School Athletic Association Major Taylor Wrestling Sectional."

The 171-pound bracket only has four seeds.

"Hank." Mom motions to me. "Come here for a second."

I jog over to her, spinning my arms. "Mom, I'm up next. What do you want?"

"I want you to at least try today."

"Okay," I say, more dismissive than responsive.

"No, I mean really try."

"It's just wrestling."

"Yeah…well, your father and I have been sitting up here talking."

"About what?"

"About spring break."

"Is now the time to get into this?"

"Son, I know you're upset about us not letting you go down to Panama City with all your friends."

"Mom, we've been through this a hundred times, and it's still January."

"And I still say you have no business going down to Florida unchaperoned when you're seventeen years old."

"Never mind I'm turning eighteen two weeks after spring break. Are you just telling me all this to piss me off again? Maybe give me some motivation?"

"Oh, I'm going to give you some motivation."

"Let me know when that starts." I jog in place, the hood of my warm-up pulled over my head.

Dad listens in on our conversation, interrupting at a no doubt predetermined moment. He puts his hand on my shoulder. "Your mother and I want you to do your best today. If you win at least one match, you can go on spring break with your friends."

I try to stifle a laugh. "You do realize I have a combined career record of something like 0–10 versus the guys in this tournament, right?"

Dad scans the program. "Taylor, Rosehaven, Prep—not exactly a rogue's gallery of wrestling powers."

"Rogue enough to beat my butt ten times," I say.

The buzzer sounds, ending the last match of the first round of the 160-pound class. It's a close match. I still have some time to kill. I turn to leave.

Dad grabs me by the sleeve. "Wait a second, son."

My father is a part-time motivational speaker. He does some seminar work on the side for Oldsmobile, even volunteers for the occasional Catholic retreat. But it's a part of him I've never seen.

I have a feeling that's about to change.

"Hank, look at me." Dad stares me down. He's never stared me down before. "You know and I know you're a much better wrestler than you pretend to be. I've watched you sleepwalk through years of wasted talent."

I shrug his hand off my sleeve. I take off my warm-ups. "What do you want from me, Dad?"

"I want you to realize your potential."

"Maybe I don't want to."

"Haughty." Dad hands me my headgear.

"Huh?" I button my chinstrap, making sure my headgear is snug.

"Haughty, Hank." Dad makes a fist, holds it in front of his face. "That's the word."

"What's the word?"

"Haughty."

"And what the heck does that mean?"

"It means knowing you will win."

"I don't know I'll win."

"Then you've already lost."

"But I—"

Dad grabs me by the front of my singlet, pulling me close to his face. "If I want to win, I win. Period."

Every hair stands up on the back of my neck. They could pipe the "Notre Dame Victory March" into the Major Taylor Memorial Gymnasium, and I wouldn't be more pumped up than I am at this moment. I've lived my life believing Dad doesn't have an ounce of conceit in him. But given that he's worked his way up from being a music teacher to owning his own car dealership, he has more than just a token dose of hubris in his schematic.

"Haughty?"

Dad grabs my shoulders, squeezes. "Haughty."

I step back and look at both him and my mother. I jump up and down a few times to get the blood flowing. I sense an opening. A *huge* opening.

"Tell you what. Forget winning just one match. How about if I win the whole damn thing today, you let me go to spring break, *and* you pay my way?"

Mom hears my counter. "What?"

"All or nothing," I say. "If I win the first match but lose in the finals, I don't go to spring break."

Dad looks at me, then at Mom. He offers me his hand. "Deal!"

I turn my back to my parents. I approach the wrestling mat, wondering how long it will take before Dad realizes he's made a sucker's bet.

My opponents are fucking toast.

I COME OUT AGAINST the second seed from Prep like a man possessed. I throw a double-leg takedown and get him on his back for a near-fall ten seconds into the match. I keep throwing my favorite move, the butcher, in which I do a cross-face, grab my opponent's elbows out from under him, and then twist him around to his back like a human pretzel. Twice he tries to put a double-arm bar on me when I'm in the down position, and twice my double jointed arms laugh at his futility. The points start piling up, and the ref calls the match in the beginning of the third period by technical fall 19–4.

The ref raises my hand in victory. My dad stands two rows up in the bleachers, cups his mouth with his hands, yelling, "What's the word?"

I pump my fist at him. "Haughty!"

Jed Pahl, the first seed from Taylor, walks onto the mat. I bump his shoulder as I pass him, and not by accident. I smile an evil smile. My head is dizzy. I'm ready to kick his ass.

I CAN'T SIT STILL waiting for the final round to begin. I warm up to a mix tape of Guns N' Roses and Van Halen songs, making sure to hit both "Paradise City"—replacing "Paradise" with "Panama" in the lyrics of course—and "Panama" on the playlist. Unlike most wrestlers, I like neither the song

"Lunatic Fringe" nor the movie *Vision Quest,* although I'd knock the back out of Linda Fiorentino.

Finally, they call us up. Jed and I walk to the center of the mat. We shake hands. I'm jumping up and down, staring at him. Jed won't make eye contact, but nonetheless seems unfazed by my posturing. He won his first match easily, pinning the third seed from Rosehaven in the middle of the second period. The ref blows the whistle to start our match.

I'm not a technical wrestler, but Jed makes me look like one. He tries to throw a standing single, and I see his move like it's in slow motion. I sprawl, the combined strength and leverage of my legs and hips sending Jed to the mat stomach first. I can hear the wind being knocked out of his lungs. I whizzer him, coming back into a quarter nelson and sneaking in a couple punches to his midsection. With the alternative being suffocation, Jed goes slack, dropping his shoulder blades.

The ref slams his hand on the mat while blowing his whistle. I have never beaten Jed in five previous tries, or even made it past the second period. On the sixth try, I pin him forty-three seconds into the match.

It's the shortest finals match of the entire Taylor Sectional. Nearly as bad as the beat down Notre Dame gave West Virginia in the Fiesta Bowl four weeks ago to win the national championship. If it's possible, Dad appears happier for me in victory than he was for his Irish. He's screaming like a goddamn girl. He points at me. I point back.

Haughty!

CHAPTER TWENTY-FOUR

Möchten sie Gegottenbush?

Ja, ich möchte Gegottenbush.

German is not my strongest subject. My dialect is Germanglish with a slight southern Indiana drawl. I can't conjugate verbs. The whole *der/die/das* noun-gender thing will forever mystify me. And I make up words when I don't know—or don't like—the German equivalent. Take for instance, the German word for sex, *Geschlectsverkehr*. Like the German language as a whole, it's unwieldy, soulless, just plain old ugly. But *Gegottenbush*? Now that speaks to me. And it's damn funny.

I am thinking about *Gegottenbush* with Beth Burke. As I sat in fourth-year German, I was tempted to ask the teacher if I could go to the restroom—to do some more intensive "thinking" about *Gegottenbush* with Beth Burke. That's about the time the school nurse interrupted the class to tell me my mom had delivered the baby.

In the wake of two miscarriages, this pregnancy was, by contrast, uneventful, sedate even, lulling my parents into a sense of security. Against doctor's orders, Dad and his eight-and-a-half-months pregnant wife made the cold February trip up to Notre Dame for their twenty-year reunion. Mom's water broke on the floor of the basketball court five minutes after the Notre Dame-USC game ended. Dad had said to me over the phone, "God knew to wait."

I PULL INTO OUR driveway. Dad's car is parked outside, the engine still rattling from the drive back from South Bend.

I walk into the family room. Mom is already asleep on the sectional along the back wall, buried beneath layers of old quilts. Grandpa George and Dad are watching television in separate chairs, my brother asleep on Dad's chest.

My *brother*. After fourteen spirit-breaking years of sisterhood, I have a fucking brother!

"Hey there." Dad's voice is just above a whisper. He starts to sit up. I wave him off. "Dad, you're fine. Stay down."

Grandpa George stands up, beaming. "Isn't he beautiful, Johnny-uh-Hank? Spittin' image of his brother if I've ever seen one!"

My father raises his fingers to his lips and turns to Grandpa. "Dad, quiet."

Grandpa sits down. "Sorry about that."

"Well, son?"

I look at Dad. "Well, what?"

"You want to say hi to your new baby brother, Jack Henry?"

Just as she did with me, Mom vetoed John Henry Junior. She came close this time, but Jack is the name on his birth certificate, not his nickname. As for girl names, I refused to look at the list. It's the late eighties, so I could guess "Caitlin" and have about a one in three chance of being right. I never even entertained the idea of a girl, convinced I could somehow will my brother into being.

Mission accomplished. "How's he doing?" I ask.

Dad rubs the back of Jack's head. "You're looking at it."

A baby sleeping on his father's chest, one of those framed moments you want to keep in your pocket. I've never seen Dad like this, save in photos. Those old, perfectly square early-seventies pictures of me as a newborn, the more rectangular ones of Jeanine. The clothes change, Mom's hairstyles are all over the place, but one thing is constant—Dad's eyes. The surrender. The contentment. The eyes of a parent falling in love all over again.

"So the trip back was okay."

"Yeah, other than when I tried to avoid the stoplights in Kokomo."

"Dad, you didn't."

"I did."

"You got lost on the back roads of Indiana with a postpartum mother and a newborn in the car?"

"Way lost. We're talking Amish country lost."

We both laugh. Dad tucks the familiar white newborn blanket with teal and pink stripes around his new son. Jack buries his head of dark brown hair back in Dad's broad chest. Another full head of hair in the Fitzpatrick line. First there was me with my comical "I-fro"—short for "Irish Afro"—that Grandma Louise teased out mercilessly, then Jeanine with what could only be described as a miniature blonde toupee.

Mom says I've always been a baby person. I shared a room with Jeanine the first six years of her life. After she started sleeping through the night a week after her birth, Mom bragged she was blessed with the greatest baby in the history of all newborns. It took Mom about a month for her to discover that every time her little girl cried, I was crawling into the crib and patting Jeanine's back until she fell asleep. I wiped baby puke off my shoulder before I even knew how to spell "puke." I changed crappy diapers before I could ride a two-wheeler. While my friends had paper routes, I had babysitting jobs.

Mom is right. I love babies. Deep down, that's what has fucked with my head the most in the aftermath of Hurricane Laura. The idea of being a father is more comforting and certainly less intimidating than being a husband. The notion of binding your heart and soul to the life of a helpless, innocent child—there's something valiant, something pure in that. But having sex with the same person for the rest of your life? Now *that* is fucking stupid.

"Okay, Dad." I hold out my hands, palms up. "Hand him over." Dad sits up. "You know the drill. Go wash your hands first."

My eyes haven't left Jack since I came into the room. I step in the kitchen, soap up my hands, rinse, and then dry them with a paper towel. I can't stop smiling. I skip over to my father.

"Here you go." Dad stands. He does that thing people do with newborns where they hold the back of the baby's neck until the baby is snug in the other person's arms. In those first few days, this maneuver is always more exaggerated, your fears more pronounced—fear that no matter what you do, this fragile creature's head will snap right off.

Jack doesn't even acknowledge the change of venue. He tries to open his eyes, his still-swollen cheeks rendering them as dark slits. I wrap his fingers around my index finger and kiss him on the forehead, inhaling his new baby smell. Tears swell in the corners of my eyes. I don't want to think about Laura and what could have been, but I do. I want to love my brother and be thankful for what my mom has gone through to get to this moment, but I'm not.

"Hank?"

Mom is awake. I turn to her. Her eyes are a little hazy. "Hey there, trooper. How's that epidural hangover treating you?"

"Hmph..." Mom tries to laugh, but it comes out as a grunt. Her attempt at a smile isn't much better. "How would you feel if you shit a watermelon out your butthole?"

"Debbie!" Dad's tone approaches scolding, then backs off for fear of the manic, drug-addled reprisal smoldering in Mom's eyes.

I tiptoe toward my mother. My steps are measured and cautious, as if I'm afraid to walk with Jack in my arms. I lean down and say, "Well, if you don't think this guy was worth it..."

Mom smiles. "You give him to me right now, Henry David Fitzpatrick!"

I hand Jack over. He stirs again. Mom whispers baby talk to him. For the first time I see Jack open his eyes. They're that black-blue color all newborn babies have. I swear he already recognizes Mom. What do they call it when they hand the baby to the mother the moment he's out of the womb and breathing? Imprinting. All the baby needs in those first moments of life is a breath of fresh air and the awareness someone loves him. Does that ever change? And if it does, should it? Why the compulsion to abandon this beautiful simplicity, all for the pretext of "growing" up?

Dad approaches the couch, sits next to Mom. He runs his hand through her hair. "You seem to be in good hands. I'm going to take my dad out for a bite to eat, maybe swing by the shop. I'll pick up Jeanine on my way home."

"Sounds good, honey. And hey..."

Mom grabs her husband by the collar, pulls him to her, and kisses him full on the lips. He kisses her back. They separate. "I love you, John."

"I love you, too, my beautiful bride." Dad gives Mom another kiss on the forehead, then kisses Jack on the top of his head. He gets up, squeezing my shoulder. He makes for the door. "Hey, George, let's go!"

Grandpa stands up. "Right behind you, son."

JACK IS ANTSY, WIGGLING in Mom's lap. "I think my little boy is getting hungry."

Awkward silence. Mom stares at me. I stare at Mom. Mom looks down at her breasts. Then at me. Then at the ceiling. Then at her breasts. Then at me.

"Oh, *hungry*. Yeah, I'll just go into the other room and, uh, do…something."

Mom shakes her head. "It's not that big of a deal, Hank. Just turn around, give me a minute to get situated."

I was ten years old the first time I saw a bare adult woman's breast. It happened when we were living in Louisville. My old babysitter, Lisa Goebel, had come down to visit from Indianapolis with her infant daughter. I was sitting on our tan sectional, the one with the sofa bed that could have doubled for a medieval torture device. My new favorite television show had just started, an Indiana Jones-inspired series called *Tales of the Gold Monkey.* I liked it because of its theme music and the fact the hero, Jake Cutter, had a dog who wore an eye patch because Jake had lost the dog's fake eye in a poker game. Jake and his one-eyed dog flew around in an amphibious airplane called The Goose. The opening credits started to roll. Pan out to The Goose flying over the horizon and the words *Tales of the Gold Monkey* emblazoned across the television set, and then suddenly there was a bare breast flopping into my field of vision, no more than five feet to the left of me. One eye on The Goose. One eye on… *The Nipple.*

Lisa might have well been an alien. Mom told me later, "She was doing what they call 'breastfeeding.'" Up until that point I had assumed all milk came from cows. And to think I was once upset at the prospect of attending a public high school and not continuing my education in my parochial cocoon.

"I'm ready, Hank."

I turn around. Jack is somewhere beneath the mammary shroud running from Mom's chin to her waist. "Mom."

"Yeah?"

"What would Jack have been named if he was a girl?"

"Oh, now you're entertaining that possibility?"

"Nope. Just gloating."

"Not that it matters…" Mom adjusts her shroud. "But she would have been Caitlin."

I'm a goddamn prophet.

I assume Dad's spot on the couch. We watch the last half hour of *Guiding Light* together, just like when I was a kid. I used to watch all the CBS soaps: *The Young and the Restless, As the World Turns, Search for Tomorrow* before it moved to NBC, even *Capitol,* which CBS later cancelled and replaced with *The Bold and the Beautiful.* David Hasselhoff was Snapper

Foster first in my mind, Michael Knight second. And Meg Ryan would always be that blonde, doe-eyed Betsy Stewart in a negligee making love to her swarthy Greek husband Frank Andropoulos on their wedding night.

"Hey, Hank."

"Yes, Mom?"

"Did you know a sixteen- and a twelve-year-old gave birth last week in Empire Ridge Regional Hospital?"

"Wow."

"Babies having babies. It's scary."

"Yep, scary."

"When you seeing Laura?"

"She's coming back in March. Bucknell has that weird winter-term schedule, so they get like a month off for spring break."

"It's been awhile since she's been home," Mom says.

"Since she left in the fall," I affirm. "She's been having trouble with the Calais and didn't want to chance it with a cross-country drive. I guess her parents made it out there for Christmas or something."

"Don't tell your father about her car. He takes that stuff personally, you know."

"I know."

"What do you plan on saying to her when she gets home?"

"What do you mean?"

"I'm not blind. I see things. You and Beth are, well…"

"Yeah, I know."

"Have you told Laura?"

"Nope. I plan on ending it with us when she gets in town. I think I owe her at least the courtesy of telling her face-to-face."

"You are your father's son, Hank. Always the gentleman."

"Hate to burst your bubble, Mom, but you might be the first woman on the planet to use my name and the word 'gentleman' in the same sentence."

"You're too hard on yourself," she says, holding Jack up in the air. "Here, take this guy off my hands for a while, would you?"

"My pleasure," I say.

Guiding Light ends. I lay on Dad's couch with my baby brother on my chest. Jack lets out a loud, satisfied burp. We fall asleep, our chests breathing in unison.

CHAPTER TWENTY-FIVE

"Hello?"

I open the front door. The lights inside the house are dimmed. Gloria Estefan is playing on the stereo. I close the door behind me.

"I'm in here, Hank."

Although we mutually agreed we could see other people, Laura and I have talked on the phone almost every night. Within days of leaving Empire Ridge, the tone in her voice changed. After a few weeks, she was being suggestive, playful even, teasing me over the phone. She started sending me photographs—one of her in her dorm room wearing a miniskirt, one of her posing at a Halloween Party dressed like Susanna Hoffs, lead singer of The Bangles—an eternal object of my self-stimulation—and one of her dressed up like Santa Claus at a Christmas Party. I could see the color and the fullness coming back into Laura's face. With each successive round of photos, I thanked the starch-filled menu of the Bucknell cafeteria for resurrecting the girl I fell in love with.

Laura came home from school today. I haven't seen her since we said goodbye in August, more than eight months ago. Her parents are out of town for the weekend, so she invited me over. I know going to see Laura will lead to trouble.

So I go to see Laura.

She's in her room. I can smell the Obsession perfume from the front doorway. I walk down the hall and open the door.

Beneath the mottled glow of candlelight, Laura is lying on the bed in nothing but her bra and panties. This night is poised to be fantastic.

Or not.

"Hello, stranger."

"Wow," I say. Laura is as close to buff as I've ever seen her. She's never carried her weight quite like this. She looks maybe five pounds heavier, but it's all muscle.

"Really?" Laura says.

Stop staring, Hank. I shake my head, trying to break the hypnosis. "Laura, we…we can't do this. Not right now."

"Then when?" Her tone is desperate. "Do you know how long I've been picturing this night?"

"Eight months?"

"Longer than that."

"Well, if you've waited this long…" I say this because at this point sarcasm is all I have to offer.

"Hank, come on."

"I haven't seen you for eight months, Laura. How about getting through first and second gear before we go straight to fifth?"

"I'm in a happy place now. I'm ready. *We're* ready, Hank." Laura jumps off the bed and grabs me. Her kisses are rough. I wish I didn't kiss her back, but I do. I feel guilty. Stopping the kiss—stopping *us*—is harder than I thought it would be.

"Laura." I push her away. "I said we can't do this, and I meant it."

She starts to cry. "What's your problem, Hank?"

I cross to the other side of the room, desperate to put some distance between me and the bare skin of a girl I would kill to make love to just one more time.

"There's no easy way for me to say this, Laura."

"Just say it."

"I think I'm breaking up with you."

Laura snatches her robe hanging off the back of her bedroom door. She opens the door and points me into the hallway. "Leave!"

"Wait a second."

"I said get out!"

"Not until you let me explain."

"Explain?" Laura shuts the door again. She folds her arms, glaring at me. She's reading my eyes, my standoffishness. She knows. She fucking knows! She opens her mouth. "It's Beth."

"Laura, I wanted to tell you before you heard it from someone else."

"Beth?"

"I don't even know how serious it is at this point."

"And I'm supposed to believe that?"

Laura sits on her bed. I sit down beside her. We listen to B-side Gloria Estefan, not saying anything.

"Laura, I'm sorry. I know that doesn't mean anything to you right now, but I am very, very sorry."

She closes her eyes, rests her head on my shoulder and sighs. "It's my own fault."

"Don't say that."

"Why not? It's the truth. I drove you away months ago. I guess, after we really started talking on the phone, I thought you wanted to make this work."

"Maybe a part of me does…uh, I mean did. I've enjoyed our phone calls, too. And I love getting your letters. But you were so far away, and I just—"

"You just fell out of love with me?"

"No, Laura. You're my first love. A part of me will always love you."

She props her chin on my shoulder and gives me a smile. She wipes her eyes. "I hate that fucking line, just so you know."

"It's not a line. You were my first love. You were the first girl who broke my heart…"

"And the first girl you got pregnant."

"Well, uh…yeah, that too."

An awkward silence, which Laura recognizes. "Too soon for jokes?"

"Yeah, probably." I'm smiling now. "My point is, aside from my family, you're the first real thing I've ever had in my life. A real love. A real breakup. A real make up. Twenty years from now, Patrick Swayze's 'She's Like the Wind' will come on the radio, and it'll take me right back to that sixteen-year-old boy crying himself to sleep because he can't imagine life without this one particular girl and because picturing her in the arms of another guy breaks his heart…over and over again."

Laura's eyes lock onto mine. She reaches up to my face. She puts her fingers on my mouth, tracing my lips. "Patrick Swayze?"

"The one and only," I say.

"Thank you for saying that," Laura says, kissing me.

I kiss her back, and I don't feel guilty about it. We kiss for a while. Her robe stays on. My hands behave. The moment is very sweet—nothing more, but nothing less either.

LAURA SHOWS ME TO the door. We hold hands as we walk through her house. "How are your parents doing?"

"Great."

"They still hate me?"

"No, they turned the corner with you a while ago."

"At least somebody did."

Her tone breaks my heart. "Most of their scorn pretty much gravitates around yours truly these days," I say.

Laura bites on the misdirection. "Don't tell me they're still pissed about you getting arrested."

"No, at least not as much as they were six months ago. My dad saw it in his heart to reduce my sentence from 'as I live and breathe, you will not have a social life' to a couple months."

"Your parents are realistic. They know the difference between having a couple beers at a party and killing somebody."

I think we both register the unintentional allusion to the abortion, if only for a split second. I wonder if it will always be in the back of our minds? Will it always hurt? Or will the pain be ephemeral and then linger on as a harmless but permanent scratch?

I have a couple of these scratches, some more visible than others.

"I think the fact I'm a minor is what really minimized the damage. It's off my record once I turn eighteen."

"And they can't print your name in the paper, can they?"

"Nope," I say. "My byline read something like, 'Minor, seventeen, Empire Ridge, illegal consumption, one-oh-seven a.m., three-eight-oh-nine Skipjack Road, by Empire Ridge Police Department, released to parents.'"

"Something like that?" Laura asks. "You saved that paper, didn't you?"

"Saved it?" I say. "I fucking framed it."

"People will still talk, you know." This time Laura's allusion is intentional. A final nod to our shared love. Our shared tragedy.

"Yeah, but we can deal with that." I say *we* for Laura's benefit. She smiles again.

"And how's little Jack doing?"

"Still the greatest gift this world has ever given me."

Laura reaches over with her free hand and rubs my arm. She opens the front door, leans in, and kisses me one more time. "Give one of those kisses to Jack for me, okay?"

I smile; Laura's taste still on my lips. I don't know what it is about this request that hits me so hard. With everything going through her head, with everything we've been through, she asks me to give my little brother a kiss? Did that really just fucking happen? It might be the most selfless thing she's ever said.

"Goodbye, Laura," is all I can muster at this point.

She runs her hand down my arm and squeezes my hand. "Bye, Hank."

I SIT IN MY Subie. I struggle to put the key in the ignition. I start the car, pull out of Laura's driveway.

A part of me wants to turn around. Wants to put down the fishing pole, walk into her bedroom, and scoop her up in my arms. We'll cry each other to sleep and start locking her bedroom door again, even when her parents are home, and they'll still pretend they don't notice.

I keep thinking about that last kiss, wondering if I've done the right thing.

CHAPTER TWENTY-SIX

Beth is waiting for me, sitting on her windowsill. I cross her front lawn and don't even bother going into her house. She's wearing nothing but my Empire Ridge High School letter jacket. No bra. No panties.

We kiss. She grabs my left hand, pulling it under the jacket, while at the same time grabs my right hand and pushes it down between her legs. Her parents are asleep in their bedroom across the hall. Dr. and Mrs. Burke are heavy sleepers. But tonight, Beth's screaming wakes them up.

I don't know if I expected screaming. But right after Beth grabbed my hands, and right before she tried to push my fingers inside her, I told her Laura and I were still in love and staying together, so screaming is what I got.

CHAPTER TWENTY-SEVEN

We've been in Panama City Beach, Florida, for three days. It's raining, again. Hatch is in the middle of throwing another party in our room attended by fifty of our not-so-closest friends. A medley of Guns N' Roses, Def Leppard, and Mötley Crüe blares out of the condo's blown speakers. I stand outside on our balcony, inhaling the ocean air. It took me a few days to get used to the smell, that blast of dead fish so shocking to the Midwestern nose, now just a pleasant salty scent. I lean over the railing. No one is on the beach.

Laura comes up behind me, taking my hand. She's wearing a florescent-yellow bikini covered up by one of my white T-shirts. "Come on," she says.

"Where we going?"

"Some place a little more private."

When you're sharing a three hundred-square-foot space with fifty people, *privacy* means locking yourself in the bathroom.

I shut the bathroom door behind me and turn to my girlfriend. She's already taken off the T-shirt. I grab her by the waist, kiss her on the lips. We take off the rest of our clothes. I notice Laura's tan lines, which appear as an upside down triangle below her waist and two milky-white crescent shapes rimming the bottom of each breast.

"You're getting some sun." I squeeze her breasts, more playful than sexual.

Laura pushes my hands away. "Stop it."

She still has a complex about her breasts, thinking they're saggy. Her low self-esteem is apparently drunk-proof.

"You should really show those things off more," I say.

"Whatever, Hank." She watches as I remove my shirt. "You're the one with the nice boobies."

I have a thing for calves. Laura has a thing for pectoral muscles. "Can you please *not* call them boobies?"

"What do you want me to call them?"

I step out of my swim trunks. "How about pecs?"

"Okay, you're the one with the nice pecs." Laura pulls back the shower curtain, stepping into the tub. She lies back and spreads her legs.

I step into the tub, but Laura raises her hand to stop me. "Wait a second," she says.

"What?"

"Do you have protection?"

"Shit! Left them in the nightstand out in the bedroom."

"That's okay."

"Really?" I ask. Knowing Laura's near-manic fear of pregnancy and her new penchant for two-plying my Johnson during her more fertile times of the month, I don't understand her insouciance. But hell, I'll run with it.

"Easy, trigger. Not in the sense that *you* think it's okay."

"What do you mean?"

"Well…" Laura fiddles with the curls dangling down the side of her head. "We could always do other things."

"Like what?"

"You could go down on me for a change."

Oral sex. As much as guys enjoy receiving it, we're reluctant to return the favor. Cunnilingus represents that tenuous line a heterosexual woman straddles (literally) between being bi-curious and full-blown lesbian—maybe even the one thing girls covet more than shoes. You would think we'd be a little less ambivalent about putting our tongues down there, and yet I've only done it a few times to Laura. Okay, maybe once if I'm being honest. And I think it was by accident.

"Sure."

"Sure?" Laura acts surprised.

"Why not?" I say.

I crawl into the large whirlpool tub. We kiss for a few seconds, but the cold, hard porcelain of the tub diffuses the notion of any extended foreplay.

I run my mouth down Laura's neck, through her cleavage, then down over her navel and in between her legs.

I ask Laura what she likes. My voice is muffled, obviously. She puts her hands on the back of my head, encourages me higher rather than lower. "I like the sucking more than the licking."

"It would help if I knew what the hell I was supposed to be sucking or not licking."

"Feel that thing in your mouth right there?"

She pushes me deeper to where all I can do is nod. And suck of course. "Good, right there! Suck on that, but do it gently. And try to concentrate on keeping your tongue more to the top right. No, *your* right, not mine. Think of it as a clock, and you want your tongue to hover around one o'clock."

After a few stops and starts, I find one o'clock. I get into a nice rhythm. Laura's knees lock my head in a vice grip. Her back arches. There's almost no circulation in the bathroom. We slip in the tub, coated in each other's sweat.

"Oh my God," Laura says.

My tongue is numb. My jaw a little sore. But I don't let on. "I do what I can to please my woman."

"*Your* woman?" Laura giggles.

"Well, yeah, of course." She giggles again. There's a knock at the door.

"Come on already!"

It's a girl's voice. Judging by her tone, she's been waiting to get in here for a while.

Laura and I slide out of the tub. I throw some soap and cold water on my face, washing Laura's scent off me as best I can. We get dressed.

I grab the doorknob. "You presentable?"

"Not really…" Laura looks at herself in the mirror. "But my face isn't going to fucking glow any brighter than it is right now."

We kiss one last time. I open the door. A petite blonde in a florescent-pink bikini bottom and a cut-off University of Illinois T-shirt stands in the doorway.

"Nice, guys," Beth says. "Real classy."

Laura takes three steps forward, nearly nose-to-nose with Beth. "What's your problem, Beth?"

"Problem?" Beth says, pointing at herself. "I don't have a problem." She looks at me. "Should I have a problem, Hank?"

Laura pushes Beth in the chest, I'm hoping harder than she intended. Beth stumbles backwards. "Your problem is with me, not Hank. You need to let him go, you fucking slut."

Out of the corner of my eye, a hand reaches for Laura's ponytail. Enter the drunk whirlwind formerly known as Claire Sullivan. Everything seems like it's in slow motion as Claire swings Laura across the room by her ponytail.

"Touch my best friend one more time, you fucking cunt," Claire says, dragging my girlfriend by her head. "I dare you."

I grab Claire's wrist just hard enough to make her let go of Laura's hair. With her free hand, Claire punches me in the groin. I fall to the ground.

"Hank!" Laura says, pushing Claire out of the way.

Beth grabs Claire just as she balls her right hand into a fist. "Easy, Sullivan."

I stand up, wincing from the pain. I look at Beth. Bowing, I offer the bathroom door to Beth with a wave of my hand. "If you need to go, then go."

Laura tugs on my elbow. "But what about me?"

"You should go get dressed," I say. "I'll take you out for some crab legs or something."

Claire flips me off. "Fuck you and your chivalry, Fitzy!"

"That's enough," Beth says. She grabs Claire, pulls her into the bathroom. She shakes her head back and forth, her eyes more disappointed in me than anyone else.

I STAND OUTSIDE ON the beachfront balcony of our condo. It's almost sunset, and my stomach is bloated with crabmeat. Laura is inside sleeping off the three-way combination of too much booze, sex, and seafood. I look down and see a tiny figure walking along the beach by herself.

It's Beth. She has on a tie-dyed tank top and denim cutoffs with a straw hat. She's barefoot, dipping her toes in the cold Gulf water, pulling them back when a wave comes too close. Every now and again, she raises her hand to hold her hat in place against the breeze.

I have to admit, Beth and I have fun together. The great thing when I'm with her is that everything doesn't have to be *everything*. With Laura, I count every second she and I aren't together. I want every moment to be ideal, even the bad ones. I want to give Laura the postcard-perfect dawn and the postcard-perfect dusk, even if it makes me miserable doing it. With Beth, maybe that postcard might not even happen, but at least I don't fool myself into believing a sunrise or sunset is any less beautiful without her in it.

Why doesn't some guy see what I see in Beth? Why doesn't someone come along and sweep her right off her feet? A decent guy. A guy who looks at Beth's subterranean self-esteem and her limitless capacity to forgive and says, "Beth, you're a fucking catch, now act like it. I love you!"

I love you.

I love you.

Wait, what?

I love Beth.

So there it is. Maybe it's always been there. But that's not the point. The point is I don't deserve Beth. I'm flawed and broken and can only bring her heartache. Laura and I make sense together almost out of necessity. Two people that self-absorbed and self-destructive can only be trusted with each other.

I place my hands on the balcony railing. Beth sees me. She stops and waves up at me. I wave back.

Fuck me. The sunset is more beautiful with her in it.

CHAPTER TWENTY-EIGHT

I'm getting kicked out of Disney World.

"Security is on its way, sir."

The Disney employee is a skinny little twerp, more nondescript than clean cut. He looks to be college age, early twenties at the oldest. I'm confident I can kick his ass. I stand near the exit of the "It's a Small World" ride, the Disney employee blocking my path.

"You've got to be kidding me," I say.

At the end of the ride, when our boat approached the final turn and just as that Orwellian menagerie of psychotic singing puppets faded from view, a bright flash went off. I noticed everyone screaming and gesticulating, so I got creative when the flash illuminated our boat. Only when we rounded that final turn and saw the massive white screen perched above the canal did I realize what was coming—a larger-than-life projected image of an eighteen-year-old-kid in a Notre Dame tank top giving the "It's A Small World" crowd of parents, pre-teens and toddlers…the finger.

Laura stands beside me, holding my hand. She's crying. I'm trying to reassure her. "Don't worry, babe. This is all one big fucking joke."

The nondescript guy gives me another look. "Kindly refrain from that language while you remain in the park, sir."

Laura won't stop crying. "Just apologize, Hank. Or at least be nice until your parents get off the ride and can talk to him."

Mom and Dad love Laura now, more than I love Laura. They insisted I invite her along for summer vacation or, as Mom declared it, "The last real family vacation with all my babies." She's such a melodramatic freak.

The end of high school came and went—spring break, Senior Prom, graduation, all that shit. After going almost an entire school year without coming home, Laura spent much of April back in Empire Ridge and then came back again for a weekend in May so we could finally get our prom night together. I made it onto the prom court, securing the Jock bloc and most of the Future Farmers of America, but I didn't have enough of the hood or bandie vote to snag the kingship. I skipped the after-prom party at Martin Neff's house because Beth was there. She and Hatch went to prom as friends. I lied and said I wasn't jealous. Hatch came to my house the next day crying because Claire lost her virginity to Bobbie the hockey player.

Graduation was a blur. I got drunk out of my mind on the last day of school. It was Hatch's bright fucking idea to raid my parents' liquor cabinet and mix everything that was clear into one giant Thermos. Several reliable witnesses informed me later I was conscious, there were balloons, and I appeared to be having a good time. I gave the senior speech at commencement, making a less-than-veiled reference to my arrest that earned a standing ovation from the senior class, a tepid laugh from the crowd, and a look of disgust on my principal's face that I will forever cherish. My father got drunk for the third time in his entire life at my graduation party. He kept shouting to everyone who would listen that he wasn't drunk as long as he could say "Johnny Mathis," right up until he burned off both eyebrows and all his forearm hair while grilling hamburgers and bratwurst.

Today is our first day at Disney World, and I'm exceptionally grumpy after yesterday's seventeen-hour road trip from Empire Ridge. At the last second this morning, literally as we stepped on the tram in front of our hotel, we decided to go to Magic Kingdom instead of Epcot. And by *we* I mean we took a vote, and I was overruled, which has made me even grumpier.

Mom and Dad arrive at the exit of the ride. Dad steps into the fray. "Excuse me, this here's my son, and I apologize for his actions. In his defense, he didn't know he was being photographed."

"That's what I've been trying to tell—"

Dad holds up his hand. "Look, I can vouch for him being a decent kid, and you have my word he'll be on his best behavior as long as he's anywhere in Disney World—Magic Kingdom, Epcot, MGM, anywhere."

There is a tenuous silence, apart from the not-so-distant chorus of multiracial animatronics. Mr. Indistinct steps aside. "Thank you for the explanation, sir. Just tell your son to watch himself. This is a family park, and we intend to keep it that way."

"Understood." Dad grabs me by the elbow. "Let's go, son."

We exit the ride to the stares of a hundred pairs of presumptuous eyes waiting in line. Apparently, they need to get in one last good dose of uninformed judgment before the cleansing redemptive power of "It's A Small World."

Laura pats my father on the back. "Thanks, Mr. Fitzpatrick."

"What are you thanking him for?" I say. "I had everything under control."

"Son, I wouldn't call getting banned from Disney World having 'everything under control.'" Dad laughs. "But it was worth it."

Mom slaps Dad in the chest. "John Henry Fitzpatrick!"

"What? You gotta admit, that was funny stuff." He makes a goofy face, raises both hands in the air, striking my same on-camera pose. Dad being Dad, he raises his two middle knuckles.

CHAPTER TWENTY-NINE

"What is going on?" Laura asks.

Today is my girlfriend's nineteenth birthday, a fact I probably should not have pointed out to my father. I shake my head. "It's out of my hands at this point."

After much whining from my sister Jeanine, we decided to attend tonight's Main Street Electrical Parade in the Magic Kingdom. I didn't notice Dad disappear into the crowd, but I sure as hell noticed his reappearance. Everybody did. He's standing in the middle of the Peter Pan float, microphone in hand, singing the Johnny Mathis rendition of the song "Laura."

"Is your dad for real?" Laura says. She blows him a kiss.

I watch my father on the stage. He's smiling at Mom and Jack, smiling at me, smiling at Laura, smiling at complete strangers as if he's known them his whole life. That's John Fitzpatrick for you. I can't help but be a shadow against a light that bright.

I almost don't pay attention to the lyrics—*she gave your very first kiss to you, that was Laura, but she's only a dream*—but how could I not?

CHAPTER THIRTY

We managed to squeeze in one more day at Magic Kingdom, a day at MGM Studios, a couple days poolside, and then today finally made it to Epcot.

Mom, Dad, Jeanine, and Jack have been asleep for the last half hour. Laura volunteered to read Jack his bedtime story and put him to bed. He's only five months old, but I could swear Jack has a crush on Laura, and the feeling seems mutual.

We're watching MTV on the pull-out couch. Laura seems distracted. I'm not exactly focused myself. "Jack go to sleep pretty easy?" I ask.

"Yeah," Laura answers. "He's such a beautiful little boy."

I nod. "The most beautiful I've ever seen."

Cheap Trick's "The Flame" comes on. Laura scoots next to me. "He gets it from his brother you know."

"He gets it from his dad," I say.

"He does?"

I'm a little shocked, maybe even flattered, with Laura's disbelief. But I appreciate her gesture. "Well, of course he does."

"Not that your Dad isn't fantastic," Laura says. "That stunt on the float was right out of *Ferris Bueller's Day Off.* Does anything fluster him?"

"That's more like it," I say, just as Laura starts kissing me on the throat.

She stops kissing me. "What did you say, Hank?"

"Nothing." I kiss her back. Laura runs her hand up my shirt. I grab her hand. "Laura, wait. There's something I need to tell you."

Laura backs up. She pulls in her knees, holds them close to her chest. "Here we go."

"Here we go?"

"Just get to what you have to say. I've seen this coming for weeks."

"You have?"

"You've been distant and cold to me. Go ahead and say it. You want to break up."

"Break up?" I reach, squeeze her hand. "I don't think I want to do that."

Laura lets go of her knees and straightens her legs. She looks relieved. That is unfortunate. I squeeze her hand again. "You might want to break up with *me*, though."

"Why?" The concern returns to Laura's voice. Concern is a good thing. Maybe she's seen this coming.

"I kissed Sheila."

Laura stands up from the pull-out couch. "My best friend, Sheila?"

"It was just one kiss," I say, ready with the justifications. "And you and Sheila haven't talked in about six months. She told me. It was no big deal."

I leave out the part about Sheila and me being in the tent together. The part where Sheila said, "I just really want to kiss you right now." The part where I obliged her request without hesitation. The part where Hatch was listening outside the tent and barged in on us only ten seconds later. The part where I knew Sheila and I would have done a lot more than kiss if not for Hatch's impeccable timing, again. (The guy fucking loses his virginity to my scraps, and he can't show the common courtesy of letting me destroy a relationship and a lifelong friendship?)

"When and where did this happen?" Laura asks.

"Two weekends ago."

"When I was back at Bucknell for early registration?"

"Yes, that weekend. We were all camping out near Empire Quarry. Everybody was pretty drunk. You should have seen Cash. He got drunk and then started tripping hard on acid. He spent half the night in a yoga position saying, 'Touch me, Hank, just touch me.' I kept having to walk over to him and touch him on the shoulder, or else Cash would start screaming hysterically. Not that big of a deal, except for the fact that the Indiana State Police Scuba Team was conducting practice night dives about two hundred yards away from us."

Cash Digsby graduated with Laura. He's a year older than me. An unmitigated stoner, he's the comic relief to almost any story in which he's referenced. Overall, I have to say that Laura seems neither amused nor relieved.

"You kissed one of my best friends, Hank."

"I realize that, Laura. I made a mistake. I'm sorry."

"Are you?"

"Of course."

"And it was just one kiss? Nothing else? Nothing more?"

"That was it, I swear."

Laura sits back down on the pull-out couch, slides her hand over to mine. "What does Beth think about all this?"

"I'll take non sequiturs for eight-hundred dollars, Alex."

"The girl is in love with you. You know that, right?"

"Apparently I don't."

Laura wipes one solitary tear out of the corner of her right eye. She sits back down on the pull-out couch, slides her hand over to mine. "Keep lying to yourself and lying to me. I probably deserve it."

"Deserve what? Am I in the fucking *Twilight Zone* or something?" I stand up, walk to the television, and turn up the volume to drown out our conversation. "Look, Laura, if you think my behavior is somehow justified by how everything went down last summer, then I can—"

"I'm not using that as justification for your behavior. Don't be ridiculous."

"Then what's up?"

"What's up is *us*. Does it hurt me to hear my boyfriend made out with my best friend? Sure it does. But at least you're being upfront with me."

"Yeah, I guess." I'm beyond confused. "Uh, you're welcome?"

"That's not what I want to hear, Hank." Laura pats the couch. "Come here, sit down with me."

"On one condition," I say.

"What's that?"

"If I sit down, you have to tell me why you're acting so weird."

"That's kind of what I was getting around to."

SHE TELLS ME HIS name is Ian Powell. He's a little older than she is. He took a few years off after high school to do some soul searching as a yoga instructor in Belize. He works nights at UPS to help pay his tuition at

Bucknell. They met last year at freshman orientation, talked a lot in those first few months, when Laura thought she had lost me. They've been close friends ever since. Nothing has "really" happened between them, but they've been talking on the phone a lot this summer. She met his family. They live in Harrisburg, Pennsylvania. Dad is a representative in the statehouse. Mom is an Episcopal priest. Come fall semester, Laura and Ian "want to give dating a shot."

She squeezes my hand. "You okay?"

"This is getting to be a bad habit with you."

"That's not fair, Hank."

I raise her hand to my lips, kiss her on the knuckles. "Yeah, I know."

"This really isn't about Beth or Ian. You know that, right?"

"You should have figured out by know that in the grand scheme of things I don't know shit."

"It's about us," Laura says. "You and I have been through a lot, more than most couples twice our age. But we're high school sweethearts. We're not supposed to make it. I'm at Bucknell for three more years. You're at Indiana University next year. We're going to be something like five hundred miles apart, right?"

"Six hundred and twenty point three-five miles."

"Exactly!" This time Laura seems unmoved by my geographic acumen. "Six hundred and twenty point three-five miles apart for more than two-thirds of the year, maybe more if I stay out East next summer like I plan to do. The odds just aren't in our favor."

"Since when did you become such the pessimist?"

"For Christ's sake, you're rooming with Hatch at IU. You've already cheated on me multiple times; you just don't know it yet."

She has a point there. If Hatch has any say in the matter—and he usually has the *only* say—there will be no shortage of liquored-up whores in our apartment come fall semester.

"You know I'm right, Hank."

"But it feels like we're just giving up," I say. "Has our relationship lost some of its spark? Maybe. Probably. I mean, of course there are times when I want to be with other girls, but there are also times when I look at you and can't imagine being with anyone else."

"And I feel the same way. A part of me will always love you. But we owe one another some time to figure out these moments when we think about other people. We're too young to start living with regrets and what-ifs. I have to do this—for me, for you, for Ian."

"I realize that, Laura. And I'm just as ready for this as you are. I just can't—well, I don't quite know how to explain this. I can't..."

"You can't what?"

"I can't imagine my life without you in it. Do I want to have the full college experience? Yes. Do I want to see other people? Yes. But do I want to just walk away from you, from us? Do I want to never touch you, never hold you again? Laura, I—"

She cuts my last sentence off. When all else fails, kissing a boy shuts him up faster than anything else.

We remove each other's clothes, oblivious of the fact that we're separated from my parents and siblings by a few sheets of drywall and a couple hollow-paneled doors.

Laura gets on top, maybe to feel in control one last time of a relationship that's never quite seemed to be in anyone's control. If only for a few fleeting minutes, our love-making is new again—naive, bold, reckless.

I push her off me. Bending her over the couch, I take her from behind. I smack her ass, maybe a little too hard.

1990-1991

CHAPTER THIRTY-ONE

Hatch and I are sitting in our apartment at Varsity Villas. We're a little drunk at the moment. What am I saying? We're *a lot* drunk at the moment. We blew off all our Friday classes to drink forties of Crazy Horse malt liquor and watch the *Star Wars* trilogy on the old LaserDisc player Dad gave me from the dealership. I have a collection of twenty LaserDiscs, fourteen of which are General Motors sales videos. The other titles comprise the aforementioned three *Star Wars* movies, *The Hunt for Red October, When Harry Met Sally*, and Chevy Chase's highly underrated *Modern Problems*.

We tried the fraternity life together, but both of us washed out as pledges. Hatch wasn't a big fan of attending compulsory study tables or washing dirty toilets. I wasn't a big fan of getting pelted by rotten pig intestines while doing push-ups and sucking on a stick of butter rolled in Copenhagen Original Fine Cut tobacco as Matthew Wilder's "Break My Stride" played on a continuous loop. Hatch quit in the middle of pledgeship. He didn't mind the hazing, just the study tables and the chores. I minded the hazing. Two weeks after I punched my pledge trainer in the face during a midnight lineup—"pledge trainer" being fraternity code for World's Biggest Cocksucker—I was blackballed. We both struggled through our freshman year, skipping more classes than we attended, and yet somehow emerged with GPAs north of 2.0.

Hatch hands me a fresh forty of Crazy Horse. "Thanks," I say reluctantly.

"Pals, Fitzy?" He offers the toast as more of a question than a declaration.

I unscrew the cap, taking a small sip of malt liquor. "What's on your mind?"

"Nothing," Hatch says.

"Bullshit."

"Promise you won't go apeshit on me."

"Nothing you do surprises me, Hatch."

"Beth Burke and I fooled around last night."

"Excuse me?" I say.

"I didn't want you to hear it from someone else. We ran into one another at a party on the other side of the Villas. One thing led to another. I couldn't help myself."

HATCH SPARES NO DETAILS, but the gist of it is they got "totally ripped," went skinny-dipping in a pubic fountain, and had "Olympic-level" sex in a hotel suite that was so expensive he maxed out his Discover Card. He doesn't shut up, rambling on for ten minutes, talking about the flexibility of gymnasts, and about sexual positions that may or may not exist.

"You finished?" I say.

"Yep," Hatch says.

"Do you even know what an iron cross is?"

"I made that part up. Sounds good though, doesn't it?"

"Sure, it sounds good, if you're fucking a dude. An iron cross is when you hold a position like a cross on the rings. It's a men's gymnastics skill."

I lift the Crazy Horse to my mouth, taking down a good twelve ounces with three swallows. I sit the bottle down on the coffee table. I pull a half-smoked cigarette out of the ashtray on the coffee table and light it.

I can tell the silence is killing Hatch. He's fidgety, agitated. Good.

"So, we cool?" Hatch says.

The stale smoke rims my head halo-like. "Why wouldn't we be cool, *pal*?"

"You know, you and Beth. You had a thing there for awhile."

"What thing? We never really dated."

"You broke her heart when you stayed with Laura."

"I did?"

"Stop playing dumb," Hatch says. "Look, as much as I'd like to pretend she's really into me, a part of Beth will probably hold a torch for you till the day she dies. You can still see it in her eyes every time your name comes up. It's disgusting."

"And yet you still fucked her?"

"Show a little respect, Fitzy."

"And there it is," I say.

"There *what* is?"

"You're crushing hard on Beth."

"Am not," Hatch says.

"I know you."

"No, you don't."

"Yes, I do. Ask me."

"Ask you what?"

"Do we really have to drag this out?"

"So you wouldn't mind if I asked Beth out on a proper date?"

"You and the word 'proper' go together like JFK and the military-industrial complex."

"Fuck you, Fitzy."

"Relax, Hatch ol' buddy." I pat him on the back. "You don't have to ask me for permission. We're not in high school anymore. Beth is a big girl now, with plenty of suitors from what I'm told."

"You're one to talk."

"Excuse me?"

"Who should we start with?" Hatch says. "Pattie, Emily, Summer, Nicole, Maria, Angelina the Untouchable, Harper, *my fucking cousin*."

"Okay, you made your point."

"Have I?"

I think Hatch loves to do the play-by-play recap of these past two years more so for his own edification than anything else. Hatch affectionately refers to the twenty-two month window between July 1989 and now as my "Monster of Cock Tour." And I will reluctantly admit, when I step outside myself, that I do look like a bit of a whore.

Laura and I broke up on the Fourth of July—well, the fifth of July, considering we didn't say the actual words 'break up' to one another until we had finished having sex for the third time in as many hours around two in the morning our last day in Disney World. She left for Bucknell and was back in Pennsylvania the very next week, the same week I started seeing Emily Kaufmann.

Emily and I first met when we were both in high school. Hatch dated her for something like a month. I think, statistically speaking, given the number of girls we've swapped, Hatch and I have all but fucked each other.

Emily was my height, the tallest girl I've ever dated—dark hair, slightly bow-legged, with a lean, athletic build. She was also on the rebound from her high school sweetheart. I caught her eye at a pool party—a party at which, drunk, stoned, and wearing only my boxer shorts, I jumped off the roof of a house into the shallow end of a backyard pool, my head absorbing most of the thirty foot fall. Emily was the first one who noticed the bleeding. She drove me home. I told her not to tell my parents. She told me she'd never seen me without my shirt on and didn't realize I was in such good shape. She held a gauze pad on the back of my head all night, every hour checking my wound and shaking me awake to make sure I wasn't in a coma. Our month or so of dating was unusual, borderline chaste. We made out for hours at a time but didn't do a whole lot beyond that. We cried in the front seat of my car to Bryan Adams's "(Everything I Do) I Do It For You" when we said our goodbyes over Labor Day weekend. Emily cried because I was "special" and "as much a friend as a lover." I cried because we never had sex.

My first night as a freshman at IU, and all of twenty-four hours after lip-synching to Emily, *"There's nooo love, like yourrr love,"* I fooled around with a full-time med student and part-time amateur boxer named Summer. To my credit, she looked a lot like an older Emily. She invited me over to her place. We started kissing, and Summer had just taken off her shirt when she said, "I'm going to slip into something more comfortable." Two minutes later, she walked out of the bathroom wearing a white V-neck men's undershirt, red Umbros, and matching red boxing gloves. She threw me an extra pair of gloves, said it would be fun to box. "It'll be like foreplay," she said. It was fun, right up until she caught me with a left uppercut to the chin that knocked me unconscious. I was only out for a few seconds, but the ensuing headache left me crippled on my couch for the rest of the weekend.

I first met Pattie Reisen the December before Christmas break 1990. She was a baseball groupie who followed around the IU players with her tongue hanging out of her mouth. I wasn't a baseball player. But I was athletic, and I pulled off the Richard Grieco look—triple-pierced left ear, long hair with bandanna, black leather jacket, ripped jeans—enough to merit an AIDS test. Pattie made her first pass at me the Thursday night before Christmas, stumbling intoxicated into my apartment wearing an IU "We're #1" foam finger. "I wunna' kith you right now," she kept mumbling, shaking her foam finger at me. At the time, she was dating a guy on the baseball team. He was a pitcher, reputed to have the meanest fastball in the Big Ten conference. With her cropped, dark brown hair and tanned skin, Pattie reminded me of Rachel Ward—more *Against All*

Odds than *The Thornbirds*, although both examples are infinitely hot. Her birdlike features—small eyes positioned close together, a petite sharp nose, tiny feet—didn't quite complete the Ward impersonation. But in concert with one another, these features just worked. If not the most beautiful, Pattie was the most striking girl I'd ever contemplated sleeping with. Still, I preferred my head attached to my shoulders as opposed to severed by a baseball traveling at a ninety miles per hour. Pattie and I "kithed" for about five minutes, then I told her to come back for more when she was single.

Nicole Chase was my Christmas fling. Dad made me take a "character building" job over winter break working third shift at a box factory. The foreman decided to give me the hardest job on the line—catching cardboard sheets out of the corrugation machine. My hands looked like raw ground beef for the first five days. Nicole's job was to assemble the finished cardboard displays. She had long, curly blond hair, big eyes, and tanned skin that gave off an unnatural sheen beneath a daily applied layer of baby oil. She was eighteen years old and had a two-year-old son. She was neither married to nor dating the birth father. I went to the circus with Nicole, her son, Nicholas, and the biological father's parents. It wasn't even weird. We had a good time. I held Nicholas in my arms while he fed the giraffe sweet potatoes. Nicole stood next to me, and the grandfather took our picture. The animal handler passing out the sweet potato slices said we were a cute family.

Okay, it was weird.

Nicole never wore panties. I'd say she dumped me, but I don't think we were ever officially dating. We were just having a lot of sex one day, and the next day we weren't. She reconciled with her high school sweetheart—also, not Nicholas's birth father. Nicole was a bit of a hose beast, I think.

Pattie Reisen came back to me when she was single, and we started dating the first week of school in January 1991. She lived two doors down from me in the Villas, and over the course of January and February we had sex more times than I thought possible. In her room. In my room. In her shower. In my shower. Outdoors. On Valentine's Day, for reasons still unclear to me, I told Pattie I loved her. In response, she did an interactive striptease for me that involved strawberries, whipped cream, and Bobby Brown's "Rock Wit'cha." Pattie is the only girl I've ever dated who woke me up in the mornings with blow jobs. On one such occasion she lifted her mouth off of me and watched as I shot my wad in my own face. She laughed, so I dumped her.

By early March I had my eyes set on Maria. Armed with no musical training, save a half year of trumpet lessons in the eighth grade, I auditioned for the Indiana University Theater Department's production of *West Side Story* solely to get in the female lead's pants. Her name was Maria in real life, which of course made her that much hotter. I landed the role of Nibbles, and I landed Maria. We made out on a kitchen table at the cast party. Between her large breasts and supple lips, Maria could give the best combination pearl necklace–blow job I'll ever receive in this life or the next. She was three years older than me, a semester away from graduating, and already talking about her plans after school: maybe law school, maybe social work, but definitely marriage and a big family. I liked her enough to even float some halfway sincere reassurances, telling her right before I left for spring break, "I'm getting used to the idea of us—of being with you—for the long haul."

Twenty-four hours later, I fell in love with someone else.

It started when I jumped on the hood of a random car idling down the strip in Panama City Beach. I had an instant crush on this olive-skinned vision who was riding shotgun. Angelina Valerio was an Italian girl from Boston. She spoke with a heavy accent and attended Florida State in nearby Tallahassee. We stayed up all night drinking and commiserating over our shared hatred of the University of Miami. We said our goodbyes, and the next morning she walked two miles from her condo just to give me fresh baked muffins that tasted homemade but, Angelina admitted, "came froom a baw-ux." We made love for the better part of five days straight, pausing only to write love letters to one another while the other one was sleeping.

When I got back to school, I walked the three blocks to Maria's apartment to tell her, "I feel like we're going too fast and this relationship thing is just too much work," leaving out the part about casting aside our two months together because I was in love with someone halfway across the country who I'd known for less than nine days.

Angelina drove back and forth between Bloomington and Tallahassee three times in four weeks. I introduced her to my parents, and they loved her. Over a four-week period, Angelina logged seventy-two hours and forty-six hundred miles in the name of love. On the Saturday night of the third weekend, I ran out of condoms, Angelina told me she was sterile, we had unprotected sex on the floor of my apartment to Depeche Mode's *Violator* album, and I dumped her the very next morning. At the end of those four weeks, without ever leaving Bloomington, I was the one who told her, "This long-distance thing is exhausting and just isn't working out for me." The truth—that I was so obsessed with her I was heartbroken at the prospect of not ever having children with her—would have just fucked us both up. To this day I don't know why I fell that hard that fast. Everyone has that one that got away, I guess. Mine just wasn't on the line that long. So it goes.

The next year or so, from roughly May 1991 to now, was a bit more of a blur. There was Harper Donovan, a girl who had a crush on me in high school and has lately become my casual sex partner. Once even, when Harper was out of town, I think I had sex with her roommate, although I still can't recall if there was actual penetration. There was Hatch's red-headed cousin—man, he was fucking pissed about that one, although he did get a chuckle out of the fact that she told me the next morning I wasn't that good in bed. There was the sorority girl—Kathy? Katie?—who was engaged the first time we had sex and then married the second time we did it. In my defense, she didn't tell me about being engaged our first time in the sack, and I didn't care to ask her when she was more than willing to make a follow-up visit. I even circled back around to Emily Kaufmann once. I fell back in love with her for about a week before I realized she still wasn't going to sleep with me.

"Hatch, what was Beth even doing in town last night?"

"Just passing through, on her way to a gymnastics meet at Ohio State."

"She's competing for Illinois, right?"

"Yep, the Illini," Hatch says just as the phone rings.

"I'll get that," I say, standing up. Dad and I have been playing phone tag the last couple days."

"Can we continue this conversation later?" Hatch asks.

"What else is there left to say? You like her?"

"It's like you're not even fucking listening to me."

"What?" I say.

"Beth is still into you."

"Call me old-fashioned, Hatch, but fucking my best friend isn't the way to my heart." I pick up the phone. "Hello?"

"Hey, son, got a second?"

"Of course, Dad. What's up?"

"You busy?"

"Nah, Hatch and I were just shooting the shit."

"Finals going okay?"

"Great. Just one more to go."

"What are your plans for next week?"

"No big plans really," I say this while noticing Hatch hasn't left the room yet.

"Dad, can you hang on a second?"

"Sure thing," Dad says.

I put the phone against my chest. "Hatch, what do you want?"

"I want to know we're okay."

"Okay?" I ask. "You're my friend, not my fucking wife. If you want to make a move on Beth, make a move. Regardless of what you think there is between her and me, that ship sailed a long time ago."

"Really?"

"Really." I start to bring the phone up to my mouth. I pause and then place it back against my chest. "But, Hatch?"

Hatch is halfway out the door. He pokes his head back inside the room. "Yes?"

"Thanks for asking," I say.

Hatch nods, leaves the room. I don't know why I'm being so gracious. Truthfully, I don't want Hatch to ask Beth out. I don't give a shit that I'm selfish. There's no rational reason for why my throat hurts, for why my heart hurts. In the words of David Coverdale, here I go again.

"Hank? Hello? Hank?"

The voice on the other end of the phone interrupts my contemplation. I rest the receiver on my chin. "Sorry about that, Dad. Where were we?"

"Your plans for next week?"

"Oh yeah. Nothing on the schedule. Just hanging out. Don't start back at the box factory until the first week of June."

"You think you might be able to set aside next week for some time with your Dad?"

"What do you have in mind?"

"Your mother just called. Turns out she can't get off work next week, last week of school and all. Says the guidance office is a madhouse."

"To be expected. So what are you saying exactly?"

"What I'm saying is I can't go on an all-expenses-paid Oldsmobile trip to the Bahamas by myself."

CHAPTER THIRTY-TWO

I hand my father a beer. "Cheers, Dad."

"Cheers, son." He takes a drink. "Good show."

I'm already halfway through my fourth beer since we boarded the ship. I'm tipsy and a little seasick. "Fantastic show," I say.

Dad and I have been getting drunk together all week. Our drink of choice is Kalik, "The Beer of the Bahamas." Dad has been cool since the moment we landed in Nassau. After we got to our hotel room, he handed me a Kalik from our mini-bar and said, "Drinking age is eighteen here, son. Who am I to defy native customs?"

It took me a solid twenty-four hours to feel comfortable drinking in front of Dad, maybe twice that long before I felt comfortable power drinking in front of him. We saw Kool and the Gang live in concert last night during the Oldsmobile gala at Merv Griffin's Paradise Island Resort. The band surprised everyone with their crispness and showmanship, reeling off an amazing set of their greatest hits: "Ladies Night," "Get Down On It," "Fresh," "Cherish," "Joanna," "Too Hot." As the evening drew to a close, this glistening embodiment of late-seventies funk segued finally into "Celebration"—the greatest song ever, although no one over the age of eight admits to liking it anymore—as I segued into a mosh pit of forty- and fifty-something car dealer wives groping me on the dance floor.

Today is our last full day in Nassau. Oldsmobile chartered us a Spanish Galleon for the day. It isn't a real Spanish Galleon, rather a diesel trawler sheathed in a not-even-close-to-authentic facsimile of a Spanish Galleon. The three masts are decorative—about half as tall as they should be—although a small sail is raised on the aft lateen rig advertising the charter company's name and phone number.

"Kool and the Gang aren't the Commodores," Dad says, "but they were fun."

In addition to being one of the few decent bands Dad likes, the Commodores have a special place in Dad's heart because the priest at Grandma Eleanor's funeral gave a eulogy in which he claimed Eleanor's life was analogous to the song "Three Times a Lady."

Talk about a reach.

"Hey, Pops, speaking of the Commodores, did you know Grandma Louise used to tell me black singers grew beards because all black men have bad acne?"

Dad chokes on a swallow of beer, coughs, and hits his chest. "She did not tell you that."

"Oh yes she did."

"She was just raised in a different time, Hank."

I look around to make sure no one is within earshot. "Dad, the other night when we all went to her house for dinner, Grandma told me that NAACP stood for 'Niggers Are Actually Colored Pollacks.'"

Dad chokes again. "Hank, Louise's sister married a Pollack!"

"So *that* is the part you find offensive?"

Dad pats me on the shoulder. "Take it easy on her, son. She took your Grandpa's death pretty hard, same as your mother."

The taint of death still sticks to all of us. Grandpa Fred, my mother's Dad, died in October. A retired Eli Lilly chemist, he had a hand in the development of Prozac, or at least I claim he did. I know Mom and Aunt Claudia were two of the first children in the country to get the Salk polio vaccine, which is almost as interesting.

The doctors said it happened at about six thirty in the morning. Grandpa Fred finished his daily three-mile walk, his seventy-four-year-old swimmer's physique easily mistaken for a man twenty years his junior. After his walk, he picked the last of his vegetables, at least the ones that had withstood the freak October blizzard earlier in the week. The vegetable garden—a half-acre plot of tomatoes, green beans, radishes, green onions, zucchini, and peppers—was where Grandpa sought refuge from my paranoid schizophrenic grandmother. Grandpa entered the kitchen through the backdoor and grabbed a cup of coffee on his way to the kitchen sink. In the middle of washing a giant zucchini, he was struck down where he stood by a pulmonary embolism. Grandma called Aunt Claudia, Mom's sister, first. She and her husband, Uncle Howard, showed up. Uncle Howard tried to administer CPR. But Grandpa was already gone.

Dad puts his arm around me and squeezes. We let the moment dissipate. A steel drum band starts up aft of us near the helm.

"Thanks, Dad."

"For what?"

"For the trip, this time with you."

"You don't have to thank me. Spending a week with my oldest son is a privilege, just as being your father for nineteen years has been a privilege."

"Laying it on a little thick there, aren't we?" I create some separation, giving him the customary you're-cramping-my-style push-off.

"Hey!" Dad says.

"What?"

He pokes me in the chest. "You too old to give your dad a hug or something?"

"No." I grab his shoulder and squeeze, leaning in for a one of those awkward man hugs. I ease back. "There, you happy now?"

Dad smiles. "We should do this more often."

"Hug?"

"Well sure, but not just that."

"We should go to the Bahamas, get plastered, and play blackjack more often?"

"No." He slaps me on the shoulder. "And remember what I told you. This weekend—the drinking, the gambling—that's between you and me."

"Got it."

"What I'm saying is we should hang out more—me and you. Father and son. Or at least talk more."

"We talk, Dad."

"Not enough. You're your mother's son. She knows things about you I'll never know."

"It's not like that, Dad."

"It isn't?"

"Oh, make no mistake. I'm a certifiable mamma's boy."

"That's my point."

"But it's not that I don't want to confide in you. You and I come from two very different worlds, and I think we're just now trying to figure each other out."

"We're not that different, Hank."

"You don't think so?"

"No."

"You were raised poor by two alcoholic parents and shared a room with your grandma until you were sixteen. You're the only kid from your fourth grade class to have a college diploma. You're hardened, yet full of conviction and hope. You're a good man."

"And you, Hank?"

"I don't even see myself as a good *anything*. I've had a great life handed to me, and I've crapped on most of my opportunities. I was drunk both times I took my SAT, I got arrested and suspended from the wrestling team, and I didn't even attempt to fill out my Notre Dame application."

"You act as if you were born with a silver spoon in your mouth, Hank. We've had some lean, tough times, especially when you were little. Uncle Mitch could tell you some stories."

"Uncle Mitch could tell us a lot of stories," I say.

"What do you mean by that?" Dad says.

Goddammit. Fucking Kalik. "Nothing," I say. "I mean, uh, is Mitch doing okay? You talk to him at all?"

"Not for at least a year."

"You miss him?"

"I guess, maybe, I don't know. Mitch is not the guy I grew up with anymore. Some things came out in the annulment proceedings, things that changed the way I looked at him."

My chest tightens. A small but noticeable panic attack. "What things?"

Dad takes a long sip of Kalik. "Things I should have seen. Things maybe I did see but never chose to acknowledge."

Is it really going to be this easy? Am I just going to say to my father here and now, "Well, my memories of childhood are tempered by the sensation of Uncle Mitch's hands cupping my balls. Are those the things you're talking about?" Or maybe I'll say to him, "My godfather used to molest me right in front of you and Mom under a blanket while we all watched *The Muppet Show* together on Sunday nights. Is that what you never chose to acknowledge?"

"Uncle Mitch is gay," Dad says.

"What?"

"He's always been gay. I just never wanted to admit it. You remember us ever joking about Mitch serving the shortest tour of duty in the history of the Vietnam War?"

"Vaguely. An accident during Army basic training or something like that?"

"If by 'accident' you mean being caught in the shower in a compromising position with his staff sergeant."

"Holy shit."

"Yep."

"Dad, I…I don't know what to say."

"What can you say?"

"So that's the reason Aunt Ophelia got the annulment?"

"Because of the Army incident?"

"Well, yeah," I say.

Dad takes another sip of beer. "Unfortunately, Ophelia has known from the very beginning about that. She got the annulment because Mitch has been having homosexual affairs behind her back for the last twenty years."

"Just affairs?" I ask, my question more of a challenge. *Come on, Dad. Connect the fucking dots.* I have to give Mitch some credit for the misdirection. He's recast his role in our little morality play. He's not a guy into little boys—he's merely a gay adulterer. He outed himself to protect himself. Yeah, maybe Dad did detect the occasional furtive glance or maybe even an inappropriate gesture or two. But it's still a whole lot easier to rationalize someone who's lost and searching than someone who relishes being the predator.

"I would think twenty years of affairs is pretty good justification, Hank."

Okay, so Dad isn't connecting the dots. Time for a new approach. "What's Mom say about this?"

"She doesn't know."

"What?"

"I'm not even supposed to know. The terms of the annulment were confidential, and Mitch and Ophelia were sworn to secrecy."

"Mitch told you the day after he was in our driveway, didn't he?"

"Closer to a week after, but how would you—"

I cut Dad's words off with a hard, chest-to-chest bear hug. I actually hug my father all the time—granted, less than he would like and more than I would prefer—but this hug is different. It's desperate, it's knowing. Dad hugs me back, like he always does, only now I'm the one who isn't letting go. I'm holding on, hoping that I can somehow tell Dad about Mitch through osmosis.

"You okay, son?"

I can't tell him. In a way, Mitch has died in Dad's eyes. That has to be enough. I can hear Mitch in my head. *"So that's what this has come down to, son? You're willing to break your father's heart, just like that?"*

No, I'm not willing to do that. Uncle Mitch still wins.

I let go and straighten my shirt. The steel drum band continues playing on the deck. Dad is marching, two fresh Kaliks in hand. He hands me my last beer on the island. "Cheers, son."

"Cheers, Dad."

"Hank?"

"Yeah?"

More questions? Has he finally figured it out?

"You were drunk both times you took the SAT?"

1992

CHAPTER THIRTY-THREE

I watch as Jack zooms down the hallway of St. Augustine's Little Sisters of the Poor on his tricycle. He's chasing Augie, a Border Collie mix and the resident nursing home mascot. Grandpa George used to be right out there with him, but not today. Maybe never again. Dad is over in the nuns' office making arrangements to transfer Grandpa to hospice care.

Our old rituals simplified drastically when Grandpa moved in with us. If I'm being honest, he was an old guy, and I had better things to do. But the one ritual we still enjoyed together was a Cincinnati Reds game.

I was sitting with Grandpa in his bedroom, the expansive room in the corner of our first floor Dad converted into a custom mini-suite for his father. We were watching the Reds play the Padres. It was a late afternoon game. Eric Davis had just hit for the cycle and drove in his sixth RBI of the game. "Man oh man, Grandpa," I said. "Davis is on fire!"

Grandpa didn't respond.

"Grandpa?" I asked, turning to him.

He looked at me with fear in eyes, tilting his head as if to say, "What's happening to me?" He couldn't speak. I screamed for Dad.

"He had a stroke," the doctors said at the hospital, "likely even two or three of them."

GRANDPA HAD AN AMAZING, albeit incomplete, recovery. He could feed and dress himself. And while his gait and speech were slower, his mind was still sharp and his incontinence wasn't any more pervasive than it had been. But Dad knew the stroke was the first domino in his father's endgame, and so he moved him to St. Augustine's Little Sisters of the Poor, a Catholic nursing home on the northwest side of Indianapolis. *"I'm jealous, Pops,"*

Dad said during the family's first visit up from Empire Ridge. "You're right across the street from the new Shapiro's location."

"Forget corn beef and cabbage," Grandpa said back to my father. "Give your Grandpa some matzo ball soup and a potato pancake, and you got yourself one happy old Irishman."

Dad smiled when Grandpa said these words, but he couldn't forgive himself. Dad believed he had abandoned his father.

Grandpa George's enthusiasm for living has never waned, but his hips didn't share in the sentiment. First one hip went, then the other. He had his last big fall in March and has been bedridden for going on sixty days. It's sad to see such a proud man go this way—too old to survive hip-replacement surgery, too stubborn to know when to die.

CHAPTER THIRTY-FOUR

At the cemetery I notice Dad staring at his parents' tombstone, the '1992' yet to be etched next to the '1906'– below 'George Fitzpatrick.' Grandpa's casket is draped in an American flag. An honor guard stands at attention on each side of the casket—two Army officers, a man and a woman, wearing olive-green uniforms and black berets. Both of them turn and salute the casket. They execute a couple more turns, saluting again.

Dad is crying. He puts his arm around me. "You and your Grandpa had some good times together."

"The best times," I say.

A third Army officer I hadn't noticed, about thirty yards away standing amongst the rows of white and gray memorials, starts to play "Taps." It makes me think of the two war stories Grandpa George would tell me over and over. One was about the time he was in charge of four German POWs—"a right decent bunch of krauts"—down at the Army Air Force base in Corpus Christi, Texas, and how they hid his rifle as a practical joke when he fell asleep under a tree. The other story was about when he served as a member of the honor guard that received the dead soldiers from overseas.

With his horrible eyesight, Grandpa was forced to remain stateside with the United States Army Air Force for World War II. I usually lie and tell people he was an airplane mechanic or even a pilot, but the truth was he spent the better part of the war painting big-breasted pinup girls on the sides of bombers. As one of the base's semi-permanent residents, Grandpa was in charge of the honor guard. One day toward the end of the war, he was intently listening to the bugler on the tarmac as they offloaded the flag-draped caskets from a C-47 transport plane. As the bugler started into "Taps," only then did Grandpa realize he had listened to the same person playing for three years. For no other reason than the fact he could carry a tune on a hollow piece of brass, this kid was never sent to the frontline.

"That's when I knew your father would be a musician," Grandpa said. "If I could get him to pick up a horn, maybe I could save him from ever having to pick up a gun."

"Taps" ends. The first two Army officers fold the flag and present it to my father. They thank him for Grandpa's service "on behalf of a grateful nation."

I see Grandma Eleanor's casket in the hole below Grandpa. I picture Grandma, a chain-smoking Methodist to the very end, chewing Grandpa George out right about now. Grandpa made sure they were buried in a Catholic cemetery. "Eleanor didn't live Catholic," he once said, "but she sure as hell is dying Catholic." I imagine the late Mr. Shapiro handing Grandpa a potato pancake dripping with applesauce—just the way he liked it—and Grandpa saying something like, "See Eleanor, I told you they got into heaven, too."

The soldiers leave. Dad is still staring at the tombstone. "You know, your Grandpa chose this precise burial site."

"Really?"

"Yes, sir. He wanted to make sure he and Mom were in walking distance of the pickled pig's feet and turtle soup at Barringer's Tavern."

"That's kind of gross, Dad."

I expect him to laugh here. Instead, he turns away from the gravesite. I reach for him. "Dad?"

He grabs me in a bear hug. His body is sweating, shaking with grief. He mumbles into my shoulder. "Promise me something, son."

"Anything."

"Promise me, when I get old and worn down, that you'll take care of me like we tried to care of your grandfather."

A flash of Dad's youthful face morphing into the face of my Grandpa—a freckled, blonde-till-the-day-he-died Irishman, with a nose and ears too large for even his whiskey-swollen face and thick bifocals that exaggerated the size of his eyes.

"Come on, Dad." I hug him back. "Like you even have to ask."

CHAPTER THIRTY-FIVE

I'm on the couch in my apartment watching a well-worn VHS copy of *The Outsiders*. Cherry Valance and Pony Boy Curtis front a vintage Coppolla pink-gray dawn that consumes the whole scene. I can't stop staring at Diane Lane's eyes. I'm freshly showered and shaved, but the sex odors of the previous night—another limbs-flailing, drunken mistake with some Varsity Villas tramp whose name I can't remember—still linger on my fingers, on my lips, on my cock. I want to say the girl's name is Greek. Athena? Aphrodite? Medusa? Fuck it. Whatever her identity, she's upstairs in my room right now, sleeping off her shame.

The answering machine is flashing. I press play.

"Hank, this is Monica…" Delete.

"Hey Hank, Monica here…" Delete.

"Hello, Hank? Monica again…" Delete.

I was hired as a waiter at Fuddruckers the first week of school. I work Thursday and Friday nights and Sunday mornings, and it beats the hell out of the box factory. Dad calls it "Mother Fuddruckers," pretending his world is the least bit profane or scandalous. Two weeks ago a coworker bet me I couldn't sleep with the "next hot box to walk in the door." Monica Ferguson was the next hot box to walk in the door, but she sat in the wrong section. I asked June if he'd trade sections with me so I could get her table, and he was happy to oblige. "June" is a gay man, my first gay friend. June is his stage name, but no one but his mother calls him Michael. When June and I go out for after-hours cocktails, I'm not above pretending to be bi-curious if it means a round or two of free drinks.

Monica had a girlfriend, a sidekick who knew what I was up to, but that didn't seem to matter. Monica ordered the Cajun chicken tenders. Six stiff rum drinks and a 40 percent tip later, she invited me to her friend's place.

We shared a cigarette on the hood of her Trans Am. She opened up to me. She had just turned eighteen, wanted to be treated like an adult. "Do I look mature to you?" Monica asked. She didn't look a day over sixteen. I told her she could easily pass for twenty-five. She was on the rebound from a three-year relationship with her high school sweetheart. "I thought he was the one." She was estranged from her parents. "They hate me, I hate them." Your standard vulnerable teenage girl. I asked Ty Wilson, the guy who made the bet with me, to come along and run interference with Monica's friend. Ty made a valiant run at the friend, working his way into her bedroom. His effort lasted right up to the point where she stopped him from putting his hand up her shirt, muttered something about "being saved," and turned on her nightstand light to reveal a hand-knit facsimile of "The Lord's Prayer" hanging over her bed.

By that time, however, I was all over Monica in the family room. When it looked like there was a definitive line Monica wouldn't cross, I forced a yawn with my mouth closed. It's a grade school trick I learned to make my eyes water—guaranteed to illicit unbridled sympathy and compassion. Contrived grief flowing, I closed on my target.

Monica noticed the tears. "What's wrong, Hank?"

"Nothing. It's just…oh, you'll think I'm cheesy for saying it."

"No, I won't." She grabbed my hand. "I can't imagine anything you ever say or do being cheesy."

Let the record show I had known Monica for all of about ninety minutes and she had made a blanket, baseless judgment about the sterling quality of my character. Apparently her three years of high school-induced monogamy occurred inside a cave. Nobody was this easy.

"You sure, Monica?" It was a preemptive question whose answer would be the presumed answer for the remainder of the night's questions, and we both knew it.

"Yes, Hank." She lifted my hand to her lips and kissed my fingers.

And that's when I closed. "The worst thing about tonight is that we've just met one another. I feel so comfortable with you right now, and it breaks my heart to think this could be our first and last night together."

I entered Monica right there on the living room floor. Both of us were clothed save for our pants and underwear pulled down to our ankles. Monica cried real tears. She told me she loved me. She gave me her keychain, one of those little plastic telescopes with a picture inside that she bought on some tacky ocean boardwalk. The picture was of her posing on a beach in a bikini. She wrote her phone number in permanent marker on my hand. I returned Monica's phone calls for the first few days, just to be nice. On day four I erased her number off my hand with acetone. I still masturbate to her bikini keychain, but I know I'll never see Monica again.

I fast forward to the next message on the answering machine:

"Hank, Dad here. I got an extra ticket for Stanford. I don't think you work Saturdays at Mother Fuddruckers, so clear your schedule and don't get drunk Friday night. Go Irish!"

The last Notre Dame game we attended was versus Michigan three weeks ago. Hopefully this one goes a little better. Notre Dame didn't lose that day, but they didn't win either. It was a 17–17 tie. It was only the second tie in Notre Dame Stadium in the last quarter century. Some fans in the stadium, including me, booed Coach Holtz as he ran off the field. But not John Fitzpatrick.

"Let's give the boys the benefit of the doubt," he said. "The way I see it, I'm standing in the parking lot outside Notre Dame Stadium on a gorgeous Saturday afternoon, surrounded by family and friends, and the Fighting Irish didn't lose."

Dad always had a way of putting things into perspective, especially under the watchful eye of Touchdown Jesus. That was all that mattered to him that day—being around the people he loved. Ever the loyal Irish fan, he wasn't interested in second-guessing or criticizing the latest in a long line of infallible leaders of the University of Notre Dame Fighting Irish football team.

"Our Lady of the Van" had its usual band of merry parishioners after the Michigan game. The only things Dad asked of them was to bring their faiths and their lawn chairs. The body and blood of Jesus Christ was served from white foam plates and red plastic cups. The body was a partial loaf of sweet Hawaiian bread left over from the spinach dip. The blood was a five-dollar box of white zinfandel, half of which my father and I had already consumed since the game ended.

Our pastor that afternoon was a tall, bald man of medium height. His name was Father Ignatius, better known to his friends as Father "Iggy." He was a bookend in my parents' lives, graduating with Dad from Ben Davis High School in the mid-sixties right before he went into the seminary, and then later in the early eighties meeting Mom when they were both faculty members at Cardinal Ritter High School. Dad always sets aside one of his tickets for a priest. He asks for but a single concession from him—he must agree to preside over an afternoon mass in the Red West parking lot of Notre Dame Stadium.

The "OLV" congregants stood. Father Iggy crossed himself. "In the name of the Father, the Son, and the Holy Spirit…"

I notice a fifth message on the answering machine. It wasn't there before I got in the shower, so someone must have just left it.

"Hank, this is Hiram Gerwin at the dealership in Empire Ridge. Please call me as soon as you get this message. It's your father. He's been in an accident."

Hiram is the dealership's longtime office assistant. He's a paraplegic. I take his car for a spin whenever he brings it into the shop. It has this metal gearshift device that allows you to work the gas and the brake with just your right hand. It took me a couple tries to figure it out, but I became a better-than-average paraplegic driver.

I pick up the phone and dial the dealership's number. An operator picks up after four rings. "Fitzpatrick Oldsmobile-Cadillac-Subaru."

"This is Hank Fitzpatrick calling for Hiram Gerwin, please."

"Oh, hi Hank. I'll get Hiram right away for you."

Hiram picks up almost immediately. "Hank?"

"What's up, Hiram?"

"It's your father. He was at the Indianapolis Auto Auction this morning. There's been an accident. He got hit by a car around eight-thirty a.m."

"What?"

"He's been admitted to Wishard Memorial in Indy, off 10th Street. You know where that is?"

"Yeah, I know where Wishard is. What happened? Is it serious?"

"We don't know too much here, Hank. Just get there as soon as you can."

I hang up the phone and tiptoe up the stairs to my room. I get dressed without waking up Cassiopeia, or whatever her name is. She turns over and mumbles something in her sleep. I see her face for a moment, before she buries herself in a pillow. I pull down the covers for a quick look at the rest of her. Dark hair. Pale skin. A smooth back knotted by the indentations of her spine. A small, somewhat bony ass. Long legs and long, high-arched feet. She's a pretty girl, although skinnier than what I'm attracted to sober. I notice the soft pack of Marlboro Lights sticking out of the back pocket of her discarded jeans at the foot of the bed. I stuff the cigarettes in my jacket.

Once outside the apartment, I start up my truck, a brand-new light blue Chevy C/K 1500 Dad gave me off the lot two months ago. The engine radiates a trace of heat from multiple runs to the liquor store a few hours earlier, and the gas gauge has dropped below a quarter-tank. The truck smells like a guy trying to impress some Grecian waif whose name he can't remember—beer, cigarettes, cheap perfume. I peer out the back of the truck, almost too afraid to look, but there it is—a V-shaped indentation on the inside of the truck bed. What am I going to tell Dad? The truth? That Persephone, or whatever her name, was blowing me while I was driving and I didn't see the red light until it was almost too late? That I slammed on the brakes and sent a pony keg hurtling across my truck bed and a girl almost bit my dick off? "See, Dad, it's like this. We're reading Irving's *The World According to Garp* in my Twentieth Century Lit class, and I was just reenacting the, uh, climactic scene."

Yeah. Right.

A PLUMP BUT SWEET-LOOKING old black nurse at the receptionist's desk ushers me forward after I tell her my name. "Come with me, Mr. Fitzpatrick." It's the third time anyone's ever called me "Mister" Fitzpatrick.

My trip up Highway 37 annoyed the fuck out of me. I got stuck behind a combine just north of Bloomington. All the traffic lights were out in Martinsville, perhaps the last town in which I'd ever want to be stuck in traffic. Then, once I was on the interstate, I-70 was one lane all the way into downtown Indianapolis. A trip that should have taken me forty minutes and three cigarettes was more like ninety minutes and a half pack of smokes.

The nurse escorts me through swinging double doors beneath a sign that reads EMERGENCY ROOM. The doors open wide on the hallmarks of suffering: white coats scurrying around in comfortable shoes, the rattle of gurney wheels on dirty tiled floors, machines that go *ping* but not in a funny John Cleese way, a piney, gin-smelling antiseptic scent that tries to mask the odor of human excrement and who knows what else.

The nurse takes a sharp left and points me to a door marked E.R. WAITING ROOM. "Have a seat in there, Mr. Fitzpatrick."

Again with the "mister." "When can I see my father?"

The nurse smiles, walking away and saying over her shoulder, "The doctors will be with you shortly."

I enter the waiting room. An unexpected sight greets me. Six people, three of whom I know, sitting in chairs along the walls. My Aunt Claudia and Uncle Howard huddle together on my far left, holding hands.

Aunt Claudia is Mom's younger sister, a loud and obnoxious pink-haired English teacher prone to gossip, overeating, and making my mother's life a living hell. Picture *Whatever Happened to Baby Jane?* reimagined in a sleepy Midwestern suburb with Mrs. Garrett from *Facts of Life* as Baby Jane Hudson.

"Thank God you're here, Hank." Aunt Claudia waddles across the room and hugs me, smothering me in perfumed cellulite. Her skin is red and splotchy from crying. "They're not telling us anything, but it's going to be all right. Okay, honey?"

"Relax, Aunt Claudia." It's all I can think to say. "I'm sure everything is fine." I nod at Uncle Howard. "Uncle Howard."

He nods back. "Hank."

Uncle Howard is the quietest man I know. The number of cigarettes he smokes in the course of our annual Thanksgiving Day dinners more often than not exceeds the number of words that come out of his mouth. I've known the man all my life, and all I can say about him is he chain-smokes, he hunts, he fishes, and he pretends to be a good golfer.

Standing across the room with his back turned to me is Saul Gorman, Uncle Howard's kid brother. Saul is an IPD officer, tall and lean-bodied compared to his older sibling and in plain clothes due to his recent promotion to detective. Saul is one of the few people I know who's had his fifteen minutes of fame, and then some. Back in '86 he was cast as an extra in *Hoosiers*. It was a non-speaking role in which he nonetheless had a solid ten to fifteen seconds of onscreen time as the gaping-mouthed newsman taking a knee during the Hickory–South Bend Central state final. Just last year he was the lead detective in the Mike Tyson rape investigation and subsequent conviction, something I didn't know until a few weeks ago when Dad blurted it out during one of our many late nights spent watching boxing on Univision, the Spanish channel. *El Mundoooooh del Box!*

Saul raises his right hand to his mouth, says something into a handheld radio. He's half-listening to the two guys seated in the chairs behind him. One of the guys scribbles on a yellow notepad, while the other makes wild hand gestures. I catch every third or fourth word of the conversation.

I try to move closer to listen in, but another man dressed liked Fred Rogers steps into my path. He reaches out to shake my hand.

"Are you Hank?"

I don't reciprocate the gesture, barely even making eye contact. "Uh, yeah."

Mr. Rogers leaves his hand hanging there for a moment, still hopeful, but then drops it. "I'm Ike Lewis, a volunteer chaplain here at Wishard."

"Oh, sorry, Father." I extend my guilt-ridden hand.

He shakes it, smiling. "Please, Hank. Call me Ike. No title is necessary. While I am a recently retired Baptist minister, we are all just humble servants of our Lord and Savior, Jesus Christ."

Jesus Christ is right, I feel like saying. The chaplain is kind enough to reiterate what I already know: my father was in an accident, they're working on him right now, and not to worry. But I'm no closer to getting some answers than I was an hour before, sitting on a couch in a post-sex haze watching *The Outsiders*. And now I have to wait here with an aunt who's volatile even under normal circumstances, a near-catatonic uncle, and a fucking Baptist who wants to be my best friend.

"Mr. Fitzpatrick?"

Five white coats enter the room. All of them doctors, I assume. All of them looking at me.

"Yes." I scan the room for anyone else who might claim the name. Where is Mom anyway? "I guess you can call me that."

"Please, Hank." The doctor is a darker-skinned Indian, the kind you imagine having a mustache and career plan since he was like six years old. His voice carries with it that half-refined, half-cartoon accent of English imperialism. "Have a seat."

I sit down. Uncle Howard and Aunt Claudia take the chairs on either side of me. I wonder what the damage is. A broken leg? A broken arm? Maybe both legs? Both arms? No matter. Mom is going to come in here worried sick, and this ominous, brooding routine from the white coats sure isn't going to help things.

"Hank..." The doctor says my name again, looks down at his chest and then back at me. He lets my name hang there for a second. "Your father had lost too much blood. We were never able to revive him."

CHAPTER THIRTY-SIX

Death sure is one creative son of a bitch. Four years after Reyes Syndrome killed my six-year-old girlfriend, I watched my father spoon-feed squashed peas to his seventy-five-pound, cancer-starved mother who spent her last days on this earth in the fetal position hurling expletives at the people she loved. *"You're a goddamn prick, George! Fuck you, Johnny! Get your slut of a wife out of my face, Johnny!"* Nine years after that, Grandpa Fred's seventy-four-year-old swimmer's physique dropped dead in his kitchen the same month his internist proclaimed he'd live to be a hundred. And now, weeks after extracting a promise at Grandpa George's grave that I would watch over him in his elderly years, my father is dead? Not just fucking dead, fucking *killed*.

No. Fuck no.

"What?" I squint and bite my lip. I clench my fingers around the oak arms of my chair. I bow my head, closing my eyes. My head is pounding. It's quiet in the room, but to me the world is deafening.

The Indian doctor pats me on the shoulder. "I'm sorry, Hank."

"No!" I bolt up from my chair. I shrug off Aunt Claudia's halfhearted attempt to either hug or restrain me, who knows which. I turn one last time to the room, staring the Indian doctor in the face. "Fuck this, and fuck you!"

I need to get out of there. I stumble out of the waiting room, tripping over an empty wheelchair. I grab the wheelchair and lift it over my head. I throw it down the hallway. It slides to a stop just short of the receptionist's desk.

"Sir, please!"

It's the plump but sweet-looking old black nurse. I'm coated in sweat, breathing hard. The sleeve on my right arm rolled up to my elbow. The sleeve on my left pulled all the way down to my wrist. My hair is all over the place from me pulling on it, my right wrist cut and bleeding from where I grabbed the wheelchair. She calls me "sir" because she doesn't remember my name. She calls me "sir" because the person standing in front of her bears little resemblance to the one she called "Mr. Fitzpatrick" thirty minutes ago. And yet that's who I am. Mr. Fitzpatrick. The only one left.

"Hank?"

The soft voice comes at me from behind. "Hank, what's wrong?"

I turn to face my mother. Jeanine stands behind her, Jack latched on to her leg. Our eyes meet. Mom knows before I can even find the words.

Mom opens her eyes. She's sitting in a wheelchair now. I'm holding her hand.

"How long have I been—"

"About ten minutes," I say. "You need to relax, Mom."

"P-please, Hank. Please, tell me this isn't happening." She stutters and gasps, like a sobbing child who's just been sent to her room—hysterical with grief and trying to sort out why a world would leave her so alone. "I can't live without him. I don't want to live without him. I have no reason to live."

Jeanine and Jack are sitting right next to me. They hear every word. I see the tears in Jeanine's eyes, the confusion in Jack's. Aunt Claudia picks up on my nod and shuffles my two siblings out of the room.

Mom sobs on my shoulder. I sit back and hold my arms out. I grab her shoulders, like I'm steadying someone in a drunken stupor. "Mom, I don't want to ever hear you say those things again."

"But it's true, Hank."

"I said '*never*!'"

I shake her. Where is this coming from? This isn't me talking, is it?

"You want reasons to live?" I say. "What about me? What about Jeanine? What about Jack?"

Like a beleaguered field general rallying the troops, I throw all I have left at her. I invoke her children a couple more times, Dad's memory, Grandpa Fred's memory. But if she counters, I'm finished. My strength is fading. If she tells me to shut up, I'll shut up. If she asks me to kill her, I'll kill her. Watching her in this kind of pain is the hard part. Ending the pain would be the easy thing to do.

Ten minutes pass in silence. Mom rests her head in the crook of my neck. "Hank."

"Yes?"

"You're the man of the family now."

Mom has an annoying tendency to recount embarrassing family moments out loud in public places. Over a deep-fried onion, she'll recount a story you've heard about a hundred times, because all she wants to do is amuse that couple in matching sweater vests in the booth behind you eating imitation crab dip. "*You're the man of the family now*"? This over-the-top cliché strikes me in much the same way. Mom looks past me as she says it, as if there's an unseen audience listening to her. Cliché or not, it's not what I expected to hear, nor a sentiment I'm prepared to embrace.

And that's when Uncle Mitch walks into the room.

He sits down beside my mother, wraps his arm around her. "I came as soon as I heard, Debbie."

"What am I gonna do, Mitch? What am I gonna do?"

"We'll get through this. I promise."

"'We'll get through this?'" I say. "Fuck you, Mitch!"

Aunt Claudia sticks her head in the room. "Jeanine and Jack want to see their mother."

I scowl at Mitch and then turn to Aunt Claudia, a mixture of fear and anger in my voice. I point at her. "Keep Jack out of this goddamn room!"

The Indian doctor returns. "Mrs. Fitzpatrick...Hank."

Mom nods to me. I guess I'm doing all the talking. "Yes, doctor."

"You can see him now."

"Can I ask a favor?" I ask.

"Certainly," the doctor says.

"Just me and my mother." I pull Uncle Mitch off my mother and push him against the wall. "Get this man the fuck out of here, or I'll have security throw him out."

"What are you doing?" Mom asks. "Mitch was your father's brother!"

I ignore her and turn to the Indian doctor. "Doctor, you will note in my father's medical records that he's an only child. Mitch is not family, period."

"But Hank," Mom says.

"Mom, don't fight me on this."

Mom apologies to Mitch as security escorts him outside. I don't even look at him. We walk down a corridor of white walls dotted with wheelchairs and gurneys, some occupied, most not. Hospital personnel scurry between rooms in their blue scrubs and white coats.

"Here we are." The doctor pushes open a set of double doors to our right marked TRAUMA CENTER in stenciled letters.

We enter the trauma center. I notice an immediate change in the smell. As you plunge deeper into hospitals, they become acute and unmistakable in their redolence: bad cafeteria food, antiseptic cleansers, urine, feces, flowery old women's perfume. But this room is different. The odor is metallic, like the smell of your hands after you stuff them in a jar of pennies. The smell of blood.

My earliest memory of blood was when I was six years old. Dad tried to install a screen door by himself. I handed him the wood chisel right before he sliced a three-inch gash in his groin. He passed out in Mom's car, a brown 1980 Datsun B210 Delux Wagon, before we even got out of the driveway. By the time we got to the hospital, the blood soaked through his shorts and shirt all the way up to his navel. Mom cried.

But it was nothing like this.

Dad lies on a gurney five feet in front of us, a utility sink to his left and a red plastic container labeled *biohazard* to his right. Black articulated arms ending in lights extend from the ceiling above him like spider's appendages. Various wheeled contraptions with tubes sprouting out of them stand watch over him, as if to say, "We're sorry, but we fought the good fight."

Mom runs to him. I stand behind her. Dad is wrapped like a mummy, from his neck to his feet in bright white sheets. He looks so peaceful. His eyes closed. His mouth frozen in a small permanent near-grin, his straight lips turned up at the corners—the signature Fitzpatrick smirk. It's the closest semblance of a frown we Fitzpatrick men can manage. I can almost pretend Dad is asleep, until we're cautioned by the Indian doctor not to touch him anywhere below his chest.

No. Fuck no.

Mom strokes Dad's hair. "John, my dear John." She kisses his cheek, again and again. I'm in shock. The seconds, the minutes are interminable. My head hurts. I'm not here. This isn't my father. This isn't happening.

"Hank." Mom reaches her hand out to me. She slides down to give me some room alongside my father.

I look at my mother. She smiles but not a good smile. It's one of those awful, lips-trembling smiles. The only expression your body can think of to convey unimaginable grief. I lean down until my forehead is resting on Dad's cheek. I raise my head. I notice a trickle of dried blood in Dad's ear.

The blood makes it real for me. My tears come. Uncontrollable. Vicious. I *am* here. This *is* my father. This *is* happening.

I press my cheek against his. He's still warm. I wrap my right arm around his head and run my fingers through his hair. I raise my left hand to his lips. "Hey Hank," Dad said to me before I went back to school on Sunday night, "you think you'll ever be too old to get a hug and kiss from your Dad?" I don't even remember what I said. Did I let him hug me? Did I let him kiss me? Did I tell him I loved him? Why wasn't I at least there on the other side of the phone to say, "Yes, Dad, I'd love to go to the Stanford game with you!"

My fingers linger above his mouth, hoping for the breath that will never come. I look to Dad's eyes, waiting for them to open. In that brief moment, I see my future laid bare before me. Hollow. Empty.

I touch his cheek with my own again. He's getting colder. Can't they give him more blankets? Something to keep him warm?

More blankets. That's all he needs. More blankets.

CHAPTER THIRTY-SEVEN

Mom wants today to be a celebration of Dad's life. In her words, "None of that dark, Catholic purgatory bullshit." She invited the Ridge Spirit Band to the funeral. Propped on the balcony of St. Isadore Roman Catholic Church, they are about two-thirds through a thirty-minute pre-funeral set of New Age jazz that's more ridiculous than celebratory. The doors to the back of the church are open wide. We're sitting with the window down in the limousine. I hear the music. As bad as it sounds—we're talking Chicago's "25 or 6 to 4" sandwiched in between Al Jarreau's not-so-greatest hits—Dad would have loved it.

I sit with my family, waiting for the hearse parked in front of us to unload the man of the hour. I pull out a stainless steel hip flask and sneak a quick sip of Rumple Minze. I'm going with a hundred-proof peppermint schnapps instead of the more predictable whiskey. The schnapps is stronger and will get me to where I want to go a whole lot faster. Also, if people smell my breath they might mistake my drunkenness for good oral hygiene.

Eight pallbearers stand at the back of the hearse. Uncle Mitch is one of them. I'm giving him today, for Dad. They slide Dad out and carry him from the hearse through the back doors of the church. The chortling of the hearse's diesel engine gives way to the sound of feet shuffling across hard pavement in soles too sad to pick them up. A cold October breeze sends eight bad neckties snaking around each of the pallbearers' heads. They deposit Dad onto a dolly and wheel him inside the church.

We follow Dad into St. Isadore, crowding in with the rest of the funeral procession into the church's small vestibule. The music grows louder. A small basin of holy water stands to my left near the door. I dip my fingers in it and cross myself. I reach up and brush back my hair, which is ambivalent about whether to frame my face or cover it. I pull on the collar of my starched shirt. The collar is tight, too tight, thanks to my slight double chin. That's the Irish in me, the genetic trait passed down through Fitzpatrick men that ensures any extra weight must first show up in your face.

My suit is ashen black and oversized, borrowed from Dad's closet. It smells like him, an earthy aroma of tanned leather that for a moment overshadows today with yesterday. Dad was heavier and taller than me. It's all my seventy-inch, 190-pound frame can do to fill the suit. Safety pins at the cuffs and hems fool everyone into thinking it's mine. We move forward into the main sanctuary, an enormous entourage preceding us. Three altar boys dressed in white robes walk at the front carrying a cross, a leather-bound book, and a gold censer of incense. Three priests follow the altar boys. Two of the priests are wearing all white, one wearing a violet stole, the traditional color for Advent, Lent, and burying people. Two of the priests are bald, and all three are wearing glasses.

Father Iggy and Father Fisher Kelly could pass as brothers. Both a couple inches over six feet tall, both middle-aged, and both sporting tanned and proudly bald heads. For years these two have jostled for Dad's extra Notre Dame season ticket.

Prior to his transfer up to St. Ambrose, "Father Fish" was a longtime fixture in the Fitzpatrick household. He was the priest who baptized your little brother. The priest you invited over for dinner Sunday nights to the envy of the rest of the parish. The priest who in the summer skipped homilies and said, "Please remain standing," because he knew even blind faith had no patience for ninety degrees and 90 percent humidity. The priest who'd hug you before he crossed you. The priest who your dad looked to as a brother. The priest in the middle of a week of mandatory bed rest prior to back surgery when he heard one of his dearest friends had been killed. The priest who, during the waning hours of your father's wake, stumbled over his faith.

"John Fitzpatrick was the greatest, most faith-filled man I ever knew," Father Fish said to me last night, sitting in a chair opposite my father's open casket. He'd been crying off and on throughout the day, and he made no excuse for his grief. "In my years of serving the Lord, I've had a lot of things test my faith, but I can't make sense of this one." He stood almost the entire day, teeth clenched. I could tell the pain was killing him.

Fuck me. I'm proud of myself, downright exultant, if I can just cut down the masturbating to once a day. And here Dad is inspiring crippled priests to mourn his passing, question their faith, and envy his piety.

Bringing up the rear of the clerical procession is Father Liam Attenbird. Father Liam is the pastor of St. Isadore, hence the stole, and Father Fish's underappreciated successor. He's the shortest one of the priestly bunch, but with a full head of hair and eyeglasses that are thin-rimmed and more stylish than his peers'. I've met Father Liam once or twice and can't say much about him, other than he looks young and women whisper behind his back that he's too handsome to be a priest.

My father is next. He appears as a seven-foot long coffin of red, hand-rubbed African mahogany. I picked the coffin out because Mom couldn't. She could barely sign the check. The same went for the design of the tombstone. I drew it up on a piece of spiral notebook paper in her bed, right after she passed out halfway into her sixth vodka gimlet.

Jeanine and I follow behind our father. Mom wobbles almost drunkenly between us, bobbing her head, tripping over her own feet. I hold tight to Mom's arm, bearing the weight of this day for her as best I can. Jeanine walks behind us with Jack.

Jack is the one I'm worried about, and not because of the ridiculous mustard-yellow, button-down sweater Mom made him wear today. He is our small miracle, the result of Mom and Dad telling the medical establishment—and their eldest son—to go fuck themselves. I guess you're allowed one miracle per family. After that, the lamb's blood on your front door just fades away.

I look over my shoulder to see Jeanine and Jack, and behind them Aunt Claudia, Uncle Howard, and Aunt Ophelia. Jack stands as he did in the emergency room—latched around Jeanine's leg, unsure of a world that had been so simple to him three days ago. People say I look like Dad, and I do. But Mom has at least a small stake in my genetic makeup, from my fuller lips and more rounded head to my big, almost-feminine eyes, complete with exaggerated curling eyelashes. Jack on the other hand carries no trace of my mother. He's all Dad—the dark brown hair, the thin lips, the square head, the smaller eyes. He cried once. It was this morning at the funeral home. We had just closed Dad's casket for the last time. Everybody was crying. I think Jack felt left out.

I refuse to let Jack be left out. I'll remind him every day about the flip-flop sound of Dad's sandaled feet in the summer. Dirt and earthworms under his nails after he baited you a hook. His laugh. His awful jokes that made you laugh. The scratchy feel of his face against yours when he'd forget to shave for a couple days. English Leather cologne. That particular smile he reserved for his sons. His limitless capacity to forgive. I cannot let Jack forget any of this. My memories, the memories of my mother and my sister, will always be of a *living* husband, of a living father. Barring our diligence, Jack's will be of a dead one.

The Ridge Spirit Band serenades us down the aisle with some Louis Armstrong. The band is off-key, the trumpets, trombones, and saxophones drowning out each other's runs, and the snare drum acting like it has better things to do than play a funeral. To make matters worse, the band starts the song about five minutes too soon. By the time the funeral procession makes its way down the aisle, the chorus of "When the Saints Go Marching In" has been played at least twenty times.

The church is standing-room only. We chose to have the funeral in St. Isadore, the nineteenth-century Romanesque-style church in downtown Empire Ridge. We almost had the service in the newer St. Benjamin across town, but Mom felt there was a certain grandeur lacking in a thirty-year-old church that looked like a limestone IHOP. With its towering barrel-vaulted walls and infantry of stained glass windows surrounding you, St. Isadore does what a good Catholic church is supposed to do: it makes you feel small and contrite.

The dolly rolls to a stop at the altar, a veined slab of white marble covered in a white cloth. The pallbearers file into the pews. The three priests take their places behind the casket. Father Iggy and Father Fish stand to the right of the casket with the altar boys and the choir. Father Liam stands behind the casket, next to the paschal candle. I'm the first to walk forward, standing alongside the left of the casket, followed by Mom, then Jeanine and Jack.

THE READINGS AND THE songs were like any readings and songs at a Catholic funeral. A whole lot of bullshit about God's plan, everything happening for a reason, and Dad being in a better place. A solid ninety minutes of people blowing smoke up your ass.

Father Iggy gave a decent homily. People seemed to react well to it. I wasn't listening. I was thinking during the homily that if God had always existed, then he didn't have a father. And if that's the case, then God is a bastard, just like me.

It feels good to say that. *You listening to me, God? You're a bastard. You're a gutless, heartless, fucking bastard.*

Father Fish approaches Dad's casket to the tune of "Be Not Afraid," a depressing liturgical ditty made more so by the out-of-tune St. Isadore choir. An altar boy hands Father the gold censer. The domed cover is dotted with small openings in the shape of crosses. Father Fish's movements are practiced, measured, in time with the music. In his right hand he holds the censer level with the top of his chest. He grasps it by the chain near the cover, while his left hand, holding the top of the chain, rests on his chest. He raises the censer upward to eye level, then swings it in an outward, ascending motion toward my father's casket. He does this a second time, the tendrils of smoke now curling out of the circle of crosses and blanketing the first few rows of the church. He hands the censer back to the altar boy, returns to the casket, and folds his arms.

"So I get this call in my office last week," Father Fish says. "My secretary says to me, 'Father, there's a John Fitzpatrick on the phone, and he wants to know if you want to go to the Holy Land on October twenty-fourth to see the Catholics beat the Mormons.' I tell her to put him on the phone, and of course it's John. And of course he keeps me on the phone for an hour, and of course when that hour ends, I hang up the phone and already miss the sound of his voice. My secretary comes in and asks me, 'How often does your friend go to the Holy Land?' And I tell her, 'Oh, about six or seven times every fall.'"

We all laugh.

Father Fish chokes up. "That was the last time I talked to John, but in my heart I know he's in a better place. And in my heart, I know the reason Notre Dame lost to Stanford last Saturday was because John, Grandpa George, and Grandpa Fred were raising so much hell up in Heaven that no Hail Mary's got through."

We all laugh again, but not as loud this time because Father Fish is crying. The incense in the church claws at my nose, like the smell of smoldering wet leaves on a wool sweater. The smell of grief. The smell of death. I place Dad's handkerchief, stained mascara blue by my mother's tears, over my mouth and nose.

Father Fish brings his arms down to the casket. He places his hands on my father. "John, my friend..." We can hear the heartbreak in his voice. "May the road rise up to meet you. May the wind be always at your back. May the rains fall soft upon your fields and the sun shine warm upon your face. And until we meet again, may God hold you in the hollow of his hand."

The altar boys and priests walk down the aisle to the tune of the "Notre Dame Victory March." The pallbearers are next, followed by my family. For most people in the crowd, this is the last time they'll see John Fitzpatrick. Like a dead autumn cornfield flanking both sides of a lonely country road, they surround me with walls of withered anguish. And to make matters worse, the band has segued into a Chuck Mangione medley. Yes, ladies and gentlemen, that is the theme song from *Cannonball Run*.

Dad loved Chuck Mangione—"Feels So Good," "Bellavia," "Fun and Games," "Land of Make Believe," "Give It All You Got," and especially "Children of Sanchez." How could anyone not like "Children of Sanchez"? The local Cincinnati Reds television affiliate used to use that as its theme music during the days of the Big Red Machine. Dave ConcepciÓn turns a double play. Cut to Pete Rose sliding head first into home. Cut to Johnny Bench picking someone off at second. Foster, Morgan, Perez—damn, I haven't thought about those old Reds teams in years. But I think about them now. I think about them because of Chuck Mangione. Dad would hop around the house snapping, singing the trumpet parts, screaming when Mangione hit that high register in "Hill Where the Lord Hides." I said trumpet, didn't I? Dad would have corrected me. "Chuck Mangione plays a *flugelhorn*, Hank." Dad could play all the brass and woodwind instruments, and even got by on percussion. "Think of a flugelhorn as a mellower trumpet," Dad would say. Then he'd squint, bob his head, hold his thumbs and middle fingers together, moving his hands with the music, conducting some unseen orchestra. A drum major reliving his glory days. And whenever Dad was into the moment, he'd stick out his tongue and bite down on it.

I crouch down into the limo with my family. I watch as the pallbearers push the end of Dad's casket into the hearse and close the doors. Jack's face is pressed against the glass. What's going through that little mind of his? I reach for him, pulling him into my lap.

"Hey, little guy, you doing okay?"

Jack wipes his nose. "My frote hurts."

"Yeah," I say. "My throat hurts, too."

"Where they taking Daddy?"

"That's his rocket ship to heaven."

"Can we go?"

"Maybe someday."

Jack smiles. "Cool!"

CHAPTER THIRTY-EIGHT

Aunt Claudia decides to "host" a reception after Dad's funeral at our house. About twenty to thirty people circumnavigate our first floor, walking from the kitchen to the dining room to the living room to the entryway. Some stop for a few minutes to gather in the living room in front of my mother, who sits in the corner like a battered prizefighter refusing to answer the bell. But most seem content to hang out in the kitchen and feast on the casseroles that keep showing up on our doorstep.

Seriously, what the fuck is up with all these casseroles?

I haven't seen Jack or my sister for hours. Aunt Claudia told me they went over to Nancy Friedman's house. Nancy babysits Jack on weekdays when Mom and Dad are at work. She's like family—better than family, if we're comparing her to Aunt Claudia.

I feel a tap on my shoulder. "You ready to get out of here for a little while?"

I turn and face her. She's wearing an understated black dress. Her hair is more wavy than curly now, not quite as dark as I remember it being. She smells the same.

"Laura?"

"Hello, Hank."

I WALK AROUND TO the passenger side door of Laura's silver Calais. The paint looks a little faded, even at night. "Still got the old girl, huh?"

"Up to my ears in student loans." Laura opens her door. "I'm driving her till the wheels fall off."

We get in the car. "Where to?"

"Liquor store?"

I nod. "My home away from home."

I WALK INTO THE liquor store. I hand the store clerk a pint of Jim Beam with my right hand, slide a ten-dollar bill across the counter with my left. "I'll also take a pack of Marlboro Lights and one of those fifty cent lighters please."

The clerk reaches up for the smokes and the lighter. "Marlboro *Lights* you say?"

"Yes, sir."

"Hard or soft pack?"

"Hard."

He slides the smokes and the lighter across the counter. He's a bald guy, in his early seventies. Wrinkles and liver spots vie for real estate on his face. "What are you doin'?" he asks, a hint of scorn in his voice.

"Just getting some whiskey and some smokes." I slide my driver's license across the counter. "Look, here's my ID."

"No, that's not what I'm talking about." He slides my driver's license back to me without picking it up or even looking down at it. "I know who you are."

"You do, huh?" I start packing the smokes against my hand, as if in affirmation of what's to come next.

"You're John's boy. Hank, right?"

"Yeah, that's me."

The old man shakes his head. "It ain't right, what happened to your dad. Just ain't right."

"No, sir, it isn't." Complete strangers presuming a level of intimacy with my family's affairs make me uncomfortable. I remind myself he's just being nice.

"He was a good man, a great man if you ask me."

"You knew him?"

"You see that El Dorado parked outside?"

"The white convertible?"

"That's the one."

"What's that, about a seventy-six?"

"I see you got your father's car sense."

"Lucky guess."

"I couldn't get qualified for a loan with the bank, so your dad set up some non-interest payment plans with me. Paid her off last month."

"Good for you." I look outside, impatient. I'm over this conversation.

The old man holsters the bourbon in a brown paper bag. "Your mother, she still working over at the school?"

"Yes, she's still at the Ridge."

"Please let her know she's in everyone's prayers."

"I will." I grab the bag, scrambling for the exit.

"Hank?"

Halfway out the door, I poke my head back in. I wish this fucking guy would stop talking to me. "Yes, sir."

"You forgot something." The old man walks up to me. He holds my ten dollar bill in front of my face. He stuffs it in the front pocket of my leather jacket. "I ain't takin' your money, least not tonight."

"Thanks." My gratitude is assured and swift. If there's one thing I never let stand in the way of free booze and smokes, it's pride.

I twist the cap off the pint of Beam before I get to the car. I tilt the bottle to my lips with my right hand, a cigarette already lit in my left hand. The woody bite of the bourbon is both sharp and soothing all at once.

Laura puts the car in reverse. "Where to now?"

"The cemetery, if you don't mind."

I TAKE FOUR PULLS off the whiskey in succession. I offer Laura a drink. She declines. Limestone columns flanked by a black wrought iron fence appear on my right. "Turn here," I say.

We pass under an engraved limestone arch that reads "Whiskeyville Cemetery," one of the few nostalgic reminders of the town's former alias. We ignore the sign that says the cemetery closes at dusk.

"Way in the back, behind the mausoleum, right?" Laura asks.

I nod. "Yeah, just behind it. How'd you know?"

"I came to the service, but I kept out of sight."

"Why?"

"I don't know. I felt weird. I know your friends have never cared for me too much."

"I would've liked for you to have been there, with me."

Laura reaches over, squeezes my hand. "Well, I'm here now."

We park behind the mausoleum. Twenty yards in front of us, a rise of fresh cut flowers sits beneath a sugar maple. Laura offers me her hand. I accept her invitation.

"Thank you."

"Please, Hank." Laura tears up. "You don't have to thank me for this."

We approach the grave. Easels of red and white carnations and baby's breath are piled on top of one another. Embossed ribbons saying things like "Dad" and "Husband" and "Uncle" and "Boss" reflecting in the moonlight. Several votive candles still lit on the perimeter of the mess.

I let go of Laura's hand and reach down to the ribbon labeled "Dad." I trace the words with my fingers. Laura kneels beside me, laying her hand over mine. She traces the words with me.

The gravestone is still weeks from being delivered. Until then, all I have are these dying flowers and a mound of earth. I take my hand off the ribbon labeled "Dad" and dig my fingers into the loose soil.

"What's the weather forecast for the next few days?" I ask.

"I don't know," Laura answers. "Chance of rain tomorrow or the day after, maybe?"

"Yeah, I think so."

I say this knowing the rain will come. It will pitter-patter through the red-green leaves of the sugar maple and pool on top of this Indiana clay. And when the rain stops, the clay will dry. And it will harden.

All I can think about is the clay.

Laura kisses me on the cheek and then the throat. I can feel the warmth of her tears on the side of my face. I think I might even be a little turned on right now.

I stand up, push her away. "Bringing you here was a mistake."

"But I want to be here."

"No, you don't."

"How can you say that?"

"We haven't so much as spoken to one another in more than a year."

"I'm not going to apologize for caring about you."

"Caring about me? Don't insult my intelligence."

The tears are now streaming down Laura's face. She doesn't even try to wipe them off. "Can't you just let me be here for you?"

Laura is still my one great love. I've wondered, to the point of obsession, why we didn't make it. Tonight, that answer is laid bare: we will never learn how to stop hurting one another. I kiss her on the forehead. "I'm sorry."

Laura wraps her arms around me. "I loved him, too, Hank."

I run my hands through her hair. "You were always Dad's favorite."

CHAPTER THIRTY-NINE

"Six thousand dollars?"

"Afraid so," Mom says. She sits at the kitchen table, her greasy, unwashed hair slicked back off her forehead, a vodka gimlet in her right hand.

Mom decided to sell the dealership three weeks after Dad was killed. Just like that. She called the University of Notre Dame athletic department to tell them we wouldn't be renewing our season tickets for the '93 season and then farmed out the remaining '92 season tickets to Dad's friends. Just like that. Next there was Halloween—Jack in a Batman costume sat in his Radio Flyer, while I pulled him around from house to house, crossing streets at inopportune times and taking shortcuts to avoid the questions and the compassion. Then there was Thanksgiving—we decided not to go to Mass, opting for ham instead of turkey, and forgetting to even watch football. Christmas came and went—Mom gave Dad's golf clubs to Uncle Howard and mailed his Smith & Wesson .357 Magnum to Uncle Mitch without asking me if I wanted either of them, and everyone overbought for Jack as if to say, "Don't worry kid, there's still a Santa Claus." After that, we had to resolve a dispute with the cell phone company over a four-hundred-dollar phone bill, because someone stealing your Dad's phone off his still-warm corpse is not a legitimate excuse for unpaid service. And now, after three months of haggling with the insurance company, a goddamn six-thousand-dollar invoice from Wishard Hospital is what we're left with.

Well, that and a fucking armed pedophile.

"Six grand for what? Dad was DOA. We're paying the hospital six grand for managing to keep him dead?"

Mom takes another swig of her gimlet. The ice rattles in her glass. "It was for the blood, Hank."

"His blood?"

"No, the hospital's blood. They pumped something like forty pints into him. He was losing it as fast as they were putting it into him."

She's crying again. I sit down beside her. I hold her left hand. "It's going to be okay, Mom." For these last few months since Dad's death it seems like these are the only words I've been saying to my mother. The thing is, I need more convincing than she does.

"That's not what's got me all torn up." Mom squeezes my hand and then lets go. "This just came in the mail this morning."

She hands me a seven-page stapled document. I read the first few lines aloud. "'Indiana University School of Medicine Department of Pathology Forensic Division. Autopsy Report. Name, John H. Fitzpatrick. Age, forty-six years. Sex, male. Autopsy number nine-two-one-oh-two-three. Date: October two, nineteen ninety-two. Time: seven-thirty a.m.'"

I start flipping through the pages. "Don't tell me you read all this."

Mom nods. "Every word of it."

"Jesus, Mom."

I run my fingers over particular words and phrases as if to make them more real: "*white blood-soaked underwear...khaki pants with blood smears... significant deforming blunt force injuries of the legs and right wrist...contusion and deep subcutaneous hemorrhage invests the tissues over the anterior pelvis, groin and upper thighs, encompassing an area of 13 x 8 inches...extensive lacerations and crush injuries of the mesentery and bowel...ruptured colon...lacerated liver...extensive retroperitoneal hemorrhage...ruptured bladder...multiple-fractured pelvis.*"

I even pause at the descriptions that have nothing to do with his injuries, the ones that talk about Dad as if he was a healthy man, as if he has every reason to still be alive.

He had a great heart: "*no softening and/or mottling of the myocardium due to recent myocardial infarction or necrosis...no myocardial fibrosis...no myocardial contusion...no defects in the arterial or ventricular septa.*"

His vascular system was that of a man half his age: "*no evidence of aneurism, coarctation, dissection, or laceration of the aorta...renal arteries are not stenotic.*"

He had the lungs of a lifetime non-smoker: *"trachea complete, without malformation, from the larynx to the carina...lungs and hilar nodes not significantly anthracotic and no emphysema."*

He wasn't even close to brain-dead: *"no hemorrhage in the scalp or galea...no evidence of herniation at any of the portals of the brain...no internal evidence of contusion, edema, hemorrhage, tumor, atrophy, infection, or infarction in the cerebrum, cerebellum and brainstem...craniocervical junction demonstrates a usual range of motion."*

His brain, his heart, his lungs, his *"genitalia of a short foreskin male adult"*—hell, even his prostate—were all given clean bills of health. Then why the fuck isn't he here? Why isn't Dad here to take Jack trick-or-treating or to tell Mom, "Debbie, nobody eats ham on Thanksgiving"?

"Well?" Mom takes the autopsy report, flips it face down on the table.

I back away from the table, a little teary eyed. I stand up, already trying to distance myself from the words. "That's not something I care to ever read again."

Mom smiles. A full-on fucking smile! She pours some Rose's Lime Juice into the glass. She shakes the glass, mixing the lime juice with whatever is left of the vodka and melted ice mixture. "Two hundred and thirty-one."

"What?"

"Your father's weight." Mom finishes her drink. "The autopsy report said he weighed two hundred and thirty-one pounds." She opens the report face up again and turns to page two. She points to where it says, *"The body is that of a well-developed white male adult appearing the stated age of 46 years. The body length is 72 inches and the body weight is 231 pounds. Scalp hair is gray."*

Mom is still smiling. In fact, she's laughing.

"You okay?" I say.

She finishes off her gimlet. Still laughing. "That son of a bitch told me he was one ninety-five."

I smile, laughing with her now. I see Dad eating his nightly chocolate-covered ice cream bar he'd have about an hour after dinner, even if he already had dessert. After he ate it, he'd lie on the couch for hours at a time until one of us got up, just so he could hand you his chewed-up ice cream stick and say, "You mind throwing that away for me, champ?"

I don't second-guess this unexpected gift of humor. Given these last few months, laughing at my father's autopsy makes sense. Mom finishes her gimlet. "I know why you were upset with Mitch."

"You do?" I say.

"Sure I do. He slept around on Ophelia with other men. You and John knew, but you never told me."

"Dad told me when we went to the Bahamas," I say. "Nobody wanted you to know. It's like we all unconsciously decided to protect Uncle Mitch, which if you ask me was disgusting."

"We all make mistakes, Hank."

"Please don't tell me you're defending him."

"Nobody's perfect," Mom says. "You haven't seen what I've seen. Kids coming into my office, struggling with their sexual identities. I feel sorry for him."

"I feel like he's a demon that needs to be exorcized from this fucking family."

"Well, you're going to need to confront those demons at some point."

"Come again?"

"Uncle Mitch is moving back to Indiana. He's looking at apartments in Empire Ridge."

1993

CHAPTER FORTY

I look in the bathroom mirror. I run my hands through my hair, lamenting my more salt than pepper coif. My wife walks into the bathroom. She begs me not to go into work. I've been fighting a stomach bug so bad I've already thrown up twice this morning. "I'll be fine, Debbie. I need to get up to the auction and buy some cars to build up our used inventory. I've told you before, that's where we make our best margins."

I kiss my wife goodbye, tell her I love her. She doesn't say it back.

When I get to the Indianapolis Auto Auction, I bypass the usual meet and greets with other area car dealers. I sneak into the restroom. I'm sweating and more than a little lightheaded, still fighting the nausea. That large black coffee I just finished off on an empty stomach isn't helping things. Maybe Debbie was right. Maybe I should have stayed home. My stomach churns. I feel like I might throw up again. I hover in the restroom. Spending even an extra five minutes hunched over a toilet could mean losing out on a deal. I swallow, forcing the acid back down my throat and into my stomach. I wash my hands, then wipe my face with a wet paper towel.

I exit the restroom, managing to trade a few handshakes and smiles. I grab another cup of coffee, plus a donut to try and settle my stomach. I check my watch. I step onto the auction floor, noticing the white GMC Sonoma pickup truck.

A wholesaler from Nashville flags me down. He's standing beside the auctioneer. "You like this, John?"

"I sure could use some trucks on my lot, Bill." I shake the wholesaler's hand. I walk to the back of the pickup, run my right hand along the tailgate, my coffee in my left hand. I take a sip.

It's 8:30 a.m. "Move 'em up, move 'em up!" the auctioneer shouts into the microphone.

I hear a high-revving engine behind me and the sound of tires squealing. I look over my shoulder and see the black Ford Bronco barreling into the garage.

Two bodies go flying like bowling pins. The Bronco is coming for me.

I drop my coffee, reach down with my right hand, trying to muster some superhuman feat of strength that might prevent the Bronco from hitting me. I close my eyes, feel the splintering pain of my wrist being crushed into a mash of skin and bones. I hear the screaming, the crashing sound of metal hitting metal, the audible cracking noise of my own pelvis being crushed. I smell the burning rubber.

I can feel the Bronco and the Sonoma colliding inside me, my groin being ripped in half. My liver exploding. The outer wall of my abdomen, my bowels, and my bladder all shredded and expelled in bits and pieces onto the reddening concrete floor. The combined wreckage of my body and the two vehicles slide six feet across the freshly painted floor. Cold steel and fiberglass tear through my skin.

A sick, desperate sound exits my throat. I start gargling and choking on wet mouthfuls of blood. The driver of the Bronco appears dazed. The Bronco is still in drive, wheels spinning, the bumpers of the two vehicles grinding away at the few tendons keeping my body from being cut clean in half. People are shouting at the driver, "Turn it off! Turn it off!"

Someone reaches into the open driver's side window of the Ford Bronco, grabs the keys and cuts the engine. I slump over the hood, arms spread. Out of the corner of my eye, a man picks my cell phone off the ground, pockets the phone, and disappears into the crowd. The wholesaler from Nashville grabs me right before I fall, lays me on the floor. He holds my hand as I gasp a few stubborn breaths.

And then nothing.

"So…" Hatch says. "You're telling me you dream about taking the place of your father in the accident?"

"That's what I'm telling you."

"And that's the same dream you've been having every night for the last three months?"

"Yep."

"Holy fucking Christ, Fitzy."

The bartender gives us our usual, a pitcher of Natty Light and two glass mugs. He pours the first glass for me, salting the cocktail napkin before he puts down the glass, an old bartender trick to keep the napkin from sticking to the bottom of the glass. His name is Shane Estes, owner and proprietor of Shane's Pub. The night of Dad's funeral, Laura dropped me off here and Shane kept the bar open until I was done drinking. "We close when you close," he said to me.

Hatch leaves with the pitcher and his mug. "Thanks, Shane."

Shane wipes the wet circles off the bar where the pitcher and mugs used to be, his lone distinctive feature an oily, untrimmed mustache. "Happy New Year?"

He says this in the form of a question. I've learned people don't necessarily want you to be happy. They want to think you're happy. "Yeah, Happy New Year."

Hatch and I have spent half the day helping Mom move the last of the boxes from the old house. I hate the new house. Yeah, living in the old house was like dipping an open sore in a pile of salt on a minute-by-minute basis. But that was preferable to a brand new house—heartless, soulless, smelling of latex paint and a family running away from something.

Tonight is the last weekend night before people start heading back to school for the '93 spring semester. Hatch and I occupy the table by the jukebox.

"You need to stop reading that autopsy," Hatch says. "That shit is going to fuck with your head."

"I think it would help if Mom stopped reminding me how Dad had the stomach flu the day he was killed and she almost talked him into staying home that morning."

"Yeah, that would help."

"The deposition is almost as bad."

"The deposition?" Hatch says. "Of who?"

"The guy driving the Ford Bronco that hit Dad."

"You've read that, too?"

"We got it from our attorney just this morning. We're pursuing a wrongful death lawsuit against the auto auction. The deposition is pretty graphic."

"I don't want to know."

I ignore Hatch. "It reads like a fucking conspiracy to kill my father. You got this Ford Bronco that breaks down like a half-dozen times while waiting in the repo line. The general manager of the auction tells his driver, this dim-witted retiree who doesn't have a driving record so much as a rap sheet, how to feather the gas and the brakes together so they can at least get the Bronco to the auction block. Next thing you know, the driver panics, stands on the gas, and cuts my—"

"Jesus, Fitzy. What part of 'I don't want to know' did you not understand? Shut the fuck up!"

God love him, Hatch has struggled being a real human being since Dad was killed. He was supportive early on, but his default assumption now seems to be that my life is like a sitcom in which you forget the dead parent after the pilot episode. Five minutes and twenty-two seconds into the show, Mr. Brady has the one conversation with Bobby about hiding his mother's picture. "I don't want you to forget your mother, and neither does Carol," Mike says. "Gee, that's swell," Bobby says. And everyone is peachy fucking keen for the rest of their lives; well, at least until the episode where Mr. Brady dies of AIDS.

We empty the pitcher in short order. Hatch stumbles back toward the bar, ostensibly to get more beer but more likely to flirt with Claire, who just walked in. I do my best to mingle, but it's more just a disinterested shuffle through the slurring, ash-scented masses. I try not to trip over the bad pick-up lines.

Left-hand wrapped around the handle of my empty beer mug, I tap the soft pack of Marlboro Lights on my left wrist. I knock a cigarette loose until it extends halfway out the pack. Extracting the cigarette with my left thumb and index finger, I bring the cigarette up to my mouth and light it with a Bic lighter I stole off the bar. Tired lungs inhale until it burns as I hover over the jukebox. It plays "Family Tradition" by Hank Williams Jr., as it does once every third or fourth song on any regular Shane's Pub playlist. With the obvious exception of the Mellencamp library, few songs get Empire Ridge locals into more of a drunken lather than this stupid fucking song. The waitress identifies me by name, tells me the jukebox is paid through the next seventeen songs. I give her a smile and a nod, pretending I know her.

"Got one of those for me?"

I turn to the familiar voice coming from the dart room. "For you, Ms. Burke, anything."

Beth smiles and slides her arms around me. She gives me a long, drawn-out hug, one of those hugs in which you squeeze almost too hard and for too long, your eyes closed, until people start staring and you end with rubbing each other's backs as if to affirm the sincerity of the gesture.

We separate. I hand Beth a cigarette, lighting it, and stare at her eyes.

Beth stares right back at me, holding the cigarette between her left middle and index fingers and raising it to her mouth. She inhales to get it started, blowing smoke out the side of her mouth.

Her eyes guide me to the table beside her. A pitcher of beer and a stack of plastic cups stand watch. Beth nods. "Want to sit down? I got next on darts, but it looks like it's going to be awhile. I could use the company."

"Sure."

Beth is still the coolest girl I know. She's come out of her shell in the last couple years, striking a balance unique in the Empire Ridge female population—nice and refined when she has to be but prone to cussing, chain-smoking, and out-drinking guys twice her weight when refinement is neither mandatory nor preferred. She's one of those women oblivious to how fucking hot she is, unafraid to go out to a bar wearing loose-fitting jeans, wool socks, and Birkenstocks.

The fact she's both hot *and* smart is what made her decision to date Hatch such a curious lapse in judgment.

Granted it was a fling to Beth and something more to Hatch. I still remember how he went all out: three months of dinners and roses, multiple mix tapes—with narration!

"Beth, love will find a way." (Cue Tesla.)

"Beth, you kickstart my heart." (Cue Mötley Crüe.)

"Beth, what can I do?" (Cue KISS.)

I was insanely jealous. Of course, I never let on about my jealousy. Even when Hatch went into graphic detail about Beth's flexibility in the sack or her prowess at giving blowjobs. Even when Mom and Dad headed to South Carolina for a week and Hatch kicked me out of my own house for an entire weekend just so he could nail Beth in my parents' bed.

Beth came to her senses eventually, dumping Hatch at summer's end. Hatch broke down and cried about it on multiple occasions. On the record, I was a loyal and steadfast friend, telling Hatch things like "You deserve better than that," and "She doesn't know what she's missing." Off the record, I was damn near exultant that the overachieving fucker's three months of nirvana were over.

"How you holding up?" Beth wraps her arm behind me and rubs my back again, exhaling a puff of smoke.

"Been better." I hunch forward, as if I can hide from my grief.

"Yeah." She leans in, dropping her chin on my shoulder. "Did you know I bought my first real car from your father?"

I sip my beer. "Who didn't?"

"Laura, too?"

Beth still spits her name more than she says its. It used to bug me. Now I find it attractive. I nod. "Yep, Laura too."

"I bet I got a better deal," Beth says. "When I got a full ride to Illinois, my dad said I could spend my college fund on a new car."

"And you picked an *Oldsmobile*?"

"Who said anything about an Oldsmobile?" Beth grabs my forearm. "Why would any self-respecting girl drive an Oldsmobile?"

"Uh, Laura drives an Oldsmobile."

Beth's eyes say to me, *I rest my case*. "Your father hooked me up with a Fiero. Said he got it for a song from a Pontiac dealership that went out of business and couldn't with a clean conscience sell it to me for anything more than cost. I'll always have that memory of your father. He was one-in-a-million."

"So everyone tells me."

"Not to mention a hunk." Beth smiles. "Like father, like son."

A compliment veiled in sympathy. I like that. I like that a lot. "How've you been?"

"Gymnastics keeps me busy."

"Sounds like it. I saw your name in the paper. You made it to nationals. That's pretty cool."

"I guess." She says this under her breath, stroking her hair with her free hand, taking a purposeful drag off her cigarette.

"You guess? Two-time state all-around champion in high school, first Illinois gymnast to ever win the Big Ten All-Around, the fourth gymnast in Illinois history to qualify for the NCAA national championships. That's pretty damn cool."

She smiles. "Why, Mr. Fitzpatrick, are you stalking me?"

"Have been for years..." I lose my train of thought, distracted by Hatch leering at me over Beth's shoulder.

"He's pissed I'm talking to you, isn't he?" Beth douses her cigarette in the ashtray on the table.

"Who?"

"Hatch."

"I would assume so, yes."

"That dude has got to just fucking let it go."

"Hey, now." My turn for a compliment. "You can't blame a guy for being pissed off at losing someone like you."

"Shut up." Beth punches me in the shoulder. "What about you?"

"What about me?"

"Whose heart are you breaking these days?"

Beth has an overinflated opinion of me as a ladies' man, partly because she always seems to catch me drunk at a bar, when my inhibitions are down and I don't know when to shut up. Like tonight.

"You know how it is, rockin' and rollin' and a whatnot."

"Nice, Danny Zuko."

"You like *Grease*?"

"I publically like *Grease*, but I secretly love *Grease 2*."

"I figured you for a Cool Rider type."

Beth raises "You want to be my Michael Carrington?"

"I don't do leather pants."

"Seriously, how long has it been since we've hung out?"

"What do you mean? We randomly run into each other all the time."

"No, I mean when did we last *really* hang out?"

"Two summers ago."

"Wow. That's what I thought. I remember you were dating that exchange student that summer."

"You mean the summer you and Hatch dated?"

Beth shakes her head. I can't tell if she's picked up on my disgust or is merely considering her own. "You remember it your way, I'll remember it my way."

"Fair enough," I say.

"Now, about that foreign exchange student," Beth says. "She was from Portugal, right?"

"Brazil." I offer her another cigarette. "But she spoke Portuguese."

Beth grabs a book of matches from under the ashtray and lights her own cigarette this time. "I remember her being quite the little hottie. I just assumed you held on to her."

"I held on to her for one date, if that's what you mean."

"You're kidding me."

"Nope. Took her to see *Pretty Woman*, got shot down later that night in my backyard when I tried to talk her into skinny-dipping."

"That's awful."

"That's nothing."

"I hesitate to say this..." Beth takes a drag off her smoke and leans back in her chair and folds her harms. "But indulge me."

The alcohol did all my talking for me. Over the last half hour I told her about almost everyone—Emily, Summer, Pattie, Nicole, Maria, Angelina, Harper, Monica. I left out the stories about Hatch's red-headed cousin and the engaged-and-then-married girl possibly named Kathy or Katie.

Beth looks at me in disbelief. "Are you finished?"

"I think so," I say.

She stands, clapping.

"Hey, I was in a bad place, okay?"

"Sounds like a good place to me. Although I would've paid good money to see that Summer chick lay your ass out."

The fact Beth continues to flirt with me tells me she's either fearless or just plain insane. "Your turn," I say.

"What do you mean?"

"You seem different."

"How so?"

"I don't know…more confident, maybe? It's not that you were ever a wallflower, but you seem to be almost glowing. Am I making the least bit of sense here?"

"More sense than you realize," Beth says. "I credit my new vibe to getting out of this town."

"You have something against Empire Ridge?"

"Not so much Empire Ridge as I do my gymnastics coach."

"You had an okay high school career, and last time I checked that coach gets The Ridge in the state finals pretty much every year."

"And for every trophy on her mantel, she has a girl in therapy with an eating disorder."

"Ouch."

"Yeah, ouch is right."

"Hey, you two, how about a picture?"

The voice startles me. Beth is unfazed. She introduces us. Her name is Sylvia, Beth's roommate from Illinois. Sylvia is holding a camera.

Beth stands up, as if this was her plan all along. She walks behind me and wraps her arms around me. She squeezes her face in next to mine. "Be a good sport, Hank." She gives me a small peck on the cheek and turns to the camera. Our faces touch. "And try not to break my heart tonight."

I put my hand on hers, smiling. "Never."

CHAPTER FORTY-ONE

Grand Prix is Purdue University's half-ass answer to Indiana University's Little 500. *Breaking Away*, Cutters, "The Italians are coming!"—yeah, that Little 500. Only instead of bikes, they race go-karts. Same as Little Five, Grand Prix is just another elaborate choreographed excuse to drink for an entire week straight.

Count me in.

My sister, Jeanine is a freshman at Purdue. She's doing pretty well, all things considered. Keeping up with her course load, pledging a sorority, not getting any STDs. Just what'd you hope for from a freshman, let alone one whose Dad recently got gutted by a Ford Bronco. In lieu of going to my classes at IU, I've been crashing at her dorm for almost a week. Today, we decided to go watch the Purdue University concert band give a free show at the Slayter Hill amphitheater, little more than an open stage in a sea of inebriated college kids.

"Easy on the wheelchair, sis."

We're splitting a joint, the contents of which we affectionately refer to as "wheelchair weed" or just "wheelchair" for its tendency to incapacitate you for long periods of time.

"How's school?"

I laugh. "Still there, I think."

"When's the last time you actually went to class?"

"Three or four weeks ago, maybe?"

"Jesus, Hank."

"It's my life, sis."

"But can't you just—"

"Talk about something else?"

"Okay, how about Lex, then?"

I choke down my smoke. "What's there to say?"

Alexandra EncarnaciÓn, "Lex" as she's known to her friends, is Jeanine's roommate. She's half-Dominican: dark hair, tall, long legs, with a toned, brown body. Lex and I have been fooling around the entire week, and Jeanine hates it.

"So we have a few cocktails and some random fun together. It's no big deal."

"Random drunken sex. Gee, that's something new for you."

"It isn't like that."

If I'm being honest, it's never like that with Lex. She's the ultimate sexual pragmatist. Anything goes, save for the actual act of sexual intercourse. I think I've managed to get everything inside her *except* my dick. And in return, she gives me frequent heavy petting, followed by a hand job and, in rare instances, a bad, overly toothy blow job. I don't think I've ever met a girl who loves cunnilingus so much. Last night she pulled me into a closet at a fraternity party, grabbed me by the ears and pushed my face down into her panty-less crotch after ten seconds of foreplay. The irony of her chosen nickname actually sounding like "lick sex" doesn't escape me.

I sneak one more toke before passing the wheelchair. "Jeanine, I think I might have feelings for Lex."

"No, you don't. You deal in impulsive emotions like I deal in verbs."

"Funny." I start giggling. "I really don't like her that much. I just wanted to see your eyes bug out. You looked like a fucking alien."

"Watch yourself, Hank. You're really vulnerable right now."

"Maybe."

"We all are—you, me, Mom, even Jack. And the drinking sure as hell doesn't help things."

"I'll figure it all out. How about you?"

"What do you mean?"

"Been to any good shows lately?"

Jeanine takes a hard toke off the wheelchair. "Shows?"

"Concerts, I mean."

"Not since the Dead show at Deer Creek."

Like any teenager on the cusp of her twenties, Jeanine's taste in music has undergone a profound change. The days of *Tiger Beat* magazine, walls plastered with Kirk Cameron posters, and New Kids on the Block concerts have been supplanted by a *High Times* subscription, Nelson Mandela posters, and Grateful Dead shows. Gone is the sister in near hysterics screaming and crying, "Jordan Knight looked at me…oh my God, he looked at me!" In her place is the sister saying, "Man, that was the first time the Dead played 'To Lay Me Down' at Deer Creek in two years…far out."

It's not always been this easy with me and Jeanine—the brother–sister mentoring, the frank discussions, the not beating the living crap out of each other. She was barely out of diapers when I sent her to the hospital with a ruler stuck in her throat. Although, in fairness to me, she already had the ruler in her mouth. I just kicked her feet out from under her. She enacted her revenge a couple years after that. I was running down the hallway, turned a corner, and there was Jeanine's foot. I tripped and the top of my head hit the corner of the wall. Went to the ER and received ten stitches. To this day, short hair just doesn't work on me because of that scar.

Jeanine and I signed our armistice when I got my driver's license. She needed someone to chaperone her at boy-band concerts. I needed an excuse to be around thousands of hormonally charged teenage girls. I got her and her best friend, Dana Black, into Color Me Badd's hotel room at the Omni Hotel on the northeast side of Indianapolis. Six months later, a couple television writers ripped off our true-life adventure for an episode of *Beverly Hills 90210*. The Omni was now the Bel Age. David Silva played me, with Brenda Walsh and Kelly Taylor passable in the roles of Dana and Jeanine. Okay, maybe they didn't rip us off—isn't saying that libel?—but talk about your fucked-up coincidences. And it doesn't end there. Shannon Doherty and I were both born on April 21, 1971. I think I might be on to something.

"Hank, Shannon Doherty was not born on the twenty-first. You always say that. She was born on the twelfth."

"Are you sure about that?"

"I'm sure you need to stop hooking up with my roommate."

"I'll try."

"And you'll fail miserably."

"Yes, I will."

"Oh well…" The orchestra is silent. She smiles and looks at me. "You ready?"

"For what?"

I haven't missed a day of Grand Prix week. It's Thursday evening, and I got here last Friday. I've been here ten days out of the last two weeks. Jeanine has me working kitchen crew at her sorority. I'm still shaking the cobwebs out from yesterday afternoon's drinking game, Century Club. One shot of beer a minute, every minute, for a hundred minutes straight. It's not the beer that gets you—a hundred ounces is barely over eight beers. It's swallowing all that air. I was an honorary Phi Kap for the day in a Century Club face-off against Sigma Chi. Most bailed out at or around a hundred. I won the competition, both barfing and pissing myself at three hundred and two shots. I beat the next closest guy by a hundred shots. A halfway serious petition was circulated to initiate me into the Phi Kap house on the spot.

Jeanine explains to me this Grand Prix tradition of charging the water fountain in front of the amphitheater when the band starts playing the William Tell Overture. She's disrobing down to her sports bra and boxers as she explains everything. I grab the wheelchair out of her hand, hoping to get too stoned to notice my half-naked sister.

The wheelchair helps. I play along, taking off most my clothes as well: the jeans I bought yesterday for two dollars at the West Lafayette Goodwill, the Minnesota hockey jersey Grandma Louise bought me in Rochester when I volunteered to chaperone her to the Mayo Clinic because no one else can tolerate her for more than twenty-four hours straight. We watch the band apply layers of plastic to themselves and their instruments. The conductor walks to the middle of the stage looking like the Gordon's Fisherman. He taps his music stand and raises his baton just as the wheelchair weed eases me into the folds of memory.

Sixth grade. Louisville, Kentucky. Christmas 1981. Dad had used his connections as former assistant band director to bring the University of Notre Dame concert band down to play a one-night, sold-out show at Trinity High School. They played a three-hour set. I sat by Dad, stood as he stood, clapped as he clapped, leading ovation after ovation. After they finished what we all thought was to be their last song, I whispered into Dad's ear, "But what about the fight song?" Then the conductor, Notre Dame Band director Robert O'Brien, stepped back from the music stand. He turned, looked right at Dad, and offered him the baton. Dad stood. The crowd stood, cheering wildly. Mom was crying. Dad smiled a smile as big as I'd ever seen. Dad grabbed the baton. He walked to the middle of the stage…

Jeanine grabs my hand. "Let's do this!" We charge the fountain in our underwear. About fifty people in similar states of undress are right there with us. Several, of course, pretend they're riding a horse down the hill, knowing the song only as the theme music to *The Lone Ranger*. They shout "High ho, Silver, away!" to the crowd. Most are armed with some type of water-emitting contrivance—squirt guns, water balloons. The full orchestra performs in front of us, raised on a stage above the fountain. Everyone, from the conductor to the bass drummer, is decked out in full, head-to-toe all-weather gear. The first-chair violinist gets squirted with a Super Soaker. The second and third chairs laugh…right before two balloons whiz by the conductor's head and nail them both in the head.

I lose Jeanine in the crowd. I look up at the conductor, already soaked to the bones. His sheet music ink-smeared and indecipherable. He's smiling, laughing. He punches the air with his hands, pointing to the brass section, pushing them, louder and louder. I close my eyes. And I pretend the "William Tell Overture" is the "Notre Dame Victory March."

CHAPTER FORTY-TWO

Adam West and Burt Ward survey the scene, striking typically heroic poses.

"Leaping libido, Batman!" Robin says. "Is that man having sex with a twelve-year-old girl?"

"No, Robin," Batman says. "That appears to be merely a young adult male in his early twenties. And the girl you speak of is in fact in her early twenties as well."

"But that's impossible."

"Impossible, Robin? Note the slight pooch in her stomach."

"Yes, what of it?"

"It is a pooch that could only come from four years of bad decisions and even worse drinking and eating habits."

"Of course, college," Robin says. "Free beer and starchy food."

"Precisely, Boy Wonder."

"But what about?"

"Down there?"

"Yes, Batman. It's just so…smooth."

"Smooth perhaps, my young sidekick. But there are traces, a shadow if you will. Logic dictates that she shaves."

"Holy bare bush, Batman!"

"Bare bush indeed, Boy Wonder."

I PAINTED A LIFE-SIZE mural of Batman and Robin on Jack's bedroom wall after we moved into the new house. At the moment, the Dynamic Duo is watching me have sex with Harper Donovan in my little brother's race car bed.

Since we were eighteen, Harper and I have been the friends with benefits, the friends that have sex, whatever you want to call it. We don't go out on dates, have never dated, and don't have any plans to date. We're the unspoken asterisks in each other's life. She'll get in a fight with her boyfriend, come over to my place, and we'll have sex. When I recall relationships with other women, I don't necessarily recall having sex with Harper during that time though we may indeed have had sex. The sex just happens. It's like eating or breathing. The arrangement makes perfect sense to us, but it offends almost every other girl I know. The guys of course want to know my secret. They want me to write a book, give seminars, but mostly just introduce them to Harper.

Harper and I almost hooked up as sophomores in high school. She transferred from Prep after winter break and flirted with me for weeks. Half the sophomore class met at the theater for the premiere of *Police Academy 4: Citizens on Patrol*. Harper offered me the seat beside her. I said, "No thanks," and shot her down before a young and mop-headed Sharon Stone even made it onscreen. Sitting next to me, Hatch said *out loud*, "Hell, Harper, I'll take you up on the offer if Hank is too stupid not to."

Later that week, when I totaled the Oldsmobile Custom Cruiser, Harper and Hatch were actually making out in the backseat. They were a couple for most of the summer.

Harper and I fooled around a little in high school, nothing major. In fact, the only significant encounter was when we *didn't* do something. We were seniors. It was Grad Night at Kings Island. I smuggled a pint of Beam and a couple joints into the park. Laura was back at Bucknell. Hatch and Harper smuggled my near-catatonic butt out of the park. The party followed us to our hotel room, at which point Hatch laid me in bed, tucked me in, then proceeded to have sex on the floor with his girlfriend. Harper passed out next to me, in my arms. Maybe I thought Harper was Laura. Then again, maybe I didn't.

There was nothing dramatic or even memorable about our first time. It happened in college, freshman year. I ran into Harper one random Thursday night in downtown Bloomington. Penny beer night at the Bluebird—penny beers, quarter pitchers, dollar well drinks. It got ugly fast. After some suggestive dancing on the dance floor, Harper took me back to her apartment room, and we just did it.

Harper lifts herself off of me. She sits on the side of the bed naked, silhouetted in the light of Jack's Batman nightlight. Harper is a very pretty girl: light brown hair that curves in at the base of her neck, large eyes, odd but strangely attractive conical breasts, and a trim if not athletic body with thin arms, the beginnings of a pot belly, and thin legs. She could have better posture, as she has a tendency to hunch forward.

Tonight was the first time we've been together since my twenty-first birthday. Easily our longest drought. She took off all her clothes, got on top of me and stayed there. Her orgasm was quick and business-like. Mine took a little bit longer, which isn't anything new for me, at least with Harper. I don't know if it's her pelvic approach, if she has a crooked vagina, or if I'm just too damn drunk whenever we get naked, but when it comes to sex with Harper, I can always count on a sore dick and hitting my target heart rate.

I HELP HARPER WITH her coat, walk her out to her car. "You going back to Bloomington?"

"Yeah," Harper nods. "My job here is done."

My job here is done. Fantastic! In many ways, Harper is my perfect girlfriend, although I'll never tell her that. I call her out of the blue, and she drives an hour from Bloomington to Empire Ridge just to have sex with me. And now she's leaving. No talking about our feelings, about my father—none of that. She knows what I want, maybe what I need, and she gives it to me.

Harper stops halfway to the car. "Hank, can we talk for a second?"

Looks like I spoke too soon. "Sure, what's up?"

"I've met someone."

"Really? That's great."

"It could be," Harper says.

"I know him?"

"I don't think you do. The name Logan Yancey ring any bells?"

"Not a one."

"He used to live in Empire Ridge. We were childhood friends, best friends actually. He and I were an item at Prep, before I transferred over to The Ridge. He moved to Michigan the middle of our freshman year. I went and visited him later that summer."

"Oh, *that* guy," I say. "He was your first."

"Uh, yeah," Harper says. "How'd you know?"

"Harp," I say. "You and I have spent way too many loose-lipped, drunken nights together."

"I guess we have, haven't we?" Harper smiles. "The point being, Logan and I want to start things up again."

"Good for you," I say. "It's like a goddamn fairy tale."

"Yeah, it *is* like a goddamn fairy tale, isn't it?" Harper moves her hand between us, pointing to herself and then to me. "But *this* has got to stop."

I smile. "I think we both knew we couldn't do this forever."

I kiss Harper full on the lips. She kisses me back. We kiss for awhile. My hands behave.

"I'll call you when I'm back in Bloomington," I say, closing Harper's car door behind her.

Harper rolls down her window and rolls her eyes. "No you won't."

I smile. "You know me pretty damn well, don't you?"

"Hank, I'll never know you well. But do me a favor, will you?"

"Anything."

"Find someone special. You deserve it."

I tap the roof of her car. "You know I can't promise anything."

"Oh, I know."

"See you, Harper."

She smiles. "No you won't."

Harper pulls out of the driveway as I walk back into the house. It's Friday evening, and no one is home. I haven't seen Mom in months. Jack is who-knows-where, most likely spending the night at a friend's house. I grab a half-eaten bag of microwave popcorn off the kitchen counter.

The old tan sectional sits in our basement, the arms and backrests indented from years of loving abuse. We've had this sectional for going on eleven years now, but its components have been reunited back into a sectional only since we moved in January. The multiple windows and bookshelves of the old house necessitated the division of the sectional into three pieces—a long couch, a loveseat, and a convertible. The convertible used to be positioned so Dad could lie down, prop his head up on a pillow, and watch the television just above his feet. From here Dad doled out his nightly ice cream stick, patted Jack to sleep on his belly, and then fell asleep to the melodic lullabies of local news broadcasters, late night talk show hosts, and of course, Mexican boxers on Univision. *El Mundoooo del Box!*

I remembered when Jack got too big for Dad's belly. He was two years old. Dad said, "Stop wiggling." This went on for a couple nights. Then Jack slid up and over to the top of the couch's backrest and propped his little body against the wall. They ended up on that couch every night—Dad on bottom, Jack on top. The night after Dad died, Jack fell asleep on the backrest. Nobody had the courage to sleep on the couch with him.

I turn on the television and start flipping through the channels. I hear the front door open and close. Mom is home.

I hear giggling. "Tommmmm."

Tom Shelden was Mom's high school sweetheart. They broke up when Mom left for college, back in like '64 or '65. Tom came to Dad's funeral. Jeanine and I encouraged Mom to call Tom a couple months later. We told her, "It'll be good for you to get out."

Apparently, I've missed a few months.

More giggling. I turn down the volume on the television. I hear the clink of ice being dropped in glasses. Pieces of the conversation:

"Watch those hands…"

"…more to drink."

"Don't tease me like that…"

"Come on, Debbie…"

"I'll be right up…"

Feet scurrying up a flight of the stairs. And the giggling. *The fucking giggling!* This isn't happening. I can't turn up the volume on the TV, can't let them know I'm here. But I can't listen to *this*.

A door shutting. Quiet. Thank God.

Thump.

What was that?

Thump, thump…

No. Fuck no.

Thump, thump, thump…

Jesus fucking Christ no.

"Ohhhhhh…"

My dad has been buried for six months, and his wife is already sharing their bed with another man, a balding, chain-smoking piece of shit who wears spandex shorts and gets his dates liquored up on vodka gimlets.

Thump, thump, thump…

Six fucking months. My mother is a goddamn whore. A goddamn, drunk, fucking whore.

"Ohhhhhh…"

I reach for the phone on the coffee table. I dial my apartment.

The phone rings. The thumping and the moaning don't stop. Dear fucking God, I hope Dad is in heaven at this very moment, watching all this and fucking the brains out of some smoking hot pussy like Helen of Troy, Marilyn Monroe, or Dorothy Stratton.

He picks up after six rings. "Hatch here."

"About fucking time."

"What's up, Fitzy? You back in Bloomington yet?"

"I will be. Meet me over at Brink's and Cash's place. I'm coming in hot from Empire Ridge. Let's get an early start on Little Five weekend."

"Fuck that. I got no interest in dying tonight."

"Come on, you don't have to get high. Just have a couple beers with me and make sure I don't do anything stupid."

"I can't be your babysitter tonight, Fitzy."

"Why not?"

"Dad got my grades," Hatch says. "I'm in deep shit if I don't turn things around."

"Then fuck you!" I say, slamming the phone down on the receiver. I hear the stairs creak.

"Hank, what's wrong?"

Mom stands halfway down the staircase. She's wearing a sheer robe I've never seen before, her face painted in equal shades of relief and embarrassment.

"I thought I heard a noise, and look what we have here. My baby's home." Her smile seems forced to me. Hell, everything about her seems fake right now. "I've been so worried about you. This weekend's your birthday. What do you want to—"

I raise my hand. "Shut up."

"What?"

"I said shut up."

"How dare you talk to me like that!"

"I heard you, Mom. Upstairs—I heard all of it."

"All of what?"

"Listening to it was bad enough. I'm sure as hell not going to rehash the play-by-play for your benefit."

"If you're going to presume to lecture me about my sex life, Hank—"

I stand up, pointing my finger in her face. "Why *can't* I presume? That fucker upstairs is the second guy you've ever slept with in your entire life. I had more sexual encounters than you by the time I was ten years old."

"What's that supposed to mean?"

I still can't believe no one has fucking connected the dots with Uncle Mitch. "I'm just saying that…that…"

"That your views on intimacy are more mature than mine?"

The introspective high school guidance counselor makes her long overdue appearance. I'm not in the mood to see her.

"Yeah, Mom, that's it. I'm mature enough. Mature enough to know that fucking an old high school flame when the love of your life hasn't even been in the ground for six months is wrong."

The color in Mom's face drains away. I could have hurt her less if I had just punched her in the stomach. She collapses onto the couch, her face in her hands, wailing.

CHAPTER FORTY-THREE

In the light of day, the drive between Empire Ridge and Bloomington is among the most scenic in the state. Southern Indiana is where the Ice Age stalled three hundred thousand years ago, the glaciers that rolled the northern half of the state and most of the Midwest flat and nondescript retreating back into the Great Lakes and Canada. You'd think people could get past the stereotypes. Corn rows as far as the eye can see. Republicans as numerous as mold spores. A basketball goal in every driveway or backyard, or better yet nailed to the side of a barn, hovering over a dusty court of game-saving shots. And yet, even after three hundred thousand years, nobody outside the state seems to know southern Indiana exists. The rolling knobs. The limestone caves carved out by underground streams. The valleys of sumac, maple, gingko, and sweet gum with their autumn hues of magenta, gold, orange, and peach. And Indiana University, one of the most liberal campuses in the country.

Not disputing basketball goals. We're fucknuts crazy about that sport.

I stop at a gas station in Nashville for some malt liquor and cigarettes. With its own "Little Nashville Opry," Nashville, Indiana, fashions itself as the next best thing to the country music capital, never mind there are six Nashvilles in America larger than the one in Indiana. John Mellencamp's home isn't too far from the city limits, but Nashville continues to hang its star on its quaint storefronts and the fact Theodore Clement Steele died here.

T. C. Steele was once apparently an American Impressionist painter of some repute. Whatever. I've seen Steele's "House of the Singing Winds" oil on canvas, and it's no *American Fool* album.

I pull into the apartment complex just off Kirkwood Avenue. My breath smells of malted hops and cigarettes from the Mickey's Big Mouths and Marlboro Lights I've been inhaling since Nashville. Brinks and Cash's place is on the first floor, steps away from where I park. I can already hear the music. Predictably, it's "Sugar Magnolia" by the Grateful Dead. I just walk in. Cash is sitting on the couch, a bag of half-eaten Cool Ranch Doritos in his lap.

"Cash, what the fuck you up to, buddy?"

"Holy shit!" Cash stands up and sends the bag of tortilla chips flying off his lap. He bounds across the room, grabbing me in an inebriated bear hug. "Hey, Brinks, we got ourselves a guest!"

Neil Brinkley is Cash's half-brother. He and I worked together at the box factory last summer. Brinks is a year younger than me, two years younger than Cash. Whereas a night with Cash is guaranteed to give you a good buzz, a night with Cash and Brinks together is guaranteed to give you an out-of-body experience. Brinks has a bad habit of slipping me LSD wrapped in rice paper during concerts. And by *slipping me*, I mean Brinks says to me, "Hey, Fitzpatrick, want to try this?" and I say, "Sure."

Brinks screams from the kitchen. "Get the fuck out of here!" He walks into the family room, a slice of pizza in one hand, a small glass pipe in the other. He hands me the pipe. "Light her up, Fitzpatrick!"

I pull my lighter out of my pocket and raise the pipe to my lips. "You sure, Brinks?"

He nods. "Take a big fucking hit off that bitch. I just packed her."

I raise the well-packed pipe to eye level, a half-dime sized nest of pungent marijuana just beyond the end of my nose. Judging by the smell of it—that strong hemp odor of sage, rope, and grass clippings mixed together—this isn't the kind of weed I should be fucking around with. I place my finger on the hole at the end of the pipe, lighting a corner of the nest rather than the whole thing to leave some of the marijuana still green for my friends. I inhale the smoke and start to feel it inside my mouth and in my nose. I release my finger from the hole at the other end, at the same time sucking hard. The smoke surges down into my lungs. Like needles on my throat, inside my chest. I cough.

"Ewwwhuuuughhhh!"

I'm lightheaded. I bend over, handing the pipe to Cash. Each hard, guttural cough intensifies the buzz.

I cough maybe a dozen times.

Brinks pats me on the back. "Dude, take it easy. We got all night." He hands me a tall ceramic cup of an unidentified steaming liquid.

"What is this?"

"Some hot tea with honey. It'll keep your throat from hurting too bad. And with tokes like that, your throat's gonna be hurting pretty bad."

"Thanks." I take a sip. The tea feels good on my throat, but there's something not right about its flavor. Even with the honey, the taste is, for lack of a better descriptor, dirty.

Before I can think on it some more, the pipe is back to me. Another cough fit hits me.

"Jesus, Hank! Brinks and I got like a half shoebox of this stuff. You don't need to try and smoke it all at once."

"Fuck off, Cash!" The marijuana is doing my talking. I sip my tea.

We continued to smoke for maybe an hour. They handed me the pipe. I coughed. I drank my tea.

They handed me the pipe. I coughed. I drank my tea. Lather, rinse, repeat.

We've repacked that goddamn bowl at least three times. Our smoke-off ends when we laugh at a Comedy Central stand-up skit so hard I swallow the teabag at the bottom of my cup.

A piece of the teabag comes back up. I spit it into my hand. It's brown, almost rubbery. I hold the regurgitated foreign object in the palm of my right hand, poking it with my left index finger. "What the fuck?"I say.

Everything starts to slow down. Time means nothing. A feeling of awkward sadness overwhelms me. I'm uncomfortable, not so much overwhelmed by being sad, but rather hyper-aware of my sadness. A total fucking puddle of melancholy.

Did I call my mom a whore today? Or did I just think it?

When are you getting back, Dad?

Everyone says you're gone for good, but the joke's over. Come home.

"Hank?"

"Dad?"

A hand on my shoulder. "Uh, no."

I lurch up from the couch, startled. "Cash?"

"Yeah, sorry about that."

"What did you give me?"

"Relax, you're not gonna die or nuthin. You just drank an entire cup of shroom tea. Given that I put two mushrooms in your tea and you're holding one in your hand, I think you might have swallowed a mushroom whole."

Brinks drops to the floor, laughing and in tears. "See you tomorrow, Hank."

CHAPTER FORTY-FOUR

Saturday morning of Little 500 weekend. For some people, Little 500 means thirty-three teams of four riders racing relay-style for two hundred laps along a quarter-mile cinder track on identical, single-gear, coaster-brake racing bicycles with flat rubber pedals. For most, it means drinking yourself into identical, multi-substance, amnesiac comas while never making it within a mile of the race.

Hatch tries to peel me off the couch. "Dude, get up."

"Where the fuck am I?"

"At Cash's place, and you smell like ass."

"Fuck off, Hatch." I stand up. I drop my nose down into my armpit. My eyes open wide, the stench shocking me awake.

"I think I'm getting high just standing here." Hatch takes inventory of the room. Empty beer cans and greasy pizza boxes frame a coffee table. In the kitchen, the odors of tobacco and pot linger over a large ashtray brimming with cigarette butts, castoff marijuana seeds and stems, and a roach we were too stoned to finish.

"Where's Cash and Brinks?" Hatch asks.

"They went out for some breakfast. I don't have much of an appetite this morning."

"Speaking of this morning. Happy fucking birthday!"

I'm twenty-two years old today. Mom usually calls me to recount the hours and minutes leading up to my birth on that "cool spring night" of April 21, 1971. How I was almost an Aries. How my great-grandma Myrtle, a former bouncer, yanked me out of the nurse's arms saying, "Nobody's going to tell me I can't hold my great-grandson." How Mom was Uncle Mitch's inorganic chemistry tutor around the time I was conceived and

Mom and Dad laughed when the doctor went in with an oversized crochet needle to break Mom's water and the needle came out with several locks of curly black Mitch-like hair wrapped around it. I can almost hear Mitch telling the story, pig-giggling while dreaming about little boys' pubes.

I don't expect Mom's birthday call. Not after yesterday. I stand up, pushing Hatch out of my way. "I'm going to go jump in the shower."

"Good call," Hatch says. "Mack just got in from Tennessee. We're supposed to meet him in an hour at the Bluebird."

"Mack, huh? What's he up to?"

"About six-nine, two-forty."

We started hanging out with Josh McKenna the summer before college. "Mack" is a Prepster with above-average hoop skills. A former McDonald's High School All-American, he got a full ride to Austin Peay. He never saw the court because of injuries. Two knee surgeries have since marked his digression from a genuine All-American to a self-proclaimed one. I don't feel too bad for Mack. He's still on full scholarship, with an expanding closet of brand-new Nike shoes he'll never wear because he still receives his annual allotment of gear whether or not he plays. Not to mention the mileage he continues to get from feasting on basketball groupies and the vast majority of eligible—and oftentimes ineligible—women who are into tall men.

I make my way to the stairs, a shuffling gait that refuses to make the effort. "Mack's pushing two-and-a-half bills?"

Hatch laughs. "On a light day."

I walk upstairs to the bathroom. I close the door behind me. I step in the shower, an old claw-footed tub that's been jury-rigged with a cheap off-brand spigot and a faded yellow polyester curtain tipped with blotches of black mold. I turn the hot water up to just below boiling. I do my usual routine—shampoo, soap, shave, and masturbate. My hangover is minimal. One of the many advantages of drugs over alcohol. The hot water helps.

Splashhhhhh!

A shower of ice water rains down on me from above. The corner of a large saucepan is perched just above the shower curtain.

"Hatch, you're a fucking bastard!"

As far as college music venues go, they don't get any more venerable than the Bluebird. Since 1973 the stage has seen acts ranging from

Dizzy Gillespie to Lou Reed to a reading by William S. Burroughs. It's that fucking cool. Like most cool college bars, it reeks of cigarette smoke, cheap beer, and underage livers.

We're early, so the Bluebird is merely crowded as opposed to crowded as fuck. Two people are leaving just as we get to the bar. Hatch orders a pitcher of Natty Light as he snags the empty seats.

I eye the stage. "Who's playing tonight?"

Hatch shrugs. "Beats me."

The bartender sets the pitcher down. He looks at me. "Why Store."

"No way," I say.

The bartender places two coasters and two empty plastic cups on the bar. "Yes way," he says.

The Why Store. Chris Shaffer on lead vocals, acoustic twelve-string, tambourine, and harmonica. Michael D. Smith on lead guitar and backing vocals. Greg Gardner on bass and backing vocals. Charlie Bushor on drums, percussion, and congas. In my opinion, they're the best thing to come out of the Indiana music scene since Mellencamp. The buzz is they're about to sign with a major record label. But I doubt they'll ever top their independent release, *Welcome to the Why Store,* one of my all-time favorite albums.

"Hatch, we're staying for the goddamn Why Store." Hatch tops off my glass, nods. "It's your birthday."

WE ORDERED SOME CHICKEN wings and a couple Cokes to delay the power drinking. But by the time Mack shows, we've still managed to down at least three pitchers and a round of Jim Beam shots.

The bartender brings us a round of tequila shots. I hand both Mack and Hatch slices of lime and place the salt shaker between them on the bar.

"Snakebites, Hank?" Mack asks, grabbing his shot glass.

"Nothing but the best."

"I ain't drinking that shit," Hatch says.

"It's my birthday," I say, handing him his contribution to the moment. "You have to let me piss in your mouth if I want to."

Hatch grabs the shot from my hand. "That's what I'm about to do."

We salt the area of our hands between our thumbs and index fingers. We lick the salt, slam our tequila, and then suck on the limes. *Three Stooges*-like, we each let out our own unique sound of disgust, gagging in unison.

"Fuckin' Why Store, Mack!" I blurt out.

"So I hear." Mack chases the tequila with a room temperature wing off my plate. He shoves the entire wing into his mouth, stripping the meat with his teeth, and swallows. Mack smells of too much cologne, which is standard for him. It looks like he just got a haircut, his dark hair close to his head but not quite buzzed. He wipes his mouth with a cocktail napkin. "You ready to get your drink on, Hank?"

Hatch pokes his head over my shoulder. He hands Mack another tequila shot. "I think you got some catching up to do, circus freak."

Mack downs the shot. He signals the bartender. "Yeah, two more tequilas please—one for the birthday boy and one for the goofy-looking fuck behind him."

We go two more rounds with the snakebites. The tequila starts to go down smooth. Too smooth.

The bar is now crowded as fuck. Hatch and Mack go in shifts, one at the stage, one at the bar holding our seats. It's my birthday, so I do whatever the hell I want. Like, for instance, right before The Why Store takes the stage, I pull the roach and handful of marijuana stems I swiped out of Cash's ashtray and shove them in my mouth. And like consuming two rounds of Sex on the Beach—heavy on the vodka—from a girl's double-D cleavage.

The Why Store comes on stage for its first set. With his lace cuffs, purple velvet jacket, and broad-brimmed hat punctuated by a large feather, The Why Store front man, Chris Shaffer, looks like a cross between Jimi Hendrix, Long John Silver, and Huggy Bear. He starts with a new song I've never heard called "Father" that's about a dad letting his son go. It's a little too preachy if you ask me.

After "Father," the band went mellow with "Oh Lord" and "Rosie," followed by their signature tune that's been getting radio play, "Everybody Holds the Future." Chris Shaffer got on his soapbox and segued into "Your World" that led to a rant on the legalization of pot. The crowd cheered its wholehearted, red-eyed approval, which is when Hatch summoned me back to the bar. He has a couple shots waiting for me, each of them covered with a lemon slice. More snakebites.

"Bottoms up, Fitzy!" Hatch hands me a salt shaker. I salt my hand. He hands me the first shot. I peel the lemon off the top, lick the salt, and shoot the tequila. I stick the lemon in my mouth.

"Next!" Hatch already has the second shot in his hand. He again hands me the shot. I do the same as before—salt, shot, lemon.

The second shot hits the back of my throat. It's not tequila. My swallow is forced. My mouth is on fire.

Hatch starts laughing. "Say 'ello to my lit'il fren."

"What did you just give me, fucker?"

"A Prairie Fire."

"What's that?"

"Bacardi 151 and Tabasco sauce."

Between the burrito I had on the way over here and the chicken wings, I don't know which comes up first. Regardless, the bar—the actual hardwood bar itself—is soon covered by both food items in various stages of digestion. So much for the coasters.

Even drunk, I'm still pretty quick on my feet. Just as I finish throwing up, I drop to my knees and crawl on the floor alongside the bar.

I pop up at the end of the bar and start to make a break for the restroom.

I see out of the corner of my eye the bartender standing on top of a stool. He points at me. "That's the fucking puker right there!"

"Let's go, son." The bouncer's hand is on my collar just as I get halfway into the restroom. He's what you would expect in a bouncer—big and bald, one diamond-stud earring, a painted-on shirt. He looks like Mr. Clean's evil twin.

Hatch and Mack block my exit. They beg for clemency.

"Sorry, fellas. You guys are welcome to stay, but I think your friend here has had enough."

"Wait a second." I have an idea, emboldened for no good reason. "What if I offered to clean up my mess?"

Mr. Clean smiles, loosening his grip on my collar. He seems struck by the novelty of my offer. He lets go of me. "Stay here."

We stand just inside the entrance to the Bluebird. A procession of college students, some twenty-one, others trying to pass for it, hand over their IDs for inspection. Mack shakes his head. "Way to go, Hank."

"Don't yell at me." I push Hatch in the chest. "Talk to this asshole who made me drink gasoline."

Laughing again, Hatch recounts the story to Mack. Mack punches Hatch in the shoulder. "That's still almost worth getting kicked out." He's laughing now, too. "Dude, you horked *on the fucking bar*!"

"I know, Mack. I was there." I can feel the post-puke sweats coming on. I wipe my forehead with my sleeve. "That shot didn't leave me much of a choice."

"Here!" Mr. Clean is back. He shoves a rag and mop in my face. "Go for it, buddy."

I walk to the scene of the crime, halfway down the bar. Mr. Clean is right behind me, followed by Hatch and Mack.

The bartender is waiting for me when I arrive. If I'm being honest, he doesn't look happy to see me. "Get to work," he says, turning his back.

The crowd at the bar gives me a wide berth, much of the vomit is still strewn about on several chairs, an ashtray, and three abandoned cocktails now spiked with stomach acid. I look left, look right, and catch a whiff of my own bile.

"Yeah…" I sigh. I look right again, look left again. Hatch and Mack are getting a kick out of this. The bartender is not. Draping the rag over one of the barstools, I try not to smile at Mr. Clean but can't help myself. I rest the mop against the edge of the bar, throw my hands up in the air like someone has a gun to my back. "You can go ahead and kick my ass out of here."

CHAPTER FORTY-FIVE

Mack is too impatient to wait in any bar lines, and Hatch and I are too drunk to stand in one place without falling over. We walk down the street to Big Red Liquors, convinced a couple more six-packs "will clear our heads."

I approach the ATM outside the liquor store knowing I have less than three dollars in my account. I type in my password. The screen gives me several options, including asking whether I want to take money from checking, savings, or do a "Fast $50" transaction.

Mack reaches over my shoulder and pushes the button. "Fast fifty, Hank!"

"You fuckhead. I don't have five dollars to my name, let alone fif—"

I am interrupted by the sound of the ATM spitting out two twenties and a ten. I grab the money. I'm thirsty, and what's one more overdraft notice?

We walk into Big Red Liquors and make our selection. I somehow get roped into paying for all of it. Two six-packs somehow becomes two cases. I'm not even out the door when I have second thoughts about my spending spree.

"No ice, no cooler, and we leave the goddamn liquor store with forty-eight cold beers. You tell me, Mack, how in the hell are we going to drink all these tonight?"

"Relax. We're going to a party."

"A party?"

"Yeah."

"Where?"

"Sheila's place. I even hear Laura's going to be there."

"Fuck you." I sit the beers down on the ground, fold my arms.

"Come on, Hank. It'll be fun."

I go Bender on him. "No, Mack, fuck you!"

Hatch steps in. "Fitzy has a point, Mack. It's his birthday, and you're taking him to see Laura Elliot?"

"Come on, guys, it'll be fun," Mack says. "The whole gang is there."

"Where's Ian?"

Mack cocks his head. "Who?"

"Laura's boyfriend."

Hatch mimics Mack, monkey-like. "Her what?"

I reach down and pick up the two cases of beer. "Fuck it, never mind. Let's just do this."

In the grand tradition of fate not even giving me a chance to catch my breath, Laura answers the door to Sheila's apartment. She's wearing a pair of form-fitting jeans and a Bucknell University sweatshirt capped by a smile that either looks shit-faced or happy to see me.

"Hey, fellas!" Laura hugs Mack. Hatch grabs the cases of beer out of my hands, walks right by her. She stops me, leaning in to kiss me on the cheek.

"Hope you don't mind us crashing your party," I say.

Laura shuts the door behind me. "I heard you and Mack were hanging out this weekend. I was hoping he'd talk you into it."

"You were?"

Laura smiles and gives me another kiss on the cheek. "Happy birthday, Hank."

I was barely in the apartment and already working on a solid trifecta: the drunk ex-girlfriend hitting on me, the drunk ex-boyfriend not doing a whole lot to dissuade the overtures, and the alcoholic-in-training best friend handing me a beer with a hole cut out of the bottom yelling…

"Shotgun!"

"Goddamnit, Hatch."

"Come on, Fitzy."

"Go into the kitchen with that mess!" Laura pushes us both out of the family room.

The sink is already piled high with at least a dozen holed-out aluminum cans. We both shotgun a beer.

And then a second beer.

And then a third.

Laura leads a round of Thumper in the dining room. It's a simple drinking game. The emcee—in this case, Laura—starts the round by asking, "What's the name of the game?" To which the group shouts back in unison while drumming their hands on the table, "Thumper!" Laura asks, "How do we play it?" The group responds, "Down and dirty!" Laura asks, "Why do we play it?" And then the group smacks their hands on the table three times in synch with the last three words, "To get fucked up!" Laura gives her hand signal—in this case, a head-bobbing imitation of going down on someone—then flashes a hand signal of another person in the group, after which that person responds with his or her hand signal, then flashes another person in the group his or her signal, and so on and so on until someone messes up. The first person to mess up drinks and gets to start the next round.

I play two quick rounds before realizing I have no business playing drinking games. My hand signal is simulating double-handed masturbation, a move tinged with both irony, given my average penis size, and revelation, given my above-average penchant for masturbation. Hatch calls me a "lightweight pussy." He tells me to "take off my skirt and strap on a pair."

"Southern Cross" by Crosby, Stills & Nash transitions into Meatloaf's "Paradise by the Dashboard Light" on the stereo.

Hatch jumps up. "Ohhh shit, Fitzy!"

The game of Thumper is suspended. The room divides in accordance with proper Meatloaf etiquette—boys on one side, girls on the other. Boys go first, remembering once again every little thing as if it happened only yesterday, followed by the girls leaving no doubt in the discussion about their respective ages and general lack of clothing.

The boys and girls go back and forth with two long solos, pausing at the bridge—an indiscernible radio broadcast of a baseball game no one knows the words to that allows for drink refills, a few drags off your cigarette, and sneaking your tongue into your ex-girlfriend's mouth.

We trade two more long solos. This segues into the guys wanting to sleep on it rather than just tell the girls they love them—you know, that polyphonic bit in which the dueling genders are tasked with singing at the same time but to different lyrics, resulting in a block of drunken noise. Enthusiasm trumps vocal ineptitude on a grand scale, rising to a testosterone-and estrogen-fueled crescendo of everyone swearing eternal love to their God on their mother's grave.

It's going on three in the morning now. Hatch and Mack are passed out on the floor in Sheila's bedroom. I've found my way to Sheila's queen bed. With Laura.

"Some party," I say.

"Sure was," Laura says.

We're both still clothed, albeit face-to-face with our arms and legs wrapped around one another. We'd been making out for about a half hour when Laura decided to take off her bra. That was about the same time I decided I was having sex with her.

"Confession time, Hank."

"Go for it."

"I have missed your soft, cushy lips."

Let the record show these two adjectives have been explicitly directed at my lips by at least three different women. Next to maybe my hair, my lips are my best feature.

"And they've missed you." I kiss her again for good measure.

She pulls away. "Hank, what are we doing here?"

"I think that's kind of obvious."

"Don't start getting all riled up." She pulls my hand out from under her shirt just as I squeeze her right breast. "You're not getting any tonight."

Laura is pretending she doesn't want this to happen. Fine, I'll play along. "How's Ian doing these days?" I say.

Laura puts her right index finger on my lips. "Can we please spend a night together without fighting?"

"Who's fighting? I think I'm entitled to know whether I'm about to be a home wrecker."

"I see you're still overconfident in your pick-up skills." She again pulls my right hand out from under her shirt. This time I manage to squeeze her left breast. "Nobody's wrecking any home tonight, Hank."

"So you're not dating Ian?"

"I didn't say that. The short story is he proposed, I got scared."

"How scared?"

"Scared enough to take a semester off from grad school at Bucknell."

"Then that's it for you two?"

"Hardly. We're just spending some time apart. I need some space, some time back with old friends and family to sort out some things. I still very much love Ian."

"No offense, but you have an interesting way of showing it."

"Let's be honest here." Laura smiles. She's drunk, very drunk. "Will anything I say stop you from trying to get in my pants?"

"Probably not..." My words dissolve into a small kiss on her throat, just under her chin. Laura takes a breath, a deep inhalation that renders her transparent. A brazen move on my part, but she responds.

Laura runs her fingers along my face, brushing my hair behind my ears. "Remember when your dad serenaded me on my birthday?"

"How could I forget?" I say. "Hard to believe it's been four years since then. You're what, twenty-three now?"

"Almost."

"You're practically my sugar mama."

"Hilarious, Hank."

"Yes, it is."

"Anyway, that serenade was the best birthday present of my almost twenty-three-year-old life."

"Next to this you mean?" I grab the plush, long-eared elephant from the foot of the bed. "What's this doing here?"

Laura wrests the elephant away from me. "I take Dumbo pretty much wherever I go."

I had won Dumbo at the Magic Kingdom, although of course my gesture was overshadowed by Johnny Fitzpatrick Mathis brilliance. I pawned it off as a belated birthday gift—the typical gesture of a shit-for-brains teenage boy. I adore Laura for holding on to it. I think about the "It's a Small World" ride. I think about Dad.

"I miss him, Laura."

She puts her hand on my face. "He's still here. I see him every time you smile, every time you laugh."

"I guess I see him, too, especially in that picture over there." I point to a small four by six framed photograph on the nightstand. It's a picture of Laura and me from our Disney World vacation. Jack is sitting between us in the crook of Laura's arm, smiling up at her just as the camera flashes.

"Oh yeah, that," Laura says.

I grab the picture. "I don't even remember when this was taken."

"Jack had just met Pluto and was on cloud nine."

"Man, that kid fucking loved Pluto. But I'm still curious about one thing."

"What's that?"

"Any particular reason you carry a framed picture of me and my brother around?"

Laura stares at the picture, almost in a trance. She says nothing. "Uh, Laura?"

She shakes her head, pokes me in the chest. "Hey now, you're not the only sentimental fool on the planet. That was a great vacation."

"Really?" I say. "I just remember being sweaty and exhausted and having crazy break-up sex."

"Getting back to my point, Hank…" Laura takes the picture from me and places it face down on the nightstand. "You're just like your father, and not just because you look like him. You wear your passion and emotion on your sleeve. You trust people. You surround yourself with a circle of friends who worship you. That's all John Fitzpatrick right there."

"Worship me? That's an overstatement. I'm just the injured, sad-eyed puppy right now. Everyone loves a puppy."

"That's about the dumbest thing I've ever heard."

"No, it isn't."

"Yes, it *is*."

"Fine, Laura, let's just assume everyone's intentions are sincere and I have all these good friends who 'worship' me. Can we stop pretending I'm a good friend in return?"

"You're a great friend, Hank." She squeezes my nose and shakes it. "Just a shitty boyfriend."

"Speak for yourself." I turn and face the wall, feigning long-term insult in the hopes of short-term gratification. I assume Laura sees right through me, but she wouldn't have brought me back here if she didn't want to do this.

The bed sits in a corner of the room. I'm curled up between Laura and the wall. The room is pitch-black. I can still identify Hatch and Mack by the sounds of their inebriated snore-off on the opposite side of the room.

I hear the rustling of blankets, of clothes being removed. A hand snakes around my belly, undoes the button on my jeans, and slides inside my boxers. I reach back with my hand. Starting at the knee, I run my hand up the inside of Laura's thigh. I press up against her, feeling her bare breasts flattening against my back. She kisses the back of my neck and slithers down the bed. With both hands, she pulls my pants and boxers down to my ankles all at once. She climbs over me. Like a puzzle piece, she positions herself just so in front of me, our bodies spooning, finding just the right fit. She takes me in her hand, guiding me toward her. She arches her back and props her hand against the wall. I enter Laura from behind.

We made love three times. It seemed, if I'm being honest, more desperate than passionate. If love were easy, then everyone would jump into the deep end of the pool and touch the drain like Jodi Foster in *Stealing Home*. But no one does that. The whole idea of drowning in the idea of someone, and what's worse, not knowing you're drowning until you're underwater and you open your mouth to take a breath and realize, hey, something isn't quite right here—well, it doesn't just *sound* fucking stupid. It *is* fucking stupid.

Or is it?

Some love can be idiotic, bumbling even, and still endure. But Laura and I lost the right to be stupid years ago. The saddest of human journeys is taken by shattered hearts dusting off old love. There is no eternal innocence for me and Laura to cling to. John Keats can take his Grecian urn and shove it straight up his ass. Truth is not beauty. Truth comes at the expense of beauty.

It's been ten minutes since Laura fell asleep. I get dressed. I walk out of the apartment.

CHAPTER FORTY-SIX

Mack, Hatch, and I are living together for the summer. Hatch and I are working as student painters, while Mack has a sports marketing internship downtown. We're sharing a duplex on the east side of Indianapolis, just off Pendleton Pike. We've nicknamed it "Sanford & Son." It's in a bad neighborhood, surrounded by refrigerator- and couch-laden porches. We blend in by purchasing a beat-up powerboat with an inoperative outboard we can't afford to fix. We park the boat in our driveway. The boat is a nice accessory to my new vehicle. Mom sold my new Chevy pickup back to the dealership, so I bought a late-seventies black El Camino to haul paint supplies. It cost me more to title it than to purchase it. We named it "The Hoopty." It has a bad alternator, which requires us to extract the battery at the end of every day and recharge it overnight. It isn't running as of Memorial Day weekend.

It was Hatch's idea to throw the Indy 500 party. The party was denoted by the ten-feet-by-three-feet number "500" I carved into the front lawn with the push mower and spray-painted in alternating black-and-white checkers. After Emerson Fittipaldi took the checkered flag, we decided to have a front lawn demolition derby with the Hoopty and the neighbor's rusted-out van. The Hoopty laughed off its injuries in typical Hoopty fashion, prompting Mack's new girlfriend from Butler to sing a sorority anthem about the El Camino that went like this:

El Camino, El-El Camino. El Camino, El-El Camino.

The front is like a car, the back is like a truck. The front is where you drive, and the back is where you…

El Camino, El-El Camino!

Sanford & Son's location affords it two advantages. One, when a southwest wind blows just right, the smells of fresh-baked bread and snack cakes waft over from the Wonder Bread Factory on Shadeland Avenue. And two, it's less than a mile from one of the best strip joints in the city, P.T.'s Showclub. I have gone to P.T.'s eight times in the last three weeks, blowing at least two hundred dollars a pop. All I have to show for my efforts are a shoebox full of free passes into the club, a small Hanes T-shirt with two blotches of fluorescent green paint, for which I paid fifty bucks after watching a stripper paint the shirt using just her bare breasts, and a stripper's phone number.

The stripper's stage name is Divine. Her real name is Amanda, although I haven't got her last name yet. Her breasts are smaller than the one who painted my fifty-dollar Hanes T-shirt, but still a decent handful. She took me to a dark corner of the club and gave me a private dance for twenty dollars. We made out and dry-humped to a Stone Temple Pilots medley, and she wrote her phone number on the back of my bar tab.

Mack told us he was playing in a softball tournament down at the Ridge all weekend. He bribed us to come down to the game with a half-gallon of his uncle's dandelion wine. We drank the entire half-gallon on the drive down. We pull into the Ridge, just beyond left field of the softball diamond.

"You're not dating a fucking stripper, Fitzy."

I step out of Hatch's truck and stash the empty wine bottle behind the front seat. "I'm telling you, she wants to go out with me."

"Let me guess..." Hatch slams his truck door shut. "She's just stripping to pay her way through med school."

"Shut up." I slam my door in kind. "Matter of fact, she is in school. Takes night classes at Marian College."

"Isn't that the Catholic school run by Franciscan nuns over by Butler?"

"That's the one."

"To *blave*?"

Hatch and I assume almost everything the other says is total bullshit. The percentages tend to be in our favor. We refer to this character flaw as "blaving," after Billy Crystal's Miracle Max bit in *The Princess Bride*. "*Sonny, true love is the greatest thing in the world. Except for a nice MLT, a mutton, lettuce, and tomato sandwich, where the mutton is nice and lean and the tomato is ripe. They're so perky, I love that. But that's not what he said. He distinctly said 'to blave.' And, as we all know, 'to blave' means 'to bluff.'*" Either Hatch or I will say something dubious, implausible, or just fabricated, to which the other responds, "Are you blaving?" Or the shortened version, "To blave?"

"Believe whatever the hell you want, Hatch."

"Hi, boys!" Mack raises his glove, yelling from his third base position. I tried to play in a summer softball league with Mack once, but he's way too fucking serious about his sports. He's almost a caricature now—the overweight former athlete with bad wheels intent on somehow reclaiming his glory years, raging against the dying of the light.

"Let's sit over there." Hatch points to the bleachers along the first base line.

I notice a familiar face sitting in the bleachers along the third base line. "I'm fine with these bleachers right here."

"I'm sure you are. See you at the end of the game, then."

I approach the bleachers. I put my hand above my eyes, shielding them from the sun. I see her sitting on the upper rung of the aluminum bleachers, casually smoking a cigarette. She's wearing a tie-dyed tank top, cutoff jeans, and Birkenstocks. Her long, blonde hair, longer than I remember it being, is pulled back into a ponytail, except for her bangs, which still end just above her eyebrows.

"Hey there. Got one of those for me?"

She flashes a tanned smile and hands me a Marlboro Light. "Well, well, well. If it isn't the infamous Henry David Fitzpatrick."

"And if it isn't the equally infamous Beth whatever-the-hell-your-middle-name-is Burke."

"You in town for the summer?"

"Nope. Just came down for the weekend for Mack's game. Maybe doing some canoeing on the Sycamore River tomorrow."

"Where you living? Indy?"

"You bet. How about you?"

"I'm in Empire Ridge until September."

"Working?"

"Waitin' tables."

"Where?"

"Casa Columbo."

"The Mexican place in the mall?"

"That's the one. You working anywhere?"

"Painting houses with Hatch."

"How's school?"

"Over for now, thank God."

"You graduate?"

"I wish. What about you?"

"I'm on the seven-year-plan."

"Seven?"

"Yeah, I decided to change my major second semester of my junior year from secondary education to nursing."

"You'll land on your feet. Of that I have no doubt."

Beth grabs my hand, holding it tight. She's staring at me.

"What? I got something on my face?" I wipe the corners of my mouth, look down at my jeans. "My fly open?"

She points at me, tapping me on my chest. "You're drunk."

"Is it that obvious?"

"No. But your cheeks are flushed. It's cute."

An unprompted flirtatious compliment. That's my cue. "Soooo, Beth, how's the love life?"

"What love life?"

"I heard you were dating somebody in town."

"Dating is a strong term."

"You sure about that?"

"Positive."

"That's interesting."

"Interesting, huh?" Beth flashes her dimples.

"Yeah..." I flash my own dimples right back at her. "Interesting."

"Jordan is his name. He tends bar at Casa Columbo. My friends call him 'The Tool,' but I enjoy our time together. Jordan just wants to have fun, no strings attached. How about your love life?"

"I fooled around with a stripper last night."

"A stripper?"

This admission doesn't carry with it the feel-good sentiment of my previous statement. She looks stunned. "What's the big deal?"

"Come on, Hank. A stripper?"

"Isn't this the type of shit we tell each other all the time? If there's a bar to close down in Empire Ridge the Wednesday before Thanksgiving, chances are you and I are the last ones standing at two a.m."

"I have plenty of drinking buddies. None of them are banging a stripper, last I checked."

"I haven't banged any stripper, Beth. She gave me her phone number. It's probably nothing. Besides, you're the one who banged my best friend, quite a bit if I remember. I also remember holding a wet rag on the back of your neck at one of Hatch's parties that summer while you projectile-vomited into a toilet."

"And I also remember finding you the very next morning at that same party passed out in your own urine after you got drunk and pissed the couch."

"Was that before or after you had sex with Hatch?"

"It was after I had sex with Hatch, which was after I had sex with you, which was before you led me on for six months and stayed with Laura."

Reunited with quite possibly my favorite girl on the planet, and I take the express train to standoffish asshole. Smooth fucking move, Hank.

"I guess I deserved that," I say, standing up to leave. "And on that note."

"Where the hell you going?"

"I'm going to go see what your ex-boyfriend is up to."

"Tell him I said, 'Hello.'"

"Yeah, I'll get right on that."

"Later," Beth says.

"Later," I say. I make a move to leave, but not really.

Beth and I have no reason to ever say goodbye like this. I have to throw out some sort of olive branch. "Hey Beth, you and what's-his-name want to join us on the river sometime? Camping, canoeing, a few cocktails maybe."

"Sounds tempting, but I don't know."

"What's to know? You can even bring The Tool."

"His name is Jordan."

"Yeah, Jordan, that's what I said."

"It's not that, Hank." Beth stands up, stretches. She kicks off her Birkenstocks, stretches her arms out from her body, head back. She stands on her tiptoes. They're painted red. My eyes linger at her calves, the best set of calves I've ever seen on a woman. "I work weekends. Big tips. Jordan and I usually just rent a movie afterward."

"Suit yourself," I say. "But the invitation still stands."

I turn to walk down the bleachers. Beth grabs me by the elbow. "Hey, Hank."

"Yeah," I say, turning back.

I'm one row down from Beth, so we're seeing almost eye-to-eye. She leans into me, kisses me on the cheek. It's a different kind of kiss on the cheek, one of those not-quite-on-the-cheek kisses that grazes the outer corner of your lips. "You really want to know my middle name?" she says.

"It's Alison, with one 'L', on top of which your first name is Elisabeth with an 'S'. You hate the affectation of oddly spelled names, so you just go by Beth."

Beth smiles. "Why Mr. Fitzpatrick, are you stalking me?"

"Do you want me to?" I ask. "Because I can."

THE GAME WENT INTO extra innings. Beth left in the sixth to make her evening shift at Casa Columbo. My head is starting to make the transition from drunk to hungover. I stop by the snack bar and order a hot dog and a Diet Coke.

The cashier rings me up. "A dollar seventy-five, please."

I reach into my jeans pockets. They're the same jeans I wore last night, the front pockets still stuffed with one-dollar bills. I pull out my bar tab from last night, the one with Divine a.k.a. Amanda's phone number scribbled on the back. I look over to where Beth had been sitting in the bleachers.

I throw the phone number in the trash.

CHAPTER FORTY-SEVEN

"Why is my mother in the hospital?"

"It's just a precaution, Mr. Fitzpatrick. She came in here complaining of an elevated heart rate. When we admitted her, her speech was noticeably slurred."

"Please, doctor, call me Hank."

"I'll call you Hank if you call me Jeb."

"No can do, Dr. Pahl. You're a doctor. You earned that title."

I haven't seen Jeb since whipping his ass at the 1989 Taylor wrestling sectionals. He looks great, maybe even a little on the thin side. Turns out he's some sort of genius. At age twenty-two, barely four years out of high school, he's the youngest first-year intern in the history of Empire Ridge Memorial.

"Have it your way." Jeb flips through my mom's chart. "Can we go over your mother's meds one more time?"

"Go for it."

"Miss Fitzpatrick, is—"

"*Missus* Fitzpatrick."

"Yes, Hank." Jeb recognizes my intent. "Mrs. Fitzpatrick is taking Lexapro for her depression, Urso for her liver disease, Ambien to put her to sleep, Elavil to keep her asleep, and Vicodin to counteract the migraines she gets from drinking alcohol with the Lexapro, Urso, Ambien, and Elavil. Does that about cover it?"

"Just about. She also sometimes takes a double-dose of Darvocet instead of Vicodin, because Vicodin gives her nausea if she mixes it with Bass Ale instead of vodka gimlets."

"Good lord, Hank. Does that woman have a death wish?"

"I think that would be fair to say. Can I see her now?"

"Sure thing. All things considered, she's fine. I'm just going to monitor her for a couple more hours. You can take her home this afternoon."

I KNOCK ON MOM'S door.

"Come in."

"Housekeeping." I force out a laugh that doesn't quite get there.

"Hank, just the man I wanted to see." Mom opens her arms. "Give your mom a kiss."

I walk over to my mother's bed and kiss her on the forehead. She's been looking better the last month or so, all things considered. Her face is a little fuller; her skin is a little less pale. "Love you, Mom."

"I love you, too. Jack at Nancy's house?"

"Yeah, I dropped him off after soccer."

"How'd he do?"

"Leading scorer."

"For both teams?"

"Like always."

"That's my boy."

"Yeah, whatever. What the hell are you doing in here?"

"I want to talk to you about my behavior, Hank."

"That'd be good."

"And I'm not talking about today, about me being here. This whole thing is just the hospital taking precautions. I want to talk about me and you, about our relationship."

"Mom, we've been down this road already. I was out of line with you about Tom, and I'm sorry. You can see whoever you want. I have no right to judge you."

"You have every right to judge me. You lost your father and both of your grandfathers in the span of twelve months. Meanwhile, your mother—"

"Jumps in the sack with her high school sweetheart in between chasing antidepressants, painkillers, and sleeping pills with vodka gimlets?

"You don't have to be such a jerk, Hank. I realize I'm failing you now, just as I failed you when you were a kid. Today more than ever, I realize this." Mom appears to sink into the bed, as if a giant weight is bearing down on her.

"Uh, come again?"

"You heard me. I'm not in this hospital by accident. I had one too many gimlets after your aunt Ophelia called me this morning."

"She called you? About what?"

"You remember how Uncle Mitch moved back, right?"

"I try not to remember."

"Well, he got hired on at Empire Ridge Middle School."

"No!" I yell, almost manic in my reaction.

"Well, yes, Hank."

The moment is here. It's now. *Tell her. Tell her!* "But, Mom. Y-you don't understand."

"I understand plenty, Hank. There's no easy way to say this, so I'll just come right out and tell you. Uncle Mitch turned himself into the police late last night. He's been sexually abusing young boys, his own middle school students. He's been charged with four counts of child molestation. He's confessed to at least three others beyond what he's charged with, but he can't be prosecuted for any of these because they exceed the statute of limitations."

"What?" I don't even know why I react. Her next words have been waiting to be said for the last twenty years. And I'm not going to get to say them.

"The three other people Uncle Mitch confessed to molesting were his two nephews and his only godson."

I let the word *godson* hang in the air, trying to give the revelation some sort of proportionality to the amount of time I've kept it buried and festering inside me. But in a weird way, I feel ripped off. I feel like I'm being outed. This was a horrible secret, but it was *my* horrible secret. Uncle Mitch the gay adulterer was, in its own weird way, palatable. Uncle Mitch the pedophile was my cross to bear. Fuck you, Simon of Cyrene. Let me face Calvary on my own terms.

"Sounds about right, Mom."

"Sounds about right?"

"Yeah."

"Dear God, Hank. Is that all you have to say? Were you just going keep this to yourself forever?"

"I had planned on it."

The plan didn't start out a conscious one, but it sure ended up that way. I protected everybody along the way. Aunt Ophelia, Dad, Mom. Even Uncle Mitch. Too bad nobody stepped up to protect me.

"But when did it start?" Mom says. "When did it end? How did we not know?"

"You don't want to know all that."

"Yes, I do."

It was the Fourth of July, 1976. I was five years old.

This was when it started, or my earliest approximation of when it started. There are some auditory and visual cues. "The Hustle" by Van McCoy & the Soul City Symphony was playing on the radio. I know it was 1976 because I remember Dad's red-white-and-blue bicentennial sunglasses propped on top of his head when he and Uncle Mitch were out on our back porch laughing about a Saturday Night Live skit while Dad grilled some burgers and brats.

Mom, Dad, Uncle Mitch, and Aunt Ophelia were playing cards at the kitchen table—euchre I think, although it might have been bridge. Mom had just sent me to my room for fighting with Jeanine.

Our house was small and cozy. A white bookcase went all the way to the ceiling in between the kitchen and the living room. A twenty-nine gallon aquarium of tropical fish sat in the middle of the bookcase. The tank was filled with swordtails, mollies, and platies—Uncle Mitch's favorites. He and I went to Animal World and picked out the very first fish for the aquarium. The fish was a large, fiery-orange male swordtail. The pet store clerk told us to get two females to go with the one male. She said male swordtails were too "horny" for one female to handle. It was the first time I heard that word used in its proper context—that is, other than the time young Arliss traded in his "horny toad" and a home-cooked meal for Old Yeller. Uncle Mitch smiled at the clerk's comment.

Of course he fucking smiled at the clerk's comment.

I heard through the bookcase Uncle Mitch telling Mom to take it easy on me. Mom said back to Uncle Mitch that he was a big softie. Everyone laughed. A chair scraped the floor. I heard footsteps.

I was lying on my bed, crying. I was embarrassed, which was how I always got after Mom yelled at me. The television was on in the other room. It was one of the *Planet of the Apes* movies. Those movies gave me nightmares because I kept hearing on the news about the "gorilla" warfare in the Middle East, and as I lived in the Midwest, I assumed these gorillas were running around Pennsylvania.

Uncle Mitch popped his head around the corner of my bedroom door. I smiled a little. Uncle Mitch slid behind me on the bed. He tickled me until I laughed, too. He nuzzled his scratchy, five o'clock shadow into the back of my neck.

My neck started to sweat beneath the heat of Uncle Mitch's three-packs-a-day breath. He always forgot to take his pack of cigarettes out of his front pocket. I heard the plastic wrap on the cigarettes crunching, again and again, as he rubbed his erection into my backside. Uncle Mitch reached his right arm around to the front of my underwear, putting his hand down my pants. His hands were clammy.

"Can you get us a clean one please?" I hand the bedpan to the nurse. It's filled with a mixture of my mother's tears and vomit.

Mom stops yelling, but I don't know if it's from exhaustion or if she's just run out of ways to describe the act of human castration. When it comes to protecting her firstborn, it's fair to say my mother's level of creativity—hell, outright sadism—is both inspiring and disturbing.

"I just don't see how any of this is possible," Mom says. "If your father wasn't dead, this would have killed him."

"Come on, Mom. You're a high school guidance counselor. You see this all the time."

"Those are my students, Hank. You're my son. I tell my students what the manuals tell me to tell them. When it involves my flesh and blood, *fuck the manuals*. We should've been there, your father and I, we should have done something."

"You're being way too hard on yourself. Uncle Mitch is a sick man, but he's also calculating and deceitful. He snowed everybody. And a guy like Dad was the perfect foil."

"Always believed in the good in everybody. Always assumed everything would work out for the best."

"Exactly. Dad was incapable of seeing a guy like Uncle Mitch for who or what he was. Dad was just never wired that way. And Uncle Mitch took advantage of him just like he took advantage of me."

"Who else knows?"

"Well, Uncle Mitch and I have known about it for a while."

"Besides us, I mean. Have you ever opened up to anyone about this?"

"Not really," I say. "What's done is done, Mom."

"But don't you want to talk to somebody? This would explain a lot about your behavior when you were younger, the situation you got in with Laura, your promiscuity."

"My *promiscuity*?" I exaggerate her words. "So you're saying that maybe my sexual activity as a young man was just a defense mechanism, a way of acting out Uncle Mitch's abuse, and that as a boy I was just never given the proper tools to be a man, and that my Catholic faith with its patriarchy and its feigned more-patronizing-than-sincere adoration of women exacerbated my skewed views of masculine and feminine archetypes?"

"Now you're just mocking me."

"You bet your ass I'm mocking you. I'm not going to sit here and concoct a bunch of bullshit armchair psychology to justify being just your average horny teenager."

"Your hormones were anything but average. And you can't dismiss Uncle Mitch's abuse as never happening."

"I'm not dismissing the fucking abuse. What happened to me as a boy, I've just chosen to forget as a man. I'm done surviving my life. I'm going to try living it now."

"That's a good line, Hank."

"That's a *great* fucking line."

"But you don't just forget stuff like that."

"You don't?"

"No, you don't."

"Then I guess you can tell me what you did, who you saw, what you were wearing on October 1, 1992?"

"That's not fair. You know I blacked out."

"So, let me get this straight. Just ten months after the fact, there are large chunks of the day Dad died that you can't recall. And yet you want me to sit here and psychoanalyze something that happened to me fifteen *years* ago?"

"I've leaned on tons of people this last year. For most of your life you've been carrying this secret inside you, alone. Nobody can go through what you went through without some scars."

"My scars are fine." I pat myself on the heart. "I somehow managed to survive my *promiscuity*, even the situation I got in with—"

I stop myself short.

"Hank?" Mom asks.

"…"

"Hank?" she asks again.

"Yes, *Debbie*."

"You okay?"

"I'll be okay after you answer me one question."

"Ask away, honey."

"What *situation* would that be?"

"What are you talking about?"

"You said earlier, 'This would explain a lot about your behavior when you were younger, *the situation you got in with Laura*, your promiscuity.' What *situation*?"

"You know what I mean," Mom says. "I'm talking about your first love, your first broken heart, your first overdose…"

"My first abortion?"

Mom bites her bottom lip, exhaling. "Well, yes. That, too."

"How the hell did you find out?"

"Laura told me," Mom says.

"When? Why?"

"Please, calm down, Hank. Laura and I talk."

"Since when?"

"Since forever. Look, these questions can all be answered in good time. Laura is here."

"She's what?"

"She's in town visiting, and she called me right before you got here. Uncle Mitch is all over the news. She tried to call you at home. Nancy answered the phone, said I was in the hospital and you were here with me. Laura is coming right now."

"Coming where?"

"Here, to the hospital."

"Are you out of your fucking mind?"

"There are things we need to get out in the open."

"No, we don't.

"Yes, Hank, we do," says a voice from behind me.

Laura is standing just inside the room, her left hand on the door. I notice the engagement ring.

CHAPTER FORTY-EIGHT

"Holy Christ," I say. "How long have you been standing there?"

"Long enough."

"Nice fucking rock. I take it the world's perfect couple is back together again?"

"That's not why I came here," Laura says. "I saw the story about your uncle on the news, and I had to find you." She looks over my shoulder and waves. "Hi, Mrs. Fitzpatrick."

Mom waves back. "Good to see you, Laura. Your parents doing well?"

"Yes, thanks. They send their regards."

"Tell them I—"

"Can we cut the crap?" I interject. "They're fine, you're fine, Ian's fine, we're all fucking fine. Laura, why the hell are you here? And since when did you and my mom get so chummy?"

"Since forever," Laura says.

"Perfect," I say.

"Laura," Mom says. "It's time."

"I know it is, Debbie."

"Time for *what*?" I ask.

Laura pulls up a chair, offering it to me. "Hank, with all due respect, I'm going to need you to sit down and shut up for a few minutes."

I sit down. My hold on the *shut up* part of the equation is precarious at best.

"You remember the day I told you I had decided to get an abortion?"

"How could I not? You said that—"

"It was a rhetorical question. Please, let me talk."

I grind my teeth, nodding.

Laura continues. "You said, in no uncertain terms, that you were opposed to the abortion. I never felt so alone. My parents would've disowned me if they found out. I turned to the one person who I knew would listen to me with an open mind and an open heart."

"You didn't," I say, running my fingers through my hair and pulling it straight up in two big horns. Debbie and Laura conspiring to just cook a fucking omelet scares me. This level of collusion and subterfuge is beyond comprehension.

"I did." Laura looks at my mother. "I called my high school guidance counselor."

"What the fuck?"

Mom reaches over and touches my knee. "Let her talk, Hank."

"Your Mom and I met for lunch," Laura says. "It was the day after you left for Hoosier Boys State. We talked for three hours. We talked about everything—you, me, us, motherhood, fatherhood, life. Debbie talked about her struggles to get pregnant, about her miscarriages, about her hopes for your future. As we talked, I saw in Debbie someone whose desperation to be a mother was matched by my desperation to *not* be one. It affirmed all the reasons I didn't want to have this baby, and your mom agreed to help me out with my situation."

I stand up, shaking my head. I turn in a half-sprint toward the door.

Mom's voice chases me down. "Henry David, where do you think you're going?"

"I'm leaving."

"No, you're not."

I turn to face the room again. "What are you going to do if I leave, Mom? Abort another one of my kids behind my back?"

"Son, you don't know what you're talking about."

"I don't?"

"No, you don't. I didn't pay for any abortion. I paid to help Laura carry the baby to term."

"Excuse me?" I say.

"It's true," Laura says. "I never got the abortion."

I turn from my mother to Laura. This isn't a fair fight. "So you lied to me?"

"Your mother talked me out of it. When I got to Bucknell, she set up a checking account that helped me pay for some of my medical expenses, for which I've since paid her back plus interest. Between Debbie's help and an assistantship Ian got me, I managed to keep my head above water until the baby was born in February."

"When in February?"

"The fourteenth, on Valentine's Day."

"So the baby was born a year after we told each other we loved—"

"Yes." Laura brushes the memory under the rug like an unsightly pile of dust.

The puzzle pieces start coming together. "Ian was there for the birth."

"Yes," Laura says.

"And that's how you two became so close?"

"Obviously."

"Laura, nothing is fucking obvious with you."

"You had to have suspected, Hank. What about all those photos I sent you? I wasn't exactly wasting away. I didn't even wear padding when I dressed up as Santa Claus."

"I just thought you were eating a lot of turkey Manhattan."

"Turkey Manhattan?"

"You know, starchy foods, the freshman fifteen. Oh fuck it, never mind." I pull on my hair again. I clasp my hands behind my head, bending my elbows toward my face. "So let me see if I got this all straight. My mother, my girlfriend, and my girlfriend's future husband conspired to fake an abortion, hide my pregnant girlfriend in Pennsylvania, and give my child up for adoption without telling me about it. Is that about it in a nutshell?"

Laura shakes her head. "There's more."

"What?"

She looks at my mother. "Debbie?"

Mom nods. "I'll take it from here."

"Holy crap, Mom," I say. "Who knows what's going to come out of your mouth. Are you comfortable? Can I get you some narcotics?"

"Just listen, son. Just listen."

"Oh, I'm all ears."

"You remember what happened after my second miscarriage?"

"I remember it being better than your first one."

"Better? How so?"

"Dad was better about it. You were in bed for a long time—almost four weeks if I remember right—but Dad was a good nurse the second time around."

"Yes, your father was a good nurse, and yes, I was in bed for a while. I was in a lot of physical pain after the emergency hysterectomy."

"Come again?"

"Hysterectomy," Mom says. "The doctors removed my uterus right after I miscarried the twins. You and Jeanine just assumed I was recovering from the miscarriage, and your father and I didn't go out of our way to correct you. When we were trying to decide when and how to break the news to all of you, Laura called me. We had our talk, and I offered to help her."

"*Help* her?" I say.

"As Laura said, it was decided she would carry the baby to term, with me helping to pick up her medical and living expenses."

"*Help* her?"

"The twenty-year reunion at Notre Dame was a convenient excuse. Dad went up to South Bend, while I picked up the baby in Pennsylvania. We handled everything through a private adoption agency. It was all very discreet."

This is the type of revelation reserved for Shakespearian tragedies or bad Mexican soap operas. This is the implausible twist in our hero's story. This is the zinger Maury Povich keeps in his pocket just so everybody can watch two tattooed bald dudes with multiple piercings throw haymakers at one another. Only I can't punch my mother.

"No, Mom." I bury my hands in my face. "No, no, no."

Jack isn't my brother.

Jack is my fucking son.

Laura pulls her chair close to mine. She puts her arm around me. "Please, Hank. You have to believe this was the best decision for all of us."

"But you were as big as a house," I say to my mother. "You looked…"

"Pregnant?" Mom says.

"Well, yeah."

"Chalk it up to some conscious overeating and a prosthetic stomach."

I raise my head from my hands, teary-eyed and red-faced. "And Dad, he was in on this the whole time?"

"Not the whole time. Your father had to be convinced. He and I had a bit of a falling out after my second miscarriage."

"But I thought you two seemed to deal with the second one better than the first."

"We were very good liars, Hank. When my milk came in after the second miscarriage, I started pumping it without telling your father. I couldn't let go of my baby."

"And that's how you could still breastfeed, Jack?"

"Yes."

"Mom, that is sick."

"That was your father's initial reaction when he caught me in the nursery at three a.m. two weeks after my miscarriage singing nursery rhymes to myself with suction cups hanging off my lactating breasts."

"Sweet Jesus."

"Hank, wet nurses provide their breast milk to total strangers. Jack is our flesh and blood."

"You mean *my* flesh and blood."

"No, I mean *ours*," Mom says. "Once I convinced your father we were sustaining Jack's life as a memorial to the twins, he was all in. Like me, like Laura, he felt we were doing the right thing. He felt as long as Jack was happy and healthy under our roof, there was plenty of time to set the record straight once you had a job and a life of your own."

"Dad was all in?"

"Yes, all in."

"So in the end, Dad wasn't a reluctant accomplice at all?"

"Hardly," Mom says, hesitation in her voice. "The prosthetic stomach was...well, it was his idea. He gave me his own empathy belly from our childbirth classes."

"Isn't that an ironic fist up the ass?" I look up at the ceiling, my right hand pointing to the sky as if I'm trying to start a fight with my father, if not the Almighty Himself. "Here I've been heartbroken for the last goddamn year about Jack living his life without you, Pops, and it turns out his dad is still fucking alive!"

I glance at Laura. "And Ian, he knows about *all* of this?"

"He knows my high school sweetheart got me pregnant. He knows I put the baby up for adoption and that I never told the father about the baby."

"But he doesn't know the part about the baby being adopted by his grandmother who faked a pregnancy with her husband's empathy belly and is now posing as the baby's mother, or the part about the baby's brother being his unsuspecting father?"

"He will."

"When?"

"Someday, Hank. And as Ian's fiancée, it's my responsibility to tell him."

I raise my hand, mocking her. "Can someone buzz the nurse for an extra bedpan, because I'm about to fucking throw up. I assume you haven't told Ian about our romp in the sheets this spring, either."

Mom looks at Laura, curious.

"You didn't tell him, did you?" I say.

"Hank, I..." Laura trails off, flustered.

In truth, my allusion is half-hearted, if that. Our assignation now seems a hundred years away, displaced from this moment, innocent when juxtaposed with the actions of the two women in this world who've simultaneously loved and hurt me the most.

"Son, I realize this is a lot to take in."

"You think, Mom?" I jump out of my chair, pulling on my hair. "I'm still your son, right? I'm not like a test tube clone of Dad you've raised in an incubator in the hopes I will one day be either the conductor of the New York Philharmonic or the CEO of Oldsmobile?"

"You're my firstborn, Hank. With John gone, you're my life now."

"Cue the tiny motherfucking violins."

"What's done is done," Laura says, "and all we can say is we're sorry."

"That doesn't fix this," I say.

"Then what else do you want from us?"

"I want nothing from you, absolutely fucking nothing. My mother is my mother. She's the only parent I got left, so I don't have any real choice but to forgive her. But you, Laura, can stay out of my way for the next sixty or seventy years."

"You oblivious fucking asshole!" Laura runs across the room. She grabs a handful of my shirt and shoves me into a wall with her right forearm. Our faces are inches apart. "You think this was easy for me to do? Remember the last night we were together, when you found that picture of me, you, and Jack?"

"Vaguely."

"Fuck off, Hank. You think I'd really carry a framed picture of you and your brother around just to remind myself about a vacation?"

"Sure, why not?"

"Newsflash, Hank. You're not that fucking fun."

"I'm no Ian, obviously."

"Please, don't do this." Laura's grip on my shirt loosens. She drops to her knees, sobbing. "I'm Jack's mother, and he can never know. You see him almost every day. You were there when he said his first words, when he took his first steps. In his four years on this earth I have read my son one bedtime story and rocked him to sleep one time."

My world is in rewind. Like an old reel-to-reel tape player I'm thrown back through the course of time to events once innocent, now portentous. Laura's weight gain. The almost too-perfect timing of Mom's pregnancy. The picture on the nightstand.

Disney World.

"That last night of our vacation?" I ask, kneeling down beside Laura.

"Yes, that last night in Disney," Laura says. "Do you know how many times I've replayed that night in my head? How many times I've cried myself to sleep because I can't imagine life without this one particular boy and because picturing him in the arms of another mother breaks my heart...over and over again."

The tears are now streaming down my face, but I don't even try to wipe them off. I frame Laura's face with my hands. I kiss her on the forehead, just as I did the day of Dad's funeral. "I'm sorry," I say.

Laura recognizes the moment. She remembers. "I love him, too, Hank."

I run my hands through her hair. "You were always Jack's favorite."

CHAPTER FORTY-NINE

"The other goal, Jack! Kick it in the *other* goal!"

Jack Fitzpatrick is a scoring machine in the Empire Ridge Ages four to five Youth Soccer League. The problem is he's indiscriminate in his goals, sending the soccer ball sailing into the nearest net *for either team*. He's resolute and consistent, and at some point everyone except me gave up trying to temper his enthusiasm. Today, like most Saturday mornings, Jack leads his team in scoring…and he leads his opponent's team in scoring. Unlike most Saturdays, we actually win.

Coach Larry shakes my hand. "Another great game by Jack Attack."

I laugh. "If you say so, coach."

"The kid can score at will, Hank."

"Problem is he usually does."

Jack runs up to me, squeezes my leg. "Mommy still sick and at the doctor?"

"Yeah," I say, "Mommy's still sick and at the doctor."

"Hank, I yisten to coach Yarry and scored all duh goals."

"Yes, Jack, you did score *all* of the goals."

"I yike scoring all duh goals."

Jack has been pronouncing all his L consonants as Y consonants. It's an adorable speech pattern. According to Jack's grossly overqualified preschool teacher, a former freelance editor who has a Master's in speech-language pathology, this is a common substitution. It's called liquid simplification, whatever the fuck that means. Apparently it's very common, and most kids self-correct by around age six. If they're still doing it by that point, that's when speech therapy may be necessary. I have a feeling it won't be Jack's first trip to a therapist in his life.

I take a knee in front of him. "You want to play a game, Jack?"

"Is it hard?"

"No."

"Is it fun?"

"Maybe."

"What is it?"

"I can't tell you unless you play it."

"Okay."

"It's just a word game."

"A wood game?"

"No, *word* game."

"Yeah, *wood*. Das what I said."

"Okay, fine. I'll give you a *word*, and you try to repeat what I say *exactly*. Got it?"

"Got it."

"Mommy."

"Mommy."

"Daddy."

"Daddy."

"Hank."

"Hank."

"Jack."

"Jack."

"Love."

"Yuv."

"Coach Larry."

"Coach Yarry."

"Luh-luh-luh-luh-Larry."

"Luh-luh-luh-luh-Yarry."

"You're a goofball." I tickle Jack until he giggles. I hoist him in the air and pull him into my chest. A vintage Hank Fitzpatrick hug. I give him a big wet kiss on the cheek, which he immediately wipes off.

"Oh, come on, squirt. You too old to get a kiss from your…big bro?"

"I yuv my big bro."

"Then don't wipe this one off." I reapply an even wetter kiss on the side of his face. I can see the crazed look in his eyes.

"You yicked me, Hank." Jack wipes the kiss off, again. "Das yucky."

"Okay, I give up. Let's go, All-Star." I hold Jack in my left arm while hitting the keyless entry to Mom's Oldsmobile Bravada with my right hand.

"What's All-Star, Hank? Do I yike All-Star?"

I strap him into his car seat and ruffle his brown mop with my hand. "Yes, little buddy. You do yike All-Star."

"I yuv my big bro," he says to me.

The words are like tonic and poison all at once. Jack is just too young to understand. His memories of a father are of *our* father, John Henry Fitzpatrick, his namesake. I don't have it in me to take that away from Jack just yet.

Or do I?

Laura returned to Ian and Pennsylvania, vowing to start her life anew. But no matter how hard I try, I can't shake the image of Laura reading Jack a bedtime story and rocking him to sleep that last night at Disney. His coffee-brown eyes staring back at this strange crying woman. He reaches up and touches her cleft chin with his hand. She kisses his tiny little fingers, smells his baby powder smell, and tastes on his skin the sweet-salty mixture of baby lotion and her own tears.

Yeah, with all due respect to dear Mom and Dad, fuck them. Laura and I aren't perfect, and I doubt we find our way back to Jack together. But we will find our way.

CHAPTER FIFTY

Hatch and I camped last night along the Sycamore River, getting blitzed despite ourselves. Claire passed out early, so she's the first one up along with her boyfriend, Derek Candela, a former Prepster and teammate of Bobbie the hockey player. That's Empire Ridge for you. We don't like to wander too far from our usual fishing holes. We decide to hit the Waffle House south of the livery.

"This World Famous Pecan Waffle isn't sitting too well in my stomach, fellas." Claire backs away from the table. "Can you excuse a girl while she goes and splashes some water on her face?"

I help her with her chair. "Sure thing, darlin."

Twenty-two years old, in her red spaghetti-strap tank top and jean shorts, Claire sticks out in a diner of old truckers and farmhands. Even hungover, she owns the room.

Claire and Derek have been a semi-casual couple for about a year now. I like Derek, even though he's known for getting drunk and playing "dick games." For example, I might be standing around a pool or a bar, meanwhile Derek will pull his penis out of his shorts. "Hey, Hank!" he'll shout. Then I'll turn, unable to prevent myself from looking straight at his penis, to which Derek says, "Stop looking at my dick, you fag."

Derek leans over the table. "I got a secret, Hank."

"Oh yeah?" I wipe some syrup off my face, then flag the waitress. "More coffee, please."

Derek shakes his head. "I shouldn't be telling you this."

"Telling me what?"

"I know somebody who likes you." Derek smirks. He's one of those hairy missing-link types, with a thick black mop for a head and dark tufts sticking out of the neckline of his shirt. He bears more than a passing resemblance to Elvis, whom he worships. There's a flea market about halfway between the livery and Waffle House. Claire and I had to talk Derek out of a hundred dollar bejeweled velvet painting of the King. "A Velvis with real rhinestones," he said. "How can I pass that up?"

"Spit it out, Derek."

"She's a buddy of yours, a buddy of mine, and a very close acquaintance of Claire's."

"No way."

"Then you know?"

"Well, I saw Beth earlier in the summer at a softball game. I even invited her to one of these canoe trips, but she's kinda been blowing me off ever since, so I figured—"

"Bingo," Derek interrupts.

"Seriously?" I say.

"Seriously. She's wanted to ask you out since the beginning of the summer. Everyone in Empire Ridge knows she likes you. She's never stopped liking you."

"Even if I concede there's still something there between us, what about The Tool?"

Derek places his hand on my shoulder. "Hank, my brother from another mother, do I really have to convince you of your chances against a guy nicknamed 'The Tool?'"

"I guess she did leave a message at my mom's house last week."

"I know she did."

"Something about getting together to see a movie."

"You return her call?"

"Didn't get the message until a few days after the fact. My mom and I aren't on the same page right now."

"But did you return Beth's call?"

"No. I didn't even recognize her voice on the answering machine at first. I thought she was just trying to get a group of us together."

"Well done, dumbass."

"Fuck off. I still say you're shitting me."

"I'm not shitting you, and don't tell Claire I told you."

A LITTLE OVER EIGHT miles long, the Sycamore River is a small offshoot of the White River. Sycamores stand as living and dead sentries along the river's edge, breaking off and drifting downstream, hence the river's obvious name. For years, drunken Empire Ridge kids have plied these not-so-treacherous waters in vessels of battered aluminum and fiberglass.

Today is one of those days.

"Hank!" Derek stands up in his canoe, which he shares with Claire. "Pass the fucking Jägermeister over here, you pussy!"

Hatch and I share the other canoe. I haven't started drinking yet. I can still feel the Waffle House World Famous Pecan Waffle sitting in my stomach, but it's starting to settle. I've brought a twelve-pack of Natty Light, but I need to catch up.

"Wait your fucking turn!" I shout, unscrewing the cap off the Jäger. I take a long, aggressive pull.

Derek raises his fist in the air. "Now that's what I'm fucking talking about."

I pass the Jäger over to Derek and Claire. I sit in the front of the canoe, dipping my paddle in the water every third or fourth stroke so as to maintain the illusion I'm contributing to our forward motion.

Hatch is doing most of the work. "I can't believe you're drinking the hard stuff already."

The licorice taste settles at the back of my throat. My cheeks puff out as I puke inside my mouth. It's just a small puke, one of those you swallow back down and try to pass off as a cough.

"You aren't going to believe a lot of things, today." My voice is gravelly with stomach acid.

"What's that supposed to mean?" Hatch says.

"Derek told me Beth wants me."

"Beth Burke?"

"No, Beth Ehlers."

"Who's that?"

"The actress who plays Harley in *Guiding Light*. Of course, it's Beth Burke, dumbass."

"What's she want you for?"

"For a date. Beth wants to go out with me on a date."

"You and Beth…dating?"

"Don't get carried away," I say. "There's a difference between *a* date and *dating*."

Hatch mumbles something under his breath. Or it might be the shot of Jägermeister I just swallowed rendering me temporarily deaf. Jesus, that shit is nasty.

"What'd you say, Hatch?"

"I said that if you guys last the rest of the summer I'll give you my fucking truck."

Hatch isn't offering much. He owns a year-old teal-green Ford Ranger rear-wheel drive pickup that has a four-cylinder engine, the towing capacity of a one-legged Shetland Pony, and a tendency to careen off the road if you so much as ask for extra ice at a fast-food drive-thru.

"Keep your truck, dickhead," I say.

I FORCE DOWN FOUR more shots of Jägermeister over the next mile and a half of river. Predictably, we fall behind Derek and Claire's canoe. We catch up to them at the exact wrong time.

"Oh shit." I try look away but not soon enough.

Hatch is also caught off-guard. "What, Fitzy?"

"It's Derek."

"Dick games?"

"Dick games. Looks like Helicopter Man."

We're in a shallow area. Hatch beaches the canoe on a patch of loose gravel. "I hate fucking Helicopter Man."

Derek has been drinking basically since the Waffle House. Claire sits in the front of the canoe. Derek just took a piss, and now he's standing up in the back of the canoe, his shorts down to his knees. Three canoes float by, including an older couple scarred for the short remainder of their lives. Derek has a beer in his left hand, a cigarette in his right hand, and in the middle hangs his naked, semi-hard phallus for the whole world to see.

First Derek moves his hips in a circle, sending his dick in a counter-clockwise spiraling motion. "Helicopter Man!"

Next he rotates each hip forward and back, his dick flipping from right to left. "Ping Pong, Ping Pong, Ping Pong!"

Then he rocks his hips forward and back, his dick flopping up and hitting him in the belly then going back between his legs and hitting him in the balls. "Jai Alai, Jai Alai!"

Claire is embarrassed, right up to the moment Derek talks her into flashing him. She thinks no one notices. We all notice. Her breasts are small but nice.

It's getting well into the afternoon. Our flotilla is crawling the last mile to the livery. Hatch has stopped trying to steer, letting the current spin us in circles. Every movement in our canoe is telegraphed by the shuffling of a carpet of empty aluminum cans.

Hatch throws an empty beer can at me.

"Jesus, Hatch. Do you have to be a constant fucking roughhouser?"

He ignores me, throwing another beer can at my face. "You going, Fitzy?"

"Going where?"

"Off the bridge."

A century-old railroad line runs through Empire Ridge. That line crosses the Sycamore in the form of a rusted iron truss bridge just northeast of the canoe livery. About twenty-five, maybe thirty feet separates the water from the railroad tracks. We've made the jump numerous times. It's harmless, assuming you avoid the rocks and tangles of tree roots you can't see beneath the Sycamore's tawny surface.

We float under the bridge. I look up, smiling. "How about I jump off the top, Hatch?"

"You're shitting me."

"Nope."

I've seen one person do it before. You climb the actual ironworks to the top of the bridge. It doubles the height from track level. This is the jump that kills people.

I find the idea of it irresistible.

We beach our two canoes at the base of the bridge on the west bank of the Sycamore. I start climbing. My right hand moves from one tree root or sapling to the next, careful to avoid the thorns of the boysenberry bushes that have naturalized along the embankment. I reach the level of the train tracks.

The hot, sticky creosote smell hits me with the force of memory. Memories of walks with Grandpa George. The railroad ties baking in the sun. The crickets chirping. The boysenberry bushes. I don't believe in messages from the grave. But if I did, somebody is talking my fucking ear off.

Hatch has followed me up. "You know, you don't have to do this. It's still quite a ways up there to the top."

I follow his eyes to the top of the bridge. "I don't have to do this, but I need to do this."

"Suit yourself, then."

Hatch jumps, but I keep climbing. I move quickly, the rusted iron hot enough to burn bare flesh. The rivets and joints give secure footing all the way up, although I cut myself in a half-dozen places. The chants of "Go! Go! Go!" urge me forward.

I reach the top. The air is heavy, motionless save for the waves of visibly humid heat coming off the bridge. That's what air does in July in Indiana—it hands you a wet fur coat and says, "Enjoy!"

My knees are shaking. I make the mistake of looking down. What's the rate of descent for a near-two-hundred–pound object from this height? I used to know this type of shit in high school. I want to say your weight doesn't fucking matter, something along the lines of your velocity in feet per second is equal to the distance you had already fallen. Fifty, sixty miles an hour—that sounds about right. Fuck. This is going to hurt.

My arms at my side, I turn my back to the water. I bend my knees, springing up and out from the bridge. I do a back flip with my eyes open. I see the bridge, the sky, the river, and then the bridge again. The fall is fast. My stomach is in my throat. The wind rushes through my ears.

I hit the water.

The force of the impact twists my right ankle, wrenches my arms up over my head like they're made of rubber. A huge booming sound slaps my ears as the water closes over the top of my head. It feels like somebody has punched me in the face.

I hit bottom.

There aren't any tree limbs or rocks. But my feet are stuck in the thick, unyielding mud.

I try to push off the bottom with both feet. My bad ankle lets me know what it thinks about that. I'm stuck a good fifteen feet below the surface of the Sycamore.

And I'm running out of air.

"Swim, Hank. Swim goddammit!"

It's a disembodied voice. My father, maybe? Jesus back to annoy the fuck out of me? Whoever it is, I listen. I open my eyes to try and see. I'm surrounded on all sides by a green-brown darkness. A ribbon of yellow, heaven-like haze dapples overhead.

A cascade of bubbles roll out of my mouth as I scream underwater, wasting precious oxygen. I swallow a mouthful of river water. As my panic begins to acquiesce to resignation, I give one last kick with my good left foot.

It's out! I've managed to dislodge my left foot from the muck. I bend down, grabbing my sprained ankle with both hands. I heave my injured foot out of the mud. Reaching, I clap my hands together as if I was an angel praying, or Susanna Hoffs walking like an Egyptian. My arms doing all of the work as I rise up. The water burns my lungs.

I break the surface to the cheers of my friends. Dirty river water and bile shoots out my mouth in multiple heaves as I crawl ashore. My ankle is already swollen. My shoulders hurt. My ears are ringing. My face is warm just above my lips, the blood pouring out of my nose.

Someone once told me your body forces you to awaken from dreams of jumping off high places before you land, because the psychological trauma of landing can kill you.

Today I landed. Death took its best shot at me, and it pussied out.

Or did it? As much as I might want this to be some type of Messianic bookend to these last few years, my sins washed away in the muddy shallows of the Sycamore River, life just isn't that perfect.

I forgot to take my wallet out of my shorts when I jumped off the bridge. There's your fucking bookend, and it isn't Messianic. It sucks.

Somewhere on the bottom of the Sycamore River, folded alongside my driver's license, my college ID, and the last seven dollars I had to my name, my faceless belly dancer is drowning alone.

CHAPTER FIFTY-ONE

"Nervous?"

"About what?"

"Your big date."

I made a jar of sun tea for Mom today. She loves sun tea. About halfway into trimming her goldmound spirea bushes, she invited me out on the back porch for a drink. We talk between sips.

"It's just Beth we're talking about."

Mom and I have reached an understanding, if not a full-on truce. And barring an actual how-to manual for dealing with all the shit of these last eighteen or so months, we just woke up one day, stopped surviving and started living. That, plus she now gives me plenty of heads-up before her dates with Tom.

"Hank, you've had a crush on that girl for years."

"I've had crushes on a lot of girls."

"This one's different. I can feel it."

In the interest of full disclosure, Mom has experienced "feelings" about every girl I have ever dated and even some I haven't. She and Angelina were all but ready to pick out china patterns. I once brought Pattie Reisen down for dinner and busted Mom commiserating with my girlfriend of a whole three weeks about how clunky the name "Pattie Fitzpatrick" sounded.

"You mark my words," Mom says. "Beth is the one."

I stand, wiping my hands on my shorts. "Oh don't worry, Mom, I'll mark your words. You don't mind if I do that in pencil, do you?"

"I talked to her, you know."

"Beth?"

"Yeah. She waited on us at Casa Columbo."

"You and the Tomster?"

"Be nice. Tom's a good guy."

"Once you get past the comb-over and the black spandex shorts you mean?"

"I said, 'Be nice.'"

"Oh, I'll admit Tom's growing on me."

"He is?"

"Like a fungus."

"That's at least something. By the way, congrats."

"For what?"

Mom hands me a white envelope with an Indiana University return address. "Your grades came in from IU."

I take the envelope from her. "And I assume you've already looked at them?"

"I figure it's my prerogative as long as I'm paying your tuition."

"Understood." I pull the folded piece of paper from the envelope.

Mom has never been one for suspense and is the absolute last person on earth I would entrust with a secret. "You avoided academic probation, just in case you're wondering."

"Well, Mom, I'm not wondering now, am I?"

I scan my grades: one B, two C's, and a D. An exact two-point-zero. At midterm I was failing every course. Finals week remains a blur to me. I have a vague recollection it involved abstinence, caffeine, nicotine, my first and hopefully only experimentation with crystal meth, and maybe some studying. The abstinence part isn't entirely accurate, given Alexandra EncarnaciÓn, Jeanine's college roommate, drove down from Purdue late in the week to sit on my face for a couple of orally stimulating nights.

"You barely made it, Henry," Mom says. "I expect to see that two-point-zero back up into the threes."

I stuff my miraculous report card back into its miraculous envelope. "Count on it, Mom."

Mom takes a sip of her sun tea then sets her glass down. "You finish sorting through all those videos?"

I repeat the gesture, finishing my tea in one swallow. "Pretty much."

I had found a box of Dad's old VHS tapes when Mom and I were cleaning out the attic yesterday. Most of it was junk—a grainy copy of the last episode of *M*A*S*H*, Season 1 of *American Gladiators*, some marching band competitions from the seventies and eighties, and an almost unwatchable eighty-six minutes of foreign soft-core called *Six Swedes at a Pump* Dad had confiscated from me and curiously never discarded. I did come across a few gems—the 1988 Notre Dame/Miami game, a local public-access cable interview of Dad, about a half-dozen of his television spots for the dealership and, of course, the vasectomy tape.

I watched *What's a Vasectomy All About Anyway?* from beginning to end. The video was at least ten years old, the actors resplendent in bad hairdos, shoulder pads, and short shorts. After an extended consultation with the urologist in which the husband and wife overact to the point of the whole thing turning into an unintentional sketch comedy, the video ends with Mom, Dad, and their two-point-three children eating dinner on their back porch. Portions of this back porch scene—most notably, the image of the father wielding tongs and an I'm-going-to-get-me-some-tonight smile as grill smoke wafts around his aura of masculinity—are shown at least a half-dozen times throughout the program, as if to ease the apparently common post-vasectomy fear men have of not being able to grill dead animals while looking like the perverted brother of Kurt Rambis.

"I have something for you," Mom says. "Come with me."

"What is it?"

"Just follow me." Mom leads me around the outside of the house. We get to the garage. She is holding the garage door opener in her hand.

"What are you up to, Debbie?"

"I hate when you call me Debbie, Hank." Mom presses the door opener. She seems pretty proud of herself at the moment. "But every prince needs a chariot."

The garage door opens, and I see my grandfather's '68 Oldsmobile 442 Coupe with a 455 CID engine backed by a modified W-45 rated at 390 horsepower retrofitted with cylinder heads from the W-30 and the camshaft from the W-31 to generate more rpms. I think I remembered that right.

"The Beast?" I say, astonished. "But I thought everything that was titled under the dealership went with the sale."

"There was one exception," Mom says, grinning from ear to ear. "John kept the Beast in my name because it was my father's car."

"No shit?"

"No shit," Mom says.

I run my hands across the Beast's hood. "She still suck down gas?"

"I filled up the tank, so don't you worry about that. Where are you and Beth going anyway?"

"Up to Broad Ripple. We're going to have dinner, see some live music. I don't want to throw anything too intimidating at her for a first date."

"A first date? The implication being you're already thinking about a second date?"

"Mom, can you let me make my own decisions and my own mistakes without the running commentary?"

"But, Hank, I'm just—"

"Getting yourself into trouble...*again*."

My tone is more casual than caustic, more casual than Mom deserves. Have I forgiven her? Have I forgiven Laura? Not hardly. All I know is Laura spared our child, and Mom has raised that child to be a beautiful four-year-old boy. These are both debts I can never repay.

CHAPTER FIFTY-TWO

I turn the corner onto Beth's street. At the end of the road, I pull into her driveway. I honk the air horn.

Beth answers the door. She's barefoot in tight khaki cargo shorts and a T-shirt. Her hair is pulled back in a ponytail, her perfectly applied makeup the lone hint she's trying to impress me. She takes my hand and guides me to the family room at the back of the house. Her parents are waiting for me.

"It's been awhile, Hank." Dr. Burke offers me his hand. "Nice car."

"Yes, Dr. Burke, yes it has. And thanks." I see a lot of Dr. Burke in Beth. The high forehead. The blond hair. His eyes remind me of my father's—trustworthy, honest. What you'd expect from a pediatrician.

"Please, Hank. Call me Stan."

I never assume this type of informality when talking to a girl's parents, even when it's insisted upon. "Thanks again, Dr. Burke, but if you don't mind, I'd like to work my way up to Stan."

"Suit yourself." The doctor smiles. He's already comfortable with me.

Go figure. I was around the car business for the first twenty-one years of my life, a solid sixteen of those years spent in a classroom with my nose up some teacher's ass. Making adults comfortable around me is hardwired into my brain.

Beth's mom hugs me. "Nice to see you again, big guy."

I flash my for-women-only smile and kiss her on the cheek. "Hi, Mrs. Burke."

She returns the smile. "Oh, you're going to call me Joan. And that's an order."

Joan looks more than a few years younger than the doc. Her hair is dark brown and cut short, but other than that, she's all Beth—her eyes, her slightly turned-up nose, her high cheekbones, her five-feet-nothing height. Joan heads up the local theater company. I see the pictures on the wall of Joan and Beth on stage together. In one of the pictures, Joan is dressed as Miss Hannigan and Beth as Annie.

Beth's parents have always been nice to me. They of course float the requisite, "How's your mother doing?" I've come to accept as the lead-in question for any random ice breaker with someone in Empire Ridge over the next decade. We will also accept "How's your little brother?" or "How's the family?" or any variations thereof.

Dr. and Mrs. Burke are good talkers. They keep the conversation going for ten minutes. I finally just interrupt them.

"We better get going if we want to get a seat."

"Ready when you are." Beth is one step ahead of me, Birkenstocks on, purse in hand. She's changed her shirt. She smells of perfume, that same subtle lavender scent she's worn since I first met her. If I could bottle innocence, that's what it would smell like.

"Let's do this."

We say our goodbyes and walk outside.

"I love this car," Beth says.

"Yeah, Mom surprised me with it."

I open the passenger-side door, holding my hand held out to Beth. "Madam," I say.

Beth takes my hand. She sits in the car, her legs sliding on the freshly waxed seats. I shut the door behind her. It takes everything in me to be cool, to not skip like a giddy fucking schoolboy over to my side of the car.

I get in the car, shut my door and stick the key in the ignition. We sit there for an awkward few seconds, each waiting for an icebreaker that refuses to bail us out.

"All set?" I say.

Beth seems to want to think about her answer. "Should I be afraid, Hank?"

"Fear not. The Beast looks ferocious, but I assure you he's a pussy cat if you know how to handle him."

"I wasn't talking about the car."

I flash her just my right dimple. "Neither was I."

Per Beth's request, we pull into the gas station just off the interstate. "You want some smokes?"

"No, thanks, I'll just bum a couple off you."

Beth leans over and looks at the clock on the dashboard. "Our first official date is twelve minutes old, and you're already presuming things?"

"I'm just not a big smoker. If you want me to buy my own pack I can—"

"Relaaaax." She smacks my knee with the back of her hand. "I'm just teasing you."

I watch Beth as she walks to the convenience store. Her gait is more of a strut, her left foot extending farther out than her right. She enters the store, approaches the counter. She points to the smokes. The bearded, overweight attendant hands her two packs of Marlboro Lights. He says something to her, followed by a toothy grin that screams, *I'd give these to you for free if I could, pretty lady*. Beth exits the convenience store, grimacing. She gets in the car.

"You okay, Beth?"

"I think so."

"Creepy dude?"

"The creepiest."

I wait for traffic to clear. As the Beast accelerates onto the highway, I point across the on-ramp to a yellow building to our left. "There's the historic Waffle House."

"Historic?"

"Maybe."

"Best waffle you ever had?"

"As a matter of fact, yes."

We drive down the interstate for about ten minutes in silence. Beth seems anxious.

"So, Hank?"

"Yes, Beth?"

"This feel weird to you?"

"A little. How about you?"

"A lot."

"A couple beers in us, and we'll be fine."

Beth winks. "I'm sure we will be. Where we going in Broad Ripple?"

"I was thinking Bazbeaux for pizza and then maybe The Vogue for some live music."

"Who's playing tonight?"

"Peter Wolf."

"You're pulling my leg."

"Nope."

"Peter Wolf, as in J. Geils Band's Peter Wolf?"

"The one and only."

"You do realize 'Freeze Frame' is my gymnastics floor music, right?"

"I might indeed realize that."

"You had no clue."

"None at all."

"You know, you handled yourself pretty well back there."

"Back where?"

"With my parents."

"Your mom and dad are cool."

"They like you. I can already tell."

"Could you tell before or after you left me alone in a room with them for fifteen minutes?"

"Hey, it was ten minutes, and you held your own." She punches me in the shoulder. "Besides, a girl like me needs time to get beautiful."

"A girl like you needs *no time* to get beautiful."

"Why, Mr. Fitzpatrick." Beth purses her lips, dips her shoulder. "Are you flirting with me?"

"Yes, I am. Get used to it."

Our conversation segues into our tastes in music. Her favorite band is "a three-way tie between Fleetwood Mac, Aerosmith, and Van Halen." Like a lot of girls, she thinks the Aerosmith front man Steven Tyler is hot. Like a lot of guys, I think she's nuts.

"How about you, Hank?"

"I don't know. It took me awhile to wean myself off the hairbands—Mötley Crüe, Ratt, Cinderella, Scorpions."

"Mötley Crüe's 'Kickstart My Heart' always makes me think of you."

"Really?"

"I picture you playing air guitar at your parents' house."

"Funny, all I think about are Hatch's mix tapes," I say.

"His what?" Beth says.

Why the hell did I just do that? I mean yes, right now I am picturing Beth having sex with Hatch. But fuck. Can't I stop being such a douche, and let myself like this girl?

"Don't mind me," I say.

"So you don't listen to Crüe anymore?"

"I listen to them plenty, but I think Guns N' Roses *Appetite for Destruction* might be the greatest album ever made."

"If only Axl would get his head out of his ass," Beth says.

"Exactly," I say. "And I did the grunge thing like everybody else, but I think the Seattle scene takes itself way too seriously, and I don't regard the music as either mind-blowing or life-altering. If I had to pick one band I've just never stopped listening to, it's Metallica."

"Sorry to hear that."

"Not a Metallica fan?"

"Afraid not. I'm right there with you on grunge, though. Our generation is supposed to worship the stuff, but I like some Soundgarden, maybe half of Pearl Jam's *Ten*, and the soundtrack to *Singles*."

"You've just described my grunge playlist almost to a tee. Give me a few Chris Cornell vocals, a little bit of *Ten* when I'm in the mood, maybe some of the old late-eighties Seattle stuff—Mother Love Bone, Green River, Mud Honey—and that's about it for me."

"And Alice in Chains, of course."

"Of course," I say. Goddamn, she's into Alice in Chains? Since when? Even her taste in music turns me on.

"Favorite singer?" Beth asks.

"Well, it sure as hell ain't Steven Tyler."

"Hey now."

"Okay, Freddie Mercury."

"Freddie, huh?"

"What's wrong with Freddie?"

"That seems too, I don't know, predictable for you."

"Fine, it's Chris Risola. You happy?"

"Who the hell is that?"

"Lead singer for Steelheart."

"One-hit wonders."

"If that," I say, "but the man has got some pipes."

"Not that I don't love obscure hairbands like any self-respecting eighties chick, but what are you into lately? Been to any good concerts?"

"GNR and Metallica about a year ago was the last real kickass show I went to. I'm looking forward to Jimmy Buffett in September. Nothing else comes to mind at the moment. How about you?"

"Well…" Beth bites her lip. "I'm told I went to a good concert this summer."

"Ahh, one of *those* shows. Got pretty tore down?"

"That's what everybody tells me."

"Which one?"

"Lollapalooza."

"Rage Against the Machine, Primus, Alice in Chains?"

"That's the one."

"Wasn't that like…"

"Last Monday, yep—a day that shall live in infamy. I even have a stack of pictures back home from the concert. I wore these low-rise cutoffs and a tiny bikini top to show off my new tattoo."

She lifts her shirt up. A daisy-like flower curves around the left side of her navel, just below her well-defined six-pack.

Beth could have been a belly dancer.

I do my best to prevent the car from swerving off the road. "A flower? That's cool."

"The flower is actually just decoration. The stem of the flower is an Indian symbol for my sign."

"Leo?"

"Very good, Hank. You've done your homework."

"You know we were kinda together in high school, right?"

"Kinda together?" Beth says. "Is that what you call it?"

"Never mind," I say. "But I will have to take a look at some of those photos—you know, strictly for research purposes."

"Be my guest." Beth pulls down her shirt, making the roads safe once again for cars in my general vicinity. "Of course, those photos are mixed in with the pictures of me urinating, vomiting, and passed out on the lawn with my hair matted to the side of my sweaty, alcohol-swollen face."

I laugh. "Hold me back."

"Yeah…" Beth laughs, too. "That's what I thought."

THE DRIVE NORTH BETWEEN Empire Ridge and Indianapolis is the Indiana most people picture—fields of corn and soybeans visible all the way to the horizon broken up by the occasional barn, an oversized billboard, a gnarled tree, an industrial park, a full-service truck stop, and of course, the omnipresent tracts of trailer homes.

There's no shortcut to Broad Ripple, so I chose the scenic route. We jumped off the interstate at Meridian Street on the north side of downtown Indy. Crossing 38th Street, we entered the old-money North Meridian Street Historic District. Smaller Arts and Crafts and American Foursquare homes gave way to massive pre–Great Depression revival mansions—Tudor, Colonial, French, Mission Style. The cozy exposed rafters, low porches, and deep overhangs recede into more intimidating facades of stucco, three-story columns, and tiled roofs.

We reached the end of the historic district just past fifty-seventh Street, hung a right at Westfield Boulevard. Westfield runs east-to-west, parallel to the old canal. No more than twenty yards wide, the canal is a beloved relic of what was to be a part of the four-hundred-and-fifty-nine–mile long Central Canal project extending from the Wabash and Erie Canal at Peru, Indiana, through Indianapolis, and back to the Wabash and Erie at Worthington, Indiana. Abandoned in 1839 when the state went bankrupt, the canal's mere eight point twenty-nine miles of waterfront is now the exclusive domain of joggers, cyclists, fishermen, and flightless geese with bad tempers and even worse bowel movements.

We followed the canal along Westfield to College Avenue, the western boundary of Broad Ripple. The canal ends just east of here, dumping into the White River at the river's widest point anywhere in the county—hence the name, "Broad" Ripple.

Broad Ripple is the closest thing Indianapolis has to an eclectic village with its shops, art galleries, outdoor cafes, and unintentional allusion to a Grateful Dead song. Save for the McDonald's on the east side of the village, corporate America concedes the place to less-than-household names like Grateful Threads, Artsy Phartsy, The Jazz Cooker, The Village Idiot, and Bazbeaux.

We find a parking spot only steps away from Bazbeaux, where I'm taking Beth for dinner. I pull into the spot. A goose guarding its nearby nest lets me know what it thinks about that.

"Oh shut up, you stupid goose," I bark, walking round to Beth's side of the car.

"I love the vibe up here," Beth says.

"Yeah." I offer her my hand, help her out of the car. "If I end up staying in Indy, this is where I want to live."

Bazbeaux Pizza operates out of an old house perched on the banks of the canal, right next to the fire station. The two main dining areas are a rickety front porch of warped cedar and exposed nails in the front of the restaurant and, in the back, a tacked-on garage that masquerades as an indoor–outdoor café in the summer months when the owner raises the doors.

"Please follow me." The Bazbeaux hostess is attractive—tall, long legs, brunette. My exact type. It strikes me right at this moment that Beth Burke is the only petite blonde I've ever dated.

Smoking still has its privileges in Indiana. The day they outlaw smoking in this state is the day I'm handed an election ballot that isn't just a list of overweight and balding white Republicans running unopposed. We bypass a line of people waiting for nonsmoking tables. The hostess seats us near the back of the garage. "Your waiter will be with you shortly."

Beth grabs a menu and glances around. "This place is cool."

"You've never been to Bazbeaux?"

"Nope."

"How does that happen?"

"Well, I've lived most of the last four years of my life in Champaign, Illinois. Between school, work, and gymnastics, I just haven't had a whole lot of free time."

Our waiter interrupts us. He's a young kid, younger than us at least. "Can I get you two something to drink, maybe a salad, or appetizer to start out with?"

Beth scans the menu. "I don't know what I'm in the mood for."

I haven't even looked at a menu. I grab Beth's hand. "You trust me?"

She squints, contemplating an answer. "Sure…for now."

"Yeah, Carl is it?" I eye the waiter's nametag.

"Call me C.B."

"We'll have a bucket of Rolling Rocks, two house salads, and a large Pizza Alla Quattro Formaggio."

"What's that?"

"Already stopped trusting me, have you?"

"Maybe I'm allergic to something on the pizza. Ever think of that, smart guy?"

"What are you allergic to?"

"Poison ivy, ragweed, and bee stings."

"Rest assured there's no poison ivy, ragweed, or bee stings on the Pizza Alla Quattro Formaggio. How do Romano, cheddar, ricotta, mozzarella, provolone, bacon, and mushrooms sound?"

"Perfect." Beth reaches over and squeezes my hand. We giggle.

C.B. shows a conscious disinterest in our cutesiness. "What kind of dressing you want on those salads?"

I cut him some slack. "What kind of dressing do you have, C.B.?"

"Uh..." C.B. looks at the ceiling. "We got ranch, blue cheese, thousand island, ballsmatic."

A laugh leaks out Beth's nose. I look at her. She knows I can't leave this one alone. It's fucking gift-wrapped for me.

"What was that last dressing?"

"Ballsmatic."

"Yeah, I think we'll go with that." I hand C.B. our menus. "Beth, you okay with *ballsmatic*?"

She nods, biting her lip.

C.B. brings us our ballsmatic salads and a bucket of Rocks in short order. I'm tempted to ask if the ballsmatic is freshly squeezed. I extract two green bottles from the ice, then hand one to Beth. I hold my beer aloft. "Cheers."

"Cheers." Beth clinks her bottle against mine. She takes a sip of beer, douses her cigarette. "I don't know about this, Hank."

"About what, the beer?"

"About us, you dummy."

"What's there to know?"

"Nothing. And that's what scares me. You know my secrets. I know yours."

"You don't know all my secrets, Beth."

"I know some of the bigger ones."

"Like what?"

"Allow me to reintroduce you to our hometown. When you drive into the city, the first thing you see is a billboard that says, 'Empire Ridge: Your Fucking Business Is Everybody's Fucking Business.'"

There is no such billboard, but I see her point.

"C.B, it's about time!"

Our waiter's timing is impeccable. He places the large Pizza Alla Quattro Formaggio on our table. We eat the whole thing. I order us another bucket of Rocks.

Beth has matched me beer-for-beer. The second bucket of Rocks is down to only two beers. Stomachs full, heads spinning, we savor our post-meal cigarettes. I'm not what you'd call a "real" smoker. I smoke when I drink. I buy one pack a week, if that. I can take it or leave it, which annoys the hell out of my smoker friends and most especially my ex-smoker friends. That being said, the post-meal smoke is still one of life's simple pleasures.

The waiter gives us our bill. I tip him thirty percent, a fair commission for adding *ballsmatic* to my vocabulary.

"Ready to head over to the Vogue?"

Beth stands up. "Can we stop by the car first?"

"I guess so."

"Why the sad face?"

"You want me to be Pocket Man."

"What?"

"Pocket Man." I open the door at the front of Bazbeaux. "You're going to put that cute little purse of yours back in the car, and then ask me to hold your driver's license, your lipstick, and either your cash or ATM card for the rest of the night."

Beth takes my arm in hers, steps out of the restaurant. "And just how do you know that?"

"Because I'm a guy, and as a guy, I know girls are genetically incapable of taking a purse into a bar where there's live music or dancing. You, of course, won't put these loose items in your own pocket, because you want guys to look at your ass, unblemished by the random bump of a wallet or cosmetic application device."

"That is totally false."

"Totally true."

"False."

"True."

Beth rolls her eyes and stops just short of the car. She hazards a look over her shoulder, at her ass. "Okay, mostly true. I have noticed the bruthas like looking at the junk in this trunk."

I shake my head. "Is this the part where I'm supposed to say, 'Beth, your butt's not that big'?"

"Yes, Hank." She smacks me on the arm. "Yes, it is."

Of course, Beth has always had one of those out-of-this-world gymnast butts—an Olympic podium–worthy piece of rounded perfection that at this moment could only be improved upon if Beth were wearing a multi-layered silk skirt fastened low on the hips with a pearl-encrusted belt and matching gold pasties. Or if she were naked, obviously.

"Beth Burke, you have a nice butt."

"And?"

"And it's not that big."

"Thanks for noticing." She throws her purse in the car, bending over in an obvious way. She stands up and closes the door. She hands me her driver's license, lipstick, and a wad of cash. "Here you go...Pocket Man."

The Vogue has been around since the late thirties, a Golden Age theater turned porn palace in the seventies, turned nightclub in the eighties. Beth and I walk under the original 1938 Vegas-bold marquee through The Vogue's front doors. Being the one with breasts and a vagina, Beth is, of course, inside the bar and halfway into a drink by the time the testosterone in the doorman subsides enough for him to relinquish my ID.

Peter Wolf has already taken the stage. The Vogue is a nightclub, so you either sit way beyond the stage in high-backed lounge chairs or else commit to standing all night on the open concert floor. "Come on, Hank. Let's try to get up front."

Wolf is playing a post–J. Geils original, a song I don't recognize. This tanned older woman next to us, a leather-skinned groupie well past her prime, claims to be Peter Wolf's biggest fan. She tells us she saw the J. Geils Band in '81 when they were the headliner and U2 was the opening act. I'm impressed. I counter by telling her I saw Bon Jovi open for Scorpions in '84. She seems less impressed.

The song ends. That synthesized opening riff comes, as we all knew it would.

"'Freeze Frame'!" Beth screams with an almost childlike joy. She pulls me closer to the stage, closer to her. She pulls my arms around her waist, twisting her pelvis into me to the beat of the music.

Peter Wolf is going into the vault tonight, pulling out J. Geils classics like "Homework," "First I Look at the Purse," "One Last Kiss," and "Night Time." And by classics, I mean songs I've never fucking heard of. I almost give up on him until "Musta Got Lost," at which point Beth tugs on my sleeve.

"Got to take a break." My date holds out her hand. "Lipstick?"

"Hurry up." I hand over her paraphernalia. "I'm sensing a major encore."

Beth kisses me on the cheek. "Then save me a spot."

Seconds later, the stage lights are doused as Wolf ends his second set. Hundreds of cigarette lighters take their place. The Vogue shakes with drunken, nostalgic noise.

TEN MINUTES PASS. AN unmistakable bass line. Where the hell is Beth?

Wolf grabs the microphone and points to the crowd. He starts into the first verse, building to the chorus.

"I've had the blues, the reds, and the pinks. One thing's for sure..."

"Love stinks!" the crowd shouts back at Wolf.

Seriously, where is...

She taps me on my shoulder. I turn my head, right into Beth's lips.

She times her kiss with the chorus. I didn't even see it coming, our date hovering all night between a good time and me wondering if a follow-up date was even in the cards. The kiss is unexpected and cathartic all at once. Like Beth.

Her kiss tastes confident, premeditated. Freshly applied lipstick. An obvious trace of a breath mint. We dance, still kissing. There's a comfort level with Beth, as if we're starting right where we left off. Our lips press and purse when they're supposed to. Our tongues attack and retreat in concert with one another.

We kiss for the whole song. The louder people scream, the more frantic, sloppy, and wet our kisses become. Our kiss is like an open act of defiance against the mob, the irony of the chorus pushing us deeper into one another's mouths.

"Love stinks...yeah, yeah!"

CHAPTER FIFTY-THREE

Against my better judgment, I drive us to Sanford & Son. We get there just before daybreak. I can hear Hatch and Mack both snoring in their rooms.

I grab us two Natty Lights. Beth bends down and peers into the illuminated fifty-gallon aquarium on the back wall. Her calves are muscular, tight.

"His name's Bobo. Mack has had him since the beginning of college."

"He's huge." Beth taps on the glass. "What kind of fish is he?"

I hand Beth her beer. "A snakehead, I think."

"Natural Light, huh?" Beth raises her blue and white aluminum can for a toast. "Cheers."

"Six bucks a case at Costco," I say, raising my can in response. "Spare no expense."

"That was a great show," Beth says.

"It was?"

Beth smiles at my sarcasm, her cheeks a little flush. We had kissed for the rest of the concert. The fact people mocked us made no difference whatsoever. The fact Peter Wolf closed with "Centerfold" made no difference whatsoever.

Who am I kidding? We stopped kissing for *that* song!

After the show, we walked, aimless and smitten, down the streets of Broad Ripple. By the time we found our way to the car, everything had closed, even the late-night burrito shack that never dims its lights until at least four in the morning.

On every date I've ever been on, there's an endpoint, a precise moment at which I say, "I'm done with this girl," or, "I'm doing this girl." This date doesn't have that moment. It comes as a comfort to me.

"What are you thinking about, Hank?"

"Nothing," I say, when of course what I mean to say is "everything."

"You're lying." Beth takes a drink of beer. She wipes her lips, pointing to my mouth with her free hand. "You stick your tongue out and bite down on it whenever you're thinking about something. You do it when you're dancing, too."

"I do?" I pull my tongue back in my mouth. I remember Dad. I grin, shaking my head.

"I say something funny?"

"Sorry, I just had a flashback of my father marching around the house to Chuck Mangione."

Beth doesn't respond, allowing the moment to carry its own weight. She grabs my hand. It's getting to the point where I'm almost too caught up in the date. I've barreled past smitten to just full-on wanting this girl more than anything else in my life.

I look around the room. "You know, Beth, my friends think I'm crazy for going out with you."

At best, it's a last-ditch, halfhearted, but all-the-way lame attempt at reestablishing control. We take our beers and our flirting out onto the front porch.

"Your friends think you're crazy." Beth kisses me. "Or just Hatch?"

I close the front door behind us and lean in and kiss her back. "He bet me his truck we wouldn't last the rest of the summer."

"Like I told you, that dude has just got to let it go." Beth kisses me again. "But if it makes you feel any better, my friends say you're a bastard."

"I *am* a bastard."

"You are?"

"Okay, maybe in the literal sense I'm only half-bastard."

"How so?"

"Fatherless but not quite rudderless."

"That's not what I'd call a bastard, Hank."

"It's not? If being a bastard means being a product of my pain as much as my joy, my vices as much as my virtues, a raised up, broken down, and raised up again mishmash of sin and sincerity, how can I *not* be a bastard? And not just a bastard, a lucky bastard."

"Lucky?" Beth's eyes perk up.

"The luckiest," I say.

"How do you figure?"

"Look at me, Beth. I'm sitting on a porch, on the eve of morning, when the world isn't yet full of itself, and after all my fuck-ups, I'm still getting to taste the lips of the hottest girl in school."

Beth grabs my face with her hands and kisses me hard. Her tongue lingers inside my mouth awhile, licking my lips on the way out. "Anybody ever tell you that you have the softest and cushiest lips?"

I lie of course. "No, never."

She sees right through me. "How many?"

"Counting you, four."

Beth smiles and grabs my lips in her fingers, squeezing. "You are the most adorable thing I've ever laid eyes on, but you know this date has to end at some point."

"What time is it?"

"Your clock inside said almost six a.m. Let's go get some breakfast. I bet if we jump in the car right now, we can find an even better view of the sunrise."

"I don't need a better view. I'm waiting right here."

"Waiting?"

"Yeah, waiting."

"For what?"

"For nothing, for everything. I'm just tired of chasing the dawn. My postcard is right *here*, and the only thing that can lessen the beauty of this sunrise is you not being in it. Wait with me, Beth."

She stands, fronting a vintage Coppolla pink-gray dawn that consumes the whole scene. I can't stop staring at her calves. She reaches down to take my hand. "Eyes up here, pervert."

I rise up, easing into her kiss. Her arms are around my neck, her lips pressed against my own. She pretends to rub her lipstick off my lips but leaves it there. She likes to mark her territory.

"I'm a sure thing," Beth says. "You know that, right?"

I smile. "Now I do."

She smiles back. "So what are you waiting for, *really*?"

"I told you what I'm waiting for..." I glance out over the pre-dawn horizon. I think about Dad, about Uncle Mitch, about Jack. I think about Mohammad El-Bakkar. I speak with a voice not quite my own but close enough to fool Beth, if not myself. "I'm waiting for the sun...to come to me."

"Then I'll wait, too, Hank."

Her response comes as reflex. For as long as I've known Beth she's exhibited an unconditional loyalty to me I've never earned and would never deserve. But hell, life has kicked me in the nutsack enough times that I'm taking this gift and running with it.

"Hey, Beth."

"Yeah?"

"You ever think about taking up belly dancing?"

PART II

1994–1995

CHAPTER FIFTY-FOUR

Hatch chatters his teeth from beneath an old blanket. He points at the coffee table. "What the hell is that?"

A white-gold 1.85-carat princess-cut diamond ring sits on the table. I must have taken it out last night when I was drunk. Like an idiot, I passed out and left the case open.

"Family heirloom," I say. "My mom's wedding ring."

"And what the fuck are you doing with it?"

"Debbie gave it to me."

"Why?"

"Why not? Just shut up and drink this." I hand Hatch a plastic bottle of orange Pedialyte that I procured from Dr. Burke's pediatric office. Short of running an actual saline IV, it's the best cure for dehydration or a hangover.

Hatch unscrews the cap, sips the bottle reluctantly. He gasps, licking his teeth. "That shit tastes awful."

"Serves you right."

Hatch and I both took our own sweet time at IU, graduating in five-and-half-years. We continued to be roommates even after moving up to Indianapolis from Bloomington. Our house is an American Foursquare tucked into a row of American Foursquares in Indy's SoBro neighborhood—as in "Southern Broad Ripple," not "South Bronx," although our house sits in the middle of a weird Gotham nexus. I can throw a rock from my front porch and hit the neon marquee of Red Key Tavern, Kurt Vonnegut's old watering hole. Wander a few blocks north, and I'm standing in the parking lot of Atlas Supermarket, where David Letterman bagged groceries as a teenager.

"M-moving a little fast, aren't we, F-Fitzy?"

Hatch is sick. He's feverish and severely dehydrated but refuses to go to the doctor. He's shivering even though he's running a one-hundred-and-three–degree temperature. He's running a temperature because he has food poisoning. Yesterday during a Patrick Swayze marathon—*Red Dawn, Next of Kin, Point Break*, and of course the one hundred fourteen minutes of cinematic perfection that is *Road House*—we each drank five forties of Crazy Horse malt liquor. I passed out and pissed myself. Hatch got the munchies, mistook a half-pound of raw bacon in the fridge for lunchmeat, and made himself a sandwich. He's been shitting blood for the past hour, insisting he's turned the corner, but the truth is his dad kicked him off his health insurance last week.

"Fast?" I cover my mouth with a closed fist, swallow down a burp. I raise my thumb and then the rest of my fingers in sequence, counting to myself. Beth and I hit a year last July, five months to December, and then four more after that. By my count, we've been together for—"

"Two years," Hatch says. "Has it been that long?"

"Twenty-one months actually."

I'm still drunk. About half of *Road House* sits unwatched on the laser disc player I appropriated from Dad's office right before Mom sold the dealership. Hatch has managed to appropriate my dead father as his own excuse to blow off life and drink himself into oblivion. After he downed his third forty of Crazy Horse last night, Hatch confessed he couldn't recall the last day he hadn't been drunk. Over the last year, he's held multiple jobs. Just out of school, he worked the early morning shift at an indoor playground on Indy's northeast side called Leaps & Bounds. His responsibilities included dusting the entire four-story jungle gym, washing the balls in the ball pit, waxing the floors, and smoking blunts with a gangbanger who was there on a work-release program. When a Pizzeria Uno opened next door the same week his Leaps & Bounds co-worker got thrown back in jail for failing a drug test, Hatch quit Leaps & Bounds to become a waiter, sobered up for almost three months before they offered him a management position, then proceeded to get fired after every bottle of Chianti in the Uno's bar somehow ended up at a Delta Gamma sorority party at Butler University. Hatch tried the waiter thing again at the Beef & Boards dinner theater on the north side of Indy, worked there just long enough to meet B.B. King, then quit the day after he touched Lucille.

I just convinced Dr. Burke to hire Hatch to paint the interior of his house, which should keep him busy through the spring and part of the summer. At present, Hatch's monthly contribution to our rent check is somewhere between ten dollars and a half-dozen late-night burritos. He disputes this number by claiming he makes up the difference by paying for most of our booze, a dubious claim seeing as (a) he drinks most of our booze, and (b) nearly all the liquor we still have in our house is the remaining contraband from Uno.

Fortunately, about a month after we moved in here, I answered an open advertisement to IU grads for "Eager and Earnest Hoosiers with English Degrees." I got on the ground floor of a start-up independent publisher all of five blocks from my house called College Avenue Press. My title is assistant editorial director. My gross income is twenty-two thousand dollars.

Hatch's affinity for the sauce has nothing to do with me or my dad. The apple doesn't fall far from the tree, and Hatch is a drunk hanging from a fucking sequoia of alcoholics—his father, his mom, his grandfather. Since I started dating Beth, I feel like I've turned a corner. Hatch still seems stuck in the straightaway.

"Beth is the best thing that's happened to me, probably ever," I say. "But who says I'm ever going to give this ring to her?"

"Keep telling yourself that." Hatch sits up, rewraps himself in the old blanket. "You know what your problem is, Fitzy?"

"Enlighten me."

"For as much as you've fucked around, you'll always be in love with being in love. You're a man whore who deep down wants the fairy tale."

"Says the King of the Narrated Mix Tape."

"Oh, fuck the fuck off, Fitzy."

"Can't you just be happy for me, Hatch?"

"I don't know. You gonna hold that mix tape thing over me forever?"

I nod. "You bet your ass. What are friends for?"

Hatch smiles, but I think it's probably the food poisoning doing the talking. He grabs a cup off the coffee table that has a swallow of malt liquor left in it. And the bastard fucking drinks it! He reaches in between the couch cushions and pulls out an unopened forty of Crazy Horse. "Qualms, motherfucker," he says.

Qualms is another one of Hatch's stupid drinking games, *Qualms* being the code word for "finish your entire fucking drink." Even sick, Hatch can find time for a drinking game. Originally intended as a power-drinking variant of the more universal "Social!" toast that allows for the occasional harmless chug with a friend, Hatch has turned Qualms into a weapon, a way to pummel people into inebriated comas. See, the loophole in Qualms is that you simply must finish your current drink in hand. So Hatch drinks down his drink—in this example, a solitary swallow of cheap malt liquor. Meanwhile, he hands you a fresh drink—in this example, an unopened forty-ounce bottle of cheap malt liquor—and proceeds to immediately yell, "Qualms!" Then, while casually burping up a mere drop of backwash, he sits back and waits to see if the foam first comes shooting out your mouth or your nose.

This time, it's my nose. My stomach is okay, though. Money being as tight as it is, the only thing I've had in the last twenty-four hours is a bag of Cool Ranch Doritos and a large Diet Coke, both purchased with my mom's Unocal 76 gas card. Forty ounces is surprisingly easy to keep down on an empty stomach.

I wipe traces of malt liquor off my mouth. "You really are a fucking dickhead."

Hatch is laughing. "Just trying to lighten the mood, Fitzy."

"Consider it lightened," I say. The ring is still sitting in its open case on the coffee table. I grab the case and take one last look at the ring.

"You sure you know what you're doing?"

I close the case, stuff the ring in my pocket. "This feels like *the one*, Hatch. It's the first relationship I can see me being in for the long term."

"The long term? When I said you'd been together two years, you immediately corrected me and said twenty-one months."

"So?"

"So? You're still programmed to celebrate month anniversaries. You're like a new parent, holding on to those month-to-month milestones with numbered onesies that go all the way up to thirty-six because deep-down you just can't wrap your brain around being a huge part of this little creature's world basically forever."

"That's ridiculous. Who ever heard of a thirty-six month onesie?"

"Don't be a smartass, Fitzy. My point is your heart is ignoring the hard-wiring in your dick. And I do mean *hard*-wiring. Twenty-one months might as well be twenty-one days. You're not fucking ready."

"Six years, Hatch."

"What?"

"There's your number. Beth and I have been on-again, off-again friends for six years. That's a long time to get to know someone."

"Just like you were on-again, off-again fucking Laura for most of the eighties?"

"I dated Laura in high school and then accidentally had sex with her one time in college."

"Oh, you *accidentally* tripped and fell into her vagina?" Hatch snaps his fingers. "God, I hate it when that happens."

"Don't go there, Hatch."

"Don't go where?"

"I'm pretty sure Laura had it coming."

"How do you figure?" Hatch asks.

First the new parent analogy and now an earnest question. I have to hand it to the guy; he's being more attentive than he's usually capable of being even when he's not hungover.

"Never mind," I say, catching myself. No one save Laura and my mother know my secret. The faked abortion. The chain of lies. The brother who turned out to be my son.

Hatch's ADHD finally bails me out: "You ever find out what happened to The Tool?"

After we started dating, Beth and I agreed to keep things non-exclusive when she went back to the University of Illinois in the fall of '93. She told me she wanted to take things slow. What she didn't tell me was her summer fling, "The Tool," quit his bartending job in Empire Ridge and followed her to Champaign. He lived in her house until Thanksgiving. Beth said she felt sorry for him and that he slept on the couch. I didn't believe her. Although by Christmas of that year we started dating exclusively, I know that tanned, white-teethed, square-jawed smile that used to stare at me from a picture frame on Beth's nightstand didn't sleep on any goddamn couch. Any mention of The Tool still pisses me off, which is why Hatch is mentioning him.

"The Tool has been out of the picture for a while."

"Define 'out of the picture,'" Hatch says. "Does he still call her?"

"Don't care."

"He still live in Champaign?"

"Still don't care."

"Has he bought Beth a ring yet?"

I grab Hatch's hand and try to shove the bottle of Pedialyte in his mouth. "Shut up and drink your Pedialyte, you fucking baby."

CHAPTER FIFTY-FIVE

Sophie B. Hawkins's "Damn I Wish I Was Your Lover" plays from the boom box on the back deck of the beach house. Beth sits on the bottom step of the deck, a cigarette in one hand, a beer in the other. She's wearing a black bikini. She flexes her bare toes in the sand, winking at me as she sings the lyrics.

Beth is set to graduate from Illinois in a little over a month. Dr. Burke decided to reward his daughter with a free spring break at the family's beach house in the Southern Outer Banks of North Carolina. Stan told Beth to invite all her friends, but she only invited me. I'm not complaining.

The beach house is one of the older houses on this stretch of sand. It's a one-story cedar-shake bungalow Stan painted pink as an ode to John Mellencamp, but it has an intimate salty charm compared to all the stilted mansions popping up like weeds from Emerald Isle on the west side of the island all the way to Fort Macon in the east.

The abodes of avarice notwithstanding, the area still maintains a semi-quirky vibe with its mix of trailer-park locals and older professionals from the Triangle. Just last night, we attended a barbecue co-hosted by a tenured, gay art professor from East Carolina University and his champion marlin fisherman husband out of Morehead City. While an "SOBX" bumper sticker doesn't have the cache of the "OBX" logo seemingly engraved into the rear bumpers of every Land Rover, the upside to vacationing far south of places like Cape Hatteras and Duck can be summed up in four words: no fucking New Yorkers.

I hand Beth a bottle of Kalik. "Still can't believe we're here."

"Believe it." Beth lifts the overpriced beer to her lips, swallows once, then twice. She pulls the bottle away, licking her lips. "Needs more lime."

I start to get up. "I can get you a bigger slice."

"Stay here." Beth pulls me down. "It's our first day on the beach together. I think I can manage without."

I smile and clink her beer with mine. "Thanks for getting me Kalik, by the way. I know you wanted Corona."

Beth kisses me on the cheek. "Last beer you and your father had together?"

"So you remembered?" I say.

"Of course I remembered." A gust of salty air rolls off the beach. I watch Beth's hair blow back and down the small of her tanned back. Beth notices me staring.

"What are you in the mood for?" she says.

I roll my eyes. "Do you have to ask?"

"For dinner, perv."

"Oh," I say. "Shrimp burgers maybe?"

We shared the bathroom when we changed out of our swimsuits. She told me not to peek, so I peeked. We went over to Big Oak Drive-In for dinner and ate a couple of shrimp burgers with French fries, then split a six-pack of Kalik while walking down the beach.

When we got back to the beach house, we argued over what movie to watch. The videos were stacked on top of the television. Beth suggested *When Harry Met Sally*. I suggested *Field of Dreams*. Somehow we decided *The Cutting Edge* was a good compromise.

The movie wasn't half bad. Beth had evidently seen it a few times, repeating the movie's signature quote—"Toe pick!"—each and every instance Moira Kelly's character, Kate Moseley, said these words to the fallen hockey star turned rebellious figure skater, Doug Dorsey. Doug, D.B. Sweeney's character, reminded me of Han Solo. In the seconds before Han Solo was frozen in carbonite in *The Empire Strikes Back*, Princess Leia told him, "I love you," prompting the greatest single line in moviemaking history, Han's cooler-than-cool comeback, "I know." Not to be outdone, when Kate Moseley finally proclaimed "I love you" to Doug Dorsey, he replied, "Just remember who said it first."

I like Doug Dorsey, although I chuckle a little bit at D.B. Sweeney's last name. Back in grade school at St. Ambrose, I had a classmate named Brian Sweeney. The girls used to tease him mercilessly, "I *saw Brian's weenie, I saw Brian's weenie!*" Only later did I find out that he actually showed it to them.

Beth and I grabbed a smoke on the back porch after the movie ended. The weather in April in the SOBX is your basic crapshoot—as likely to be forty degrees on any given day as it is eighty—but we still threw on our swimsuits and jumped in the ocean again for a late-night dip. Beth is scared of sharks.

"Come on," I say, grabbing Beth's hand and pulling her up out of the water. "No more shark jokes."

"Promise?" Beth says.

"I promise."

"What do you want to do now?"

I try to be sweet but obvious with my intentions. "How about a shower?"

Beth kisses me on the lips. She stands on her tiptoes in the sand, reaches around and squeezes my ass, pulling me in to her. She steps back. "How about a nightcap first?"

I wrap a towel around my waist. Beth throws on her Illini Gymnastics sweatshirt. We walk back into the beach house. A bottle of cheap wine sits on the table, flanked by two empty glasses.

"What's the special occasion?" I say.

"Don't start thinking you're too special," Beth says. "I picked it up while you were jogging on the beach earlier today. I asked the guy at the liquor store what's the best cheap drink he could recommend. He gave me this."

I pick up the bottle, drag my thumb over the label. "Cisco? Isn't this the stuff that sent a bunch of sorority girls to the hospital because they pounded them like wine coolers?"

"That it is," Beth says, retrieving the bottle from me. She unscrews the cap. "The liquor store guy told me one of the big bottles should be enough for both of us."

"So I assume you bought two of the big bottles?"

"You assume correctly, Mr. Fitzpatrick." Beth drinks the cheap wine straight from the bottle.

"How is it?" I ask.

She licks her lips. "Tolerable."

"Terrible?"

"Tall-ur-uh-bull."

Beth puts on Aerosmith's *Toys in the Attic*, pours me a glass of Cisco.

"Fancy," I say as Beth laughs.

As of five minutes ago, we've opened the second bottle of Cisco. I pour Beth a full glass from the new bottle. "You feeling this?"

"Yeah," Beth says. "Quite a bit actually."

"Me, too."

Beth's eyes rotate to the right and then back to the left, like she has something on her mind. "You remember senior year spring break?"

"In high school?"

"Yeah."

"Pretty drunk week. Not a whole lot that I do remember."

"Oh, come on," Beth says, punching me in the arm. "Play along with me."

"Okay, there was you and Claire with those parking signs."

"I gotta pee!"

"Exactly," I say.

It was late in the week in Panama City Beach, at which point Beth and Claire's blood supply had been replaced by Southern Comfort. They stole our condo unit's parking signs, two metal plaques with a block letter P on them. For the remainder of the vacation they'd hold them up whenever they had to go to the bathroom and announce to the room, "I gotta pee. Get it? I got a *P*?"

"You know what I remember about you, Hank?"

"What?"

"I remember interrupting you having sex with Laura in the bathroom."

"Was that before or after Claire kicked Laura's ass?"

"Definitely before, but not by much." Beth tries to disguise her sigh, a muffled sound of disappointment tinged with jealousy around the edges. "How long did you two end up dating anyway?"

I don't like where this line of questioning is going. Beth isn't in on my little secret, at least not yet. I proceed with cautious ambivalence. "Can't really remember exactly. A year maybe, not as long as you and I have been together."

"You sure about that?"

"I think I just established that I'm not sure."

"I could've sworn I heard that you two hooked up occasionally in college."

"Not *occasionally*," I say. "Once."

"When was that?"

"Doesn't matter."

"I want to know."

"You're going to make a bigger deal out of this than it needs to be."

"When?"

I put my Cisco down. "About two years ago."

"*About* two years?"

"Fuck, Beth. It was April twenty-second, nineteen ninety-three. Is that what you want to hear? It was about three in the morning, the day after my birthday at Sheila Fleming's apartment."

"So it was before we started dating?"

"Of course. A little less than three months, actually. She was the last girl I had sex with before I started dating you. There, you happy?'"

"Wait a second," Beth says. "Laura was the last girl you had sex with before me?"

"Isn't that what I said?"

"But that was in April of ninety-three, and we started dating in July of ninety-three."

"Yes, three months. We just went over this."

"And you're sure Laura was the last girl you had sex with before me?"

"Why would I fucking make that up?"

"But we didn't even start dating exclusively for another five months after that, in December."

"Yes, over winter break," I say. "I was there, you know."

"Yeah, I know." Beth has many facial expressions: sad, happy, pouty, coy, seductive. I've never seen guilty, until this second. An unspoken affirmation hangs in the air.

"Fuck me!" I say.

Beth gets up from her seat, walks around to my side of the table. "Hank, please. What's past is past."

"Who was it?" I'm shouting now. "When was it?"

Beth is crying. "It was the fall semester at Illinois, when Jordan came to Champaign and I—"

"The Tool? The fucking Tool?"

"But Hank, you told me you were still dating around."

"Guess what, Beth? I was lying!"

"Seeing other people was what we both decided was best at the time."

"Nice to see you embraced the concept with such enthusiasm. So you fucked The Tool in September..."

"And once in October."

"What the fuck, Beth?"

"But you and I weren't even dating exclusively un—"

"Until after you made sure you got in a few more good fucks with The Tool. Yes, thanks so much for pointing out this technicality to me. Man, that's a load off my fucking mind."

"Baby, wait," Beth says, grabbing my elbow.

I wrench my arm from her hand, grab my glass of Cisco. "I'm going for a walk on the beach. Do not follow me."

I down my glass of Cisco. The breezy spring night hits me in the face as I step outside. A part of me wants to be the old Hank. Wants to jump in the car, head to the nearest strip club, and make a bad night even worse. Beth owes me that, right? This is what relationships are: tit-for-tat ledgers in which every kindness or transgression is returned with interest. Accountability is measured only by checkmarks on an internal grocery list of mistakes. Why was I promiscuous as a young man? Because my godfather made me that way. My therapist even told me so. It wasn't immoral. It wasn't personal. It was just me getting even.

Getting even. Is that what this is all about? Really? Here's a thought, Hank. Why not tear up that fucking grocery list? Maybe there is something to the Golden Rule. The difference between happiness and despair, between love and hate, could just be the difference between a mistake forgiven and a mistake avenged.

Yeah, if life could be distilled into a formula that simple, I've wasted a lot of years being an asshole.

I walk back into the house. Beth sits at the kitchen table. She's crying. "Beth…" I say, my tone purposely measured. I sit down next to her at the table. "I'm sorry for yelling at you like that. It's not like you violated my trust. You just hurt my pride."

Beth stands up, wipes her eyes with the sleeve of her sweatshirt. She walks over to me and pushes my chair out, sitting on my lap. "I love you, Henry David Fitzpatrick, and I'm sorry for hurting you. I just wanted everything out in the open. Nothing else before us matters to me anymore."

I kiss her, my lips lingering on hers. "Do me a favor, Beth?"

"Anything," she says.

"Look down at your left hand."

Beth's eyes open wide. She looks like she might pass out.

I hadn't planned on slipping the 1.85-carat princess-cut diamond ring set in white-gold onto her finger. It just sort of happened.

"Wait, what?"

I drop to one knee. "Beth, you're the best thing that's ever happened to me. We're moving too fast and everyone will say we're insane, but I say we prove them all wrong and live happily ever after. Elisabeth Alison Burke, will you marry me?"

The tears return to Beth's face. She drops to her knees and kisses me. "Yes, yes, a thousand times yes."

"You sure?" I say, wiping her tears off my face.

"Henry David Fitzpatrick..." Beth says. "I've been in love with you since I was sixteen years old."

We start to undress one other right there at the kitchen table. I undo her bikini top from behind, watching her reflection in the sliding glass door as I cup her small breasts in my hand. She turns to face me, pulls my shirt over my head.

"You ready for that shower now?" Beth says.

We kiss a little longer in the bathroom, awkwardly reluctant to cross the threshold. With some encouragement from Beth, I finally slide my hands down the back of her bikini bottoms, squeezing her butt and sliding her bottoms off in one fluid motion. She returns the favor. I open the shower curtain.

"Uh, Beth."

"Yeah, babe?"

I point inside the shower. It's one of those three-by-three fiberglass stalls tacked into a bathroom as an afterthought. Barely large enough to fit both of us standing motionless, hands at our sides, let alone what we're envisioning.

"I know you're a tiny girl and all, but—"

"Hey." Beth laughs. "I'm game if you're game."

From Casanova to the latest paperback smut, there are a myriad of sordid tales of young lovers in the throes of passion. The story of the girl bent over in a shower stall while her fiancé tries to tag her from behind while propping his foot on the edge of a toilet seat and untangling his penis from a shower curtain is probably not among these accounts.

"This isn't working," I say.

Beth looks like a baseball infielder waiting for the next pitch, her hands on her knees. She says to me over her shoulder, "I realize that, Hank."

We give up on the shower and towel each other off. Beth's hair is wet, much longer than it usually looks. It falls all the way down to just above her bare nipples. Beth grabs me by the back of the head and brings my lips to her breasts. She grabs my hand, turning away from me, her breasts leaving my mouth.

"Hey," I say. "I was just getting started."

"I know you were," Beth says. "So let's go out back and finish."

I lead us out to the beach. Beth follows close behind with a blanket. She unfurls it on the sand.

"Lie down," she says.

I lie down. Beth straddles me, the ocean at low tide gently humming in the background. She leans in to kiss me on the lips, pulls away. She leans in again, her hair falling over her shoulders and onto my face. She moves down, her hair and her breasts grazing my throat, my chest, my stomach. She takes me in her mouth.

I've always struggled to be both sexual and emotional at the same time. That's just how I'm wired. Sex fills a physical need in me, like eating. Hunger more than desire. It's a release.

Not now. Tonight, I am electric. The hair stands on the back of my neck. Goose pimples. The salty fishiness of the ocean in my nose. Beth's skin on my skin.

A few minutes pass. I push her away.

"What?" Beth says, raising her head. "That doesn't feel good?"

"Too good, actually."

Beth crawls back up my body, spiderlike, straddling me again. She runs her thumb across my cheek. "Are you crying?"

"No," I say, embarrassed.

"It's okay," Beth says.

"Doesn't feel okay," I say.

"It's actually kind of a turn-on." Beth kisses me softly on the lips. She reaches down with her left hand, her right hand propping her up. She executes a quick shimmy motion with her hips and guides me inside her.

I TELL BETH NOT to peek when I tiptoe naked across the back deck to retrieve the remaining Cisco, so she peeks. I'm too lazy to go inside to retrieve the glasses. I hand her the bottle.

"That was some crazy sex," I say.

Beth tilts the bottle up to her lips, swallows. She hands the bottle back to me. "Babe, I've never had an orgasm like that before."

I hold up two fingers. "I think I counted two of them."

"That you did."

"When you started playing with yourself and you did that thing—"

"You liked that?"

"Hell yeah I did!"

"What about when you used your tongue—"

"Didn't see that coming, but I dug it, too."

"You sure?"

"Positive, Ms. Burke."

"That's Mrs. Fitzpatrick to you."

"It is?"

"Why wouldn't it be?"

"Beth Fitzpatrick," I say. "The name doesn't exactly roll off the tongue. Beth Burke is a cool name, and calling up the credit card companies and all that stuff sounds like a big hassle to me. If you want to keep your name, go for it."

I wait for her smile. For her gratitude. For her admiration for a boy raised in a fairly conservative Catholic household standing before her now as this enlightened hunk of a man and shining beacon of gender equality.

Instead, Beth kicks me in the shin. I crumple to the deck in a naked heap.

"Well, thanks for giving me fucking permission!" she says, storming into the beach house with her fists clinched.

I compose myself and follow her inside the house. "What is wrong with you?"

"Nothing, dickhead." She kicks me in the shin again, although not quite as hard. She fumes across the family room, slams the bathroom door in my face.

I'm trying to figure out what the hell just happened when I swear the bottle of Cisco sitting on the table starts laughing at me.

I grab the bottle, looking at the label to see if "distilled belligerence" is tucked somewhere in the ingredients between the grapes and the sulfites. I walk into the kitchen, pour the remaining half bottle down the drain. My apologies to the bacteria in the sink, for they will soon be trying to beat the living shit out of one another.

CHAPTER FIFTY-SIX

Harper Donovan and I stand in the front room of my American Foursquare. "She's yours now," I say, handing her the house keys.

"Thanks, Hank."

Hatch and I moved out of the Broad Ripple house after Beth accepted my proposal. To save up for the wedding, I'm living with my mother in Empire Ridge and commuting to my job at College Avenue Press. Hatch didn't seem to care. He just packed up his shit and moved into a small loft apartment with Mack along the Broad Ripple canal that Mack has already nicknamed "Crack House" after the vagrants who mill around the canal looking for a score. My landowner waived the penalty for breaking our rental contract because I convinced Harper to take over the lease.

Whether by accident or fate, Harper and I have continued to keep in touch—the occasional run-in at a bar, a phone call every now and again to check in on each other—but our relationship, or whatever you want to call it, is long over. Though we didn't know it at the time, it ended that moment two years ago as Batman and Robin watched Harper's conical breasts and shaved snatch bounce up and down on me.

I actually tried to hook up with her one more time later that summer, right before Beth and I started dating. It was Skinemax night at Sanford & Son. I was watching soft-core porn and got struck by a fit of nostalgia. I called Harper, invited myself over to her place on Pennsylvania Avenue. She let me in, but she didn't let me *in*. While she had long since broken up with her high school sweetheart from Michigan, she was now in a long-distance relationship with some guy from New Jersey. We watched a movie. She went to bed. I showed myself out of Harper's apartment, and out of her life.

"You getting some roommates?"

"Yeah," Harper says, swinging the keys around her index finger. "Peter's going to move in with me. Maybe Lila, too."

Peter was a high school classmate of ours. A little on the odd side. Bad hair. Glasses that didn't go with his face. Not the best dresser, just came out of the closet, but a good guy as far as unfashionable homosexuals go. Delilah Prestwich, or "Lila" as we all call her, is Harper's half-Armenian best friend. Perfect skin, dark hair, big breasts, a gorgeous body hovering between the athletic and the voluptuous. Lila's parents moved to Empire Ridge right after high school. She went to college up in Indianapolis, so outside of me and Harper, she's largely steered clear of the Prep and Ridge social circles. She says she's Mormon, but I've seen Lila drunk enough times to know she's just going through the motions. In an alternate bachelor universe, I'd have hit on her years ago.

I make a motion for the door. "Tell Peter and Lila I said hello."

Harper looks at her watch. "They'll be here in about an hour. Why don't you tell them yourself?"

"Sorry," I say. "I'm already late meeting a couple friends out in Broad Ripple for dinner. We're going to hit the bars after that."

"Anyone I know?"

"Claire Sullivan and Derek Candela."

"Claire and Beth are pretty good friends, right?"

"Best friends."

"Speaking of whom, where is your new fiancée?"

"On vacation with her family."

"Still hard to believe you're getting married."

"Most of the time I don't believe it."

"When's the big date again?"

"August twelfth."

"So you still got a good year and a half to screw things up?"

"No, Harper. August twelfth, nineteen ninety-five."

"You mean this year?"

"Yep," I nod. "About four months from now."

"I suppose I can't talk you out of it."

"Correct me if I'm wrong, but your ship sailed to Jersey a long time ago." I say these words with a shameless, almost expectant flirtatiousness.

Harper leans in and kisses me on the cheek. "That it did, Hank."

I'm still attracted to Harper. As I open the front door to leave, a tiny rush of hormones courses through my body and reminds me of that attraction. "You guys think you'll make it out to Broad Ripple tonight?"

Harper shakes her head. "Probably not. I have a lot of unpacking to do. We might sit around and have a few cocktails, nothing too crazy."

"We'll be dancing at Mineshaft if you change your mind."

"I doubt I'll change my mind, but thanks for the invite."

"See ya, Harper."

"See ya, Hank."

I walk down the steps of my former porch. The front door swings open.

"I forget something?" I say.

"No," Harper answers. "Just wanted to extend my own personal invite if you get too drunk tonight."

"Your own *personal* invite?" I smirk.

"For a place to crash," Harper says. "Get your mind out of the gutter."

"I should be okay, but thanks again." I walk to my car, step on the street, and circle around to the driver's side door.

Harper follows me part of the way, stopping at the curb. "It's a long drive back to Empire Ridge. And you are prone to doing stupid-ass stunts, the least of which would be driving drunk. I've got photos, you know."

"That's not my gig anymore." I open my door, shouting over the roof of my car. "That's not *me* anymore."

"Nevertheless," Harper says, "the invitation still stands."

Claire and Derek are already drinking and halfway into a basket of garlic cheese bread when I show up at Bazbeaux. Turns out Claire and Derek don't like cheese as much as I do, so we pass on the Pizza Alla Quattro Formaggio and go with the barbecue chicken. We devour the pizza. Claire is the designated driver and drinks only two beers, but Derek and I still make it through the two buckets of Rolling Rock by the time we're out the door on our way to Mineshaft.

Mineshaft is a confection of loud music, bright lights, smoke machines, drink specials, and wannabe pickup artists. We carve out a spot near the end of the bar, close to the dance floor. I order a round of tequila for me and Derek. We are well on our way to a night of suspect music and even more suspect decisions.

"Come on, Derek," Claire says, holding out her hand. "Dance with me."

"Hold up," Derek says, turning to me. "Cheers, Hank."

We do our tequila shots. Derek and Claire disappear. I pull up a stool to the bar. Two hands side around my face and cup my eyes.

"Guess who," a female voice says from behind me.

I play along. "Blonde or brunette?"

"Brunette."

"Crotchless panties or magic underwear?"

Her hands slide off my face. "There's no need to be gross, Hank."

I turn just to catch Lila's round ass walking away from me, scolding me almost. I reach out and grab her hand. "Come on now, Lila. You know I'm kidding."

She turns. "Make it up to me, then. Buy me a drink."

A quick glance over to Claire. She and Derek are already on the opposite end of the dance floor. Already mangling the lyrics to Alanis Morissette's "You Oughta Know."

"Sure, why not." I give Lila the once-over. Her straight dark hair hangs loose over a short white dress that extends just below—and I do mean *just below*—her hips. "What's your potion?"

"Two kamikaze shots."

"Two?"

"One for me, one for you."

"Look, Lila. I probably shouldn't be—"

"Drinking with a friend?" Lila grabs another barstool, scoots up next to me.

"A friend who I'm attracted to."

"You're attracted to me? Since when?"

"Since Harper introduced us like three years ago."

"So why have you never hit on me?"

"Blame it on Harper. She's pretty much posted the 'No Fishing' sign around you. She doesn't want me corrupting you."

"Corrupting me?" Lila eyes the pack of Marlboro Lights on the bar, points to them. "Yours?"

"Nope," I say. "I quit a few months ago. I think they're the bartender's."

On cue, the bartender slides toward Lila. He grabs the hard pack, flips open the lid, and offers her a cigarette in one deft motion.

Lila pulls out one cigarette with her long fingers. The bartender immediately reaches out and lights the cigarette with a Zippo and a loaded smile. Lila inhales long and deep, then exhales the smoke through her nose. She leans her elbow on the bar. "Seriously, Hank. I'm a little disappointed here."

"Disappointed?" I hold two fingers in the air, nodding at the bartender. "Two kamikazes, please."

"Yeah."

"Why?"

"That you didn't try harder."

"Like I said, Harper didn't want me corrupt—"

"Oh, don't give me that bullshit." Lila exhales a puff of smoke. "You had your chance."

"When?"

"That night you showed up at the dorms for sex with Harper and she ended up being snowed in at her boyfriend's house and couldn't make it."

"That night you and I watched a movie together?"

"So you do remember?"

"I remember it being pretty innocent."

"Innocent? We watched the unrated version of *Wild Orchid*, and I wore a pink negligee."

"And I didn't hit on that?"

"No," Lila says. "You didn't."

"Sorry about that."

"You should be."

"How can I make it up to you?"

"You can help me set our parents up on a date."

If I didn't know Lila, I would think she's batshit crazy. But really, she's just a dreamer who believes in impossible things like fate and true love. Her mother was a nurse who fell asleep at the wheel driving home after a twenty-four-hour shift. Ever since Harper told Lila how my father died, Lila believes our parents are destined to be together simply because they were both widowed by automobile accidents. There's one flaw in Lila's master plan: her father is Mormon, and my mother is Catholic.

"Yeah, Lila. I'll get right on that."

"You just need to give my dad a chance."

"No I don't."

"Two kamikaze shots," the bartender says, rescuing us from ourselves. He sets down two large glasses of vodka, Triple Sec, and Rose's Lime Juice that are clearly doubles.

Lila is the first to raise her glass. "To the soon-to-be-married man."

I nod, raise my glass. "To great friends."

We drink our shots, slam our glasses down on the bar. I wipe my mouth. "So you're living with Harper now?"

"Just for the summer," Lila says. "Heading for New York in the fall."

"Work?"

"Postgraduate studies at NYU."

"What are you studying?"

"Getting my MFA in Creative Writing."

"I'm jealous."

"You're jealous of someone drowning in debt for a worthless post-graduate degree just for the privilege of not making any money?"

I shouldn't grab Lila's hand, but I do it anyway. I shouldn't rub my thumb up and down her hand and then give it an affirming squeeze, but I do it anyway. I shouldn't wink and say, "Something tells me you of all people will find a way to make it work," but I do it anyway. An attention whore? A guy who likes the smell of a pretty girl? A glutton for punishment? All of the above.

The DJ spins Alanis into Salt-N-Pepa's "Whatta Man."

Lila takes my hand. "Dance with me, Hank."

"No way," I say, almost too quickly.

"That's an order, not a request."

Claire and Derek have disappeared in the crowd, so I let the half-dozen Rolling Rock and two kamikaze shots do my talking for me. "Okay, one dance, but under one condition."

"What's that?"

"Get your story straight." I grab Lila by the waist, pulling her off her bar stool and onto the dance floor. "You were wearing a peach negligee."

One dance led to two. Two dances led to three. We were about halfway into Boyz II Men's "I'll Make Love to You" when Lila Prestwich and I started making out. I don't know if Lila instigated the kiss or if I instigated the kiss. But that's not important.

The fact Claire was watching me kiss her? Yeah, that's probably important.

CHAPTER FIFTY-SEVEN

I wake up with a monster hangover. I'm in my old bedroom on College Avenue. And I'm in bed with Harper and Lila.

"Morning," Harper says to my right, her head resting on my chest. "How's the head treating you today?"

Lila rolls toward me on my left side. Still asleep, she lifts her arm around me.

"Harper…what did I…what did you…what did we do? I don't know what happened last night, but I—"

"But you need to relax is what you need to do."

"Relax?" I say.

"Look under the covers," Harper says. "See anything unusual?"

I lift up the covers. "No."

"Exactly. You're fully clothed from head to toe."

"Wh-what happened to me?"

"Apparently you stumbled the entire ten blocks from Broad Ripple at two in the morning. I'm surprised your ass didn't get mugged. You stormed into the house crying about kissing Lila, and then you passed out on my bed. In lieu of sleeping on stacks of cardboard boxes, Lila and I slept here with you. And I do mean *slept*."

"I wish I could say that comes as a relief." I jump up out of the bed. Fuck, my head hurts.

"What's the big deal, Hank?"

"The big deal, Harper, is that I'm a ticking time bomb. I'm a ticking time bomb with a penis hardwired to fuck things up."

"You and your penis time bomb are being a tad melodramatic."

I grab Harper's hand with an exaggerated shake. "Hi, have we met? My name's Hank Fitzpatrick, the guy you had consensual sex with for three years *while* we were dating other people."

"But that's not you anymore. You said so yourself."

"Yeah, and last night I kissed Lila, and then I slept in the same bed with two girls I am extremely attracted to while miraculously not fooling around with either of them. The law of averages says I don't have too many of those miracles in my pocket."

"You're *extremely* attracted to me?" Lila says, apparently awake.

"Go back to sleep, Lila," I say.

CHAPTER FIFTY-EIGHT

"Hank, this is Leon Ramsey. Leon, this is my son, Henry David."

Leon extends his hand. "Hello, Henry. If you don't mind, I prefer Mr. Ramsey."

So much for first impressions. I take his hand in mine, squeezing a little too hard. The tops of his hands are exceedingly hairy, sticking out of his plaid oxford shirt in brown tufts like Michael J. Fox in *Teen Wolf.* I am reminded of a review I read for its uninspired sequel, *Teen Wolf Too* starring Jason Bateman. I think it was in *The Washington Post.* It said teen werewolf and vampire movies exist as "metaphors for preadolescents who are about to turn into adults—monsters just like their parents." Ain't that the fucking truth?

"Well, Mr. Ramsey, you can just call me Hank."

Mom invited me down to Empire Ridge tonight to meet her latest and not-so-greatest boyfriend, Leon Ramsey. This clown makes me miss even Tom the Spandex Love Machine, although he might be better than Marky Mark, the corporate pilot who was only three years older than me. I had a soft spot for Robert Ware, the assistant football coach from Prep who insisted Jeanine and I call him "B-ware."

Where to begin with Leon? For one thing, he's an ugly son of a bitch. His hair is a sad grayish-brown color, like a dead carp. Instead of a tangible chin, he has folds of skin covered in a patchy beard that runs from his upper lip to his chest and makes his face look like a big vagina. Mom told me he teaches economics at IU's Empire Ridge campus, that he's an atheist, and that he doesn't like kids but he loves his two Siamese cats, Ayn and Rand. Fucking perfect.

Leon, Mom, Jack, and I sit down for dinner. Mom cooks everyone chicken, save for Leon. He doesn't eat chicken because the smell of white meats—chicken, pork, and fish, but not turkey burgers—makes him gag. Mom grills him a large New York Strip that costs more than the rest of our meal put together.

I don't like Leon and can feel myself itching for a fight, so I turn to face the only person in the room whose company I can tolerate. "How's my big and bad first grader?"

"Good," Jack says.

"You like school?"

"Yep."

"You like your teachers?"

"Yep."

"You have a girlfriend yet?"

"Noooo!"

"You like anybody?"

"Noooo!"

"What's your favorite class?"

"Recess."

"Recess?" Leon says, dropping his fork and knife on his plate in mid-cut. "As stimulating as this conversation is, could we kindly have a little peace and quiet during our meal?"

Jack look downs at his plate, as if he's been scolded by Leon before. I wipe my mouth with my napkin and turn to face him. "Excuse me, *Leon*?"

"Hank, what he's trying to say is—"

"Debbie," Leon interrupts. "I can fight my own battles, thank you very much."

"Then do it," I say.

"All I'm asking is to come home from a long day of work and not have to—"

"Home? This isn't your fuhh-freaking home."

"Good job saying 'freaking,' Hank," Jack says.

His squeaky voice is like a good fart joke, an irresistible force that disarms me instantly. How can I possibly stay mad with those dimples staring at me? I ruffle his hair. "Thanks for the support, little buddy."

"No problem."

I look down at Jack's plate. "Why don't you eat your asparagus?"

"I hate asparagus," Jack says. "It makes my pee smell."

"You'll eat it and like it," Leon says.

"Yeah," I say. "This conversation is over. Jack, give me your plate."

I stand up from the dining room table and take Jack's plate to the kitchen. I rinse off his dish and put it in the sink. Like a miniature shadow, Jack follows me into the entryway.

"And just what do you think you're doing?" Leon says. Mom sits beside him quietly, her usual straight-lipped and vacant-eyed self.

"I'm taking Jack for some pizza," I say, opening the front door. "And getting the freak out of this freaked-up house."

"You will not—"

"The hell I will, Leon."

I notice Jack arch his eyebrows. "Hank, you said H-E-L-L."

"Head outside, little buddy, I'll be out in a sec. I need to have a grown-up talk with Leon."

I shut the door behind Jack, turning back to the room. Mom still sits at the kitchen table in silence. Leon is standing, red-faced.

"What's wrong, Leon?" I say.

"I have never been disrespected like that."

"I find that hard to believe. Someone as miserable and as unlikable as you?"

"Hank, please," Debbie says.

I bow. "Oh, welcome to the party, Mom."

"You just need to get to know Leon."

"No, what I need is a strong mother. What I need is someone who doesn't whore herself out to the first man who shows her affection. What I need is someone who doesn't waltz into our lives and presume to be a patriarch. Newsflash, Leon—the position is filled, you stupid fucking cocksucker."

Leon steps around the table and makes a move toward me. I raise my finger, pointing at him. "Better be sure, asshole. You lay a hand on me, and I will thoroughly enjoy driving my fist through the back of your head."

CHAPTER FIFTY-NINE

Claire never told my fiancée about Lila. With the notable exceptions of my slipping my tongue down a half-Armenian Mormon's throat and Vagina Head's continued courtship of my mother, it's been a blissful few months.

Beth graduated from Illinois at the end of May. That same month, we signed a lease on a house in Rocky Ripple, an incorporated river town of hippies just northeast of Butler's campus. I was promoted from assistant editorial director to editorial director at College Avenue Press, and Beth got a job teaching gymnastics at a private club after her first day at the hospital confirmed everything she hated about clinicals: being around death isn't for her. Beth's dad still isn't over the quitting nursing thing, but her mom is so supportive of the whole living-in-sin arrangement she helped us move. Being the devout, condoms-and-cohabitation-for-everyone, Vatican II Catholic that she is—not to mention too hopped up on narcotics to give a shit—my mother of course gave us the hearty thumbs up.

Beth has her face buried in one of her five hundred wedding magazines. I'm trying to wrap up a phone conversation with Hatch, about a third of which Beth hears thanks to Hatch's booming voice that dominates conversations even from the other end of a telephone line.

"If you need anything, call me," I say.

Beth puts down her magazine. "Don't know what you were talking about, but it sounded ominous. What's up with Hatch?"

I hang up the phone. "You don't want to know."

"Sure I do," Beth says, her curiosity genuine. Somehow, she and Hatch have become civil acquaintances if not friends.

"Apparently, Hatch went on a bender after we got engaged and I broke the lease on our apartment. He said he pretty much bottomed out the night he went bar-hopping in downtown Indy and woke up the next day in Buckhead not knowing how he got there."

"Buckhead? As in Atlanta, Georgia?"

I nod. "He woke up in a strange woman's bed, went out for some air, and actually said to her, 'When did Indianapolis get so fucking humid?'"

"Jesus."

"But wait, it gets better. Hatch gets in his car and then drives back to Indy and straight into rehab."

"Rehab?" Beth says. "What kind of rehab?"

"AA," I answer. "He's been clean and sober for six months."

"Six months? And this is the first you've heard of it?"

"I told you we had lost touch."

"But six months? If it was my friend, I'd have been worried."

"We're dudes," I say. "Most of our mistakes come down to the fact that we just don't pay attention."

Beth puts down her wedding magazine. "You know what? Good for Hatch. We should throw a party for him to celebrate."

"Uh, yeah. That's not gonna happen."

"It'll be fun, Hank. No booze. Just some good movies and good friends."

"I can already tell you Hatch won't be able to make it," I say.

"Why?" Beth says.

"Hatch enlisted in the Navy."

"You're pulling my leg."

"Finished the twelve-step program and then went straight to boot camp. Says he's hoping to get sent to Bangkok and check out some Thai hookers."

"Now that sounds more like Hatch," Beth says, sorting through the pounds of wedding-related parcels on our coffee table.

"How many invites we get back?"

"Most of them," Beth says.

"How many are coming?"

"Most of them." She holds a nearly square envelope up to the ceiling lights, trying to see through it. "Hey, what's this?"

"What's what?"

"A letter addressed to you," Beth says. "No return address. Looks like a wedding invitation or something. Anyone we know getting married?"

"I don't think so," I say. "Open it."

Beth opens the envelope. She removes the card, reads it aloud. "Dear Mr. Fitzpatrick, thank you for your condolences. Regards, Tammy Elliot and Laura Powell."

"What?" I say. "That's all it says?"

"Who are Tammy Elliot and Laura Powell?"

"That's fucking bullshit!"

"Uh, Hank?" Beth raises her hand. "Remember me? Your fiancée here, a little concerned about her soon-to-be husband being all cryptic about a card from two mystery women."

"Sorry," I say, I grabbing the card from Beth in disbelief. "No mystery here. Powell is Laura's married name. Tammy is her mother."

"Laura Elliot? Your ex-girlfriend?"

"Whatever," I say, handing Beth the note. "It's no big deal."

"Condolences?"

"Arthur died of a heart attack a couple weeks ago."

"Laura's father?"

"Yep."

"I'm sorry."

"Me too. And I wrote her what I thought was a pretty nice letter. I told her I knew what she was going through and said she could call me anytime to talk about it. I told her what a good man Arthur was and how I thought he would have been an awesome grand…"

"What's that?"

"Nothing," I say, catching myself. "You're not mad?"

"Why would I be mad?"

"Because I didn't tell you about the letter. I sure as hell felt guilty about it."

"She used to be an important part of your life, Hank. And now she's going through something you have a uniquely personal perspective on. I'd be disappointed if you *didn't* write her a thoughtful letter."

"Really?"

"Hank, your ex-girlfriend sent you a generic thank you card. So what? Where was your head at when your dad died?"

"There's more to it than that, Beth."

"Then what is it about?"

I want to tell Beth that Laura is more than an ex-girlfriend. She was more than just my first love. She's the spurned mother of my first-born son, like that Virgin Mary statue all Catholic boys treasure for the first decade of their lives only to stash away once they hit puberty and religion becomes spectacularly uncool. In the two years since Laura and Mom told me I was my brother's father, I've mailed Laura three large envelopes stuffed with pictures of Jack and some of his drawings from school. She never wrote me back until today. Laura has always worn guilt well.

"Can we sit down for a second?" I say. "I need to tell you something. You deserve to know before we get married."

"Sure," Beth says.

We walk into the living room and sit down on the couch. Beth reaches over and grabs my hand. "Hank, I—"

"Please, let me finish before I chicken out."

"But I—"

"I told Laura in the letter that I always thought Arthur would have been an awesome grandfather."

"That's a sweet to thing to say, given what you and Laura went through."

"You mean the abortion?"

"Should I mean anything else?"

"Yeah, about that. See, the thing is, that's not exactly how it all went down. When I talk about Arthur being an awesome grandfather, I'm not speaking metaphorically. There's no easy way for me to say this, so here it goes."

Beth is still holding my hand. I look at the analog clock on the wall. The second hand ticks menacingly. My throat starts to close.

"Laura faked her abortion," I say, finally. "She carried her baby to term, and then my mother secretly adopted the baby. My brother, Jack, is actually—"

"Your son," Beth says. "I know."

I stand up, shake her hand loose. "Excuse me?"

"A part of me has always known, or at least suspected. The way you look at him, the way you act around him. Your paternal instinct just kicks in. You can't help yourself."

"Beth, being fatherly is a long way from being *a father*. There's no way you could have known unless—"

"Your mom told me."

"She didn't."

"She did and she didn't."

"Huh?"

"Remember last fall when you were at the book fair in New York?"

"Vaguely."

"And I called telling you I went out to dinner with your mother and she had a bad reaction to her medication."

"Rings a bell," I say. "Was that the time she chased three Class IV Narcotics with a vodka gimlet?"

Beth nods. "Bingo."

"You said she signed her home address instead of her name on her credit card bill and that she started—"

"Speaking in tongues. Exactly."

"And I take it you understood at least some of what she was saying?"

"It was all slurred gibberish at first. The restaurant manager almost called an ambulance. But eventually I got her stabilized with a little food and water. I got her back home, put her in bed, and that's when she started becoming a little more lucid. When I was tucking her in she said to me, 'Beth, I always knew you'd be a better mother for Jack.'"

"What did you say?"

"What do you think I said? I told her I could never replace her as Jack's mother. And then she put her hand on my face and said, 'I'm not talking about me. I'm talking about Jack's real mother, Laura.'"

"And then what happened?"

"She passed out."

"I'm so sorry, Beth." I sit back down on the couch, grab my fiancée's hands. I raise them to my lips and kiss them. "Why didn't you say anything to me after you found out?"

"I had no way of knowing."

"Knowing what?"

"If you even knew," Beth says. "And I sure as hell wasn't going to be the one who told you."

"So you're not mad at me?"

"Well, of course I'm a little upset you didn't trust me enough to tell me earlier, but I can't fault you for keeping it from me. The fewer people who know, especially in a gossipy town like Empire Ridge, the less chance there is it gets back to Jack. You need to tell him on your terms. I get that."

"And if the day comes when he lives under our roof as my son?"

"Then I'll welcome *our* son into *our* home with open arms. Hell, I'd do the same for Jack even if he were your brother. That's what you do for people you lo—"

I cut her last sentence off. When all else fails, kissing a girl shuts her up faster than anything else.

Beth's lips purse around my own. She relaxes, backs away. "Like I said, I don't want you feeling guilty about writing a letter to Laura. This is the type of crap married couples or very nearly married couples are supposed to talk to each other about."

"So you're giving me permission to write letters to ex-girlfriends behind your back?"

"I didn't say that." Beth puts her wine down, points to our bedroom door.

"What?" I say.

"Get in that room right now, smartass!"

"Why?"

"Because I'm going to tie you up, rip your clothes off, and then proceed to punch you in the balls a few hundred times."

"If you don't mind," I say, "I'd just settle for a cold, dispassionate grudge fuck at my expense."

"I'm sure you would."

Like I said, with the notable exceptions of my slipping my tongue down a half-Armenian Mormon's throat, Vagina Head's continued courtship of my mother, and telling my fiancée I have a secret love child, it's been a blissful few months. As Beth throws me on the bed, strips me naked, ties me up with four silk scarves, and drizzles hot candle wax onto my nipples, I feel like everything is going to be okay. There's no way I'm fucking things up.

CHAPTER SIXTY

I'm fucking things up.

The guys at work decided this morning to take me out for "lingerie lunch" at Legzz, a seedy strip club down on Meridian Street. A mini-bachelor party, they called it. We left the office at noon. It's now three o'clock. All of us—me, Aaron, Chuck, and Hector—are anywhere from slightly tipsy (Aaron, he's Jewish, and a lightweight) to quite nearly tanked (that would be yours truly, the bachelor).

Aaron Rosner is the publisher of College Avenue Press. An import from West Bloomfield, Michigan, with eyes too small for his face and a head of tight curls, he's the only Jew I know in Indianapolis. His close relationship with the Borders corporate office up in Ann Arbor—I think he's sleeping with the fiction buyer—has almost singlehandedly kept us in the black. Aaron's real claim to fame is that he was the high school classmate (confirmed) and childhood friend (alleged) of Elizabeth Berkley from *Saved by the Bell*. He reminds me of this incessantly, to the point where I've started calling him "Jessie" or "Spano" as the mood suits me. Rounding out the trio are College Avenue's sales and marketing director, Chuck Gill, and Chuck's dark-haired, vaguely George Clooney–looking roommate, Hector Rush.

"A toast to Jimmy Chitwood," Hector says. That's his nickname for me. It's an ironic reference to my lack of basketball skills. Hector never fucking shuts up. He's the media relations director at the US Hardcourt Championships in downtown Indianapolis, and over the last half hour I've learned more than I have ever wanted to know about professional men's tennis. In no particular order: Jim Courier generally keeps to himself, Bud Collins drinks beer during rain delays, Goran Ivanisevic loves to go clubbing, and Stefan Edberg is a nice guy who practices perpetually with his shirt off in front of the ladies.

"How about just a toast to bachelors?" Chuck says.

We hold our beers up. "To bachelors!" we shout.

Hector slaps a ten-dollar bill on the table. I eye it skeptically. I've avoided the customary lap dance up until now. "I thought you said you didn't have any bucks to tuck?"

Hector smiles. "I saved one for you, Chitwood." He signals a dancer to approach.

The lunch crowd at Legzz is comprised of escapist truckers and second-shift factory workers getting a buzz on before they clock in. The clientele is reflected in the dancers, a cast of toothless, stringy-haired drug addicts with bad skin. The one who approaches me has no breasts, no ass, and even worse, no calves. She's wearing a cowboy hat and cowboy boots along with G-string panties, all of which suit the song, Bon Jovi's "Wanted Dead or Alive."

"A dance for the bachelor?" she asks, straddling me.

"If you'd be so kind," Hector says. He reaches over, stuffs the ten-dollar bill down the front of her panties.

Aaron, Chuck, and Hector are laughing their asses off. I can honestly say this is one of those rare times I'm not enjoying a mostly naked woman writhing on top of me. She's ugly, but not as ugly as we are. I miss Beth, but I don't miss being this guy.

CHAPTER SIXTY-ONE

I pull into my driveway. It's six o'clock, and I'm mostly sobered up. Beth is standing on the front porch smoking a cigarette. She smells of cheap wine and belligerence.

"How was work?"

"Work," I say. "Work was good."

"What'd you do today?"

"Nothing."

"You sure about that?"

"Yes."

"So, if I happened to run into one of your coworkers at Target earlier today, and if she happened to tell me, 'I can't believe you're letting those guys take Hank to a strip club,' you'd deny that, too?"

"Shit," I say.

"Yeah, shit is right. *You're* a shit."

Beth hates strip clubs. *Hates* them. I think it all goes back to my "I fooled around with a stripper last night" comment right before we started dating, which thereafter planted this notion in Beth's head that (a) all strippers fool around with their customers and (b) I possess some kind of preternatural attraction to strippers, neither of which is remotely true. Last month, when Mack orchestrated a weekend rafting trip in West Virginia for my bachelor party, Beth told me the wedding was off if she heard there were strippers. Mack had wanted to get a couple of West Virginia's finest to show up at our campsite, but that fell through—thankfully—at the last second.

"The wedding's off," Beth says.

"What?"

"You heard me."

"It was the guys' idea. I didn't know about it until today."

"And I assume they knocked you unconscious and dragged you to the strip club?"

"No."

"That's the only acceptable excuse."

"It was no big deal."

"You know how I feel about those places."

"It was a joke. The women are grotesque there."

"I bet they are."

"No, really. The place is called Legzz. It's a dump. I'll take you there. If you can find me one attractive girl in the place, I'll give you a hundred bucks."

"That's not the point."

"Then what *is* the point?"

"For one, you think tucking dollar bills in ugly women's G-strings is funny. What's that say about your respect for women overall?"

"Oh, come on, Beth."

Beth starts to cry. "But more importantly, you just stood in front of me, five days before our fucking wedding day, and lied straight to my face."

Beth grabs her keys and makes like she's leaving.

"Where do you think you're going?" I ask.

"Out."

"Out where?"

"To get drunk maybe. Maybe I'll even hook up with The Tool."

"Beth, please." I grab her hand, take her keys away from her. "I messed up, and I'm sorry. I'm sorry I went there. I'm sorry I lied to you about it."

"Why *now*, Hank? Why *today*? You know what I did today? I started packing for our wedding and our honeymoon. There isn't a day that goes by where I'm not messing with some detail about this wedding. It's all I think about. *You* are all I think about."

"And you're all I think about, too," I say, but it comes across as reactive rather than heartfelt.

"Evidently not," Beth says. She grabs the door with her free hand, opens it.

"Where are you going to go without your car keys?" I ask.

"I'll fucking walk."

"No you won't."

"Watch me."

I slam the door shut with my forearm, squeeze Beth's hand hard. Maybe a little too hard. "Beth, this is what couples who've been together for a while do. They fuck things up sometimes. And they don't leave to avoid confrontation, or go crying to mommy, or kick their significant other in the shin. They work it out. I didn't want to be there. Yes, I could've said no, but I didn't, and that's all on me. But the whole time I was there, I was..."

"You were what?" Beth says.

"I don't know...sad, I guess."

"How much of a fool do you think I am, Hank?"

"I'm being dead serious. I was sad for me, sad for the girls on stage, sad for letting you down."

"But you didn't know I had found out yet."

"Just me knowing was enough." I point back and forth between us. "I signed up for the long haul with us."

Beth's arm goes noticeably slack. "So these girls were grotesque?"

"Hideous."

Beth lets go of the doorknob, turns around. "I still would really like to kick you in the shin right now."

I reach down, raise my pants leg. "Go ahead. One free shot."

"I have a better idea."

"What's that?"

"I got a list of follow-up calls to make for the wedding." Beth reaches down to the veneer desk just to the right of the door. She picks up a piece of paper, hands it to me. "Why don't you make the calls?"

I grab the list. I bite my lip, wincing. "Sure you don't want to just kick me or have some angry makeup sex?"

"You and your libido."

"I'd like to think I'm pretty normal."

"Normal?" Beth says.

"Yeah."

"Since when is a compulsively masturbating sex addict who lies to his fiancée about going to strip clubs classified as 'normal?'"

I raise my hand. "I'll take hyperbole for eight hundred dollars, Alex."

"What did you say to me the very first time I told you I wasn't in the mood?"

"You remember that?"

"Well, you've said it a few times since then."

"Well, you've not been in the mood a few times since—"

"Just answer the question, Hank."

"I said, 'I'm going to have an orgasm every day with or without you, so you might as well be along for the ride.'"

"Okay then, if you could have only one superpower, what would it be?"

"That's not fair, Beth. The last time we had this discussion, we weren't even dating yet."

"*What* superpower?"

"Invisibility," I say, sighing. "I would want to be invisible."

"And why is that?"

"So I could spend my days hanging out in the showers of hot chicks."

"And when you board an airplane, what's the one thing you look for?"

"Now you're just taking stuff out of context."

"It's a simple question, dear fiancé. What's the one thing you hope for when you get on a plane?"

I shake my head, powerless. "I hope there's an attractive woman sitting next to me."

"And why oh why would you do that?"

"Because I want to know that if the plane starts to crash, there's a chance I might have sex with her right before I die."

"That's not normal, Hank."

I look at my watch, a beat-up digital Timex I've had since *Playboy* published those naked photos of Madonna as brunette with armpit hair. "Considering we'll be husband and wife in less than one hundred and twenty hours, you don't have whole lot of time to figure if you want to be abnormal with me."

CHAPTER SIXTY-TWO

While Mom again felt there was a certain grandeur lacking in a thirty-year-old church that looked like a limestone IHOP, we nonetheless decided to have the wedding at St. Benjamin. St. Isadore downtown is where I buried my father, and I intend to give it that lone distinction. I will never again step inside that church.

Our wedding photographer is a dead ringer for Kenny Rogers. He was Dad's roommate at Notre Dame. At this precise moment, I think I hate him.

"And we're done, gentlemen," Kenny says. "See you inside."

The pre-wedding photos are done roughly ninety minutes after they started. Even by Indiana standards, the humidity is withering. The heat index is pushing one hundred degrees. The groomsmen head into the air-conditioned confines of St. Benjamin. In need of a moment to myself, I decide to hang outside for a few minutes.

"Hank, can I talk to you?"

He approaches me from the bushes, lying in wait. He looks awful, a good twenty pounds lighter since I last saw him. His once salt and pepper hair has faded into a washed-out gray. He's wearing blue jeans beneath an untucked short-sleeved plaid button-up shirt. Nervous sweat visibly blooming from his armpits. As always, he smells of cheap aftershave and cigarettes.

"*Mitch…*" I spit his name more than I say it. "What in God's name are you doing here?"

"Nervous?" he says, reaching for my arm.

I take a step back. "Why would I be nervous? The people I can trust in my life are few and far between. Being able to give myself to one of these rare individuals is a gift."

"I suppose I deserved that."

"This isn't about deserving anything, Uncle Mitch. Now is not the time for us to have this conversation. This is my wedding day. Are you really that delusional and self-absorbed to think you can presume to wash away your sins on today of all days?"

"You just called me 'uncle' again. I like that, Hank. I like that a lot." Uncle Mitch smiles, reaches to me again, but this time I don't back away. I let him grab my arm. He squeezes, smiles even bigger. A part of me is afraid of him. A part of me feels sorry for him. A part of me hates him. A part of me loves him. I start to smile.

Really? A smile? Fuck that! I tug my arm loose. I back away from him. "Again, why are you here?"

"Ask me, Hank."

"Ask you what?"

"Ask me why I did it."

"I don't want to know why you did it."

"It's my penance," Uncle Mitch says, his eyes moistening with tears. "I have to tell you. I have to acknowledge my moral weakness to those whom I've aggrieved and accept your anger and hopefully your forgiveness."

My fist connects with his nose before I realize I'm even throwing it. Uncle Mitch falls to one knee. The years of repression and guilt channeled into the hardest punch I've ever thrown.

"There's my anger," I say. "Your forgiveness is waiting for you in hell, you goddamn motherfucker. This is still about you and your satisfaction. You're not looking for penance. You're just looking for another fucking orgasm."

I turn. Uncle Mitch reaches out and grabs my hand. Just as I raise my opposing closed fist for another blow to his face, he places something in my palm. It's a familiar gold Tissot watch with a brown alligator leather band. My father's watch.

"Your mom gave this to me when John died," Uncle Mitch says. "But it belongs to you."

I take the watch in my hand. I walk away without acknowledging his gesture.

CHAPTER SIXTY-THREE

I'm petrified. The pre-ceremony pint of blackberry brandy that Mack made me drink served only to make me drunk and petrified. Two blackberry-smelling beads of sweat roll parallel down my body from each armpit. My stomach isn't helping. I try to concentrate on bending my knees. If they lock up on me, I'm dropping hard.

The groomsmen fan out behind Father Fish. With Beth being an only child and me only having one sibling, we struggled to fill out the wedding party. My groomsmen are Aaron Rosner and Mack, while Beth's bridesmaids are Claire and my sister Jeanine. Mack is best man, serving as Hatch's stand-in while he's doing God-knows-what to a Thai prostitute. Claire is the maid of honor, and still uncomfortably attractive. The groomsmen and I stand at attention, hands clasped behind our backs, just like we practiced at rehearsal last night. True to form, Mack forgets and folds his hands in front. I elbow him, eyeing his hands.

What? Mack mouths.

"Your hands," I say through gritted teeth and a half smile.

"Oh," Mack says, gritting his teeth and wincing. "I forgot."

Aaron meets Jeanine halfway down the aisle, escorting my sister to her seat. Kenny Rogers snaps a shot of both bridesmaids as they enter the church. The best man and maid of honor, Mack and Claire, are next. Mack meets Claire halfway down the aisle, escorting her all the way to the altar. Separating in front of Father, they both wink at me.

Jack is up. He's the ring bearer. We don't have a flower girl, not that it seems to faze this six-year-old. "*Walk slowly,*" we all told him last night. "*This isn't a race.*"

He listens to our advice. I'm guessing he covers the length of the church in about twice the time it took the entire wedding party. Jack gets to me and smiles. I smile back. As I give him the thumbs up, I look at my father's watch on my wrist. I'm proud of Jack and maybe even a little proud of myself.

The trumpets go silent.

The rustling of wedding programs. Someone coughs.

Wagner explodes out of the pipe organ. Everyone stands.

The double doors at the back of the church open wide. I see Beth on her father's arm. The hairs on the back of my neck stand on end. But I'm not nervous. I don't feel sick or even faint anymore.

Usually when a moment is bigger than me, it involves someone getting hurt, someone dying, someone getting buried. But not today. This is living. This is me rising up, spitting the dirt out of my mouth, and telling my demons to kiss my ass. I'm not one for religious moments, but if this is what true grace feels like, sign me the fuck up.

Beth looks radiant. Her dress is simple but elegant. The top of the dress is off the shoulders, slowly dipping to a V in the front with a hint of embroidery and beading. Her bouquet is made of white and peach roses to tie in to the color of the bridal party's dresses.

Did I mention she looks radiant?

Father Fish steps forward into the aisle. I follow him. We meet Beth and her father just as the music stops. Mom stands in the pew next to us. I'm the only one who seems to notice her wobbling.

Mom is intoxicated. She's wearing an inappropriately white dress of course, accessorized by an oversized strand of pearls that gives her a flapper throwback look—and not in a good way. Beth caught her this morning chasing a couple Darvocet down with a pitcher of mimosas. Several people have asked me why Leon decided not to come to the wedding. My answer to all of them has been, "Because he's a dick."

Father folds his arms, careful not to bump his cordless microphone. "Deborah," he says to my mother, "you and..."

The pause we all knew would come.

"...your husband, John Fitzpatrick, gave life and love to your son Hank. You watched him grow into manhood. Today, he's chosen to marry. I ask that you accept his choice of a bride into your own family, that you give your blessing to him as he continues life now in a very different way, that you give consent to this marriage."

Father extends his hand, palm up, and bows his head. Mom says, "We do."

Father Fish smiles when Mom says "we." He turns to his right, walks a couple steps until he's halfway between Beth's parents. "Joan and Stan," he says, "you gave Beth life and love. You taught her how to get along in this world. And also, today, she has chosen to marry Hank. I ask that you now give your blessing of her choice of a husband, and that your home will always be open to your daughter and your future son-in-law."

Joan and Dr. Burke say, "We do."

Father steps back toward the center of the aisle. "And now, Stan, I ask that you offer your daughter's hand in marriage."

Dr. Burke kisses his daughter. He turns to me, nods. We hug.

The gesture is scripted. Dr. Burke and I had been working on it since last night. He came up with the idea at the rehearsal dinner, saying to me, *"A hug instead of a handshake would add something special to the moment, don't you think?"*

I said, "Sounds like a plan to me, Dr. Burke," if only because it seemed more appropriate than, *I'm a not-so-closet narcissist about to experience a day in which I'll be overshadowed to an almost obscene degree, and you're asking me if I'd mind making a play for the spotlight?*

The hug is perfectly executed: a firm backslapper in which we each bury our head in the other's opposite shoulder. I can even hear the muffled *awwwwwwws* in the crowd.

Stan puts his daughter's hand in mine.

Beth smiles at me, her hand shaking a little. I look into her eyes, but of course stray down to her cleavage. A single strand of pearls and two matching pearl teardrop earrings offset her tanning bed–bronzed skin. I give her hand a squeeze. I look back into her eyes, winking at her.

There's a pause. A brief moment of silence. I can hear my father's watch ticking.

CHAPTER SIXTY-FOUR

The wedding party pulls up to the reception in the limousine, a stretch Cadillac Deville. I help Beth out of the limo. A guy wearing a white oxford with rolled-up sleeves, a black tie, and earphones walks up to us. I guess him to be the DJ.

The ceremony was a blur. What did I say? What did Beth say? I remembered Jeanine serenading us with a stirring rendition of "Edelweiss," but that's only because I heard her practicing the song at the rehearsal. Didn't Beth's cousin give one of the readings? Yeah, that's right. The unemployed thespian cousin as opposed to the heavily medicated celebrity vegan chef cousin who introduced me to Woody Harrelson.

Woody had come back to his alma mater, Hanover College, to star in a play called *The Diviners*. I cornered him at the cast party at the buffet table. He was wearing a tall cowboy hat to compensate for the fact he was much shorter (and much balder) in person than he appeared to be on camera. We talked while shoving handfuls of pan-fried tofu in our mouths. I couldn't recall a word I said to Woody. Much like my own fucking wedding.

All I genuinely recall is looking into Beth's eyes and putting things on cruise control for about an hour. In the limousine ride to the reception I asked Mack—*three times*—if he and I remembered to sign the wedding license.

"Yep, we signed it…" Mack said. "Still."

Beth and I decided to have the reception at Beaver Stick Golf Club, a refined but understated club overlooking "one of America's premier public golf courses." I don't golf, so I'm impressed merely to the degree Beaver Stick affords Beth and our wedding guests a nice backdrop for getting hammered. The clubhouse is a contemporary design—clean lines, a gray-shingled roof broken up by white columns, walls of glass surrounded on three sides by an expansive redwood deck pitted by golf spikes.

"Just count to sixty and then come inside," the DJ says to us, his pocket already lined with a fifty I spotted him in exchange for a promise that he not play "The Chicken Dance" under any circumstance.

The glass walls of Beaver Stick, an anemic air conditioning system, and a guest list thirty percent longer than the fire department legally mandates for this particularly sized building conspires with the one hundred-degree heat index to turn our reception into an oven. My mother-in-law walks around with a linen napkin filled with ice cubes, massaging the necks of the older folks. The younger folks—well, they're just drinking themselves into an oblivious stupor.

"Again, I apologize." I tip the manager a fifty as he starts to walk away from me. "Thanks for being so understanding."

"What was that about?" Beth asks.

"No big deal," I say, sipping on my third or fourth beer in the last half hour. "Somebody got busted peeing off the balcony."

"Already?" Beth swipes my beer, tilts the pint glass into her mouth. She hands the glass back to me. "That's not a good sign."

I set my beer down, take her hand in mine. "You ready?"

"Does my answer really matter at this point?" Beth says.

We thought long and hard about what our first dance together would be. We thought about being sentimental old fools. But honestly, how do multiple generations of newlywed couples continue latching on to "Unforgettable," "What a Wonderful World," and "Unchained Melody" and still with a straight face call their wedding song *special*?

Beth and I had no recourse. I escort her to the dance floor. The DJ pops the CD in the player.

With a little love, and some tenderness…

Damn straight. Hootie and the fucking Blowfish, baby!

For seemingly as long as Beth and I've been dating, there's been Hootie. We loved Hootie before anyone else loved Hootie. We never get tired of Hootie. I pledge to get some Hootie from Beth while she's still wearing her wedding dress. It's an hour's drive up to the airport hotel. We'll have a couple glasses of champagne, feed each other chocolate-covered strawberries. I'll casually raise the privacy window between us and the limo driver. Then I will slip my hands beneath her dress and—

"What are you thinking about?" Beth asks.

"Hootie," I say.

In the wake of the BoDeans's breakout hit "Closer to Free," people forget that Hootie and the Blowfish's "Hold My Hand" was the actual theme music of the *Party of Five* pilot episode. Granted, gliding across the dance floor lacks the dramatic flair of Scott Wolf and those impossibly dreamy dimples sweeping a nubile, pre-boobs Jennifer Love Hewitt off her feet, but Beth and I do our best. I dust off some of the old cotillion standbys.

"Debbie, I think Hank's doing the foxtrot," Grandma Louise says to Mom. Grandma is here with her nurse after we secured her a day pass from the Franklin Community Alzheimer's & Dementia Care Center, so this will likely constitute her solitary coherent sentence of the afternoon.

I dip Beth again.

"Easy there," Beth says, blowing a few stray curls out of her face. "This champagne's kind of getting to me."

I furrow my brow, give Beth my close-mouthed, I'm-up-to-something smile while grinding my pelvis into her. "Isn't that the idea, honey?"

Beth pokes me in the chest. "Someone needs to hose you down."

I take note of the guests surrounding the dance floor, none of the men wearing their coats, all of the women barefoot and wrapped in dresses so drenched with sweat they look glued on. Jeanine crouches in the corner of the dance floor capturing the moment with her camera and her black-and-white film. One of Beth's Illinois friends quietly dry humps his date, a raven-haired minx in a tight-fitting, snakeskin-patterned dress with a slit that goes halfway up her thigh.

"Someone needs to hose all of us down," I say.

"Good point," Beth says. "Still, it's been a good reception."

"Mack's speech was funny. Claire rambled a bit."

"That's what Claire does when she's nervous."

"Then she must have been terrified."

"Be nice," Beth says. "And thanks, by the way."

"For what?"

"Not stuffing the cake in my face."

"Oh, you're welcome, I guess."

"You guess?"

"I thought you were going to say something romantic like, 'Thanks for being my husband' or 'Thanks for saying yes.'"

"Do you want me to say that?"

"No, at least not now that I've prompted you to say it."

Contemplative pause.

"Okay, Beth, go ahead and say it."

The song ends. She leans in, nibbles my ear. "Thanks for being my husband," she whispers.

I kiss her on the neck. "You're welcome."

I LOST BETH AFTER our dance together. First she danced with her father, then I danced with my mother, apparently thereafter Beth snuck out for a cigarette—to the extent a five-foot mound of billowing white could "sneak" at anything. The party felt like it was starting to wind down, although Dr. Burke was still trying to strong-arm the Beaver Stick manager into tapping into a fourth keg.

"I miss anything?" Beth asks.

"Where'd you come from?"

"The ladies' room."

I sniff, detecting a generic floral air freshener and a whiff of spearmint all but subsumed by tobacco. "That's not what it smells like to me."

Beth and I are "mostly" non-smokers now, both of us still in that post-college transition phase in which we have to teach ourselves how to drink without smoking. We've tried using straws for a few months, pretzel rods after that, but sometimes there's just no stopping that first cigarette once you have three or four cocktails in you.

"Cut a bride some slack." Beth chews furiously on a stick of spearmint gum. "It's been a stressful day."

"Sure has," I say. "You and your dad have a good dance together?"

"It was nice," Beth says. "How about you and your mother?"

"It was good, all things considered."

"What's that supposed to mean?"

"Oh, I don't know. Maybe that given a choice between hitting me in the face with a frying pan for three and a half minutes or dancing to an unbelievably heartbreaking song, my mother went with the more painful option."

"The song?"

"Yep."

"Dan Fogelberg was pretty rough."

"'Leader of the Band'?" I shrug my shoulders. "Rough? Hell, how about borderline incestuous? Mom was glued to me like a second suit."

"Her desperation on full display."

"Debbie unfiltered."

"You should really help her."

My mother isn't equipped to be by herself. I realize that, but at this point in my life I have better things to do than babysit a fifty-year-old woman. She is the most tragic of widows, the kind who goes from high school to college to marriage to family without breaking stride and so never learns to discern between being *alone* and being *lonely.* The kind whose happiness will forever labor beneath the yoke of lost love.

"Why do I need to help her, Beth? She's got her mimosa pitchers, narcotics, and Leon to get her through the day."

"Leon came?"

"He's out in the parking lot in the car listening to a Cubs game. He told Mom he'd drive her home, but he doesn't want to come into the reception."

"What a dick," Beth says. She rests her head on my shoulder. "But at least Jack is eating all this up."

"You think?"

"Being his big brother's ring bearer is the biggest day of his life. He told me so. Your mom said he tried that tux on yesterday morning and hasn't taken it off since. The kid is over the moon for you."

"His *brother's* ring bearer, huh?"

Beth smiles, brings her head into my chest. "Like I said, you need to tell him on your terms. I get that."

I continue to live a lie with Jack—my brother, my son, my whatever. He's happy. Isn't that enough? With a mother teetering on the precipice of abject despair, who am I to push her over the edge?

I reach down, straighten Beth's dress. "After we finished dancing, Mom said to 'make sure to ask Jack where babies come from.'"

Beth giggles, more than a little tipsy. "Well, have you asked him?"

"Not yet. But speaking of the place where babies come from, one of the Kornatowski boys tried to feel up Callie."

Grandma Louise's sister, Great Aunt Joy, married into the Cleveland-based Kornatowskis. Kornatowski is a surname that evidently in Polish means, "He who fucks like rabbits." They have ten kids, separated by fourteen years, and an exponentially larger number of grandkids. Six of the ten Kornatowski brood have been the reception's main entertainment for the last few songs, assaulting the dance floor—and some of the female guests—with moves and gesticulations more Miller Lite than measured.

"My cousin Callie?" Beth says.

"No, honey, the Kornatowski boys tried to feel up the entire state of California."

And there you have it: the first recorded smartass remark as husband and wife.

"Ouch!" I say, reeling from the first recorded physical reprisal in response to said smartass remark as husband and wife.

"Callie probably had it coming," Beth says.

"I highly doubt it."

"What makes you say that?"

"Because the Kornatowski boys are so drunk I caught one trying to hit on my mom."

"Isn't Aunt Joy your grandmother's sister?"

"Yep."

"So that means your mom and Aunt Joy's sons are—"

"First cousins."

"That's gross."

"Nope," I say. "That's a Catholic wedding reception."

The DJ transitions into Meatloaf's "Paradise by the Dashboard Light." What am I saying? Of course the DJ transitions into Meatloaf's "Paradise by the Dashboard Light."

The dance floor divides in accordance with proper Meatloaf etiquette—boys on one side, girls on the other.

Thanks to Meatloaf, the reception found its second wind. The song's fade-out is interrupted by the high-pitched feedback of a microphone being switched on.

"I'd like to take this moment to congratulate Hank and Beth," Mack says. The big man is sporting a full-on lather. Pools of sweat rim his shirt at the armpits and chest. He holds the microphone in his right hand, a sweat-drenched towel and a pint of light beer in his left.

Mack continues. "Darndest thing, Hank. I was sitting on the toilet just a few seconds ago, about ready to pass out, when I looked underneath the stall next to me and saw a pair of rhinestone shoes. DJ, if you wouldn't mind cuing the music up for me. Ladies and gentlemen, it's my pleasure to introduce, all the way from Memphis, Tennessee, THE KING!"

The back door flies open, and in walks Derek Candela dressed from head-to-toe in his authentic replica "Vegas Elvis" costume—a white polyester jumpsuit covered in gold and silver costume jewelry topped off by Derek's exposed hairy chest, a butterfly collar, multiple Hawaiian leis hanging from his neck, and a white cape extending down his back.

Elvis grabs the microphone from Mack. "Hey, cameraman," he says to Kenny Rogers, "you mind taking a picture of me and the lucky lady?"

Elvis takes a knee, offering Beth a seat on his other knee. She accepts the invitation. Kenny Rogers snaps the photo while Elvis keeps playing to the crowd.

"Oh man, oh man," he says. "This is one pretty lady. I-I-I-I could see me leaving Priscilla for this hot number. You hear that, Hank...*HUGHHH*!"

Beth stands up, laughing. Everyone is either (a) laughing, (b) screaming, or (c) drunk, with most of us more like (d) all of the above.

I'm thinking Elvis might be close to a (d) himself.

"So I'm down in Memphis with Mickey Gilley and the Gatlin Brothers. Hey, can somebody get the King a beer? These peanuts here are making me thirsty. Anyway, like I was saying, I-I-I-I was hanging with Mickey and the Gatlin Brothers, about halfway through a fried peanut butter and banana sandwich. Oh man, oh man, those things are so good...*HUGHHH*! And I said, 'Mickey, I need to make it up to Empire Ridge, Indiana, to see my friends Hank and Beth get hitched.' And I gotta tell you, now that I'm here, I-I-I-I feel a lot of love in this room. Put your hands together if you feel it, too."

The crowd responds with applause, shouts, and random song requests.

The King stands between me and Beth. "I-I-I-I just want to introduce the lovely couple here. I met Mr. Fitzpatrick during my '68 comeback album. This guy was one of the greatest bodyguards the King ever had, and he could go into a bar and pick up women left and right. It even made the King jealous."

This is one of those offhand comments meant to be funny but inevitably misinterpreted by half the audience as inappropriate. Fortunately, the drunken half of the audience is loud enough to overcome the uncomfortable handclaps of the reasonably sober half. Unfortunately, the tribute to my pickup skills elicits a brief but obvious straight face from Beth.

Elvis picks up the vibe.

"What's even more impressive," he says, "is not only how Hank managed to steal away my biggest groupie, Beth, here, but how this lovely lady managed to wrap him around her finger. I-I-I-I'd like to therefore dedicate my first song today…to the crowd."

The girls in the audience scream like inebriated, sexed-up groupies, which is cool to me in a nostalgic, perverse sort of way. I think it's their bare, pedicured feet getting to me. I like good feet almost as much as good calves.

"And of course," Elvis adds, "I-I-I-I dedicate the song after that to the happy couple. Hit it, Jimmy."

The King strikes the pose, his hand in the air, knees bent.

You ain't nuthin' but a hound dog…

Elvis grabs Beth out of the crowd, twirls her a few times. The King escorts Beth back to me as the procession begins.

Callie jumps onto the middle of the dance floor. For someone so recently victimized by my Polish cousins, she seems to have recovered to the point where she can hump the King's leg. She stands and backs up into the crowd.

Elvis gives the ladies what they want: more pelvic thrusts. Aunt Joy is the next to respond. It's the first and hopefully last time I ever see dirty dancing by a couple separated by a half century.

Aunt Joy cedes the floor…to my mother. The screaming is deafening. I shield my eyes for fear of reopening the psychological scars of a son still holding fast to the image of his mother as an asexual being.

The song ends abruptly. The girls can't get enough.

"It's been a long time since I've done a live show," Elvis says. "I-I-I-I was screamin' for that teleprompter. But I'm going to do a romantic number to close things out today. I'd like the women to all come gather around me."

Per the King's instructions, all the women at the reception surround him. "Okay, Jimmy," Elvis says. The DJ cues up the song.

Wise men say only fools rush in…

"Why aren't you out there?" I say to Beth, her head leaning on my shoulder.

"I got my king right here."

I shake my head, somewhere between embarrassed and appreciative of the compliment. I push her onto the dance floor. "Get out there!"

Kenny Rogers stands with his camera between me and the King. "Wait for the bride!" someone shouts.

Beth lifts up her skirt. Her eyes scan for an opening in the King's harem. She shrugs her shoulders, saying, "Here goes nothing." She slides in front of the group while flashing the peace sign and doing the splits.

Again, the screams are deafening. Beth smiles as the cameras flash. It's the best picture of the day, no doubt destined for a shelf in the Fitzpatrick household for years to come. But the picture will only tell half the story. The picture won't tell you a third of the girls in the photo are under twenty-one and sauced out of their heads. The picture won't tell you the girl to the left of Jeanine and right above Beth is the only twenty-year-old I know with double-F breasts and that she plans to get a breast reduction. The picture won't tell you that even though Claire is on the King's arm and laughing out loud, she just wishes Derek would propose to her already.

Someone grabs at my shirtsleeve. I turn around. No one is there. "Down here!" the voice says.

"Hey, little bro," I say.

Jack is the cutest person in the room. People call him Dad's tow-headed clone, but only because they don't know any better.

The fact Jack even comes out of his room is a minor miracle, let alone the fact he's as well-adjusted as any six-year-old on the planet. After the accident, Mom held him back for another year of kindergarten. The teachers said "he couldn't concentrate" and that "he lacked focus." On behalf of all the sons in the world whose fathers were gored by a Ford Bronco's front bumper, allow me to say to those kindergarten teachers, go fuck yourself.

"Hank," Jack says, "I wanted to tell you something."

"Go for it, buddy."

"Uhhh..." He rolls his eyes, like he's lost the words and is trying to find them. In one breath, lacking any inflection or pause between words, he says, "I-just-wanted-to-say-congratulations-I-love-you-and-I-hope-you-have-fun-on-your-honeymoon."

Rehearsed? Probably. Prompted by Mom? Undoubtedly. But the tears start to well up in my eyes nonetheless.

Let's get one thing straight. I have not been a second father to Jack, not by any stretch of the imagination. But I've done my best. I lift him in the air and pull him into my chest. I give him a big wet kiss on the cheek that he of course immediately wipes off. I set him down, ruffle his blond mop with my hand.

"Hey, Jack, I want to ask you a question."

"Okay," Jack says, his face flushed with the typical embarrassment of a kid who realizes he's about to have a conversation with an adult.

"Where do babies come from?"

"That's an easy question."

"Then tell me," I say. I grab a random full beer off the table next to me, take a sip.

"Babies start in the mommy's esophagus," Jack says, "then they grow in the Eucharist, and then they come out the mommy's butthole, as an egg."

The beer shoots out my nose. I laugh. I laugh hard. So hard that I nearly miss seeing my mother-in-law being held upside down by Mack over the newly opened fourth keg of beer.

Aside from our parents and the Kornatowski boys, there are maybe a handful of people left at the reception over the age of twenty-four. The DJ cues up "December, 1963 (Oh What a Night)" by the Four Seasons. I stand up, pulling my wife out of her chair and back onto the dance floor.

"One more dance?" I say.

She takes my hand in hers. "How about we keep that number a little more open-ended?"

"Forever then?"

"Forever it is," Beth says.

CHAPTER SIXTY-FIVE

"These things are good," Beth says with her mouth full. She's wearing a bright yellow bikini and picking brownie crumbs out of her navel.

"Probably my favorite wedding present," I say, my mouth also full.

My sister Jeanine made a batch of fun brownies for the honeymoon. We baked them together the night before the wedding. She had held court in my kitchen, channeling the illegitimate daughter of Julia Child and Jerry Garcia.

"The key is to mix your weed in with the butter reduction," she said while stirring the pot of melted butter and marijuana with her right hand and chain-smoking Marlboro Lights with her left hand. "Too many people just mix the weed in with the brownie mix and throw it in the oven. You know what that does, right?"

"Uh, sure?" I said to her, not having a fucking clue.

Jeanine pointed at me, smiling. "You'll thank me for these tips someday."

"If you say so," I said. "But just for kicks and giggles, remind me again what's wrong with mixing the dope into the mix."

"Pretty basic knowledge, really." Jeanine poured the hazel-colored gelatinous ooze in a mixing bowl. She grabbed the dry brownie mix and dumped it into the bowl. She added an egg and about a third of a cup of water, stirred the mix with a wooden spoon. "You only get a fraction of the THC if you just cook the weed into the mix."

"Basic knowledge indeed," I said. "What's THC again?"

"Come on now, Hank," Jeanine said. "Tetrahydrocannabinol. It's the shit that gets you high."

"Oh, so you're saying cooking weed in the brownies gets you less high?"

"Bingo."

"We don't want that."

"Hell no, we don't!"

Beth and I couldn't afford a honeymoon. We were up to our eyeballs in student loans, and Dr. Burke's beach house was booked through the end of the summer. At the last minute, Dr. Burke's partner offered us a three-day weekend on his houseboat on Lake Cumberland, free of charge. The eighty-foot-long houseboat is more like a condo on water, with six bedrooms, plus a full wet bar and hot tub on the roof and a two-story curly slide extending off the stern of the boat.

With over twelve hundred miles of shoreline and a maximum depth of 250 feet, Lake Cumberland in southern Kentucky is the largest lake east of the Mississippi. The great thing about Cumberland is that no one west of the Mississippi or east of the Appalachians seems to know it exists. The man-made reservoir is a vast flooded valley, surrounded on all sides by public parkland. Dr. Burke's partner told us we could quite possibly go all three days without seeing another boat on the water.

It's a theory I'm prepared to put to the test.

We finish our last bites of brownies. I smile. Beth is lying on a sun lounger. I'm sitting at her feet. The Divinyls's "I Touch Myself" starts up on the houseboat sound system, which immediately compels me to massage her calves.

"Freak," Beth says.

I give her calves a good squeeze. "How stoned are you right now?"

My bride giggles. "Way stoned."

Beth and I have spent the past half hour taking turns coating one another from head to toe with Palmolive—softens hands while you're doing your wife—and sliding down the curly slide. Montell Jordan reminds us both that "This Is How We Do It," although I can't imagine many people in South Central do it this way.

"I'm over the slide," Beth says, climbing out of the water. She grabs a towel, wraps it around her hair.

"What do you want to do now?" I say, stepping aboard the boat's deck.

Beth removes her towel from her head, throws it at me. "I want to fool around."

"Uh…" I wipe my face with the towel. "Isn't that what we've been doing?"

"No, I mean *really* fool around."

"If you insist." I throw the towel on the ground. I rush to Beth, my left hand on her right breast. My free hand, seemingly of its own volition, reaches between her legs.

Beth pushes me away. "Easy, tiger."

"But I thought you said—"

"How about a little foreplay before you go stampeding toward the clitoris?"

"I can do that, too," I say, sprouting a full tripod at this point.

"Then go up top," Beth says, pointing at the aluminum stairs next to the slide. "I have a surprise for you."

Montell Jordan defers to TLC. Beth walks downstairs. She turns up "Waterfalls." I peer down the steps. "Can I come?"

"You stay up there," Beth shouts back. TLC is cut off in midstream, replaced by the beginning of Van Halen's "Summer Nights."

Fuck yeah!

Beth just put on the *Super Sexy Six Metal Mega Mix*. It's a six-song "boner block" of music that gets me going: Van Halen's "Summer Nights," Mötley Crüe's "Girls, Girls, Girls," Def Leppard's "Pour Some Sugar on Me," Led Zeppelin's "Whole Lotta Love," Jackyl's "Dirty Little Mind," and Scorpions' "Tease Me, Please Me." Beth made the mixtape for my twenty-fourth birthday back in April and proceeded to do an eighteen-minute striptease that quite nearly made my dick explode.

"Close your eyes," Beth says.

I close my eyes. I can hear her coming up the steps to Sammy Hagar's scratchy serenade.

"Okay, you can open them."

I open my eyes. Beth is standing in front of me. In place of her bikini bottom, she's wearing a multilayered silk skirt fastened low on her hips. She is topless, save for two small, golden teacup-like pasties.

"Oh my God," I say. "Are you a…a belly dancer?"

CHAPTER SIXTY-SIX

The conservation officer seems like a nice guy. He speaks with a lazy southern drawl, and he keeps the back of his squad car exceedingly clean.

"That thar wuz uh sumthin' I ain't uh never seen."

His name is Don. He arrested us on charges of indecent exposure. Our houseboat was tucked away in a fairly isolated cove, but our music had attracted his attention. I was having sex with Beth—still wearing her belly dancer costume and Scorpions's "Tease Me, Please Me" echoing in my ears—when Officer Don tapped me on the shoulder.

Beth sits in the front passenger seat, trying to talk Officer Don out of taking us to jail. For being eternally mortified and braless, wearing a belly dancer costume covered only by one of my V-neck T-shirts, she's amazingly composed. She asks Don about the fishing on Cumberland, about where he's from. She looks like she's getting somewhere. It's time for me to step in and close the deal.

"Flossie!" I blurt out, less sober than I expected to sound.

"'Scuse me, son?" Officer Don says.

"Aunt Flossie," I say. "She lives, or should I say lived, in these parts. Campbellsville, or was it Mannsville?"

Officer Don nods. "Both those towns ur in this county."

I pretend not to notice Beth shaking her head. "My aunt Flossie lived there her whole life. We used to come down and stay on her farm. There was this huge barn across the street where they'd hang tobacco leaves to dry."

"Makes sense," Officer Don says. "Tobaccuh's a big crop 'round here."

"Yeah," I say. "Big crop."

"Son?"

"Yes sir."

"Your aunt Flossie. She got a last name?"

"Last name?"

"That's whut I said."

"She was my great-aunt, my dad's aunt."

"Great-aunts don't have last names?"

"I'm sure they do," I say. "I just can't remember mine."

For all my earnestness, my name dropping goes about as well as if I had told Officer Don that Jesus was a black homosexual democrat who hated Adolph Rupp. He escorts us into the Columbia County Jail.

BETH AND I HAD to wait to be processed after a three-hundred-pound bald man who was arrested for a DUI on a riding lawn mower. The lady who books me, an old, haggard, Bea Arthur look-alike, speaks with an accent bordering on indecipherable.

"Have uh seat," she says, nodding to the chair beside her desk. "Nyeeem?"

"Hank Fitzpatrick," I answer.

"Birth-dye?"

"Four, twenty-one, seventy-one."

"White?"

"Huh?"

"White?"

"One more time?"

"White?"

"Uh, yeah, I'm white."

"*Weight*, Hank," Beth says from the other side of the room. "What's your weight?"

"Oh, sorry," I say. "One seventy-five."

I haven't been one seventy-five since the eighth grade, and Bea Arthur notices. "You show 'bout that?"

I throw my thumb over my shoulder. "If John Deere over there can get away with saying he's two forty, I can get away with one seventy-five."

I swear Bea Arthur smiles. "Y'all kin go now," she says.

"What?" I say, looking at Beth. She shrugs her shoulders. I look back at Bea Arthur.

"Your bail's posted," she says, enunciating for my benefit. "Wuz only five bucks uh piece. Officer Don went easy on y'all."

"Define 'easy,'" Beth says.

"You two ain't hurtin' nobody, so we're giving you deferrals. Long as y'all pay a seventy-five-dollar fine within the next sixty days, we'll just say today never happened."

"And that's it?" I say.

Bea Arthur shakes her head. "Not exactly. Y'all are on probation. Best keep your noses clean for the next eighteen months, and *then* we'll forget about today."

"Sounds good to me." I stand up. "Now, do we pay you the ten dollars for bail, or do we pay it on the way out?"

Bea Arthur shakes her head. "Like I said, your bail was posted. Paid for a half hour ago."

"By who?"

"He's outside uh waitin' for y'all. Says he's your uncle."

CHAPTER SIXTY-SEVEN

"What the fuck are you doing here?"

"Please, Hank, let me explain."

I stand in the middle of the Columbia County Jail in a tie-dyed tank top, swimsuit and flip-flops, my fists clenched. Uncle Mitch stands opposite me, unshaven and smelling like body odor, still in the same pitted-out button-down and blue jeans from our wedding two days ago.

Beth grabs my elbow. "Hank, let's just leave."

I yank my arm free of my wife. "Answer me, Mitch. What the fuck are you doing here?"

He steps tentatively toward me, his outreached hand nearly touching my arm. "I couldn't let things end like they did the other day. I had to see you. I overheard someone going into your wedding say where you were going for your honeymoon, so I got a room at a motel down here and just waited things out. The moment just kind of presented itself when I was having a cup of coffee on the town square and saw you being taken in handcuffs into the police station. Indecent exposure? I can only imagine what you were—"

I poke him in the chest. "You can only imagine *what,* Mitch? Being there with me, just like old times, so you can grab hold of my little pecker?"

Uncle Mitch stumbles backward. "Hank, I—"

"You *what*?"

"I only want your forgiveness."

"Never."

"You don't mean that."

"I don't?"

"You are your father's son. His capacity to forgive is inside you. I know it is."

"And what the fuck is that supposed to mean?"

"You don't think he knew?"

"Knew what?"

"About me?"

"Fuck you!" I shout. Officer Don walks back into the station just as I pin Uncle Mitch against the wall, my elbow in his throat.

Beth is crying. Uncle Mitch gasps for air. "W-we were teenagers. He caught me with another guy, one of his bandmates. I swore to him it was a one-time thing. He promised to never tell anyone, but he had to have known. He just had to have known, Hank."

I knee Uncle Mitch in the groin. He falls like a sack of potatoes. I reel back my foot for another blow. Just as my foot connects with his exposed ribs, Officer Don checks me into the wall.

He spins me around, pins my arm behind me, immobilizing me. "Mr. Fitzpatrick, that's enough. There'll be none of that in my station, yuh hear?"

Both of our backs are turned away from Uncle Mitch. Beth is the one who sees him reach into his pocket.

"Gun!" she screams.

Bea Arthur is already on the com in the other room. "*We have a four-seventeen in progress at the Columbia County Jail. I repeat, a four-seventeen. Officer on the scene. Request backup.*"

Beth drops to the floor. Officer Don lets go of my wrist. We both turn to the assailant.

"Sir, I'm going to have to ask you to put that gun down," Officer Don says. "We don't want to see anyone get hurt here."

"Spare me your bullshit, officer," Uncle Mitch says, waving the handgun in our faces. "I know how this works. I just pulled a loaded gun inside a fucking police station, plus I'm a convicted sex offender. The math just isn't working in my favor on this one."

I reach out to my godfather. "Uncle Mitch, please..."

"Going with *Uncle* Mitch again, huh? Smart boy." He motions toward me with the handgun. "Come here."

I walk toward him. "This is just between you and me, so let's have it out, then."

"Yes, Hank," Uncle Mitch says. He places the barrel of the gun directly between my eyes. "Let's have it out."

I raise my hands, recognizing the gun. I'm suddenly short of breath. The room goes black for a split second. When I open my eyes, I feel like a part of me is outside my own body, hovering above the scene, watching Uncle Mitch force me to undo his life, to absolve his sin. But I'm not afraid anymore. I'm pissed off.

"Humor me, *Uncle* Mitch," I say, trying not to sneer. "How can we make this right?"

"It's simple, really. Say you forgive me."

"And that's all?" My hands are raised. Beth is sobbing now.

"Yes, Hank," Uncle Mitch says. "That's all. I need your mercy. I need your father's mercy. Please, set me free."

"No," I say.

"What?" Uncle Mitch pushes the handgun harder into my forehead.

"You heard me. I know you're a monster, but I also know there's a small part of you who was my godfather and Dad's best friend. You're a sick fuck. But you're not a killer."

He steps closer to me, drops the barrel down from my forehead and pushes it beneath my chin so we can stand face-to-face. "You don't think I'm a killer, huh? What if you're wrong?"

"If I'm wrong, then I'd rather die knowing I never forgave you than live knowing I offered you even an ounce of hope for your miserable existence."

Uncle Mitch's eyes open wide, manic-like. He grabs me by the shirt with his free hand, pushes the handgun harder up into my chin. The room is spinning. We're both sweating. His three-packs-a-day breath is stifling.

Then, as suddenly as he grabbed me, Uncle Mitch just backs away.

"You aren't your father's boy, Hank."

"What?"

"You heard me," he says. "John Fitzpatrick forgave everyone, but forgiveness doesn't come easy to you. Your dad was always too busy being humane to be human. You're tougher. And in a weird way, I feel like I had something to do with that. Thank you."

"For what?"

"For setting me free…*son*."

Uncle Mitch sticks the barrel of the gun in his mouth. The bullet is through the back of his head before Officer Don can even raise his sidearm.

A godfather's love measured by the diameter of his exploded brain matter.

THEY'VE MOVED US TO another wing of the building, away from the carnage. Beth and I sit in Officer Don's office.

"You okay, honey?" Beth says, squeezing my hands.

I squeeze back. "Some honeymoon, eh?"

Officer Don enters the office. "You two can go now. Paperwork is pretty much done here. We have to hold the assailant's gun until the investigation is officially closed, but I assume you'll eventually want it back."

I stand up. Beth follows my lead. "Want it back?" I ask.

"Yeah," Officer Don says. "The gun is nice, all things considered. It's a Smith & Wesson three fifty-seven Magnum. We did a trace on it, and records show it's still registered to—"

"John Fitzpatrick," I say.

"You knew?"

I rub my mouth. "I knew it the moment he pulled the gun on me. That's why I didn't do it."

"Didn't do what?"

"Forgive him."

"You didn't forgive your uncle because he had your father's gun in his hand?"

I open the door to Officer Don's office. Beth walks out of the room. "I didn't forgive Uncle Mitch because I knew my father was about to kill him."

On cue, my wife vomits in the hallway of the police station.

1996

CHAPTER SIXTY-EIGHT

"I can see the head. I can see our baby's head."

"Blond?"

"Dark hair, and a lot of it."

Beth is propped about a third of the way up in her bed, her legs spread. Beth's ob-gyn Dr. Martha Florio sits on a chair between Beth's legs, exhorting her to push. Dr. Florio is short, thick but not fat. Dark hair. Always smiling. She has the look of a Greek mother, always ready to smother you in kisses and oddly pronounced pastries. I stand just behind and to the left of Dr. Florio, looking over her shoulder. Bob Marley's *Legend* CD plays in the background. We're coming up on 8:00 p.m., nearly twenty-seven hours after my wife's first major contraction.

"It's not coming," the doctor says under her breath.

"What?" I say.

We're not calling the baby "it" by accident. Beth and I decided to bring our first into the world the old-fashioned way. Even after four ultrasounds—which Beth insisted upon, convinced she had drunk and smoked the baby stupid on our honeymoon—we refused to know the gender of our child, hamstringing the grandmothers into buying an almost exclusively yellow wardrobe.

"The baby," the doctor says. "It doesn't want to come out this way."

Dr. Florio is from the new school of childbirth and delivery. She doesn't believe in using suction or even forceps. That is unfortunate for Beth. After all these years of self-deprecation in regards to her wide "birthing hips," it turns out Beth has an extremely narrow pelvis. "I see it a lot in gymnasts," Dr. Florio tells us, as if that makes what she's about to say any easier.

"Hey kiddo," the doctor says. Since the day Beth had her first ultrasound, Dr. Florio has addressed her as "kiddo." Her informality and comfort with the word makes me think it's a catchall nickname she uses with most of her patients.

Beth is exhausted. "Yes, doctor?" she says.

"We're going to need to deliver your baby via C-section. The combination of your narrow pelvis and the baby's large head makes a vaginal delivery problematic."

I adjust my fitted seven-and-five-eighths-inch Notre Dame ball cap, silently cursing the long line of Fitzpatrick fiveheads. I tip the manager a fifty as he starts to walk away from me.

"Whatever you need to do to get my baby out happy and healthy, do it," Beth says. She accepts the news better than I expected. Must be the drugs talking.

I smile at my wife. I lean down next to her face. "Everything's going to be okay, honey," I whisper, patting her belly. Her hospital gown barely contains the seventy-plus pounds she's put on during pregnancy.

Twenty pounds of that weight gain is in her formerly A-cup now D-cup breasts, one of nature's cruel jokes on men. As suckable as they might look, milk-swollen breasts are rendered too sensitive to even think about fondling, let alone the full-on pearl necklace you fantasize about roughly twenty-seven hours a day.

I kiss Beth on her sweaty, oily forehead. I run my hand through her unwashed hair. She is dirty. She smells like body odor. I just saw her take a crap in the bed when she tried to push the baby out.

All in all, Beth is as beautiful as I've ever seen her.

Dr. Florio instructs two nurses to "prepare for an emergency C-section." *Emergency?* I have to stay calm, for Beth's sake. God, I fucking hate hospitals.

Beth reaches up, squeezes my hand. "Do you think we should tell everyone what's up?"

"I guess so," I answer. "But I don't want to leave you."

Dr. Florio looks at me. "It'll be a few minutes until the operating room is prepped, kiddo. We have some time."

I still don't want to leave Beth. But she nods, pushes me. I kiss her again, this time on the lips. I've been spoon-feeding her ice chips for the better part of a day, but her lips are still horribly chapped. "I'll be right back," I say.

I WALK INTO THE waiting room. An episode of *Beverly Hills 90210* plays on the room television. It's a repeat of this season's two-part finale. Steve Sanders is having a twenty-first birthday party on the Queen Mary with the Goo Goo Dolls as the house band. David Silver and Donna Martin are getting back together, which is predictable. Brandon Walsh is dumping Susan Keats, which is unfortunate given how insane Emma Caulfield looks in a bikini.

Stan and Joan are seated in the waiting room across from Mom, my sister Jeanine, and Jack. Jeanine has been Beth's enabler over these last nine months. After we moved back to Empire Ridge last year, she had a front-row seat to most of the pregnancy, living with me and Beth while completing clinicals toward her physical therapy certification. She has a PT job lined up in Portland, Oregon, but she got her start date deferred six months so she could help out during Beth's maternity leave. The two have put on an ice cream-eating display, the likes of which I have never seen nor will ever see again. I'm almost surprised there's any Edy's French Silk Light ice cream left in the greater southern Indiana area, given that they've been going through the stuff at a gallon-per-week clip.

"Hey Doc," I say.

Stan stands up. "Yeah, Hank?"

"I could really use an assist in here."

"What is it?" Joan asks.

"Is Beth okay?" Jeanine adds.

"Everything is fine," I say. "Looks like they're going to have to perform a C-section. Very routine. Beth is doing great."

Joan knows better. I can see the skepticism in her face. "Then why do you need Stan in there?"

I'm as scared as my mother-in-law is, but I don't let on. "The hospital's on-call pediatrician probably won't make it here in time," I say calmly. "Dr. Florio asked if Dr. Burke wouldn't mind keeping us company."

THE NURSE HANDS DR. Burke and me our gear. Together we suit up: scrubs, surgical gowns, caps, masks, and shoe coverings. The nurse shows us to the operating room. My surgical mask doesn't seem to fit, positioned just so on the bridge of my nose that it deflects all exhaled air out the top of the mask and straight into my eyes.

"Here," Dr. Burke says. He reaches over and pinches the metal band running along the ridge of my mask, sealing the mask to my face.

"Thanks…Stan." My voice cracks a little.

"It'll be okay, Hank." My father-in-law pats me on the back. I don't know if I've earned his love yet, but he's giving it to me anyway.

I hand Stan the video camera. "Sure you don't mind filming?"

"Not at all," Stan says. "You worry about Beth. I'll worry about saving the moment for posterity. Besides, the more things to keep me distracted and out of the way in there, the better."

I read somewhere that C-sections were formerly only used to save the baby's life. The survival of the mother wasn't even considered until the early 1800s, at which time they figured out you could stitch the mother back up as opposed to leaving her to die from infection or massive hemorrhaging. As much as I know Beth appreciates my grasp of random useless trivia, I think it's best not to bring up this factoid.

Stan and I enter the operating room. Beth is lying on a table in the middle of the room, her swollen belly exposed to the bright surgical lights overhead. Dr. Florio and a nurse stand to the left of her belly, a second nurse stands to the right. The second nurse is swabbing Beth's belly with what I assume to be some kind of antiseptic. A tray of gleaming surgical instruments hovers over Beth's chest: various scalpels, scissors, and clamps. A light blue screen is raised just below Beth's chin, preventing her from seeing the actual procedure. I take a seat on a stool beside Beth's head. Stan positions himself just beyond the screen with the camcorder.

Ten minutes pass, maybe fifteen. Scalpels and scissors are constantly exchanged just above the rim of the blue screen. A stream of instructions pass between Dr. Florio and the nurses. Their words are drowned out by the ambient noises of an operating room. The classical music on the PA system. The beeping of the heart monitor. That high-pitched whistling coming from the suction machine, a noise that haunts me with images of multiple cavities, pulled permanent teeth, root canals, and five years of braces, retainers, rubber bands, and headgear.

"How you feeling?" Dr. Florio asks my wife.

Beth blinks, looks at me. She has that powerless look on her face, like the look my Grandpa Fitzpatrick had after he had a stroke.

"Beth?" I say.

She closes her eyes and inhales. "Having…trouble…breathing," she quietly stammers.

"You need to relax, kiddo," Dr. Florio instructs. "That's just your epidural doing its job, maybe a little too well. It's numbed you to where you can't feel yourself breathe."

"I'm here, honey," I say. "So's your father. And pretty soon our baby will be here, too. Just stay calm and focused, feel yourself breathing in… and out."

I repeat this mantra over and over—*in…and out, in…and out*—until I can feel her breathing steady.

"Thanks, Hank," she says.

"They're just getting the head out now," Stan says.

I turn to my wife. "Can I watch?"

A moment of clarity from Beth. "Can you witness the birth of your first born? What the hell kind of question is that?"

I stand up, an expectant father not expecting…*this.*

Of course, there's the tattoo: a dainty daisy-like flower to the left of Beth's navel that has long since been stretched to the size of an actual sunflower. But it's her stomach that gets me. It's peeled back in layers of skin and muscle. The hypodermis layer is most pronounced, like a line of tapioca pudding set against a backdrop of blood and amniotic fluid. I want to be disgusted. But I'm not.

"Look at all that hair," Dr. Florio says. She and the two nurses are wrenching the skin around the baby's head, trying to dislodge it from Beth's uterus. One of the nurses sticks a tube in the baby's mouth. The baby chokes, coughs up some fluid, and begins to cry.

"Hear that?" Stan says from behind the camcorder. "That's what you want to hear."

Dr. Florio gives the baby one hard tug, and then it's out. And it's purple. And its head looks like an eggplant.

"Now comes the verdict," Dr. Florio says, turning the front of the baby toward us.

The moment of truth. Five sets of eyes all trained on one baby's genitalia.

"I was right!" Stan exclaims.

"What?" Beth says.

I walk behind the screen, lean down and tell my wife the news.

It's a girl.

Like Stan, I always knew it would be a girl. Some people would even go so far to suggest if there's any justice in this world I will have nothing but daughters.

Some people? Who am I kidding? *A lot* of people would go so far to suggest this. The birth of a daughter is a father's great reality check, the giant "fuck you" to guys like me who look back at their formative years with shamelessly wistful naivety. Newsflash, Hank: Every girl you've ever been with is someone's daughter. And about fourteen years from now, your daughter is going to be dealing with pricks just like you.

Taking cues from great-grandmothers on both sides of the family, we name her Sasha Grace. It's been about five minutes since they wiped her down, drained the fluids from her nose and mouth, and placed her in an incubator. Sasha is already pinking up. Stan is still recording. Still crying, Sasha opens her eyes for the first time.

"She's looking all around, Beth," Stan says. "Sasha is looking for her mommy."

Stan appears restless. Dr. Florio is still busy on the south side of my wife sewing things up.

"How about we wheel the incubator to where Beth can see her baby girl?"

"Good idea, Hank," Stan says.

I reach for the camcorder, starting to pull it off Stan's shoulder. "I'll take this off your hands and go update the troops. Why don't you give your granddaughter her first checkup?"

Stan pulls the camcorder shoulder strap over his head, thrusts the camcorder at me. "That's an even better idea."

I kiss Beth on the lips. She's still a little drugged, trying to maintain consciousness on the off chance the hospital might change its policy regarding the handling of newborns by catatonic patients.

"You did it, sweetie," I say. "Get some rest. I love you."

She musters a response through her haze. "I love you, too, Hank."

I hand the camcorder to the throng of new grandparents, aunts, and uncles. They huddle around the small view screen for a first glimpse of Sasha.

I sneak outside for a smoke. Neither Beth nor I smoke anymore, so I bummed one off Jeanine.

"I thought you quit."

Mom stands there, tears streaming down her face in mauve tentacles.

I exhale a puff of smoke. "Needed a cigarette today."

"I'm sorry, son."

"Sorry for what?"

"I'm sorry he couldn't be here."

Leon refused to come tonight. Married six months to my mom, and he's still the same old dick.

"I'm actually happier that Leon isn't here."

"Not Leon." Mom buries her head in my shoulder. "Your father. I'm sorry he couldn't be here to see the birth of his first grandchild."

"But technically didn't he get to see the birth of his first grandchild?"

"Not really."

"But you and he were there when Laura—"

"No, don't you remember? Your father was up at Notre Dame for his reunion."

"Oh, that's right."

"I drove to Pennsylvania and back by myself in a rental car, and then I dropped off the car in northern Indiana. Your dad picked me up in Angola. When he saw Jack for that first time, the look in his eyes made all my guilt and fear about our deception just go away. I saw that look in Stan's eyes tonight. I just wish I could have seen it one more time in John's."

It's the first time I've heard her talk about Dad since she started dating Leon. My tears follow hers. "Yeah," I say. "I wish he were here, too."

"What's next?"

"Next?"

"Gonna go for more?"

"Mom."

"Two is just as easy as one."

"I think we'll have our hands full with just the princess for now. Maybe a dog will be next."

"Still holding on to that dream, huh?"

"Not everyone hates dogs like you do, Debbie."

"I don't hate dogs."

"No, you *loathe* them."

Mom grabs the cigarette out of my hands, takes a small toke, coughs. She hands it back to me, her fist to her mouth, still coughing.

"Friendly advice, Mom."

"Yeah?"

"Don't inhale."

"But you do," Mom says.

"Took me about two years of smoking to work my way up to inhaling."

"It was your father, you know."

"What are you talking about?"

"No dogs," Mom says. "That was his rule."

"Dad loved dogs," I say. "We'd go to the park and he'd play with them all day if we let him."

"I know."

"But you said—"

"You remember Snooper?"

"Dad's beagle. The one he had as a kid."

Mom nods. "Grandpa George used to go foxhunting with Snooper. Turns out Snooper stunk at foxhunting, but he was a great family pet, and fiercely loyal to your dad. One day, John came home after school with two black eyes and a missing front tooth. He had got in a fight on the playground."

"Dad in a fight?" I say. "I can't picture that."

"He was eleven years old, and at recess saw three teenage boys ripping a black girl's dress off behind the school. He stopped them and probably saved the girl from being raped or worse. While they roughed him up pretty bad, he managed to get in a few good shots. John walked home from school. Two of the three teenage boys left school in an ambulance."

"Sounds like he got in more than a few good shots."

"So John gets home from school and tells his mother what happened."

"Where was Grandpa George?'

"Out of town at an American Legion function."

"And what did Grandma Eleanor do?"

"She took John out back underneath the willow tree."

"Not the switch."

"You know about that?"

"Dad had permanent scars on his back."

"That was the day he got those scars," Mom says. "Grandma Eleanor tied her son's wrists to the willow tree and started whipping his bare back. He was screaming and bleeding, and at one point she hit John so hard she broke a switch in half and he nearly passed out from the pain. Just as Eleanor was about to lay into him again with a new switch, Snooper broke through the screen door on the back of the house. He had been locked in a kennel in the basement, and when he heard John's screaming, he ripped the metal door off the hinges of his kennel. He had broken all four canine teeth in the effort."

"Holy shit."

"Those busted teeth clamped down on Grandma Eleanor's arm, the one holding the switch. With her free hand, she grabbed a baseball bat lying in the yard and hit Snooper in the head. She knocked the dog unconscious, but she didn't kill him. Eleanor untied her son and went into the house. John ran to Snooper. He put his ear on his muzzle and was relieved to hear him breathing. That's when Eleanor came outside with Grandpa George's double-barreled shotgun. "

"No, Mom. Please don't tell me she shot Snooper and made Dad watch."

"She didn't."

"Thank God."

"She made John shoot him."

IT'S NEARLY DAWN NOW. Beth is sleeping. I stand at the window of the bedroom, looking down at the sidewalk that curls around the front of the hospital. An old man walks his dog along the sidewalk. Sure enough, the dog is a beagle. Sasha's head rests on my shoulder. I hold her tight with both arms. I lean my nose into her soft, innocent-smelling skin—that spot just behind the ear on a baby's neck. I hold this seven-pound-fourteen-ounce glimmer of hope against my chest.

"Hey, don't hog her," Beth says. Her voice is like a lifeline to me. As she's done so many times before, often without even knowing it, my wife saves me from myself.

"You awake?"

Beth reaches her arms out. "Yes, now give her here."

"Patience, Mommy," I say.

Beth sits up. She pulls down a flap on the left side of her shirt, revealing her bare chest. I position our newborn daughter in the crook of her right arm. Beth squeezes her nipple between her left index and middle fingers as I help guide Sasha's head toward her mother. Beth is still weak from the C-section, so I help support Sasha with my left hand. With my right hand, I help Beth squeeze her nipple to get the colostrum going. The fact I'm massaging a woman's swollen breast without being the least bit turned-on is a big step for me.

1997–1999

CHAPTER SIXTY-NINE

The dirty little secret about life is that it speeds up as you grow older. You put things in cruise control and watch the miles tick by without stopping to look at the scenery. It's a secret no one bothers to tell you until you've actually succumbed to the time warp, feckless and coma-like, as people younger than you have "retro" eighties parties and DJs label your favorite songs as "classic" rock. Why is it an eternity between Christmases for a child? Because the time between Christmases is half of a two-year-old's life, a third of a three-year-old's life, a fourth of a four-year-old's life, and downward it goes until you can't distinguish one holiday from the next. Hell, I'm twenty-eight years old, so my next Christmas is a mere thirty-six hundredths of my life away. Think about thirty-six hundredths of a second. It's an eye blink, a flash of light, an impulse. Time is all about context. Years become days. Miles become inches. Life becomes death. You start taking things for granted, at least the things that matter. You fail to notice your wife's new haircut—again—but Catherine Zeta Jones's major motion picture debut in *The Mask of Zorro* leaves you smitten. Seriously, can somebody prescribe me a fucking pill to slow this shit don? Like Rip Van Winkle, I feel like I've missed a significant part of my life, or at the very least 1997 and 1998. Sasha turned three today. I don't believe it, but that's what Beth keeps telling me. Jack played her "Happy Birthday" on his recorder. Is there a reason school systems still insist on imposing the recorder on our troubled youth? Throw in its archaic cousin, square dancing, and I'd rather take my chances with methamphetamines, bullying, and hate crimes.

Mom called me today to say the divorce was final. It started when Leon tried to get Mom to sign all her financial assets over to him after we won the wrongful death lawsuit against the Indianapolis Auto Auction. He told Mom that he was "just better at moving money around" than she was. Then Leon's mother died, and he sued his siblings for their inheritance—at the funeral. But I think the last straw was when she caught him not only hitting up Jeanine for some weed, but hitting on her with a four-hour erection powered by Canadian pharmaceuticals.

Mom and Leon were married, and then they weren't. Vagina Head just disappeared. Yesterday he hopped on a plane to Amsterdam with a cashier's check for one-point-five million dollars, roughly half of my father's estate. I'm trying not to be too hard on myself, but I keep thinking that my ambivalence and hostility toward Mom cost our family half of Dad's blood money.

Sorry, Dad. I let you down again.

CHAPTER SEVENTY

Beth pushes open the door to the restroom. She looks at me over her shoulder. "I have to pee. Wait for me?"

"Sure," I say.

The door swings behind her. A whiff of her perfume wafts out in the hallway, that same subtle lavender scent she's worn since I first met her. I close my eyes and inhale deeply, like I always do when a pretty woman who smells good walks by me. I leave my foot just inside the door, cracking it open. I can hear the faint trickle of my wife's urine.

I think I've got a thing for women urinating. Not in a sick way. I'm not talking I want a golden shower or anything like that. But the image of a woman's pale cheeks on cold porcelain makes me yearn to be a toilet seat. I picture the goose bumps starting to rise on Beth's bare ass. The toilet flushes. I listen close to hear the elastic snap as she pulls up her panties.

Okay, maybe it's a little sick.

"All done," Beth says.

We're attending our ten-year high school reunion. Beth had the idea to have a combined Ridge-Prep reunion. As Empire Ridge High School Class of '89 president, I was tasked with doing much of the field work.

"Pretty big turnout," I say.

"See," Beth says. "I told you Prepsters weren't snobs. We Ridgies are the ones with the chips on our shoulders and the inferiority complexes."

Beth and I approach the bar. I raise two fingers.

"What are we having tonight?" the bartender asks.

"What do you got?" I say.

"Just Bud and Bud Light," he answers,

Beth shakes her head. "I can't do straight-up Budweiser."

"Not in the mood for the Heavy, huh?" I say. "The Heavy" is a popular nickname for Budweiser. The judges will also accept "Diesel" and of course the standard "Bud."

Beth places her hand on her waist and strikes a pose. "I have to watch my girlish figure, you know."

"Is this the part where I'm supposed to say, 'Beth, your butt's not really that big'?"

"No, Hank." She smacks me on the arm. "This is the part where you make an innocuous statement that has nothing to do with my butt, because by specifically singling out my butt, you reinforce my insecurities and subconscious belief that my butt is in fact big."

"Uh, come again?"

"We've been married for four years," Beth says.

"I realize that."

"So you should realize when to talk or not talk about my ass."

"There are times when I can't talk about your ass?"

"Sir," the bartender interrupts. "You know what you want yet?"

I place a ten-dollar bill on the bar top. "I guess make it two Butt Lights."

"Excuse me?"

The joke escapes the bartender. At some point over the last decade Bud Light eclipsed Miller Lite in popularity, which is unfortunate because Bud Light tastes like plastic and gives me diarrhea to the point where I've taken to calling it Butt Light. I'd even settle for a Natty right about now.

"Bud Light is fine, and keep the change." I slide the ten-dollar bill across the bar. The bartender slides two amber bottles back at me.

I hand Beth hers. She sips the beer, nursing the bottle and her ass-driven self-esteem. "Anybody interesting on the walk-in list yet?"

"Chip Funke is here," I say. "You just have to get past his groupies."

"Really?" Beth says, starstruck.

I'm still amazed at Chip Funke's meteoric rise from McDonald's third shift manager to teenage weekend warrior to NASCAR phenom. For about eighty years Empire Ridge has been home to the limestone quarries that built the Empire State Building, the Pentagon, the Biltmore Estate, the St. Anthony Society Chapter House at Yale, the entire University of Chicago campus, and the Washington National Cathedral—and yet the city was finally put on the map because one of its citizens possessed a high aptitude for making left turns.

"Chip had to attend a friend's wedding in North Carolina this afternoon, but a friend of a friend of a friend told me he was going to bust his ass to get here."

"Not bad for the bandie who always talked about his go-karts."

"The what?" I say.

"Your words, not mine, when I said we should invite him to the reunion."

"I never called him that."

"You most certainly did call him that," Beth says. "I asked if you knew Chip Funke in high school, and you said that he was quiet, pretty much kept to himself."

"That's not the same as calling him a—"

"And then you added, 'I really just remember him as being a bandie who always talked about his go-karts.'"

"Fucking bandies."

"Wasn't your father a bandie?"

"Yeah," I say. "But Dad didn't cost me prom king."

"After ten years you're still sore about that?"

"I couldn't get the hood or bandie vote to save my fucking life."

"You're a pretty boy, Hank. Always have been, always will be."

"But I went to pig roasts, I got in fights with Prepsters for no reason. I had street cred."

"Street cred," a disembodied voice says from across the room. "That's fucking hilarious."

Like the parting of the Red Sea, the crowd separates, cleaved neatly in half by Elias Hatcher's booming voice.

"What's a guy got to do to get a ginger ale around here?" Hatch grabs me and Beth in a full bear hug. We haven't seen each other in four years. His cutlass bangs against my leg. I can feel his hardened, sinewy body underneath his Full Dress Navy Whites, and I'm more than a little envious.

"Nice uniform," I say.

"And how," Beth adds.

Hatch stands at attention, salutes. "Petty Officer Third Class Elias Hatcher at your service."

I grab Hatch by the shoulder. "Color me fucking impressed."

"But wait, there's more," Hatch says. "Claire, you can come out now."

The Hottest Girl I Never Tried to Sleep With comes around the corner. Beth screams, runs to Claire, and about knocks her over. They hug, scream a little more, make a couple quick excuses for why they haven't kept in touch.

Claire comes up to me, winks, and gives me a big kiss on the lips. "I've missed you, Hank."

Maybe it's because I'm standing in a room of former classmates whose bald heads and multiple chins don't seem to give a shit about life, but I think Claire looks better than she did in high school. A silver sequined cocktail dress accentuates legs I don't remember being that long and an ass that's as exactly as tight as I remember. I wink back, and I mean it. "Feeling's mutual, Claire."

"What the hell is that on your ring finger?" Beth says. "Is that what I think it is?"

Claire looks down at her left hand, smiles. "Yes, it is."

"We got hitched in Vegas last night," Hatch says.

Beth, Claire, and I have spent the last hour doing tequila shots. Not our best decision. I tried to talk Chip Funke into being our designated driver, but he said he needed to fly back that night to Charlotte. Something about wrecking his car in practice and being on "Bill Junior's shit list." Apparently Bill Junior is someone I should know, so I nodded and said, "That's the last guy you want to piss off." I had Beth take at least five pictures of us together. I'm pretty sure I was a total ass.

Depeche Mode's "Somebody" starts playing on the dance floor.

"Where the hell is my husband?" Claire says.

"He's walking around being Hatch," I say. "You can take the guy out of Empire Ridge, but you can't take the Empire Ridge out of the guy."

"Still the social fucking butterfly, isn't he?"

"Always," I say.

"I love this song." Claire grabs my hand. "How about a twirl with the new bride?"

I look to Beth. She nods. "Go on. I'm in no shape to dance."

Claire and I are reasonably hip people. And given that we spent our formative years as drinking buddies in the late eighties and early nineties, it's written in stone that we must worship Depeche Mode. "Somebody" is an awkwardly intimate song, a point of fact I fail to remember until I get on the dance floor.

Claire runs her hands through my hair, because she's Claire. "You surprised?"

"That's an understatement. You and Hatch? When did it start?"

"About six months ago. I had a layover in Heathrow. Hatch was in London on leave. We kinda just hit it off."

"Kinda? What happened to Derek?"

"You know and I know he was never going to settle down."

"True. But Hatch?"

"What's wrong with Hatch?"

"Nothing. I just always thought of you two more as siblings than lovers."

"Me, too."

"Then what gives?"

"Things change. Feelings change. Plus, neither of us wants kids, and with him being a naval officer and me a flight attendant, our hectic schedules just somehow fit together."

"That doesn't sound like love to me."

"It'll get there," Claire says. "I'm sure you know what I mean."

"No, I don't know what you mean."

"Don't play dumb with me, Hank. I remember that night at Mineshaft."

"I wondered how long you were going to hold that over me."

"Hold it over you? You know that's not my style."

"But Beth is your best friend."

"And so are you. I knew the day you two got engaged you weren't fucking ready. I figured you'd mess up along the way, but with a little luck you'd get there. Nobody's perfect, except for maybe your father."

The DJ grabs the microphone, stumbles through a contrived segue into Richard Marx's "Right Here Waiting." It's another overly personal love song, but Claire and I keep dancing, unfazed.

"Claire, my dad was far from per—"

"What's it been now, six years?"

"Seven years in October."

"I miss him, Hank."

"Take a number."

"I sense a little resentment. You okay?"

"My dad had his faults. Why can't people just love him without fucking canonizing him? Did you know he was a draft dodger?"

"What?"

"Back in the late sixties, Dad got his draft notice for Vietnam right after he and Mom got engaged. He ended up failing his physical for the military."

"Flat feet?" Claire looks down at my feet, remembering my own personal deformity.

"No, smart gal." I roll my eyes. "A hernia."

"Easily fixable."

"Exactly! But guess what? The government can't order you to have the surgery. Dad refused to get the operation until he was too old for the draft."

"So you have your dad's weak groin to thank for being alive?"

"I guess you could say that." I laugh, but only a little. I'm struck by the role Dad's balls have played in my life. A cough here, a snip there. Gaming the system. Learning how to be a man after someone has lost the instructions or else read them to you in fucking Spanish.

"Speaking of fathers, congratulations. Sasha, right?"

"That's right," I say. "Sasha Grace."

"Two years old?"

"Just turned three."

"Any sisters or brothers planned?"

"One or two more, depending on what Beth can handle. Sasha was a C-section."

"Ouch."

"And my wife might be the meanest pregnant woman on Earth."

"On behalf of all past, present, or future pregnant women, go suck a dick."

"I'm not kidding. Hitting, screaming, cursing—you name it. If my wife were a dude, I could've had her arrested."

"And yet you kept coming back for more."

"Of course I did."

"Why?"

"Because I love her, Claire."

"I can see that, Hank." A wistful, almost envious look from the ever-guarded Claire Sullivan Hatcher. She runs her hands through my hair again. "You're very sexy when you're in love—have I ever told you that?"

I smile at Claire. She positions herself closer to me, my knee now firmly between her legs. I place my hand on the small of her back, maybe even a little lower than that. Low enough to know she's not wearing any panties. If her hemline were any higher, my knee would be buried in her bush right now. Tanned a soft gold and rock-hard, Claire's calves flex with every step she makes.

Claire and I have always had great chemistry. But in lieu of attempting anything that could be deemed a relationship—sexual, casual, or otherwise—we long ago settled into a flirty but harmless cat-and-mouse game.

At least this is what I keep telling myself. What Claire and I engage in is definitely flirty, but hardly harmless. A failed relationship or lost love is a maypole of life, for a brief moment the absolute unyielding center of everything but in time dismissed as something not worth getting that excited about. Far harder to escape the semi-permanent shadows of an affair that never was.

"Mind if we dance with yo' dates?"

The combination of the *Animal House* reference and Richard Marx giving way to Poison's "Every Rose Has Its Thorn" snaps me back to reality.

"What?" I say.

Hatch and Beth stand in front of us on the dance floor. "May we cut in?" Hatch says.

I step back, bow. "Be my guest."

Claire winks at me again. "Thanks for the dance, Hank."

Not only do I not wink back, I don't even make eye contact. "You're welcome."

Beth reclaims my empty hand. She straddles my leg, more obvious with her dry humping than Claire was, being my wife and all. "You two looked pretty cozy," she says.

"You know Claire is like a sister to me."

Beth shakes her head. "In West Virginia maybe."

"She's your best friend."

"That's never stopped her from hitting on my boyfriends—or my husband apparently."

"What do you want me to say, Beth?"

"How about 'I love you, honey'?"

"I love y—"

Beth puts her hand on my mouth. "It doesn't count if I have to prompt you."

I take her hand away. "It seems like it doesn't count regardless."

"And what's that supposed to mean?"

"It means that maybe I'd enjoy dancing with Claire a little less if you showed more interest in me."

"More interest? We had sex last night."

"Yeah, for the first time in eight weeks."

"I'm sorry. Apparently you've been living in a cave for the last three years. Have you seen my stomach? Ever since the C-section, my abs look like a fat old person's ass. I don't feel pretty."

"But you *are* pretty. You're fucking hot. We've had this conversation before. I'm a very vain guy. If you get ugly and fat, I'm divorcing you."

"You really know how to make a gal feel special, Hank."

"That's what you don't seem to get. You're still in twice as good a shape as almost any twenty-eight-year-old woman I know, let alone tonight's episode of *The Bald and the Bloated.*"

"Except for Claire."

"Fuck Claire! She's got her high school body because she's never been pregnant, and she's too self-absorbed to ever get pregnant."

Beth leans in, kisses me on the lips. "You really think that?"

"Hell yes, I think that." I lick my lips, tasting both Claire's and Beth's lipstick on my tongue. I'm pretty fucking turned on right now.

"You're just buttering me up."

"No I'm not," I say. "The butter comes later tonight."

2000

CHAPTER SEVENTY-ONE

Beth and I sit in Dr. Florio's office. My wife flips through the March 2000 issue of *Parents* magazine. She's uneasy, rifling through the pages without looking at them.

I grab her hands, take the magazine away. "Will you just relax, honey?"

She inhales deeply, turns and looks at me. "Bite me."

We're here for the eighteen-week ultrasound. This time around we're finding out the baby's gender—that is, if my wife doesn't have a heart attack in her OB's waiting room.

I left Jack at home with Sasha. Jack is staying with us for a few days. Mom is up in Indianapolis with Aunt Claudia getting all of Grandma Louise's affairs in order.

Grandma died last week. I tried to cry at the funeral and play the part of the heartbroken grandson, but it's hard to get past the fact she was such a psychotic, racist bitch. Jeanine brought her fiancé, Marcus. They met in Portland when Jeanine was his physical therapist. Marcus is a professional basketball player for the Idaho Stampede of the Continental Basketball Association, and he's black as coal. Grandma would have hated him, and I loved Jeanine for bringing him.

There's a lot riding on today's OB visit. One girl and one boy is the master plan. This pregnancy has no other option but a boy. Our new gay neighbors, Oscar and Marshall, told us to load up on red meat and salty snacks and for me to pound a pot of coffee before sex to get the Y-chromosome sperms swimming faster. Beth's thong-wearing aerobics instructor with the store-bought breasts—I think her name is Shena, but I might just have Tone Loc's "Wild Thing" in my head—told her to have "as much sex as humanly possible" because more boys are conceived during the honeymoon phase of a relationship. Needless to say, I'm a fan of Shena. Beth's hairdresser, Jodi, told her to let me initiate sex and focus on my pleasure because "if the man climaxes first, you almost always conceive a baby boy." I like Jodi, too. Her hair is two-toned, blonde with dark roots. She has these wild sky-blue eyes that give her a hot, older-woman vibe, like Julie Christie in *Afterglow.* A lot of people say if they had a time machine, they'd go back two thousand years and meet Jesus Christ; personally, I'd just go back to 1965 and fuck Julie Christie. Jodi has been pumping out kids since her teens and sneaks out for a smoke every fifteen minutes. When she washes my hair, it feels so good I feel like I'm cheating on my wife.

Putting aside our friends' learned advice, and Beth's father being a pediatrician and all, we've done our homework on this one. There are fifty-one boys born for every forty-nine girls, so we know math is on our side. We flirted with trying the Shettles Method, which mandates "deep, penetrative intercourse no more than twenty-four hours before ovulation and no more than twelve hours past ovulation." The Chinese Conception Method showed some promise, right up until we realized all our dates were wrong because we were using the Gregorian calendar instead of the Chinese lunisolar calendar. Ultimately, we settled on the Whelan Method—i.e., having sex at the beginning of Beth's cycle up until four-to-six days before ovulation. Whelan doesn't specify the level of depth or penetration like Shettles does, so I improvised. (I've narrowed it down to somewhere between "fuck me harder" and "fuck, that hurts.") All I know is the Whelan Method involves more sex than most any other approach, so I'm willing to make the sacrifice—you know, for the children.

The door to the waiting room opens. A nearly attractive nurse with pinned-back hair and comfortable shoes holds a clipboard and smiles at us. "Mrs. Fitzpatrick?"

Dr. Florio smiles at my wife, her hand on her belly. "How you feeling, kiddo?"

"Not so good, to tell you the truth," Beth says. "I've had a lot more nausea and a lot less sleep with this pregnancy."

"Interesting." Dr. Florio squirts the ultrasound gel onto my wife's bulging abdomen with her right hand, follows up with the transducer in her left hand. "Let's take a look, shall we?"

We eye the black and white sonogram. There's only so much you can see four and a half months into a pregnancy, at least that's what I remember with our daughter. With her translucent spine and huge head, Sasha looked more like a cross between a baby dinosaur and Patrick Ewing.

"Whoa!" I say. "That popped up fast."

We see the back of our baby. It turns. We see a beating heart. "Hmmm…" Dr. Florio says.

Beth turns to her. "What?"

"Your husband was right. He did pop up fast."

"*He* popped up fast?" I say.

Dr. Florio points to the baby's now-obvious phallus. "Oh, he's definitely a boy."

Beth raises her hand. I give her a high five. She notices Dr. Florio's pensive look. "Is there something you're not telling us, doctor?"

"There's a reason he popped up fast," Dr. Florio says. "I'm going to turn the probe ninety degrees here and let you see for yourself."

"Holy shit," Beth says.

"What?" I say. "What am I looking at?"

Dr. Florio adjusts the transducer. "You're looking at two heartbeats, Hank."

"Come again?"

Beth puts her hand over her face. "I'm pregnant with twins."

"That's why you poked out so quick at eighteen weeks."

"And that's why you're sicker," I add, "and not sleeping compared to when you were carrying Sasha."

"It certainly explains a lot," Beth says. "I got the hormones of two boys raging inside me."

"Exactly," Dr. Florio says.

I shake my head. "Are you sure, Doc?"

She points to the video monitor. "There are clearly two babies, kiddo. The second one is just lying across the bottom, hiding almost. And they both look to be boys."

"And this would explain the abnormalities in my AFP tests a couple weeks ago?" Beth asks.

Dr. Florio nods. "It totally explains it."

I have no idea what the hell "AFP" means, but I give a confident, affirmative nod as if everything in the world now makes sense. I can barely get past page twenty of *What to Expect When You're Expecting.* My interest always starts to lag in the middle of the Fibroids section, and I completely jump ship at Incompetent Cervix.

My wife is crying.

"Beth," I say. "You okay?"

"I'm fine. Just a little scared is all."

"These two boys look perfectly healthy, kiddo."

"It's not that, doctor," Beth says. "It's just that I've been reading up on vaginal births after a cesarean. I was really hoping with this pregnancy that I could at least try to—"

"VBACs aren't for everyone. They're not for most people, quite frankly."

"I know that."

"Least of all gymnasts and their narrow pelvises."

"As you've told me before."

"Let's just cross that bridge when we come to it." I run my hands through Beth's hair. Brushing her bangs back, I kiss her on the forehead. "You'll be fine. I promise."

CHAPTER SEVENTY-TWO

"I hear congratulations are in order."

Lila Prestwich stands at the entrance to the College Avenue Press office. She's wearing tight jeans and a sleeveless knit top that barely contains her always-ample bosom. Her hair is cropped just below her chin, her skin giving off the somewhat off-putting black currant scent of Ralph Lauren Safari perfume. A printed tote with a Strand Bookstore logo hangs over her right shoulder.

I walk over to Lila. She gives me a casual hug. "How long have you been standing there?"

"Long enough," Lila says.

"So you heard that phone call?"

"Was that Beth?"

"More like her evil doppelganger."

"Trouble in paradise?"

"That's an understatement. I once told someone that my wife might be the meanest pregnant woman on Earth. I take that back—she is the meanest pregnant woman on Earth."

"Sorry to hear about that. Still, congrats. Twin boys, huh?"

"Who told you?"

"Your boss."

"Fucking Rosner. When was that?"

"It was when he was in New York last month. He came by my apartment and took me out to celebrate."

"Yeah, celebrate."

"*College Avenue Press, an imprint of the Random House Publishing Group.* That isn't worth celebrating?"

"It's just 'College Ave' now, per an edict from some marketing department idiot who thinks branding means anything in publishing. They even got really cute and changed our logo to a navy blue rectangle with the word 'COLLEGE' in white caps."

"Like John Belushi's sweatshirt in *Animal House*?"

"Exactly."

"Very cute."

"Aaron took the money and ran. Meanwhile, I'm afforded a slightly bigger paycheck with a lot less editorial freedom. Forgive me if I don't join in the merriment. But enough about me. To what do I owe this visit?"

"Just flew in today. I wanted to stop in and say hello before I drove down to Empire Ridge."

"Well, hello."

Lila reaches out and gives me a much improved hug followed up with a kiss on the cheek. "Hello, Hank."

"Here, have a seat." I smile, offering her a chair. "How's New York treating you?"

"Best city in the world."

I sit in the chair opposite her. "Still working for that literary agency?"

"Not anymore. I took a job with Little, Brown and Company just last month. I'm their new director of foreign rights."

"Nice."

"It sounds nicer than it pays."

"And who's the lucky guy in your life these days?"

"Chris."

"Next time I'm in New York you should introduce me to him."

"I'll introduce you to *her* if you'd like."

"Come again?"

"Hank..." Lila says, patting my hand. "I'm a single Mormon woman pushing thirty. You figure it out."

"I guess I just never figured you for a—"

"Lesbian?"

"Yeah."

"Chris is the hardcore lesbian. I'm still solidly in the bisexual camp. We're living together in one of her father's brownstone rentals on the Upper Westside. She's the lead singer of an all-girl band called Femshack."

"How very New York of you."

Lila nods, raised her eyebrows. "Yeah, Dad is really pleased."

"How is Papa Prestwich doing these days?"

"You'd know better than me, Hank."

"I doubt it."

Actually, I do know better. Mom and Gillman Prestwich have been dating for six weeks. After Mom's rogues' gallery of suitors, I figure a guy who doesn't drink, doesn't swear, and goes to church too much is probably a safe option.

"They're so cute together, Hank."

"I'll take your word for it. Now, I'm assuming you didn't come here just to chat about the Odd Couple and tell me you've started playing for the other team."

"Astute observation as always." Lila reaches down into her shoulder bag, pulls out a manuscript. She hands me the tightly bound pages. The first page is blank. The second page has a W.B. Yeats quote from the poem "The Second Coming" that says,

The darkness drops again; but now I know That twenty centuries of stony sleep were vexed to nightmare by a rocking cradle,

And what rough beast, its hour come round at last, Slouches towards Bethlehem to be born?

"WHAT IS THIS?" I say.

"It's my book."

"That thing you've been working on for like five years that you won't tell anyone about?"

"All one hundred and twenty thousand words of it. The working title is *The Messiah Project*."

"Quick synopsis?"

"It's a near-future dystopian novel that asks the question, What would happen if someone traveled back in time, obtained the genetic material of Jesus of Nazareth, came back to the future, and foisted the Second Coming on the world by creating a cloned Christ?"

"Holy shit, Lila. I love it! It's very commercial. Plus you have this great angle as this attractive, well-connected, fall-away Mormon. I assume your agent is sending it out to the big boys—Random House, Simon and Schuster, Penguin, or at least your own people at Little Brown."

"He wants to, but I don't know."

"Lila, come on now. Bunts aren't your style. You need to swing for the fences on this one."

"Like I said, I don't know."

"What's to know?"

"I feel like the big New York houses just aren't for me. I work for one, so I have a pretty good idea how much they suck. My book has to pique the interest of an editor, who then submits the manuscript to an ed board meeting in which a room full of editors with disparate literary tastes must somehow come to a consensus that the book is publishable by spending an hour vetting the author's platform and sixty seconds vetting the author's actual writing acumen."

"Sounds about right," I say. "At some point in the last ten years, the word 'platform' went from meaning 'a raised horizontal surface' to 'the degree to which one manages to blow smoke up an editor's ass.'"

"Exactly," Lila says. "Which is why I've been trying to focus on some midsized—Norton, Houghton Mifflin, Harcourt, Bloomsbury."

"And what's the word?"

"Most editors seem to enjoy the book, to a point."

"What point is that?"

"The point at which the protagonist obtains Jesus Christ's *genetic material*. I've been told the scene is somewhat blasphemous."

"Oh, come on, seventy-five percent of your editor friends are Jews. How bad can it be?"

"Let me preface this by saying the protagonist is a theoretical physicist and recovering crack addict who discovers time travel at about the same time she becomes a born-again Christian."

"I love her already."

"An angel visits our protagonist in her sleep and tells her she must travel back to ancient Jerusalem to procure the seed of the Son of David and bring it back to the future to fulfill the prophecy of the Messiah's return."

"Procure the seed?"

Lila nods, points at me. "That's the tricky part. She drugs Jesus and gives him a handjob."

"Why not go all the way and have her give him a blowjob?"

"Well, she starts off doing just that but is worried her saliva might taint the semen."

"Fantastic! What happens next?"

"She travels back to the future intent on inseminating herself with Jesus's sperm, only to misplace the sample at a local sperm bank, and then—"

"Madcap hilarity ensues from there?"

"More or less."

"And you're telling me no publisher will touch this?"

"Are you really surprised, Hank? This is the new millennium. Clinton is out, Dubya is in, and the publishers see the writing on the wall. Like Moses's golden calf, Christian fiction is a huge cash cow just waiting to be suckled."

"And imagery like that is exactly why you should have a publishing deal."

"Oh, I signed with a publisher," Lila says.

I scratch the winter stubble on my face. "Who is it?"

"I'm looking at him right now."

"Huh?"

"Aaron and I had two things to celebrate. He signed with Random House, and then he signed me as College Ave's newest author, with you as my editor."

I grab Lila's shoulders and squeeze her tight. I kiss her right on the lips. "Well, hot damn!"

Lila looks flustered, and she never looks flustered. "So you're okay with this?"

"Why wouldn't I be?"

"Well, Aaron and I kind of took the decision out of your hands."

"Lila, it's not like I don't know you're a good writer. I've been asking to see your stuff for years."

"And now you're going to see probably too much of it. Just promise me you'll be brutally honest."

"I have no intention of patronizing you. The first step in becoming a good writer is allowing people to tell you you're a bad one."

"That's a good line, Hank."

"That's a *great* fucking line. Now, before we get started, I only ask for one concession."

"What's that?"

"Change the title."

"What's wrong with *The Messiah Project*? It's an allusion to the Manhattan Project."

"Uh, yeah, I get that, which is kind of my point."

"And what is your point exactly?"

"The title isn't subtle enough. Leave the hitting-the-reader-over-the-head allusions to C. S. Lewis."

"What problem could you possibly have with C. S. Lewis?"

"You mean, other than the fact Aslan basically introduces himself by screaming, 'Hey readers, Jesus Christ in da fuckin' house!'"

"Easy, Hank." Lila raises her hands in submission. I can almost see the Mormon in her wincing as I pepper her with heresy. "Any suggestions, oh wise editor?"

"Just one."

"Lay it on me."

"It's perfect."

"I'll be the judge of that."

Magician-like, I unfurl the imaginary marquee with my hands. "*Sperm Bank Messiah*," I say.

Jesus doesn't talk to me anymore—hell, he probably never did—but I can almost picture Aslan standing behind Lila, shaking his head in disgust. Lila assumes I'm joking, just as I assume God doesn't notice me go through a box of Kleenex every other week without ever having a cold.

CHAPTER SEVENTY-THREE

The moment we got back from Beth's OB with the news of the twins, I started running, and I haven't stopped. I don't know why I'm running: excitement, fear, uncertainty. I'm running five, seven, sometimes ten miles a day, six days a week. I'm at one hundred and eighty-four pounds, down from my wedding peak of two-fifteen. My wife passed me on the scales this morning at one eighty-five. She has packed on nearly sixty-five pounds during the pregnancy.

I sip my coffee. "Would you stop crying already?"

Sasha is still sleeping. Beth sits at the kitchen table. She's wearing my robe because her robe doesn't fit her anymore. Her hair is wound tightly on top of her head beneath a white cotton towel. She's been crying for about twenty minutes straight.

This is pretty much our standard third-trimester breakfast. This morning in bed, I came at Beth with my 6:00 a.m. erection, assumed the spoons position, and squeezed her milk-sodden circus boobs. She rejected my advances, and then I went into my commensurate emotional shell and ignored her as she tried to explain how her lack of a sex drive had nothing to do with her feelings for me. I went downstairs, put on some coffee, and masturbated to Internet porn, which afforded Beth just enough time to shower, look at herself in the mirror after getting out of the shower, and crank up the self-loathing.

While I'm on the subject of porn, I simply couldn't imagine being a teenager in the Internet age. Instant gratification with the click of a mouse: holy hell, I would've been blind and dead by age sixteen. Barring a cooler older brother or an oblivious father with a hidden stash, porn in the eighties was acquired through a mix of subterfuge and raw tenacity. Even then, it usually amounted to only bad soft-core videos and ten-year-old hand-me-down magazines.

"Fuck you, Hank!"

"Is this still about your weight?"

"I'm heavier than you!"

"It's just a number."

"Husbands are supposed to be supportive."

"I'd like to think I'm doing a pretty good job at that."

"You're not supportive. You're fucking one eighty-four!"

I shake my head in disbelief. I run my hands through my hair. "That's what's bothering you? The fact I'm not a goateed, pinheaded lard ass like most of your friends' husbands? Go ahead, call up your gal pals. Ask them if their husbands make a pass at them every morning and night, even when they weigh a hundred and eighty-five pounds."

"Having the libido of a sixteen-year-old boy doesn't make you a good husband."

"But it doesn't me make a bad one either."

"I didn't say that."

"Maybe not in so many words. What do you want me to do, Beth? Do you want me to apologize for being attracted to you?"

"No."

"Then what?"

"I want you to apologize for not being my friend."

"Oh Christ."

"Wanting me is the easy part for you."

"I got a thing for my wife," I say, shrugging my shoulders. "Guilty as charged."

"It's *liking* me that you struggle with."

"Well, I'm sure struggling with liking you right now."

"Stop being so fucking glib."

I touch her shoulder. "Look, that came out wrong. I'm sorry."

Beth looks at my hand, then down at the table. "Do you even know what you're apologizing for?"

I remove my hand from her shoulder. "Not a clue."

"Then why apologize?"

"Because I rarely know what I'm apologizing for."

"Fuck you, asshole!"

I stand up from the table, turning my back on her hostility. The kitchen opens up to the family room. I walk to the side table along the far wall of the family room, grab the dog-eared copy of *What to Expect When You're Expecting*. I walk back to the kitchen, open the book, and slam it down in front of my wife.

"Show me," I say.

"What?"

"Just show me, Beth."

"I don't know what you want me to—"

"Maybe I missed a section. Maybe somewhere between gastrointestinal ills, rubella, toxoplasmosis, cytomegalovirus, fifth disease, group B strep, Lyme disease, measles, UTI, hepatitis, mumps, and chicken pox, I missed the part about abusive wife syndrome."

Beth is crying again. "Y-you just recited those diseases off the top of your head?"

"Of course I did." I grab my coat off the coat tree in the hallway leading to the garage door. The coat is an olive double-breasted London Fog trench that used to belong to my father. It's a little dated, but I'll wear it forever.

"How did you know all of them?"

"Because I read the goddamn book," I say, buttoning my coat. "Chapter fifteen lists all the shit that can go wrong with your body during pregnancy."

"But why did you read it?" Beth says.

I open the door to the garage, turn to my wife. "I read it because you're my friend, because I like you."

CHAPTER SEVENTY-FOUR

Mom got married, again.

She and Gillman Prestwich dated for a whole twelve weeks before eloping. They got married in Nauvoo, Illinois, which I'm told holds some sort of sacred significance to Mormons, but to Mom's credit, she refuses to convert. Once a Catholic, always a Catholic, I guess, although I'm not allowed to swear or bring alcohol into her house.

Son of a bitch, that really fucking sucks a goddamn ass-ramming moose cock.

Phew. I feel better now.

CHAPTER SEVENTY-FIVE

Basic Search
First Name **Angelina** Last Name **Valerio**
City or ZIP / Postal **Boston** State / Prov
MA
What the fuck am I doing?

I've considered a lot of reasons as to why I've decided to contact my Spring Break '91 fling—the most meteorically intense but brief love of my life and, in fact, the only other woman besides Beth I had ever considered marrying—when my wife is nearly nine months pregnant with twins. Being in a sexless, emotionally abusive marriage for the last six months might have something to do with it, but the reason I seem to have settled on is actually a rhetorical question: what's wrong with a guy on the cusp of being a father again taking stock of his past and wanting closure with someone who used to be important to him? And by rhetorical, I mean I don't want anyone to answer that question, because the obvious answer is nothing's wrong with that—if you're an insensitive douche pump.

"What are you doing, Hank?"

"Nothing, Urwa."

Urwa Mashwanis is College Ave's silver-haired, middle-aged Pakistani IT director. He's a nice guy, annoying as hell but forever well-intentioned. He constantly and, too often, graphically whines about his marital woes, a typical conversation with him going something like this: "How's Beth doing with her pregnancy? My wife put on a hundred pounds with our baby and never lost it, and now she refuses to have sex doggie style because she doesn't want me to see her cellulite ass. Only missionary, only missionary. She doesn't even like the cunny-lingus. You want to grab lunch?"

Urwa looks at the top of my computer screen, reading aloud. "Whitepages.com? Who you looking for?"

"Nobody."

"Angelina Valerio doesn't sound like nobody to me."

Aaron Rosner tends to err on the side of apocalyptic—maybe it's a Jewish thing—so in anticipation of Y2K, he hired Urwa away from Eli Lilly's patent division for twice the salary. Predictably, Y2K amounted to a whole lot of nothing, but Urwa was retained at the same level of compensation. This pisses me off a little. While, yes, my family's seven-figure settlement with the Indianapolis Auto Auction has paid for three cars and half the mortgage on my house, my actual salary still skirts IRS tax brackets with the reckless abandon of someone who, minus a dead father, would be flirting with abject poverty.

"You want to grab some lunch?"

"We've been through this before, Urwa. You don't eat lunch."

"Sure I do. Large fries. Best deal in town."

Urwa insists that the $1.75 the MCL Cafeteria down the street charges for a Styrofoam box filled to the rim with French fries is the steal of the century. "I figure I get about a thousand calories for less than two bucks," he is fond of saying.

I just need to stop arguing with Urwa and let the potato-addicted Pakistani face his maker—probably sooner than he's likely anticipating—on his own grease-laden terms. "Fine, Urwa, eat your damn fries."

"You still haven't answered my question."

"What question?"

Urwa points at my computer monitor. "Who's Angelina Valerio?"

"She's nobody."

"She's not nobody. I've seen the letters you typed to her."

"How about you get back to your desk and mind your own business? It wasn't multiple letters. There was just one."

"I counted at least four."

"Damn, Urwa," I say. "You are one nosy fucking Pakistani. There was only one letter. I sent copies of the same letter to four different people."

"Oh," Urwa says. "Why did you do that?"

"Angelina Valerio is an old friend who I lost track of is all."

"Friend?"

"Fine, an old *girl*friend. Beth and I have had a rough go of things the last couple months."

"Beth's body is going through lots of changes," Urwa says, empathetic apparently as long as it doesn't involve the prohibition of doggie style and the cunny-lingus.

"Don't you think I know that?" I say. "It's not like I'm going to do anything stupid. I'm just real lonely and want to talk to an old friend. I've spent the last three weeks searching the Internet for any Angelina Valerios along the East Coast."

"The East Coast?"

"Angelina was from Boston."

"Got it."

"I found four Angelina Valerios in the greater Boston area and sent four duplicate letters out to these women."

"What if they call you back and Beth answers the phone?"

"Won't happen."

"How do you know?"

"I listed my office phone number and office return address on the letters."

"Smart thinking."

"I thought so."

"Deceitful thinking, but smart thinking."

"You can shut up and listen to my story, or you can be an asshole. Your choice."

"Sorry," Urwa says. "Go on."

"Three of these Angelina Valerios have returned my call, all of them telling me the same exact thing—'I'm not the Angelina you're looking for, but your letter was so beautiful I wish I was her.'"

"Some letter I take it."

"I thought so."

My phone rings. The caller ID on the phone flashes *Out of Area*. "You going to answer that?"

"Nope," I say. "Probably just Cindy again."

"Aaron's former secretary?"

"Admin assistant."

"Yeah, whatever. I thought Aaron fired her."

"He did."

"She still calls you a lot."

"That's because she still wants my dick."

"You have a highly inflated opinion of yourself, Hank."

"That's a fair comment," I say. "But in this case I'm not exaggerating. Remember when Aaron, Cindy, and I went to that Canadian bookseller convention in Windsor?"

"Vaguely."

"Well, the three of us went out on the town one night. We ended up at Jason's."

"Jason's?"

"A famous high-end strip club."

Urwah's face practically lights up. "Continue," he says.

"Cindy had never been to one, so we took her. She got really drunk."

"*Really* drunk?"

"Really drunk."

"What happened?"

"Aaron disappeared into one of the back rooms with three girls and a wad of hundred dollar bills, so Cindy and I took a cab back to the hotel. The moment we got back, Cindy stuck her tongue in my ear in the elevator, told me she was going to her room to draw a bath, and asked me to join her."

"So she didn't really come right out and say she wanted your dick."

I shake my head. "You're right, Urwa. She didn't say that. I guess she could have just been implying that my personal hygiene left something to be desired and that in the interest of being environmentally conscious we do some innocent tandem bathing."

The phone starts ringing again. Again the caller ID flashes *Out of Area*. "Just pick it up, Hank."

"Fine," I say. I pick up the phone. "Hello, this is Hank."

"Hank Fitzpatrick?"

"Yes."

"Hank, how ah yuh?"

My chest hurts. Hearing that deep Boston inflection for the first time in nine years makes me dizzy, short of breath.

"Angelina?"

"You muss think I'm so wid callin' yuh like this."

"Weird?" I say. "I'm the one who wrote a letter and mailed it to four random Angelina Valerios in the greater Boston area."

"Foh-uh?"

"Yeah, Angelina." I close my eyes and smile, inhaling the memories. "Foh-uh."

"Yuh always knew how to sweep a gal off huh feet."

Urwah hovers over my desk. "Angelina, can I put you on hold for just one second?"

"Shu-uh."

I stare down Urwah. "What?" he says.

"Aaron coming in at all today?"

"Not that I'm aware of," Urwah says.

"I'm taking this in Aaron's office."

He swats his hand at me. "You're no fun."

CHAPTER SEVENTY-SIX

elcome to Indianapolis International Airport."

I make my way through security to the Delta terminal. I take a peek at the arrivals listed on the video screen. Her plane landed at Gate A7 ten minutes ago.

"Smoking is prohibited in the main concourse of Indianapolis International and is restricted to designated smoking areas."

The automated voice over the PA sounds strangely familiar, but I'm too nervous to think about that right now.

"I'd be nervous, too, if I were you."

"Who said that?" I say, turning around. People are staring at me.

"I think you know who this is, Hank."

"Jesus?"

"It's been a while. How about we go somewhere a little quieter so all these nice people don't get freaked out by the guy talking to himself?"

I hold my cell phone up to my mouth. "I'll just pretend I'm talking to someone on the other end of the line."

"Suit yourself. Before I forget, what's with that book Lila is writing?"

"Sperm Bank Messiah?"

"Yes. You really make it hard for me to like you sometimes."

"Sounds like somebody needs to reread his Sermon on the Mount."

"Don't throw that back in my face."

"Hey, you're the pacifist."

"What are you doing here, Hank?"

"Relax, Jesus. Angelina has a short layover in Indy on her way to see some old college friends down in Tallahassee. She's here for an hour, and we're just having a coffee."

"Boston to Tallahassee by way of Indianapolis? Help me out with that one."

"It was like two hours out of her way, and we wanted to catch up."

"And your nearly nine-months pregnant wife knows about this?"

"I'm not hurting anyone."

"Keep telling yourself that."

"Look, these last few months with Beth have sucked. I don't have anything to feel guilty about."

"You apparently feel guilty enough to imagine your conscience as the voice of Jesus Christ who's talking to you from the airport PA system although curiously no one else can hear me."

"Hank, izzat you?"

"Uh, I gotta go." I hang up my phone.

Angelina drops her purse, runs over, and hugs me as if we just said goodbye yesterday as opposed to nine years ago. She steps back, smiles. "Look at yuh, Hank. Yuh haven't aged a day. Yuh might even be a little skinny-uh."

I smile as I listen to the *r* disappear off the end of her words. "I've been running lately."

"It shows."

"You're not so bad yourself." I wish I was just being nice, just as a part of me wished on the drive up here from Empire Ridge that Angelina had let herself go. I'm convinced the two main reasons old flames are rarely rekindled are time and gravity. The passage of years makes you forget why that beautiful young woman was special, while gravity conspires with bad eating habits and a sedentary middle-age lifestyle to distort her figure until you start believing she never was.

None of this has happened with Angelina Valerio. With the exception of some faint crow's-feet, she's still a knockout. Her hair is dark brown, nearly black. She's petite but not rail-thin, reminding me vaguely of Cynthia Gibb, Rob Lowe's love interest in *Youngblood*, but more reminiscent of Lisa Dean Ryan, a.k.a. Doogie Howser's high school sweetheart, Wanda.

"Want to grab a coffee?" I say.

Angelina looks at her watch. "I only have about forty-five minutes. How's about a Bloody Mary?"

"Twist my arm."

We sit down at the bar. We both order our Bloody Marys extra spicy. Angelina clinks my glass. "Chih-uhs."

"Cheers," I reply.

AND JUST LIKE THAT, the forty-five minutes is over. We talked about our lives since we said our goodbyes. About how Dad died. About how she was my last girlfriend who really knew my father and that this fact had always stuck with me. She told me she'd saved every one of the letters and poems I wrote her in a shoebox beneath her bed. She told me she's been bisexual for the better part of the last eight years for reasons I couldn't quite understand, but that now she was "way in-tuh dudes again" and engaged to a "Bah-stun cahp." She told me about her fiancé. I told her about Beth, Sasha, and the twins.

I escort Angelina back to her gate. She leans in and hugs me again, kissing me on the cheek.

"You know, Hank, yo-uh writin' still makes me cry."

"What part?" I say, ever the sucker for validation.

"All of it." Angelina reaches into her purse and pulls out my letter. "'As I stand once mo-uh on the vudge of fathuhood, about to again become that which I miss so much in my life, I want to find closhuh with someone who was once close to my haht, someone who knew me as just the fehlessly precocious son of Hank Fitzpatrick, and not the flawed, insuhcuh man I've become.'"

"Did I write that?"

"Don't be so modest. Yo-uh one in a million, Hank. Yo-uh the one that got away."

"Right back at you, Angelina. But I have to say, the new guy sounds like good people."

"Uh, yeah, Hank. He's good people."

We giggle, acknowledging a moment from our shared past. Myrtle Beach in just the early cusp of spring. Air temperatures still dropping into the thirties after the sun goes down. We ran naked out of the ice-cold ocean. I gave her my towel even though I had lost all sensation in my extremities. As we warmed up in the hot tub, she kissed my shivering, purple lips and said, "Yo-uh good people, Hank." Never hearing this phrase before in my life, I of course looked around to see if my family had magically teleported into the tub with me.

"I read him yo-uh lettuh, you know," Angelina says. "Pulled out the shoe baw-ux and read a couple of 'em."

"Really?"

"Yo-uh not mad, ah yuh?"

"No, no," I say. "Not at all."

"You shuh-uh?"

"Yeah, I'm sure."

"Well, okay. Call me outta the blue and let's do this again sometime."

"Sounds like a plan," I say.

I kiss Angelina on the cheek and watch her board the plane. The tone of our goodbye is too casual, both of us pretending like we'd talk again, maybe as soon as tomorrow. But I know better. As happy as I was for these forty-five minutes, this is all I'm entitled to. Angelina is like the Notre Dame football autographed by the '88 National Championship team I keep on my mantel—unblemished, tanned and oiled to a bright sheen, perfect. Never to fade in the sun. Never to be left out in the rain. Never to be thrown and bounced off blacktop until its dimples wore smooth. Never to be touched. Never to be carried to bed under the arm of an adoring child who dreamt of being the next Joe Montana.

Huh. Go figure.

I'm not jealous. I don't love Angelina Valerio, or even the idea of her. As it turns out, I'm still very much in love with my wife.

In all honesty, Beth probably doesn't give a fuck either way at that moment. Regardless of my long-overdue epiphany, she's two weeks from praying that modern medicine finds a way to stuff two watermelons inside her husband's bladder and make him shoot them out the end of his penis.

2001 – 2002

CHAPTER SEVENTY-SEVEN

Aisha adjusted the turban wound tightly to her head, her long hair bound up and dripping rivulets of sweat down the small of her back. She pulled the rough excess of her collar over her face, trying to shield herself from the drifting sand. The fake beard only added to her discomfort.

Sand snuck into the folds and various openings of her drafty garment—little more than a burlap toga, tied at the waist by a rope. It had been a birthday gift from her sister, years ago, back when their parents thought they were merely recreational hookah users and not the biggest marijuana dealers in Dearborn, Michigan. Aisha was happy she wore the thing, actually. She was far from home, in need of a touchstone.

She was six months clean, not that this helped her gain her bearings. It was just after daybreak. Strangers passed her on the streets of Jerusalem. A steady stream of Pesach pilgrims filtered into the city. A merchant towing along a caravan of camels laden with spices, fabrics, and dried figs. A peasant driving a small, curiously stoic flock of sheep—too hardy to die, too lean to ever make a profit. Three women balancing atop their heads baskets of donkey and camel dung to be later used as fuel for fires. Aisha rubbed shoulders with strangers dead two-thousand years in her world: *Sadducees, Pharisees, Phoenicians, Babylonians, Arabians, Roman soldiers, tax collectors, merchants, craftsmen, peasants, beggars, slaves. Aramaic, Hebrew, Greek, and Latin were spoken intermittently, mixing in her head and rendering translation difficult.*

While pursuing her doctorate in theoretical physics, Aisha had befriended an exiled seminarian—exiled presumably for being too deist and too heterosexual—who tutored her in Greek and was familiar with the colloquial, first-century dialect. In exchange for Ecstasy-fueled, exceedingly non-missionary sex, Aisha had mastered the language from the modern Greek all the way back to Mycenaean, plus a little Aramaic, Hebrew, and Latin.

The smell of incense, the sound of trumpets and Psalms, the oxen, sheep, kids, and doves being sold for sacrifice. All carried with them a poignancy she had never felt. The sun danced over the Mount of Olives, brighter than any sun she had ever seen. The Antonia Fortress and Herod's Temple veiled most of the city in their imposing shadows. Aisha reached down, pulling a weed from the ground outside the abandoned amphitheater. She smelled the weed, inhaling deeply and imagining troupes performing Homer, Aeschylus, Sophocles, or perhaps another even greater Greek tragedian history had forgotten. Two Jewish rabbis cursed at her in Hebrew, remembering the theater's more sinister raison d'être as a gladiatorial killing field for thousands of pious men.

"Shabot shalom," she said to them in a plaintive but consciously masculine tone.

Aisha made her way to the western edge of the city, keeping to herself as the day progressed. After the encounter with the rabbis she spoke aloud only once to buy a loaf of bread and some pressed olives. She waited outside Herod's palace for her cue from the Roman soldier. He was a handsome man, a well-muscled legionnaire in his early twenties with medium-length hair that curled out from under his helmet. His armor comprised overlapping strips of iron that hugged his torso in two halves and fastened on the front and back by a system of brass hooks and leather laces. He carried a shield and a short sword.

Late last night, Aisha had bribed him with several gold pieces and a handjob. She needed the practice. The legionnaire unlocked the palace gate and walked away.

She checked inside her hip pocket for at least the tenth time in as many minutes. Everything was still there: the half-dozen empty vials, the cryoprotectant semen extender, the plastic gloves, the small bottle of mead laced with roofies. A hundred yards down the corridor, He sat in His prison cell...

I STACK THE PAGES neatly on my desk. Trimmed down from one hundred and twenty thousand words to an even seventy-five thousand, *Sperm Bank Messiah* has taken up most of my professional time these last few months. I'm late for my twin boys' first birthday party today. I assume Beth will understand, just like Beth assumes it's perfectly normal for a couple married seven years to have sex once every two months.

"Very nice," I say.

I can hear Lila breathing on the other end of the speakerphone. "You think?" she says.

"Yeah, I do. You have a way with character and setting. I felt like I had a front-row seat to Passover in ancient Jerusalem. Obviously, the handjob scene with Jesus needs some more work."

"Agreed, but the general setup is better?"

"Yeah, more or less."

"What do you mean by that?"

"I'm still torn overall on Aisha."

"But I thought you were into exotic looking women."

"That's beside the point," I say, trying not to smile or picture my stepsister in a peach negligee—failing at both. "Why did you give your protagonist, who's supposed to be a born-again Christian, an Islamic name?"

"Truthfully?" Lila says.

"No, just make something up. Yes, truthfully."

"I wanted to piss off all those misogynist fuckers in the Middle East."

"Okay, I'll buy that. But you couldn't come up with a better name than Aisha?"

"What's wrong with Aisha?"

"It makes me think of little black kids doing the running man in single-strap airbrushed overalls."

"Come again?"

"You know, Another Bad Creation, aka the boy band ABC? *Iesha, you are the girl that I neva had, and I want to get to know you bettah!*"

"Still nothing."

"You disappoint me, Lila."

"My profuse apologies, but other than my protagonist reminding you of early nineties hip-hop artists, what else don't you like?"

"Your setting."

"What's wrong with Indianapolis? You love Indy."

"If you want this book to make any kind of commercial or critical splash, at least move Aisha out of the Midwest."

"Why?"

"Because unless you're Jonathan Franzen or Jeffrey Eugenides, the Midwest just doesn't sell. It's the *Saved by the Bell* factor."

"The *what*?"

"The *Saved by the Bell* factor. Ever watch those old reruns of *Saved by the Bell*?"

"Maybe."

"Come on now, Lila. Either you have or you're lying to me. It's fucking *Saved by the Bell*."

"Okay, I've seen a few episodes."

"A few episodes?"

"And by that I mean every episode at least four times over. I guess I was just hoping we had reached our nostalgia quota with Another Bad Creation."

"That's better," I say. "You remember the first season?"

"Barely. It's been a while."

"The series actually debuted on the Disney Channel in 1988 under a different title, *Good Morning, Miss Bliss*. The focal point was Miss Bliss as opposed to the students, and the setting was John F. Kennedy Junior High School in Indianapolis, Indiana. After one season, the show was retooled as *Saved by the Bell* and quietly relocated to Los Angeles and the now-familiar Bayside High School. The acting never got better. The stories never got better. There was always the laugh track and predictable 'ooos' and 'ahhhs' whenever Zack and Kelly kissed. But that one small tweak to the setting made a horrible show legendary."

Lila looks unimpressed. "That's sixty seconds of my life I'm never getting back."

"What do you mean?"

"I like the Midwest, Hank. It has an everyman quality that readers can relate to—like John Hughes's Illinois and Judd Apatow's Michigan."

"Readers don't want to relate anymore, they want to escape. Why the hell do you think *Freaks and Geeks* got cancelled after one season? Not to mention, you have the critics to think about. And there's only one surefire setting for the preening literati."

"Cue the New York rant."

"It's been that way since Nick Carraway partied with Jay Gatsby in West Egg, and you know it, Lila. You make Aisha a Manhattanite, and critics will eat that shit up."

"How about Brooklyn?"

"Even better. Hell, go for the jugular and put her in Williamsburg, Bed-Stuy, or Dumbo—the more indie you can make the setting the better. And if you're thinking about working in a Midwest anecdote about basketball, change it to something completely esoteric that nobody west of the Hudson gives a shit about, like cricket or cribbage."

"What's cribbage?"

"My point exactly. And if you can get a critic thinking that only he will get your references, that's a guaranteed rave review."

"And by rave review you mean three pages of a pseudo-literary celebrity showing off before spending maybe three sentences actually talking about my book?"

I stand, grabbing my sport coat off the back of my chair. I extend my arms through my coat sleeves. "Is there any other kind of rave review?"

"What's all that jostling going on in the background? You got somewhere to be?"

"It's the twins' birthday."

"Give Burke and Johnny a kiss from their Aunt Lila."

"Give Chris a kiss from your brother Hank."

"Behave," Lila says. "Although Chis and I aren't really what I'd call 'a couple' at the moment."

"Trouble in paradise?"

"Trouble in paradise, trouble everywhere. I feel like I've lost control."

"I'm guessing a lot of people in New York don't feel like they have control over much of anything right now."

I can hear Lila start to tear up. She blows her nose into the phone. "It's been eight weeks since the Towers fell, Hank. Eight weeks! And you can still smell it on the streets, on your clothes, on your soul. The city is just so…sad."

"Hang in there, Lila. My recommendation for you and Chris would be not to do anything rash."

"Are you my editor or my therapist?"

"Depends."

"On what?"

"Will you let me flirt with you or keep playing that stupid sister card?"

"Go to your boys' party, Hank."

The phone line goes dead, and I'm a little sad not to hear Lila's voice anymore.

CHAPTER SEVENTY-EIGHT

Principal Denise Lobrano runs through the afternoon announcements at St. Benjamin Catholic School. She leads the school in a closing Hail Mary. I can hear the pious mumble of the two hundred or so students echoing her prayer down the musty hallway of nineteen-seventiees carpet and eighteen-seventies ideals. She motions for Jack and me to enter her office.

"Good afternoon, Principal Lobrano," I say, shaking her hand.

"Please, Mr. Fitzpatrick, call me Denise."

Jack's principal is an obvious gym rat. She's in her forties and has that overly fit, emaciated look that belies her femininity: almost perfect half-spheres for breasts poking from a striated overly tanned chest, hollowed-out cheek bones, arms so lean I can make out every veined curve of her triceps and biceps. If her muscle tone was just a shade softer, she'd be hot. As it is, much like Demi Moore, Madonna, and the female cast of *Friends*, she's let the one-two punch of divorce and the fear of aging scare her into looking like a starving triathlete.

"Okay, Denise," I say, trying not to ignore the painful, bony firmness of her handshake. "But only if you call me Hank."

"Deal," Denise says. She motions to the two curiously out of place floral-print wingback chairs across from her desk. "Please, have a seat."

"Look, I'm sorry our mother couldn't be here today."

"A belated honeymoon, I hear?"

"So she tells me."

"No big deal," Denise says. "You're listed as his emergency contact anyway. Quite a gap in age between you two."

Jack joins in on the conversation. "Eighteen years."

"He could be your father," Denise says.

"Wish he was."

"No you don't, little brother." I pause to quietly note the irony. I feel like my inflection on *little brother* was a little too loud and compensatory. How great would it be if I just ended the ruse here, Jack? Sitting in a floral-print wingback chair in your principal's office.

"You'd be better than Gillman," Jack says.

"That's not exactly a high bar you're setting there."

My brother—at least for a little while longer—can't help but chuckle. Once again, I've lived to fight another day.

"Hank," Denise says. "I don't mean to interrupt, but this is a fairly routine disciplinary issue. I'd like to get you in and out of here as painlessly as possible."

"Disciplinary?"

"Yes. See, the seventh graders went on a field trip up to the International Festival at the Indianapolis Convention Center today."

"I ate baklava for the first time," Jack chimes in again.

"Did you like it?" I say.

He shrugs his shoulders. "Not really. Too dry."

Denise sighs, shuffling her papers. "Jack, can you wait outside in the administration office lounge?"

"Be glad to." He gets up, leaves the office. I try to pretend I don't see him winking at me.

Denise closes the door and turns to me. "I didn't want to embarrass him, Hank."

"Uh-oh," I say. "This is going to be interesting."

"Apparently, Jack bought one of those water wiggler toys at the festival."

"Water wigglers?"

"They're those trick hoses filled with gel that are hard to hold on to because they keep rolling in on themselves."

"Oh yeah, I know what you're talking about. They kind of look like an artificial, well, you know—"

"Let's just say sex toy."

"Yes, let's say that. What was he doing with it?"

"He was in the hallway outside Mr. Winsome's seventh-period history class simulating, uhhh…"

"Masturbation?"

"Among other things, yes."

"I'll talk to him. What's the damage?"

"A slap on the wrist. Jack's a good kid. We've confiscated the item, and he'll have a week's detention."

"That's fair," I say, standing up. "Is there anything else you need?"

"Just keep an eye on your little brother. He seems lost."

"Thanks, Denise. Would I be a bad role model if I said, 'That makes two of us'?"

"Nah, Hank. You'd just be human."

I say my goodbyes to Denise. Jack is sitting in the administration office waiting room flirting with a redhead. And she's cute.

"Who's your friend?" I say.

"Oh, uh, this is, uhhh…"

The redhead offers me her hand. "My name is Brooke, Mr. Fitzpatrick."

"Please, Brooke." I shake her hand. "Mr. Hank, or just Hank, is fine."

She starts to back out of the room. "Anyway, call me, Jack?"

Jack nods. "Yeah, sure."

"Great," Brooke says, blushing. "Nice to meet you, Mr. Hank."

"Same here, Brooke."

I smack Jack on the shoulder. "Not bad."

"Shut up."

"Just teasing you, buddy. Let's get out of here."

Jack stands up from his chair. "How bad is it?"

"Detention for a week. You're lucky."

"You going to tell Mom?"

"Nope," I say. We walk down the hall to the front doors of the school. I open one of the doors, and we walk outside. "I have a better idea."

"What's that?"

"Let's leave the car here and take a walk."

"Where?"

"Home."

"But that's like three miles."

"And I feel like we're going to need all three of them."

We're about a mile from the school when I summon enough courage to broach the subject. "Okay Jack, let's do this. Has Mom ever had the talk with you?"

"What talk?"

"You know, the sex talk."

"Hell no!"

"What about Gillman?"

"Gillman needs to have the sex talk with himself."

"Good point," I say. "But all joking aside, have you ever talked with anyone about, you know, sex?"

"I had sex ed last year and the year before that, in fifth and sixth grade. I know how to do it."

"That's not what I asked. Have you ever sat down and talked with anyone about any questions you might have?"

"Questions? What kind of questions?"

"Anything," I say. "If you want to ask something, ask me. That's what I'm here for."

"Hank, this is really weird."

"We could always go back and have this chat with Principal Lobrano if that would make you feel more comfortable."

"Hell no!"

"Then talk to me. If my twelve-year-old brother gets caught simulating masturbation with a sex toy, I'm thinking he has some issues."

"I don't have issues."

"Are you masturbating?"

"Hank, shut up!"

"Well, are you?"

Even though we're at least a dozen blocks from school, Jack still looks around as if to make sure no one can hear him. "Yes, I masturbate."

"Good."

"Good?"

"Don't believe anything people tell you about the evils of masturbation—Mom, Gillman, Father Liam, or for that matter, anyone at St. Benjamin. It's going to keep you sane. Did you know that masturbating five times or more a week reduces your chances of getting prostate cancer by thirty percent?"

"Looks like I'm probably not getting prostate cancer, then."

"That's the spirit," I say. "When you can't stop thinking about a girl, masturbate. When you can't stop thinking about what you want to do with that girl, masturbate. If you're upset, if you can't concentrate, if you're anxious, if you're depressed, if you can't sleep…"

"Masturbate?"

"Exactly!"

"This is officially the grossest sex talk ever."

I haven't even skimmed the surface of gross, but I'll keep that to myself. I still remember the first time I masturbated. It took me three nights to muster the courage to go through with it. The first two nights, I would get just to the precipice of my climax and then chicken out because of the cramping. For a forty-eight hour period, I almost convinced myself masturbating *was* evil, otherwise why would it hurt so much? On that third night, I brought the album cover of *Exotic Music of the Belly Dancer* into my bedroom. I propped up the faceless beauty on my bed with two pillows and stood over her. The overhead lights cast a glare on her breasts, so I turned them off and used my desk lamp. I had planned on using Kleenex so I could flush the evidence, but the toilet paper was too rough, so I used the legs of my old teddy bear. I can still picture the teddy bear riding my cock and my ejaculate covering his face.

"Jack..." I say. "You have no idea what gross is."

"I bet I do."

"I bet you don't. But the bottom line is, don't be afraid of yourself, of what you're feeling. Masturbate as much as you want, and if you have any questions, just ask me."

"Really?" Jack looks around again, still convinced someone is eavesdropping. "Anything?"

"Yes, please. What are kids your age into these days?"

"Well, I haven't had sex, if that's what you're fishing for."

"You're twelve, Jack, so I'd hope not."

"You'd be surprised with what's going on with kids my age."

"Really?"

"Well, maybe not at St. Benjamin. But I hear stories, you know, about what they do at the junior high."

Ah yes, the dark specter of public schools. I'm guessing the stories Jack hears are overblown, if not complete bullshit. Vilifying public schools and their demonic minions is a time-honored Catholic school tradition. I think back to my parochial schooling, back to those Monday mornings we'd come into class and everyone would open their desks and summarily claim all their pencils had been stolen. They hadn't been stolen, of course, but we all knew the CCD kids had been in our classroom for Sunday school. CCD, aka the Confraternity of Christian Doctrine, or simply "Catechism," as it's more commonly called today, is the religious education program provided to kids who don't attend Catholic schools. In my childhood, CCD was basically the mark of Cain. It meant your parents were too poor to send you to Catholic school, and so you couldn't help it that you were a pencil thief or that you never showered, which was why our classroom stunk only on Monday mornings. Curiously enough, I don't recall any priests, nuns, or teachers trying that hard to correct our misconceptions.

"I don't care about the stories you hear, Jack. What are *you* doing?"

"Nobody, I mean nothing. Nothing at all really."

"Good to hear," I say. "I assume you've kissed a girl."

"Well..."

"What?"

"When I say 'nothing,' I mean *nothing*."

"No kissing at all?"

"A little. The occasional game of kiss and tag at a birthday party. Lately I've kissed a few girls because somebody dared me to at the..."

"Skating rink?"

"Yeah, how'd you know?"

"Open skate night taught me a lot of things, too."

"Good, so you know where I'm coming from."

"Not exactly," I say. "My life wasn't quite as sheltered as yours. Just so we're clear, you've never French kissed a girl?"

"Nope."

"Okay then, time for your first lesson."

"What are you talking about?" Jack starts walking double time ahead of me.

"Come back here, you idiot! I'm not going to freaking kiss you."

Jack slows down. "Then what are you gonna do?"

"Teach you how to practice." I hold my right fist close to my mouth. "Raise your hand to your mouth like I'm doing."

"No way!"

"Do it!"

"Okay," Jack says, mimicking my motions. "Whatever."

"Now, you know when it's cold outside and you blow air through the opening in your hand to stay warm?"

"I guess so."

"That's basically the same principle we're going with here, only instead of blowing through your hand you'll be puckering up and sucking."

Jack drops his hand away from his mouth. "I was wrong, Hank."

"What?"

"*Now* this is officially the grossest sex talk ever."

I grab his hand and lift it back toward his face. "Do you or don't you want to learn how to kiss a girl?"

"I do," Jack says, rolling his eyes.

"Instead of a perfect circle like you'd normally use to warm up your hand, make it more of an oval so the opening in your hand is shaped like a mouth."

Jack shows me the lemon-shaped opening in his hand. "Like this?"

"Perfect." I press my mouth against the side of my hand. "Now, pucker your lips and kiss the opening of your hand like this."

Jack follows my directions to the letter. "Like this?"

"That's pretty good," I say. "Remember, it's all about balance. You're not trying to swallow your hand, but at the same time you don't want to stab the opening of your hand with your mouth. That's when you slip in the tongue. Just like your lips, there's a give and take to it. Imagine you're kissing a girl. Don't fight her tongue, but at the same time don't let your tongue just hang there limp in her mouth."

"How will I know if I'm being too aggressive or not aggressive enough with my tongue?"

"Believe me, you'll figure it out. And whatever you do, don't use your teeth. Don't bite her tongue, don't lick her teeth, just keep the teeth out of the whole equation."

"Why?"

"Because that just encourages her to keep biting. And biters are the worst kissers, among other things."

"What other things?" Jack asks.

I pat my naïve student on the shoulder. "That's not in today's lesson plan, buddy. I just want you to know one thing."

"What's that?

"No matter what situation you find yourself in, you can come to me. If things are getting too heavy or out of control—at a friend's house, at a party, wherever you are—I'm just a phone call away. I will come get you, no questions asked."

"No questions asked?"

"None," I say as we approach a busy intersection. I don't notice the "Do Not Walk" sign.

"Easy there, big bro." Jack holds his arm out to prevent me from stepping into the street. My protector. "So, we done with the sex talk?"

"Do you want to be done?" I ask.

"I didn't want to start."

"What do you want to talk about?"

"Music maybe?

"Perfect. What's everyone into right now?"

"Train, Matchbox Twenty, Destiny's Child."

"Yuck."

"Tell me about it," Jack says.

"No Staind or Incubus in there?"

"So you know what everyone is into right now?"

"I have a radio, fool."

"I don't listen to the radio." Jack smirks. "I'm pretty much all about the Dave Matthews Band."

"Still?"

"What's not to like?"

Jack spent two weeks with Jeanine in Portland last summer, and she effectively brainwashed him. Gone was our shared love and shared CD collection of Metallica, Scorpions, Guns N' Roses, and Mötley Crüe, and in its place were cassette bootlegs of various live Dave Matthews shows and mind-numbing deconstructions of the band's "transcendent visual imagery and musicianship." Jack's words, not mine. I even caught him listening to one of Jeanine's bluegrass bootlegs. Seriously, sis. Fucking bluegrass?

"Do we really have to go over this again?" I say. "There are three reasons I don't like the Dave Matthews Band. Reason number one, too many drunken frat boys at their concerts. Reason number two, they've become the fallback band for Deadheads who still haven't come to terms with Jerry Garcia's death, getting a job, or personal hygiene."

"I like the Grateful Dead."

"Of course you do."

"What's the third reason?"

"They don't rock."

"Don't rock?" Jack says. "Have you even listened to them?"

"I've listened plenty, and I can't envision going to a Dave show and banging my head, pumping my fist, or feeling my heart about to explode out of my chest."

"That's your main criteria for music? Whether or not it makes you violent and gives you a heart attack?"

"When I want to rock, I want to rock, not do the stoner shuffle to safe, uninteresting folk music."

"I wouldn't call Carter Beauford safe or uninteresting."

"He's Dave's drummer, right?"

Jack nods. "And probably rock 'n' roll's greatest living percussionist."

I shake my head in a dissenting motion. "I'm never leaving you alone with our sister again."

"Name someone better."

"He's practically in our own backyard. Does the name Kenny Aronoff ring a bell?"

"Should it?"

"He's John Mellencamp's drummer."

"Is it possible for you to have a musical discussion without referencing Mellencamp?"

"Okay then, what about Neil Pert?"

"Neil *who*?"

"Dear Lord, I have failed you as a big brother."

"Relax, Hank." A car honks as it passes by us. Jack waves. "I know who Neil Pert is. I just don't think he's as good a drummer as Carter Beauford."

"Neil Pert could eat a bowl of drumsticks and crap a better solo than Carter Beauford."

Jack laughs at me. I laugh right back at him to spite myself. I'll never be a Dave Matthews fan, but if the guy can deliver me more of these moments with Jack, I might just jump on that Phish-wannabe frat-rock bandwagon. Talking about music is something I always wanted to do with Dad, but by the time I had formed an opinion one way or the other, he was gone forever. I think Dad would have been on Jack's side in this argument, but I don't tell him that. Blues harps, fiddles, a full horn section: that was John Fitzpatrick's kind of music.

Thank you, Dave Matthews. If somewhere in between smoking dragons with your girlfriend, getting stung by bumblebees, and wearing pineapple grass bracelets, you can make the world smile, who am I to disparage a twelve-year-old's cassette bootlegs?

CHAPTER SEVENTY-NINE

With my late nights working at College Ave and Mom being an absentee parent to Jack in the midst of her newly wedded bliss, I feel like I'm neglecting my wife and children.

Well, I *know* I'm neglecting my wife.

Beth and I are struggling. It started after the twins were born. At first, I chalked it up to the same thing she went through with Sasha: another bout of post-partum depression. We talked through it, or pretended like we did, for about a year. Raising a toddler and two infants was a convenient distraction. I stopped counting the weeks and months that would go by without having sex with her. Beth stopped asking how my day was. The idea of even striking up a conversation intimidated me. I felt like a stranger in my own house.

Nothing prepares you for this in a marriage. For the doldrums. For those moments when your sails stall and the ship flounders. A part of you wants to look to the horizon, hoping for that wind that will carry you home or at least to kinder shores. But a part of you also just wants to jump off the boat.

"Hello again, Vanessa."

She bows her head. "Good morning, Hank."

Beth and I sit on the couch across from the old woman. Her name is Vanessa Sheed. She's our couples therapist. In her fifties, soft in the middle, and pear-shaped, with auburn hair sprinkled with strands of gray and an authoritative, borderline-sneering Margaret Thatcher countenance. Beth, of course, corrected me this morning, saying the woman "isn't so much old as she is just older than us" and that my choice of adjectives is "further indication of your emotional immaturity."

Whatever. If I'm a kid masquerading as an adult, then Beth is counting the days until she can apply for an AARP card. The disapproving sneers. The constant rejections of her "sex ogre" of a husband. The lamentations about how she's lost her womanhood to motherhood. Beth didn't lose anything; she gave it away enthusiastically.

We agreed I should see Vanessa for a couple sessions on my own prior to meeting in a group setting. And by "we" I mean Beth ordered me to do it. All things considered, our conversations have gone pretty well. I started opening up. I uncorked a bottle of resentment about my sainted father. I talked about Jack in the context of being my son and not my brother. I wrote a letter to my dead godfather asking him why he felt compelled to massage my balls and stick his finger up my butthole. Great stuff all around. Turns out this last bit about my butthole was a repressed memory that my therapy only now brought to light. I can't say I'm particularly grateful or that I've become a better person for now having a conscious memory of my godfather knuckle-deep in my anus, but I leave that to the professionals to decide.

Barring the anus revelation, a part of me almost thinks the worst is behind us and that we might be turning things around. There's no way we're going to throw all this away, are we? Life with Sasha and the twins is pretty close to perfect. Beth and I even had sex twice recently, *in one week!* At one point, I almost went forty-eight hours without masturbating to Internet porn. My streak came to a crashing halt when the new neighbors moved in. The wife, this full-breasted half-Vietnamese woman named Lang who works in the healthcare industry, had me searching on the Internet for a few hours, dick in hand, for *Busty Asian Nurses*. There's a revelation for you, Vanessa: I didn't even know I was into Asians.

"Hank," Vanessa says. "Would you agree with your wife's assessment?"

"What?"

"My assessment of you," Beth says. "Do you agree with it?"

"I don't know." I shrug my shoulders. "What's this about anyway? I thought we've been in a good place lately, even in the bedroom. Haven't we?"

Beth shakes her head. "He wasn't listening, not that I'm surprised."

"Please, Beth," Vanessa says, holding her hand up.

"Hank, your wife thinks you're in a state of arrested development. That the sexual abuse you suffered as a child was compounded by the sudden death of your father and essentially froze you, emotionally and psychologically, at twenty-one years old."

I turn to my wife. "So that's it? We've circled all the way back to that?"

"Our problems aren't going to be solved simply by rolling around in the sheets a couple times."

"Did I say they were solved?"

Vanessa raises her hand to interrupt. "So you don't agree with your wife, Hank?"

"That's just it," I say. "A part of me agrees with her implicitly. My childhood, my boyhood, that brief period of my life in which I had a father, is a moment frozen in time for me. A part of me will always want to stay in that moment. But that doesn't mean I'm not working to be a better person, a better father…"

"A better husband?" Beth says.

"Of course, a better husband." I bite my bottom lip, my finger raised to my wife's face, almost touching her nose. "You didn't let me finish, and that's my problem with *you*, Beth."

"Let's assume a less aggressive posture, Hank," Vanessa says. "But I like where this is going. Keep talking to Beth, not me."

"Yeah, Hank, talk to me." She reaches for my hand as I lower it. I pull my hand away.

"My problem with you is that you don't want to fix things. You seem to take some sort of perverse pleasure in exposing my faults. I've never seen someone try so hard to dislike another person. You are the one person who laughs least at my jokes."

"That's because I've heard all of them."

"No, it's because you don't want to give me a break. Anything that might possibly fragment your view of me as a completely flawed human gets cast aside. I know I'm not the world's best listener. I know I'm not good with money and I don't think about the future enough. And I know I publish books instead of saving sick kids."

"Saving sick kids?" Beth says. "What are you talking about?"

"I'm not your fucking father, and you resent me because of it."

"That's absurd."

"Is it? You're here today to fix me, not us and certainly not you. You don't want me to be the man of the house, you want me to be *your idea of a man*. Your idea of a man balances the checkbook, watches the stock ticker all day, alphabetizes his family videos, and knows his children's vaccination schedules by heart."

"What's wrong with that?"

"Nothing, I guess. But your idea of a man has also spent the better part of the last thirty years as a glorified roommate to his spouse. Your idea of a man hasn't kissed his wife in public since Jimmy Carter was president."

"You've made your point, Hank," Vanessa says.

"Your idea of a man doesn't even hold his wife's hand, never mind have sex with her."

"I said that's enough."

"Don't worry, Vanessa." My wife reaches over and touches the therapist's knee. "I can handle this."

"Then handle it," I say.

"Do you like your life?" Beth asks me.

"What?"

"It's a simple question. Do you like your life?"

"I guess so."

"You guess so? Let's see. You have your perfect little family. You have a job you love. Meanwhile, I'm the one taking care of the kids. I'm the one who, on top of being a mom and a good housewife, goes to work in the evenings to take shit from entitled teenage gymnasts who reek of smelly feet and dirty tampons. Your life has turned out exactly the way you wanted it to turn out. And I'm just a stay-at-home mom with a worthless nursing degree and no marketable skills."

"You're being a little hard on yourself, Beth."

"Am I?"

"If you want to do more with your life, then do it. But don't sit here and act like I'm the bad guy or try to tell me that your parents raised you right."

"Better Stan or Joan than Debbie."

"Nice misdirection."

"How so?"

"My mom lost her reason for being a good partner to someone nine years ago when her husband got stabbed in the liver by a truck. What are your parents' excuses?"

"At some point you're going to have to start realizing there's an expiration date on grief."

"And at some point you're going to have to start fucking me more than once every three months."

"Okay, you two," Vanessa says, standing. She extends her arms between us, like a referee. "This session is no longer productive."

Beth sits in the car, still crying. I approach the driver's side door. Inhale. Exhale. I open the door, slide behind the wheel. I shut the door, forcing a half smile.

"That was productive, all things considered," I say. "Looks like we might have a few more of those in store for us. Thank God for Random House medical benefits."

"Hank..." Beth says.

"Unlimited ten-dollar co-pays for therapy. I confirmed our appointment for next month."

"Hank..." she repeats through a veil of mascara and tears. "I want a trial separation."

My wife's request is hardly shocking. She's played this card close to a dozen times in our seven years of marriage. My standard response is to grovel, say something about how "we need to think about the kids first," then spend the next thirty to ninety days working our relationship back to a semi-tolerable equilibrium. Lather, rinse, repeat.

I turn the key in the ignition.

Lather, rinse, repeat? Not today. Maybe not ever again. I just don't have anything left for her, for us.

"A trial separation, huh?"

Beth nods.

I put the car into drive. "Fine by me."

CHAPTER EIGHTY

From: Fitzpatrick, Hank [mailto:hfitzpatrick@collegeavepress.com]
Sent: Tuesday, April 16, 2002 11:26 AM
To: Prestwich, Delilah [mailto:di_prestwich@yahoo.com]
Subject: Advance Praise for SPERM BANK MESSIAH

Dear Lila,
They love you! The last review is my personal favorite. Hank

P.S. Until my situation with Beth gets settled, I'm working mostly in New York at my satellite office in the Bertelsmann Building. An author friend is letting me crash at his place in Hell's Kitchen for free. I'll be here for the rest of the week. Come by for lunch?

"A sardonic yet endearing confection of Ian Frazier humor, Paul Theroux travelogue, and Karen Armstrong theological progressivism."

—*Publishers Weekly*

"Think Monty Python's *Life of Brian* by way of *Doctor Who,* its unbridled self-awareness, mordancy, and aleatoric narrative arc derailed only by the occasional and unfortunate homage to Anita Diamant's *Red Tent.*"

—*Kirkus Reviews*

"Thank God for Lila Prestwich! Other critics might take a few potshots at her almost consciously derivative protagonist, but I have to think Dickens and John Irving would get a kick out of the baton being passed from Oliver to Garp to a time-traveling born-again crack whore. *Sperm Bank Messiah* is crass, vulgar, and inappropriate. Needless to say, I loved it. Recommended for all serious fiction collections."

—*Library Journal*

"With American fiction heading into an inevitable post-9/11 morass, Lila Prestwich reminds us of what the world used to be like, vacillating between willful enervation and ambivalent immurement. She dares to be contumelious, her ribald yet perspicuous prose challenging the reader on every page."

—*The New York Times*

"Modernism and its wicked doppelganger secularism have reached their zenith with *Sperm Bank Messiah*. Soon-to-be excommunicated Latter-Day Saint turned homosexual activist Lila Prestwich piggybacks on the mainstream media's virulent hatred of all things Christian and masculine and gives us perhaps the most willfully offensive and wicked tome in the history of English (and I use this term loosely) literature."

—*Salt Lake Tribune*

CHAPTER EIGHTY-ONE

From: Fitzpatrick, Hank [mailto:hfitzpatrick@collegeavepress.com]
Sent: Tuesday, April 30, 2002 8:14 AM
To: Prestwich, Delilah [mailto:di_prestwich@yahoo.com]
Subject: Young Lions Fiction Award Nominees Announced

Dear Lila,

What did I tell you about kissing New York's ass? Hank

P.S. Dinner tonight?

Young Lions Fiction Award Nominees Announced
Posted Monday, Apr 29, 2002

The New York Public Library announced six nominees for its second annual Young Lions Fiction Award [YLFA], which recognizes the work of authors aged thirty-five or younger.

Nominated for the YLFA top six are: *The Muse Asylum* by David Czuchlewski (Putnam), *The Miracle Life of Edgar Mint* by Brady Udall (Norton), *John Henry Days* by Colson Whitehead (Doubleday), *Esther Stories* by Peter Orner (Mariner Books/Houghton Mifflin), *Paradise Park* by Allegra Goodman (Dial Press/Random House), and *Sperm Bank Messiah* by Lila Prestwich (College Ave/Random House).

The ceremony will be held May 11 in the Celeste Bartos Forum at the New York Public Library's Humanities and Social Sciences Library. The winner will receive a $10,000 award.

"[YLFA] is run by avid readers and formidable writers who believe in, and are committed to, the cultural necessity of the written word," Mark Danielewski, last year's winner for the novel *House of Leaves,* said in a statement. "It's essential for writers in the early part of their publishing lives to have opportunities for support and ratification."

YLFA stemmed from the Young Lions group, a membership organization for library supporters in their twenties and thirties. The nominees for YLFA were selected by a Reading Committee of Young Lions members, writers, and librarians, including Rodney Phillips, director of the New York Public Library's Humanities and Social Sciences Library.

CHAPTER EIGHTY-TWO

The bad news is that Colson Whitehead's *John Henry Days* won the Young Lions Fiction Award. The good news is, on the heels of Lila's nomination, Michael Pietsch, publisher and executive vice president of Little, Brown and Company, outbid Random House's own paperback imprint, Vintage, for the trade paper rights to *Sperm Bank Messiah*, singlehandedly putting College Ave in the black for the rest of the year. Mr. Pietsch heard I was in town visiting Lila and asked that we both attend the party he was hosting for Alice Sebold, one of Little Brown's new authors. The party is being held at Flûte, a champagne bar on West 54th Street.

Lila and I emerge from the bowels of the subway. She had wanted to take a taxi from her apartment, where I've been crashing off and on since Beth kicked me out of the house. I wanted to take the 1 train, seeing as it dumps you at 50th and Broadway, all of a five-minute walk from the bar. In a rare fit of acquiescence, Lila agreed to take the train.

"See, that wasn't so bad, was it?" I say.

Lila smiles. She straightens her cocktail dress, a black sleeveless number with a plunging neckline that dares me to stare at her cleavage. As usual, the sight of me walking down the street with her on my arm provokes multiple *How the fuck did he land her?* sideways glances.

"Loosen up, Hank."

"Easy for you to say. These are your co-workers."

"Can we at least go over this one more time?" Lila says.

"Sure," I say.

"This is a party for who?"

"Alice Sebold."

"And she wrote what?"

"*The Lovely Bones*, her debut novel and a follow-up to her memoir, *Lucky*. Alice is married to Glen David Gold, author of *Carter Beats the Devil*, an ambitious novel of Roaring Twenties pre-Depression era America that reads like *The Great Gatsby* as viewed through the lenses of Michael Chabon-slash-Daniel Wallace American postmodern fiction."

"Well done, Mr. Fitzpatrick. You've been studying."

"Maybe a little," I say.

"And what's *The Lovely Bones* about?"

I stop walking. "Uhh..."

"You mean to tell me you remembered all that about her husband, and you can't give me just a simple one- or two-sentence overview? You're a publisher, for God's sake."

"I don't read other people's books. I want to say there's a...murder?"

"Good guess."

"Of a little girl."

"Now you're getting somewhere."

"And her name is Eliza Naumann."

"No."

"No?"

"You're thinking of the protagonist from Myla Goldberg's *Bee Season*."

"Bone Boatwright, maybe?"

"And that's Dorothy Allison's *Bastard Out of Carolina*."

"Scout? Moby?"

"And now you're just being a smartass."

"Why am I picturing a fish?"

"Because her name is Susie Salmon."

"Susie, that's right. Now it's coming back to me. Susie is murdered, and then her skeleton narrates the book. Hence the title."

"Hank." Lila shakes her head, pulls on my arm. "Just leave the talking to me tonight, okay?"

If you didn't know the exact address of Flûte, you'd walk right by it. A former speakeasy, the bar is tucked down in the basement of a Theater District high-rise and by way of signage is afforded little more than a small marquee at the top of an unlit stairwell. The only giveaway tonight is a smartly dressed blond woman holding a clipboard and a muscular gentleman in a tight black tuxedo standing in front of a red velvet rope.

"Name?" the blond woman says.

Lila gives her a fake smile. "Delilah Prestwich and Hank Fitzpatrick."

The blonde nods at the muscular gentleman. He unclips the velvet rope, motions down the stairwell. "Ma'am, sir," he says, nodding in between each missive.

As far as New York publishing parties go, the atmosphere at Flûte is predictable. The lights dimmed to the point of near-pitch. Cozy surrendering to indulgent. Too many conversations competing for floor space. Publishing executives who've been told to watch their bottom lines toasting to million-dollar deals with two-hundred-dollars-a-bottle champagne in lieu of paying their copy editors living wages.

Lila and I settle in quickly at two open seats at the far end of the bar.

"Who's your friend, Lila?" a voice says over my shoulder.

I turn. The voice belongs to a petite woman—thin and no more than five feet tall, about Beth's height. Her hair is cut short. There's no telling with any certainty in this light, but I'm guessing it's some shade of brown. Standing next to her is a gentleman in dark-rimmed glasses with a consciously unkempt swirl of over-gelled hair .

"Hi, Amber," Lila says. "Hank, this is Amber Pate, Director of Subrights for Little Brown. We're officemates."

I shake Amber's hand and proceed to lie. "Oh, *that* Amber Pate. I've heard a lot about you."

"Same here," Amber says. She hooks the arm of the gentleman standing next to her. "This is Brian Sweeney, Director of Acquisitions for audiobook publisher Talk Hard Media."

"Brian Sweeney?" I say, shaking his hand. He's aged well, a little fuller in the face maybe. "As in St. Ambrose Brian Sweeney?" "Do I know you?" Brian says.

"St. Ambrose, nineteen seventy-six to nineteen eighty. We were in Mrs. Anderson's and Mrs. Whitcomb's first and fourth grade classes together."

"I'm not quite placing the name with—"

I sing it more than I say it: *"I saw Brian's weenie, I saw Brian's weenie!"*

"Excuse me?" Amber says.

"Long story." Brian shakes his head. "It's something the Catholic school girls used to tease me about. It appears my ghosts have tracked me down."

"I didn't mean anything by it, Brian."

He waves me off. "Hank, I'm just teasing you. How've you been?"

"Not bad," I say. "You?"

"Can't complain," Brian says.

I notice his tailored though not quite fitted suit and his slightly expensive though not pretentious Hamilton Khaki Field wristwatch. "Books on tape seem to be paying the bills."

"Uh oh," Amber jumps in.

"What?" I ask.

"You said the three no-no words, Hank."

"Books on tape?"

"Yeah," Brian affirms. "It's a common mistake. In 1975, Books on Tape became the first company to produce and sell audiobooks to consumers and then to libraries and retailers. Talk Hard, my company, opened its doors three years later. *Books on tape* has since become the generic term for audiobooks, but saying *books on tape* to me is like telling a Puff sales rep to pass you a Kleenex or a Panasonic rep to go Xerox some copies. Fortunately for us, Random House bought Books on Tape and allowed them to be absorbed by Random Audio, sacrificing one of the only true brand names in all of publishing just to stroke their own egos."

"Random Audio?" Lila says. "Whoever heard of Random Audio? "

"Exactly my point," Brian says.

All things considered, I don't try too hard to defend Random House. In fact, I don't try at all. Brian is absolutely right. Random House is the biggest publisher in the world, and nobody walks into a bookstore asking, "Hey, what's the latest from Random House?" Fuck branding. With the exception of Books on Tape, Harlequin, Little Golden Books, the Dummies books and maybe Penguin Classics, the only thing consumers recognize is the author.

"Oh well," Lila says, grabbing my arm. "As fascinating as this topic is, I need to pull Hank away for a bit and work the room."

"Wait a second," Amber says to Lila. "I need your powers of persuasion."

"For what?"

Amber puts her hand on Brian's shoulder. "I'm trying to convince Sweeney here to buy the audio rights to *In the Hand of Dante.*"

"The new Nick Tosches book?" I say.

"That's the one," Amber says.

"I thought you already had an audio deal," Lila says.

"That's the problem," Amber says. "A competing audiobook publisher paid me a lot of money for the rights, and then they spent even more money renting a recording studio in Paris and hiring Johnny Depp as the narrator."

"Johnny Depp?" I say. "That's pretty sweet."

Amber nods. "You would think so, right? Problem is, over the last month they've salvaged about an hour of usable audio at most. Apparently Depp and the author keep showing up at the studio blitzed out of their minds on red wine. The audio publisher wants out, and I'm trying to convince Brian to pick up the tab."

Off to the side of Amber, Brian shakes his head again. "Let the record show I love both Depp's and Tosches's work and think the idea of these two characters pounding wine in Paris is cooler than anything I've ever been a part of." He finishes his glass of Dom, cutting himself off in mid-sentence. "And let the record also show that I'm not touching this project with a ten-foot fucking pole."

I tilt my head, raise my champagne flute. "You're a smart guy, Brian. I don't care what those St. Ambrose girls said about your wiener."

THE PARTY ENDED. I got to meet Alice Sebold and Glen David Gold. Alice was unbelievably nice, her husband generous with his time and quick with anecdotes that keenly played off my uninteresting stories. I can't imagine they cared too much about my life as a small-time editor, but I appreciated their efforts to suggest otherwise.

Michael Pietsch never spoke to me.

"Don't take it personally," Lila says. "Michael has a lot on his mind these days."

"I'm sure he does." I slide my Metro Card through the subway turnstile, once for Lila, who walks through, and then for me.

"You're in publishing, you know how it is. Sales are flat across the board. Guys like Michael are under the gun to find new customers, new markets, new sources of revenue, the next big thing."

The 1 train approaches the station. We take a seat in the middle of the second car.

"The next big thing," I say. "You mean like *The Lovely Bones*?"

"I'm talking bigger than just one author or one book," Lila says. "You didn't hear this from me, but Michael had some execs from Gemstar in the office today."

"Is that name supposed to mean something to me?"

"You don't know Gemstar?"

"Nope."

"It's the company that manufactures the Rocket Book."

"That electronic book reader thingy?"

"Yes," Lila says. "They want to format the entire Little Brown catalog for their Rocket Book."

"I think Michael is barking up the wrong tree with that one."

"How so?"

"Electronic books? I just don't get it. Books are something you touch, something you smell, something you hold in your hands—keepsakes, heirlooms. Reading a book on a computer screen is never going to catch on."

"You're probably right," Lila says.

"Trust me on this one," I say.

WE EXIT THE SUBWAY at the southeast corner of Seventy-ninth and Broadway, the closest station to Lila's place. My friend's couch on Forty-second Street was only temporary. Lila was the one who talked me into moving into the spare bedroom in her Upper Westside brownstone. She didn't have to try too hard.

"Enough publishing talking," Lila says. "How about a nightcap?"

"Chris not waiting up for us?" I ask.

Lila hooks her arm in mine. "She left this afternoon for Georgia. Femshack is playing at a music festival down in Savannah. You knew that."

"I did?"

"You did."

"Well…" I say, pulling Lila's waist in to mine, "having you all to myself is really going to suck."

"Behave," Lila says, pushing me away.

"Hey now, you know no one is happier than me that you two worked it out."

"Nothing to work out, really. Chris and I never should have broken up in the first place. Last year was a weird time for everyone, I think. After 9/11, instead of holding on tight to those we loved, it seemed like a lot of us tried to just run away, myself included."

"I know the feeling."

"I'm glad I stopped running, Hank. She was just too perfect to let go."

"And I'm sure living rent-free in a brownstone within walking distance of Central Park doesn't exactly detract from Chris's perfection."

"Listen here, fucker." Lila smacks me in the ass. "You about ready to stop talking and start drinking?"

We cross the street to the Dublin House, a narrow taproom smelling of Guinness and mildew. The mustachioed bartender nods at Lila when she enters.

"Tony, two rounds of the usual," Lila says. He slides us two pints of Guinness and two shots of Jameson in short order.

We toast, slamming our shots of Jameson in concert. I chase the shot with a small sip of Guinness, letting the creaminess of the head massage my tongue. I return my pint to its loyal coaster. "Great bar," I say.

"The best," Lila says. "Hasn't once shut its doors since the day Prohibition was lifted."

"Where'd Chris get the idea for the name of the band?"

"You really want to know?"

"What else do I have to do?"

"Chris started up her band right out of high school back in her hometown of La Plata."

"California?"

"Rural southern Maryland. They used to play out of an old army barracks. They nicknamed the place 'The Femshack,' and it became kind of a hangout for all the hip DC lesbians. When they got their first real paying gig in Georgetown, Femshack came with them."

"And that's it?"

Lila nods. "That's it."

I grab my pint, holding it up to the lights tinged yellow by a century of cigarette smoke. "Did you know Guinness used to be prescribed to post-op patients, pregnant women, and nursing mothers, and that new research suggests a daily pint can lower your risk of a heart attack?"

"Okay." Lila grabs my pint, sets it on the bar. "Spill."

"Spill?"

"What's on your mind?"

"Nothing."

"My ass. When you start in with the random useless trivia, that usually means you're trying to work up the courage to ask me something. Let's just dispense with the bullshit and get to it."

I grab my pint of Guinness, finishing it in three swallows. Tony seems less than impressed. I clear my throat.

"She's been calling you, hasn't she?" I say.

"Who?" Lila asks, as if she doesn't know exactly who I'm talking about.

"Beth."

"She wants you back, Hank."

"Bullshit," I say. "Beth started talking divorce almost immediately after we were separated. I hear she's even be dating."

"Jealous?"

"Should I be?"

"No."

"You're telling me, after six months of trying to fast-track me out of her life, now she has a change of heart? I'm not buying it."

"You've given people a second chance who deserved it a whole lot less than Beth."

"Maybe."

"At least just call her back, if only because I'm tired of being your fucking answering service."

"I think I'm going to tell Jack."

"Wait...*what*?"

"I'm going to tell Jack that I'm his father."

Lila has known for years. I can't remember when I told her, only that she didn't act surprised. No one seems to act surprised when I tell them. For someone who struggles mightily with being a father, I seem to at least wear it well.

"How'd we get on this subject?" Lila says.

"I'm drunk," I say. "Felt like talking about something else."

"I'll accept drunk as your excuse, then."

"My excuse for what?"

"For being out of your goddamn mind."

"The boy is thirteen years old, Lila. He's nearly in high school. I have Sasha and the twins, and apparently my wife again if I want her. Jack deserves to know."

"Your mother should be the one to tell him, Hank. Not you."

"But he needs a father."

"Jack *has* a father."

"Who, Gillman? That looney tune is no father to Jack."

Oh shit. Did I really just say that out loud? Lila's bottom lip is quivering. Her eyes well up with tears. "Lila, I'm sorry. I didn't mean it."

"Oh you meant it, dickhead!"

Tony approaches, his mustache leering at me menacingly. "You got uh problem here, laddie?"

"I'm fine, Tony," Lila says, waving him off. "I think you know by now I'm a big girl."

Tony leaves. I grab Lila's hand. "I'm sorry for what I said, really I am. I know Gillman means well."

Lila grabs a cocktail napkin, wipes her eyes. "Hank, he just comes from a totally different world than most people. His grandparents were polygamists, his parents were glorified drill instructors, and he thought the answer to undoing all their damage was to just seek out very atypical women—first my mother, a barely practicing LDS Armenian, and now your mother…"

"A loud, obnoxious Irish Catholic with a taste for narcotics-tinged melodrama?"

"Your words, not mine," Lila says. "Problem is, Gillman Prestwich is his father's son. Dad needs a passive woman. He needs a wife who doesn't laugh at him when he asks her to wear shirts with sleeves and capri pants instead of shorts because it makes her look like a harlot."

"You have to admit that was pretty hilarious. He called her a harlot. I mean, come on, who uses that fucking word anymore? Hey, Gillman, the nineteenth century called, and it wants its thesaurus back."

Lila laughs, the last swallow of her pint shooting out her mouth.

I raise two fingers. "Tony, a couple more Guinness here." He stands at the other end of the bar, unmoving.

Lila leans into me. "Uh, you kinda have to earn your way up to calling him Tony." She raises her hand. "Hey Tony," she says in her best fake Irish brogue. "Two pints o' the black for me and Henry David Fitzpatrick."

"Fitzpatrick?" Tony says, his eyes and mustache perking up in unison. "Why didn't yuh say so?"

Lila struggles to find the lock with her house key. I'd offer to help her, but I see three doors to the apartment.

"Shhhhhhh," Lila says, putting her finger to her mouth.

"What?" I say.

"Weeft."

"Weeft?"

"Weef to be quiet."

"You're the only who's talking."

"Shhhhhhh," Lila says again.

Nothing good happens at four in the morning, so we made sure to stay at the Dublin House until 4:30. The rounds of Guinness and Jameson blurred into one another. How many rounds did we have? Five? Six? Seven? Eight? I know I blew through at least twenty bucks on the jukebox, all eighties hairbands of course. Tony put an exclamation point on the night for us, buying us a round of Tullamore Dew right before we left.

Lila opens the door, walks into the apartment. I follow her inside, shut the door behind us.

"Wuuna sleep inna yuroom or inna mine?" Lila says.

"In my room or yours?"

"Yeah, zwut I said."

As is customary with my constantly raging libido, my penis does a half-salute inside my pants as if to say, *Can we, pleeeeease?*

"My room is fine," I say.

"Zoot yerzelf," Lila says. She walks up to me, kisses me full on the lips, with tongue. She stumbles back. "Mmm, you taste good."

"You're not so bad either," I say.

Lila pats me on the chest. "Can I tell yuz one thing?"

"Sure, Lila."

"You do whateverz you thinks is best for Jack. Yours hiz dad. Gillman isn't."

I grab Lila by the hand, pull her into me. We kiss. I feel her pelvis lean into mine. My road to redemption deserves at least one tap on the snooze bar, doesn't it? Just as I start to slide my hands down the small of Lila's back, she appears.

"What are you doing, Daddy?"

Lila doesn't see her. Only I can see her. She's a figment of my imagination, but in every way that counts, she's very real. She is my six-year-old daughter, Sasha.

When I was a teenager, my father and I had precious few man-to-man conversations. But the one I remember most was the lecture on fidelity. I was twenty years old and had just screwed up my fourth relationship in as many months.

"How do you do it?" I remember saying to him.

"Do what?"

"Stay with one woman...forever."

"Masturbation and patience," Dad said. *"But mostly masturbation."*

His candor surprised me. Genuine off-color humor from John Fitzpatrick? I didn't know whether to congratulate him or run screaming to Mom. *"Uh, yeah..."* I said, still off balance. *"I think I got a pretty good handle on the masturbation, Dad."*

Dad grinned. *"Truthfully, Hank?"*

"No, just make something up. Yes, truthfully."

"Jeanine helps me."

"Come again?"

"Your sister."

"Yeah, I know her name."

"Whenever I'm in a potentially compromising position, I picture myself with the compromising woman, and then I picture my daughter watching everything I'm doing. It's like a built-in monogamy kill switch."

And so, here I stand, on the verge of quasi-incestuous Armenian Mormon sex, when my daughter Sasha appears.

I unhinge my lips from Lila's face. "Good night," I say abruptly.

"What's wrong, Hank?"

"Nothing," I say, giving Sasha a quick smile. She smiles back.

"Sure about that?"

I reach into my pocket, pull out my cell phone. "You were right, Lila. I should call my wife."

CHAPTER EIGHTY-THREE

I open the front door, walk into the house without knocking. Gillman and my mother are in the family room watching television.

"Hey, son," Mom says. "Back already? I thought you wanted to stick around and spy on Jack a little bit."

"It's an eighth-grade dance, Mom. He made me drop him off a block away from school. I'll live if I miss creeping on a bunch of thirteen year olds." I slap the application to Empire Ridge Preparatory Academy on the coffee table in front of Gillman and my mother. "Now, do either of you mind explaining this?"

"That's a Prep application," Gillman says.

"No shit," I say.

"Hank, a little respect for your father, please."

"Gillman's not my fucking father. He's barely a father to his own daughter."

Gillman stands up. I move toward him until we're standing face-to-face. He's my exact height but outweighs me by a good seventy pounds. For a guy who abstains from alcohol and caffeine, you think he'd exhibit a modicum of temperance with sweets and fried food.

"Debbie," Gillman says, turning away from me. "I don't have to stay here and take this in my own house."

"Running away already?" I say. "Come on now, Gillman, I know you want this fight. I can see it in your eyes and that donut-stuffed face. You're ready to go all Mountain Meadows Massacre on me, aren't you?"

"Hank!" Mom shouts.

"It's okay, Debbie." Gillman waves my mother off. "I got this."

"Sure you do," I say.

"Why would you think I'd run away, Hank?"

"Everyone runs away."

"Open your eyes, son."

"Don't call me—"

"Spare me the martyr routine," Gillman says. "Look around you. I'm the only one who *hasn't* run away. Your sister moved to Portland the day she graduated college. We're lucky to get a Christmas card from her. You're in and out of Jack's life when the mood suits you, teaching him how to masturbate and French kiss but not teaching him the difference between right and wrong or what it means to be a Christian. Meanwhile, your marriage is falling apart and you spend months at a time in New York away from your family just so you can flirt with my daughter."

"Excuse me?" Mom says.

"That's an oversimplification of things," I say. "And you know it."

"What exactly am I 'oversimplifying'?"

"First off, let's just leave Lila out of this. She confides in me more than she'll ever confide in you, and that's your problem, not mine. As for Jack, if I didn't have that talk with him, no one would. The kid was scared shitless. He was turning into an emotionally and socially dysfunctional freak. He was turning into *you*, Gillman."

"Give me a break, Hank."

"If you could only see yourself in social situations, Gillman."

"I am plenty social."

"No, I'm talking when you have to get down and dirty with the unwashed Gentiles. Seeing you with your fellow Mormons at a Catholic wedding reception is priceless. You guys all huddle together around one table with this panicked, bug-eyed look as if you're witnessing an orgy."

"To be fair, if it's anything to do with you Catholics, I usually am witnessing an orgy."

"'*You Catholics*,' huh? Oh good, let's go there next. Let's talk about you teaching Jack what it means to be a Christian."

"What about it?"

"You fucking suck at it."

"Hank!" Mom shouts again.

"Debbie, I said I got this." Again Gillman waves her off. "Okay, Hank. Take your best shot."

"You don't want my best shot."

"Try me."

"Okay, Gill-*man*. First off, the next time you have a spare moment, open a fucking dictionary. Stop calling non-Mormons 'Gentiles'. A 'Gentile' is a non-Jew. Mormons are just as much Gentiles as Catholics, you idiot. And I realize the Catholic Church is far from perfect, but an apostasy? My ass, you intellectually dishonest and morally hypocritical prick. Let's not forget for the first thousand years of Christianity my imperfect church was a goddamn one-man show. If not for that millennium of kicking ass and taking names, there wouldn't even be a Christianity for your church or anyone else's church to break away from. Hell, I got T-shirts older than your religion. Suck on that fucking revelation, Joseph Smith."

I'm short of breath. Face red. Pulse racing. Perspiration drenching my shirt. But I've won. I know it. I can see it in Gillman's eyes. I can taste it in the sweat dripping down into my mouth like liquid vindication.

Mom abruptly stands up and leaves the room. Strangely, Gillman hasn't budged.

"Have you said all you wanted to say, Hank?"

I wipe my brow with the sleeve of my shirt. "I guess so."

"Are you familiar with the term *putative father*?"

"Should I be?"

"If I were in your shoes, yes." Gillman nods. "A putative father is defined as the presumed father of an illegitimate child."

Gillman knows I'm Jack's father? Well, fuck. I guess the joke is on me, eh, Joseph Smith?

"When did Mom tell you?"

"The first night we went out on a date, and I didn't run away."

Fortunately, Mom's complete inability to engage in subterfuge has lessened the blunt force trauma of this revelation. There are only so many ways you can bring characters into the story, make them interesting and necessary to the narrative arc, and then find plausible ways to drop the big reveal on them. Quite frankly, I'm a little disappointed here. Mom telling Gillman over a basket of breadsticks at a shitty Italian restaurant is rather pedestrian.

"Well, go on," I say.

"You sure you want to hear this?" Gillman asks.

"It's becoming increasingly clear that it doesn't matter what I want."

"A putative father registry is a state-level legal requirement for all non-married males to document through a notary public with the state each female with whom they engage in heterosexual sexual intercourse in order to retain parental rights to any child they may father."

Gillman has practiced this speech. His words sound like they're being recited more than said.

"The putative father registry is intended to provide legal recognition to the non-married putative father of a child, provided he registers within a limited timeframe, usually any time prior to the birth or from one to thirty-one days after a birth."

"But all bets are off," I say. "If I never even knew he was my—"

"I'm not finished, Hank." Gillman's eyes roll up into his head and then back, as if he's scrolling down the page to the last sentence. "Lack of knowledge of the pregnancy or birth is not a legally acceptable reason for failure to file."

I bite my lip in disbelief. Gillman has won, big time. He's called my bluff. I won't say anything to Jack, at least not yet, and Gillman knows that. I've been Jack's age. The kid is an emotional and hormonal powder keg, and I refuse to be the one to light the trail of gunpowder.

"So that's it?" I say.

"Hank, I'm—"

"You're pulling the rug out from under me?"

"I don't want to shut you out of Jack's life."

"Then don't!"

"Answer me this," Gillman says. "When's the last time your mother had a drink? When's the last time she took a sleeping pill? Where is Jack graduating in his class?"

"I don't know."

"Your mother hasn't had a sip of alcohol or so much as one narcotic in almost three years. Jack is graduating first in his class. First! Do you know how proud that makes me feel? I messed up with Lila. I know that, and I hope she can learn to forgive me. But with Jack, I have a chance to make things right. He and your mother are the lights of my life. I know I come across to you as old-fashioned and weird, but I'm a good man. I don't want to change your mother or your brother."

"Jack is not my brother, Gillman. He's my son."

"I know he is, and I can't begin to fathom what you've gone through. All I'm asking is for a little more time. You and I are never going to be father and son, and I think we're both fine with that. But I'm not going anywhere, and I hope for Jack's sake you don't go anywhere either. Just let me be his father for a little while longer. I promise you there will come a time when I won't stand in the way."

Conveniently, Mom pokes her head around the corner and walks into the room. She and Gillman sit back down on the couch. I pick up the Empire Ridge Preparatory Academy application off the coffee table.

"Is he going to have friends there?" I ask, looking at just my mother.

"Yes, baby. Tons of friends. Almost half his eighth-grade class is going to Prep."

"That's good, I guess." I hand her the application. "I know you don't need my permission or anything, but I think he'll be okay there."

My stepfather grabs me by the crook of my arm. "We don't need your permission, Hank, but we want it."

A smile tries to fight its way through my straight-lipped visage, but it's not going to fucking happen. I jerk my elbow free of Gillman's fat, clammy hands. "Don't get to thinking we're picking out china patterns anytime soon, asshole."

CHAPTER EIGHTY-FOUR

I pull into the driveway in my blue Subaru Outback. The odometer is at 175,000 miles. The engine rattles as I turn off the car, reminding me I'm about five thousand miles overdue for an oil change. Beth sits barefoot and tanned on the front porch steps, just back from a girls' weekend in Las Vegas with Claire, Lila, and Chris. She's wearing a white tank top and her favorite old pair of cutoff jeans, a glass of red wine in her left hand and her right hand cocked just enough to suggest it might have been holding a cigarette only a split-second ago.

I step out of the car, Sasha trailing behind me. She slams her car door. Dad hated when we slammed our car doors. "Those doors are on loan from the dealership," he'd shout at us. "There's no need to slam them into next Tuesday."

"How were the kids?" Beth asks in between sips of wine.

"Fantastic," I say.

"I hate my brothers!" Sasha screams as she marches toward the house. She is her mother's six-year-old clone, right down to her blond hair, her high cheekbones, her obstinacy, and even the way she struts, her left foot extending farther out than her right.

"Fantastic, huh?" Beth finishes off her wine, sets the glass on the porch, stands up, and makes her way toward the car.

"We had a bit of an incident." I point to the two sleeping balls of fat known to the outside world as Johnny and Burke. "The boys kind of barfed on their big sister."

We named the boys after their grandfathers, the "Burke" name almost an inside joke in honor of the Cisco Shin-kicking Affair of 1995. They are identical twins, their only distinguishing features being their moles: Johnny has a single mole centered on his forehead, while Burke's two moles appear like a vampire bite on the right side of his neck.

Beth recovered nicely after her second C-section in four years. I would like to credit my bedside manner for her recovery, but as I haven't been in her life or in her bed for the last six months, I'm indebted more so to the post-cesarean umbilical hernia that forced the insurance company to cover the entire cost of Beth's tummy tuck. She lost her tattoo along with a few inches of loose skin. She even lost her navel. The fake navel looks real enough, and I've caught Beth enough times staring at her bare stomach in the mirror to know she's pretty pleased with the results. The surgeon also gave her a breast lift at a reduced rate. Even though we're separated, Beth has caught me staring at her cleavage enough times to know I'm pretty pleased with the results.

"Both of them barfed on her?" Beth says.

"She wanted to take them on the merry-go-round. I advised against it, but you know Sasha when she gets an idea in her head. I sat the boys on each side of her and made sure to not spin them too fast, but it didn't take much for them to start spewing."

"Is it bad that I'm picturing our daughter covered in her brothers' vomit and wanting to laugh out loud?"

"Go for it," I say. "I sure as hell did when it happened."

Beth walks into the study just off the front hallway. She places Johnny in one of the two cribs pushed up against the hardwood bookcases. She tucks Johnny in, points to the other crib. "You can just put Burke in here for now."

I lay Burke in his bed, swaddling him in a similar fashion to his brother. My eyes dart from one corner of the study to the other. A diaper pail vies for space with a fax machine. A changing pad sprawls over the antique mahogany desk I bought at an estate sale. My first-edition library of Fitzgeralds, Steinbecks, Hemingways, and Faulkners share space with Dr. Marc Weissbluth's *Healthy Sleep Habits, Happy Child*, Rachel Simmons's *Odd Girl Out: The Hidden Culture of Aggression in Girls*, Rosalind Wiseman's *Queen Bees and Wannabes: Helping Your Daughter Survive Cliques, Gossip, Boyfriends, and the New Realities of Girl World*, Dr. Dan Kindlon's and Dr. Michael Thompson's *Raising Cain: Protecting the Emotional Life of Boys*, Dr. William Pollack's *Real Boys: Rescuing Our Sons from the Myths of Boyhood*, and

Steve Biddulph's *Raising Boys: Why Boys are Different—and How to Help Them Become Happy and Well-Balanced Men*.

"I like what you've done with the place."

"I thought you might," Beth says.

I grab the paperback copy of *Real Boys* off the shelf, cracking the spine. I read aloud the first few lines of the introduction: "'Boys today are in serious trouble, including many who seem "normal" and to be doing just fine. Confused by society's mixed messages about what's expected of them as boys, and later as men, many feel a sadness and connection they cannot even name.'"

"Agree or disagree with the premise, Hank?"

I close the book, return it to the shelf. "Yeah, I'll buy that."

"Technically, you did buy that."

Beth reaches over, squeezes my elbow. I don't smile.

"Too soon for child support jokes?" she asks.

"Yeah…" I say. "Probably."

"Would you like to stay for dinner?"

She has asked me over for dinner at least once a week since I closed my satellite office in New York and started working full time again out of College Ave's Indianapolis headquarters. I've been promoted to publisher. Last month, Aaron Rosner's father helped him secure a seat on the board of directors at Domino's Pizza in Ann Arbor. Aaron always hated Indiana anyway. "*Too many goddamn Gentiles*," he said, using the word "Gentiles" in its proper context. I've been sleeping on a cot in the copy room. My clothes smell perpetually of warm paper and ink.

I have yet to accept my estranged wife's invitation. "I don't know, Beth."

"Where do you have to be tonight?"

"Nowhere really, but with you just getting back from Vegas, I thought you might like some quality decompression time with the kids."

"I do want some quality time, Hank…*with my family*."

"Your family?" Her words chase me to the front door, Beth trailing close behind. "Not to bust your bubble or anything, but I haven't been a part of this family equation for almost a year now."

Beth wheels around me, blocking my path to the front door. "Please, Hank. I want you to stay. I want you to want to stay. It's not like we're divorced."

"Legally separated, divorced—it's just semantics, isn't it?"

"Is it?"

"What is it you want from me?"

"It's not about what I want."

"Okay?"

"It's about what I don't want."

"Enough with the mind games, Beth. Just—"

"I don't want to be separated anymore." She reaches out, grabbing me in a desperate bear hug. She buries her head in my chest, tears welling up in her eyes. "I don't think I ever wanted it."

I try to push her away, my heart wanting both literal and metaphorical space. But she won't let go. "Where's all this coming from?"

"What do you mean?" Beth says.

"I know you've been dating."

"Who told you that?"

"People."

"Well, those people are full of shit. I've been thinking about us for a long time, and the Vegas trip pushed me over the edge. Those girls just move at a different speed than me."

"Let me guess," I say. "Claire, Lila, and Chris ended up in various states of undress with strippers and/or each other, and you sat in a dark corner thinking, 'What the fuck is going on?'"

Beth looks over both shoulders, then back at me. "How'd you know?"

"Chris and Lila will always be Chris and Lila, especially when you get some cocktails in them. As for Claire, she's the consummate attention whore. She'll latch on to the coolest guy in the room or stick her tongue down the hottest girl's throat without thinking for a second about Hatch. And why is that?"

"Don't know," Beth says.

I wipe the tears out of my wife's eyes. "Because Claire Hatcher would rather be noticed by a hundred men than loved by just one. You've always wanted to know why it is we never once fooled around in all those years. Well, there's your answer."

"Every guy has his one Hottest Girl I Never Tried to Sleep With, and Claire Sullivan has been your undisputed titleholder for as long as you've known her."

"Where did you hear that?"

"At a bar, from you, before we ever started dating." Beth pokes me playfully in the stomach. "My question to you, Henry David Fitzpatrick, is when did you get so fucking perceptive?"

"Let's just say I've had a lot of free time on my hands lately."

"So you'll stay for dinner?"

I shake my head. "I still don't think that's a good idea."

"Why not?" Beth says.

Holy Christ. Is she crying again?

"Look…" I say. "Just because I have keen insight into your girlfriends doesn't mean my insight when it comes to you has improved."

"Can you let me be the judge of that?"

"How about a rain check?" I say in my best paternal voice, rubbing Beth's arms for good measure.

"Fuck you, Hank!" Beth says, punching me in the chest. "Fuck you!"

My instinct is to run away. But let's be honest here: lately, my instincts have sucked balls.

I wrap my arms tightly around my wife. I can feel her start to relax in my embrace. She fights me, but only for a second. "Beth," I whisper.

"Yes?" she whispers back.

"There's something else you're not telling me, isn't there?" Silence.

The wall clock ticks off the tension one second at a time. "My mom and dad got divorced," Beth says.

"They filed for divorce? When?"

"No, they *got* a divorce. It's over. They filed sixty days ago and didn't tell anybody about it. They were afraid I'd try to talk them out of it. They broke the news to me in a fucking e-mail!"

I stroke Beth's hair. "Honey, I'm so sorry."

"What are you apologizing for?" she says, wiping her nose with the back of her hand. "Being right?"

"No," I say. "I'm apologizing for not being a better husband."

Beth smiles. She leans in, kisses me on the cheek. "A wise man once told me, this is what couples who've been together for a while do. They fuck things up sometimes."

I ACCEPTED MY WIFE'S dinner invitation. Later that night, as I rolled off her naked body, sweating and spent, I accepted her breakfast invitation.

2003–2004

CHAPTER EIGHTY-FIVE

I open the door for my wife to the urologist's office. "Ladies first."

Beth pokes me in the ribs. "And soon-to-be-not-so-manly men last."

"Hey now," I say, looking at my watch. "I can always walk right back out this door."

My vasectomy is scheduled for 10:00 a.m., but this day began more than a year ago, back when Beth gave birth to the boys. The attending nurse came in and checked on her prior to the caesarian. The nurse was an exceedingly chatty woman with pendulous breasts who claimed to know Peyton Manning and who I remember as being named Jill. She talked Beth out of the tubal ligation. She said to her, *"Don't let the doctor feed you that 'while I'm down there I might as well' bullshit. If you want to be up and about tomorrow, tell them to kiss your ass. If you want to be bedridden for a week, get your tubes tied."* And then Nurse Jill looked at me and said, *"He looks like a tough guy. I think one small snip is a fair trade for cutting open a six-inch gash in your abdomen*...twice."

They sewed Beth up, her tubes intact. The vasectomy issue remained unsettled, largely because the state of our marriage remained unsettled. After we got back together, it became a once-a-month dance with us:

"When are you going to make an appointment with the urologist?"

"Soon."

"How soon?"

"As soon as I'm comfortable with the idea of my nutsack getting sliced open."

I was prepared to do the vasectomy two-step for as long as she let me get away with it, which turned out to be about six months. She backed me into a corner with one simple gesture: she went off the pill.

Marriage is the toughest job in the world. It requires patience, compromise, and the humility to acknowledge there are very few nonnegotiable items when it comes to the marital covenant. A couple of my nonnegotiables are: one, nothing interrupts the Notre Dame game on Saturdays; and two, my immutable right to make love to my wife without ever wearing a condom. Some would call that a very shallow outlook, but I'm too busy having mind-blowing, latex-free sex with my wife—who for purposes of this analogy is doing a reverse cowboy wearing nothing but a tight Notre Dame polo and plaid knee-highs—to give a shit.

Beth signs me in. The waiting room is unusually crowded—well, not so unusually, but I'll get to that later—so we stand shoulder to shoulder against a wall.

"Nervous?" Beth says, turning to me.

"No," I say, looking at my watch again.

"Why do you keep doing that?"

"Doing what?"

Beth nods at my watch. "We're ten minutes early. Relax."

"I'm kinda hoping we'll get in and out."

"Where you gotta be?"

"Nowhere," I say. "Just want to get it done and get home."

"And get on the couch with me waiting on you hand and foot?"

"Doctor's orders."

"Yeah, doctor's orders," Beth says. That's when her eye catches a glimpse of ESPN Sportscenter on the waiting room television. "Wait a second."

"What?" I say, fully aware I'm busted.

"Today is Thursday."

"That's right."

"As in the first day of the college basketball tournament."

"Really?" I say. "That's a weird coincidence."

"Is it?"

"Kind of funny how many guys are in here today, don't you think?"

"Hank, please don't tell me this is the reason you've procrastinated about this for six months."

"Well, it's not the *only* reason."

"You son of a—"

"Oh come on now, Beth. This is a once-in-a-lifetime opportunity. Four days and forty-eight games of basketball, during which time you're actually under strict doctor's orders to be at my beck and call. How could I not pass that up?"

There's a knock at the door between the waiting room and the examination rooms, a door we happen to be standing in front of. We move away from the door.

"You ready, Hank?"

The nurse's voice is casual, familiar even. Her jet-black hair is pulled back in a tight ponytail, but the perfect Asian bone structure and the slightly mushy lilt on the end of her voice are dead giveaways. Well, that and the familiar D-cup Asian boobs staring back at me.

It's Lang, my full-breasted, half-Vietnamese neighbor. She always wears shorts and never wears shoes. I make up excuses to go over to her house just to look at her tight calves and perfect bare feet.

And I really need to move to a bigger fucking town than Empire Ridge.

Beth doesn't recognize Lang, partly because she looks distinctly different with her hair up, but mostly because Lang is part of that exclusive subset of pariahs in my insecure wife's social circle known as The Perfectly Nice Women Who Will Never Be My Friends Just Because They're Hotter Than Me Club. In a way, the club is a godsend, as it helps me behave, but it gets annoying when we're vetting the invite list for vacations and couples weekends and "Does she look better than me in a swimsuit?" is Beth's one nonnegotiable item. In recent years, it's also really cut down on the quality of the traffic in our hot tub.

My wife kisses me on the cheek, still a little miffed, I think. "Bye-bye, balls," she says, unapologetically, grabbing an open seat in the waiting room. I leave her to watch ESPN break down today's basketball games with the eight other wives.

CONSENT FOR VASECTOMY

I, the undersigned, request that Empire Ridge Urology, Inc., perform a vasectomy on me. It has been explained to me that this operation is intended to result in permanent sterility, which means that I would not be capable of fathering a child.

I agree to the administration of local anesthetic (medicine to numb the area of the surgery) or other medications before, during, or after the procedure.

I understand that vasectomy is not immediately effective and that I must use another method of birth control until a semen test proves that my vasectomy was successful.

I recognize that, as with any operation, there are risks, both known and unknown, associated with vasectomy, and that no guarantee has been given to me as to the results of this operation. Possible complications include, but are not limited to, the following:

a) Inflammatory reaction in the epididymis or vas deferens (5%)
b) Excessive bleeding into the scrotum (hematoma)
c) Painful nodule or scar (sperm granuloma, neuroma)
d) Infection
e) Allergy or adverse reaction to an anesthetic or medication
f) Emotional reactions that could interfere with normal sexual function
g) Impaired blood flow resulting in loss of a testicle
h) Failure to achieve or to maintain sterility

I understand and accept that these or other conditions may necessitate further treatment, tests, another operation, procedure, and/or hospitalization, at my own expense. I request and authorize Empire Ridge Urology, Inc., to perform such treatment or procedures as required.

I have read and understand the contents of the Informational Booklet, including the alternative forms of birth control for both men and women. I understand and will abide by the instructions for care after vasectomy, and I have received a written copy.

I hand Lang my signed consent form.

"Excessive bleeding into the scrotum? Loss of a testicle? That's comforting."

She tries not to laugh. "Those are extreme worst-case scenarios, Hank."

I'm trying to make small talk, given that I'm pants-less and Lang has just dropped to her knees and is about to grab my balls. It's all I can do to not get an erection, but the mental image of my scrotum bleeding excessively helps.

"This should only take a second," Lang says. She grabs the can of Barbasol off the counter with her right hand. She squirts a dollop of shaving cream in her left palm. She gently massages my scrotum with the shaving cream.

Memo to any guys considering a vasectomy: make sure your urologist has a hot nurse, and shave poorly.

"Soooo…" I say, "is Lang a family name or something?"

Her face only inches from my junk, Lang shaves with a deft touch. "It's a Vietnamese name."

"Meaning what?"

"It's a little embarrassing."

I look at my balls and then at Lang. I arch my eyebrows. "Uh, *you* are worried about being embarrassed?"

"Good point," Lang says. She rubs my bare balls with a wet, warm towel. "All done."

"So I can go?"

"Don't you wish."

There's a knock at the door. The door to the exam room opens. A big black man in a small white coat enters. His nametag says, almost unbelievably, *Dr. Balzac*.

The doctor nods at us both. "Nurse Lang, Mr. Fitzpatrick."

"Good morning, Doctor," we chime in unison.

"Let's get to it, shall we?" He reaches his open hand out to Lang. Lang hands him a syringe. He points the syringe at my balls. "You take a Valium before you got in here?"

I nod. "Two of them."

"Oh boy," Lang comments.

"This is the lidocaine," the doctor says in a monotone voice. "Just some local anesthesia to numb the skin and vas deferens. You're going to feel a tiny prick."

"That's what she said," I say.

Lang laughs. The doctor doesn't.

"Fuck me!"

"Sorry about that, Mr. Fitzpatrick. Did I get you?"

"That was more than a little prick," I say. Suddenly, I feel short of breath. My chest is tight. I'm sweating.

Lang notices immediately. "Hank, what is it?"

My eyes are open wide. The room is shrinking. "I think I'm having a heart attack."

"Nonsense," the doctor says nonchalantly. "Probably nicked a blood vessel. You're just getting a small dose of adrenaline in your heart right now."

"In other words, a mini-fucking heart attack?" I say.

Impassive, the doctor nods. "It'll pass."

"Please..." I say, grabbing Lang's hand. "Just talk to me."

"Sweet potato," Lang says.

"What?"

"Lang is Vietnamese for sweet potato."

I nod. "Keep talking."

Lang wipes my forehead with a towel—a fresh one, not the one that was wrapped around my bag five minutes ago. "My mother's parents were sweet potato farmers just outside of Saigon. My father was a US Marine. He was married to my mother in the US Embassy the day Saigon fell."

"Wow, that's kind of awesome."

"Yeah, it is."

"I'm feeling better now, save for the fact the ceiling looks like it's made of Jell-O."

"That's the Valium kicking in."

"Cool," I say.

And then it hits me: the urge to sing.

"They're called Bui-Doi..."

Lang shakes her head. "Here we go."

"The dust of life! Conceived in hell! And born in strife!"

"Nurse Lang?" Dr. Balzac says.

"They are the living reminder of all the good we failed to do..."

"Sorry about this, Doctor," Lang says. "Hank is on a little bit of a Valium bender right now. Apparently my Vietnam story has him singing the big emotional anthem from *Miss Saigon*, the one about the lost generation of Vietnamese children conceived from Vietnamese women and US soldiers during the war."

"We can't forget, must not forget that they are all our children, too!"

I think the doctor actually smiles this time, although to be honest the whole world looks like it's smiling at the moment. "Well..." he says, "that's different."

Lang wheels me out of the exam room in a wheelchair. Beth is standing there waiting for me near the exit door.

"How did it go, honey?"

I throw a thumb over my shoulder. "I got my balls shaved by this sweet potato!"

Beth puts her finger to her pursed lips. "Shhhhhh..."

"What?!"

"You're screaming, Hank."

"My urologist's name was Doctor Ballsack! Can you fucking believe that?"

Beth looks at Lang. "Is he going to be like this all day?"

"Ballsack!"

Lang shakes her head. "He's been hallucinating a bit from the anesthetic. It should wear off soon."

"Thanks, Miss…"

"You can call me Lang, Beth."

"Have we met?" my wife says. "You look familiar."

"Just in passing," Lang says. "I'm your neighbor."

"Get out of here."

"No, really."

"Ballsack!"

"I can't imagine why we haven't crossed paths yet." Beth laughs without a trace of earnestness in her voice.

"Oh, oh, oh, I know," I say, sticking my hand in the air like Arnold Horshack from *Welcome Back, Kotter.* "It's because you're too insecure to have friends who are hotter than you."

An uncomfortable, almost standoffish silence hangs in the air between Beth and Lang. If I could feel my tongue, I'd probably try to articulate some sort of mediation. What the hell, I'll give it a try:

"They're called Bui-Doi! The dust of life! Conceived in hell! Born in strife!"

"Uh…" Beth says. "What's going on?"

Lang smiles. "I find it's best to just let him finish."

"We owe them fathers and a family, a loving home they never knew. Because we know, deep in our hearts, that they are all our children, too!"

CHAPTER EIGHTY-SIX

"Ty Detmer is the least-deserving winner of the Heisman Trophy in the history of college football. That's a fucking fact, Gillman!"

"Hank, language!"

"My car, my rules."

My stepfather and I sit in my Subaru, arguing as we drive up Highway 31. We're attending the Notre Dame-Michigan game together. Last week, Gillman hosted a viewing party for Notre Dame's opening game in the 2004 college football season because they were playing his alma mater, Brigham Young University. They were playing BYU in Provo, I got tired of Gillman harping on about BYU's supposed "tradition," and at some point during the game I declared, *"You want to see tradition, Gillman? Tell you what, if the Cougars beat the Irish, I'll buy us tickets to next week's Michigan game and personally drive us up to South Bend. Just you and me taking an old-fashioned father-and-son road trip."*

Final score: BYU 20–Notre Dame 17.

"Rocket Ismail better than Ty Detmer?" Gillman says. "Is that a joke?"

"Ty was just another overrated stats machine destined to flame out in the NFL, while Rocket was probably the most electrifying player of the decade."

"Says you, Hank."

"Says me and everyone who doesn't live in Utah. And what happened to Detmer the first game he played after winning the Heisman?"

"Oh no, here we go."

"Two broken arms, Gillman!"

"It was two separated shoulders, actually."

"Whatever," I say. "If that isn't God coming down and smiting him, I don't know what is."

"So your theory is that Ty Detmer's shoulders were not separated by a Texas A&M defensive player, but rather by God as vengeance for Rocket Ismail not winning the Heisman Trophy?"

"That's no theory." I shake my head, my left hand on the steering wheel and my right pointing at Gillman. "And you've got a lot to learn about Notre Dame football."

GILLMAN AND I WALK just past the northwest entrance of Notre Dame Stadium. "And right here was where I stood as an extra when Ned Beatty got off the bus. I remember he had on a faded brown trench coat and dark brown cap pulled over his ears and tufts of silvery-gray hair poking out of the bottom of his cap that made him look like my Grandpa George."

"So you were here when they filmed *Rudy*?"

"For some of the scenes, yeah."

"That's quite a memory, Hank."

"It's kind of hard to forget that season."

"What year was it?

"Nineteen ninety-two."

"Oh, sorry."

"Yeah. Me, too."

"We don't have to talk about it if you don't want to."

"I don't mind. After Mom canceled our season tickets, she gave me two tickets for each of the remaining home games. I missed the Stanford game because of the funeral, but I went to BYU, Boston College, and Penn State.

"Dad had told me the *Rudy* story a hundred times before Hollywood ever got a hold of it. An old classmate tipped him off that they were going to be filming most of the campus scenes during the BC and Penn State games. I remember he had the dates, November seventh and November fourteenth, circled on his office calendar. I brought Jack with me to the BC game, but he was four years old and didn't know what was going on. We made it to our seats right before kickoff, but we missed all the pageantry: the gold helmets coming out of the tunnel, the band's high-step routine to *Hike Notre Dame*, the *Notre Dame Victory March*, even the national anthem and 'America the Beautiful.'"

"Your father would have been pissed."

"Totally," I say. "At six–one–one Notre Dame was ranked number eight in the country. They had tied Michigan back in September and lost to Stanford the Saturday after Dad was killed. BC came in with a seven–oh–one record and a number-nine ranking. It was the highest both teams had ever been ranked when facing one another. I saw a guy holding a poster that said *The Pope Needs Four Tickets*. ND won the coin toss, deferred to the second half, and Boston College chose to receive. The Irish defended the south goal, and I expected a great game."

"And did it meet your expectations?"

"Depends on what my expectations were."

"A win maybe?"

"Maybe," I say. "Two BC fans arrived late, toward the end of the first quarter. There was a TV timeout on the field, so the teams were huddled on opposite sidelines. The two BC fans sat down next to Jack and me, and one of them complained that he didn't realize there was an hour time difference between Chicago and South Bend. They parked on the opposite side of the campus and had no clue what had just happened. The guy asked me, 'What did we miss?' and I pointed to the scoreboard. It was twenty-one–zero Notre Dame with four minutes still left in the first quarter."

"Ouch," Gillman says. "Still, it had to be a fun day with Jack."

"Like I said, he really didn't know what was going on. The highlight of the game for me was halftime. A bunch of extras in vintage nineteen seventy-two Notre Dame and Georgia Tech football uniforms stormed the field. They executed about a dozen plays, we were given cues to cheer, and at the end, the Notre Dame players carried Sean Astin off the field."

"So you get to see that scene essentially replayed every time you watch *Rudy* now?"

"Yeah, I guess I do. But that game was bittersweet. Not just the circumstances of why I was there, but the game itself. The whole day left a bad taste in my mouth. Coach Holtz called a fake punt when the Irish were leading thirty-seven–zero. They won fifty-four–seven, and no part of me felt good about rubbing it in BC's face. It was like Notre Dame had become as ugly and embittered as I felt. When I got home, I pulled out my shoe box of Notre Dame ticket stubs dating back to the first game I ever attended."

"Which game was that?"

"Georgia Tech nineteen seventy-eight. Vagas Ferguson ran for a school-record two hundred fifty-five yards."

"Don't tell me you threw out all your tickets."

"Nope."

"Good."

"I burned them."

GILLMAN AND I HALF-SPRINTED across the west side of campus. He watched as I crossed myself beneath Touchdown Jesus. As I patted Number One Moses on the head. As I saluted Fair Catch Corby. As I crossed myself again at the steps of the administration building and Our Lady atop the Golden Dome. By the time we got to the stone steps behind Sacred Heart Basilica, Gillman was hyperventilating.

"You okay, old man?"

We reach the bottom of the steps. Gillman hunches over, panting. "I sure hope…this was…worth it."

I pat my front pocket. "These things have to be done just right."

Tucked in a small hillside just behind Sacred Heart, the Grotto is a one-seventh scale replica of the original Grotto of Our Lady of Lourdes, France, where the Virgin Mary is said to have appeared to St. Bernadette. Dozens of white votive candles are perpetually lit inside the cobblestoned sanctuary, with that number hovering closer to a few hundred today, given that we're playing those Godless, Catholic-hating secularists known as the Michigan Wolverines.

I light a candle and drop a dollar in the collection box. A kneeler and a wrought iron fence run the full width of the Grotto. I wait for a small, elderly nun to vacate her spot and kneel in her place, convinced the kneeler will of course retain a little extra Catholic mojo.

I pull the rosary out of my pocket. It belonged to Grandpa George. He carried it with him during the war. Oxidized brass links connect fifty-nine beads of black onyx. Fifty-four of the beads converge into a brass Sacred Heart pendant, from which hangs the remaining five beads and a brass crucifix. I wrap the rosary twice loosely around my left hand. Using my right hand, I hold the crucifix in between my index finger and thumb. I recite the Apostles' Creed.

"I believe in God, the Father almighty, creator of heaven and earth. I believe in Jesus Christ, His only Son, our Lord. He was conceived by the power of the Holy Spirit and born of the Virgin Mary. He suffered under Pontius Pilate, was crucified, died, and was buried. He descended to the dead. On the third day he rose again. He ascended into heaven and is seated at the right hand of the Father. He will come again to judge the living and the dead. I believe in the Holy Spirit, the holy Catholic Church, the communion of saints, the forgiveness of sins, the resurrection of the body, and life everlasting. Amen."

I grab the larger bead just above the crucifix. I recite the *Our Father*.

"Our Father who art in heaven, hallowed be thy name. Thy kingdom come, thy will be done, on earth as it is in heaven. Give us this day our daily bread, and forgive us our trespasses, as we forgive those who trespass against us, and lead us not into temptation, but deliver us from evil. Amen."

I grab the second smaller bead. I say a *Hail Mary*.

"Hail Mary, full of grace, the Lord is with thee. Blessed art thou amongst women, and blessed is the fruit of thy womb, Jesus. Holy Mary, Mother of God, pray for us sinners, now and at the hour of our death. Amen."

I grab the next bead and repeat the *Hail Mary* prayer.

"Hail Mary, full of grace, the Lord is with thee. Blessed art thou amongst women, and blessed is the fruit of thy womb, Jesus. Holy Mary, Mother of God, pray for us sinners, now and at the hour of our death. Amen."

And again.

"Hail Mary, full of grace, the Lord is with thee. Blessed art thou amongst women, and blessed is the fruit of thy womb, Jesus. Holy Mary, Mother of God, pray for us sinners, now and at the hour of our death. Amen."

I move to the fourth bead.

"Hail Mary, full of grace, the Lord is with thee. Blessed art thou amongst women, and blessed is the fruit of thy womb, Jesus. Holy Mary, Mother of God, pray for us sinners, now and at the hour of our death. Amen."

Finally, I throw in a *Glory Be* at the fifth bead.

"Glory be to the Father, and to the Son, and to the Holy Spirit, as it was in the beginning, is now, and ever shall be, world without end. Amen."

I stop. Shoving the rosary back in my pocket, I know this is all I have in me. There are people who make it through a full rosary every day, and that's not just one time around. A full rosary is three rotations. It comes out to something like seventy-five *Our Fathers*, one-hundred-and-fifty *Hail Marys*, and another seventy-five *Glory Bes*. Grandpa George tried making me sit through a whole rosary once. I got about halfway before my knees went numb and I had to pee. Glory be to the Father, and to the Son, and to the Holy Spirit for eight-year-old bladders.

"About an hour until kickoff." Gillman whispers from behind, hushed and respectful. "Probably should think about making our way to the stadium."

"I'm ready, Gillman." I stand, offer my kneeler to another nun—for bonus points, of course.

On our way back across campus, the Young Republicans talk us into bratwursts in front of Doyle Hall. Gillman hands me the mustard.

"Thanks," I say.

"No, Hank, thank you."

"For what?"

"For sharing today with me. I know Notre Dame games were you and your father's thing."

"That they were, Gillman. But don't start getting soft on me. You're a decent guy and all, and you're real good to Mom and Jack, which in the end is all that matters to me. But I still think you're a total whack job."

"I'll take that as a compliment."

"You would."

"Well, Hank, you're one to talk."

"What do you mean by that?"

"For someone who isn't the biggest fan of all the pomp and circumstance of organized religion, that was a quite a show back there at the Grotto."

"I'm a fan of organized religion, Gillman. Just not *your* organized religion."

"You're a true believer, my friend. Against every impulse in your body, you have faith. Just admit it."

"Faith?" I finish off the last bite of my bratwurst and discard the wrapper. "The only goddamn thing I believe in is Notre Dame football."

"Hank, language!"

"My campus, my rules."

CHAPTER EIGHTY-SEVEN

The rain is cold and ferocious. I can't see out the front of my Subaru. The water veils my station wagon in a sideways sheet of foreboding. Jack is standing outside, waiting for me. He runs to my car, his clothes soaked through to his wiry teenage frame.

"Need a ride?" I say, opening the door.

Jack slides into the car, shuts the door. He runs his hand through his wet hair and pulls his Prep letter jacket around his face, trying to shield his bloodshot eyes from me.

"Can we just go?" he asks.

"Where?"

"Somewhere, anywhere."

Jack is about an inch taller and twenty pounds lighter than me. Fifteen years old, a month and a half into his sophomore year in high school, his jacket bears his athletic accomplishments: a block-letter P on his left chest; two chevrons, one in soccer, one in golf; a couple all-conference recognition patches in each sport.

"Where are Mom and Gillman?" I say, shifting the car into reverse.

"They went to Brown County for the weekend."

"Car still in the shop?"

"Yep."

In the great Fitzpatrick tradition, Jack's car seems to spend more time in the body shop than on the road. He only has his permit, and he's already wrecked his car twice.

"So how stoned are you?"

"Whatever happened to 'no questions asked'?"

"I guess I forgot about that after I picked up my brother standing in a monsoon in front of a strange house with liquor and marijuana on his breath."

"You can smell all that?"

"I'm guessing Jim Beam and a couple rounds of bong hits in a small enclosed room."

"How the hell did you—"

"The Beam was easy," I say. "Cheap bourbon has a fairly distinctive smell, and I still drink it enough to recognize it almost immediately. As for the bong hits, your eyes are redder than Ben Johnson at the '88 Seoul Olympics, and the cannabis smell coming off your skin, clothes, and hair is way too strong to be delivered by just a joint or bowl."

"Who's Ben Johnson?"

Man, I'm getting fucking old. "Never mind," I say.

We head to Wagon Wheel, the late-night greasy spoon on Central Street that's frequented by no one under the age of seventy-five. I used to take Grandpa George here when I was a teenager, a few months before I learned it wasn't cool to hang out with your grandfather in public and a few years before his death taught me I was a dipshit. The waitress brings us two plates of biscuits and gravy.

"Not hungry," Jack says, pushing his plate away.

"Like hell you aren't." I push his plate right back at him. "Now eat and talk to me."

"I can't do it anymore, Hank."

"Can't do what?"

"Live under the same roof as Gillman."

"Come on, Jack. He means well."

"Does he?"

"So he's a little controlling."

"Last night he found a couple of those little travel bottles of whiskey in my nightstand."

"And I assume he grounded you, which is what parents are supposed to do."

"He grounded me all right. He said when he and Mom get back from Brown County I'm losing all cell phone privileges for the rest of the semester."

"Damn!" I say. "That's like cutting off your arm."

"I know, right?"

"I'm kidding, buddy." I sip my black coffee, slowly and with intent. I return my coffee cup to its saucer. I have to get these words right. I'm more than his big brother, and I need to start acting like it. "Look, as much as I want to back you up, I've gotten to the age where I'm not allowed to be on your side sometimes. Does that make any sense to you?"

"No."

"I didn't think it would, so tell me, what's *really* bothering you?"

"What do you mean?"

"Saying you have problems with Gillman is like saying the sky is blue. We all have problems with Gillman. He's a dick."

"What happened to 'he means well' and he's just 'a little controlling'?"

"I was being nice. So come on, fess up. You having problems at Prep?"

"No, Prep is awesome. The Ridge sucks, dude."

"Excuse my French, little brother, but fuck you."

"Ha." Jack's first smile of the night. "I love getting you all amped up."

"Well, it's working."

"Like I said, Prep is cool. I just had an issue tonight, at the party."

"What kind of issue?"

"It's a little embarrassing."

"Try me."

"There's this game kids at Prep and the Ridge are really into right now. It's called a lipstick party."

"Never heard of it."

"It's big in New York and LA, I guess. Last year somebody transferred in from Culver and brought the game with them."

Culver is a military academy in northeastern Indiana that could have been ripped right out of a Bret Easton Ellis novel. An oasis of old East Coast money, its alumni include George Steinbrenner and Roger Penske. I took a weekend tour of the campus when I was a sophomore in high school and saw somebody snort cocaine out of a girl's cleavage at a party involving a lot of kids with Roman numerals at the end of their names. Whatever a lipstick party is, if it came from Culver, it can't be good.

"I'm listening, Jack."

"A lipstick party is when a bunch of girls put different colored lipstick on their mouths and then give guys blowjobs in the dark. When the lights are turned back on, the guys try to guess which girl gave them the blowjob."

"You got to be kidding me."

"Nope."

"That's not just a plot for a bad TV show on Fox or an exploitative YA novel?"

"It's very real, Hank."

"So you were at one of these lipstick parties tonight?"

"Yes."

"And what did you do?"

"What do you mean, what did I do? I chickened out."

"And?"

"And everyone is going to make fun of me at school on Monday."

"Not everyone."

"You don't know, Hank."

"Don't tell me what I don't know. In fact, I'd be willing to bet almost no one makes fun of you."

"I don't believe you."

"What I'm telling you is not for you to believe or disbelieve. It's a fact. There will be a couple douche bags who give you a hard time, but high school is like an all-you-can-eat douche bag buffet. And sure, maybe a few sluts will no longer look your way at a party. But is empty validation and a sexually transmitted disease really something to lose sleep over? Trust me when I say there will be a lot of girls who are going to respect you more for doing what you did, and out of those girls, you're going to find one who will run through fire for you. Maybe you don't find her tomorrow, or even next year. Maybe you don't find her until college. Or maybe you find her, and for whatever reason the timing just isn't right for you two. But when you do find her, and when the timing is right, hold on to her. A real man only needs one tube of lipstick."

"Why would I need a tube of lipstick?" Jack asks. "I'm not gay."

"You know, little brother, you really suck at metaphors."

Jack smiles. I can almost see a little bit of Dad in him. It's a wise look bordering on mischievous. "And you, big brother, seem to think everything in life needs one."

2005

CHAPTER EIGHTY-EIGHT

A family road trip from Indiana to North Carolina with a nine-year-old and two five-year-olds: what the fuck were Beth and I thinking?

The Southern Outer Banks are about eight hundred miles away from Empire Ridge. Our Honda Odyssey minivan's DVD player kept the kids occupied nearly all the way to Raleigh, but at this point, as we pass over the White Oak River Bridge in Swansboro, I'm halfway considering chucking all three of them into the White Oak River.

"Daddy," Sasha says.

"Yes, honey?"

"The boys keep farting, and it stinks back here."

"Then open a window."

My wife had tried to put this drive off as long as possible. Stan still owns his pediatric practice in Empire Ridge, but he's pretty much retired at this point, spending eight months of the year at the pink beach house, which he got in the divorce. This is the first time we've brought the kids back to the place since Stan and Joan separated, and we're worried how they'll react. During the holidays, Beth's parents are acutely skilled at pretending they like one another—"I've had decades of practice," Joan told me last Christmas—so up to this point, the kids really haven't been affected by the situation.

"I tried opening a window," my daughter says. "It doesn't work."

"Boys," I say. "Stop it."

"Stop what?" Johnny says.

"You're suffocating your sister."

"What's suck fuck kating?" Burke says. Johnny giggles.

"Burke said the f-word, Daddy."

"I know what he said, Sasha."

"You have to give him one squirt. Those are the rules."

Burke starts crying. "It was an accident, Daddy. No squirt! No squirt!"

I notice my wife eyeing the glove box. "No, Beth. Like he said, it was an accident. And it's vacation."

"Don't complain to me," Beth says. "You made the stupid rule."

Sasha and Burke are referring to the most feared weapon in our parent arsenal, the doomsday device: a squirt of liquid hand soap. We keep the bottle of orange retribution in the glove boxes of both vehicles. One cuss word equals one squirt on your tongue. Like Tina Turner telling Mel Gibson as he entered Thunder Dome, "Two men enter, one man leaves," the squirt is the law.

"Bust a deal, face the wheel," I say to my wife.

"What's that mean?"

"You know, *Mad Max: Beyond Thunderdome*?"

"That post-apocalypse movie with Mel Gibson?"

"Yes!"

"Never seen it."

"What? So when someone says to you, 'This is Thunderdome, death is listening, and will take the first man who screams,' that means nothing to you?"

"Up until just this moment I have never heard those words used in a sentence together, and I've certainly never heard that bad of a Tina Turner impersonation."

"It was good enough that you recognized it."

"This isn't Thunderdome, Hank. It's a Honda Odyssey."

"I know that, honey." I look at my red-eyed son in the rearview mirror. "Hey, Burke, bust a deal, face the wheel."

He wipes his nose. "What?"

"You broke the agreement we had for cuss words, but because I'm on vacation, I'll let you choose your punishment."

"What are my choices?"

"I'll go easy on you. You can either eat soap or be nice to your sister for the entire vacation."

Burke looks at me in the rearview mirror. Looks at his sister. Looks at me again. He closes his eyes and sticks out his tongue.

Burke is on his third juice box in as many minutes, trying to get the hand soap taste out of his mouth. We're about through Emerald Isle and nearing Stan's place in Salter Path.

"Promise something, Hank?" Beth both says and asks simultaneously.

"Depends on what that 'something' is."

"No working vacation this week. I want my husband off the clock."

"You know I can't promise that. I have a lunch with Margaret on Wednesday that I can't miss."

"A lunch appointment? Since when?"

"Since we booked this trip."

Margaret is Margaret Maron, the author of the North Carolina-based Judge Deborah Knott mystery series. I've been trying to woo her away from her print publisher Mysterious Press for years, but Random House has given College Ave increasingly less acquisitions money to work with. I have it on good authority Margaret has already re-upped with Mysterious—well, her agent just flat out told me—and that Margaret is taking this lunch with me more out of guilt. I figure the least I could do is put a couple bottles of red wine and some shrimp and grits on my Random expense account.

It's not that my relationship with Random House hasn't been fruitful. Far from it. I've made a lot of money off being more lucky than good. I was gifted Lila's book, *Sperm Bank Messiah*, which she managed to stretch into a trilogy. Each successive book in the series—the middle volume, *Mrs. Jesus*, and the finale, *Viva Leviticus*—was more critically panned while at the same time more commercially successful than its predecessor. And then, just last year, a flavor-of-the-year graphic novelist at Comic-Con agreed to adapt one of my own short stories, "Plaid & Plasma," into a tongue-in-cheek fusion of contemporary vampire fiction and Scottish Highlands romance called *Blood, Sex, and Kilts* that hit the *New York Times* bestseller list and was optioned by Showtime for a cable TV series.

"You got one lunch," Beth says, holding up her left index finger. "But if at any other point in the week I see you bust out that stupid laptop, I'm chucking it in the ocean. Deal?"

I grab her hand and kiss it. "Deal."

We pull into Stan's driveway. The pink paint on the cedar shake has faded to salmon. A white sign hangs over the front door with the words *Little Pink House* burned into its surface.

"Let's unpack later," Beth says. "Dad hasn't seen his grandkids in months."

We unharness Sasha and the twins. Beth leads the way. A wind chime serenades us as we walk across the white-railed front porch and into the house. My wife walks in without knocking.

Busted.

"Dad!" Beth shouts. With her left hand she covers Sasha's eyes, with her right forearm she shields the eyes of the twins.

A tanned woman in an orange bikini, a little older than Beth but not by much, is in the kitchen with Stan. She's on her knees, giving my father-in-law a blowjob.

The woman bolts upright, wiping her mouth.

"You're early," Stan says, pulling up his swim trunks and scolding his daughter, as if she's the one who needs the lesson on decorum.

"Apparently not early enough," Beth says.

I reach my hand out to the tanned woman in the orange bikini. Much like Jack's old principal, she's more fit than attractive. Upon closer inspection she also looks more mid-fifties than mid-thirties. "Hi, my name is Hank."

The woman accepts my gesture. She shakes my hand, outwardly not the least put off by what just happened. There's not even a hint of blushing in her face, although granted that would be hard to see against her leathered, paprika skin. "Hiya, darlin'," she says. "My name is Marilyn, but all my friends call me May-May."

"May-May?"

"Yeah, darlin'. I used to have a twin sister named Margaret, ya see. But she died as a baby, on account of havin' a weak heart. We were born in May, so after Ma lost her, she took to callin' me 'May-May' 'cause she couldn't bear to forget her little Margaret."

"That's…interesting," I say.

"You Yankees and yuh manners," May-May says, pulling her hand away from me and backhanding my arm. "It's downright morbid, s'what it is. I just cain't never imagine bein' called anythin' else."

"Well, May-May"—Beth elbows me out of the way—"if you need someone to be rude to you, I'm happy to oblige."

"Easy, little girl," Stan says, stepping between the two women.

"I'm not your fu—" Beth cuts her expletive in half, realizing her kids are well within earshot. "I'm not your little girl, Dad. But if I were, that would probably be cool, because given her age, May-May and I would probably be into a lot of the same things."

"You think?" May-May says.

"That's not a freaking compliment!" Beth shouts.

"Hey, May-May," I interject. "Can you do me a favor and take the kids out back?"

"Sure thing, darlin'," she says, turning to Sasha and the twins. "Have any of you ever seen a jellyfish before?"

"Is it made out of real jelly?" Burke says.

"No, stupid," Sasha answers.

"Zip it, Sasha," I say. "Just go outside with Miss May-May and your brothers for a few minutes. We have to talk to Grandpa about something."

"Children, y'all can call me Aunt May-May."

"No, *y'all* can't," Beth says.

In between yelling at her father for the last twenty minutes, my wife has consumed a pitcher of margaritas. I'm standing on the periphery, a bottle of Carolina Blonde Ale in my hand as I watch my Indiana blonde pace between the kitchen and living room, still pissed as hell.

"I'm sorry for what you saw," Stan says to his daughter.

"Apology not accepted."

"Who's apologizing? I'm not sorry for it happening. I don't owe you an explanation for being in a relationship."

"A relationship?" Beth points out the back window. "Is that what you call that orange dick sucker out there?"

And there's my cue. "Come on, babe. That's a bit harsh."

Beth sends me another slightly more obvious cue. "You stay the fuck out of this, Hank."

"Baby doll, please," Stan says. "We're not going to fix this today. Just tell me what you want from me."

"What do I want from you?" Beth wipes one lone tear from her right eye. I have a feeling that's all she's giving him today. "I want my dad back."

"But I haven't gone anywhere."

"You know what I mean."

"How about if for now I just ask May-May to go home?"

"How about if you just ask her to go to hell?"

"Home is good for now, Doc," I say.

Stan walks out the back door. Beth turns and faces me. "Don't tell me you're on his side."

"I'm not on anybody's side. So your dad has a girlfriend. There are worse things in the world. Quite frankly, I'm a little put off by your behavior at the moment."

"What did I do?"

"Not that I'm surprised, but you seem more possessive and jealous about your father than you ever are with me."

"You're not barking up that tree again, are you?"

"You kind of invite the barking."

"A woman half his age was giving him head in his kitchen!"

"First off, last time I checked your father isn't a hundred years old. Secondly, good for him. He's starring in his own rom-com."

"His own what?"

"Romantic comedy. There's you, the daughter, losing touch with her femininity under the heavy burden of motherhood while dealing with the broken marriage of your empty-nester parents. There's Stan, the exiled father, rediscovering his masculinity in the arms of an attractive and confoundedly endearing woman."

"Confoundedly endearing?"

"I know you don't see it, Beth. But May-May is ripped right out of a screenplay. She's like Bess Armstrong in *The Four Seasons* and Sarah Jessica Parker in *LA Story*.

"Or like Natalie Portman in *Beautiful Girls* and Mena Suvari in *American Beauty.*"

"Jesus Christ, it's not like your father is pining after Lolita. He and May-May are two consenting adults. They just want to have a little—"

Beth raises her hand. "Let me stop you right there, hubby."

"What?"

"When I say 'stop,' that means stop talking. You know how you like to do that thing where you distill a scene into something insightful or clever, as if you have an invisible audience watching you?"

I don't respond.

"Uh, hello?"

"So I can talk now?"

"Just nod your head, smartass."

I nod my head.

"Well, I fucking hate it."

"Sorry."

"No you're not," Beth says. "Now wipe that faraway look off your face and stop thinking about Natalie Portman in *Beautiful Girls*, you pervert."

Busted.

CHAPTER EIGHTY-NINE

Easter Vigil is the service held traditionally after sunset on Holy Saturday before the sun rises on Easter Sunday. This service engenders wildly disparate reactions in Catholics. The devout regard it as the most important mass of the liturgical year, while the majority of Catholics—i.e., those of us who have two-point-three children because we wear condoms and pop birth control pills like Tic Tacs, think abortions should be rare but legal, and would rather watch George Carlin in *Dogma* than Jim Caviezel in *The Passion of the Christ*—well, we fucking hate it.

Very simply, Easter Vigil is when the real Catholics get their Jesus on. The service is anywhere from three to four hours long and is an all-you-can-eat sacramental buffet. There are Baptisms, First Communions, Reconciliations, Confirmations, even weddings. Easter Vigil is interminable to the point where in the pantheon of old school Papist rituals I'd rather sit through a Rosary, watch a Mother Angelica marathon on EWTN, or read an entire issue of *Latin Mass* magazine.

The first Easter Vigil service I remember attending was in 1983. We were living in Louisville, Kentucky. Our next-door neighbor was the team doctor for the University of Louisville men's basketball team, a dynastic program of the early eighties. He got Dad and me in to see closed practices in which we met the players, and so names like Milt Wagner, Lancaster Gordon, Scooter and Rodney McCray, Charles Jones, and Billy Thompson supplanted the latest Fighting Irish football players at the dinner table. Granted, Dad and I appropriated the Cardinals more as a temporary distraction from the Gerry Faust era at Notre Dame, but our passion and commitment was real enough to us.

Louisville was playing Houston in the Final Four the Saturday night before Easter. CBS promoted it as "the Doctors of Dunk versus Phi Slamma Jamma." Dad had the bright idea to go to church on Saturday afternoon so we could stay up late and watch the game while not having to worry about getting up early for church. We attended Holy Trinity. An eighteen-year-old parishioner by the name of Mary T. Meagher was the cross bearer, still a year away from winning gold in the pool at the Summer Olympics in Los Angeles. We missed almost the entire game, although about halfway into the four-hour Vigil service, Dad excused himself to go to the restroom, never to return. Just as my feet and knees had gone numb and I shouted my first "Alleluia!" in forty days, Dad was in the car screaming at his radio, "Crum, get a body on Olajuwon!"

Today's Easter Vigil service is passably tolerable, as I have a vested interest. For one, my old friend Father Fisher Kelly presides over today's Easter Vigil. For another, Beth and Sasha are receiving the sacrament of First Communion together. Father Fish wears the traditional Roman Catholic alb, a white linen liturgical vestment with tapered sleeves. The stole around his neck is reversible, purple on one side and white on the other, which allowed him to symbolically flip it from purple to white at the beginning of the service to symbolize the progression from Lent to Easter. He stands behind the altar. A large ceramic bowl of communal wafers sits to his left, a gold chalice of wine to his right.

"Blessed are you, Lord, God of all creation," Father Fish says. "Through your goodness we have this bread to offer, which earth has given and human hands have made. It will become for us the bread of life."

The congregation responds, "Blessed be God forever."

"Blessed are you, Lord, God of all creation," Father Fish says again. "Through your goodness we have this wine to offer, fruit of the vine and work of human hands. It will become our spiritual drink."

We again respond back to him, "Blessed be God forever."

Father Fish walked us through the requisite rituals: the singing, the bell ringing, the bowing, the reaffirmations we say by rote more than faith. After about ten minutes, Beth and Sasha approach the foot of the altar with the other catechists. My wife wears a sheer black dress, my daughter a floral print that, because she's nine years old, I can still get away with calling cute instead of pretty. An altar boy stands in front of Father Fish, holding open a leather-bound book. Father looks down intermittently at the book, but the way he maintains eye contact with the congregation tells me he isn't reading it.

"The holy Eucharist completes Christian initiation," Father Fish begins. "Those who have been raised to the dignity of the royal priesthood by Baptism and configured more deeply to Christ by Confirmation participate with the whole community in the Lord's own sacrifice by means of the Eucharist.

"At the Last Supper, on the night he was betrayed, our Savior instituted the Eucharistic sacrifice of his body and blood. This he did in order to perpetuate the sacrifice of the cross throughout the ages until he should come again, and so to entrust to his beloved spouse, the Church, a memorial of his death and resurrection: a sacrament of love, a sign of unity, a bond of charity, a Paschal banquet in which Christ is consumed, the mind is filled with grace, and a pledge of future glory is given to us."

This is the part about the Eucharist that usually freaks out non-Catholics. Protestants regard the consumption of Jesus's body and blood as symbolic, while Catholics are supposed to believe in a process called transubstantiation, by which the bread and wine are mystically transformed into the literal body and blood of Jesus. That's right, Catholics are actively practicing cannibals. The doctrine is disgusting, but the truth is most Catholics don't obsess about it too much; with all due apologies to Pope John Paul II and St. Peter, we don't buy into it any more than our Protestant friends.

Father Fish continues. "The Eucharist is the source and summit of the Christian life. The other sacraments, and indeed all ecclesiastical ministries and works of the apostolate, are bound up with the Eucharist and are oriented toward it. For in the blessed Eucharist is contained the whole spiritual good of the Church, namely Christ himself, our Pasch.

"The Eucharist is the efficacious sign and sublime cause of that communion in the divine life and that unity of the People of God by which the Church is kept in being. It is the culmination both of God's action sanctifying the world in Christ and of the worship men offer to Christ and through him to the Father in the Holy Spirit.

"Finally, by the Eucharistic celebration we already unite ourselves with the heavenly liturgy and anticipate eternal life, when God will be all in all. The Eucharist is the sum and summary of our faith: our way of thinking is attuned to the Eucharist, and the Eucharist in turn confirms our way of thinking."

If the Lord works in mysterious ways, the fact Beth came around to "our way of thinking" is as mysterious as it gets. How does the wife of the world's worst Catholic, not to mention the daughter of a divorced atheist, decide that a world of rhythm methods and fish fries is the smart move? In the decade prior to Beth starting catechism, I could count on one hand the number of times we'd been to church that didn't involve a holiday, wedding, or funeral.

Sasha is mostly to blame. Firmly ensconced in the Empire Ridge Public School system, she's now more than two years behind her Catholic friends who received their First Communion at age six or seven. It got to a point where we didn't go to church just to avoid explaining why she was the only one her age required to approach the altar for the Eucharist with crossed arms and a closed mouth. Barring that, we've deferred to the ultimate rationalization of thirtysomething closet agnostics that, our intellectual faculties be damned, we're giving Sasha "a good foundation."

Like most parents in their mid-thirties, Beth and I have talked ourselves into believing that in lieu of relying on our own reasonably competent parenting skills, it is up to an imaginary bearded old man in the sky to teach our kids right from wrong. Furthermore, he's not even teaching them right from wrong; rather, he's teaching them there's no point in worrying about right or wrong as long as you bathe in the soul-cleansing afterbirth of his kinda-but-not-really-dead son.

Like I said, I'm the world's worst Catholic.

"WELCOME TO THE FINE young cannibals," I say, hugging my wife.

"Aren't they a band?" Beth asks.

"Or so you thought."

Sasha looks up at me. "Daddy, why do grown-ups drink wine? It tastes horrible."

I smile. "Check back with me in about ten years."

Beth wraps her arm around my waist. "If we're that lucky."

"I thought that was you," a voice says from behind us. Before I can even turn to face him, Father Fish has me in a full bear hug.

"Been a while, Father," I say.

Father Fish grabs Beth and Sasha and brings them into the hug. "Too long," he says.

"I can't breathe," Sasha says.

Father Fish talks to us in between greeting the polyester brigade exiting the church. Glad-handing the procession of retirees is of absolute necessity. They will forever regard him as their pastor, seeing to it that Father never pays for a meal, eighteen holes of golf, a ticket to a Notre Dame football game, or a car. If Dad were alive, he'd be their ringleader.

"What are you doing here?" I say. "I thought you're retired."

"Semi-retired," Father says. "I've been doing missionary work in Central America for the last three years and just needed some time to recharge the batteries. With Father Liam on sabbatical in Rome, I thought I'd come back to my old stomping grounds for Easter. I assume you're going to be at the birthday party in a few weeks."

"Birthday party?"

My master scheduler pipes up behind me. "Jack's 'Second Sixteenth' party, husband."

"Oh, that," I say. "You mean the birthday party Mom is throwing for Jack two months after the fact because she was too busy back in February sitting on her ass in a ski lodge in Utah."

"Show a little respect, Hank." Father crosses himself, and then me. "For your church and your mother. She's the only mom you got."

"Don't remind me."

"Hank!" Beth says, smacking my shoulder.

"I'm kidding," I say. I rub my shoulder, looking at Father Fish. "Of course I'll be there. I take it Mom invited you, Father?"

He flashes me his toothy white grin. "Not really. I kind of invited myself. I have a little surprise for Jack."

"What is it?" Beth and I say in unison.

A liver-spotted wrinkly hand squeezes my shoulder. I notice out of the corner of my eye that Father still wears a gold claddagh ring on his left ring finger, the heart turned inward as a sign of his commitment to the Lord.

"Your guess is as good as mine," Father says.

CHAPTER NINETY

It's Friday night, April 22. Although Jack's birthday was technically in February and mine was yesterday, Mom decided to throw Jack a "Second Sixteenth" party after missing his actual birthday. With Father Fish here and Jeanine in town from Portland, Debbie was conveniently rewarded for being a shitty mother. As for me, well, I'm left with a quieter thirty-fourth celebration over Sunday brunch.

My passive-aggressive behavior toward my mother notwithstanding, I have to admit, sobriety suits Mom. She's managed to throw quite a party tonight, rounding up conceivably everyone who's ever met Jack. As I look around the backyard, it's a who's who of our family history. Gillman sweats over the charcoal grill, flanked by Lila and Chris. Mom sips on a glass of sparkling water while chatting up Aunt Claudia and Aunt Ophelia. Uncle Howard and Father Fish try to make small talk, pretending they have anything in common. Jeanine stands next to them, just in from Portland and newly single after her long engagement to Marcus ended with him taking a Euroleague front office job in Barcelona with Winterthur FC Barcelona. Nancy Friedman, Jack's old babysitter and surrogate mother, nibbles on a plate of cheese and crackers. Aaron Rosner is down from Ann Arbor with a Monster Energy Drink supermodel on his arm. Hatch and Claire stand on opposite sides of the yard from one another, still happily married, although in typical Hatch and Claire fashion, you'd think they barely like one another. Beth's parents, Stan and Joan, are also on opposite sides of the yard, not having to pretend. And of course there's my brood, Sasha and the twins. They are playing a game of girls-versus-boys touch football, with Jack and the twins on one side and Beth and Sasha on the other.

The party has already had its requisite awkward moments. Gillman judged Chris with his eyes whenever she touched Lila in an affectionate manner, after which he caught me with a bottle of Miller High Life and gave me his "not in my house" speech. Stan and Joan tried and failed to not hate one another with Beth as the conscripted referee. Aunt Ophelia remained firmly entrenched in her tenth year of stonewalling me, somehow convinced I'm partially to blame for that pedophile rotting in the ground with a hole in his head. Claire relentlessly flirted with Jack—well, at least to the point where Hatch subbed for Beth in the game just so he could "accidentally" nail Jack in the balls with the football.

"Burgers are up," Gillman says.

"About time," I say, the ice rattling as I sip the soda from my red plastic cup. Rather than endure Gillman's Mormon wrath, I stashed the High Life, but the joke is on him. I'm still making do with a hip flask of Jim Beam, which I use to top off my Diet Coke, and the eleven-pack of High Life sits wrapped in a bow in the mini-fridge in Jack's room.

"Boys rule, girls drool!" the twins shout.

Their sister doesn't appreciate the gloating. "Mom let you win, you dummies."

Beth taps Sasha on her shoulder.

"What?" Sasha says.

"No dessert for you."

"But Mom, there's cake!"

"I know."

"That's not fair!"

"It's fair for sisters who call their brothers dummies."

Beth and the kids enter the house. I hang back with Jack. He seems leaner than usual, although all I have for a control group is my former sparkplug wrestling build.

"Soccer start up yet?" I ask.

"Just finished the indoor season," Jack says. "I'm taking a few weeks off. Prep tryouts are in June."

"Tryouts? I thought you were hoping for team captain."

"I am. Coach has everyone try out just for appearances. No individual player is more important than the other. You know, all that team-building rah-rah shit."

"Don't let Gillman catch you with that mouth."

"Fuck Gillman."

"You got some game out there."

"Where?"

"Out there, with Beth and the kids. You got some moves. Quick feet. You throw a nice, tight spiral. Why didn't you ever try out for the football team?"

"No offense, but I was playing against a nine-year-old girl and a middle-aged woman."

"If you call Beth middle-aged to her face, she'll do worse than what Hatch did to you."

"What's with that guy?"

"Maybe stop making googly eyes at his wife."

"Claire was coming on to me."

"She just loves the attention, and she especially loves getting under Hatch's skin."

"So he's not a dick?"

"Nah," I say. "He comes on a little strong, but he means well."

"Did he mean well when he threw me in our pond when I was three years old and didn't know how to swim?"

"You still remember that?"

"I remember Dad wanted to kill him."

"Yeah, buddy, that narrows things down to roughly two dozen moments in Hatch and Dad's relationship."

"They had a relationship?"

"More parasitic than symbiotic."

"More what?" Jack asks.

"Never mind," I say. I open the back door, ushering Jack inside the house. "Like I said, he means well."

Between the Beam and Cokes, what I estimate to be a half of a cow, and the red velvet birthday cake made with butter cream icing, I need a nap. Sitting at the patio table on the back porch, surrounded by his loved ones, Jack seems pleased if not overwhelmed by his second round of gifts in the last eight weeks. Mom and Gillman got him an Indiana University soccer jersey to go with the week of summer soccer camp, which disappointed me. I gave Jack a secret "present" earlier in the day: my driver's license that I had claimed as missing to the Indiana Department of Motor Vehicles. I said to him, "On the record, I strongly discourage underage drinking, and if you get caught with this I'll claim you stole it. Off the record, if you can find an out-of-the-way, hole-in-the-wall liquor store, this should do the trick."

Officially, however, Jeanine and I already went in together on a used Trek road bike we found on eBay. To go with the roundtrip ticket to New York they bought him in February, Lila and Chris bought Jack box seats and backstage passes to the musical *Rent*, a gesture Gillman seemed not to appreciate. Everyone else left it up to Jack, giving him a mixture of cash, checks, and gift cards.

"Is that it?" Jack asks.

"I guess I'm up, then." Father Fish stands up from his chair and walks across the back porch to Jack. He's wearing a red cardigan sweater and underneath that the standard black-on-black attire of a Catholic priest, his white clerical collar showing at the neck.

"Father, you didn't have to get me anything," Jack says.

"I didn't." Father Fish reaches into his sweater, pulling out a manila envelope. "This is a letter, from your dad."

"What?" Jack says, as shocked as we all are. The backyard suddenly feels a whole lot smaller. Everyone has stopped eating, drinking, talking, or even breathing.

"I guess an explanation might help," Father says.

Jack leans over in his chair. He rubs his mouth with his hand. "Uh, it wouldn't hurt."

"When you were about two years old, your father came to see me in my office." Father looks at Mom. "You remember that, Debbie?"

"I think so," Mom says. "That was after the motorcycle accident, right?"

"Exactly."

Something Mom neglected to tell us until just recently was that three years before he was killed, Dad almost died in a motorcycle accident. Back in '89, Dad was out riding motorcycles with a couple of his buddies. It had started raining, they were on a bridge, and the semi-truck driver never saw them. My father barely avoided the truck only to see one of his best friends crushed between the trailer and the side of the bridge. The guy died in Dad's arms.

Dad owned a motorcycle most of his adult life. His baby was a Candy Super Blue 1978 Kawasaki KZ900, just like the motorcycle used by Ponch and John in the TV show *CHiPs*. He used to sneak me out for rides when I was little, making me promise not to tell Mom. I could smell the collusion of father and son as we barreled down the highway, the wind a mixture of sweat, exhaust fumes, and English Leather cologne. I still have a scar on my right calf from burning my leg on the Kawasaki's exhaust pipe.

Dad let Uncle Mitch on his bike just once. I can still remember Dad handing him the keys and Uncle Mitch sneaking one last drag off his cigarette before flipping it into our front lawn. It was a Kool, not a Merit, and Uncle Mitch was still everybody's favorite, so it had to be back in the seventies. Uncle Mitch had only completed one lap around the neighborhood when he took the last turn right before our driveway a little too fast. He panicked, gunned the engine. The Kawasaki spun out, slid sideways a good five or six feet, throwing Uncle Mitch face-first onto the concrete. Everyone cried but me. Uncle Mitch managed to escape with only a busted lip. For a raging closet pedophile, the guy lived quite the charmed life.

Dad never told anyone why he sold the motorcycle. Three days after the bridge accident, I just noticed our next-door neighbor Calvin Franks riding it and never cared to ask. Mr. Frank had a miniature schnauzer, six saltwater aquariums, and two cockatiels. He liked to drink Pepsi, build radio-controlled airplanes, and light illegal fireworks on the Fourth of July with his cigarettes.

"John was white as a sheet," Father recounts. "He told me about the accident, how he kept having nightmares, premonitions even."

"Premonitions?" Jack asks.

"That he would die young," Father says.

"Oh my God," Mom says.

I stand up, waving my arms. "Okay now, take it easy. Let's not make this out to be anything more than what it really is."

Mom looks at me, her mouth still agape. "And what's that, Hank?"

"A random coincidence," I say. "Please, Father, continue."

"Very well," he says. "So John tells me that he isn't afraid of dying—rather, he's afraid of not getting to grow old with Debbie and most of all not getting to know Jack. He felt like he was so busy with getting into the car business that he missed Hank and Jeanine growing up. He saw Jack as his second chance, his new lease on life, his blank canvas, and he was afraid he wouldn't be there to help paint it."

"Hence the vasectomy reversal in his forties?" I say.

"Exactly," Father affirms.

"And he told this all to you?"

"Every word of it, Hank." Father slides the manila envelope across the patio table. Jack stops it with his hand. "Inside that envelope is a letter from John Henry Fitzpatrick to you, Jack. I was instructed by John that if he died prematurely, I was to deliver it to you on your sixteenth birthday. Well, here I am. Granted, I'm a couple months late."

I shoot Mom a look. "His excuse was missionary work in Third World countries. What's yours?"

Jack grabs my arm, shaking his head at me. "Some other time, Hank."

"Agreed," Father Fish says. "Anyway, there's your letter. May God bless you."

The wise old priest turns on his heels and walks toward the house to leave.

"Wait, Father," Jack says. "You don't want to know what he had to say?"

"Yeah, Father," I echo Jack's sentiments. "It's not like you're Moses and I'm going to be the ass who kicks you out on Canaan's doorstep right before the party gets started."

Father closes his eyes, purses his lips, and sighs. He opens his eyes, nodding at the letter. "Jack, those words are for you and your father."

Almost everybody gets the hint. We spend about a half hour saying our goodbyes and thank yous. Gillman leaves with Lila and Chris on an evening drive. (Mormons do that a lot.) Joan and Stan take the grandkids out to see a movie. Jack asks Mom, Jeanine, Beth, and me to stay.

Jack has yet to move from the patio table. We sit down next to him. I stop the pretense and bring up the Miller High Life from the mini-fridge, sitting it on the patio table.

"Where'd you get that?" Mom asks.

"Jack's room," I say.

Mom turns to Jack. "Young man!"

"It's not my beer, Mom."

"Relax, Debbie," I say, unscrewing a cap off the fluted beer bottle. "They're mine."

"Well..." my sister says, taking one of the beers and handing another to Beth. "Are you going to read it or what?"

"I can't," Jack says, his eyes welling up with tears. "Hank, you read it for me."

"I-I don't think I should, buddy."

Jack slides me the manila envelope. "Either you're reading it or no one is."

I take the envelope in my hand. Straightening the clasp through the hole, I run my finger under the flap. "You sure about this, bro?"

"No," Jack says. "But do it anyway."

Slowly, I peel back the flap, careful not to rip the envelope. I pull out the white unlined letter. It's written on Fitzpatrick Oldsmobile-Cadillac-Subaru letterhead and dated February 11, 1991, Jack's second birthday. The handwriting is unmistakably Dad's, his capital letters sweeping, confident, and nearly illegible. It's probably best I'm doing the reading, as I was one of the only people I knew who could ever translate Dad's Sanskrit.

I begin to read…

Dear Jack,

If you are reading this letter, it means I am no longer in your life, and for that I am profoundly saddened. The circumstances of why I'm not there are irrelevant, but know that I am sorry and that if it were in my power I would never leave you.

I love your brother and sister, but I feel like I missed their lives. While their mother taught them how to do things like walk, talk, tie their shoes, write in cursive, do long division, and not pee their pants—granted, Hank is still working on that one—I was working sixteen-hour days selling Oldsmobiles, Cadillacs, and Subarus. The fact I missed both Hank and Jeanine say their first words and take their first steps just so Mr. Spangler would be happy with his Coupe DeVille sickens me. If I had to do it all over again, I would have stayed a music teacher.

You were my reset button, Jack. You were my chance to make things right. I saw you take your first steps. I taught you how to walk and how to tie your shoes. When you took your first big-boy poop in the potty, I was there cheering you on harder than if Notre Dame had won another national championship. You were the only Fitzpatrick whose first word was "Daddy" instead of "Mommy." While your mother still gets credit for teaching you cursive and advanced mathematics—two skills I admittedly lack—I feel like you were really and truly, more than Hank or Jeanine, all mine.

Choosing to reverse my vasectomy and try for a second family was the craziest and most wonderful choice I ever made in my life. While it did not give me or Debbie the gift either of us expected, it did bring us to you. You may not be of me, but you're of us, and that is more than enough. It is more than I deserve. And I will always call you my son.

I almost forgot. Happy sixteenth birthday, and here's to many more. Don't be too hard on Hank. I fear this fatherhood thing won't come easy to him, but I know in my heart he'll be a great dad to you.

Love, Dad

I don't know why I read the whole letter. It's not like I hadn't already looked ahead and knew what was coming. Maybe I let it happen. Like a subconscious switch, my brain just shut everything down and said, *Fuck it, let's finally get this over with*. I've told Beth more than once I was tired of carrying this burden. But that's not the point. The point is that, just like with Uncle Mitch, it was my burden to bear and my burden to relinquish. Right or wrong, these were my choices to make. Yet here I stand again, outed from the fucking grave by my goddamn father.

"Please," I say. "Let me explain."

"No!" Jack, my brother no longer, stands and walks around the table. He rips the paper out of my hand and holds it in front of my face. He screams through his tears. "This isn't possible."

Though galactically inappropriate, an *Empire Strikes Back* allusion sneaks into my brain. I try to snuff it out, but the Beam and the High Life don't let me. It's the only thing I can think to say. "Search your feelings, Jack. You know it to be true."

Jack pushes me to the ground. He stands over me with his fists clenched, the letter balled up in his right hand. "Fuck you, *Dad*. And fuck you too, *Grandma*." Jack throws the letter in Mom's face, giving her a forearm to the chest as he brushes by her. He walks out the patio gate that opens directly to the front yard.

"Where are you going?" Mom shouts after him.

"Let him go. Nothing we say right now is going to help."

"You okay, honey?" Beth reaches for my hand, helping me to my feet.

I lean in, kiss her on the cheek. "Better than I've been in a while actually."

Mom makes toward the patio gate. "We have to stop him."

I reach for Mom, grabbing her elbow as she runs past me. "Don't make a bad situation worse."

"But you don't understand."

"I think I understand plenty."

That's when I hear it: the throaty growl of a 390-horsepower '68 Oldsmobile.

"The Beast?" I release Mom's elbow. "But she was in storage. We haven't been able to get her started in years."

"It was Gillman's surprise," Mom says. "He rebuilt the engine himself. Did you really think I was just going to get Jack the same old soccer camp gift for his sixteenth birthday?"

"Of course I thought that, Mom. You're not a considerate person."

"You have to go after him, Hank."

"I'm not going anywhere."

"The hell you aren't."

"I'm drunk," I say, sitting in Jack's recently vacated chair. "Besides, I have an idea where he's going. He'll be fine."

Mom starts crying. "You don't know that."

"The hell I don't." I say, purposely snickering for effect. "Jack has about twelve years' experience making it on his own."

CHAPTER NINETY-ONE

Beth and I took the kids home after the party. Later that night, we had wildly inappropriate but erotic sex, first in the hot tub, then in the shower, and finally in front of the standing mirror in the corner of our bedroom. On second thought, it was very appropriate; it was like makeup sex even though we weren't the ones who had the fight. I got maybe four hours of sleep before jumping in the old Subaru Outback for the drive north.

If Hansel and Gretel left bread crumbs for their father, Jack is leaving loaves of bread for me. He picked up a twelve of Natural Light and a pack of Parliaments in a dive bar in between Hope and Shelbyville. I found the empty twelve-pack and the nearly untouched nineteen-pack of cigarettes—Jack doesn't smoke—in a rest area in Greenfield.

Later, sometime around two in the morning, Jack went to the Hiphugger strip club in Kokomo. The Hugger's longtime bouncer—a soft-spoken, smiling giant of a man by the name of Pappy—turned him away at the door. "Gotta love the balls of a sixteen-year-old trying to pass himself off as a thirty-four-year-old," Pappy told me. "But he might want to check beforehand and make sure the original owner of the driver's license didn't spend most of the early nineties in this bar."

Like I said, Pappy has been there a long time.

At some point after striking out at the Hugger, Jack doubled back to Tipton. He booked the Jacuzzi Suite with some of his birthday money at the Flamingo Motel. In the morning, he went to Sherrill's, the diner and gas station right off US 31 with the famous marquee that reads *Eat Here And Get Gas*. He tried to buy everyone in the diner breakfast, but Sherrill thankfully refused the gesture.

I knew where Jack was going the moment he left Mom's house. He's a Fitzpatrick, and there's only one place we drop everything to visit in the middle of April: the campus of the University of Notre Dame, for the Blue & Gold Game spring scrimmage.

The Notre Dame Stadium usher hands me my ticket stub. "You might want to buy some gloves and a hat at the gift shop," he advises me. "They're saying this is the coldest Blue and Gold Game ever. Game time temps in the thirties, thirty mile-per-hour wind out of the northwest, maybe even some snow."

"I'll take that under advisement," I say.

After a couple false positives, I find him. Jack is sitting by himself, about two-thirds the way up in Section 23, corner end zone, the section that had a front-row seat to Pat Terrell batting down Miami's two-point attempt in '88. To the west, he's afforded a clear view of Touchdown Jesus. He's decked out from head to toe in brand-new ND gear, the campus bookstore apparently the beneficiary of his remaining birthday funds.

Jack doesn't notice me until I'm three rows away from him. "How did you know that I would—"

"Give me a little credit, Jack." I sit down next to him but not too close. "I may not be your favorite person right now, but I know you better than just about anyone on this planet."

He doesn't respond. The silence is uncomfortable.

"Montana and Zorich honorary captains for the Blue team?" I ask, trying to make small talk.

"Yep," Jack says, trying to make it even smaller.

"And Theismann and Tim Brown are captains of the Gold team?"

"Yep."

"Brady Quinn looking good?"

"Yep."

"Darius Walker running well?"

"Yep."

"Come on, Jack, talk to me."

"Isn't that what I'm doing?"

"I mean really talk to me."

"What do you want me to say, Hank? Is there a proper reaction here? You've let me believe my father was dead for sixteen years."

"Technically, about eleven and a half years."

"What?"

"I didn't know you were my son until you were four-and-half years old. Mom kept it from me, too."

"And I'm supposed to believe that? How could you have not known?"

"My girlfriend lied to me. She and your mother—or should I say, she and your grandmother—faked the abortion, and then Debbie adopted you."

"Wait a second," Jack says. "My mother is your high school sweetheart, Laura Elliot?"

"Wow, you put two and two together pretty quick. How'd you know about the so-called abortion?"

"Jeanine told me that summer I visited her in Portland."

I run my hands through my hair, shaking my head. "Of course she did."

"And Dad—Grandpa, whatever the hell I'm supposed to call him—he knew all about this?"

"Yes," I say. "He was initially reluctant, but considering that aborting his grandson was the only alternative, he went along with it. After a while, the deception got easy for most of us, but in hindsight I don't think it ever got any easier for Dad."

"He was just never wired that way," Jack says.

I sigh, my mind on rewind to that moment in the hospital I told Mom about Uncle Mitch's deception, right before she doubled down on the lies. "It was after Dad died that things started spiraling out of control. In the end, I think he gave his family way too much credit."

"Credit for what?"

"For doing the right thing."

"What makes you say that?"

"You don't have to suddenly pull punches for my benefit, Jack. The tone in Dad's letter was pretty obvious, especially those last few paragraphs. He just assumed we would have told you by now. I feel like I let him down again."

"Look, Hank, uh, I mean Da—"

"Please, don't start calling me that. I don't deserve that. I might never deserve it."

"Okay, whatever…Hank. Can you just give me some time to process this?"

"Take all the time you need."

"It's not that I'm letting you off the hook for this, because I'm not."

"I don't expect you to."

"But really, at least with you, what are we talking about here? A debate over semantics? You've basically been my father since I was four years old, since before you even found out I was your, you know, your s—"

"Yeah, you don't have to use that word in conversation either."

Jack flirts with smiling. "Thanks," he says.

"You're welcome, bro." Jack looks at me. I say "bro" out of habit, but for the very first time, the word feels strange in my mouth.

"Hank, I have a lot of questions. I don't even know where to begin."

"How about at the beginning?"

"Okay," Jack says, his eyes starting to water. "Can you tell me about Laura? What was my mother like?"

"Jack," I say, standing and patting him on the shoulder. "Let's get out of here."

"Where we going?"

"I'd rather not associate any of this with Notre Dame Stadium."

"Good call. Where to?"

"How about we have this chat over beer and wings at Hooters and go watch the NFL Draft on some big screens?"

"Beer?" Jack says.

"Why not? We're just two thirty-four-year-old dudes knocking back a few pitchers of brew."

"A *few* pitchers?"

"You got somewhere you need to be?"

"Well, there's your birthday brunch tomorrow."

It's hard to resist the way Jack's eyes suddenly light up, reminding me he's still like any sixteen-year-old boy—ready and willing to break the law for little more than a mild buzz. And today at least, I'm more than happy to oblige him.

"You know what, Jack?"

"What?"

"Fuck 'em."

CHAPTER NINETY-TWO

Jack and I ended up getting too drunk to drive. We spent the night sleeping in our cars in the Hooters parking lot, but we made good time this morning on the drive back from South Bend.

I pull into my garage. Jack parks the Beast behind me in the driveway. He steps out of his car. "So you're really not going to your birthday brunch?"

"Are you going?" I ask.

"Hell no," Jack says.

"Then that makes two of us."

Jack points to the empty stall next to the Subaru. "Where are Beth and the kids?"

"At church."

"Church? Since when?"

"Since about a year ago."

"Any particular reason?"

"Don't think we need a reason to be closer to God."

"Hank, this is me you're talking to."

"Yeah, so?"

"I know you're trying especially hard to set a good example for me right now, but you finding religion is like you waking up with a vagina instead of a penis. It just ain't natural."

I can't help but laugh. "Okay, you got me. We're doing it for Sasha."

"Ah, yes. Giving her that good foundation."

"Bingo."

"I guess it beats having your ass dragged to a Mormon service."

"Gillman do that to you?"

"Every Sunday. Three hours of hell on earth."

"Sounds like Easter Vigil."

"What?"

"Nothing," I say.

"It isn't so much the length that bothers me. The last couple hours are usually just Sunday school and administrative stuff. Debbie and I skip that a lot."

"Debbie?"

"You call her that when you're pissed at her, so I think I've earned the right to call her that for eternity."

"Fair enough."

"Anyway, it's that first hour that always wigs me out. The bishop invites members to come up and testify in front of the congregation. Kids my age come up, but sometimes there are even nine and ten year-olds who do it. They start talking about their love for the Lord, all this holy roller shit, and they are bawling their eyes out. We're talking full rapture mode."

"Sounds like you're a few venomous snakes and a mason jar of strychnine away from a genuine End Times party."

"I know, right?"

I point at my face, trying to be stoic. "See this, Jack?"

"What?"

"This is me not looking surprised."

"Well played," Jack says. He approaches the garage. "So, we done for now?"

"Done?" I slide open a small panel to the left of the garage door, type in the security code. The door begins to shut as I walk back out onto the driveway. "We're just getting started."

"Why am I not liking the sound of that?"

"If the lies are going to end, then let's end them all." I walk to the passenger-side door of the Beast. "But you're driving."

Jack walks around to his side of the Oldsmobile, opening his door. He looks over the roof at me. "And to where exactly am I driving?"

We slide into the car, shut our doors. Like most cars back then, the '68 Olds 442 Coupe came equipped with only lap belts, so neither of us buckles our restraints. Plus, I think we've established that no matter what we do to actively or passively protect ourselves, automobiles are nothing but randomly dangerous motherfuckers.

"You sure you don't just want to be surprised when we get there?" I ask.

Jack starts the car. "I think I've reached my quota on surprises."

"Fair enough," I say. "We're going to go visit your grandma."

"Debbie?"

"No, Tammy. Laura's mother."

CHAPTER NINETY-THREE

Tammy has company, and it's the worst kind of company. A white Suburban with Pennsylvania plates sits in her driveway.

"Stay in the car," I say to Jack.

"But why?"

"Laura is here."

"Here? Now?"

"Yeah," I say. "I'm just afraid things might get ugly, and I'd rather keep you out of the line of fire."

"Roger that," Jack says.

I knock on the front door. Three little mounds of curls, each of varying heights, peek out the picture window to the left of the door. They look at me, stick out their tongues, and then scurry away giggling wildly to one another. I knock on the door again.

Someone fiddles with the lock as the doorknob starts to rotate. The door swings open.

"May I help you?" the man says.

He's a little taller than me and a whole lot heavier—not morbidly obese, more your typical middle-aged thickness around the face and torso, like Kevin James in *The King of Queens*. Much like Doug Heffernan did with the sassy-hot (cue *Saved by the Bell* reference) Stacey Carosi, this guy outkicked his coverage by landing Laura Elliot. He's what we used to call in high school and college "OC," as in "over-cheeving."

I offer him my hand. "I'm guessing you're Ian Powell.

To Ian's credit, he accepts my gesture. His large flesh mitt swallows my childlike hand. "I don't have to guess who you are, Hank."

"Look, if we came at a bad time—"

"You most certainly did."

"Ian, behave!"

Her voice is like an emollient, instantly diluting the testosterone in the room. She comes around the corner, steps around Ian's left side, and gives me a hug.

"Hi, Hank."

Laura's curly hair is pulled back in a tight ponytail, so her bare cheek brushes upside mine as she pulls me in. I put my chin on her right shoulder. I could swear her sweater smells like movie theater popcorn. As inappropriate as it might be for me to respond with one of those long, swaying, eyes-closed hugs in which both people exhale audibly as if they've been holding their breath waiting for this one embrace, I do it anyway. I can't help but notice Ian is still staring me down. This pisses me off. In retribution, I decide to cop a little bit of a feel. With my right hand hidden from Ian's view, I give a quick squeeze just above Laura's waistline—partly to make sure she's done her best to keep off the back fat but mostly so I can reach down and sneak my pinky finger just inside the rim of her jeans. As I pull away, with Ian still staring me down with his oblivious, bloated face, I brush my index and middle fingers subtly underneath the curve of Laura's left breast.

"Hello, Laura. What are you doing here?"

"Ian and I just got back from seeing *Robots* with the girls. Good movie."

This at least explains the popcorn smell. "That's not what I mean. What are you doing *here*, in Empire Ridge."

"Wait," Laura says. "You haven't heard?"

"Heard what? It's not like you and I are pen pals."

Laura's voice cracks. "It's my mother, Hank. She died last night."

"B-but how?"

"Cancer."

"Not leukemia?"

"Yes."

"But I thought she beat the disease way back when you were a kid."

"You remember that?"

"You told me she went into remission when you were like twelve years old."

"That's right. But it came back. It was too fast this time, too strong. She just couldn't fight it. We didn't even get here in time to see her conscious. She was on a ventilator, and my brother is stuck in China on a jobsite."

"Oh God, Laura. I'm so sorry."

"I was the one who took her off life support. I was the one who had to pull the..."

Laura buries her face in her hands, sobbing. My instinct is to comfort her, but I step back, conceding her personal space to Ian. He nods in vague appreciation of my gesture, wrapping his arm around her. Laura turns her face away from me.

"Maybe come back later, Hank?" Ian says.

I nod. "Uh, yeah. That's probably best."

Ian shuts the door behind me. I see Jack in the car. He looks at me, shrugging his shoulders with a typical teenage what-the-fuck expression.

The front door opens. "Hank, please, wait!"

I turn to her. "Now is not the time for this, Laura."

"For what?" she says, grabbing my arm. "You came here to see my mom. Why?"

"It can wait."

"Until when? She rises from the dead?"

"I didn't really come here for Tammy's benefit. I came here for—"

"Jack!"

"What?"

"Is that my..." Laura's left hand is on her mouth, her right hand pointing at the sixteen-year-old boy now standing behind me in front of the car. "Are you, Jack?"

I lean in toward Laura, my chin tilted. "He knows," I whisper.

Laura shoves me out of the way, practically bounding toward Jack. But then she stops suddenly. They stand there, face-to-face, both afraid to speak. This moment is exactly as awkward as I imagined it would be.

I step between them. "Jack, this is Laura. Laura, this is Jack."

Jack reaches out with his right hand. Laura grabs it with both of her hands. She looks at Jack's hand, rotating it like an archaeologist carefully studying a lost artifact. She continues looking at his hand, then his face, then his hand again.

"It's wonderful to meet you...Jack."

"Uh, uhhh..." he mutters. "Same here, Mrs. Powell."

"Can you at least call me Laura?" she says, wiping away her tears.

"Depends," Jack says.

"On what?"

"Can you give me my hand back?"

Laura laughs. She releases his hand. "You came at a difficult time, Jack. My mother, your, uh…"

"My grandmother?"

"Yes. It's just that…well, we lost her yesterday. It's been a rough twenty-four hours on us."

"I'm sorry."

"You and Hank want to come inside for a little bit?"

"Oh no," Jacks says, shaking his head. "I don't…I-I don't want to impose."

Laura looks at me, then back at Jack. "Jack, I think you've earned the right to be an imposition for a very long time. Besides, I want you to meet a few people."

Jack steps back cautiously, his hands in the air like someone is holding a gun to his back. "Look, Laura, this is all happening a little too fast for me. Like you said, it's been a rough twenty-four hours. I don't think I'm ready to jump right in and chat up your relatives just yet."

"I totally understand and respect that," Laura says. "All I'm looking for is a guy who'll wear a dress and drink some tea."

"Excuse me?" Jack says.

Laura nods toward the front door. "You got three half-sisters in that house who are going to love you."

CHAPTER NINETY-FOUR

"This is the worst idea in the history of ideas."

"Oh shut up and paddle," Beth says to me.

Jack was the one who suggested the canoe trip the day after Tammy Eliot's funeral, and of course nobody was in a position to tell him, "No way in hell!" or "Are you fucking insane?" A seven-mile combined Fitzpatrick and Powell family float down the Sycamore River. Two husbands who can barely stand to be in the same zip code. Two wives who've hated one another for going on two decades. What could possibly go wrong?

The twins and Laura's two youngest daughters were deemed too young for the trip, so we left them with Mom and Gillman. Our flotilla comprises four canoes. Beth and I lead the way, followed by Laura and Ian, Jeanine and Sasha, and then Jack and his half-sister Cassie. Cassie is the same age as Sasha. With their sandy-blond hair and gymnast builds, they could pass for cousins if not sisters. Jeanine and Jack have paddled a good half hour ahead of us by now; probably already out of their canoes and raiding the picnic baskets.

"Hey, Hank, when you taking your skirt off?"

We've covered about five of the seven miles. Ian has been harassing me since about mile two. He started the trip with a twelve-pack of Yuengling and just cracked open his eleventh lager.

"You got me, Ian. I'm obviously a woman."

"Seriously," Ian says. "Who goes canoeing without drinking beer? That's like cookies without milk, or a Philly steak and cheese without cheese."

"Or Pennsylvania without assholes," I say under my breath.

"What did you say?"

"I said, 'I think I see some tadpoles.'"

"Hey now," Beth says, splashing me with her paddle. Some of the water runs down the small of her back. Although it's spring and there's still a chill in the air, she's wearing denim shorts and a bikini top. The goose bumps on her skin are incredibly distracting. "You need to behave."

"If you only knew," I say, grinning more than smiling.

We round the bend just northeast of the canoe livery. Thirty feet up, the rusted iron-truss bridge casts a stern, judgmental shadow over the rippling echoes of my past sins. I feel like it's even mocking me a little.

Then again, that might just be Ian's drunk ass.

"This bridge is sweet!" he says. "Anybody ever jump off it?"

"It's illegal," I say.

"That's not what I asked."

"Plenty of stupid kids have jumped off the thing."

"You ever see it?"

"I've done it."

"No way. Your scrawny little ass has jumped off those train tracks?"

"Not the train tracks."

"That's what I thought."

"I jumped off the very top of the bridge."

"Stop it, Hank," Laura says. She's also wearing denim shorts but with a one-piece bathing suit minus the distracting goose bumps, thank God.

"Stop what?" I say.

"Encouraging him."

"Who's encouraging him? I do believe I explicitly said that jumping off this bridge is stupid."

A giant splash interrupts our argument as Ian swims for shore.

"Ian, no!" Laura shouts.

"Do something," Beth says to me.

"What do you want me to do?"

"Go after him."

"I'm not jumping in there. It's April. South Bend was still having snow flurries *last week*. If Ian wants to get hypothermia, that's his business."

Beth points up at the bridge. "Hypothermia is the least of his problems."

Ian stands on the bridge, already at the level of the train tracks.

"Just jump from there, buddy," I shout.

"You'd like to see me do that, wouldn't you? That way you can always say that you were the one who made the real jump while I pussied out."

"You think this is a contest? Really?"

"Well, isn't it?"

"Step into my world, Ian. My life has sucked—a lot. It's getting better now, and I'm not wasting my time getting in a pissing contest with you or anyone else. I'm fine with the cookie-cutter house in the suburbs and the minivan. I'll fucking hit from the green tees all day long and not give a shit. Hell, come down here, let's drop our pants and just whip it out. You probably have a bigger dick than me. You don't need to prove anything."

"You don't get it," Ian says.

"Then tell me—what am I missing?"

Ian stands on the edge of the tracks, looking down at the water thirty feet below. "I don't need to prove anything, huh? Step into my world, Hank. For sixteen years my wife has had a son by another man. Up until a month ago, I thought she had given the baby up for adoption, not shipped him off to her high school sweetheart's mother for safekeeping."

I turn to the other canoe. "What is he talking about, Laura?"

She ignores me. "Please, honey, just come down from there!"

"You didn't tell him who Jack's father was until *last month*?"

"Surprise!" Ian shouts. He moves quickly up the ironworks. The rivets and joints give secure footing all the way up. He reaches the top. "But that's not all. Hey, Roddy, tell our contestant what he's won. Well, Bob, in addition to Ian's wife never telling him about her little bastard, she's also still carrying a torch for the birth father."

Holy shit.

Laura looks mortified. Beth looks like she wants to rip Laura's mortified face off. And here I am, my hands cupped around my mouth, still trying to talk down this sauced idiot.

"Ian!" I shout. "How about you just shut the fuck up?"

"What did you say to me?"

I sneak a glance at my audience. Laura has her face in her hands, hiding from the world. Beth is still staring daggers into the back of Laura's head. Looks like I'm on my own.

"I said, shut the fuck up. First off, if you ever call Jack a bastard again, I'll drive my fist so far down your throat you'll be shitting my fingernails. Secondly, you have a wife who loves you, and three beautiful daughters. Is it worth throwing all that away doing some drunken stunt just because you got your feelings hurt?"

"Didn't you hear what I said, Hank? She still loves—"

"I heard what you said. So fucking what? Newsflash—she's got no shot with me. But there are three girls out there who love their mommy and daddy, who love their family. Answer me this, Ian—do you love your wife?"

"With all my heart."

"Then get down here and tell Laura to get over herself."

"It's not that easy."

"It's not that hard either."

IAN STANDS IN SILENCE atop the bridge.

"How long has he been up there?" Laura says. I look at my watch. "Ten minutes."

"I can't just sit here. I need to do something."

"I think you've done plenty," Beth says.

"Stay out of this," Laura says.

"Make me, you stupid—"

"Ladies, please," I interrupt. "Not that I haven't dreamed about you two getting in another half-naked catfight, but now is not the time." I cast my eyes upward, nodding. "Besides, look."

Ian has backed away from the edge.

"Hey, Hank," he says.

"Yeah, Ian?"

"I'm sorry. Jack is a great kid."

"Apology accepted, and I know he is."

"I'm also sorry this got so out of hand."

"It happens."

"I think I'm coming down now," Ian says.

"Good to hear." I take off my hat and run my hands through my hair. Closing my eyes, I let out an exhausted sigh.

"Hey you," Beth says.

I open my eyes. She stands above me, having somehow traversed the length of our canoe undetected. I bury my face in her cleavage, wrapping my arms around her waist and clasping my hands behind her. She kisses the top of my head.

"Hey there, fellas," I say into my wife's breasts.

"I think your dick is probably bigger," she whispers.

CHAPTER NINETY-FIVE

"I mean, really, who stays married for *ten years*?"

"Apparently we do."

I dip Beth on the dance floor. After surprising her at St. Benjamin with a vow renewal ceremony—highlighted by Father Fish, our entire wedding party, and Joan and Stan being nice to one another—I rented a limo and took everyone up to Indianapolis for the night.

We're partying at the Rathskeller, a pseudo-German *biergarten* tucked on the backside of the Athenaeum Building, which was designed and built in the nineteenth century by Kurt Vonnegut's grandfather. We've had a lot of beer to drink and even more food, the latter of which has adhered to the four main Bavarian food groups: breaded meat, sausage, potatoes, and gravy. Tonight's band is Polka Boy, a bunch of middle-aged white dudes armed with accordions, trumpets, keyboards, guitars, bass players, and drums that do a polka twist on just about every conceivable music genre. At this moment, fulfilling my request, they're muddling through a bizarre rendition of Hootie and the Blowfish's "Hold My Hand."

"Ugh," Beth says. "I don't think I can look at another schnitzel for the rest of the night."

I twirl her away from me, then back. "Hopefully you'll change your mind when we get to the hotel room."

She kisses me. "I'm a sure thing. You know that, right?"

I smile. "Now I do."

"Did you see my mom and dad earlier?"

"You mean the laughing?" I ask.

"The laughing, the flirting."

"What's going on there?"

"I don't know, but they need to cut that shit out."

"Why is Joan and Stan's being nice to one another such a bad thing?"

"You don't understand, Hank. I've *never* seen them like this. Remember our therapy sessions?"

"Do I have to?"

"You said my parents were nothing but glorified roommates. I hated you for saying it at the time, but you fucking nailed it."

"I'm sorry, babe. I didn't mean to—"

Beth douses my lips with a kiss. "No, no. You were right. Don't apologize. I blame them for a lot of our problems, for not knowing how to love you."

We ease into our customary slow dance position, my left hand holding her right hand against my left shoulder, my right hand guiding the small of her back, her torso swaying in unison to mine. Every third or fourth beat of the song I pull her a little closer, bending at the knees just enough for my unabashed erection to rub between the insides of her thighs.

"So, what you're saying is, all our problems are your fault?"

My wife raises her knee into my crotch. "So what you're saying is, you don't want me to suck your schnitzel when we get back to the hotel room?"

I move my hand from her back to the bottom crease of her ass, pulling her up onto her toes and into me. "You've been quite the minx lately."

"To be fair, you've been quite the good husband."

"You're rewarding me, then?"

"No," Beth says. "You're rewarding me."

"You know my motto."

"What's that?"

"Ladies first."

Beth eases back down to the balls of her feet. "I know and very much appreciate your motto."

"Okay, lovebirds, break it up." Claire separates us with her arms like a referee in a prizefight. "I swear, whatever you two have going on here, you need to bottle and sell it."

"Where's Hatch?" I ask.

"He just got here," Claire says. "In fact, he's right behind—"

"Hank, my boy!" Hatch grabs me from behind, lifting me at the waist. "Good lord, man. Fucking eat something. What do you weigh now?"

"A lot less than you."

"What's your secret?"

"Still just running."

"Here, take this," Hatch says. "Maybe it will put some fucking weight on you."

Hatch hands me a pint glass filled to the rim with a dark amber beer. I hold it to my nose, catching a strong smoked meat scent.

"What is this?"

"Bartender called it *rauchbier*, which literally translates as—"

"Smoke beer, I know. My four years of high school German weren't completely useless. What's in it? Smells like bacon."

"Evidently all beers used to smell like this. The kilns would dry the green brewer's malt over open fires, and so the grains picked up the smoky flavors of the wood and passed them on to the beers. Nowadays the process is much more controlled and breweries tend to just use clean malt. *Rauchbier* is such a lost art that only one town in all of Germany—Bamberg—brews *rauchbier* anymore."

"And you just learned all that from the bartender?"

"Learnin' ain't nothin' but listenin', Hank."

"Which is why I'm surprised."

"Surprised?"

"Hatch, if you ain't talkin', you ain't listenin'."

"Drink your beer, asshole."

"Don't mind if I do." I hold the pint glass just under my nose. "There's more than just bacon going on here. There's beech wood and charcoal, various cooked meats—bacon of course, but also grilled hot dogs and smoked sausage."

"Hey, Hank, are you going to drink it or fuck it?"

"I'm getting there." I lift the glass to my mouth, letting the amber liquid slide down my tongue. Like most quality beers, it's served and tastes better at a temperature more cool than cold.

"Well?" Hatch says.

"I like it, a lot."

"What do you like about it?"

"It's a deceptive beer. The meat smells are not nearly as pronounced in the mouth. The finish is surprisingly clean and almost a little too thin, especially for a beer that initially portends something closer to an Islay Scotch."

"What's that like?"

"It's like a campfire, a dense, barley-infused smoke bomb."

"And you smell all that in the beer?"

"Initially, yes. But for all that smokiness that hits you upfront, the flavor profile on the backend is actually very accessible."

"Good to hear."

"Why? Do you owe the bartender a full report?"

"No," Hatch says. "I just like to know that my company is brewing good beers."

Beth sits naked on the executive table, sipping a glass of champagne. It's four in the morning. We've had sex twice, and we're contemplating a third time.

Our next-door neighbor down in Empire Ridge—Lisa, the retired Colts cheerleader turned divorcée turned Hilton regional manager—hooked us up with the employee discount on the corporate suite. It's a three-room suite, with a large main room flanked by two bedrooms. The front of the main room is the lounge area, with a wet bar, a television, a couch, a loveseat, and two Barcaloungers. The back part of the main room is dominated by a long executive table surrounded by eight chairs, and a floor-to-ceiling picture window overlooking Monument Circle and downtown Indianapolis. I feel we're going to need to tip the maid service some serious cash, because we have really fucked this place up. Beth spilled almost an entire bottle of red wine while dancing on the boardroom table to the Black Eyed Peas' "My Humps." We broke one of the Barcaloungers when we rented *Ass Worship 7: Assphyxiation* on pay-per-view and tried to mimic some of the moves. And the executive table is covered with a thin layer of edible, Creamsicle-flavored massage cream.

"Now take me through this," Beth says between naked sips of champagne. "Hatch and his father, both of them alcoholics, went in together on a microbrewery up in Indianapolis?"

"They're more like silent partners really." I walk over to the executive table, similarly naked. Beth hands me a glass of champagne.

"What happened to the Navy?" Beth asks. "I thought he was looking at being a career officer."

"He was, up until about six months ago. Says he saw some things he wasn't supposed to see over in Afghanistan, and the Navy paid him a lot of money to shut up and be honorably discharged."

"And that's all he told you?"

"That's all I wanted to hear."

Beth jumps up from the executive table, her breasts bouncing. She stumbles forward, spilling her alcohol, again. "How about a toast?"

"To what?"

My wife of ten years raises her champagne flute. "To no secrets."

"To no secrets."

"I love you, Hank."

I sip my champagne, the bubbles tickling the back of my throat. I start to return the affirmation, but apparently there's a disconnect between my brain and my mouth.

"Right after we got engaged, I made out with Lila on the Mineshaft dance floor, but it didn't mean anything. Before the twins were born and you hated me, and I hated you, I had a Bloody Mary with Angelina Valerio when she had a layover at Indianapolis International Airport. Nothing happened, and it was a stupid thing for me to do. I also kissed Lila once more when I was living in New York when you and I were separated, but I didn't really like it, and all I thought about was Sasha sitting on the end of the bed."

Beth spits more than a little champagne in my face. "Hank, what the fuck?"

"Hey, it was your toast. You said no secrets. Do you have anything you want to say to me?"

"No!"

"Nothing at all?"

"You know I have a lot of eyes and ears in Empire Ridge, right?"

"Good grief," Beth says. "It was like two or three horrible blind dates when I thought we were getting divorced."

"Two *or* three?"

"Three."

"You sure about that?"

"Yes."

"So we're done here?"

"I don't know," Beth says. "Are we?"

"I'm getting conflicting vibes."

"What are they telling you?"

"One vibe says we're sleeping in separate bedrooms tonight, the other says I'm supposed to bend you over that executive table and fuck your brains out."

Beth finishes her sparkling wine and throws the empty glass over her shoulder. It shatters against the wall. She grabs the freshly opened champagne, taking a generous pull straight from the bottle.

"We've been married for ten years," she says, wiping the champagne from her lips with the back of her hand. "Figure it out."

2006

CHAPTER NINETY-SIX

"Maybe we should slow down," Jack says.

"Slow down? We're like five blocks from home."

"You're pretty fit for an old man."

"I'm thirty-five, Jack."

"You're closer to seventy than you are to the day you were born."

"Thanks for that dose of perspective, asshole."

"Ha!"

"But at least I can take my wife to see an R-rated movie without having to show identification every time."

"Barely," Jack says. "What is up with that anyway?"

"With what?"

"Our baby faces, you still getting carded for booze."

"Chalk it up to good genes and large pores."

"Huh?"

"That oily skin and bad complexion you hate right now is a gift."

"A gift from whom? The Devil?"

"Oily skin now equals fewer wrinkles later. All the Fitzpatrick men looked fifteen to twenty years younger than they really were, at least in the face."

Jack moved in with us late last summer, several months after everything went down at his sixteenth birthday party. It was Beth's idea, but our transition from siblings to something else was surprisingly seamless.

My wife has been very supportive, and not just because we have a full-time free babysitter. And by "free" I mean I slip Jack money when Beth isn't looking. We still haven't quite figured out how to tell Sasha and the twins that "Uncle Jack" is actually "Half Brother Jack," so we haven't told them. Debbie and Jack are still struggling to define their new mom-turned-grandma / son-turned-grandson relationship. He only just started talking to Mom again a few weeks ago.

Gillman, for all his LDS quirks and fundamental flaws as a human being, has actually been my go-to mediator in this. He was the one who suggested that, with Jack now less than a year from being of legal majority age, we just keep a lid on everything. "Your choice, Hank," he said to me. "Sue your mother for paternity rights and make the next year a living hell for everyone you know, or just be quiet for twelve measly months and Jack is yours anyway." I think I might need to send Gillman a gift basket. Or maybe a can of red wheat for that weird-ass food storage he keeps in the basement because Joseph Smith told him to do it.

Jack and Laura have grown close—or at least as close as the distance between them will allow. Ian took their daughters back to Pennsylvania a couple weeks after the funeral while Laura spent some time in Empire Ridge settling up her mother's affairs and getting to know her son. She went back to Pennsylvania a couple months ago. Ian has a new job with PNC Bank in Philadelphia. Last I heard, he and Laura were in counseling and doing well. Jack says they've moved into an eighteenth-century townhouse in the Old City district that they're restoring, and that it has a spare bedroom for when he visits.

I'm not particularly happy at Gillman being a confidante in family matters or Laura managing to forge a connection with our son by being little more than his goddamn instant messenger buddy for a few months, but I've kind of lost the right to bitch about it.

"How's the college search going?" I say to Jack.

"It's going," he answers in typical non-committal fashion.

"You narrow down the list yet?"

"The usual subjects," Jack says. "IU, Purdue, Butler, Wabash, Notre Dame, a few others."

"Others?" I ask. "What others are there?"

"We'll see," Jack says. "I feel like it's all going to come down to Notre Dame."

I smack him across his back shoulder. "Damn right it is, but Mom tells me I might need to chip in for tuition."

"Yeah, so?"

"Since when has that been part of the master plan?"

"Oh, I don't know, since you stuck your penis inside Laura's vagina?"

"Bitter much?"

"You were the one who asked."

"I doubt you're going to need my help. When was the last time you got anything less than an A-minus on a report card?"

"The second grade."

"And how much money is coming to you via the annuity settlement with the auto auction?"

"Twenty-six thousand dollars a year until I'm twenty-six years old."

"After taxes?"

"Yes sir."

"Hell, I'm the one who's going to be hitting you up for a loan."

We approach our house, stopping at the end of the driveway. Beth is backing out. She rolls down her window. "Good run, boys?"

"Yeah," I say.

"I'm dropping the kids off at school," she says to me. "See you for lunch?"

"Not today, honey. I have to drive up to the Indy office."

"I thought you were working from home this week."

"I wish. The boss is flying in from New York this afternoon. He's really on my ass about hitting my numbers this year."

"What are your chances?"

"Slim to none. As they say in publishing these days, down is the new up."

"Well, good luck, babe."

"Thanks."

Beth rolls up her window. Just as the window is about to seal shut I hear her shout, "Stop licking your sister!" She backs the minivan into the street, then drives away.

"Let's go inside and get some coffee," I say to Jack.

"I don't like coffee."

"Since when?"

"Since forever."

"Can I blame Gillman's caffeine-free Mormon ass for that?"

"If you want."

"I do."

"I could go for a hot chocolate, though."

We walk inside the house. I start some water in the kettle for Jack's hot chocolate, pour myself a cup of coffee.

"Honey," Jack says.

"In your hot chocolate?"

"No, you called Beth 'honey.'"

"Yeah, so?"

"You two seem to be in a happy place lately."

"I guess."

"You don't sound particularly optimistic."

"I'm as optimistic as the sacrament of marriage allows me to be, Jack."

"Gee, that's cheery."

CHAPTER NINETY-SEVEN

Granted, most people associate the Deer Creek Music Center with July 2, 1995, the day three-thousand jackoffs tore down the back fence of the sprawling outdoor amphitheater at a Grateful Dead show and got in a rock, beer bottle, and tear gas brawl with local law enforcement. But for me, Deer Creek is the oasis of my youth. Back when I was younger, it stood alone among acres and acres of farmland. That iconic photo of Jerry Garcia standing in a wheat field, wearing all black and holding a guitar with his head bowed? That was taken at Deer Creek. I've seen at least three KISS "farewell" tours here and more than a dozen Buffett concerts, none of which I was sober enough to remember. The best live show I ever saw here was Metallica's '94 Shit Hits the Sheds tour, and the worst by far was Coldplay's Twisted Logic tour last year. The younger kids call the place by its shiny new corporate name, Verizon Wireless Music Center. All the farmland has long since been paved over. Deer Creek is now merely the "you are here" dot near the top of the Hamilton Town Center map. And Jerry Garcia's wheat field is a Bed, Bath & Beyond parking lot.

Hatch pulls the minivan into the Deer Creek parking lot. We're here for the Journey–Def Leppard concert, and Hatch is the only sober one in the vehicle. The rest of us—Claire, Beth, and I—are both drunk and stoned. We've been passing around a half gallon of Jim Beam and a two-liter of Diet Coke for the entire ride up from Empire Ridge. Claire fired up a joint just south of Indianapolis, which we proceeded to smoke before we even got to the Marion-Hamilton County border. Hatch is in the middle of trying to give me a music history lesson.

"I'm telling you 'Song and Emotion' by Tesla was a tribute to Def Leppard guitarist Steve Clark."

"Bullshit," I say. "You just love Tesla because they remind you of that sappy mixtape you made for my wife."

"Fuck you, Hank!"

"Okay, boys," Beth says from the backseat. "Let's settle down."

"When do we eat?" Claire asks..

Hatch turns the car off, reaches for the door handle. "You guys have got to get it together."

"What are they gonna do?" his wife snaps back at him. "Arrest us for being hungry?"

"Just bring the volume down is all."

"That's hilarious," I say.

"What?" Hatch says.

"You asking someone else to watch their volume."

A few words about Journey and Def Leppard. Like many adults in their thirties and forties, I regard these bands as two of our generation's touchstones. I associate songs from both their catalogs with various determinative moments of my youth. Journey's weepy ballad "Open Arms" reminds me of two things. One is the night I first got my hand up a girl's shirt during a slow dance. Her name was Molly Alden, my favorite partner in our sixth-grade evening cotillion class. I snuck my hand up the back of her sweater to "Open Arms," and my hand stayed there for both Neil Diamond's "Heartlight" and "Up Where We Belong" by Joe Cocker and Jennifer Warnes, the latter of which, just as an aside, never fails to induce a flashback of Richard Gere boning the shit out of Deborah Winger in *An Officer and a Gentleman*. The other event I associate with "Open Arms" is when I snuck down to my grandparents' basement to watch *The Last American Virgin* on HBO just because it was rated-R and had *virgin* in the title. I woke up the entire house crying when Diane Franklin's character ends up back with the asshole that got her pregnant, while the sweet-natured nerd who loved her and nurtured her through her abortion is left broken and defeated just as the movie ends with both his tears and the credits rolling in parallel lines down his face. Saddest ending to a movie. Ever.

"Wheel in the Sky" reminds me of my Uncle Mitch's peach and custard pie.

"Any Way You Want It" reminds me of the first time I saw *Caddyshack*.

"Send Her My Love" reminds me of my seventh-grade girlfriend's breasts.

"Only the Young" reminds me of Linda Fiorentino's ass.

"Separate Ways" reminds me of bad tank tops.

"Don't Stop Believin'" reminds me of Dad's smile.

Where to begin with Def Leppard? The first time I ever got stoned was to a scratched LP of *High 'n' Dry*, which I still consider to be the band's best album. I got my *Pyromania* Velcro wallet as a Confirmation gift—oh, the irony—and later that year for Halloween I wore a white scarf and sleeveless Union Jack T-shirt and dressed like lead singer Joe Elliott in the "Autograph" video. The morning after the *Hysteria* concert—Tuesday, October 27, 1987, to be exact—at least half of Empire Ridge's student body showed up to school with Def Leppard concert tees reeking of sweat, tobacco, and pot. Beyond that, however, Def Leppard was bigger than any single moment. While ostensibly more meaningful bands like The Police, Talking Heads, or U2 vied for a mere sliver of my memory, I was hard pressed to remember a day in the eighties when I didn't hear at least one Def Leppard song on my radio or cassette deck. Whether in my car playing air guitar with Hatch or in my room masturbating to Dad's *Playboys*—the volume always surreptitiously turned up to mask my moaning—the arena rock kings from Sheffield, England, defined my teenage years. Okay, co-defined. Bon Jovi's *Slippery When Wet* album was a big fucking deal, too.

I stopped listening to Def Leppard in the nineties, partly because Steve Clark died, but mostly because the band became incapable of making music that didn't suck. I ostracized friends who thought *Adrenalize* was anything more than a steaming pile of shit, with the exception of a girl I had sex with several times—her name escapes me at the moment—who included "Have You Ever Needed Someone So Bad" on a mixtape she made for me.

"Hank?" Beth says. She grabs my hand as we walk across the parking lot toward the amphitheater. Claire and Hatch are about ten yards behind. Claire is mad because Hatch didn't let her bring the other joint into the concert. Hatch is mad because it's an hour before the show and his wife is already a puddle.

"Yeah, babe?" I say.

"What are you thinking about?"

"Nicole Chase!"

"Who?"

"An old summer fling, back when we were kids. 'Have You Ever Needed Someone So Bad' was our song."

"That's a beautiful story, Hank," my wife says.

"Sorry, I just couldn't remember her name."

"Why did you need to remember her name?"

"Because of Def Leppard and sweet potatoes, of course."

"And now we're back on sweet potatoes. Great."

"You think this is about Lang?"

"I see you staring at her calves."

"Well, at least you acknowledge that she exists. That's a big step for you."

"We're not going to be friends, and, no, you're not getting her in our hot tub."

"This isn't about Lang at all," I say.

"Good," Beth says.

"It's about feeding giraffes at the zoo."

"Uh, how much dope have you smoked?"

Hatch is shouting in the middle of "Lovin', Touchin', Squeezin'"—and he's pissed off. "Who the hell is that? Where the fuck is Steve Perry?"

Our seats are in the lawn. Claire proceeded to smoke the joint by herself before Journey even came on stage. She's passed out right now, fetal and sweaty at her husband's feet.

"You know, Hatch," I say, dry-humping my wife—because come on, "Lovin', Touchin', Squeezin'" *demands* that you dry-hump the closest available female with a grindable ass. "For being sober, you're a real fucking idiot sometimes."

"What do you mean?"

"Perry hasn't been with the band since like the late eighties. That's Steve Augeri up there. Looks and sounds just like Perry."

"That guy looks nothing like Steve Perry."

"You're both wrong," Beth says into my shoulder. "Perry rejoined Journey for some reunion gigs in the nineties then left the band for good in 1998, which is when he was replaced by Steve Augeri."

I smack Hatch's arm with the back of my hand. "See, I was right. That guy up there is—"

"*Is not* Steve Augeri," Beth says, preempting my boast. "He dropped out of the band before this tour with some chronic throat problems. That mop-headed guy up there on stage sounds like Perry and Augeri, but he doesn't look anything like them. His name is Jeff Scott Soto."

"Who the hell is that?" I ask.

Hatch smacks my arm with the back of his hand. "Journey's lead singer, dumbass."

I CONVINCED HATCH AND Beth to leave before Def Leppard started into their encore. Being thirty-five years old, I hate bad traffic more than I like a good show. With the exception of Guns N' Roses' original lineup reuniting or Roger Waters fronting Pink Floyd again, there's no band on Earth that justifies me stewing in a car for two hours at the mercy of rent-a-cops and traffic cones.

"Who's ready to party?" Claire shouts from the backseat. She was unconscious for the entire concert. Hatch had to carry her over his shoulder back to the car. About halfway back to Empire Ridge, she woke up. And she's ready to party.

Claire offers me the nearly empty bottle of Jim Beam. I wave it off. "Not all of us napped for the last three hours, Claire Bear."

"You're no fun, Hankie," she says to me in her usual shamelessly flirty tone.

Beth picks up on the tone. "Claire?"

"Yeah, Beth?"

"Shut up."

CLAIRE FOUND AN OLD New Year's bottle of unopened champagne in the back of the refrigerator. She's cornered Jack in the kitchen with booze and estrogen.

"Mrs. Hatcher, I really don't think I should."

"Oh poo, Jack, have a sip. And call me Claire. When I hear someone say 'Mrs. Hatcher,' I look around for my mother-in-law."

"Lay off the kid," I say, stepping between them.

"The kid can handle himself," Hatch shouts from the living room.

"It's not the kid I'm worried about," I shout back. "Hey, Claire, go torment your husband instead of my seventeen-year-old son."

She shakes her head. "That's still so weird to hear you call him that."

Claire exits the kitchen. I hand Jack a couple twenty-dollar bills. "How were the kids?"

"Twins were demons, Sasha was perfect."

"Typical."

"Yep," Jack affirms.

"Did I hear you were going to brunch with Mom tomorrow?"

"With Debbie, you mean?"

"So that's her name for good now?"

"Well, it ain't Mom, and she certainly doesn't deserve Grandma."

"At least you're talking. That's a start."

"I suppose so."

"You can go to bed now," I say. "Thanks for watching the brood."

Jack leans in and hugs me. "Thanks for letting me...Dad."

The hug suddenly goes from sweet to suffocating. "Look, you don't have to call me—"

"Just trying it on for size," Jack says. "How does it fit?"

"Like a shmedium T-shirt on a fat guy," I say.

"Black bandanna, sweet Louisiana, robbin' on a bank in the state of Indiana!"

It's approaching two o'clock in the morning. Beth and Claire are standing in the middle of the hot tub. They're drunk, dancing and singing to the Red Hot Chili Peppers.

Hatch plugged his iPod into the stereo and is running through his "Indiana mix"—i.e., a shitload of John Mellencamp and any song that uses the word "Indiana" in the lyrics. The mix began with Mellencamp and India Arie coming up from Indiana down from Tennessee, which when you think about it doesn't make any fucking sense. Next up was the Jackson Five's "Goin' Back to Indiana," which segued into Tom Petty telling us all about Mary Jane growing up in an Indiana town with Indiana boys and Indiana nights. I almost bailed on the mix entirely when it took a dreary turn with Melissa Etheridge's "Indiana," but Hatch rallied with the Dixie Chicks talking about their brothers finding work in Indiana and now the Chilis.

There's something melodic and soulful about the word *Indiana*. Four syllables flowing into one another, almost like a poem contained within a single word. The state itself might not be much to look at, but she has a beautiful singing voice.

Beth had offered Claire a swimsuit. Claire being Claire, she winked and said, "I couldn't possibly fit into one of your suits," when what she really meant was, *Bitch, please, I'm so much skinnier than you*. With her best friend reasonably demoralized, Claire then just stripped down to her bra and panties and jumped right in.

Hatch and I sit off to the side of the tub in two Adirondack chairs. I'm nursing a High Life, my best friend a cup of decaffeinated coffee.

"About time to shut this down," I say.

"Why?" Hatch sips his coffee. "You don't like the view?"

It's hard not to stare. Beth and Claire have two different body types—one petite and muscular, the other tall and lean. They complement one another very well, though, especially when half-naked and wet. I'm reminded vaguely of the lesbian sex scene between Anne Heche and Joan Chen in the underappreciated soft-core flick *Wild Side*.

You would think after sleeping with the same woman for thirteen years that broaching sexual intercourse would be old hat.

You would think.

The hot tub dance party lost its mojo quicker than I expected. By 3:00 a.m. Hatch and Claire headed down to the basement for the night. Before she crawled into bed, Beth changed out of her swimsuit into an old shirt and cotton pajama pants, the chastity belt of middle-aged married women. But I'm not giving up that easy. Not tonight. Not after watching my wife dirty dance half-naked with the Hottest Girl I Never Tried to Sleep With.

And so begins the dance.

After Beth turns off the lights, she always tries to first fall asleep on her back. If that happens, then the dance is over. Posted no fishing.

Beth rolls to her side facing away from me. Step one accomplished. *It's on!*

I slide across the bed behind her for step two, the spooning. This is the toughest step in the dance. It can make or break the deal and must be exercised with patience and care. Move too slowly, and she grabs your arm and pulls it tight around her for the all-night cuddle. Move too fast—say, go immediately for a boob squeeze or slip your hand down the back of her panties to grab her bare ass—and it's the dreaded shutdown: not only no sex tonight, but also likely some lingering resentment that will keep you out of the T & A trade at least through her next menstrual cycle.

To avoid this confrontation, you move to step three, the foot test. While fully spooned and your hand placed casually on your partner's waist or the side of her thigh, you slide the top of your foot lightly against the arch of her foot. There's potential for disaster even with this innocuous move. Tread too lightly, and by the time you've mustered the courage to move to step four, she's in full REM sleep. Tread too aggressively, and you end up tickling her, which annoys her and sends you back into the whole lingering resentment shame spiral.

Beth pushes gently back on my foot. *Green light!*

The foot push isn't a guarantee, so it's usually best to go to step four just for confirmation. There are a couple options. One, slide the hand under the shirt and do a finger swipe beneath her breasts. Or two, slide your hand inside the back of her panties and give a light brush of her butt just below her panty line. I'm an ass man, so I think I'll—

"You going to do me any time this century?" Beth says.

"You're awake?" I ask.

"Kind of hard to sleep with your erection stabbing me in the back."

"But you put on PJ pants. I thought that meant you didn't want to—"

"I didn't."

"But now you do?"

"I could easily be talked out of it."

"I don't want your pity."

"You want something that starts with a P."

"You're a cruel woman, Beth."

"A cruel woman with an awesome rack."

"Well, yeah."

"And I noticed."

"Noticed what?"

"You looked at me in the hot tub."

"Of course I did."

"No, you looked at me *instead of* Claire."

"I did?"

"Hank, I love Claire to death, but we both know she sucks the air right out of a room. You had tunnel vision tonight, and I just wanted to say I appreciated you appreciating me."

"So we *are* having sex tonight?"

Beth reaches down, pulling her PJ pants and panties down to her knees. She reaches her hand into the slit of my boxers. "Would you prefer an all-night cuddle?"

"Only if it involves my dick inside you."

"You almost don't deserve to get some after that pickup line."

"Hey, you're the one with my dick in your hand."

"And don't you forget it."

CHAPTER NINETY-EIGHT

Lila and Chris broke up, again. Lila is still in New York, living right now with a friend from work in the West Village. I'm in town for a week of meetings at the Bertelsmann building, so Lila asked me to meet her at Sweet Revenge, a cupcake, beer, and wine bar on Carmine Street.

Lila is already at the bar when I arrive. I can tell something is up the moment I walk inside. She stands up, kisses me on the cheek, and exhales right when we hug, as if she's been holding her breath for just that moment.

"Hey, girl," I say, kissing her back. "Everything okay?"

Lila smiles. "It is now."

We order a couple peanut butter cupcakes, which our waitress advises to pair with a glass of Malbec.

I reach over, squeeze Lila's hand. "You up for some red wine this early?"

She squeezes back. "Already a glass ahead of you."

I nod to the waitress. "Red wine it is, then."

I'm on my second glass, Lila her third. The cupcakes—peanut butter cake with a ganache center and peanut butter fudge frosting—were so decadent that we ordered two more.

"Sorry to hear about Chris," I say, taking a bite of cupcake.

Lila reaches over with her napkin, dabbing at the frosting on my upper lip. "What's to be sorry about, Hank?"

"I know you loved her."

"I loved the idea of her, but let's face it—Chris was an exhausting girlfriend."

"True, but still, you two were a couple for a long time. That's not something where you just turn the page and move on."

"Who's turning the page?" Lila says. "I walked in on her doing a nineteen-year-old Columbia coed with a strap-on. That's not an image I'm forgetting anytime soon."

"Wow. I-I'm sorry."

"Oh shut up, Hank."

"What did I say?"

"You didn't have to say anything. I can see it in your expression."

"What can you see?"

"Your conscience wrestling with whether or not you should be sympathetic or turned on."

I hide my guilt in an aggressive swallow of wine. I place the empty glass on the table. Lila smiles. I smile back. "You ever wonder what would have happened with us if our parents never got together?"

"I don't follow," Lila says.

"I don't know. It just seems like, well, we've always been so compatible."

"Don't kid yourself."

"Why do you say that?"

"I love you to pieces, but we are *not* compatible."

"That's a little harsh," I say.

"Is there chemistry? Sure there is. But true compatibility? No offense, Hank, but the idea of waking up every day with you and wrestling with all your psychological repression, sexual dysfunction, and emotional transference just sounds exhausting. Beth deserves a medal, not a fucking ring."

"Speaking of emotional transference," I say, "I'm not Chris. You know that, right?"

"Sorry, Hank." Lila rubs my arm. "That just all kind of came rushing out."

I respond to her gesture by grabbing her hand. I rub it between my thumb and index finger. "Maybe you just need to get out of here for a while. Get away from the New York scene."

"No arguments from me."

"You've done all you can do here: the editing thing, the writing thing…"

"The lesbian band aid thing."

"Yeah, that too."

"Funny you should say that." Lila pulls an envelope out of her purse. She hands the envelope to me. It's addressed to her, and the top line of the return address reads *Brigham Young University–Hawaii.*

"What's this?"

"You don't want to read it?"

"I'm sorry, have we met? Why would I want to read anything from BYU?"

"They've offered me a teaching position in the English department. Full benefits, and I could get tenure as early as seven years."

"But it's a Mormon university, in fucking Hawaii."

"I've made my peace with my church after those wretched books I wrote."

"Wretched? Those things put food on both of our plates for the better part of the last decade."

"Money and notoriety isn't everything, Hank. I want stability. I want to put down roots. BYU–Hawaii is offering me all of that and more."

"Why do I suddenly feel like you're telling me this is happening as opposed to asking if I think you should do it?"

"Because you know me, and we're compatible."

"See, I knew it!"

"Come on, Hank. Be happy for me."

"I am, Lila."

"You are?"

"If this is what you want, I'm ecstatic."

"Thanks. Now what about you?"

"What about me?"

"You seem to be losing your steam at College Ave."

"Is that what you call it?"

"What do you call it?"

"I call it tired of being a figurehead for a shitty list. I'm not an editor anymore. I'm just a paper pusher."

"Then do something about it."

"Like what?"

"I think you know that answer."

"Right now, I'm having a hard time even figuring out what the fucking question is."

"You need to be a writer, Hank."

"Are you insane? I have three kids and a mortgage."

"So?"

"Now isn't exactly the opportune time to explore a hobby. Besides, what the hell am I going to write about?"

"Tell *your* story."

"My story?"

Lila stands up from the table, closing her eyes. "'My morning gets off to its usual start,'" she recites. "'I wake up. Masturbate. Eat some bacon and eggs. Drink a cup of creamed and sugared coffee. Have a frank discussion with my father about his testicles.'"

"How in the hell did you—"

"I read it on your laptop one of those various nights you passed out on my couch."

"So you're suggesting I write a memoir? Uh, hello, welcome to two thousand six. Did you see James Frey on *Oprah*? It's not exactly a growth industry in publishing right now."

"Hank, I'm not telling you to quit your day job or pen the next great memoir. I'm just telling you to write. Just sit down with your computer, a pad of paper, whatever, and write something. All that shit that's in your head? Just let it out. There's a story there. I know there is. I can feel it wanting to come out."

"Problem is there are a lot of people who would probably prefer that this story stay in my head."

"Fuck 'em."

"Debbie would certainly need to take a long hard look in the mirror."

"And that's her problem, not yours. Besides, what's Debbie care now that she and Dad are essentially abandoning you?"

"What do you mean by that?"

"You know, with the move and all. I mean, converting to LDS is one thing. I pretty much saw that as inevitable with your mother. But actually moving to Salt Lake City? Debbie is in for one hell of a culture shock."

I prop my elbows on the table, burying my forehead in my hands. Grinding my teeth, I look up and hold my right index finger in the air. "Waitress, we'll take our check now."

"Wait," Lila says, finally picking up on my body language. "You didn't know?"

I shake my head. "That's a negative, Ghostrider."

CHAPTER NINETY-NINE

Mom invited Jack and me over for dinner. I brought a box of red wine, mostly just to piss Gillman off. He invited me to say grace prior to the meal, but I declined. The four of us sit around the long Amish table Mom found at an antique store in Gnaw Bone, a peculiarly named bend in the road about halfway between Bloomington and Empire Ridge.

"What exactly are we eating here?" Jack asks me under his breath.

I eye the spread: cubed steak, Spanish rice, and green beans stewed in bacon grease. "It's a Fitzpatrick specialty."

Jack shakes his head. "No it isn't."

"Yes it is," Mom says. She ladles mushroom gravy over the cubed steak on Jack's plate, following it up with the rice and green beans. "This meal was an old staple when Hank was a kid. Try it. You just might like it."

Jack sticks his fork in the Spanish rice, dissecting it more than eating it. He eats a small bite.

"Well, what do you think?" Mom says.

"Isn't this just white rice mixed with tomatoes?"

"Eureka!" I say. "Someone has finally cracked the code. Four-star restaurants everywhere are now doomed to irrelevance by this seventies culinary masterpiece."

"Give it a rest, Hank," Gillman says. "Your mother made this meal especially for you."

"Yeah, I kind of assumed that." Grabbing the napkin from my lap, I reach up and wipe my mouth. I place the napkin to the side of my plate. "Truthfully, though, I don't really have an appetite right now."

"You sick or something?" Mom asks.

"Or something," I answer. "Can we just get on with this?"

"Get on with wh—"

"Utah, Mom?" I say.

"Oh."

"Fucking Utah?"

"What about Utah?" Jack says.

I nod in my mother's direction. "Your grandma is moving with Gillman to Salt Lake City."

"It has the highest quality of life of any major metropolitan area in the continental United States."

"Says who, Mom? Your oh-so-impartial husband?"

"Says a Gallup poll for the fourth year in a row," Gillman chimes in.

"Gillman, shut the fuck up."

"Hank, you will not talk to your stepfather like that in front of me."

"I think I just did, Debbie."

"It's just time."

"Time for what? To run away?"

"I don't see this as running away from anything," Mom says. "I see it more as running *to* something—to a new life, to some place where I'm wanted."

"Oh bullshit. You're not just moving to another state. You're moving to another planet. A planet of weird white people, weird white gods, and weird white underwear. You're moving to fucking Honkeytown."

I back away from the table. Standing, I turn and walk into the living room, my back to the kitchen. Gillman follows me.

"When was the last time you really included your mother in anything, Hank?"

"What are you talking about? I include her. We see each other for the holidays, and I always take her out for a birthday dinner."

"What about the other three hundred sixty-odd days of the year?"

"I call Mom all the time."

"You call Debbie for three things..." Gillman says. He moves close to me, now nose to nose, holding up three fingers. "You call her when you need a last-minute babysitter, on your father's birthday, and on your parents' wedding anniversary."

"That's not true."

"It is true. In fact, that's one of the reasons we're moving. It's time to lay John Fitzpatrick to rest."

"Fuck you!"

Gillman sticks his finger in my face. "I think I've earned the right not to stand in his shadow anymore."

"Careful, Gill-*man*."

"I'm tired of being careful, *Hen*-ree. I'm tired of hearing about the perfect John Fitzpatrick. He was a flawed person who struggled at being a husband, a father, and a man just like you and me."

"I would seriously shut your piehole right about now if I were you."

"Heck, Hank. Far as I'm concerned, John failed you. He shielded you from the truth about his abusive mother. He lied to you about Jack. When Uncle Mitch abused you all those years, it was on John's watch. His death didn't mess you up. His life did."

Because of the way Jack is positioned at the kitchen table, he's the only one who has a clear view of my right arm, which is partially hidden behind my back. He sees me clench my fist, but by the time he stands up he's already too late.

I underestimate Gillman's substantial gut. I land a solid punch into his midsection that I assumed would knock him off his feet. Instead, he's merely doubled over and gasping for air.

"Gillman!" Mom shouts.

"I'm okay, Debbie." Gillman waves her off with one hand, his other hand on his knee.

"Holy shit, Hank!" Jack says to me, trying not to laugh. It's just the distraction Gillman is looking for.

A word about my stepfather. He was an all-state linebacker in high school and walked on at BYU before blowing his knee out.

Gillman crouches low, his feet shoulder-width apart. He slides his head to the side of my waist and reaches his arms around my thighs. He wraps my legs, raises me up in the air, and slams me through the coffee table. It's a textbook tackle.

My wrestling instincts kick in about halfway through the spray of glass and splintered wood. Right before I hit the ground, I turn my right shoulder in just enough so I won't get caught on my back. I secure Gillman's right arm with my left while bringing my right elbow down on his right ear. His grip grows slack from the blow, his ear bleeding profusely. I slide out from under him, raising my right fist for another shot.

"Dad, stop!"

Jack's hand squeezes my wrist, my fist hovering inches in front of Gillman's face. I think Jack might be stronger than I am, although I'm not going to admit it to him anytime soon.

"Please," Jack says to both of us. "No more."

Mom helps Gillman to his feet. She leans his head over the kitchen sink, cleaning his ear with a cold washcloth.

Jack offers to help me up, but I refuse. "I can take care of myself."

"I know you can," Jack says. He still grabs my elbow, steering me toward the couch. We both sit down.

"Nice move," I say.

"What move was that?"

"Calling me 'Dad.'"

"Snapped you out of your fucking 'roid rage, didn't it?"

"That it did."

"Hank?" Gillman says, walking up to us.

"I think we've said all we need to say to one another."

"I just wanted to let you know I didn't mean what I said. I'm sorry."

"Fuck you and your apology."

"I suppose I deserved that."

"Come on, Hank," Jack says. "Be nice."

"Be nice?" I stand up, walking into the kitchen where Mom sits stone-faced and silent at the Amish table from Gnaw Bone. "Someone just accused my dead father of enabling a pedophile. You call that being nice?"

"I said I was sorry, Hank."

"And I said 'fuck you and your apology, Gillman.'"

"Just get out of here," Mom says, tears now running down her face.

"What?" I say.

"I think you and Jack probably need to leave now," she reiterates. "Some of the things Gillman just said to you were cruel and unnecessary, and I'm sorry for that. But his heart is in the right place. I love you and Jeanine and Jack more than life itself, but I also love Gillman. And for him and for me, I can't be Mrs. Fitzpatrick anymore. It's time for me to be Mrs. Prestwich."

"But, Mom, you can't go."

I don't say these words. They come from the family room—from Jack.

He runs across the room crying and into Mom's arms, just like when he was a little boy and the tornado watch would flash across the television.

"There, there," Mom says. Jack sits in her lap. She strokes her seventeen-year-old boy's hair. "You know the difference between a tornado warning and a tornado watch, right?"

"Yeah, Mom," he answers. "A warning means a tornado has been spotted in the area, and a watch means the conditions are right for a tornado."

"So when there's a watch?"

"There's no tornado."

Mom kisses Jack on the forehead. "And when there's a warning?"

"It doesn't matter, because you'll always keep me safe."

CHAPTER ONE HUNDRED

Jack and I are in the driveway playing a game of H-O-R-S-E that's just recently morphed into a game of S-T-U-P-I-D.

"How late is she?"

"About three weeks," Jack says.

"What's her name again?"

"Her name is Caitlin."

"Of course it is. Please at least tell me she spells it with a 'C' and not a 'K'."

"That she does."

"Good," I say. "And she isn't sleeping with anyone else?"

"No, Hank. We're in love."

"Oh, I'm sure you are."

Whenever you hear someone characterized as a "player's coach," it's really a pejorative cloaked in a superlative. The players love him because he "speaks their language" and because "he's a mentor first and a coach second" who "knows how to put them in the best possible position to succeed both on and off the field."

Translation: He's a shitty coach that loses a lot of fucking games.

I think that as a father, I make for a great player's coach. A player's coach who at the moment is trying to wrap his head around the fact that exactly seventeen years after his own conception, Jack has apparently decided to double down.

"I feel like I gave you the information you needed so you wouldn't get into a situation like this."

"You did."

"So what happened?'

"I don't know," Jack said. "I guess we just got caught up in the moment."

Statements like this should scare the living shit out of parents. In the nearly two decades since I was Jack's age, nothing has fucking changed. Sex education still usually devolves into on-the-job training. All those parents, teachers, and taxpayer dollars assailed against the ignorance of youth, vanquished in one split second because *I guess we just got caught up in the moment*.

"What are you going to do?" I ask.

"Caitlin is taking a pregnancy test today, so we'll cross that bridge when we come to it."

"You're not thinking about keeping it, are you?"

"What if I was?"

"Then you're a dumbass."

"Gee. Love you too, Dad."

"What's that supposed to mean?"

"So you regret that Laura didn't abort me as planned?"

"Apples and oranges, Jack."

"All I see are fetuses and fetuses, Hank."

He still bounces back and forth between "Hank" and "Dad" as the mood suits him: the former if we're having a bad day, the latter if we're having a good one. It doesn't take a player's coach to figure out where this day is heading.

"Can I give you one piece of advice?"

"Go for it."

"No matter what happens, you let this be her decision."

"I think I have the right to—"

"You have the right to keep your mouth shut."

"But that baby inside Caitlin is half mine."

"And a dude presuming a prenatal fetus to be 'half his' is like the guy who sold paint to Leonardo da Vinci being called the co-creator of the *Mona Lisa*."

"I dispute that analogy," Jack says.

"It's not an analogy for you to dispute. It's a fact. You're not the one carrying another living organism inside you for the next nine months. You're not the one whose body is going through a physical and chemical metamorphosis. You're not the one who has to endure the stigma of being a pregnant teenage girl day after day. Look at Caitlin as the owner of a bank and you as a depositor who will never be allowed to own a bank. All you did was deposit your money in the bank and walk away. And if I'm not being clear enough, the bank is Caitlin's vagina."

"Uh, yeah, I got that part."

Jack's phone vibrates in his pocket as he shoots the basketball. It ricochets off the back of the rim to give me the undisputed H-O-R-S-E driveway title yet again.

"You going to get that?"

"Yeah." Jack reaches inside his pocket. He flips open his phone, reads the text message.

"Well?" I say.

CHAPTER ONE HUNDRED ONE

I offered to help, but Jack insisted on paying for the abortion. He gathered some items from the attic and sold them on eBay. Most of the items were mine—one complete collection of late seventies Mattel Shogun Warriors, one unopened 1980 Kenner Star Wars Droid Factory, one well-used Atari 2600 game console—but I didn't make a big deal out of it. He was up to two hundred seventy-five dollars, still twenty-five short of where he needed to be, with nothing but some old comic books—also technically mine—left to his name.

We pull into the parking lot at Sal's Comic Barn, a giant aluminum-sided box in Greenwood. Empire Ridge is just too damn nosy for something like this. Local boy tries to unload some things in a pawnshop, and people talk. Here in Greenwood, Jack is just a nameless kid trying to scrounge up petty cash.

Sal's Comic Barn is a familiar place to me. I was an avid comic book collector beginning in second grade and ending in puberty. My last two years of collecting in the seventh and eighth grade were largely spent arguing with Sal, his store only two blocks away from Our Lady of Perpetual Help.

The comic books are individually wrapped in clear vinyl sleeves. We each carry a stack tucked under our arms as we enter the store. Sal sits behind the counter, a middle-aged paradox with an old-man comb-over and teen-profuse acne.

"Hank Fitzpatrick?" Sal says, brushing the remnants of his barbecued pork sandwich off his face. He sticks a toothpick in his mouth. "Is that you?"

"Been a while, Sal."

"Twenty years if it's been a day. How's it going?"

"My son here is just looking to unload some comics."

"Your son?" Sal says, looking at Jack, then at me, then at Jack again. "Looks to me like he could be your brother."

"Yeah," I say. "We get that a lot."

I nod to Jack. He nods back and places the comic books on the counter. Sal eyes them one by one. He retrieves one book, then another, and another. He slides seven of them back across the counter.

"How much for these?"

I grab the comic books, shuffling them as I pretend to assess their worth when I already know their value down to the penny. "Detective Comics numbers three hundred thirty-seven through three hundred forty-three. Good picks, Sal."

"They're okay, I guess." He shrugs. "I'll give you twenty bucks for all of 'em."

"Twenty bucks?" I say. "How stupid do you think I am?" I drop the comic books on the counter one at a time, smacking them with the back of my hand to emphasize each point.

"The first appearance of Martian Manhunter." *Smack*.

"...winner of six awards for comic book excellence." *Smack*.

"...both Archie Goodwin and Walter Simonson were recognized for their work in this series." *Smack smack*.

"...the artwork, some of Simonson's earliest stuff, continues to be hailed as a masterpiece of page layout and storytelling." *Smack smack smack*.

"Yeah yeah yeah." Sal waves a dismissive hand. "Take it or leave it."

We could have easily got fifty for them if we had the time or inclination, but like most seasoned comic book collectors, Sal's superpower is smelling desperation.

"Come on, Sal. Can you at least come up to thirty? For old time's sake?"

"I'm running a business here, not a charity." Sal rubs his patchy attempt at a goatee. He cracks a smile, a barbecue-stained row of what I like to call "summer teeth": some are here, some are there.

"Then how about twenty-five?"

"Deal!" Sal says with shamelessly obvious haste, as if to let me know he fucked me over. He throws the money on the counter. "Nice doing business with you, Hank. Try not to be such a stranger."

"See you in twenty years, Sal."

He laughs us out the door.

CHAPTER ONE HUNDRED TWO

We picked Caitlin up at 8:00 a.m. The hour-long drive north to the clinic in Indianapolis passed in complete silence save for *The Bob & Tom Show* on the radio. I tried to laugh at some of the jokes. Jack and Caitlin didn't.

Ours is only the third car in the parking lot. Save for the nearby hum of morning rush hour on the interstate, there's an eerie quiet to the place. With its mustard-painted vertical siding and faux fieldstone, the clinic reminds me of our family pediatrician's office. Jack only switched from his pediatrician to a general practitioner last year. Babies having babies.

I open the door for them both. The inside of the clinic is also like any other doctor's office. The required minimum six tropical plants. A faint antiseptic odor. Old copies of *Glamour*.

"Are you eighteen years of age, miss?" the nurse at the front desk asks. I can hear her voice just above the din of Christopher Cross's "Sailing" that crackles out of a blown speaker on the ceiling. The nurse has a large jaw and big breasts, with wide hips perched on oddly lean legs, kind of like Sally Spectra in *The Bold and the Beautiful*.

"Yes, I'm eighteen," Caitlin says. She produces her driver's license from her back pocket. With her free hand she reaches over and gives Jack's hand a squeeze. Jack tries to give her a reassuring smile, but he doesn't quite get there.

For a few seconds, I see myself in Jack's place. Laura standing at the counter handing the nurse her identification. The nurse giving her a clipboard of papers and saying, *Thank you, Ms. Elliot. I'll go make a photocopy of this. You can have a seat and fill out these papers.*

"What is all this?" Caitlin asks.

The nurse points to the clipboard. "The top two sheets are your patient history and your written consent to perform the procedure. The third is the consent to administer anesthesia, which you'll take in with you and sign after the anesthesiologist explains everything to you. They'll call your name shortly."

Caitlin fills out the forms, Jack sitting beside her. I flip through a worn issue of *Glamour* with Britney Spears on the cover. Between the how-to pictorials on breast exams and the underwear ads, I used to find *Glamour* to be a surprisingly adequate visual aid.

"Caitlin," the nurse says from a cracked-open door to our left.

"Yes," she says.

Caitlin stands up, squeezes Jack's hand one more time. He wants to go with her, but he knows that is impossible. His eyes start to well with tears. When it matters most, he can't be there for her, and it's breaking his heart. Jack seems to have figured out the part of the equation I was always missing as a teen: the part about how to do a little more honoring and a little less coveting.

Caitlin lets go of his hand, disappearing behind the door. The nurse sits back behind the front desk. "Sir," she says to Jack.

"Sir!" she says again, louder this time.

"Huh?" Jack says. He looks down to realize he's standing there with his hand on the doorknob.

"You can't go back there."

"I wish I could."

"No you don't."

"It'd be nice if someone would at least tell me what was going on."

I stand up from my chair. "You mean you don't know, Jack?"

"Not a clue."

The nurse shakes her head. I look at her. "Can I have a copy of that third form you handed Caitlin?"

"Why?" she says.

"Do I need a reason?"

She hands me the form. I hand it to Jack. "Sit down and read this."

I sit next to Jack, looking over his shoulder. I try to imagine what Caitlin is going through. Is this what Laura would have gone through had she not chosen to deceive me? Dear God, how can I be mad at her now? She didn't betray me. She saved me.

CONSENT FOR ABORTION

I hereby direct and request the physician from Women's Freedom, LLC to perform a suction aspiration abortion. If any unforeseen circumstances arise, or are discovered during the course of the abortion, which call for procedures in addition to, or different from those contemplated, I further request and authorize the physician to take whatever measures he/she deems medically necessary.

I assume the first thing Caitlin does when she enters the operating room is take off her clothes.

I understand that the purpose of the procedure is to terminate my pregnancy, but that no guarantee has been made to me regarding the outcome of this surgery.

Caitlin is repulsed by her own body. More than that, she thinks to herself as she rubs her ever-so-slight pooch belly, it has betrayed her.

It has been explained to me that, in rare instances, the pregnancy is not terminated and, if that happens, further treatment may be necessary at my expense.

The anesthesiologist enters the room. "Hello, Caitlin," he says. He offers a limp-wristed handshake, an empty gesture on behalf of a palatability this situation can never have. He explains what he's about to do to her. She signs the consent form, hands it to him.

I understand the procedure is done by suction aspiration of the uterus.

Ten minutes later, the doctor and the nurse from the front desk enter the room. "Good afternoon, young lady," he says to Caitlin, dispensing with the pleasantries and getting right to it. "This will be a lot like a pelvic exam or Pap test, so I need you to lie down on the exam table, please."

I understand that the risks involved include, but are not limited to, perforation of the uterus with possible damage to abdominal organs...

"Just relax. I'm inserting a spectrum inside your vagina."

Hemorrhage...

"I'm now going to clean the vagina and cervix with an antiseptic solution."

Blood clots in the uterus...

"You should be feeling the effects of the local anesthetic that was administered."

Allergic reaction to the local anesthesia...

"You will notice a numbing sensation in your cervix."

Cervical tear...

"And the Misoprostol should be kicking in any second now to dilate your cervix."

Infection...

"Okay, I'm inserting a thin, hollow tube into your cervical canal."

Hysterectomy...

"The cramping is unavoidable, but it'll all be over shortly. I promise."

Sterility...

"Your cramping should gradually subside now that the tube is out. What's that? You need to throw up? Nurse! Please help her."

Emotional reaction, both long and short term, to the termination of my pregnancy...

"Feeling better? Let's run through our recovery checklist."

If I experience any complications that require emergency medical care, I understand that I am financially responsible for the cost of said care.

"You'll have irregular bleeding and more cramps for the next two to three weeks. You should only use sanitary pads for the first week. No tampons, got it?"

I agree to see additional care promptly, if advised to do so.

"You're welcome to take ibuprofen or acetaminophen for the cramping and the pain, but absolutely no aspirin."

I have been told that, as an alternative to abortion, I may choose to continue this pregnancy and either parent may have custody of the child or elect adoption.

"No sex for one week."

I agree to read the aftercare instruction sheet and contact Women's Freedom, LLC if I experience any of the symptoms listed on said sheet. I further consent to the disposal of any tissue removed from my body during the abortion.

"Other than that, I think we can agree that this was a fairly painless procedure, right?"

I hereby release the physician and staff from any and all claims arising out of, or connected with, the above procedure or any resulting complications and expenses.

"Have a nice day."

I certify that I have read and fully understand this consent. I further state that consent is given without coercion or duress.

"Bye now."

After about a half hour, Caitlin was wheeled back into the waiting room. Hunched over, limp, like she had been poured into the chair. Jack pushes the wheelchair to the car. I open the rear passenger-side door and offer my hand to her. She grabs my hand and stands, her knees wobbling. She steadies herself, looks over her shoulder at Jack.

"Paperwork," she says.

"What's that?" Jack asks.

"Forgot to fill out the paperwork. Gotta go back. The receptionist said I need to fill out something else."

"You two get in the car," I say. "I'll take care of this."

I throw open the door to the clinic. The nurse is standing there with a piece of paper in her hand, evidently expecting me. "I apologize for the inconvenience, but we need to just—"

"Inconvenience? That's what you call this?"

"Please, sir, calm down."

"Listen, lady, I don't need to calm down. I want to know why it is you want that young woman out there to fill out more goddamn paperwork."

"We don't need her to fill out anything."

"You don't?"

"No."

"Then what's this about?"

"It's her blood type. Ms. Caitlin is Rh-negative, and so we had to administer a shot of RhoGAM after the procedure."

"Roe what?"

"RhoGAM."

"What's that?"

"It's short for RHO immune globulin. We administered it to Caitlin because the fetus was Rh-positive. If some of the red blood cells of the fetus leaked into her system, her body could produce antibodies to the Rh D factor—a condition called sensitization. Without the RhoGAM shot, these antibodies would cross the placenta and potentially destroy the red blood cells in the next Rh-positive baby she has, killing the child."

"Look, I just want to get out of here. What can I do to take care of this?"

The nurse hands me the invoice. "I'd prefer to just bill Ms. Caitlin and not bother her about this today, but she won't give us a mailing address."

I look at the invoice. "So basically you need fifty more dollars."

"Yes," the nurse says. "That covers the cost of the RhoGAM shot."

I pull out my wallet, extracting two twenty-dollar bills, a five-dollar bill and five one-dollar bills. I slam the money on the counter. "Take it."

Caitlin is the second person I know with an Rh-negative blood type. The other person is my mother. Mom discovered her blood type on the day I was born; Caitlin discovered hers on the day someone wasn't.

2007 – 2008

CHAPTER ONE HUNDRED THREE

When I was a child, Dad kept a Laser in our garage. It wasn't the five-megawatt weapon of mass destruction like the one invented by Chris Knight and Mitch Taylor in *Real Genius*, the greatest Val Kilmer movie no one remembers; rather, it was a small fiberglass cat-rigged sailing dinghy. Dad taught me to sail when I was six years old, and for one perfect summer, we went out at least twice a week on Eagle Creek Reservoir, the long and narrow man-made lake on the west side of Indianapolis that had strict horsepower limits, which kept away all the beer-swilling, nautical-illiterate powerboaters.

Later, that following spring, Dad took the Laser down to the Gulf of Mexico for our family's spring break. We went out sailing one day on the front end of a storm. Mom watched as Dad and I came flying into a lee shore, the shore that was facing into the wind. The storm front was closing, wind and salt spray roaring over our backs. A wave caught the bow just right, pitch-poling our boat. The Laser flipped end over end, the aluminum mast snapping in half after getting stuck upside down in a sandbar. I nearly drowned. When we drove back to Indiana, the boat—and Dad's nascent hobby—stayed in Florida.

A lot went through my mind when I saw my gay neighbors Oscar and Marshall park the beat-up sailboat in their driveway with a For Sale sign. What were two gay guys who were both afraid of the water doing with a sailboat? What was the over-under on how long it took the HOA to send them a strongly worded warning letter? Was she seaworthy? And most importantly, how pissed was Beth going to be after I bought her?

As it turns out, Oscar and Marshall were selling the boat for a friend. The HOA waited a whole two business days to send the letter, which when you factored in the time it took to actually mail the letter meant it was sent out almost the instant the boat appeared. Not only was she seaworthy, she sailed beautifully. And yes, Beth was way fucking pissed.

The boat is called a Highlander. Twenty-feet long, with about two hundred seventy-five square feet of sail between the jib and main, plus a three hundred–square foot spinnaker, she's a lot beefier than Dad's old four-meter, one-sail Laser. I named her *Heather*—after Connor MacLeod's first wife in the movie *Highlander*, obviously.

I've been trying to turn Beth into a sailor, but she's having none of it. We're a month into the summer. This is already our third weekend on the water, and I think it might be Beth's last. I'm skippering the helm at the moment, doing my best to guide my first mate.

"What do you mean, grab the sheet?" Beth says. "The only sheets I see are the sails."

I point to the left side of the boat. "The jib sheet to port. Just cleat it off."

"What side of the boat is port again?"

"The left side," I say. "Remember, 'port' and 'left' have the same number of letters."

"Oh yeah."

"So grab the sheet already!"

"*What sheet?*"

I take my hands off the tiller and grab the line running from the clew of the jib back into the cockpit. I attach it to the portside cleat. "This sheet."

"You mean the rope?"

"Sailboats have lines or sheets, not ropes."

"Hey, Hank."

"Yes, honey?"

"Nautical douche bag know-it-all is not a good look on you."

THE WIND DIED, AS it's prone to do in the summer in Indiana. Beth yelled at me for not bringing along the electric trolling motor. I said something about being a sailing purist and quoted Joshua Slocum's *Sailing Alone Around the World*. She called me a douche bag again. As we crawl into the marina, I see Jack sitting on the edge of the dock, his shoes off and his feet in the water.

Mom and Gillman came back to Empire Ridge last month for his high school graduation. It was the first time they had been back since they moved to Utah a year ago. Jack's grades fell off a little during the tail end of high school, but he still made the National Honors Society and graduated in the top five percent of the Prep Class of 2007. He broke up with Caitlin after the pregnancy scare, got back together with her, then broke up with her again. I still rarely see them apart, although Jack insists they're just casually dating, which I take to mean they're still casually having sex with one another. *With all due respect, son, this isn't my first rodeo.*

I throw the line at Jack. "Look what the cat dragged in."

He catches the line, cleats me off at the dock. "How's the sailing today?"

Beth rolls her eyes. "Ask Captain Douche Bag."

"Ha!" Jack laughs. He offers Beth his hand. "Milady."

My wife accepts the offer, stepping out of the boat and onto the dock. She kisses Jack on the cheek. "At least one of you knows how to be a gentleman."

"Where are you going?" I ask. "We still need to break the boat down."

"I'll leave that to you two," Beth says. "If you need me, I'll be up at the marina bar drinking margaritas."

I shake my head. *Prima donna*, I mouth silently to Jack.

"I heard that," Beth says.

Jack laughs. I squeeze his shoulder. "Ain't love grand, buddy?"

"Don't be so hard on yourself," Jack says. "You two make it look easy. How long has it been now?"

"Married twelve years this August. In fact, doing some quick math in my head, next year will be twenty years since we first, uh..."

"Kissed?"

"Exactly."

"You talk to Laura recently?"

"Uh, no," I say. "What the hell kind of a question is that?"

"I don't know. Just thought I'd ask."

"I mean, I know you two have been talking."

"You do?"

"I see the letters in the mail and the occasional text on your phone. Just because I do a lot of idiotic things, doesn't mean I'm an idiot."

"So you're not mad?"

"Why would I be mad? She's your birth mother."

"That's good to know. In fact, it's kind of the reason I came out here today." Jack hands me an envelope. Another fucking envelope? Really? It's addressed to Jack. The top two lines of the return address read, *University of Notre Dame, Admissions Office.*

"What's this?"

"You don't want to read it?"

"I'm sorry, have we met? Hell yes, I want to read it!"

I unfold the off-white paper. Before I read the letter, I hold it to my nose. It carries with it the smells of expectations: fresh-waxed floors, leather chairs, a professor's aftershave, the mustiness of an old textbook tempered by the chemical-sweet note of the book glue binding its pages together. Where's the *Rudy* soundtrack when I need it?

"Uh, what are you doing?" Jack asks.

"Just give me a moment." I close my eyes, then open. I begin to read.

Dear Jack,

The Committee for Admissions has completed its review of your application for admission. I am pleased to report that your academic achievement and personal qualities have earned you a place in Notre Dame's 2007 Freshman Class. I trust that you will view this offer of admission as a special recognition of your accomplishments during the past four years and as a vote of confidence in your potential for success during your college years.

To confirm your enrollment at Notre Dame, please follow the instructions on the enclosed sheets, noting all the important dates and deadlines. If you have not already done so, please forward a copy of your final transcript when it is available. If you have any questions or need some personal attention, please call us and ask to speak with one of our counselors.

Those who love you must be proud of you—who you are and what you have accomplished. We at Notre Dame are eager to have you with us because your intellectual and spiritual growth will continue here.

Sincerely,

Sister Vivian Rose Morshauser, O.S.F.
Assistant Provost for Enrollment

"ARE YOU FUCKING KIDDING me?" I grab Jack in a bear hug, heaving him up in the air. "You did it!"

"I take it you're excited, then?"

"Best day ever."

"Come on, really?"

"Okay, there's the day Mom brought you home, the day I married Beth, and the days Sasha and the twins were born, but this has to be a solid number five on that list."

"Wow."

"You don't understand, Jack. This was Dad's dream for me, and I let him down. I never even filled out the application. He's up in heaven right now looking down at us with the biggest ear-to-ear grin, and I bet Grandpa George and Grandpa Fred are right there with him."

"What about Grandma Eleanor and Grandma Louise?"

"Yeah," I say, folding the letter carefully into the envelope and handing it back to Jack. "I think those two might be living the afterlife in a different zip code."

"I'm glad you're happy, Dad."

"Aren't you?"

"I guess so."

"You guess so?"

"It's just that, well, Notre Dame was…like you said. It was Grandpa John's dream for you, and it became your dream for me. But it's never been my dream."

"Then make it your dream, Jack. Opportunities like this don't come around every day."

"I realize there are a lot of rare opportunities in life."

"Good."

"And that's why I'm not going to Notre Dame."

"Wait…what?"

"You heard me. I'm not going to Notre Dame."

"Slow down, son. Let's not rush things."

"That's just it. I've been thinking about this all year, during the entire college application process. Laura has really been there for me. She's talked me through it."

"Oh no."

"I was hoping the Notre Dame Admissions office would make my decision a little easier by declining my application. I purposely slacked off a little over these last two semesters just to stack the odds against me."

"This isn't happening."

"I'm going to attend Temple University in Philadelphia. Laura and Ian live within walking distance of campus, and they have a spare bedroom."

"Jack!" I shout.

"What?"

"I need you to stop talking."

We break down *Heather* in silence. I make sure she's tied fast to the dock and her rainfly fits snug over the cockpit in anticipation of some rain later in the week. I finish the breakdown by buffing out a couple of scuffmarks on her stern with a small shoeshine cloth.

"*Heather*…" Jack says, watching me. "Where'd that name come from again?"

"*Highlander*."

"Second-greatest movie ever?"

"That's right. Second only to?"

"*Road House*, of course."

"Of course."

We both smile, the tension subsiding.

"Dad?"

"Yeah, son."

"You know this isn't about you, right?"

"I wish I could believe that."

"You'll always be my number one—my teacher, my friend, my father. But this is about building a relationship—building at least something—with Laura. You've had me to yourself for eighteen years. She deserves to get to know me. I deserve to get to know her."

"Not to mention those three sisters of yours."

"I know, right?"

"Good luck with that."

"Their boyfriends don't stand a chance with me."

"I would expect nothing less." I stand up, shove the shoeshine cloth in my pocket. "When did you get to be such a grown-up?"

"I had a great teacher."

"Can I meet him?"

"Get in line," Jack says. "There's a lot of people who love him, so I'd have to check and see if he could fit you into his busy schedule."

Reaching across to Jack, I grab his arm. "Thanks for that."

He returns my gesture, squeezing my opposite arm. "I still don't get it."

"Get what?"

"Why *Heather*? Why not something cooler from the movie like *Ramirez* or *MacLeod* or even *Kurgan*?"

"You don't name your boats after guys."

"Why not?"

"Some people say it's bad luck. I don't really know. That's just the way it's always been. When you're ready to take a boat out, you'd never say, 'Let's take *him* out,' would you?"

"No, I suppose not."

"I guess there's just something inherently feminine or maternal about a boat. It's comforting to know *she* is there for you when you're out at sea and all alone."

"So a sailor is just a boy who needs to be by his mother?"

Mom watched as Dad and I came flying into the lee shore, the shore that was facing into the wind. The storm front was closing, wind and salt spray roaring over our backs. A wave caught the bow just right, pitchpoling our boat. The Laser flipped end over end, the aluminum mast snapping in half after getting stuck upside down in a sandbar. I nearly drowned.

A father and son obliviously living in the moment. A mother not caring about the moment, wishing nothing more than for them to be safe and in her arms.

"Yeah, Jack," I say. "That's exactly what a sailor is."

CHAPTER ONE HUNDRED FOUR

I hate my fucking boss.

Dean Zacharias is one of the lingering legacy hires at Random House. A direct descendant of Frank Nelson Doubleday, the nineteenth-century founder of Doubleday Books, he still brandishes the staunch Roman Catholicism of the Doubleday family like a badge of honor. He's the guy who gives good Catholics a bad name: gives Opus Dei half his income, thinks women are merely receptacles for his kid-producing man juice, a poor man's Mel Gibson. Not only is he a raging misogynist, he's grossly underqualified for his job. He doesn't read. He thinks all librarians and women writers—save for Ayn Rand and Ann Coulter—are lesbian socialists and that the Crusades were invented by the liberal mainstream media. He's the worst kind of manager, the type who is so small-minded and unintelligent that the only thing he can do for validation is micromanage menial tasks. His favorite ritual is to bring employees into his office and yell at them about their To Do lists. Never mind the fact that you've managed the only imprint under the Random House umbrella to stay in the black every quarter for the last decade; you e-mailed him your To Do list three minutes late, so you're a lazy, uncommitted employee.

I'm sitting in Dean's office. Random House flew me in this week with no explanation, other than it was urgent. We're in the midst of our sixth reorganization in as many years, a bloodletting I've managed to avoid by being profitable while most other New York publishers stare down the barrel of a once-in-a-lifetime recession that is shrinking wallets and shuttering bookstores.

"You know what your problem is, Hank?" Dean pretends to read one of my spreadsheets through his reading glasses. He wears the glasses on a chain around his neck, raising them to his eyes and dropping them to his chest intermittently, trying to create the impression that he has so much as an ounce of intellectual curiosity.

"Enlighten me, Dean."

"You got no clangers."

"Excuse me?"

Dean stands up. He grabs an unlit cigar out of the ashtray on his desk, sticks it in his mouth. He quit smoking ten years ago, but he still chews through a box of cigars every month. A woman hater with an oral fixation: yeah, like that's a fucking surprise.

"You got nothing swinging down there between your legs." Dean points at my midsection. "No fucking clangers!"

"I don't know what you're getting at, but I don't think this is an appropriate conversation to be—"

"What's with all these books you're buying?"

"What do you mean?"

Dean grabs a hardcover novel off one of his shelves. He throws it on his desk. "Like this garbage."

I pick the book up and read the title aloud. "*Teaching Yoga in Belize.*"

"What the fuck is that?"

"It's a great memoir. Won a lot of awards."

"I'm sure it did. I'm sure a bunch of intellectuals got in a room and agreed this book was the next *Atlas Shrugged*."

"Dear God, I hope not."

"See, that right there is what I'm talking about. No fucking clangers."

Dean's rant continues. I tune him out, flipping through the first few pages of *Teaching Yoga in Belize*. I lean my face into the book, smelling the rough-cut pages. This particular copy carries some unusual notes—freshly ground coffee buffeted by something almost familiar and intimate. It reminds me of that oily-haired smell of the inside of my father's baseball hats. I kept a half dozen of them in a cardboard box in my closet for about four or five years after his death. Every now and then, when I had a day that knocked the wind out of me—and I had a lot of those days after Dad died—I'd take out the hats and bury my nose in them.

As I place the book back on my boss's desk, I think about that son who just needed to smell his father's hats. "Dean," I say.

"Don't interrupt me, Hank."

"Oh, that's okay. I haven't listened to a word you've said for the last five minutes."

"Now you listen here, you disrespectful son of a—"

"Fuck you, you sanctimonious buffoon. I quit."

"What?" Dean says. "Now wait just a second."

"Good luck finding somebody who will keep College Avenue Press in the black for another ten days, let alone another ten years."

I stand up and make for the door. Dean gives chase. "Calm down, Hank. You're making a rash decision here."

"And that's exactly why I know it's the right decision." I open the door to his office, smiling. "There's just one thing I have left to say, Dean."

"What's that?"

"Pope John Paul II is fucking overrated."

CHAPTER ONE HUNDRED FIVE

Beth and I sit in a dorm room in St. Francis Hall on the campus of Marian College. We're playing a drinking game with some nursing students. Beth's mother is babysitting Sasha and the twins for the night.

"Ladies," I say. "Before we're all too far gone to remember, I want to make a toast to my brave and beautiful wife, Beth Fitzpatrick."

After I quit College Ave, things got a little tight, but we managed. I called Brian Sweeney at Talk Hard, and he hooked me up with a job as the Midwest library sales rep. This past year I've put close to fifty thousand miles on my Subaru Outback, peddling audiobooks to librarians in Indiana, Ohio, and Illinois. It pays the bills, and I still get to be around book people, so I can't complain. I've also started writing again.

Beth is the real story here. Unwavering in her support of my decision to quit my job, she decided to follow my lead and turn her own life upside down. She retired from coaching gymnastics, a career that essentially began when she was thirteen months old in a Mommy & Me class and ended at the age of thirty-seven when she came to the long overdue realization that no amount of money was worth babysitting moody teenage girls—never mind their overbearing mothers—ten hours a day. She enrolled in the accelerated nursing program at Marian College in Indianapolis. Within eighteen months, she had graduated from nursing school, passed her board exams, and accepted a job in hospice care. Depending on my monthly bonus or lack thereof, Beth's take-home pay will be at least as much as mine.

We toast to my wife. Beth wipes a trace of beer off her bottom lip, looks at me. "Drink, Asshole."

If there's an official card game in the state of Indiana, it has to be euchre. But honorable mention, especially when drinking is involved, has to go to Asshole. Numerous variations of the game exist, but we stick to the basics tonight: fifty-two cards, four players, suits are irrelevant, cards are ranked high-to-low two, ace, king, queen, jack, ten, and so on. All the cards are dealt. First one out of cards is President. Last one out is Asshole.

In the first game I am summarily dismissed to the bottom of the Asshole hierarchy, President Beth issues edicts from her throne: "I said drink, Asshole."

I lift the cold, cheap beer to my lips. Thirteen years after my graduation, Keystone Light has apparently supplanted Natural Light as the beer of choice of the frugal collegiate drunk.

Each person has to know his place in the hierarchy. As President, Beth can tell anyone playing to drink for whatever reason and is beholden to no one. Each successive player has varying levels of executive authority, save for Asshole, who obeys the whims of all who precede him and inevitably drinks the most.

"Shit!" I throw my cards down on the table in disgust. I'm the last one out. Asshole again.

I'VE MANAGED TO BE Asshole for five consecutive hands—a dazzling feat of ineptitude. Beth has been President twice already, VP the other three hands. To Beth's right sits Vicky Elstrom. Vicky is an attractive redhead in her early twenties. Slim-figured, she's been debating getting a boob job and about a month ago was wine-drunk in our hot tub when she asked if she could feel Beth's breasts. Beth said, "Of course," and took off her bikini top while Vicky fondled her for a good five minutes.

This is all hearsay of course, as I was out of town on business. Because God is a fucking dick.

The other coed in the room is average-looking at best, with the personality to match. She has dirt-brown hair, and her name is Susan. Vicky plays two tens on Beth's two eights. Susan plays two jacks, and it's to me. I pass. Beth jumps on the two jacks with two aces. No one can match. Beth puts that pile aside and starts a new deal. She leads with the three cards she has in her hand—three fives—and is out. President once more.

"Shit!" I say.

"Drink for being a sore loser, Asshole!" Beth says.

I do as she commands. Smiling, I put my cup down. I show my cards: three sevens. Hello, Vice Presidency!

I point to Vicky and Susan. "Drink, bitches!"

Beth and I bowed out of the game gracefully, and by that I mean she tried to sit on my lap, slid her leg across my torso, and her right foot knocked a beer over, soaking the playing cards. The entire room, including someone I wrongly assumed was passed out on the bed behind us, screamed, "Party foul!"

Two more beers and a Southern Comfort shot later, Beth and I decide to take a walk across Marian's campus.

"Where we going?" I ask.

Beth points to the northeast corner of campus at the large Tudor-style home on the hill. "Allison Mansion."

"Built in nineteen-eleven by automobile magnate James A. Allison."

"So you know the guy?"

"Dad used to talk about him. He co-founded the Indianapolis Motor Speedway and Allison Engine Company."

"I know," Beth says.

"You know?"

"Got the five-cent tour from the nursing school director last week." Beth hooks my arm in hers. "Allison Mansion has been on the National Register of Historic Places since 1970. It has a one-ton German silver chandelier, a staircase built of solid hand-carved walnut, a music room encased on carved mahogany paneling, an aviary lined with white Italian marble crowned by a Tiffany stained-glass ceiling, and a two-story foyer made from now-extinct Circassian walnut that was imported from Czarist Russia."

"Did you memorize all that useless trivia for my benefit?"

"I sure as hell didn't memorize it for mine."

"You really do love me, don't you?" I close my eyes and smile, leaning in for a kiss.

She pushes my mouth away. "It's a dirty job, but somebody's got to do it."

"Now, what exactly are we going to do once we get to the house?"

"Go skinny-dipping," Beth says.

"What?"

"Something else Allison Mansion can claim is the Midwest's first-ever indoor pool. It's in the basement."

"So you're serious?"

"You bet I am."

"How are we getting in? I assume a place that nice is locked up as tight as a drum."

"You would think so."

"Yes, I would."

Beth looks around. We're standing at the bottom of the hill just south of Allison Mansion, still a good two-hundred yards away from the house. She crouches down, feeling around for something. Her arm disappears. "There it is."

"There what is?"

"Our ticket inside." Beth removes her arm from the black hole in the ground. She sits on the ground, scooting her butt toward the hole until her legs suddenly disappear.

"What's going on?"

"It's the tunnel between Allison Mansion and the Alverna Hall student center."

"Why would they have a tunnel between Allison and the student center?"

"The student center used to be the caretakers' quarters for Allison before a group of Franciscan nuns established Marian's campus here in the nineteen thirties. Nobody ever bothered to block the tunnel, so sometimes students sneak into Allison and Alverna after hours."

"Beth, this is trespassing."

"I'd be happy to compare arrest records."

"Funny."

"I thought so," Beth says. She raises her hands in the air. "Now help me down."

"This can't be safe. Plus, there have to be security cameras in the mansion."

"Oh, there are."

"Then what the hell are we doing?"

"In exchange for a really nice bottle of Scotch, campus security gave me one hour."

"Bullshit."

"You might find this hard to believe, but you're not the only charming person on the planet. Now, help me down."

"Almost there," Beth says. She leads the way with a small pen light attached to her car keys. "There's the entrance to Allison."

"Is it unlocked?"

"Let's hope so," she says, turning the handle on the large oak door.

The door opens to an ornate room dimly lit by security lights. There's a sloping Gothic ceiling of what looks to be carved, pressed leather. The windows on the south side of the room are stained glass set in wrought iron. A large stone fireplace anchors the room.

"What is this place?"

"Looks almost like a basement den or something."

"A den?"

"Yep."

"Sweet," Beth says. "That means the pool is right around the corner."

The smell of chlorine lets us know we've arrived. Beth shines her pen light into the cavernous room and then down at the water. The large tiled pool is rectangular shaped and runs from east to west, with the deeper water in the east end.

"Well, it's full." I reach down, sticking my hand in the water. "And it's fucking cold."

"Oh, don't be a wuss," Beth says, already undressed. She jumps in.

I'm a little more deliberate. I take off my shoes and socks, then my shirt, then my pants, then my underwear. I sit on the edge of the pool, my feet dangling in the water.

"Today, Romeo." Beth splashes me.

Finally, I jump in. I swim underwater with my eyes open. The chlorine burns, but I can barely make out Beth's shadowy form in front of me. My hands reach around and find her ass. I pull her toward me. As I start to come up for air, I blow a stream of bubbles between her legs, then up her belly and between her breasts until I finally break the surface.

"Is that better, Juliet?"

"Quiet," Beth says.

"Oh, *now* you're being cautious?"

"Someone's here."

"I thought you said security gave you the run of the place for an hour."

"Not security." Beth points her finger in the air, tilting her head. "You hear that?"

"I don't hear any—"

"Shhh..." Beth holds her finger to her mouth. "*That*."

My hair stands on the back of my neck. I hear the sound of a little girl crying.

"What the fuck, Beth?" I whisper.

"It can't be true," she says.

"What can't be true?"

"Legend has it this pool is haunted by a little girl who drowned here in the nineteen-twenties. I never believed it—until now."

"Holy shit," I say, still whispering. The girl's crying is getting louder. "I've tried to talk you into more spontaneous acts of nudity than I can possibly count, and the first time you go out on a limb, you pick a haunted pool?"

"Maybe she'll just go away."

"She's been here for ninety years. I don't think she's going anywhere."

"What are we going to do, Hank?"

"Don't look at me," I say. "This is your show."

"I guess it is, isn't it?" Beth smiles. "You can come out now, Vicky."

Vicky walks around the corner, a Coleman lantern in her left hand and a handheld tape recorder in her right. "That...was...awesome!"

I splash Beth. "You suck."

"Hey, lovebirds, you want me to leave the lantern?"

Beth smiles again. "It's a big pool, Vick. Why don't you come join us for a swim?"

"You sure?" Vicky says.

"Wouldn't bother me. How about you, Hank?"

As I try to string together a few coherent words, I notice Vicky already has her pants and underwear off. "I, uh, well, um, it, I guess, uh..."

"I'm not sure, Vicky," Beth says, "but I think that's a 'yes.'" Vicky jumps into the pool.

Okay, God, maybe you're not a dick after all.

2009

CHAPTER ONE HUNDRED SIX

Lila sits at the wet bar in my basement. I've just poured her a Beam and Coke. I drink mine on the rocks.

"Cheers," I say.

"Cheers," Lila says, raising her glass. She sips the bourbon, sets the glass down. "Thanks for letting me crash at your place this weekend."

"Don't mention it. When's the wedding?"

"One thirty tomorrow afternoon."

"Down at the Mormon temple in Louisville?"

"Yep."

"Who's getting married again, a cousin?"

"A friend."

"Same thing."

"No, it isn't."

"Sorry, the jokes kind of write themselves."

"Not the funny ones."

"Come on, Lila. Laugh a little."

"I'll try laughing if you try being funny."

"Fair enough," I say. "One thirty, huh?"

"Yep."

"Seems aggressive for a wedding, given that you'll be kicking off the party around three. But I guess we are talking a Mormon wedding reception."

"You'd be surprised."

"At what?"

"LDS receptions can get out of hand."

"And by 'out of hand' you mean aggressive square dancing, lemonade bongs, and innocently suggestive love anthems by David Archuleta?"

"Hey now, David Archuleta rocks."

"No, he doesn't. What the hell, Lila? Two years removed from being a lesbian band aid, and now you're into Honduran-American LDS bubble gum pop?"

"Honduran?"

"On his mom's side. I watch *American Idol.* I'm not a fucking communist."

"So you thought the best singer won?"

"David Cook could belch a better song than David Archuleta could sing."

"That's not nice, Hank."

"Whatever," I say. "How much you want?"

"What do you mean?"

"For your lame-ass LDS wedding reception. A bottle of bourbon? A hip flask?"

Lila shakes her head. "I'll take a hip flask."

"And?"

"And the bottle."

"That's what I thought."

"Do you have anything besides Jim Beam?"

"What's wrong with Beam?"

"Nothing, if you're nineteen."

"I got something for you," I say, turning to the glass shelves behind me. I grab a bottle, hand it to my stepsister. "Jameson 18 Year Reserve. I've been saving it for a special occasion, but you'll have to do."

"I'm flattered you think so much of me."

"Do you want it or not?"

Lila grabs the bottle. "So what's up with you?"

"Nothing really."

"Jack is good?"

"He's great. We don't talk or see one another nearly as much as I'd like, but he loves it out East."

"You okay with that?"

"Laura and Jack deserve all the time they need to figure things out."

"Wow."

"What?"

"That's such an adult thing to say, Hank."

"I'm thirty-seven years old. At some point I need to act the part."

"Is it acting?"

"I hope so," I say, grinning from ear to ear, Cheshire-like.

Lila leans in and kisses me on the cheek. "There's my Hank."

"He makes an occasional cameo."

"Where's your beautiful wife?"

"She and the kids are out shopping for the Christmas party."

"You hosting?"

"Yes, unfortunately. Stan got us a killer deal on the caterers who did his office party."

"He's back in town?"

"More than he has been. He and Joan are actually talking about making another go of it."

"No way."

"Beth is deliriously happy about it."

"And you?"

"I think Stan and Joan are two of the least compatible people on the planet."

"You tell Beth that?"

"Hell no."

"Good boy," Lila says. "And the job at Talk Hard is going well?"

"Well enough."

"I wanted to talk to you about that."

"About audiobooks?"

"About your career. How's the writing going?"

"It's going."

"It is?"

"Sure."

"So you're writing?"

"I'm dabbling," I say.

"Define 'dabbling.'"

"I got about seventy-five thousand words down of a memoir. Signed with an agent about a month ago just based on the first three chapters."

"That's exciting. You got a title yet?"

"*Waiting for the Sun.*"

"Oh, I like that. Double entendre, great metaphor for the story of a boy figuring out how to be a man."

"All of the above."

"You could even open with that Doors song."

"I wish."

"Why not?"

"The Morrison Estate is controlled by his dead girlfriend's parents."

"The Meg Ryan character in the movie?"

"Pamela Courson was her name. She died of a drug overdose three years after Jim Morrison, and all rights to Jim Morrison's music passed to her parents. They hated Jim and blamed him for their daughter's death. They consider any advances or royalties related to the Morrison Estate to be their daughter's blood money and subsequently charge exorbitant licensing fees."

"You blame them?"

"I applaud them."

"Thought you might," Lila says.

"Hawaii treating you well?"

"I guess."

"Trouble in paradise?"

"Chris has just been, uh, writing and texting and calling me lately."

"Oh God."

"I miss her, Hank."

"Of course you do."

"What do you mean?"

"She's your Laura. She's your fucking stupid."

"My what? Listen, you pompous ass, my life is not a reflection of yours."

"I didn't say it was. Everybody has a Laura, that one person you have no business being with that you keep going back to until the meat is completely stripped from your bones."

"That's pleasant."

"That's Laura."

"So I should ignore Chris?"

"Hell no."

"What?"

"You gotta let it play out."

"Has anyone ever told you that you're a fucking lunatic, Hank?"

"Pretty much everybody I know. Look, Lila, you're a big girl. My advice to you is to not do anything half speed, good or bad. Half speed equals regrets. Full speed equals results."

"Full speed equals disasters."

"Yeah, but they're awesome disasters. And if you give up on Chris, if you two give up on each other, it's not like you're going to walk down the next block, turn a corner, and find a better brownstone."

"You're doing that thing you do," Lila says.

"What thing?"

"Where you start jumping from metaphor to metaphor, sounding all cool and evolved."

"Hey now, occasionally I'll use a simile or two."

"Same difference."

"Lila, love is like walking the streets of New York City."

"And here we go."

"Sometimes it's beautiful, sometimes it's little more than controlled chaos. Sometimes, the chaos is where the real beauty lies. But no matter what, there will always be scaffolding. There will always be building, rebuilding, demolition, renovation—often on the ashes of those who've failed before you. Perfection is for fairy tales. All you can do is buy the ticket, take the ride."

"'Buy the ticket, take the ride.' I like that." Lila drains her Beam and Coke, chews on an ice cube. She sets down her glass, arching her eyebrows at me for another round. "Hunter S. Thompson, right?"

I nod. "I'm sure as hell nowhere near that fucking brilliant." Doing my best Tom Cruise impersonation in *Cocktail*, I top her glass off with a quick two-handed pour from both the liter of Jim Beam and the Coke can. All that's missing is Elizabeth Shue and "Kokomo" by the Beach Boys playing on the stereo. I wish I could remember the name of that actor who played Cruise's bartending mentor. I think he was Australian. I can picture him shearing sheep and bedding Rachel Ward—more the long-haired, loss-of-innocence Rachel Ward from *The Thornbirds* than the steely-eyed *Against All Odds* Rachel Ward, although both examples are infinitely hot.

"Don't sell yourself short, Hank," Lila says, raising her right hand to my face. She cups my face in her palm, rubbing my cheek with her thumb. "Never fear, we may let the scaffolds fall, confident that we have built our wall."

I hand Lila a hip flask full of Jameson. "Pink Floyd?"

Lila pockets the flask, casts a dual shrug with her head and shoulders. "It's Seamus Heaney."

"Really?"

"And you call yourself an Irishman?"

"Right about now I'd like to call myself the lunchmeat in a Rachel Ward-Elisabeth Shue sandwich circa 1984."

Lila chokes on a swallow of Beam and Coke. "Uh, what?"

"Yeah, sorry about that," I say, laughing. "The metaphors inside my head tend to be a lot more bizarre than the ones on the outside."

"Not to mention weirdly graphic," Lila says.

CHAPTER ONE HUNDRED SEVEN

Never fear, we may let the scaffolds fall, a nineteen-year-old girl is playing with my balls.

"Your shot," she says, handing me the wet Ping-Pong ball.

The game is beer pong. It's played on a conventional table tennis surface, with ten cups lined up in an ascending triangle like bowling pins on opposing ends of the table. Each cup is filled halfway with beer, although I hear there's a variety of the game involving a quarter-cup of beer played by people who aren't binge drinkers. There are two players to a team, a turn involving each player getting one shot at the cups on the opposing end of the table. Beyond these basics, everyone seems to have their own individual rules. My rules tend to err on the side of drinking more. Every time you make a lob shot, an opposing player has to chug that cup. A bounce shot into the cup is a double bonus, meaning two cups must be consumed; however, a bounce shot can be legally blocked by the opposing team. This is a rarely attempted shot, reserved only for those nights when you find an opponent who's already drunk, exceedingly chatty, easily distracted, or all of the above. First team to eliminate all ten cups wins the game.

An eleventh cup sits off to the side of the table. It's filled with water, to rinse your balls. The theory is not only does the water keep your balls clean, it cuts down on the drag from the beer. Like many theories—creationism, compassionate conservatism, a woman's sex drive peaking in her thirties—it's total bullshit.

Tonight I'm playing the game with three young women. Two of the women are nineteen, the other is twenty. They're dressed in matching black pants and white oxfords with black bow ties. I force myself to call them young women in the hopes of feeling a little less dirty-old-mannish about being twice their age and wanting to bone them. Plus, calling them girls would be to imply they contextually belong in the same discussion as my thirteen-year-old daughter.

"Score!" I say, sinking the ball into the tenth and final cup. "Game, set, and match, bitches!"

The other nineteen-year-old, my teammate's twin sister, grabs the cup and lifts it to her lips. "Well, fuck me up the ass."

I half-consider responding, *That could be arranged*, if only because her ass is very fuckable. Aside from a small chicken pox scar on my teammate's forehead, the twins are identical: same plum-colored hair, same fuckable Goth asses.

Beth's sudden appearance at the bottom of the staircase tempers my enthusiasm somewhat.

"Hank, what the hell are you doing?"

"Hi, honey," I say, trying not to slur. "Just playin' a li'l beer pong."

"With the caterers?"

We hired them on the recommendation of Beth's father. They had catered Dr. Burke's office Christmas party the night before. About fifty of our friends are upstairs right now debating the authenticity of Obama's birth certificate, bitching about their jobs (or lack thereof), and trading pictures of their children. Which is why I'm down in the basement getting drunk with nineteen-year-olds.

I start toward the stairs. "You told them they were off the clock."

"Yeah," Beth says, glaring over my shoulder at the three caterers, especially the twenty-year-old, a petite blonde who looks a lot like a younger version of Beth. "That doesn't mean they can go play drinking games with my husband."

I try to walk alongside her up the stairs. "You need to lighten up."

Beth makes sure to stay a couple steps ahead of me. "Sorry, Hank, but one of us has to be the responsible host."

"Says the woman who broke into a private pool for some three-way skinny-dipping. Talk about mixed signals. The kids are at your mom's house. Why don't you relax and live a little?"

She stabs me with her eyes. "I *am* living a little. I just don't need to pound twelve beers to do it."

"Twelve beers?" I shake my head unapologetically. "I've had maybe ten or eleven, tops."

My wife doesn't acknowledge my response, walking up the rest of the stairs. I watch as she sinks into the mumbling crowd of low expectations and dead-end lives. I open a new bottle of Jim Beam.

Like most parties involving people in their late-thirties, this one loses its steam right around eleven-thirty. The ice buckets of cheap white wine now filled with room-temperature water. The brie solidified. Beth's iPod Party Time playlist now on its third rotation. Our remaining few guests closing the night with their predictable excuses.

"The babysitter is going to cost me a fortune if I don't get out of here," Lisa says.

Lisa is our next-door neighbor. She's a divorced single mother, with long legs and unusually perky breasts sprouting from her tall, stick-thin figure. She's also a former Indianapolis Colts cheerleader. I was hoping to talk her into the hot tub with me and Beth tonight, holding on to that perpetual fantasy of all married men that one day, in a moment of weakness, curiosity, and one too many glasses of bad Riesling, my wife would dive face-first into another woman's snatch while I tagged her from behind.

As if somehow sensing my descent into heterosexual ecstasy, my gay neighbors, Oscar and Marshall, chime in unison, "Great party, Hank."

If you overlook their seven Chihuahuas, Oscar and Marshall are pretty damn cool. They get inappropriately drunk on craft beer and enjoy football and basketball as much as any guy with a properly oriented penis—plus they harbor my same burning hatred for Roy and Bonnie.

Roy and Bonnie, or "R&B" as we call them, are a retired empty-nester couple on our cul-de-sac who think being older than fucking dirt and not having kids entitles them to never pay any taxes that go toward public schooling. It's a notion I'd concede if they were willing to refund the government every cent of social security they've collected over the last ten years.

R&B also think that Homeowners Association dues are more a suggestion than a mandate and have convinced enough neighbors to follow suit. Thanks to them and their brain-dead lemmings, the street lights in our neighborhood haven't been lit for three years because we don't have money to pay the electrical bill. Meanwhile, every school referendum has been met by an R&B remonstrance ensuring underfunded schools and plummeting enrollments to go with our dark streets.

I think Bonnie might be paranoid schizophrenic. Two or three mornings a week she comes outside in a faded aqua bathrobe. With an eye patch on her left eye, a surgical mask fastened snugly over her mouth, and a feather duster in her right hand, she proceeds to dust the boxwoods lining her front porch for a good fifteen to twenty minutes.

I've attempted to talk to Bonnie and even to Roy, her pathetically enabling wallflower of a husband, but they're just too far gone. They once tried to have Sasha and the twins arrested for trespassing when they took three steps into their front yard to retrieve an errant kickball. If not consciously malicious, R&B are two of the more accidentally evil people I know.

"Got to get up early for church," Hatch says. "You know how it is, Hank."

"No, I don't," I say.

Elias Hatcher has to get up early...*for fucking church*? When the hell did everyone become such goddamn squares?

"Come on, buddy. Five minutes." I grab Hatch by the elbow. "Just give me that."

He starts to unfasten his trench coat before the word "buddy" is hardly out of my mouth. "Okay," he says.

I catch Beth leering at me one last time from across the room. "Keep your coat on. Let's go outside and get some fresh air."

"Suit yourself," Hatch says. "But I'll give you five minutes under one condition."

"What's that?"

"Turn this shitty music off."

In all fairness, Beth's playlist isn't that horrible. It just happens to be playing Owl City's "Fireflies" at the moment, quite possibly the most insipid song written in the last twenty years. And given that with the exception of maybe the Black Keys, post-grunge rock and roll is the vinyl track housing of music, that's saying something.

"*Houses of the Holy* maybe?"

"Perfect," Hatch replies.

I queue up the CD. Hatch and I love this Led Zeppelin album above all others. Well, actually, Hatch does. I think it's a tie between *House of the Holy* and *Led Zeppelin II*, the latter being Zeppelin's loudest and therefore best album. At the very least, we don't worship *Led Zeppelin IV* just because everyone says we're supposed to.

"That better?" I ask.

"Go to the next track," Hatch says before stepping outside. "We need to chill out with some 'Rain Song.'"

We walk out onto the back porch, a patchwork of loose bricks and crumbling mortar. Jimmy Page's guitar and Robert Plant's vocals echo across the backyard from the outdoor speakers mounted on the back of my house. I have a glass of Jim Beam on the rocks in my left, a now half-empty bottle of bourbon in my right. I take a sip of the bourbon, inhaling the aroma. My nose burns a little. Just for a second, as the charred oak smell curls up my nose and down my throat, I miss being a smoker.

"Still drinking Beam, Hank?"

It's been at least fifteen years since Hatch started calling me Hank and stopped calling me Fitzy. I guess joining the Navy and more than a decade of sobriety made him put away childish things. He's gone from being my constant enabler to my constant rock: critical without being judgmental, supportive without being pandering, fun without being drunk. In other words, boring.

"What's it to you, lightweight?" I like to make fun of his sobriety, only because it detracts from the more pathetic reality that I still drink Beam because it reminds me of high school.

"Just figured you would have upgraded after all these years to maybe a small-batch bourbon or single malt."

"Oh yeah?" I shake my head. "And I just figured I wouldn't get lectured on my alcohol choices by a guy who's been sober since the Clinton administration."

"I'm just fucking with you, Hank."

"Yeah, I know."

"Then chill out."

"Sorry," I say. "How long is Claire going to be out of town?"

"Another week or so."

"She still with US Airways?"

"Did you really bring me out here to talk about Claire?" Hatch hands back my glass of bourbon but holds on to the bottle.

I take a swallow as opposed to a sip. Exhaling, I let the caramelly bourbon warm my insides. "Somebody called me 'sir' today."

"What do you mean?"

"I mean Beth and I went to the mall to do some last-minute Christmas shopping for the kids. We were walking through the front doors at Macy's, and some teenage girls were trailing behind us. I opened the door for Beth, and then I held the door open for the teenagers. One of the girls turned and looked at me, and I swear she was about to wink."

"I guess you still got it, Hank."

I wave him off with my glass of Beam. "Wait, I'm not finished. I smiled back at her, and she said to me, 'Thank you…sir.'"

"So?"

"So, Hatch? She called me 'sir.' I'm not a sir. I'm not even a mister. I'm a Hank. I'm a Fitzy."

"Fitzy," Hatch says. "When's the last time anyone called you by—"

"The point is I was fucking despondent. Beth noticed, asked me what was wrong, and said I looked like I was going to pass out."

"And what did you say?"

"I said, 'That girl might as well have just punched me in the nuts.'"

"Man," Hatch says, shaking his head. "I don't envy Beth."

"Why do you say that?"

Hatch points the bottle of Beam at me. "Because for the next ten years you're going to be one shitty fucking husband."

"When did you get to be so insightful?"

"When I stopped depending on brewed hops and distilled corn for insight," Hatch says, patting me on the back. "But speaking of shitty fucking husbands, how's your mother doing?"

I try not to grimace. "She's fine."

"I'm still trying to wrap my head around how Debbie ended up marrying a Mormon."

I take another sip of Beam. "He's actually not that bad."

"Plus that daughter of his is one fine piece of ass."

"Lay off Lila. That's my stepsister you're talking about."

"Oh, it's 'Lila' now?"

"It's always been Lila. She hates being called Delilah."

"Of course she hates it."

"What do you mean by that?"

"Let's see, a hot half-Armenian Mormon in her late thirties, who likes to drink, and isn't married."

"She's not even dating at the moment."

"Exactly!" Hatch says. "That's total LDA right there."

"Okay, now you've officially lost me."

"What I'm saying is, your stepsister is not a Latter-Day Saint. She's a Latter-Day *Ain't*."

"I seriously have no idea what you're talking about."

"Don't be dense, Hank. If she's LDS, she's dyed-in-the-wool. No caffeine, no swearing, no sex, Jesus talked to the Indians, beam me up to the planet Kolob, all that crazy shit."

"And if she's LDA?"

"Then she's probably one freaky-ass slut."

"Fuck you, Hatch."

"You remember Maeve, right?"

"Sure," I say. "You dated her before you enlisted."

"We didn't date so much as screw each other's brains out."

"And I suppose you're going to tell me Maeve is Mormon?"

"Born and raised."

"And she's a Latter-Day Ain't?"

"Well, not anymore. Thirty days after I was deployed, she got married to a Mormon named Babe, proceeded to squeeze out four kids in three years, and I suspect she's not living in Salt Lake City for the beachside vistas."

"Babe?"

"It's his nickname," Hatch says. "He's the youngest of six Abrahams. His grandfather is called Senior, his dad is called Junior, and his four brothers are Abraham, Abe, and Bram."

"So he's Babe, literally the baby Abe?"

"Awesome, right?"

"If by 'awesome' you mean the dumbest fucking thing I've ever heard of. But I mourn your loss."

"You and me both." Hatch looks up to the sky and rubs his chin, his face practically glowing in the winter night.

"Cat got your tongue?"

"Just remembering some good times," Hatch says. "Maeve loved her sex two ways, dirty and filthy-stinking dirty."

"And on that note…" I offer my glass to Hatch. "How about a refill?"

Hatch unscrews the cap off the bottle, tilts the bottle down toward my empty glass. "No more ice?"

"Nah," I say. "At this point water would just be getting in the way of my buzz."

"That's the spirit. Now, as I was saying about Maeve."

"Your Mormon girlfriend who was into weird sex."

"I didn't say weird." Hatch screws the cap back on the bottle of bourbon. "I said dirty."

I take another sip of Beam and fight off another compulsion to smoke a cigarette. "Correct me if I'm wrong, but weren't you stationed in Thailand?"

"Technically I was stationed in Hawaii, but we went to Thailand all the time."

"Lila is moving to Hawaii," I say.

"Oh really?" Hatch says. I can hear the change in his voice, that detached tone he uses when he's not genuinely listening to you—the one where all he wants is for you to stop talking just so he can tell a better a story.

"What did I just say, Hatch?"

"Huh?"

"Exactly," I say. "Back to Thailand. If I recall, that place pretty much cornered the market in dirty and filth-stinking dirty. Isn't that the place where pimps used to sell you two girls and a beer for how much?"

"'Two-girl, one-beer…ten-dallah,'" Hatch says in his best offensive Asian voice.

"So much for inflation," I say. "And that's also where you met a prostitute in Bangkok who stuffed her vagina with colored Ping-Pong balls and could eject each individual color upon request?"

"She was a very skilled woman, Hank."

"I can't imagine Maeve being any dirtier than Ms. Ping-Pong Pussy."

"Ms. Ping-Pong Pussy wasn't addicted to butt sex like Maeve."

"Excuse me?"

"Maeve put the A in LDA. I mean, I don't know, maybe it's a Mormon thing. But that girl loved her some anal."

"Oh, Jesus."

"And I'm not just talking your standard ramming the penis up the poop shoot."

"I think I get the picture."

"I mean any foreign object that was within a ten yard radius of her asshole. Anal beads, fists, large vegetables…"

"I got it, Hatch."

"In fact, she was fairly ambivalent about her vagina. It got to where she didn't even let me go down on her because she'd much rather have me lick her asshole."

"And on that not," I say, throwing back yet another glass of bourbon, "you can show yourself out."

Hatch tries to muffle a laugh. He pats me on the back again as he turns to leave. "Good talk, Hank."

IT'S BEEN ALMOST AN hour since Hatch left, my whiskey my only companion. The winter cold is starting to seep through my overcoat. My bourbon glass raised to my mouth with one hand, the bottle of Beam in the other, I can't see where I'm going and trip over an old tree root I've tripped over a hundred times before.

An old black walnut tree canopies our porch, its limbs as stark and judgmental as the look on Beth's face tonight, its roots as dangerous as her distrust in me. My childhood home in Clematis Gardens had a black walnut tree much like this one. It stood near the back of our property, fighting for space with ash saplings along an old farmer's fence line.

When I was five years old, Dad put an aluminum swing set under that black walnut tree. He ordered it out of the Sears catalog, back when Sears actually printed catalogs and I viewed the toy section in their Christmas edition as the most sacred tome on Earth. Dad and Uncle Mitch put the swing set together. It was painted blue with diagonal green and white stripes on the bars. The directions said, *Assembly time approximately sixty minutes.* It took them four hours to build it. I used to have a picture of Uncle Mitch pushing me on the swing, my face plastered with this fake grin. Pretending as always to trust him. Pretending as always to love him.

The swing set teased me with illusions of childhood, my naïve bare feet bruised and cut by the jagged walnut shells that littered the ground. It was a vicious cycle, my feet building up just enough calluses through the summer only to go soft and vulnerable over the winter months. Later, in college—in a botany class I took as an elective because the teacher was a smoking hot peroxide blonde with fake tits who quit her job as a weather girl in the eighties to get a doctorate in plants—I found out black walnut trees were poisonous. They give off a toxin that causes certain plants to exhibit symptoms such as—and I can still remember watching the teacher's walnut-hard calves as she wrote this on the chalkboard—"foliar yellowing, wilting, and eventual death."

The music stops, right in the middle of "The Ocean" of all places.

"What the fuck?" I say to no one. "That's the last song!"

"Oh, don't get your panties in a bunch!" Beth shouts from inside the house.

Jessie James's "Wanted" starts up on the outdoor speakers.

"Come on, Beth. You cut Zeppelin off for this?"

"No..." my wife says. "For this."

She steps out of the shadows into the flickering light of the Tiki torches rimming our back porch. She's wearing a multilayered silk skirt fastened low on her hips. She is topless, save for two small, golden teacup-like pasties.

My belly dancer has returned.

Beth starts dancing, shimmying her hips in rhythm with the song. She grabs the glass of bourbon from my hand, finishes it off with one swallow.

"Speaking of panties," I say, "are you wearing anything under that skirt?"

Still dancing, she hands the glass back to me, pushing it into my chest. "What do you think?"

"So, I'm forgiven?" I say, backing up as my wife advances.

"No," Beth says. "But fortunately for you, I'm too horny to think about it."

"Can I at least say I'm sorry?"

"Apologizing won't make me any more or less horny."

"Well, I'm still sorry."

"Just shut up, Hank." Beth continues to push me backward, steering me toward the chaise lounge, just a few feet away under the black walnut tree. In a few seconds, she will push me down on to the chaise. She will straddle me, take me inside her, and then pleasure herself while I watch. It's her favorite move. It's in my top two or three as well, trailing only reverse cowboy and early-morning spoon sex. There's a good chance I'm too drunk to have an orgasm. There's a better chance she doesn't give a shit.

"Uh oh..." I say, my words trailing off like a word balloon in a comic book as my heel catches on a black walnut root. I stumble backward, tripping over myself.

"Hank!" Beth shouts.

She lunges for me, but it's too late. My bourbon glass shatters. The last thing I see before I black out is that my feet are suspended in the air above me. The last thing I hear is my wife's scream punctuated by the blood-wet thud of the back of my head hitting our brick porch.

CHAPTER ONE HUNDRED EIGHT

Although I've never told Beth this, the reason I always hope I'm sitting by a beautiful woman on an airplane goes beyond just having sex with her as we plummet to our doom. Since I was about sixteen years old, my favorite fantasy has involved a deserted island and a beautiful woman. The woman is never a celebrity; rather, she's someone I know. Usually, she's the hottest girl at that moment with whom I have a platonic relationship. Nowadays, it could be a neighbor, a co-worker, a friend of Beth's, someone from high school or college I've stayed in touch with, one of my kids' barely of age babysitters. By some strange coincidence, we end up sitting next to one another on a commercial airliner. The plane crashes, and miraculously we're the only survivors. Even more miraculously, we crash within swimming distance of a deserted tropical island. We swim to shore, take off our wet clothes so we don't die of hypothermia. We start a fire with some coconut husks, the sun, and her glasses she just happened to be wearing even though she usually wears contacts. (I realize there's quite a bit of minutiae here; I've had this dream a lot.) We spoon naked by the fire, trying only to raise our body temperatures, but in the heat of the moment have sex on the beach. We awake in the morning, lamenting our impulsiveness. Over the next few weeks and then months, we distract ourselves with finding food, water, and shelter, but then irrevocably fall in love and spend our days and nights fucking each other's brains out. It's at this point we get rescued and are reunited with our significant others, forced to live a life we're no longer comfortable living, forced to love someone we're no longer comfortable loving. Like the TV show *Lost*, our lives become reduced to finding a way back to the island.

Has my life become just some great big lamentation? A ponderous slog from one expectation to the next? Marriage, fatherhood, work. Long stretches of lonely depression allayed only by sporadic drunken make-up sex and chronic shower masturbation. The button on my jeans pinching my beer gut. Reading *Slaughterhouse-Five* for the first time just because Kurt Vonnegut died. Feeling guilty about that third glass of red wine, social smoking, and being attracted to teenage girls.

I miss teenage girls. I miss *Headbangers Balls*. I miss the Brat Pack and *Miami Vice*. I miss the Cold War, back when good was good and evil was evil and Rocky saved the world by cutting down the giant Russian and giving a prescient speech at the center of the ring. I miss Dick Clark and his giant white wand of a microphone on *American Bandstand*. I miss big hair, shoulder pads, pumps with lacy ankle socks, Susanna Hoffs' fuck-me eyes, John Hughes' dialogue, and a how about a nice game of chess.

I miss that deserted island.

I miss my father.

I CAN'T OPEN MY eyes. They're crusted shut. How long have I been asleep? My head is fucking killing me. I'm swearing off Jim Beam forever, and this time I mean it. Okay, probably not. My tongue has a layer of fuzz on it. Jesus Christ, did I smoke last night?

I rub my eyes until I can open them, reach my arm up to my nose and smell my shirt. Marlboro Lights, and something else. Oak moss and lavender overlaying an odor that's sweaty, distinctly feminine. I smell my fingers. Well, that answers my next question. Apparently Beth and I had sex last night, or at the very least some rigorous foreplay.

Beth turns over and mumbles something in her sleep. I see her face for a moment, before she buries herself in a pillow.

What the fuck?

It's not Beth.

I sit up, look around the room. Two posters hang on the wall opposite the bed. Sharon Stone stares at me menacingly from one of the posters, her claws digging into Michael Douglas's naked shoulder. The Dream Team smiles at me from the other poster. Check that. Ewing, Laettner, and Barkley aren't smiling. Ewing is as stoic as ever. Laettner, the consummate Duke turd. It's Barkley that gets me. He has this what-the-fuck look on his face like he just had a birds-eye view of my hairy ass as I did a girl doggie style.

Below both posters is my dresser. On top of my dresser sits a television; we forgot to turn it off last night before Beth and I, or this girl and I, before we did whatever it is we did. The screen of the Panasonic TV/VCR combo stares at me with its big blue eye, the video cassette sticking out of the horizontal slot on the bottom of the set like a tongue. A tongue that's labeled, *The Outsiders*.

Fucking great. This dream again. I'm in my apartment on October 1, 1992, the day my father died. I suppose now I'm going to get up, shower and shave, take my well-worn VHS copy of *The Outsiders* downstairs to watch on the couch, and wait for that phone call that changes my life forever.

"Hank?" the strange woman says, stirring. She turns her head to me.

Well, what do you know? Genuine discourse. This is a new approach for my subconscious.

"Heeey…you."

"It's Eleni," she says, turning away from me in an exasperated huff. She pulls the sheets tight around her.

"Eleni," I say, snapping my fingers. "Of course! It's a Greek name, just like Eleni Andros, Melina Kanakaredes' character in *Guiding Light*."

She turns back to me. "Are you still drunk, Hank?"

"I don't think so," I answer. "But cut me some slack. It only took me sixteen years to remember your name."

"What?"

"Never mind."

"You want to go get some coffee?" Eleni says. "Sounds like you might need some."

I grab Eleni's jeans from the foot of the bed, toss them next to her pillow. "Starbucks on me," I say.

"Star*what*?" Eleni asks.

"Oh, that's right," I say. "It's nineteen ninety-two. Starbucks won't be in Indiana for another seven years."

"Hank, you are really weirding me out right now."

"Ahhhhhhhhhh!"

Eleni jumps, startles. "What the hell was that?"

"I can hear myself scream."

"The whole apartment complex can hear you scream."

"But that's impossible."

"You've lost you mind."

"Hold that thought, Eleni." I stand, only then realizing I'm completely naked. I drop to the floor.

"It's a little late for modesty," she says.

A pair of used boxers sit crumpled beneath the bed. I grab them. Lying on my back on the floor, I slide them up my body. It's awkward but effective.

Eleni peaks over the side of the bed. "What are you—"

"There, that's better." I jump to my feet.

"What's better?"

I raise my right index finger. "Just hold on. I'm trying a little experiment." I concentrate on my feet. Right, left, right, left, right, left. I walk in place, then jog in place. I circle the bed, pacing back and forth around the room.

"What is this?" Eleni says. "Your morning calisthenics?"

"I can walk, I can jog, I can run."

"So?"

"My feet are doing what I tell them to. That never happens. It always feels like I'm on ice, or walking in Jell-O."

"You sure you're not still drunk?"

"Don't you get it, Eleni? I can't do any of these things, in my dreams I mean. I'm always a prisoner to the dream. I can't scream. I can't consciously walk or run. I can't even have an orgasm in my dream. This all seems so, so real."

"You can't have an orgasm in your dreams?"

I shake my head. "Never had a wet dream in my life. I always wake up, you know, right before."

"So how about we put your dream to the test?" Eleni pulls back the covers, stopping me in my tracks. She's as naked as I just was, only far less modest. Dark hair. Pale skin. A smooth back knotted by the indentations of her spine. A small, somewhat bony ass. Long legs and long, high arched feet. She's a pretty girl, although skinnier than what I'm attracted to sober. I notice the soft pack of Marlboro Lights sticking out of the back pocket of her jeans.

"Eleni, I can't."

"You didn't say that last night."

"I wasn't married last night."

"Married?" Eleni says. "Since when?"

"Since about thirteen years ago."

"So you got married when you were eight?"

There it is again. That weird feeling. Something isn't right here. I feel so present, so knowing. That oak moss and lavender smell? It's Drakkar

Noir cologne. From 1986 through 1993, I bathed in that shit. I've never smelled it in my dreams. I've never smelled anything. Is this what they call lucid dreaming? What am I supposed to do?

"Earth to Hank," Eleni says, waving her hand in front of my spaced out eyes. I shake my head, snapping out of it.

"I'm here," I say. "Wherever here is."

"Sit down," Eleni says, guiding me back to the bed until we're seated side by side. She swings her legs over mine.

Now that I look at her, Eleni is pretty fucking hot. She still hasn't bothered to put any clothes on. If I'm going to relive the worst day of my life, I guess I could start it off with having sex with a beautiful woman.

She grabs my hand, places it on her breast. Her breasts are tiny but workable. Her skin, so smooth, unwrinkled, and almost baby soft. Holy Lord, I had forgotten how soft girls could be. How new this could all feel. Alcohol or no alcohol, cigarettes or no cigarettes, my head is buzzing. I'm hard almost instantaneously.

Eleni spreads her legs, guides my other hand to the tangle of dark pubic hair between them. I try not to look, but who am I kidding? I look. My fingers almost inside her, leaning in to kiss her. Still looking. I can't remember the last time I saw such a proudly unshorn puss—

"Is that clock right?" I say over her shoulder, dropping my hands abruptly to my sides.

"What clock?" Eleni says.

"The one on my night stand."

"Yeah, I guess." Eleni grabs my hands. "Now where were we?"

"But it says seven o'clock."

"Yeah, so?"

"In my dream, I always wake up after it happens, not an hour-and-a-half before."

"Before what happens?"

"I relive the day from A to Z, just like in real life. There is no prologue. Unless…"

"Unless what?"

The room starts to spin. I'm short of breath. I can feel a panic attack coming on. I am terrified. I am excited.

I am not dreaming.

I am awake.

Somehow, someway, I have awoken on October 1, 1992, twenty-one years old, armed with the knowledge of my thirty-seven-year-old self. And I can save my father.

"Eleni, it's been fun." I kiss her on the cheek. "But I have to go."

"Go where?"

I rifle through my dresser, finding my favorite old raggedy Notre Dame sweatshirt, only it's brand-new again. I put on a pair of blue jeans over my boxers, stash the soft pack of Marlboro Lights in my pocket while Eleni isn't looking. "I'll be back later. Or at least I think I will. Or somebody who looks like me will."

"Hank, you're scaring me."

"Don't be scared," I say, opening the door to the hallway. "Be happy. I've been given a miraculous gift this morning."

"And what gift is that?"

"Salvation!"

I exit the room. But just as I close the door, the smallest pang of guilt tugs at my heart. Be a gentleman, Hank. Salvation can wait ten more seconds.

I open the door. Eleni is still sitting there. Still naked.

"Forget something?" she asks.

"There's a good man out there for you, Eleni, but I'm not him."

"Spoiler alert!"

"I'm serious. Be kind to others and to yourself, and don't worry about all the other bullshit."

"Thanks for the tip. Anything else?"

"Yeah," I say. "Put all your money into tech stocks in nineteen ninety-seven, then take all your money out of tech stocks in nineteen ninety-nine. When the new *Star Wars* movie comes out, prepare to be very disappointed. If nine years from now, you find yourself planning a trip to New York City on September eleventh, two thousand one, cancel it. And in two thousand five, right before the Kentucky Derby, place a two-dollar trifecta bet on Giacomo, Closing Argument, and Afleet Alex, in that order."

"A two-dollar trifecta?" Eleni asks. "What is that?"

"Just buy the ticket, take the ride."

"I don't follow."

"It's a meta—oh, never mind."

"I understand metaphors, Hank. I'm not one of your usual airheads." Eleni stands. She finally wraps a sheet around her lithe body, a gesture for which I'm grateful, although my penis doesn't share in the sentiment. Backlit by the morning sun that peaks through the mini-blind, she almost looks like the Virgin Mary. Or Laura on the night I resigned from the Virgin Mary's club.

"Want a co-pilot on this ride?" she asks.

"Thanks, Eleni." I kiss her on the forehead, wondering yet again how it is that a jackhole like me attracts the sweet ones. "But I have to take this trip alone. You're welcome to sleep in, have some breakfast, lunch, whatever. I'm going to be awhile. There's coffee in the pantry, eggs in the fridge. Lock the door behind you."

"Will I see you again?"

"I don't know."

"You don't want to see me again?"

"I don't know if it's up to me."

"You can say 'goodbye,' Hank. I'm going to say 'see you soon.'"

I walk out the door, for good this time. "Goodbye, Eleni."

"See you soon," she says with a delicate wave of her hand.

I SHOW MYSELF OUT of the apartment. Parked out front is the brand-new light blue Chevy C/K 1500 Dad gave me off the lot two months ago. I start the truck. The engine radiates a trace of heat from multiple runs to the liquor store a few hours earlier, and the gas gauge has dropped below a quarter-tank. The truck smells like a guy trying to impress a Grecian waif named Eleni—beer, cigarettes, cheap perfume. I peer out the back of the truck, almost too afraid to look, but there it is—a V-shaped indentation on the inside of the truck bed. What am I going to tell Dad? The truth? That Eleni was blowing me while I was driving and I didn't see the red light until it was almost too late? That I slammed on the brakes and sent a sixteen-gallon keg hurtling across my truck bed and a girl almost bit my dick off?

Hell, maybe I *will* tell him the truth. What do I have to lose? We'll talk it out man-to-man. So the owner's son is sending another car to the body shop. So what? I'm saving his fucking life. I figure that earns me a little clemency. He's technically only nine years older than me, my peer more than my parent. If only I had played Powerball all these years; I could do some real fucking damage. Maybe I'll go put some money on Stanford to upset Notre Dame two days from now.

What's that smell? Probably Doc Brown shitting his pants and muttering something about the space-time continuum.

CHAPTER ONE HUNDRED NINE

I could have used a flux capacitor on the drive from Bloomington to Indianapolis, or at the very least a Delorean. I had a lot of time to think about what I'm going to say to Dad. More time than I wanted. There was an accident on Highway 37, a little past Martinsville. I tried sneaking around it by heading west on 144 and then up 67. Problem was, everybody else had the same idea. Apparently, I'm a little distracted. Almost wrecked twice. Stopped into a backwoods filling station, left the filling station with the gasoline hose still lodged in the side of my truck. Blazed through that pack of Marlboro Lights. And if there's such a thing as a profanity quota, I am set for life.

The digital clock in my truck reads 8:20 a.m as I pull into the auction parking lot. This is going to be tight. I know Dad was killed "around" 8:30, but I can't remember if it was before or after 8:30.

I don't have a watch on. I reach into my jeans pocket for my BlackBerry to check the time. Force of habit, I guess. My hand halfway into my pocket, I check myself; IBM will release the world's first smartphone, oh, about a year from now.

Again, I'm too present and knowing for this to be a dream. Feet mill to and fro on each side of me. The number of tasseled loafers unnerves me. Head down, I'm not looking where I'm going.

"Excuse me," I say into a man's chest as we run into one another.

"Hank?" the man says.

I look up. He's dressed in his usual business casual attire for the auction: polo shirt pulled tight against his middle-aged belly, khakis about an inch too short above his loafers. He's wearing the nylon blue jacket that sixteen years from now still hangs in my coat closet—"JOHN" in gold block letters on the right front, and on the left front the interlocking corporate logos of

Oldsmobile, Cadillac, and Subaru overlaid by the words "Fitzparick-Olds-Cadillac-Subaru." He holds a cup of coffee in his right hand, a half-eaten donut in his left.

"Dad!" I shout. I grab him, my left arm under his ribs and my right arm over his shoulder, pulling him into a hard, chest-to-chest bear hug. Sixteen years of depression and despair pouring out in an embrace I can't release, I won't release.

Dad hugs me back, like he always does. I bury my face in his shoulder to hide my tears, nuzzling his throat as I inhale his English Leather cologne.

If I'm being honest, the only reason I never became an atheist is that I couldn't reconcile myself with any belief system that told me I wouldn't see my father again. I believe in heaven more than I believe in Jesus. Does that mean I'm not a Christian? Do I give a shit? Maybe I'm just Ray Kinsella, that little boy wanting to have one last catch with his dad. What's the scripture quote, that one from Corinthians about faith, hope, and love? It's as if all three have coalesced into this one moment, putting me back in the arms of my father. And that's enough for me.

"Easy there, son," Dad says, trying to pry himself away from me. "Are you okay?"

"What?" I wipe the tears from my eyes. "You too old to give your son a hug or something?"

"Never," Dad says. "You're just usually not this—"

"Affectionate?"

"Well, yeah."

"First time for everything."

"Shouldn't you be in school?"

"Mid-terms," I say. "Got the rest of the week off. Thought I'd surprise you."

"Consider me surprised. Want to come home for dinner tonight?"

"Maybe," I say. "How about breakfast right now?"

"Gee, I'd love to, Hank." He holds up his half-eaten donut. "But this is the first thing I've been able to keep down all morning."

"You sick?"

"I think so."

"Then go home." I can hear my voice. It sounds anxious. It *is* anxious. "You got a wife and little boy waiting for you. Take the rest of the day off."

Dad pulls back the left sleeve of his jacket, eyes his watch. "I wish I could, son, but the dealership is really short on its used truck inventory right now. I have to do some major wheelin' and dealin' today."

I look at the analog wall clock just over the entrance to the restrooms. It reads 8:25 a.m. I need to stall him maybe five minutes, ten at the most.

"You want to come with me?" Dad asks.

"Where?"

He points with his coffee hand toward the garage area, his index finger extended from the cup. "Out on the auction floor. See your father in action."

"That's the last thing on earth I want to do."

His shoulders slump. I've hurt his feelings. But maybe there's an opportunity here. I can keep this contained. I have read the police report, the depositions, and the autopsy enough to know exactly how and where this accident happens. I can describe the vehicle. I can even describe the driver. If I'm there, with my father, it'll be as easy as walking him over to another garage stall a minute or two prior.

I punch Dad in the shoulder. "Just kidding, Pops. Lead the way."

We walk out onto the auction floor, a flurry of flesh and steel. Auctioneers babbling gibberish into their microphones, sweaty handshakes, cars going in and out. "How about this truck, Dad?" I point to a bright yellow late seventies Chevy Luv. It's not a GMC Sonoma, and that's all that matters.

"That piece of crap?" Dad says. "Ain't nothing but a rebadged Isuzu."

I look into the front window, pretending to be interested. "I don't know. I see a lot of potential here. Maybe put a light bar on the roof, some graphics on the side, a roll-up tonneau cover on the bed."

"That's just putting lipstick on a pig, Hank."

"Move 'em up, move 'em up!" the auctioneer shouts into the microphone. I flinch, but I don't see the GMC Sonoma in line. Not yet.

The Chevy Luv's anemic four-cylinder engine rattles to life. It lurches past us, its rear bumper asking us, *What would Jesus do?*

"That's a trick question, you know," Dad says.

"What's a trick question?" I ask.

"That bumper sticker." Dad nods at the Chevy Luv. "'What would Jesus do?' is a trick question."

"Why do you say that?"

"It's not what Jesus *did* that is important."

"You know I think most Christian theology is bullshit, Dad."

"I'm not saying you need to agree with the dogma. Just understand the message."

"Which is?"

"It's not enough to be born and to live as a Christian. You have to be born *again.*"

"Like I said, bullshit."

Dad pokes me in the chest. "Listen with your heart, not your head."

"I'm trying."

"What would Jesus do?" Dad asks.

As my father asks this question, I can see the white GMC Sonoma two cars back in the repo line, and behind it the black Ford Bronco. The Bronco stalls. A manager walks over to the driver's-side window. He pushes his hands forward as he barks out instructions to the driver about how to feather the brake and the gas to keep the engine running.

I have to make my move, and soon.

"I can tell you what Jesus would do, Dad."

"Yeah, Hank?"

"He'd tell his father to shut the hell up and go out to breakfast with him."

"It's not what Jesus *did* that was important."

"Yeah, you said that already."

The GMC Sonoma pulls forward, now only one car away from the auction block. The Bronco stalls again.

"You just don't get it, Hank. It's not how Jesus lived that saved the world. It's how he died."

"…"

"Hank?"

"…"

"Son?"

"…"

The edges of Dad's face start to soften, like Christopher Reeve when he pulled that 1979 Lincoln penny out of his pocket in *Somewhere in Time* and lost Jane Seymour forever. Again, the room spins. Shortness of breath, panic attack. Only this panic attack is different. It's not like the one I had earlier, when I woke up sixteen years in the past. This isn't a panic attack born of disbelief. It's one of clarity.

I am a bastard.

Fatherless but not quite rudderless, I am a product of my pain as much as my joy, my vices as much as my virtues, a raised up, broken down, and raised up again mishmash of sin and sincerity. I am someone who has loved, who has married, who has helped bring three beautiful children into this world not in spite of losing my father…but *because* I lost him.

I've shoved my hand down my pocket and found my fucking 1979 penny. For me to be saved, for me to be born again, Dad has to die.

"I think I get what you're saying," I say. The words feel hollow in my mouth, each syllable from here to the moment I turn my back on my father hammering that nail deeper into his cross. Soon his groin will be ripped in half. His liver will explode. The outer wall of his abdomen, his bowels, and his bladder all shredded and expelled in bits and pieces onto the reddening concrete floor. That one Lincoln penny now a jar of pennies. The metallic smell of blood. And I'm the prophet who's going to let it happen.

"So you understand?" Dad says.

I nod, grabbing his elbow. "I understand more than you know."

I hug him again, one last time. I'm holding on, hoping that I can somehow warn him what's about to happen. Through osmosis.

He doesn't hug me back this time. I wish he did, but he doesn't. It's not like he knows. How could he? And of course, it's not that he doesn't love me. He's just a guy in the moment, caught in an awkward hug, even by John Fitzpatrick's overly affectionate standards.

I can feel Dad trying to navigate the awkward silence, just like any good car salesman would do. Waiting for the right words. Refusing to "umm" or "uhh" his way through conversation. An Oldsmobile man to the end.

"You in for Notre Dame-Stanford on Saturday?" Dad asks.

"Wouldn't miss it for the world."

"Dinner tonight?"

"Yeah," I say, choking on the lump in my throat. "Dinner would be great."

"Burgers and beer?"

"Think your stomach can handle it?"

"I got to cash in on this kinder and gentler son thing while I can."

"Sounds perfect." I lean in again, still not ready to let go of this moment. I kiss him on the cheek. "I love you, Dad."

He reacts to this moment a little less awkwardly, rubbing the back of my neck and giving me a gentle headbutt. "Love you too, son."

The GMC Sonoma pulls up as I leave my father forever. Somebody tries to flag me down on the way out of the garage, a friend of Dad's, but I ignore him. I pass by the analog wall clock just over the entrance to the restrooms. It reads 8:30 a.m.

People are giving me strange looks as I walk across the auction parking lot. By the time I get to my truck, I'm not just crying. I'm sobbing.

My heart hurts. I sit in my truck. My arms collapse over the steering wheel. Just as I am about to close the door, I hear a high-revving engine. Tires squealing. A vehicle getting away from its driver. The screams. The crashing sound of metal hitting metal.

I slam the truck door shut, and peel out of the parking lot.

CHAPTER ONE HUNDRED TEN

My trip back to Bloomington is taking forever. I've had to pull over three times because I can't see the road through my tears. I about sung myself horse when Scorpions' seminal power ballad "Still Loving You" came on the radio. First, the tears were for Dad, but then, they were for Beth. Only for Beth. I thought about the time we first stood in that hallway at Martin Neff's house and talked about led singer Klaus Meine's accent, about how he could rhyme two completely different words. In "Still Loving You," Klaus is on his A-game, singing, *"If we go again all the way from the start, I would try to change the things that killed our love,"* while somehow managing to rhyme *"start"* with *"love."*

Going again all the way from the start. I never quite knew what that meant until this very moment. A few Christians, albeit not many, still espouse the doctrine of predestination. It is the belief that all things are willed by God, that our fates are inevitable. It's become wildly unpopular with mainstream Christianity because it takes free will completely out of the equation. It's the lyrics to "Dust in the Wind" by Kansas, only more hopeless. Even certain scientific circles hold to this notion, though stripped of its theistic underpinnings. They believe that time is static—absolute and self-correcting. You can try to change things, but you can't fight time any more than you can change the tides or deny the existence of Pop-Tarts. Fate just finds a way.

Is time static or is it pliable? Will I wake up tomorrow with my 1992 month-to-month lease or my 2008 thirty-year, low-interest mortgage? If it's the former, which I feel like it might be, have I already set events in motion that change everything? Will Eleni be waiting for me when I get back to my apartment? Instead of a nameless Grecian girl in my mind's eye, does she become my touchstone, that person who gets me through my darkest moment? Do I wake up in 1992 and somehow still find a way back to Beth, falling in love with her all over again? Do I go again all the way from the start, trying to change the things that killed our love? Like the guy who sits through a movie he's already watched before and tries to pretend he's never seen it just to make his date happy, is it possible that I can't fall in love with Beth all over again—that I might not be able to fake it? New love is naïve and bold, living in the moment. It's about not knowing what the fuck you're doing. It's like spring, the season that the poet E. E. Cummings called "puddle wonderful." It's about reckless discovery, horny belly dancers, buying the ticket and taking the ride. It's not self-aware. It's not rewinding a clock and trying to pretend that life has a rhythm or rhyme or that you haven't already spent the last decade and change fucking and not fucking the same person.

The person you miss.

The person you love.

The person you just killed for.

Come back to me, Beth. Come back to me Sasha, Burke, and Johnny. I can't do this by myself. Not again. When I wake up tomorrow, please let it be back in 2008.

Tomorrow. It comes at me like a blind turn on a dark mountain road. What is my fate? Where are my puddle wonderfuls? At this point, all I can do is go back to my apartment in Bloomington as if nothing has happened. Maybe Eleni will be there waiting for me, or maybe not. I will check my answering machine. I will call the dealership and rush back to Indianapolis. I will hold my mother's shattered heart in my arms. I will identify my father's shattered body. Hatch will come over later that night, and we'll drink our sorrows away. And then I will go to sleep, afraid to wake up. And then I will wake up, afraid to love. And then I will love, afraid to be alone.

BRIAN SWEANY has spent the last sixteen years as acquisitions director for audiobook publisher Recorded Books, working with such varied authors as Diana Gabaldon, Dean Koontz, and Alice Walker.